Robert Barr (16 September 1849 - 21 October 1912) was a Scottish-Canadian short story writer and novelist. Robert Barr was born in Barony, Lanark, Scotland to Robert Barr and Jane Watson. In 1854, he emigrated with his parents to Upper Canada at the age of four years old. His family settled on a farm near the village of Muirkirk. Barr assisted his father with his job as a carpenter, and developed a sound work ethic. Robert Barr then worked as a steel smelter for a number of years before he was educated at Toronto Normal School in 1873 to train as a teacher. After graduating Toronto Normal School, Barr became a teacher, and eventually headmaster/principal of the Central School of Windsor, Ontario in 1874. While Barr worked as head master of the Central School of Windsor, Ontario, he began to contribute short stories—often based on personal experiences, and recorded his work. On August 1876, when he was 27, Robert Barr married Ontario-born Eva Bennett, who was 21. (Source: Wikipedia)

Literary works:

"The Face And The Mask" (1894)
In the Midst of Alarms (1894, 1900, 1912)
From Whose Bourne (1896)
One Day's Courtship (1896)
Revenge!
The Strong Arm
A Woman Intervenes (1896)
Tekla: A Romance of Love and War (1898)
Jennie Baxter, Journalist (1899)
The Unchanging East (1900)
The Victors (1901)
A Prince of Good Fellows (1902)
Over The Border: A Romance (1903)
The O'Ruddy, A Romance, with Stephen Crane (1903)

THE SPECULATIONS OF

JOHN STEELE

&

THE MUTABLE MANY

A NOVEL

ROBERT BARR

PRINCE CLASSICS

PRINCE CLASSICS

First Printing: 2020

ISBN 978-93-90209-00-2 (paperback)

ISBN 978-93-90209-01-9 (Hardcover)

Published by Prince Classics

www.princeclassics.com

Contents

THE SPECULATIONS OF

JOHN STEELE

&

THE MUTABLE MANY

A NOVEL

THE SPECULATIONS OF JOHN STEELE

CHAPTER I—A NARROW ESCAPE

IT was a nasty night, with a drizzling rain nearly as thick as a fog—a rain which obscured the signals and left the rails so slippery that a quick stop was almost impossible—yet just the sort of night to make a quick stop imperative if disaster were to be averted.

Young John Steele, station-master, telegrapher, ticket-agent, and man-of-all-work in the lone shanty known on the railway map as Hitchen's Siding, ignored by all other maps, stood beside the telegraph instrument wondering whether the rain had affected the efficiency of the wires, or whether the train despatcher had gone crazy. Here was Number Sixteen, the freight from the west, coming in, and there were no orders for her. Number Three, known to the outside world as the "Pacific Express," the fastest train on the road, was already forty minutes overdue, tearing westward through the night somewhere, and John did not know where. All he knew was that she was trying to make up lost time as well as the greasy metals would allow, and here he stood without orders!

Once more he seized the key, and calling the despatched office in Warmington again demanded: "What orders for Sixteen?" Then he went outside, and on his own initiative kicked away the iron clutch that released the distant semaphore. The red star of danger glimmering through the drizzle to the east might hold the express if the driver saw it in time.

Number Sixteen had drawn up to the platform, and as her conductor came forward Steele ran to meet him, shouting: "Sidetrack your train, Flynn! Sidetrack her on the jump!"

"Where's my orders?" asked the conductor.

"There's no orders. I order you. Get her off the main line at once."

"Your orders! Well, for cold cheek——"

Steele lost none of the precious moments in argument, but, turning from the angry conductor, yelled to the engineer: "Whistle for the switch, and kick her back on to the siding. Number Three may be into you any moment."

No youth in Steele's position has the right to give a command to an engineer over the head of a conductor, neither should his orders to the conductor be oral—they must be documentary. Steele was shattering fixed rules of the road, and he knew it.

The conductor of a perishable goods train thinks himself nearly as important as if he ran an express, so Flynn was rightly indignant at this sudden assumption of unlawful authority by a no-account youth at a noaccount station. But a conductor is usually in a comparatively safe place, while the driver of an engine must bear the brunt of a head-on collision, so the grimy Morton at the throttle did not stand on etiquette, but blew the whistle for an open switch and backed his train into the siding. Steele watched the switch light turn to safety again, heaved a sigh of relief, then put his stalwart arms to the lever and slowly pulled off the danger signal to the east, and left the main line clear for the through express.

"What's all this sweat about?" cried Flynn. "Where's Number Three?"

"I don't know," replied John quietly.

"You don't know? Well, I'm blessed! I'll tell you one thing, my impetuous youngster. If Number Three has lost more time, and I'm ordered on to the next siding, you'll lose your job."

"I know it."

John turned in from the platform to the telegraph-room, and Flynn followed him. As they advanced the instrument began a wild rataplan, and Steele paused, raising his hand for silence. Even Flynn, who did not understand its language, felt that the machine was making a frantic, agonised appeal.

"Listen to that!" cried Steele, a note of triumph in his voice.

"What's it saying?" whispered the conductor, awed in spite of himself.

"'Sidetrack Sixteen! Sidetrack Sixteen! In God's name sidetrack Sixteen!' There's your orders at last, Flynn. It's lucky you didn't wait for them."

The final words were obliterated by a roar as of a descending avalanche, and the express tore past, ripping the night and the silence; fifty miles an hour at the least; the long line of curtained windows in the sleeping-cars shimmering in the station lights like a wavering biograph picture—there and away while you drew your breath. In the stillness that followed, the brass instrument kept up its useless, idiotic chatter. A heavy step sounded on the platform, and the engineer appeared at the door, his face ghastly in its pallor, the smudges on it giving a heightening effect of contrast.

"God, Flynn," he gasped, "that was a close call."

The conductor nodded, and each man strode forward as if impelled by a single impulse to grasp hands with the youngster, who laughed nervously, saying:

"They're pretty anxious in the city. I must answer." Then he went to the instrument and sent the most undisciplined message that had ever gone over the wires from a subordinate to a superior.

CHAPTER II—PROMOTION

IN the train despatcher's office at Warmington, one hundred and twenty miles to the east of Hitchen's Siding, the force was hard at work under the electric light. Philip Manson, division superintendent, strolled in, although it was long past his office hours, for he was one of those indefatigable railroad men loth to take his fingers off the pulse of the great organisation he controlled, and no employee of the road could be certain of any hour, night or day, when Manson might not be standing unexpectedly beside him. As this silent man surveyed the busy room, listening to the click of the telegraphic sounders, which spoke to him as plainly as if human lips were uttering the language of the land, he was startled by a cry from Hammond, the train despatcher. Hammond sprang like a madman to the sender, and the key, at lightning speed, rattled forth—"Sidetrack Sixteen. Sidetrack Sixteen."

Instinctively the division superintendent knew what had happened. To the most accurate of men, faithful and exact through years of service, may come an unaccountable momentary lapse of vigilance. The train despatcher had forgotten Number Sixteen! Instantly the road spread itself out before the mind's eye of the superintendent. He knew every inch of it. The situation revealed itself to his mathematical brain as a well-known arrangement of men and pawns would display to an expert what could or could not be done on the chess-board. He knew where Number Three would lose further time on the up-grades, but now, alas! it was speeding along a flat country, where every minute meant a mile. Nevertheless, there was one chance in a thousand that the express had not yet reached Hitchen's, and his quick mind indicated the right thing to be done.

"Tell him to stop Number Three," he snapped forth.

The despatcher obeyed. Where disaster was a matter of moments, there was little use in awaiting the slow movements of a heavy freight-train when the express, a demon of destruction, was swooping down on the scene. There came no answer to the frenzied appeal. Every man in the room was on his feet, and each held his breath as if the crash and the shrieks could leap across one hundred and twenty miles and penetrate into that appalled office. Then the sounder began, leisurely and insolent:

"I sidetracked Sixteen on my own, and set the signal against Three until Sixteen was in. Are you people crazy, or merely plain drunk?"

The tension snapped like an overstrained wire. One man went into shriek after shriek of laughter; another laid his head on his desk and sobbed. Hammond staggered into a chair, and an assistant held a glass of water to his ashen lips. The division superintendent stood like a statue, a deep frown marking his displeasure at the flippant message that had come in upon such a tragic crisis. But the assurance that the express was safe cleared his brow.

"The man at the siding is named John Steele, isn't he?"

"Yes, sir."

"Send down a substitute to-morrow, and tell Steele to report to me."

"Yes, sir."

And this is how our young man came to be Philip Man-son's right-hand helper in the division superintendent's office of the Grand Union Station at Warmington City.

The Grand Union Station is a noble pile of red brick, rough and cut stone and terra-cotta, adorned by a massive corner tower holding aloft a great clock that gives the city standard time. The tower is the pride of Warmington—a pillar of red cloud by day and a pillar of fire by night, with the hours distinct a mile away. The tower may be taken as a monument to the power and wealth of the Rockervelts, although in larger cities they possessed still more imposing architecture to uphold their fame.

The Manateau Midland, which made this immense structure its eastern terminus, was merely a link in the Rockervelt chain of admirably equipped railways; but, as the title, Union, implied, other roads, mostly bankrupt lines or branches of the Midland, enjoyed running rights into the Grand Union Station.

The transferring of a country youth at an enhanced salary, from a lone pine shanty on the prairie to this palatial edifice in the city seemed to John like being translated bodily to heaven. Now he had his chance, and that was all he asked of fate. He delighted in railway work. The strident screech of the whistles, the harsh clanking of cars coming together, all the discordant sounds of the station-yard, were as orchestral music to him, and he never tired of the symphony. He speedily became the most useful man about the place, and was from the first the most popular. He had a habit of dashing here and there bare-headed, and to heat or cold was equally indifferent. There was not a trace of malice in the lad, and he was ever ready with a cheery word or a helping hand. He seemed able to do anything, from running an engine to tapping a wire, and was willing in an emergency to work night and day, without a grumble, till he dropped from fatigue. Silent Philip Man-son watched Steele's progress with unspoken approval, and loved him not the less that for all the lad's witty exuberance not a word had ever passed his lips about that sinister blunder at Hitchen's Siding. Those things are not to be spoken of, and even the general manager knew nothing of the crisis. The train despatcher had retired, nerve-broken, and the newspapers never guessed why.

But there was one man who did not like John, and that was no less important a personage than the general manager himself. His huge room in the lower part of the tower was as sumptuously furnished as an eastern palace. T. Acton Blair, general manager of the Manateau Midland, was supposed to be related to the Rockervelt family, but this was perhaps a fallacy put forth to account for the placing of such a palpably incompetent man in so responsible a position. He was a bald-headed, corpulent personage, pompous and ponderous, slow moving and slow speaking, saying perfectly obvious things in a deep, impressive voice, as if he were uttering the wisdom of ages. His subordinate, Philip Manson, as everybody knew, was responsible for the efficiency of the road; and when he wanted a project carried out, he always pretended it was Blair's original idea, so the general manager got the credit if it was a success, and Manson shouldered the blame if it was not.

One morning, as Philip Manson was about to leave the general manager's room, after the customary daily interview with his chief, the latter said: "By the way, Manson, who is that individual who rushes about these offices at all hours, as if he thought he were running the whole Rockervelt system?"

"I suspect you refer to John Steele, one of my assistants, sir."

"I don't like him, Manson; he seems obtrusive."

"I assure you, sir, he is a most capable man."

"Yes, yes, I dare say; but, as I have often told you, the success of our organisation is in method, not in haste."

"Quite so, sir."

"That person always gives me the idea that something is wrong—that a fire has broken out, or a man has been run over. I don't like it. His clothes are untidy and seem to have been made for some one else. I shouldn't like Mr. Rockervelt to see that we have such an unkempt person on our clerical staff."

"I'll speak to him, sir; I admit his manner does not do him justice."

When Manson next encountered John alone, he spoke with more than his usual severity.

"Steele, I wish you would pay some attention to your clothes. Get a new business suit and take care of it. Remember you are in the city of Warmington, and not at Hitchen's Siding."

"Yes, sir," said John contritely, looking down with new dismay at his grease-stained trousers.

"I wish also you would abandon your habit of running all over the place without a hat."

"I'll do it, sir."

The catastrophe came with appalling suddenness. The Pacific Express Steele had saved, but himself he could not save.

Tearing down the long corridor at breakneck speed, he turned a corner and ran bang into the imposing front of the general manager. That dignified potentate staggered back against the wall gasping, while his glossy silk hat rolled to the floor. John, brought up as suddenly as if he had collided with a haystack, groaned in terror, snatched the tall hat from the floor, brushed it, and handed it to the speechless magnate.

"I'm very, very sorry, sir," he ventured. But Mr. Acton Blair made no reply. Leaving the culprit standing there, he put on his hat and strode majestically to the division superintendent's room.

"Manson!" he panted, dropping into a chair, "discharge that lunatic at once!"

The division superintendent was too straightforward a man to pretend ignorance regarding Blair's meaning. His face hardened into an expression of obstinacy that amazed his chief.

"The Rockervelt system is deeply indebted to Mr. Steele—a debt it can never repay. He saved Number Three last November from what would have been the most disastrous accident of the year."

"Why was I never told of this?"

"For three reasons, sir. First, the fewer people that know of such escapes, the better; second, Hammond, who was responsible, voluntarily resigned on plea of ill-health; third, Hammond was your nephew."

Mr. T. Acton Blair rose to his feet with that majesty of bulk which pertains to corpulent men. It was an action which usually overawed a subordinate.

"I think you are making a mistake, sir, regarding our relative positions. I am general manager of the Manateau Midland, and as such have a right to be informed of every important event pertaining to the road."

"Your definition of the situation is correct. Both you and Mr. Rockervelt should have been told of the narrow escape of the express."

There was a glitter as of steel in the keen eyes of the superintendent, while the inflated manner of the manager underwent a visible change, like a distended balloon pricked by a pin. Mr. Blair knew well the danger to himself and his vaunted position if the event under discussion came to the knowledge of the great autocrat in New York, so he tried to give his surrender the air of a masterly retreat.

"Well, well, Mr. Manson, I don't know but you were right. The less such things are talked of, the better. They have a habit of getting into the papers, and undermining public confidence, and we should all try to avoid such publicity. Yes, you did quite right, so we will let it go at that."

"And how about Mr. Steele?"

"After all, Manson, he is in your department, and you may do as you please. I should rather see him go, but I don't insist upon it. Good afternoon, Mr. Manson." The great man took his departure ponderously, leaving Manson somewhat nonplussed. As soon as the door to the corridor closed behind Blair, the door to Manson's secretary's room, which had been ajar during this conversation, flew open, and the impetuous Steele came rushing in.

"Excuse me, Mr. Manson," he cried, "but I was waiting to see you, and I could not help hearing part of what you and Mr. Blair said. I did not intend to listen; but if I had shut the door it would have attracted attention, so I didn't know what to do. I suppose he told you we had a head-on collision, round a curve, with no signals out."

The young man tried to carry it off jauntily with a half nervous laugh, but Manson's face was sober and unresponsive.

"It was all my fault, and you had warned me before," continued Steele breathlessly. "Now you stood up to the old man for me, and made him back water; but I'm not going to have you get into trouble because of me. I've discharged John Steele. I'm going in now to Mr. Blair, and I'll apologise and resign. I'll tell him you warned me to quit rushing round, and that I didn't quit. I'm sorry I telescoped him, but not half so sorry as that I've disappointed you."

"Nonsense!" said Manson severely. "Go back to your desk; and let this rest for a day or two. I'll see the manager about it later on." He noticed the moisture in the younger man's eyes, and the quiver of his nether lip, so he spoke coldly. Emotion has no place in the railway business.

"No, sir, I'd never feel comfortable again. There's lots of work waiting for me, and it won't have to wait long. I'm going for it as I went for Mr. Blair's waistcoat. But I want to tell you, Mr. Manson, that—that all the boys know you're a brick, who'll stand by them if they—if they do the square thing."

And as if his disaster had not been caused by his precipitance, the youth bolted headlong from the room before Manson could frame a reply.

The division superintendent put on his hat and left the room less hurriedly than John had done. He made his way to that sumptuous edifice known as the University Club. The social organisation which it housed had long numbered Manson as a member, but he was a most infrequent visitor. He walked direct to the cosiest corner of the large reading-room, and there, in a luxurious arm-chair, found, as he had expected, the Hon. Duffield Rogers, an aged gentleman with a gray beard on his chin and a humourous twinkle in his eye. Mr. Rogers was a millionaire over and over again, yet he was president of the poorest railway in the State, known as the Burdock Route, whose eastern terminus was in the Grand Union which Manson had just left. Rogers occupied a largely ornamental position on the Burdock, as he did in the arm-chair of the club. He was surrounded by a disarray of newspapers on the floor, and allowed the one he was holding to fall on the pile as he looked up with a smile on seeing Manson approach.

"Hallo, Manson! Is the Midland going to pay a dividend, that you've got an afternoon off?"

"What do you know about dividends?" asked Manson, with a laugh. He seemed a much more jocular person at the club than in the railway-office, and he was not above giving a sly dig at the Burdock Route, which had never paid a dividend since it was opened.

"Oh! I read about 'em in the papers," replied the Hon. Duffield serenely. "How's that old stick-in-the-mud Blair? I'm going to ask the committee of this club to expel him. He has the cheek to swell around here, in my presence, and pretend he knows something about railroading. I'd stand that from you, but not from T. Acton Blair. He forgets I'm president of a road, while he's only a general manager. I tell him I rank with Rockervelt, and not with mere G. M's."

The old millionaire laughed so heartily at his own remarks that some of the habitués of the reading-room looked sternly at the framed placard above the mantelshelf which displayed in large black letters the word "Silence." Manson drew up a chair beside the old man and said earnestly:

"I came in to see you on business, Mr. Rogers. There is a young fellow in my office who will develop into one of the best railroad men of our time. I want you to find a place for him on your line."

"Oh! we're not taking on any new men. Just the reverse. We laid off the general manager and about fifteen lesser officials a month ago, and we don't miss 'em in the least. I've been trying to resign for the past year, but they won't let me, because I don't ask any salary."

"This man will be worth double his money anywhere you place him."

"I am not saying anything against your man except that we don't want him. The Burdock's practically bankrupt—you know that."

"Still, John Steele, the young fellow I'm speaking of, won't want much money, and he understands railroading down to the ground."

"If he is a valuable man, why are you so anxious to get rid of him?" asked the wily president, with a smile.

"I'm not. I'd rather part with all the rest of my staff than with Steele; but Mr. Blair has taken a dislike to him, and——"

"Enough said," broke in the president of the Burdock. "That dislike, coupled with your own preference, makes the best recommendation any man could ask. How much are you paying Steele?"

"Ten dollars a week."

The old man mused for a few moments, then chuckled aloud in apparent enjoyment.

"I'll give him fifteen," he said. "Will that satisfy him?"

"It will more than satisfy him."

"But I pay the amount on one condition."

"What is that, Mr. Rogers?"

"The condition is that he accepts and fills the position of general manager of the Burdock Route."

"General manager!" echoed Manson, "I'm talking seriously, Mr. Rogers."

"So am I, Manson, so am I. And don't you see what a good bargain I'm driving? You say Steele is first class. All right; I know you wouldn't vouch for him unless that were so. Very well. I get a general manager for fifteen dollars a week; cheapest in the country, and doubtless the best. I confess, however, my chief delight in offering him the position is the hope of seeing old Blair's face when he first meets in conference the youth he has dismissed, his equal in rank if not in salary. It will be a study in physiognomy."

If the staid Philip Manson thought that Steele's native modesty would prevent him from accepting the management of the Burdock Route, he was much mistaken. When Manson related quietly the result of his interview with the Hon. Duffield Rogers, the youth amazed him by leaping nearly to the ceiling and giving utterance to a whoop more like the war-cry of a red Indian than the exclamation of a Scottish Highlander. Then he blushed and apologised for his excitement, abashed by Manson's disapproving eyes.

"I tell you what it is, Mr. Manson, I'll make the roadbed of the old Burdock as good as you've made the Midland, and I'll——"

"Tut, tut!" said Manson, in his most unenthusiastic tone; "you can do nothing without money, and the Burdock's practically bankrupt. Be thankful if you receive your fifteen a week with reasonable regularity. Now, here is a letter to the Hon. Duffield Rogers. Give it to the doorman at the club, and Mr. Rogers will invite you in. You will find the president a humourous man and you have a touch of the same quality yourself; but repress it and treat him with the greatest respect, for humourists get along better with dull people like myself than with one another. Although you are leaving the jurisdiction of Mr. Blair, do not forget what I told you about paying attention to your clothes. You will be meeting important men whom you may have to persuade, and it is better to face them well groomed; a prepossessing appearance counts in business. Prepossession is nine points in the game. Here is the letter, so be off." The division superintendent rose and extended his hand. "And now, my boy, God bless you!"

The tone of the benediction sounded almost gruff, but there was a perceptible quaver underneath it, and after one firm clasp of the hand the divisional superintendent sat down at his desk with the resolute air of a man determined to get on with his work. As for John, he could not trust his voice, either for thanks or farewell; so he left the room with impetuous abruptness, and would have forgotten his hat if he had not happened to hold it in his hand.

To the ordinary man the Burdock Route was a badly kept streak of defective rails, rough as a corduroy road. To John Steele it was a glorious path to Paradise; an air line of tremendous possibilities. He went up and down its length, not in a private car, but on ordinary locals and freight trains. He became personally acquainted with every section foreman and with nearly every labourer between Warmington and Portandit, the western terminus. He found them, as a usual thing, sullen and inert; he left them jolly and enthusiastic, almost believing in the future of the road.

He proved an unerring judge of character. The useless men were laid off, while the competent were encouraged and promoted. He could handle a shovel with the best of them, or drive in a spike without missing a blow. In a year he had the Burdock Route as level as a billiard-table without extra expenditure of money, and travelers were beginning to note the improvement, so that receipts increased. He induced the Pullman Company to put an up-to-date sleeper on the night trains, east and west, and withdraw their antiquated cars hitherto in use.

But there was one thing Steele was not able to accomplish. He could not persuade the venerable president of the road to regard it as anything but a huge joke. The Hon. Duffield Rogers absolutely refused to leave his comfortable chair in the club and take a trip over the Burdock. The president delighted in Steele's company, and got him made a member of the club, setting him down as a graduate of the Wahoo University, which was supposed to exist somewhere in the remote West. Rogers was a privileged member and a founder of the club, so the committee did not scrutinise his recommendation too closely.

"It's no use, John," he would say, when his fervent assistant urged him to come and see what had been done on the Burdock. "Life is hard enough at best without my spending any part of it in a beastly place like Portandit. I hear you have done wonders with the road, but you can't accomplish anything really worth while with a route that has no terminus on the Atlantic. As long as you have to hand over your Eastern traffic to the Rock-ervelts at Warmington, and take what Western freight they care to allow you, you are in the clutch of the Rock-ervelts, and they can freeze you out whenever they like.=

```You may grade, you may ballast your road, if you will,

```But the shadow of Rockervelt's over you still."=

Thus Steele always received his discouragement from his own chief, and with most people this would ultimately have dampened enthusiasm; but John was ever optimistic and a believer in his work. One day he rushed into the club, his hat on the back of his head, and his eyes ablaze with excitement.

"Mr. Rogers, I've solved the problem at last!" he cried. "I tell you, well make the Burdock the greatest line in this country."

He shoved aside the heaps of magazines from the reading-room table and spread out a map on its surface. The Hon. Duffield rose slowly to his feet and stood beside the eager young man. A kindly, indulgent smile played about the lips of the aged president.

"Now see here!" shouted Steele (they were alone together in the room, and the "Silence" placard made no protest). "There's Beechville, on the Burdock Route, and here's Collins' Centre, on the C. P. & N. Between these two points are sixty-three miles of prairie country, as level as a floor. It will be the cheapest bit of road to build in America; no embankments, no cuttings, no grade at all. Why, just dump the rails down, and they'd form a line of themselves! Once the Burdock taps the C. P. & N., there is our route clear through to tide-water, independent of the Rockervelt System."

Steele, his face aglow, looked up at the veteran, but the indulgent smile had taken on a cynical touch. Mr. Rogers placed his hand on John's shoulder in kindly fashion and said slowly:

"If that were possible it would have been done long since. You could not get your charter. Rockervelt would buy the Legislature, and we in the West haven't money enough to outbid him."

Steele's clenched fist came down on the map with a force that made the stout table quiver.

"But I've got the charter!" he roared, in a voice that made the doorman outside think there was trouble in the reading-room. The Hon. Duffield Rogers sank once more into his arm-chair and gazed at John.

"You've got the charter?" he echoed quietly.

"Certainly, and it didn't cost me a cent. The Governor signed it yesterday."

"Out of the mouths of babes and sucklings—" murmured the old man, who had years of experience behind him in the bribing of law-makers. "In Heaven's name, how did you manage it?"

"I went to the capital, became acquainted with the legislators—splendid fellows, all of them—personal friends of mine now; I showed them how such a link would benefit the State, and the bill went through like that." John snapped his fingers.

"Well, I'm blessed!" ejaculated the old-time purchaser of valuable franchises.

"Now, Mr. Rogers, you understand financiering, and know all the capitalists. I understand the railway business. You raise the money, I'll build the road, and we'll be into New York with a whoop."

For one brief instant Steele thought he had conquered.

Like an old war-horse at the sound of the bugle, Rogers stiffened his muscles for the fight. The light of battle flamed in his eye as the memory of the conquest of millions returned to him. But presently he leaned back in his chair with a sigh, and the light flickered out.

"Ah, John!" he whispered plaintively, "I wish I had met you thirty years ago; but alas! you weren't born then. What a team we would have made! But I'm too old and, besides, your scheme wouldn't work. I might get up the money, and I might not. The very name of the Burdock is a hoodoo. But even if the money were subscribed and the link built, we would merely be confronted by a railroad war. The Rockervelts would cut rates, and the longest purse is bound to win, which means we should go to the wall."

Steele sat down with his face in his hands, thoroughly discouraged for the first time in his life. He felt a boyish desire to cry, and a mannish desire to curse, but did neither. The old gentleman rambled on amiably: "You are a ten-thousand dollar man, John, but your line of progress is on some road with a future. Follow my advice and take your charter to that old thief Rocker-velt himself. There lies your market."

"How can I do that," growled John from between his fingers, "when I am an employee of the Burdock?"

"Technically so am I; therefore, as your chief, I advise you to see Rockervelt."

"All right!" cried Steele, springing to his feet as if his minute of deep despondency had been time thrown away that could not be spared. He shook hands cordially with the president, and returned his genial smile.

## CHAPTER III—-WAYLAYING A MAGNATE

ON the steps of the club he was surprised to meet Philip Manson, who, he knew, rarely honoured that institution with his presence.

"I was just going up to see you, Mr. Manson. I want you to do me a favour. I'm off to New York, and I'd like a letter of introduction to Mr. Rockervelt."

The brow of the division superintendent knitted slightly, and he did not answer so readily as the other expected.

"Well, it's like this, Steele," he said at last: "I am merely a small official, and Mr. Rockervelt is an important man who knows his own importance. Etiquette prescribes that I should give you a letter to the general manager, who is the proper person to introduce you to Mr. Rockervelt. So, you see——"

"Oh, very well," exclaimed Steele, sorry he had asked. This rebuff, following so closely on the heels of his disappointment, clouded his usual good nature. He was about to go on, when Manson detained him, grasping the lapel of his coat.

"Don't be offended, John; and I'll tell you something no one else knows. I'm going to quit the railway business."

"What!" shouted Steele, all his old affection for the man surging up within him as he now noted the trouble in his face. Manson quit the railway business! It was as if he had calmly announced his intention to commit suicide.

"That old fool Blair has been making trouble for you?" he cried.

"Oh, no! That is to say, there always has been a slight tension, and it doesn't grow better. I've made a little money—real estate has risen, you know, and that sort of thing—and I've been working hard, so I intend to resign. I take it you have some scheme to propose to Mr. Rockervelt?"

"Yes, I have."

"Very well. Your scheme, if it is a good one, will prove your best introduction. He's an accessible man; but plunge right to the point when you meet him. He likes directness. And, by the way, he will be in Warmington on Wednesday morning. The big conference of railway presidents begins Thursday afternoon at Portandit, and he will be there, of course. We attach his private car to Number Three, Wednesday night, and your best time to see him might be in his car during the four miles he's running to the Junction. The express waits for him at the Junction. You haven't much time, but it will prove all the time he'll want to allow you if your project doesn't appeal to him."

"Say!" cried Steele, a thrill with the portent of a sudden idea, "couldn't you persuade Rockervelt to hitch his car to the Burdock 'Thunderbolt'? I'll run him through to Portandit, and save him that dreary daylight trip from Tobasco."

Manson shook his head.

"No; Mr. Rockervelt would not go over any other road than his own. I could not propose such a thing, and Mr. Blair would not."

Steele walked down to the Grand Union Station deep in thought. He had determined to take Rockervelt's private car from its place with one of his own pony engines and attach it to his own express, and he was formulating his plans. Once away from the Junction, the Government itself could not stop him. And now we need a railway map to explain the situation. From Warmington to Portandit or to Tobasco is a long night's ride. The "Thunderbolt" leaves the Junction on the Burdock Route at 8 p.m. The "Pacific Express," on the Midland, departs at 8.20; one train from the south side of the station, the other from the north.

At ten minutes to eight Philip Manson received a telephone message asking him to remain within call. A short time after, when the men were coupling the private car to the west-bound train, Steele rushed in to the telephone cabin and shouted:

"That you, Mr. Manson?"

"Yes; who are you?"

"Steele. I've just coupled Rockervelt's car to the 'Thunderbolt.' Release Number Three, for she will wait in vain. Telegraph all those people that Rockervelt was to meet at Tobasco to-morrow morning to take the midnight train for Portandit and meet him there."

"Steele, are you out of your senses?"

"No. It's all as I say. Nothing can stop us."

"I haven't the list of the men that——"

"Then call up Blair. He's in his private car on Number Three, which of course you know. You must get the list."

"John Steele, I implore you to stop before it is too late. This is an outrage. It's kidnapping—brigand's work. You are breaking laws that will——"

"I know, I know. Good night, Mr. Manson."

"Just one moment, John, I've something important to tell you. Mr. Rockervelt telegraphed to me——"

But the young man was proof against all blandishments, determined to go his own way, so he rang off before his friend could finish the sentence.

Steele rushed out to the platform, nodded to the waiting conductor, swung himself on the Pullman car, the conductor swung his lantern, and the "Thunderbolt" swung out into the night.

When the deft and silent negro had cleared away the breakfast dishes next morning and removed the tablecloth, Mr. Rockervelt leaned back in his chair and lit a cigar. There was much to think of, and he was thinking much. The car rolled along with gratifying smoothness, and the great man paid no attention to the scenery, otherwise he might have been startled, for he knew well the environment of his own line. As for the negro, all roads were alike to him, and he attended solely and silently to his master's comfort. He hovered about for a few moments, then said deferentially:

"Day's a gennelman, sah, in de sleepah ahead's been asking for you, sah, two or three times dis mawning, sah. He'd like to have some conversation with you, sah, if you's disengaged."

"Who is he?"

"Here's he's cawd, sah."

Mr. Rockervelt glanced at the card, murmuring: "John Steele, General Manager, Burdock Route. That's strange." Then aloud: "Show Mr. Steele in, Peter." The magnate did not rise as John bowed to him, but waved his hand toward a chair, a silent invitation of which his visitor did not avail himself. He recognized the great man at once from the many portraits he had seen of him.

"I hope you have slept well, Mr. Rockervelt," began the new-comer.

"Excellently."

"And I trust you found the road-bed in good order." Mr. Rockervelt raised his eyebrows and looked with some surprise at the polite inquirer before him.

"My own bed and the road-bed left nothing to be desired, since you are so kind as to ask."

"I am delighted to hear you say so, sir," cried John with enthusiasm. His host began to fear some demented person had got into his car, and he glanced over his shoulder for Peter, who was not visible.

"Why should you be delighted to hear me praise my own road?" he asked in tones that gave no hint of his uneasiness.

"Well, sir, to tell you the truth, I wished a few minutes' talk with you, and that's not as easy come by as you may think. You are not on your own road, but on the Burdock Route, now rapidly approaching Portandit. I took the liberty last night of attaching your car to this train, sir, instead of to your own Number Three."

Rockervelt sat up in alarm, glanced out of the windows, first on one side, then on the other. Bringing back his gaze to the man before him, hot anger added colour to the usual floridness of his countenance.

"You took the liberty, did you? Well, let me tell you, sir, it is a liberty you will bitterly regret."

"I am sorry to hear you say that, sir," replied John humbly.

"The liberty! Curse it, sir! you have disarranged all my plans. There are three men in Tobasco whom it is imperative I should meet this forenoon before the convention opens."

"Quite so, sir. I had them telegraphed to take the Midnight and meet you at Portandit instead. They'll be waiting for you when you get in, sir."

"The devil you did!" gasped Rockervelt, sinking back in his chair.

"You see, sir, it's an uneasy conference you would have had on that rocky road to Dublin, the T. and P. A long forenoon's ride, sir, with a line as rough as a rail fence. It would be like coming down the Soo Rapids, only you wouldn't travel so quickly. You are too good a railroad man, sir, not to hate a day journey, and I counted on that."

"It's a minor matter, but you happen to be right."

"I have a carriage waiting for you, sir. You can drive to your hotel at your ease, hold the conference in your room, and drop in to the convention whenever it pleases you, sir."

"Have you also arranged my return to New York, Mr. Steele? By what route do you intend to send me back?" John laughed that cheerful, infectious laugh of his. He realised that the danger point was passed.

"I hope you will get safe back to New York whatever route you take, sir."

"Thank you. How long have you been general manager of this road?"

"About two years, sir."

"Where did you learn the business?"

"In the greatest railroad school of this world, sir—the Rockervelt

System."

The faint shadow of a smile passed over the face of Mr. Rockervelt for the first time during the interview.

"That I take as a handsome return for my testimonial to your road-bed. Why did you leave us?"

"I failed to please Mr. Blair, sir."

"In whose department were you?"

"In the division superintendent's."

"Did you please Philip Manson?"

"I think I did, sir."

"Um! Well, now, you did not waylay me for the purposes of pleasant conversation. I don't like to see good men leave us; and if your object in kidnapping me was to come back to us, I may at once admit I am willing to entertain a proposal."

"No, sir. That was not my object, although I make bold to say that an offer from Mr. Rockervelt would exact respect from the greatest in the land, and I'm no exception to my betters. What I wanted, sir, was to persuade you to cast your eye over this map. The red line represents sixty-three miles of level country, and——"

"I see; if a railway were built along that red line, your road would have access to New York independent of me. Well, young man, don't let that red line worry you. I could not allow you to get a charter."

"You're quick to see the possibilities, sir."

"Yes, but here are no probabilities."

"I'm not so sure of that, sir. Like the other fellow's fifteen dollars, I've got the charter in my inside pocket."

"Do you mind showing it to me?" asked Rockervelt, unconsciously finishing the line of the song referred to. John handed him the documents, and the great man scrutinised them with the quick care of an expert; then he folded them up again, but did not offer to return them. He gazed out upon the flying landscape for a few moments while Steele stood expectant.

"How did you overcome Blair's opposition?" he inquired at last.

"There was no opposition."

The president frowned, and a glint of anger appeared in the cold, calculating eyes.

"I expect Blair to watch the Legislature as well as the railway."

"He watches neither, sir."

Rockervelt glanced sharply at the confident young man who thus dared to asperse one of the minor gods of the Rockervelt System.

"Then who looks after the Midland?"

"Philip Manson, and does it quietly and well."

"Where did you get the money to put this through? A syndicate?"

"No; I didn't need any money. All I needed was that one of your general managers, should be sound asleep, and time to make personal friends of the members of the House."

"I see you are prejudiced against Mr. Blair."

"I am, sir."

Rockervelt pulled himself together as one who has had enough of badinage and now prepares for business. His impassive face hardened, and the onlooker saw before him the man who had ruthlessly crushed opposition, regardless of consequences.

"Now, young man," he began, in a voice that cut like a knife, "do you know the value of these documents?"

"Yes, sir; they're not worth a damn!"

"What!" cried Rockervelt, suddenly sitting bolt upright. "I thought you had kidnapped me to hold me up, as is the genial Western fashion. Don't you want to sell this charter?"

"No, sir. I offered the charter to the Hon. Duffield Rogers, president of the Burdock, as was my duty, but he said you could beat any combination that might be formed in the long run."

"Yes, or in the short run. Sensible man, Rogers. Well, sir, you do not expect an exorbitant price for a worthless charter?"

"I want no price at all. The charter is yours. But I'd like to offer you a hint as well as the charter, and the advice is to make Philip Manson manager of the Midland."

"I see; and what for yourself?"

"Only bear me in mind when you have a vacancy for a well-paid official down east."

The young man had been standing during this long colloquy, but now Mr. Rockervelt asked him to be seated, and there being a suggestion of command as well as of request in his tone, John Steele, drew up a chair to the table that divided them.

"You have quite definitely made up your mind, I take it, that T. Acton Blair is unfit for the position of general manager of the Manateau Midland," said the chief with quiet irony.

"Yes, I have," replied Steele, defiantly, "and so has everybody else who knows him."

"And yet you admit the Midland is a well-managed road?"

"Certainly, but that is because of Philip Manson."

"Quite so. 'The page slew the boar; the peer had the gloire,' as the old poet said, and the peer, too, has the bigger salary, as a modern writer might remark. You never heard any reason given, I suppose, why Blair holds a better position than Manson?"

"Oh, yes, I did," cried the impetuous young man, "it is said that Mr. Blair is a relative of your own."

The expression of displeasure that clouded the face of the railway prince gave instant intimation to Steele that his reply had been tactless.

"I imagine you have a great deal to learn, Mr. Steele, and I predict before you are as old as Mr. Blair you will receive some sharp lessons in diplomacy. You have shown yourself competent to smooth out the roughnesses that formerly characterised the Burdock route, but those same capabilities may not be equal to removing obstacles in your own path of life. The Midland is a well-managed road, and you say the credit belongs to Manson. Very good. I put Manson in his place, and so my purposes are fulfilled. If I made him general manager, as you suggest, he might or might not be a success, yet we are both agreed that he is a success in his present position. Now you, I see by this card, are general manager of the Burdock route. Does the Burdock, therefore, take a high place in the railway system of America?"

"It does not," candidly admitted John Steele. "Why?"

"Because there is no money behind it."

"Exactly. My excellent friend, the Honorable Duffield Rogers, has plenty of money, but he knows enough to take care of it. He doesn't waste any of his wealth in trying to make the Burdock route all that his capable general manager may wish it to be. So you see, Mr. Steele, finance has to be considered as well as good road mending. In that department T. Acton Blair occupies a high position among the railway men of the West. If you ever accumulate a little money, and doubt my statement, venture your cash in a contest where Blair is your opponent, and, I venture to say, you'll regret it. On the other hand, if you should happen to become a friend of Mr. Blair, and he cared to give you a tip or two in higher finance, you may grow rich in following his lead. In this very matter of the charter there is a possibility that you have entirely underestimated the general manager of the Midland. It is on the cards that he agrees with you and me regarding the worthlessness of the charter."

"I'll swear he knew nothing about it," persisted Steele, knowing as soon as the sentence was uttered that again he had let his tongue run away with his judgment.

"Perhaps he did, and perhaps he didn't. I strongly suspect he knew all about it, and hoped you would entangle old Rogers into a railway war, in which case I venture to assert, Blair would have crushed both you and your chief. Of course you tried to get Rogers to take up the struggle?"

"Yes, I did."

"And he very politely, but quite definitely, refused?"

"That also is true."

"Well, you see, Mr. Steele," said Rockervelt, with something almost approaching a laugh, "there is more wisdom in grey hairs than most young persons are willing to admit. Would you be surprised if I told you that I have determined to ignore your advice, and so will not remove Mr. Blair from his position?"

"I am not in the least surprised, now that I know your opinion of him."

"Maybe then I can astonish you by admitting that I intend to remove your friend, Mr. Manson, from the situation he so worthily fills."

"To place him in a better position, I hope?"

"Oh, yes. I have been in need of him for some time in our New York office. I should have taken him long ago, if I'd had the right man to put in his place. The other day I received Philip Manson's resignation, and without either accepting or declining it, I telegraphed him to let me know whom he suggested as his substitute. Yesterday I received his reply, and although I have been unable to follow the advice you have tendered me so far, I may accept it regarding the new candidate."

With this Mr. Rockervelt pressed an electric button, and an alert young man answered his call.

"Meldrum, bring me that last letter of Manson's about the division superintendency of the Midland."

The secretary returned a moment later with the document, which he handed to Rockervelt, who tossed it across the table towards Steele. The letter read:

*Dear Sir:*

*In my opinion the best man to appoint as division superintendent of the Manateau Midland is John Steele, at present general manager of the Burdock route. He was formerly employed on the Midland in various capacities, and was promoted entirely through efficiency. Although the position he occupies on the Burdock is nominally higher than that left vacant by my resignation, yet I think Mr. Steele would be content with less honour and more money.*

*Yours faithfully,*

*Philip Manson.*

As Steele looked up from the reading of this letter Rockervelt said sharply:

"I think you are the man referred to by Manson?"

"Yes, sir."

"It is rather strange that you should have taken all the trouble to attach my car to your train when I had left word with Manson to get into communication with you, and arrange an interview between you and me at Portandit."

"I was merely anticipating your wishes, Mr. Rockervelt. It is lucky I rang off Philip Manson last night so abruptly at the telephone, for I imagine this is what he was about to tell me."

"How much are they giving you on the Burdock route?" asked Rockervelt abruptly.

"Fifteen dollars a week."

Instead of expressing his surprise at the smallness of the amount, Rockervelt merely said:

"Do you get your money?"

"Oh, I see to that," replied Steele with a laugh; "I am general manager, you know."

"What salary do you want to take Philip Manson's place?"

John Steele cast down his eyes, and meditated in silence for a few moments.

"Would fifty dollars a week be too much?" he asked in a tremor.

"It's rather a jump," said Rockervelt calmly, "but I think the organisation can stand it, if it is satisfactory to you."

"It is more than satisfactory to me," replied Steele, earnestly. He was to learn later that modesty was its own reward. He could as easily have had double the money, and perhaps more. Multi-millionaire as he was, however, Rockervelt was not the man to throw away needless cash.

"We will take that as settled," he said, and this ended the interview.

## CHAPTER IV—A CONSPIRACY

THE greatest blessing that Providence can bestow upon a young man is self-knowledge. Success comes to those who know their own powers while it is yet day. To learn for the first time at eighty that you have immense capabilities in any given direction is futile. To possess that knowledge at twenty is better than to own a gold mine. It is the old adage exemplified: "If age but could; if youth but knew."

Steele's two years' management of the Burdock route should have given him confidence, but his bargain with Rockervelt showed it had not done so. If he had been shrewd enough to allow Rockervelt himself to name the compensation that should have gone with his new position, he would have made a much better financial deal than that which he accomplished. If he had then added a little shrewd bargaining, he might have bettered himself still further, but John Steele had endured an early life of poverty, and the salary he now received seemed to him munificent.

The same qualities of under-estimation which caused Rockervelt to chuckle with satisfaction at a sharp bargain driven interfered with the young man's success as new division superintendent of the Midland. When he was duly installed, his immediate chief, T. Acton Blair, quaked. Blair was well acquainted with the ruthlessness of Rockervelt, and he trembled for his own position. He wondered how much Rockervelt knew. Was he aware of Blair's years of tyranny over the capable Philip Manson? Did he know how nearly the premier train of the road had come to being wrecked through the incompetence of a relative of his own, whom he had forced into the train despatched office in spite of the protests of Philip Manson? Now Manson was gone to New York, promoted to a position of greater power and influence than any he had hitherto held, and instead of Blair's being allowed to place some favourite in the vacant office, Rockervelt himself had intervened to appoint the very man who had saved the Pacific Express: a man whom Blair had practically dismissed two years before. If Blair possessed, as Rockervelt alleged, an acute brain in other directions than that of practical railway management, this brain was deeply perturbed when its owner, with overdone warmth, welcomed the new division superintendent of the Midland on his return to the great company. Innocent John Steele accepted this cordiality at its face value, and his own kind heart prompted him to let bygones be bygones, and to make the new condition of things as pleasant as possible for his nominal chief. At first this bewildered Blair; then he came to the conclusion it was merely deep craft on the part of the young man, and finally he reached the fact that Steele was quite honestly endeavouring to do his duty, and trying to please his superiors, a fact which a more alert mind would have assimilated months before. When, after weeks of doubt and fear, Blair at last realised that John Steele had in reality buried the tomahawk; that he had no knife concealed up his sleeve; that he was honest, straightforward and capable as his predecessor had been, the general manager felt like a man who had been taken advantage of. Instead of being thankful that his former fear was groundless, his resentment burned all the brighter, and he brought his genius for intrigue into play, determining to trip up the young man on the first favourable opportunity. But while he waited for that opportunity, he resumed the old tactics which had been so successful in pushing Philip Manson to a resignation, and proceeded to make John Steele's place as uncomfortable for him as possible. There is no tyranny like the tyranny of a coward, and before John Steele had been six months in his new position, he learned what it was to live under the heel of a despot.

Nor did he enjoy the consolation which must have sustained Philip Manson, who possessed the enthusiastic loyalty of his subordinates. Manson was a born master, who had risen step by step into the position of division superintendent. Added to this, he was quiet, taciturn and unemotional. John Steele, on the other hand, was the embodiment of good-fellowship; talkative, humourous, genial; who believed every one around him as honest and wholehearted as himself. But there were those beneath him who had regarded themselves quite properly in the line of promotion, and whose ambitions had been stirred when it became known that Philip Manson was about to retire. Then, to their chagrin and dismay, an outsider had been chosen for the place who, two years before, was little better than an office boy among them, and their friendliness for him at that time had been merely a tribute to his unfailing good nature; his willingness to help. This universal liking, however, was perhaps unconsciously tinged with contempt. Their feeling was rather admiration for a joyous soul than respect for a young fellow of talent. No one had an inkling of Steele's real merit except Philip Manson, and this silent man never volunteered information. When Blair wished Manson summarily to dismiss Steele, he got information he had not expected about the latter. When Rockervelt telegraphed regarding Manson's successor, he also received information, but Manson made no confidant of any of his subordinates, and perhaps if one of them had been shrewd enough to guess how good a man Steele was, that person might have been thought worthy of the recommendation which the former division superintendent had bestowed upon Steele.

When an insider is promoted, he not only steps into the vacant place, but the one beneath him advances to the position he formerly held, and so it goes down along the line, until the lowest grade is reached. Each man gets his little move upward, and universal joy is the result. But when an outsider is brought in, he stops the move as effectually as a jammed log arrests the progress of all the timber further up the stream. Although the genial John met smiling faces among his subordinates, there was nevertheless envy and hatred behind the smiles. Things began to go wrong; he could not give his orders explicitly enough to be sure that they would be understood. He met no open opposition, but the most annoying things happened in spite of all his precautions. A little harshness and injustice here would have acted as a tonic upon the whole clan. If he had flung out of the office the first man who misapprehended an order, whether that man were guilty or not, his path would have been smoother from that time forward; but here his own proneness to blame himself rather than to censure others was his worst enemy, and the office became honeycombed with negligence, apathy, incompetence and sullen insubordination. There was no sympathy to be expected from T. Acton Blair; in fact, the stout man saw with secret satisfaction that the division superintendent was not getting on. He would condole with Rockervelt on this regrettable failure next time he met him, instilling the poison very subtly, and assuming a tone of deep regret and disappointment. Meanwhile, his whole attitude towards the young man had changed. He was querulous and fault-finding; he magnified the failures, and slighted the successes. John Steele found himself between the upper and nether millstones that were grinding his nerves to rags. Day and night he worked like a Trojan to bring the necessary order out of the chaos that had somehow come to enshroud him, and underneath was the gnawing distrust of his own endowment properly to fill the place to which he had been appointed. He was working to the very limit of his powers, and preparing for himself an inevitable breakdown. He supplemented every one, instead of making every one supplement him. It never occurred to him that the chaos against which he contended was deliberate, for a railway business differs from any other on earth, in that carelessness or neglect is juggling with men's lives. A mistake comparatively innocent in any other branch of commercial activity may mean the massacre of a score of men and women on a railway. Many a night he sat disconsolate in his office when every one else had gone, and yearned for half an hour's talk with Philip Manson. The whole difficulty was not one which he could commit to writing, and even if he attempted that, he might fail in making Manson understand the situation; a situation so completely the reverse of that which had obtained during Manson's own reign. At last he determined to take a few days off, visit New York, and consult with his former chief. This brought about his first open conflict with T. Acton Blair, and then he weakly succumbed.

"Mr. Blair," he said one day, after the formal morning's interview was at an end, "I'm going to take a run down to New York."

"Oh, are you?" replied Blair. "For what purpose, may I ask?"

"I wish to talk with Philip Manson."

"About what?"

"Well, about a great many things; about the general situation here, for instance."

"Offhand, I should say I am the proper person to consult on such a subject," said Blair, with some acidity.

"Of course," replied Steele, mildly, "but you see, Man-son was my predecessor. He has probably been through what I am going through now, and I should like a few hints from him."

"Who is to fill your place while you are away?"

"Johnson could do that."

"Do you think he is competent?"

"Oh, quite competent."

"Then can you explain why Mr. Rockervelt put you in the place of Manson, if Johnson was capable of filling it?"

"You had better ask that question of Mr. Rockervelt," suggested Steele, his temper rising.

"I shall certainly do so if you leave your post. You are either necessary here or you are not. If you begin to suspect that you are not the man for the position, then you should resign."

"I am the man for the position, Mr. Blair; still, even the best of men, which I do not pretend to be, needs a little advice now and then, and I intend to seek it from Philip Manson."

"A man who knows his business neither seeks nor acts on advice. If you go to New York you go in spite of my prohibition, and I shall take your departure as an act of resignation, and proceed accordingly. I am either general manager of this road or I am not."

Now this latter phrase was one which Blair was exceedingly fond of using, and it had done duty several times during Philip Manson's régime, who had invariably shown Mr. Blair in exceedingly few words that, when it came to the point, he was not the autocrat he pretended to be. Manson would have made an excellent poker-player. He could have been beaten by better cards, but never by a bluff, and Blair's pet phrase was pure bluff.

"Oh, very well," said John Steele, rising and leaving the table, while his opponent raked in the chips. Steele did not know he had reached the climax where a determined answer would have given him the game, nor did he realise how disastrous was his defeat. A poltroon is a bad man to run away from.

John Steele retreated to his own room, and a sweet smile overspread the chubby face of the corpulent man he had left victorious. A week later came the second encounter, which although it carried a second apparent defeat for John Steele, proved, nevertheless, to be the most important turning point of his life.

The division superintendent entered the general manager's room with a telegram in his hand. Blair, looking up, noticed the agitation of his manner, and the paleness of his face.

"Mr. Blair, I have just received a telegram which says that my uncle is dying. I wish to go to him, and intend to leave by to-night's train. He lives in the north of Michigan. I have therefore come to let you know that I shall be absent for a few days, perhaps."

Blair continued to gaze at him with a winning smile on his cherubic face.

"Would it not be a simpler matter, Mr. Steele, if you were to write to Philip Manson, and ask him to take a trip to his old home? You are a member of his club, I understand, and could quite readily hold your conference there if either of you did not care to discuss the state of affairs in this office."

"I don't understand what you mean, Mr. Blair."

"Oh, yes, you do. The dying uncle device, or the funeral of a relative device, have all been tried upon me before. I am proof against such schemes, and really, Mr. Steele, I paid you the compliment of believing you to be more original."

"Do you think I am lying to you?" asked John indignantly, taking a step nearer the general manager's table.

"We don't call it lying, Mr. Steele; we may term it diplomacy, or what you like. A week ago you requested leave of absence to consult Philip Manson. I refused my permission. Now you come to me with the story of a dying relative. I am bound to believe you, although I made a friendly suggestion a moment since which apparently you do not intend to accept, so we will get back to the original situation. Your uncle is very ill, and I am very sorry. There are doubtless at this moment many excellent persons in extremity, yet nevertheless the trains of the Midland must run, and even if Mr. Rock-ervelt or myself were removed to a better land, not a wheel would cease turning on our account. Therefore, hoping you will accept the expression of my deep sympathy, which I hereby tender to you, I must nevertheless refuse to allow the office of division superintendent to remain vacant for one hour."

"But this is the only relative I have in the world," protested John, earnestly. "Here is the telegram I have received. Read it for yourself."

Mr. Blair, still smiling, waved his stout hand gently to and fro, but refused even to glance at the paper laid before him.

"I do not doubt in the least that the despatch comes from Michigan. I can even guess that it is worded in the most urgent terms, and that the signature is perfectly genuine. Nevertheless, Mr. Steele, it is better we should understand each other. As I told you a week ago, if you leave your position without my permission you will find that position permanently filled on your return. This is a free country, and you are entitled to go or stay as you please. If you hand me in your resignation, as your predecessor did, I shall say to you as I said to him, 'Go, and prosperity be with you,' but while you are a member of my staff, you are under my orders. Do I make myself sufficiently plain?"

"Yes, you do," replied John Steele, picking up his telegram and leaving the room.

Once more at his own desk he sat there for a long time with his head in his hands. At first it was his determination to resign forthwith. The situation was growing as intolerable for him as it had been for his predecessor, but the longer he thought over what had happened the more he realised the impossibility of surrender. If he resigned now, he left the Rockervelt system a failure. He would be compelled to begin at the foot of the ladder again, handicapped by practical dismissal; to strive as an unsuccessful man, his years of experience counting for nothing. But even if that consideration did not harden his resolution to remain where he was, the thought of his uncle would alone have been sufficient to turn the balance. Bitterly he accused himself of his neglect of the old man who, as he had just said, was his only relative on earth. While he was escaping from the hopeless poverty in which they had both lived, the struggle for existence had become so interesting that it had obliterated the fact that Dugald Steele was still where he had left him, and not a penny of money had the young man ever forwarded to him. Up to the time his salary was made fifty dollars a week he had not only saved no money but had run into debt. These obligations were now liquidated, and he had a few hundreds in the bank; the nucleus, he hoped, of more to follow. The old man had brought him up, after a fashion, allowing him to go to school during the winter months, but every waking hour the uncle forced the nephew to work almost beyond the limit of his youthful powers, and at last had driven him forth with blows and cursings during one of those periodical fits of temper which had made Dugald Steele a terror to the neighbourhood. One letter, indeed, John had written to his old home, when he got his situation at Hitchen's Siding, but that had remained unanswered, and he had taken it for granted that his uncle's anger was permanent. Nevertheless, the telegram showed that the uncle had kept the letter, or remembered the address, for the despatch had been sent to Hitchen's Siding, and from there forwarded to John Steele's office in Warmington.

However, there was little profit in bemoaning a state of things he could not remedy. It was certain that Blair would carry out his threat, if Steele left his place without permission, so there was nothing for it but to sit tight.

With a deep sigh the young man pulled himself together, drew toward him a sheet of paper and wrote a letter that proved to be more important than its wording would have led a casual reader to suspect.

## CHAPTER V—A FAVOURITE OF FORTUNE

DUGALD STEELE cordially hated his neighbours, and evinced little hesitation in telling them so, whenever opportunity offered. He lived apparently in the depths of extreme poverty, occupying a dilapidated wooden, unpainted house at the northern outskirts of the village of Stumpville, Michigan. He kept no servant, but cooked his own meals, and if any trespassers dared to set foot on his property, he threatened them with a shotgun. He was a cantankerous, crabbed old Scotsman, snarling like an unowned dog, and going about in shabbier clothes than the most ragged tramp that had ever honoured Stumpville with his fleeting presence.

Dugald and his younger brother Neil, the latter then newly married, came out of the highlands of Scotland to the lowlands of Michigan. It was not that the life in the American backwoods was harder than life in the northern part of Scotland, but the hardships were different, and they affected the health of the young wife; she died because of a falling tree—a tree she had never seen, and whose final crash she had not heard. Her husband was felling oaks in the forest, and one of them lodged in the branches of another, resting there at an angle of forty-five degrees. Neil, unaccustomed to forestry in its gigantic American form, not knowing the danger he ran, set himself to chop down the impediment, when the half-fallen tree suddenly completed its descent and crushed him, face downward and lifeless, into the forest mould. To the elder brother fell the grim task of chopping through the fallen timber and rolling the log from off the dead man. The wife died from the shock, and their little boy was left to the care of his taciturn uncle.

No one is alive who knew Dugald Steele in his youth, and so none can tell what early experiences may have warped his character. Perhaps the stinging poverty of those days gave him an exaggerated idea of the necessity of hoarding money; perhaps the tragic death of his brother, whose rude coffin he made with his own hands from slabs of the tree that killed him, crushed out his natural affections instead of ripening them; but, be that as it may, he was, during the latter part of his life, a hard man, whom no tale of pathos could move into the expenditure of a penny; a gnarled, cross-grained, twisted specimen of humanity from whom all emotion, except that of hatred, seemed to have departed.

When he died a will was found leaving all his property to a neighbouring town simply, as he said in the document, written by his own hand to save a lawyer's fee, that he might wreak posthumous revenge upon his neighbours, who would understand, now that it was too late, what they had missed by not being decent to him. But this will was invalidated by a later one, which shows how a man with a kind heart may sometimes do well for himself when he little understands what he is about.

Nemesis comes to all of us, and it is strange that it should have rested on old Dugald, as the result of the hard, honest work in his young days. Seeing no smoke from his chimney, a kindly woman neighbour, with fear and trembling, penetrated to his dwelling, and found him knotted on the floor with rheumatism, snarling and waspish as ever, but helpless. The woman ran for assistance, and he was lifted into his bed, where he lay when the doctor came, while the old man protested that he had no money to pay him, and would not pay him if he had. The doctor, however, did the best he could for him, and told the neighbours that the old man was stricken with his last illness, which indeed proved to be the case. The doctor said to his patient that if he had any relatives he wished to see he had better send for them, offering to write if the old man gave him an address. All his life Dugald Steele had distrusted medical advice, but it is likely that on this occasion something within him corroborated the verdict which had been passed upon him. He lay there for a long time in silence, the doctor waiting, and at last said, in a hoarse whisper, that he would like his nephew to know he was ill, giving the address as John Steele, Hitchen's Siding; but, he added, with a return of his cantankerousness, that the doctor was to tell his nephew he need not come unless he wanted to. The doctor at his own cost sent a telegram, and late that night received a long answering despatch from John Steele which deplored the impossibility of the sender's going to Stumpville at that time, begged that no expense should be spared in getting the old man what comforts he needed, and concluded by saying that a check for a hundred dollars had been posted to the physician for the purpose indicated.

The young man knew his uncle well enough to be aware that if he sent the money direct to him, that miserly person would hoard it, rather than spend a penny on whatever necessities he required. He also knew the delight his uncle experienced in handling money, so when he sent the letter he enclosed two crisp new ten-dollar bills.

*My Dear Uncle,—he wrote,—I am deeply grieved to hear from the doctor of your illness and sincerely hope it is not serious. I would come to you at once if I could, but, alas, there is over me a severe taskmaster who refuses me even a day's leave, yet my position here is so good that I dare not jeopardise it by absenting myself without permission, for if I lose my job I lose also the chance of assisting you. Please accept the twenty dollars which I send you, and get for yourself whatever you may need. Procure the best physician in the place, and a nurse. I will send you more money right along, and if it is not enough, refer creditors to my employers, and they will, I think, guarantee that I can pay any debt you may incur. Please do not stint yourself, but order what you want, or whatever the physician thinks you should have, and do not imagine that the spending of money will leave me short, for I have several hundred dollars in a bank, and will send it to you as you require it. So, dear uncle, keep up a good heart and take every care of yourself.—Your loving Nephew.*

The woman sitting at the bed-head read this letter to the old man, wondering if he was paying attention, for his eyes were closed. Presently she saw a tear trickle down his withered cheek and she thought his heart was softening, but the first remark he made did not seem to verify that conclusion.

"Give me the money," he demanded in a harsh whisper.

The bills were handed to him, and his long, yellow fingers, like talons, closed avariciously upon them; lingeringly dwelling on their smooth texture, thumb and finger rubbed them up and down. His next remark was more encouraging.

"Read the letter again," he said, and the woman did so, although anger was in her heart that affection should be wasted upon one so unworthy. There was a long silence after she had finished the second reading, and at last she asked him:

"Shall I send for another doctor?"

"No," growled the old man, "doctors can do me no good. Go and tell Lawyer Strathmore I want to see him. Tell him I have just received twenty dollars, else he won't come."

The lawyer came on the strength of the woman's assurance that the money had arrived, and on his return to his office his partner said: "Well, what struck the old Highlander? Wanted to make his will, I suppose. I hope he hasn't left his ancient suit of clothes to me."

"Oh, he's gone clean crazy," replied Strathmore, "but I secured ten dollars all right enough, so it doesn't matter. He seems to think he owns Michigan. Two hundred thousand dollars Michigan Central Railway stock are deposited in the vaults of the Wayne County Savings Bank. Seventy-nine thousand dollars Northern Pacific stock deposited somewhere else. Cash in the bank over thirty thousand dollars—amounting all in all to something like three hundred thousand dollars, which is left to a nephew of his, a railway man on the Manateau Midland."

"By Jove, Strathmore," cried the partner, who had been a newspaper man in his youth and saw a sensation in this, "I wouldn't take my oath that it isn't all right. He's just the sort of a dilapidated old miser who would turn out to be a rich man."

"Impossible," said Strathmore.

"Improbable, perhaps, but a telegram to Detroit would soon let us know."

And it did let them know. The inhabitants of Stumpville learned next morning that an old man had died in one of their most ruinous shanties who could have bought and sold each of them, and all of them combined.

When the telegram came announcing his uncle's death John Steele rose from his desk, locked the door, and paced up and down the room with bent head. He had not expected this outcome, for although his uncle was old, he had weathered so many gales, it had not occurred to the young man that there must come one storm which would lay the gnarled old oak level with the ground. Unavailingly did he regret that a consideration for his own position had kept him from the bedside. With a sigh he stopped his walk, pulled himself together, sat down at his desk, and wrote a brief note to Blair, saying he had just received a telegram informing him of the death of his uncle; that he intended to start by the next train for Michigan, and would put Johnson temporarily in his place. He might be gone as long as three days, but anything addressed to Stumpville would find him. Pinning the telegram to this, and folding up the documents, he sealed them into an envelope addressed to T. Acton Blair, and sent the letter by a messenger to the general manager's room. He knew that official was in his office, but until the time John took his train there came no response to his note. He called in Johnson, and briefly placed him in transient command. The young man received his appointment with a smug satisfaction that he found it impossible quite to conceal, and although his departing chief noticed this, he made no comment upon it.

During his journey to Stumpville John Steele meditated upon his plan of campaign. The sense of injustice he had felt ever since Blair refused him permission to visit his uncle was now crystallised into a determination to use the iron gauntlet rather than the velvet glove in future. Naturally he was of a conciliatory disposition, but the exercise of forbearance had resulted in failure and disorganisation. The next move lay with the general manager. If Blair persisted in dismissing him, he would appeal to Cæsar, for Cæsar himself had placed him in the position he held.

Arriving at Stumpville, he went direct to the telegraph office, and found awaiting him a despatch which, he was well aware without opening it, came from the general manager; no one else knew his address. The fact that he telegraphed instead of sending a messenger to his room in the same building, which he had had ample time to do, seemed to Steele the first sign of weakness. Blair wished to settle this matter at long range. Tearing open the envelope he read: "I am amazed that you should have left your post without at least personal consultation with me. I have made your appointment of Johnson permanent, but will hold his former office open for you unless you decline to accept it."

Steele smiled grimly as he read these words. They showed that Blair had not the courage definitely to dismiss him. The general manager was afraid to burn his bridges behind him, hoping possibly that Steele would telegraph his resignation or his indignant refusal of the subordinate position.

Before leaving the city, John Steele had withdrawn from the bank several hundred dollars in order that he might pay any debts his uncle had contracted, and in order also that his funeral should be as imposing as if the old man had been the leading citizen of the place. Then to his amazement he learned that Dugald Steele had made him comparatively a rich man, but this independence made no difference in Steele's projects for the future. He liked work for its own sake, and he was particularly attached to the duty which chance and good fortune had assigned to him. He was not going to allow that task to be interfered with by a pompous wind-bag like T. Acton Blair, and much less so by a gang of undisciplined subordinates who needed to hear the crack of the whip over their heads.

On the journey back to the city, however, a germ of thought formed in his mind, for the present to lie dormant, but in the future to develop into marvellous things, watered by circumstance, fertilised by disaster. Pondering on the strange, almost repulsive character of the old miser who was gone, it occurred to John Steele that mere hoarding could never have produced the sum of money he had accumulated. In his uncle's mental equipment there must have been a shrewd understanding of the world's affairs, of which he secretly took advantage to his own enrichment. Quite unsuspected by his neighbours this recluse had played a game of finance that proved marvellously successful. This could not have been done in Stumpville. Dugald Steele had evidently worked through a broker in some large city, and John Steele began to wonder if he, too, had inherited this seventh sense of money-making which has produced those bulky unearned fortunes for which America is celebrated or notorious.

John resolved to watch the markets in future and learn some of the rules of the game; then he would venture in a small way, so that it did not matter whether he won or lost, and thus put his suspected hereditary abilities to the test. He was very sure from what he remembered of his uncle that the cautious old man had never plunged blindly into speculation. Unless he was very much mistaken, there had been nothing of the gambler about Dugald Steele. He surely amassed his wealth because of a well-informed belief in the continued progress of his adopted country, placing his money here and there where he believed it would secure the advantage of a rise in values. Thus the glow lamp of sweet reasonableness shed its mild rays upon the entrance of a path new to John Steele; a path which offered alluring vistas, but led into a wild and dangerous country—the path of speculation.

When Steele opened the door of the division superintendent's room, Johnson, seated in the division superintendent's chair, whirled round abruptly with the frown of high authority on his brow, apparently annoyed that any one should have taken the liberty of entering without knocking.

"Ah, Steele, it's you, is it?" cried Johnson airily, neglecting to prefix the word "Mr." which he would have used a week before. "How-d'e-do, how-d'e-do? When did you get back?"

"My train arrived just three minutes ago," replied John Steele calmly. He closed the door behind him, and stood there, while Johnson remained seated, palpably uneasy, evidently determined to carry off the situation with an air of bonhomie. Mentally he had no doubt rehearsed it several times during the past few days, but the man now confronting him was not the anxious, worried individual who had left the chair he continued to sit in, or the genial, good-humoured youth of former years. For the first time in their intercourse Johnson saw before him the stern demeanour of one in authority, and inwardly he quaked, though outwardly he endeavoured to maintain the guise of airy indifference which appeared fitting for the encounter.

"You received Mr. Blair's telegram, I suppose?" said Johnson at last, becoming more and more embarrassed by the frigid silence. Somehow the crisis was not evolving exactly as he had pictured it. He was de facto division superintendent, yet somehow this new, quiet man before him did not appear to recognise his elevation.

"Everything has gone right since I left, I take it; otherwise I should have heard from you," remarked Steele, ignoring the question just put to him.

"Oh, yes," said Johnson, "everything has gone smoothly. Look here, Steele," cried Johnson in a burst of candour, "why didn't you reply to the old man's telegram? You know how touchy he is on questions of discipline. He very generously offered you the position I held, and you didn't even take the trouble to acknowledge his kindness. I can assure you, John, it has been all I could do to keep the old man from promoting Car-ruthers into my place, but I succeeded in persuading Mr. Blair to take no further steps until you returned. I said I was sure you would have some satisfactory explanation to offer."

"You were quite right; I have. And now, Mr. Johnson, you will reap the reward of your own kindness. The place you have so generously kept open for me I take pleasure in bestowing upon you; but in return for the counsel you have been good enough to give me, I warn you that unless I get a little better service than has been rendered for some months past you will not hold the position."

Johnson threw back his head and laughed loudly.

"Steele, my dear boy, that's a good bluff, but it won't work. I have been made division superintendent by the general manager of this road. Mr. Blair and myself have both been very patient over your unauthorised desertion of your post, but I tell you frankly that my patience is at an end. I offer you the position which I formerly held. If you do not at once accept it, I shall call Car-ruthers in and give him the vacant place."

"Do," said John Steele.

Johnson's hand hovered over the electric button, but he forbore to press it, looking anxiously toward the impassive man who had made such a curt reply to his threat.

"I dislike exceedingly to call Carruthers. I want to give you every chance,

Steele."

"That is very good of you, but don't hesitate on my account. I may say, however, that if you touch that button, or issue any further orders in this room, you will automatically have dismissed yourself from the service of the Midland Road."

"Oh, that's it, is it? You're going to show fight, are you? I'll very quickly convince you that you haven't the slightest chance of winning. I have behind me the general manager of this road, and he has the owners of the system behind him. If you bring on an unnecessary contest, in which you have no possibility of victory, I shall then not allow you to be employed on this line, even in the meanest capacity."

"I quite understand, Mr. Johnson, that either you or I must leave. Now, press the button, and make your promotion without further talk."

All this time Johnson's hand had been hesitating over the ivory knob. It trembled slightly, but at last it took the plunge, and made the signal. Presently there came a knock at the door, and James Carruthers entered, glancing uncertainly from Steele to Johnson, apparently undecided whom he should first address. Johnson's voice was extremely urbane, and it brought joy to the heart of his former colleague.

"Carruthers," he said, "you will now take my place in the other room, and with your new position I am happy to say there will be an addition to your salary."

"Thank you, Mr. Johnson," replied Carruthers, very humbly, meanwhile glancing timidly at the silent man standing there. Perhaps James Carruthers would have been more certain of his promotion had John Steele made the announcement. The latter's kind heart was not proof against this mute appeal, and a smile came to his lips as he said: "Have no fear, Carruthers. It gives me great pleasure to sanction your appointment. Now, just step around to Mr. Blair's room, and ask him to come here for a moment."

"You will do nothing of the sort, Carruthers," cried Johnson truculently, springing to his feet with clenched fist. It was neck or nothing now, and he knew it. "I am division superintendent, and in this room you take orders from no one but me."

Poor Carruthers stood with his hand on the door knob, wishing himself safely back in his own room, while Johnson took a determined step toward him, seeing the youth's hesitation, and resolved to overcome it in his own favour. Then a quite unimportant incident happened which caused him to face the other way, and to feel that somehow he had lost a point in the game. Without any hurry John Steele had seated himself in the division superintendent's chair. Steele, momentarily ignoring both commander and commanded, rang a bell at the private telephone which communicated with the general manager's room, and placed the receiver at his ear.

"Is that you, Mr. Blair? This is John Steele. I have just returned, and I want you to step round to my room, as I wish to make a rather important communication."

There was a momentary pause, and so intensely still did the room become that the two men standing there looking at John Steele could hear the indefinite murmur of the voice coming over the telephone.

"No," said Steele firmly, "the conference must take place in this room, and it must take place now. Otherwise the complaint I have to make against you will go by telegraph direct to Mr. Rockervelt, and I shall leave by to-night's train for New York."

Again there was a pause, and a ghostly suggestion of a whisper. Then Steele said: "Oh, I am not on the war-path at all. In fact, such is my deep respect for yourself that it rests entirely with you to say whether there will be a war-path or not. Personally I see no necessity for it. Just step round, and we'll talk it over in the most amicable way. Yes, Johnson's here." With that Steele hung up his receiver, swung round on the swivel chair, the usual winning smile on his lips as he met the gaze of two very anxious young men. His voice, however, was sharp enough when he spoke.

"Carruthers, clear out," whereupon Carruthers opened the door and disappeared as if by magic.

"Johnson, sit down. You are just about to learn a lesson on the value of all this backing of which you have been boasting."

Before Johnson could either accede to the request or disobey it the door opened and the stout gentleman entered. There was a severe frown on his brow intended to denote resolute strength, but an expression of uncertainty in his lower face which hinted at weakness.

Steele waved his hand amiably toward a deep leather-covered easy chair, and into its luxurious folds the fat man sank, drawing forth a handkerchief, which he passed across his brow, and somehow the action appeared to obliterate the frown.

"You said in your telegram, Mr. Blair, that I was in fault because I left without personally consulting with you, but I think you will forgive my error when you remember that having applied for permission to leave when my uncle was dying, and being refused, it would have been futile for me to appear before you with proof of his death and a further request for leave of absence. You would have been bound in consistency to refuse, while I was equally determined to attend my uncle's funeral. If you disbelieved my words when I told you he was dying, you could not have so stultified yourself as to credit the news of his death."

"I did not disbelieve your word," protested Blair, timorously.

"I understood you to do so. If you did not, then your action was at once cruel and tyrannical. However, that is past and done with, so we will say no more about it, unless you choose that it should come up later on. Now, I may inform you that my late uncle has left me a legacy that approximates three hundred thousand dollars. As the interest on this, even at one per cent, is more than I receive as division superintendent of the Midland, you will easily understand that I do not retain my position merely from mercenary motives. I am to-day in a position of independence which makes the outcome of any struggle we may engage in a matter of perfect indifference to me."

"I am happy," said Blair, again mopping his brow, "to be the first of your old colleagues to congratulate you on your improved prospects. John Jacob

Astor once said that a poor man with a hundred thousand dollars might make a fortune in this country. Although times have changed since then, still, a poor man with three times that amount has numerous opportunities denied to more poverty-stricken individuals. As for the struggle you speak of, I really see nothing on earth that either of us would gain by engaging in it."

"I am quite at one with you there, sir, and indeed you will find me the least belligerent of individuals if I but get my own way, which I intend to insist on hereafter, so far as my immediate department is concerned. While I have no fear of the struggle I suggested, neither have I any desire to engage in it. You see, Mr. Blair, you would be too severely handicapped from the start to give you a chance. Your task would be to show that Mr. Rockervelt is a fool, while all I should need to do would be to prove that he is the wisest of men. You are too shrewd a judge of human nature to doubt the outcome of such a contest. Mr. Rockervelt prides himself on two things. First, the unerringness of his judgment regarding men; second, the excellence of his various roads, and he reaches the second by means of the first. Now, he placed me in this chair. If he had wished you to choose the occupant, he would have delegated that duty to you. If he had desired the estimable Mr. Johnson here, he would not have had the slightest hesitation in enlisting Mr. Johnson's co-operation. Now, if you stood to gain anything by forcing a hopeless issue I could comprehend your attitude, but anything you wish you can have through good will, so where is the use of coercion or of a fight?"

"I assure you, my dear Mr. Steele, that I have no desire whatever to bring on a fight. I have said so all along."

"Very well, Mr. Blair, there's no more to be said, and I predict you will find me the most deferential, accommodating subordinate that ever worked in your office."

"But where do I come in?" ejaculated the panic-stricken Johnson, whose face had become paler and paler as this colloquy went on.

"My dear sir, you don't come in," said John Steele urbanely. "I told you that at the beginning, when I counselled you not to enter a contest where you were bound to be the loser. I commend to you in future the sensible attitude assumed by Mr. Blair."

"Mr. Blair," persisted Johnson, "you appointed me division superintendent, and assured me you would stand by that appointment."

"Oh, well," explained Blair, "you see how it is yourself. I did so under an entire misapprehension. I thought that Mr. Steele had openly defied my authority, which I now understand was not the case. Am I right in that, Mr. Steele?"

"Perfectly right, sir. I had no desire to impugn your authority, and I apologise for my abrupt action, which certainly bore that complexion."

"There, Johnson," said Blair, almost pleadingly, "you must see that puts a different face on the matter entirely."

It certainly put a different face on Johnson, who stood there with dropped jaw, gazing pitifully at his backboneless chief.

"I am very sorry there has been any misunderstanding," said Blair soothingly. "Such, of course, occurs in all offices, but luckily discipline is so perfect here that a few words will adjust things in their right proportion to each other. You have done very well, Mr. Johnson, during your short occupancy of this room, and when you resume your old place you may be certain that both Mr. Steele and myself will remember you when a chance for promotion occurs."

"I regret to say," remarked Steele casually, before Johnson had an opportunity of speaking, "that Mr. Johnson's last act during his temporary occupancy of this chair was to promote Carruthers into his vacant place, and this promotion I myself confirmed. I recommend Mr. Johnson to take a vacation for a month, and if during that period he secures another situation, I shall be happy to recommend him, and probably you, Mr. Blair, would not object to do the same."

"Certainly not, certainly not," muttered Blair hastily. "If, at the end of a month," continued John Steele, "you have not suited yourself, Mr. Johnson, you may return to me, and I'll see what I can do for you. I am going to rearrange my staff, and give most of its members a step upward. Some of them, however, will take a step downward, and some will be promoted over the heads of their seniors. All this will require a little thought and manipulation, but, as Mr. Blair truly says, discipline is everything, and I am determined to carry out his wishes in that respect."

"Well, Mr. Steele," said the general manager, rising with a deep sigh of satisfaction, as if everything had gone exactly as he planned it, "anything I can do to help on the good work will not be stinted. Call upon me when in any difficulty, Mr. Steele, and be assured of my most whole-hearted support," and with that the great man held out his hand, which Steele, springing to his feet, clasped cordially. Without a glance at the crest-fallen Johnson, T. Acton Blair strode majestically from the room.

John Steele turned to his desk.

"May I have a word with you, Mr. Steele?" asked Johnson.

"Yes, this day month," said John Steele without looking up.

## CHAPTER VI—"THERE'S NOTHING HALF SO SWEET IN LIFE"

JOHN STEELE now entered upon a period of his life which was most interesting and enjoyable. The numerous petty and annoying incidents which had heretofore been the cause of friction between himself and his numerous subordinates disappeared as the mist fades before the rising sun, and he found himself at the head of as willing and energetic a staff as any man could wish to have co-operate with him. With his chief even the most captious of men could have no fault to find, and Steele was far from being captious. T. Acton Blair seemed a changed man. No one could be more genial and considerate. He even drifted into the habit of calling his division superintendent "John." Their business conferences were of an exceedingly friendly and amiable character, and yet John frequently censured himself when he detected deep down in his own nature remnants of distrust still lingering regarding his urbane superior. Once when Blair was gone rather longer than usual on a visit to New York, some inquiries that came through caused him to surmise that Blair was undermining him at headquarters, but on Blair's return John felt rather ashamed of himself. That good man had indeed mentioned him to the powers that be, but the mention had been entirely to his advantage, with the result that John got ten dollars a week added to his salary, quite unsolicited. Blair almost apologised for his action, saying by way of excuse that the road was really getting so prosperous, and had been so free from disaster ever since Steele had joined it, that Rockervelt was pluming himself on having chosen the right man once again.

"By the way," said Blair casually, "Mr. Rockervelt informed me he had read in the newspapers of your windfall. He asked me in what your money was invested, but I was unable to tell him."

"Most of it is in railway stocks," replied Steele.

"Ah, that would have interested him. Are any of the Rockervelt stocks in your safe deposit vault?"

John laughed.

"No, I don't think I possess a single share, even in the Manateau Midland. Perhaps it wouldn't be a bad idea to make a transfer."

"Oh, I don't know," replied Blair, impartially. "Unless a man is a professional speculator he generally loses in transferring his stock from one interest to another. The broker usually gets a slice when this happens. Still, I am sure Mr. Rockervelt would be rather pleased to hear that you own stock in the Midland. He encourages that sort of thing, especially among his higher officials, imagining quite rightly, perhaps, that they are just a leetle more careful if they are part owners of the road they operate. I think it's a very good idea, myself; still, at the present moment all the Rockervelt lines are booming, and I don't know any investment I could more cordially recommend. Still, I'm prejudiced in the matter, so don't let what I say influence you in the least. But if you should buy a block of Midland, for instance, I wish you'd let me know, so that when I am next in New York I can answer Mr. Rockervelt's former question. It certainly wouldn't do you any harm with Rockervelt, and there's no better security on the market."

The newspapers had made much of John Steele's luck in falling heir to a considerable sum of money. The circumstances and unexpected nature of the legacy gave the item a semi-sensational value which was not neglected by the reporters, and even if the amount was in many cases exaggerated, the reputation of being a wealthy man revealed an entirely new world to the young superintendent—the world of social life. He was taken up by society with a warmth that was peculiarly gratifying to so modest a man as John Steele, and for this taking-up T. Acton Blair was largely responsible. On two or three occasions he invited John to dinner, where the young man met many delightful people. He now saw a side of Blair that had heretofore been entirely hidden from him, and, in spite of Rockervelt's former warning, quite unsuspected. Blair as a host was one of the most charming of men; debonair and polite as a Frenchman; a very prince of good fellows. His house was a veritable palace, and when first John was ushered into the midst of its magnificence, it seemed scarcely credible that a young nobody like himself, but a few years past occupying a miserable position on the railway in the prairies, should actually have browbeaten and defeated the owner of all this wealth.

Blair evinced no rancour over this defeat, and Steele esteemed him a human nettle, dangerous only when timorously handled. Steele was too shrewd a man not to have recognised that he had discovered the weak spot in Blairs armour, which was a fixed aversion against being brought into conflict of any kind with the great Rockervelt, and this knowledge gave the young man assurance that his position on the staff of the gigantic corporation was more stable than he had hitherto regarded it. He now saw Blair as a genial, easy-going man, who always took the line of the least resistance, avoiding unnecessary trouble, which was wise in one-so well to do in the world's goods, and as John himself was imbued with the most kindly feelings toward even his enemies, he had the gratification now of beholding his future extend before him like a well-ordered railway line: a clear right-of-way, and no signals against him.

One morning Mr. Blair entered the division superintendent's room, accompanied by a man so much like himself that he might almost be taken for his younger brother.

"Mr. Steele," cried the general manager, in his most amiable manner, "I wish to introduce you to Colonel Beck, an officer of the company, who keeps us all out of prison. Colonel Beck is Mr. Rockervelt's chief legal adviser, who knows so much about the law that he can enable any one with money to evade it. Colonel Beck, this is Mr. John Steele, our youngest, and I believe I may add, our most capable division superintendent."

The Colonel laughed pleasantly as he shook hands with the young man.

"Mr. Blair gives you a better character than he bestows upon me," said the lawyer, with a good-natured twinkle of the eye. "If there is one characteristic more distinctive than another in the Rockervelt system, it is the unvarying respect it holds for the law."

"Oh, that's true enough," rejoined Blair. "Why shouldn't we respect the laws when the Colonel here makes most of them pertaining to railways?"

"Are you then a member of the Legislature?" asked John innocently.

Both of the fat men laughed, and Colonel Beck replied: "No, I am not so restricted as all that. A member of the Legislature possesses one vote. In the secret sanctity of this room, now that my friend Blair has given a hint in that direction, I may say I control many votes in the various Legislatures, and perhaps a few in the National Capitol as well. Still, that's all among ourselves, Mr. Steele, and, getting to safer ground, I may add that I esteem this meeting a pleasure, for you are one of the few men I have heard Mr. Rockervelt speak highly of, and when Mr. Rockervelt praises a man I like to know that man and make him my friend if possible, for he is sure to go far. I think," continued the Colonel, turning toward Blair, "that Mr. Rockervelt said the superintendent here was rather a considerable shareholder in the Midland."

"Mr. Rockervelt was a trifle premature if he said that," replied the general manager. "He spoke to me about it last time I was in New York, but I was unable at the time to give him definite information."

"He is not in the least premature," Steele intervened quietly. "Since our conversation a while ago, Mr. Blair, I have sold out all my Michigan Central Stock with some of my Northern Pacific, and have invested in Manateau Midland."

"Ah, then you are one of us," cried Beck, with enthusiasm; "I wish I had known you before you made the transfer, because I could have introduced you to brokers who would have done the job at the same rate they transact business for us, which I may add is a considerable shade lower than the general public pay. In future if you have any dealings on the market, I shall be glad to give you the benefit of both advice and introduction, which may result in your saving money."

"I am an investor, rather than a speculator," replied John, "and more anxious to get good securities than exorbitant dividends."

"A very wise rule of conduct," said the Colonel, nodding his head sagely several times; then, abruptly changing the subject, he once more expressed his pleasure at making the acquaintance of John Steele.

"I live part of the year in New York, and part in this city," continued the

Colonel, "for I am a native here. I arrived a week ago, and to-morrow night we give a little house-warming which I should be glad, Mr. Steele, if you would attend. Not a great crush, you know; a homely gathering rather than a fashionable function, but you shall meet very choice people there, eh, Blair? You'll corroborate me in that, I'm sure?"

"Yes, Colonel," responded Blair, "you are altogether too modest. Your dinners might well form a model to Lucullus, and I can assure Mr. Steele that he will meet people whom it may be a great advantage for him to know. Now, there's a handsome, unsolicited testimonial."

"No, by Jove, it was solicited, wasn't it?" cried the genial Colonel, rubbing his hands together. "Well, Mr. Steele, may I depend on you? You will forgive the shortness of the notice, because of the shortness of our acquaintance."

John Steele accepted the invitation with a cordiality equal to that with which it was tendered.

The prediction of both the stout gentlemen that John Steele would meet interesting people whom he should be glad to know was more than fulfilled, although his joy of new acquaintance was concentrated on one person.

Miss Sadie Beck was the most beautiful girl Steele had ever seen. Her face was sweet and innocent; her complexion of purest ivory tinted with dawn, the colours that go with hair of Californian gold, profuse and waving; the whole entrancing picture being lighted up by eyes as blue as a June sky.

The portals of the Beck mansion proved to be the gates of Eden, with Eve awaiting him within the Paradise. John, hitherto all unused to the society of women, found himself in the presence of Sadie Beck thrilled with emotions of which he knew nothing, and life quite unexpectedly presented possibilities that dazzled him.

Colonel Beck was a widower, and the only child of his only brother was mistress of his household. The Colonel had been too busy a man to think of marrying again after his wife had died, but circumstances solved the problem which his own immersion in great affairs prevented him from grappling with. His elder brother had been as unsuccessful in business as Colonel Beck was the reverse, and dying, he left his daughter to the care of her wealthy uncle, who had given her the most fashionable education money could procure, and then had installed her as the fascinating hostess of his home, a position which she amiably filled to the delight of his guests, and to the complacent satisfaction of himself.

The effect of this new-born friendship upon John Steele was instantaneous and permanent. All the counsels which Philip Manson had formerly tendered to him, urging a greater care in his personal appearance, and a stricter attention to the niceties of dress had made but ephemeral impression upon the object of Manson's solicitations; but now, without a word being spoken, John became almost a modern dandy. The hairdresser's constant attention worked wonders with his head covering, and the most expensive tailors found him an exacting customer.

John discovered suddenly that the onerous duties of division superintendent required a far wider outlook than he had so far bestowed upon them. He must know the law pertaining to his profession, and therefore he found frequent consultations necessary with the adviser to the corporation, and that urbane gentleman did his best to enlighten so diligent a student. Frequently, as was bound to happen with a man on whose shoulders rested a portion at least of the legal business pertaining to a wide-spreading railway system, Colonel Beck was occupied in his own study, compelled to refuse himself to any visitor, and great as should have been the disappointment of so earnest a pupil, John, nevertheless, could scarcely conceal his delight that the niece rather than the uncle should be his entertainer upon these occasions. The elderly lady who acted as chaperone in the Beck household was a placid nonentity, whom even a less strenuous person than John Steele might easily have ignored. She always contented herself with reading the latest book or magazine in a corner under the shaded electric light, while Sadie sat at the piano at the further end of the large room, and played most divinely certain soft, clinging, sentimental harmonies which might be carried on in conjunction with whispered conversation.

Sadie was a deservedly popular young lady, and often, to his chagrin, John found others in the drawing-room, claiming a share of her attention, and to do Miss Beck justice, she bestowed her favours with impartial charm upon all alike, although as time went on John Steele flattered himself that there was reserved for him a tone slightly more confidential than any of the others received. If the old Colonel saw what was going forward, almost, as one might say, before his eyes, he made no sign, and certainly treated the young division superintendent with an even cordiality that would have proved flattering to a man of much higher standing in the company's service than was John Steele.

During this interesting period of his existence the young man lived in an intoxicating, rose-hued atmosphere. "Lucky in love, unlucky in war" was proving itself false in his instance. Never before had he been so successful in his business; never so popular with superiors and subordinates alike. Difficulties appeared only to vanish before the magic wave of his hand. His suggestions were adopted, his plans prospered, and perhaps most inspiring of all, his sagacity and his energy met unasked appreciation. His salary was raised to a hundred dollars a week, and Blair, when he announced the fact, referred almost apologetically to the ever-increasing prosperity of the road, due largely, he was good enough to say, to the efficiency of the division superintendent.

And yet there was one pebble in his shoe. With increase of means, curiously enough, there came the increased knowledge that intrinsically he was a poor man. The property which a few months before had seemed wealth, now appeared what Blair had actually suggested it to be, merely the nucleus around which an energetic man might accumulate a fortune. He was in the social class of the millionaires, but not in their financial class. No matter what dividends were paid on two or three hundred thousand dollars' worth of railway stock, that income, added to his salary of five thousand a year, would never support a palace such as Blair lived in, or even a mansion similar to the one inhabited by Colonel Beck. Sadie, with the demeanour of a queen, needed also the income of a queen. John had no delusions on that score, and furthermore, being proud, he could not ask her to step down, but to step up. The germ that had remained dormant in his mind since his uncle's death now developed into the belief that he might become as prosperous in speculation as he proved to be in all other walks in life. Often in after years he remembered the coincident conjunction of necessity, development and opportunity. Any two of the trinity would have been inactive without the presence of the third, but the trio travelling by different highways met at the crossroad, and then important things happened.

One eventful evening he dressed for dinner and dined early at the club; then he strolled up the avenue to the residence of Colonel Beck. Ushered into the drawingroom he found Sadie standing by the open piano, idly touching the upper keys with the tips of her fingers, standing there as if she were waiting for him, yet he knew she was waiting for some one else, for her opera cloak hung over the back of a chair beside her, and she was arrayed superbly for dinner, ball or reception. Never afterward could John give to himself any lucid description of what she wore, except that she looked like a radiant angel garbed in white. Her raiment was diaphanously, airily beautiful. Her gleaming, snowy shoulders, superb neck, and crown of golden hair made up a vision almost unearthly in its loveliness, which at once entranced and startled the young man. She turned toward him that superbly poised head, with the arched brows of surprise at his entrance mellowed by a seductive smile of a welcome not to be misunderstood. John himself was one of those well-set-up young men who look their best in evening dress, and as he came rapidly forward down the long room the girl could see the soul shining in his eyes, and the sight brought added colour to her own fair cheeks.

"Sadie," he cried, taking both her hands in his, although she offered him only one, "if but a painter could place on canvas even a hundredth part of your adorable beauty to-night, his fame would ring down the ages."

The girl laughed.

"Is it so striking as all that? Then I am sorry I can give you but fifteen minutes of it, for my uncle is taking me out to dinner, and man-like he is late, having just arrived home and gone upstairs to dress."

"Fifteen minutes! What is it the poet says of fifteen minutes as compared with a cycle of Cathay? Fifteen minutes, Sadie, with you, is worth an eternity with any one else on earth. Why, bless my soul, the Declaration of Independence was signed in ten!"

Again the girl laughed, trying, not very strenuously, to disengage her hands.

"Do you wish me to sign a declaration of independence?" she asked.

"Yes, a declaration of independence from all the world except me."

"In other words, a declaration of dependence on you rather than independence of the rest?" she corrected.

"Sadie, I've adored you ever since I met you. The picture on canvas that I spoke of is impossible, for there is not genius enough existent to do it justice. But there is a picture I ask you to look at," and he swung her round almost rudely until she saw the reflection of two young people holding each other's hands in the tall pier-glass.

"If you appreciate that Princess as she deserves, you will wonder at the conceit of the man standing beside her, that he dares to ask for the original."

Sadie looked at her counterpart with a certain complacency, for doubtless she was a girl who had received many proposals, and was not to be swept from her feet even by one so impetuous as this. But that she was gratified by the young man's earnestness, one needed but a glance at her sparkling eyes and rosy cheeks to see. She turned from the glass to him.

"Is it the girl from New York or the gown from Paris you so warmly admire?"

"Answer me, Sadie, answer me," he cried.

"Hush, hush," she whispered, "I hear my uncle coming," and now she struggled in earnest to release herself, but strenuously he held her firm.

"Answer yes or no."

"Which word will release me most speedily?" she demanded.

"The first."

"Then it must be yes. A fine masterful lover you are!" she cried with pretended indignation, as she whisked herself free from him.

It was a maid who came in, and taking up the white cloak, she adjusted it over the fair shoulders of her young mistress. A moment later the Colonel, rubicund and beaming, entered the drawing-room.

"Ah, Steele, is that you?" he saluted his visitor, shaking hands in the most friendly manner; "has my niece told you that we must enact the inhospitable savage tonight, and turn you forth in a cold and pitiless world?"

"Yes, Colonel," laughed John, who was in such a state of joyous exaltation that he would have laughed, no matter what his host had said, "yes, and I must confess that it is like being turned from Paradise."

The Colonel, smiling, allowed his eyes to pass from the exuberant young man to the downcast face of his niece, who seemed absorbed in the rearrangement of her white cloak. If the Colonel suspected anything, he said nothing that might give a hint of his surmise.

"Do you know that Mr. Rockervelt is in town?" he asked.

"No," replied the young man, in some astonishment.

"He arrived here by the noon train," continued the Colonel, "and all this afternoon we have been in close session at Blair's house. Mr. Rockervelt spoke of you, and said he was sorry he could not see you this trip. We are dining with him to-night at Blair's, but ladies being present, no business will be talked. Mr. Rockervelt leaves by special at ten o'clock."

"Rather a short stay," commented Steele.

"Short, but important," replied the Colonel, as he led the way to the door.

John Steele had the advantage of escorting Miss Sadie to her carriage, and the felicity of pressing her hand before he made way for the Colonel to enter. He stood there for a moment, watching the receding back of the carriage, and then walked uncertainly down the avenue, treading not upon hard flagstones, but on clouds, his mind far aloft in the realms of romance, while his body bumped heedlessly against innocent passers-by, or those who hoped to be passers-by until he ran into them, interrupting their course and causing one stranger to remark that it was a pity to see a young man so drunk this early in the evening

## CHAPTER VII—THE FIRST CAST OF THE DICE

NEXT morning John Steele was startled to receive a rather peremptory message from Colonel Beck requesting him to call at once at his residence. The young man instantly obeyed, and mounted the steps with some trepidation, wondering whether Sadie had made a confidant of her uncle, and fearing that the uncle's designs for his niece excluded a division superintendent from any discussion regarding her future. He was shown into the Colonel's study, a large room on the first floor at the back of the house. The Colonel greeted him with what might be termed absent-minded friendliness. He was evidently perturbed about something, and after requesting his caller to sit down, himself paced up and down the room two or three times with a shade of perplexity on his brow. At last he threw himself into his office chair, and sitting back, interlocked his hands behind his head, and bent his looks upon the visitor he had summoned.

"I thought it best, Mr. Steele, to ask you to come here, as what I have to say is extremely private, and I wish to incur no interruptions, and to obviate the possibility of eavesdroppers."

"Yes?" interpolated John, thinking this opening must certainly pertain to the episode of the previous evening in the room beneath.

"You said to me once," went on the Colonel, "that you were an investor, not a speculator."

"Yes," repeated his listener.

"Has it ever occurred to you that a man may be both, or rather, that he may indulge in all the advantages of successful speculation without any of the risks that occur through playing in the open market?"

"If such a thing could be done," said John with a smile, "it would be the very heaven of financiering."

"Such a thing not only can be done, but it is done, every day. It is the outsider who speculates, and who must incur the uncertainties which accompany speculation. Those on the inside do not speculate, but operate in a security as absolute as that of a bank which receives a certain amount from a depositor. Now, I told you last night that although Mr. Rockervelt's visit was brief, it was important. Its importance lies in this. The financial year now drawing to a close—the financial year, I mean, so far as the Rockervelt system is concerned—has been far and away the most prosperous in its existence. Manateau Midland stock to-day stands at 162 1/2, which is much under its intrinsic worth. But before I proceed with this exposition of values, I should like to ask you a question or two. Am I right in surmising that you owe your position entirely to Mr. Rockervelt?"

"Yes, to him through Philip Manson's recommendation."

"Ah, Philip Manson! I believe he is one of Mr. Rockervelt's favourites, too. He was your predecessor, wasn't he?"

"Yes. Mr. Rockervelt took him to New York, and put me in his place here."

"The chances are, then, that Mr. Manson will get his tip straight from Mr. Rockervelt himself, and, if he takes advantage of his knowledge, will doubtless operate through our brokers in New York. Well, the position is just this, Mr. Steele: Times have been good, and I tell you in confidence, what perhaps you have already guessed, that never has the Rockervelt system enjoyed a more prosperous year. The various roads, thanks to efficient men like yourself, have been remarkably free from disaster, and in truth during the twelve months now closing there has been no serious accident at all. In spite of our determination to let the actual state of affairs be known only to those on the inside, among whom Mr. Rockervelt, without saying it in so many words, evidently reckons yourself, the general public has arrived at some inkling of the facts. Stock which a month ago could be got for a hundred and fifty-two sells to-day at over a hundred and sixty. Still, the public has no real idea of how prosperous we have been, and I venture to predict that our next declaration of dividends, which is less than a month away now, will come as a complete surprise, and those who previously possessed inside knowledge will benefit accordingly. Of course, your duties heretofore have not brought you into contact with the finance of a huge corporation like the Rockervelt system, so I may tell you that after the annual meeting is held and a good dividend is declared the real owners of the railway, such as Mr. Rockervelt and his colleagues, sell their stock to the general public, buying it back during the ensuing year at a lower figure, in time for the next election of officers. We are now all loaded up with as much as we can carry, and it has been agreed that the time is ripe for the introduction of a very select few, like Manson, yourself and one or two more, into the inner circle. We take into our confidence only those who are actively engaged in the management and working of the various roads; men on whom we depend for our continued success. Now, our brokers have just been in communication with a man who wishes to sell stock to the amount of something like half a million, and I have asked them not to part with it or to seek a customer until I had communicated with you."

"Colonel," said the young man, his face aglow with excitement at the chance offered to him, "that is very kind of you, but you see, my money, or at least most of it, is already in Midland stock to the amount of between two hundred and three hundred thousand dollars."

"Yes, I was aware of that, but our brokers will arrange everything for you. If, instead of buying the stock outright—and by the way, what did you pay for it?"

"I got it at a trifle less than a hundred and fifty."

"Why, there you are. Suppose you had, instead of buying it outright, taken an option, say, on a million, you would already have made a hundred thousand dollars on the rise. Our brokers will arrange the financial details and you can secure the stock you now possess and the half million block as well, with ample margin to spare. Then, when you have taken your profits, you can do as you please: reinvest if you like, or wait until the inevitable reaction comes and buy in at a lower figure a much larger amount than you now possess."

"All right, Colonel, I'll do it. In fact, I leave the matter entirely in your hands to arrange with the brokers."

"Thanks. I don't attempt to conceal from you that it is a great opportunity, and I need not ask you to hold in strict confidence all I have told you, for we don't care to see the price go much higher until after the dividend is declared. There's just one request I must make which perhaps you will have no hesitation in granting. We should like to secure the voting proxy of this stock against the general meeting, to be used in the Rockervelt interest."

"Oh, certainly," cried John, delighted.

The Colonel selected some blank forms from the receptacle on his table before him, rapidly filled them in, and passed them across for John to sign, which he did almost without glancing at them, Colonel Beck in somewhat legal language pointing out the purport of each instrument.

"Well, that's all right," said the Colonel, as he gathered up the signed papers. "I'll see the brokers at once, and get the deal put through."

As John Steele came downstairs, he realised that these were business hours, but considered himself justified for the first time in his life in filching a few moments from them. He determined to see Sadie, and learn whether or not it was her wish he should at once communicate with her uncle on a matter which did not concern the buying or selling of stock.

Sadie received him in a morning room that was partly library. Her first utterance rang with a tone of imperiousness that was new to him.

"Why have you been shut up with my uncle so long in his study this morning?"

"Because he sent for me."

"Why did he send for you?"

"To make some arrangements about the future." Sadie's blue eyes were scintillating with excitement or anger; the young man could not quite tell which. "What arrangements?" she demanded.

"Well, our conference was strictly confidential, and your uncle asked me not to mention the subject to any one."

The girl almost stamped her foot.

"You know very well what I mean," she said. "Did he send for you because of—because of—last night?"

"No, Sadie, he didn't. To tell the truth, when I received his message this morning I thought perhaps he suspected something last night, and wished to question me, and I assure you I felt very uneasy meeting him before speaking first with you and learning your views upon the matter. However, his conversation was entirely about the railway business, and some new features of it, which arose through Mr. Rockervelt's visit yesterday."

"Then you said nothing to him about last evening."

"No, Sadie, I could not take such a liberty without your permission."

"Ah," sighed the girl, with evident relief, "you did give me a fright when I learned you had gone to my uncle's room so early in the morning, and when you stayed so long."

"Don't you want me to speak of our engagement, then?"

"There is no engagement. You were so boisterous standing there by the piano that I had to say 'Yes' to release myself, otherwise my uncle would have come in upon a fine tableau."

"I hope you are not going back upon that 'Yes,'" said the young man earnestly.

For a few moments the girl did not answer. She seemed in an uncertain temper that morning, and rather inclined to pout, yet to the ardent young man she appeared more entrancing than ever.

"I am going neither back nor forward," she said at last. "I desire to remain just where I am. I am not sure of myself. I think you took an unfair advantage of my dilemma last evening with your obstreperousness; and there are many reasons why I should not wish to be bound by the answer you forced me to give."

"You shall not be bound," replied John very seriously; "everything must be exactly as you wish it to be. You, doubtless, have been and will be sought by lovers richer than I, but you will never find one more devoted to you."

"Oh, I wasn't thinking of riches," explained the girl petulantly; then after a pause she added: "though I may as well confess I am quite unsuited to be a poor man's wife. The cottage with roses clambering over it looks very beautiful in a painting, and a description of it reads well in a magazine story, but when I was a small girl, I endured the reality of poverty and I don't want any more of it. I suppose you think that very sordid?"

"No," rejoined John Steele gravely, "I think it very sensible."

"I should loathe a house in the suburbs with two servants, or its alternative, the middle-class hotel or superior boarding-house down town. My education and my bringing-up haven't fitted me for these delights."

"You incur no danger from a cheap house in the suburbs or its alternative. I am at present earning five thousand dollars a year, and am only on the threshold of my profession. I own absolute cash-producing property to the extent of about three hundred thousand dollars, and if you will consent to our engagement being made public when I am a millionaire, I guarantee that the announcement will take place before two months are past." Up to this point the girl's eyes had been fixed on the floor; now she raised them level with his, and he saw that all resentment had fled from them, leaving in its stead a sparkle of mischief and merriment.

"Why," she laughed, "one would think that the financial conversation upstairs with the uncle was resumed in the morning room with the niece. I suppose these monetary revelations arise because of the business suit you are wearing in this hard morning light; but I think I like you much better, John, in evening clothes, under the radiance of shaded lamps. I am sure neither of us thought of money last night, and I certainly did not this morning until you began talking about it."

She held her hand out to him, and he took it with enthusiasm.

"I do not wish anything said of our engagement at the present moment," she went on. "There is nothing very terrible about such a proviso, is there? I have many friends in this city, and I don't wish them all set gossipping, as will be the case if any announcement is made. We will let the 'yes' stand where it did, but you must give me a little time quietly to learn how my uncle may regard the news. You will come here, I hope, just as if nothing had happened, and if I receive you as crossly as I did just now, I give you leave to scold me. Is that a bargain?" she concluded brightly, smiling up at him, and giving him freely what he had taken the night before, her two hands in his.

"It is a bargain," said John with content, drawing her suddenly toward him and kissing her, an act to which she submitted half with reluctance, half with acquiescence.

And so for a month everything went on as before, except that John was perhaps the most frequent visitor at the Beck household. He thought more of his love than of his money, as it is right and proper a young man should, for youth is the time of optimism, and everything was progressing smoothly.

A week before the general meeting Blair departed for New York, and before he left he appointed Steele acting general manager pro tem., which had the effect of making John the busiest man in the city, giving him little opportunity to think of either femininity or finance. Colonel Beck accompanied Blair to the metropolis, but had returned the day before the annual meeting was held. There were large interests in the West, he said, which would require his unremitting attention during the next few days, and this proved a true prediction.

On the evening of the day of the general meeting Steele left his office late, intending to snatch a hasty meal at the club and return to his work. He found the streets in unusual commotion; newsboys were rushing frantically here and there yelling at the top of their voices: "Great panic in New York."

Steele bought a paper, and the glance he bestowed upon the black headlines rooted him to the pavement.

"Financial Thunderbolt," he read. "No dividend for Rockervelt shareholders. Panic on the Stock Exchange this afternoon. Heavy drop in all securities. Rockervelt stocks leading the rout. Are we on the verge of a crisis?

Fall of twenty-eight points in Rockervelt holdings when the Stock Exchange closed. Fears for tomorrow."

"Twenty-eight points," muttered the grave young man to himself. "That means a loss to me of nearly two hundred thousand dollars!"

Without reading further particulars, Steele thrust the paper into his pocket, and continued his journey to the club. His mind was in a whirl, but clenching his teeth, he strove to rearrange his thoughts and settle upon a course of action. It was too late that day to do anything. If he had only known of this disaster as soon as it occurred; if he had had word as early as was possible after the passing of the dividend, he might have got out without a loss of more than thirty or forty thousand dollars perhaps. What an innocent lamb he had been; almost begging to be shorn. Not a single precaution had he taken. It needed but a word to Philip Manson in New York, and a telegram would have apprised him at once of what had happened in the general meeting; yet here he had remained buried up to the eyes in the business of this corporation, which had evidently been engaged in a gigantic game of thimble-rigging; working like a fool while all the world knew of the topical item except himself. The reason of this complete absorption in duty suddenly struck him like a blow in the face, and he stood still at the thought of it. Blair had put upon his shoulders the burden of general manager without relieving him of the task of division superintendent, and he had been struggling to fulfil adequately the obligations of both offices. Had Blair done this for a purpose? One suspicion led to another. Might not the whole net in which he found himself enmeshed be of the general manager's weaving? If so, Blair had found him an easy victim.

His meal at the club, instead of being snatched as he had intended, was a most leisurely one, but his appetite was gone and he ate little. He did not go back to his office, but walked up the avenue to Colonel Beck's house, only to find that the Colonel and his niece had gone out for the evening.

John Steele was at his broker's office the moment it was opened. A crowd was collected before the place, but only those were allowed in who had dealings with the firm.

"I was just about to telegraph you," said the junior partner, who received Steele in his private office. "I rather expected you in yesterday, but as we had no instructions we held on."

"Why didn't you telegraph me yesterday?"

"Why?" asked the broker, justly indignant at such a childish suggestion. "You left no instructions, and as every ticker in town announced the news, I did not think it necessary. The fact is that as soon as the announcement came we were so busy here that no one in the office had time to turn round. The crash was so unsuspected we were not prepared."

"It seems to me," said John bitterly, "that a firm like yours, intimately connected with the Rockervelt interests, should have had some idea of what was coming."

"Oh, well, so far as that goes," said the junior partner airily, "I might be equally justified in saying that an official like yourself, holding an important position on the Rockervelt staff, would have been much more likely to get the straight tip than we."

"Oh, I got a tip all right enough," replied John, grimly, "but it seems to have been a crooked rather than a straight one."

"Ah, well," said the broker, with the easy nonchalance of one whose withers are unwrung, "these mistakes happen now and then. The outlook in New York this morning is very-gloomy. Of course things may rally before noon, but we can't count on that. I was going to telegraph you that we must have margin put up; not less than twenty-one thousand dollars, and even that will only give you three points lee-way when your present margin is absorbed."

"Do you think twenty-one thousand would save me?"

"Who can tell?" answered the junior partner with a shrug of his shoulders. "It all depends. If you can inform me what Mr. Rockervelt will do during the next two hours, I can predict what will happen with the stock. I expected he would support it, but apparently he is letting it go smash."

"Why shouldn't he? He is the cause of it all," said John. "I know the road earned a dividend, even if Rockervelt didn't declare one."

"Well, there you are," said the broker. "The public always loses its head at a time like this. Rockervelt stocks are now away below their intrinsic value, but that fact won't prevent their going lower if the panic continues."

"What would you advise me to do?" asked Steele.

"I don't give advice; I take instructions. We'll hang on just as long as we can, but if the decline continues, we must sell your block before it gets below the margin."

"I hold three times twenty-one thousand, face value in Northern Pacific Stock. Can you tell me if there is any chance of raising twenty-one thousand dollars on it?"

The broker shook his head.

"You might have done that two days ago, but now? with gilt-edged stock like Rockervelt's on the toboggan how can you expect to raise a loan on Northern Pacifics? I don't believe any one would venture a thousand dollars on that security to-day. Those who have money are sitting on it, waiting for the clouds to roll by. This may be merely a little financial flutter and a quick recovery, or it may prove the beginning of a commercial crisis that will last for two or three years."

"Yet these devils in New York heedlessly run the whole country into such a risk to make a few more dirty dollars for themselves, who are already millionaires."

The veins in Steele's forehead were swelling, and his hair bristled with indignation, but the broker merely threw back his head and laughed.

"Satan reproving sin!" he cried. "What were you doing, a man with a quarter of a million or so, but trying to add a few dollars, dirty or clean, to that amount."

"True, true," said John, calming down suddenly, "you are in the right.

Well, good morning; I see there's a host waiting for you, and as you have no advice to give, and no money to lend, I'll see what I can do outside." He walked to the nearest telegraph station, and sent a message to Philip Manson in New York:

*"Can you telegraph me twenty-one thousand dollars? Will forward as security sixty thousand par-value Northern Pacific."*

This handed over, he returned to his office, opened the safe, took out the Northern Pacific securities, and placed them on his desk. For an hour and a half he was busy giving directions to this man or that, then a telegram was brought in to him from Philip Manson.

"Very sorry, but have lost everything I possessed in yesterday's panic."

"Poor old Manson," mused Steele sadly. "So he was caught in the trap too. Well, after all, when an old and experienced man is nipped, there is some excuse for myself." He thrust the securities in his pocket, put on his hat, and paid a visit to Colonel Beck. That benign gentleman received him with beaming effusion.

"Ah, Mr. Steele, I am so sorry we were out when you called last evening. It was a little dinner to which I had accepted an invitation more than a week ago, little dreaming that such a financial storm was about to break over our heads. Sit down, Steele, sit down. What can I do for you?"

"You can lend me twenty-one thousand dollars."

The smile faded from the cherubic face of the Colonel, and a shade of melancholy took its place.

"You mean, then, that your margins have all but disappeared?"

"That is exactly what I mean."

"Would twenty-one thousand save you?"

"You can tell that better than I, Colonel, being more in the confidence of the Rockervelts. I offer you as security nearly three times the amount in Northern Pacific stock."

The Colonel slowly shook his head.

"I shouldn't ask for security at all, Mr. Steele, if I had the ready money, but this unexpected crisis has tied up all the funds at my disposal."

"Unexpected! Do you mean to tell me you did not know the dividend was to be passed?"

Colonel Beck placed the tips of his fingers together, and gazed across the apex before him at the young man, more in sorrow than in anger.

"My dear Mr. Steele, I have no doubt you heard the news before I did. As I told you in this very room, large dividends had been earned, and of course I came to the conclusion that they would be declared. Then you say, quite justly, if a dividend was earned, why was it not declared? The reason is a most convincing one, and I am expecting every moment Mr. Rockervelt to give it to the public. When he does so, people will learn how senseless is the panic which has ensued over what is, after all, an exceedingly simple matter; one of those exigencies of business which are constantly occurring.

"While I was in New York I was consulted about the case; indeed the main lines of the deal were settled, although the method of payment was left open. You may be aware that Mr. Rockervelt is aiming at the Pacific coast, and gradually extending his lines to the west. Very well. About a week ago he got a private offer of the L. S. & D. Road, for which at the present moment he has no use, but which in a few years' time, when he makes certain connections, will be a most valuable link in his chain to California. Now, Mr. Rockervelt seeks advice, and listens to it, but no man can tell whether he will follow that advice or not. The information I have received from New York is to the effect that at the last moment Mr. Rockervelt made up his mind that instead of declaring a large dividend, as he might have done, he would put the amount in the L. S. & D. Road. Of course, he could have explained this at the meeting, but he did not do so, and there I think he was wrong. However, as you know, he works along his own lines, and perhaps his announcement might have raised difficulties before all the papers were signed. I imagine this is why he has made no statement. The truth is that just after the meeting he left in his private car for the West, intending to go over the L. S. & D. Road, but I am sure that when he realises the effect of his reticence on the business affairs of the country, he will be prompt to make his explanation, and save any further depreciation of securities. His manifesto will doubtless appear in to-night's papers, or in the morning sheets at the latest."

"I'm afraid that won't help me, Colonel Beck, and as you are yourself unable to accommodate me with the money for a few days, I suppose it would be useless to ask if any of your wealthy friends would accept my securities and hand me over the money."

"I fear not, I fear not," said the Colonel, with an air of inexpressible sadness. "At times like these every one pulls tight the purse-strings. If I went to the richest friend I have and asked to be accommodated with a loan, telling him the true story of the passing of this dividend, I am very sure I should not be believed." John rose to his feet, a wry smile on his lips.

"It is rather deplorable, Colonel Beck," he said quietly, "that people should so distrust their fellow men, and even though you say so, I find it impossible to believe that any one should suspect you of setting a trap."

"Ah, well," sighed the Colonel, "we must take life as we find it, you know, and not as we would have it. Time sets all things right, and I am old enough to be philosophical. Must you go? Well, drop in when you can, and if the financial tension relaxes, I may be able to be of some assistance."

John went downstairs and, as on a former occasion, expressing a wish to see the young lady of the house, was conducted into the morning room, where she greeted him, as it seemed to his now over-sensitive nerves, somewhat distantly.

"Sadie," he said, "I told you in this room that I was worth three hundred thousand dollars; that I was earning a salary of five thousand dollars a year, and that within two months I expected to be a millionaire. I must now inform you that all my money has been swept away, that I am about to resign my five thousand a year, and that I shall probably never be more of a millionaire than I am at the present moment."

"Oh, I'm so sorry," said the girl, with the breathless haste of one who is confronted by a condition, and does not know the exact words that fit it.

"I am sorry too," said John simply.

He stood there for a full minute, and there was silence between them, until at last the girl appeared to force herself to speak.

"Still, you are young, Mr. Steele, and this is a country of great opportunities, is it not?"

"I think it is," said John, with a grin; "yes, it is generally understood to be a land of excellent chances, and, as you say, I am young, much younger than when I was in this room last time. I knew as a general proposition I was young, but I had no idea I was the infant I have found myself to be."

As he spoke the girl drew herself up, and tried to assume an air of haughty indignation.

"If you are laughing at me," she said, "I think it is very unkind."

"I give you my word, Miss Beck, that I do not feel much like laughing, and least of all at you. I merely came in to bid you good-bye."

He held out his hand, and she took it gingerly, at arm's length, as it were.

"Good-bye," she said, "and I wish you luck."

"Thank you," replied John simply.

## CHAPTER VIII—AN IMPENDING CHANGE

TO borrow money at any time is difficult; to borrow during a panic is impossible. John Steele spent the first half of the second day of the crisis in attempting the impossible. Every man to whom he applied seemed to be in the same position as himself. All stocks had come down in sympathy with the Rockervelt slump, and it seemed as if every person supposed to be rich was then engaged in a frantic endeavour to prevent ruin by putting up all the ready money in hand, or else trying, like John himself, to borrow.

About half past twelve he gave up the quest, and made a second call on his brokers. It was the junior partner again who received him.

"Ah, Mr. Steele," cried the broker, "here you are, eh? They say all things come to him who waits."

"That isn't true in my case," replied John. "I've been waiting all day for money and couldn't get it. It didn't come."

"Well, I've been waiting for you," rejoined the broker. "I have had messengers after you all over town. Called at your rooms, at your office, at your club; found any number of people who had just seen you, but not one of the searchers caught sight of you."

"What's the news?" asked John, without much hope.

"We hung on to your stock till ten minutes to twelve, and then we had to let it go. We were lucky enough to get a purchaser for the whole block at a price that just cleared us, but I can tell you I spent a bad quarter of an hour before I got into touch with him."

"When you say cleared, I suppose you mean that I'm entirely wiped out, but you got from under without loss."

"I don't know a better way of putting it than that," replied the broker.

"I didn't think there was a man in town with ready money enough to make such a purchase to-day. I wish I had managed to encounter him. Perhaps I might have detached twenty-one thousand dollars from him."

"It is very likely, for he is a friend of yours, and from your own office. He said there was no secret about it; so I may as well tell you the purchaser is Mr. Blair, general manager of the Midland."

"Oh, he's back from New York, is he?"

"Yes, he returned this morning; haven't you seen him? Haven't you been at your office at all today?"

"No, I've been calling on friends and acquaintances. I suppose the stock is going up now?"

"Well, such a large purchase had first the effect of putting the brakes on its downhill course, and now it has recovered two points. Then the news from New York is encouraging. It seems that the Rockervelt forces, both in New York and Chicago, are buying all that is offered. You see, Mr. Rockervelt himself left for the West just before the scare, and I imagine he didn't realise how serious it was."

"Quite so. I heard he had gone West. Pity there are no telegraph wires to the West, isn't it?"

The broker laughed.

"Oh, I guess Mr. Rockervelt is as foxy as they make 'em. I don't suppose he's lost anything over this shake-up, and perhaps he thought it was a good time to squeeze a little of the dampness out of the stock. I expect a very rapid recovery. The country is prosperous, and from the way things look this last hour or two we've been going through a little squall, but not entering upon a financial crisis."

"That's a blessing," said John with a sigh; "still, the squall has upset my canoe, even if the big liners ride through it. Good-bye."

Once outside, instead of feeling depressed, as he had expected, John experienced an unaccountable thrill of elation. The disaster was complete;

complete beyond recall; complete in spite of anything he did or did not do. The very finality of the catastrophe seemed to lift a weight that had been oppressing him for a night and a day. He remembered that he had had practically no dinner the evening before, and no breakfast that morning, and now a fierce and healthy hunger which seemed to have been biding its time sprang upon him. A glance at his watch showed that it was nearly two o'clock. He walked rapidly to the University Club, noted for its excellent cuisine, and wrote on an order card the menu of a sumptuous meal. A deferential servitor approached silently to his elbow.

"Mr. Steele, No. 1623 wants you on the telephone."

"All right, ring him up, and tell him I'll be there in a moment, and if he is impatient, inform him I am at present engaged on the important choice between camembert and brie."

Sending his order upstairs, he went into the little telephone cabin. He knew the number meant the general manager's office.

"Hello, is that you, Blair?—Yes, this is Steele.—What's that?—Oh, no, now that you mention it, I haven't been there last night or this morning. How's the old road running?—What? It isn't doing so well outside.—Oh, if it comes to that, I've been general manager and division superintendent for the past week, so surely you can act Pooh Bah for a day. To tell the truth, it seemed to me that a road whose stock was falling so rapidly wasn't worth general managering or division superintending.—Levity? Bless you, no! I'm the most serious man in town.—Oh, I'm sorry you think my remarks flippant. Have you had lunch? I've just ordered a meal for a millionaire; come down and have a bite with me.—Oh, had it, eh? You're an early bird. I've ordered a late bird grilled upstairs. Sure you won't drop round, and have a cup of coffee and a liqueur?—Yes, I see, you're quite right. Somebody must attend to business.—Well, I'll drop round on you at four o'clock. Good-bye."

John Steele allowed himself a good hour and three-quarters for his luncheon, then he strolled down to the Grand Union Station, and, exactly as the big bell in the tower tolled four he walked into the general manager's room.

Mr. Blair was seated at his broad table, and as he looked up his chubby face was a study in various emotions. Superficially it wore the conventional, official frown which a great man may call to his aid when a subordinate's conduct has been such as to merit disapproval. The severity of the frown, however, was chastened by the expression of the just man, who, although righteously offended, is nevertheless prepared to listen to an explanation, and perhaps accept an apology. The lips were prepared to censure, or even, in a last resort, to condemn, although, if the case merited leniency, one would not be surprised to hear them admonish and advise. It was the face of a simple and honest man, willing to forgive, yet not afraid to punish.

The eyes, however, rather gave the situation away. In them twinkled triumph and glee, and lurking in their depths was a background of malice and hatred.

"Mr. Steele, I was amazed to find on my return from New York that you had absented yourself without permission from your duties," began Mr. Blair, in a sincere more-in-sorrow-than-in-anger tone.

"Oh, that's all right," said John airily. "I was general manager pro tem., you see, and a general manager may do what he pleases. But I was division superintendent also, so I asked the general manager for an hour or two off, and permission was granted me."

"As you know, Mr. Steele, I am the most forbearing of men, but such a tone as you have adopted will not do. As I told you over the telephone I was surprised at the flippant manner you thought fit to adopt, but I expected a satisfactory explanation when we met face to face."

"If that is the case, sir, I shall be so sorry to disappoint you. The satisfactory explanation I beg to offer for my absence is that I was busily engaged in gambling."

"Gambling!" cried Mr. Blair in astonishment; "this is shocking. It is my opinion that a man cannot be an efficient servant of a great railway and a speculator at the same time."

"I quite agree with you, Mr. Blair, and we are two shining examples of the truth of your aphorism. You are the most inefficient railway servant I ever met, and at the same time the most successful gambler. I am an excellent railway man and the most idiotic speculator there is in the country at the present moment. What's the use of wasting that sanctimonious 'holier-than-thou' look of yours? You know, and I know, that you don't care a hang about my being away a day. What you want me here for is to gloat over me. You've got my three hundred thousand dollars as slick as any bunco man ever achieved a much smaller sum over a green farm hand from the country. I'm here, not to receive any censure or to make any apology, but so that you may enjoy the effects of my humiliation and defeat. I am the last person in the world to deprive another of innocent amusement. Here I am, therefore. I have just come out of the tail end of the threshing machine, and have brought the remnants for your inspection. What do you think of them?"

"I am exceedingly sorry to hear that you have been unfortunate in your financial transactions."

"Of course you are. Thanks ever so much."

"Did you succeed in raising twenty-one thousand on your Northern Pacific stock?"

"No, I have it with me yet. That N. P. stock sticks to me closer than any friend I have in town. You don't want to buy it by any chance?"

"No," said Blair smoothly. "I have quite recently made a very large investment in Midland shares, re-buying a block that I was fortunate enough to sell at its highest point, and have therefore no desire to acquire further securities at the present moment."

"You're just in the same fix as all the rest of my acquaintances, Mr. Blair, so your refusal does not disappoint me."

"You lost also the thirty thousand you had in the Bank at Detroit?"

This was said very quietly, and for a moment amazed the listener by the accurate knowledge the elder man possessed of his affairs. The next instant John Steele gave utterance to a shriek of laughter, smiting his thigh with his open palm as if he had just heard the best joke in the world. The young man strode up and down the room giving way to shout after shout of hilarity, while the elder, all trace of humbug vanishing from his face, rose to his feet in alarm, believing that misfortune had turned the other's brain, and fearing a transformation into a sudden savagery that might make his isolated position one of danger. His eyes rested longingly on the door, while his hand nervously sought the electric button. John, seeing these premonitions of interruption, controlled himself with an effort, and stammered: "Sit down, Blair; it's all right. Don't get frightened. I'll explain in a minute. You see, it was this way," said John, coming up in front of the table again, and resolutely crushing down his bubbling tendency to merriment; "that thirty thousand was deposited in the Detroit bank by my late uncle. I possess my own little bank account here, which I have been adding to week by week. Consequently, I never needed to draw a check upon Detroit. Now, the funny thing is that I have been searching this town from cellar to garret that I might borrow twenty-one thousand dollars, and all the while I could have drawn my own check for the amount, and had nine thousand odd left over."

"Do you mean to say, then," said Blair, visibly disappointed, "that you didn't put in the thirty thousand as margin?"

"I did not. Do you feel you ought to have a check for that thirty thousand? You remind me of the hotel keeper at a summer resort down East, whose customer said: 'You have made a mistake in my bill,' and when the proprietor denied that there could be any error, the guest explained: 'Oh, there must be, for I have still ten dollars left.' The beautiful part of it is, Blair, that if I had thought of my thirty thousand I would have put it in; so I am mighty glad I didn't think of it, for it would not have saved me. I was looking over the figures of the decline on the tape at the club, and found that the stuff reached its lowest point at about half-past eleven, and that point would have not only wiped out my thirty thousand, but another thirty thousand as well. The brokers told me they had hung on till ten minutes to twelve, but they evidently knew their customer, and got out on the rise. I am afraid, Blair, that even brokers are not truthful men. It's a wonder that staunch, true hearts like you and me can make a living in this deceitful world. Well,

Mr. Blair, I have come to bid you good-bye, and I venture to predict that I'll have more fun out of that thirty thousand dollars than I had out of the three hundred thousand. Wealth isn't everything here below. Meanwhile keep on living a virtuous life, and you will reap your reward by and by. Never become discouraged in well-doing. Ta-ta."

With that John Steele took his departure from the Grand Union Station, packed up his traps, and took train for Detroit, where he lifted his money from the bank, and left on the night express for New York.

Here he rented Drawer 907 in the Broadway Safe Deposit Vaults, and in this drawer he placed his Northern Pacific stock and locked it up. He next turned his money, all but a thousand dollars, into a letter of credit on Europe; then bought a first-class ticket to France on the biggest boat sailing that week. He determined to burn his bridges behind him before he called on his old friend Philip Manson, for he knew instinctively that Manson would strongly disapprove of the course he had laid out for himself, and, remembering his great esteem and affection for Manson, he was not sure enough of himself to venture within the circle of his influence without some extraneous aid to hold him to his purpose.

It was nearing twelve o'clock when he went up in one of the half-dozen elevators of the huge Rockervelt building, and was ushered into Philip Manson's room.

"Hello, Mr. Manson, how are you?" he cried cheerily, as his former chief rose to greet him. Although he called the much more important general manager plain "Blair," he never was able to drop the prefix "Mr." from Manson's name. His respect for his solemn friend was as deep as his affection, and the strong regard manifested itself unconsciously in this manner. Manson's appearance gave no indication that he had passed through a crisis which had ruined him. He was the same quiet, reserved man he had always been, and a touch of grey at the temples was all the change John noticed as having taken place since he saw him last. The stern face relaxed into a bright expression of welcome as he shook hands with the young man from the West.

"I am very glad to see you," said Manson. "Did you get my letter?"

"No, I left Warmington the day I telegraphed you."

"Ah, well, it doesn't matter. It was merely about your telegram I wrote. I am very sorry indeed that it proved impossible for me to send you the money, and I merely wrote a fuller explanation than my telegram contained."

"You got caught in the crash, then?" said Steele.

"Yes, everything I possessed was swept away. It serves me right for doing what I never did in my life before, which is to dabble in stocks. Was I right in supposing from your telegram that you also had become involved?"

"Yes, and if you had sent me the money it would have been lost; so you see, you don't need to regret that you didn't have it. The funny thing is that I had myself thirty thousand dollars in the Detroit Bank, which, in the excitement of the day, slipped my memory as effectually as if it had been only thirty cents."

"And did you save it?" asked Manson, with as near an approach to eagerness as he could show.

"Oh, yes, but the saving was an act of Providence, as we always try to make out our accidents are, and not through any sanity on my part. How did you come to put everything in stocks? I thought you never gambled?"

"I didn't, up till about a week ago. Colonel Beck gave me the straight tip, which I understood came direct from Mr. Rockervelt, and I was foolish enough to act upon it."

"He did the same kind office for me, but he's merely a stool-pigeon for old Blair. Blair was the man behind the gun."

"We have no proof of that," said Manson, judicially.

"I have proof. Blair didn't hesitate to confess as much after he had raked in my money. Blair's one of those oily hypocrites who smile and smile, and remain the villain. He never forgives, though he may appear to do so."

"You were always inclined to be prejudiced against Mr. Blair, John," said Manson meditatively. "Still, there's little use in talking of what is past. I suppose you read Mr. Rockervelt's statement in the papers?"

"Admirable piece of virtuous indignation, isn't it? What a beautiful sermon against all speculation! And yet it is stated very freely that those on the inside have made millions by selling the road and buying it back again. I wonder what fool it was that said you couldn't have your cake and eat it too."

"Well, let's think no more about it. When are you going back West, John?"

"I leave to-morrow, at noon, but I don't go West; I go East."

"East?"

"Yes, I sail on the first out-going liner to-morrow, and hope to drop off in France."

"Why, you've never given up your situation, have you?"

"Oh, yes, it was impossible for me to remain. I'm done with railroading."

"Nonsense. What's your purpose?"

"Mr. Manson, I don't exactly know. Reason tells me that I'm no worse off than I was the day my uncle died, when I had little thought of coming into any money I didn't earn. Indeed, I am very much better off. My salary has been doubled. I have thirty thousand dollars in cash, and a bundle of Northern Pacific securities which has just been placed in the Broadway Safe Deposit. I don't understand myself in the least. Reason tells me that I ought to get angry and slaughter somebody, yet I feel no resentment. I am hurt, rather, that I was sand-bagged in the house of my friends. Still, even that fact doesn't appear to affect me much. Nevertheless, there's a change. I suspect it's the beginning of dry-rot. I fear that from being a useful man I have become a useless one. The utter folly of hard work, faithful service, reasonable honesty, and all that, has been brought home to me."

"Nonsense, nonsense, John," expostulated Manson.

"I am not theorising, Mr. Manson, but am merely trying to explain something to you which I do not myself understand. My uncle managed to get together a certain amount of money during thirty-five years. I lost that money in as many hours. If I worked honestly like a beaver for the next ten, fifteen or twenty years, it is unlikely I could save that much; yet my dear friend Blair, during, say, half an hour's silent meditation, evolves a plan, perfectly legal, by which the money is transferred from my bank account to his—transferred beyond possibility of recall. You will say perhaps, as my broker said, that I am just as bad as he is. I expected to place some one else's money in my bank account, beyond recall, and didn't succeed. Therefore I make a row. But the truth is, I am not making a row. I admit all any critic may say of my folly, but I realise that being an honest, hard-working efficient man doesn't pay in this country. At least, it pays only in allowing you to scrape together a modest competency, which may be quite lawfully filched from you in ten minutes. You will add I am a fool to throw over my shoulder a situation worth five thousand a year. You may even mention the hundred thousand young fellows of my age who would jump at my chance. I admit all that; I admit I'm a fool; I admit anything. I am the most open-minded person on earth at the present moment, and the least argumentative. I am like a boat that has been tied to a pier until somebody has cut the rope, sending it adrift. If you ask the boat where it's going, it doesn't know. I don't know what I'm going to do. I am only aware that I've got close on thirty thousand dollars in a letter of credit. I can have a high old time on that money for a year in Paris. I can have an hilarious time on it for two years in various capitals. I can study in Germany with the greatest luxury for five or ten years on that amount, or I can live thirty years in Europe in some quiet out-of-the-way place and be sure I shan't die of starvation. I'm all at sea, like the boat I was speaking of. I thought I knew John Steele pretty well, but I find I don't know him at all. All his ideas of morality, energy, industry, have turned somersaults. I am going over to Europe, where it's quiet, to get acquainted with the new John Steele."

Philip Manson had been regarding him with almost painful concentration while he spoke, and when the harangue was finished he said, soothingly, persuasively, looking at John: "Come with me up to the Adirondacks and enjoy a week's fishing, or to Maine, and put in two weeks, or to Canada, and stay three weeks."

Steele laughed heartily.

"Oh, yes, I know. Why don't you advise me to go to some sanitarium and consult a physician on mental aberration? I want to fish, but it is to fish out the secrets of John Steele. By this time to-morrow I shall be kissing the tips of my fingers to the statue of Liberty."

"John," said Manson, solemnly, "you are taking a false step. If you go to Europe in this frame of mind you are making a grave mistake which may not be easily remedied. Opportunities come once, twice, thrice, but they don't come always, and if they find a man persistently not at home, they pass on. In a year or two this little set-back you have experienced will have almost completely passed away from your mind. Look at me. I am a much older man than you. I have lost everything I succeeded in accumulating, yet I set my face toward re-earning it. You are on the threshold of a great success; you have in you the making of a first-class general manager. Now, I can well understand that you don't care to be in an office that contains Mr. Blair. I cannot say I blame you for that, but Mr. Rockervelt will be back here the day after to-morrow. You wait till he comes; I'll go in and see him, and I am sure you will be offered a position that will give you ample scope for the powers we both know you to possess."

Steele shook his head slowly.

"I have told you, and evidently you don't believe it, that I have no desire to develop any powers of usefulness I may possess. I suppose I am in the state of mind that makes a labouring man become a tramp. You are a stalwart oak of the forest, Mr. Manson, and the gale that has merely ruffled your branches has uprooted the sapling."

"Nonsense, John; it has simply given the sapling a bit of a twist."

"That may be so. It is quite possible that by the time I touch at Southampton or Cherbourg I may be yearning for that stolid old statue of Liberty again, and perhaps I shall take the next steamer back. In that case Mr. Rockervelt will have had the disadvantage of endeavouring to run his system without me for three weeks or thereabouts, and so we will deal with him more effectually than we would the day after to-morrow, when he doesn't know what a vacuum my absence has caused."

"Don't try to be cynical, John. It doesn't sound convincing from the lips of so sensible and capable a young fellow as you are."

"On the other hand," John went on unheeding, "it may be that I have taken to the road; that I am in reality the tramp I feel myself to be. Perhaps there has been a mistake in the outset, and Europe is really my country, not America. My father was born over there, and who knows but that thousands of years of ancestry are calling to me. That is a question Europe will settle. I half suspect that I shall feel so out of it after a month over there that you'll find me again coming up this express elevator before you realise I've been away. Any how, my steamer ticket is in my pocket, and I am off to Cherbourg or wherever they like to land me, in the morning. And now, Mr. Manson, you know this wicked city better than I do. Let's get out to some good eating house and enjoy a substantial meal. What's the best restaurant in town? It isn't every day a capitalist asks you to lunch with him. I'm the prodigal son, so we'll reverse the ancient parable and kill the fatted calf before I start on my travels."

## CHAPTER IX—LOVE'S SPECTRE

JOHN STEELE sat at one of the little round tables in the Café Germania, where a customer may have brown Munich beer in a big stone mug with a white metal lid. The café was very full, so also were some of the habitués; and on a raised platform at the corner were seated the members of a Viennese band, giving forth music in the smoke-beclouded room. Steele was waiting for a friend, and had turned a chair face forward against the little table, that a place might be ready for him when he arrived. With his fountain-pen the young man had just written a cable despatch, in answer to a transatlantic message that lay before him, mutilated somewhat in its English, as is the habit of Italian telegraph offices, but still understandable, which was lucky, for more often than not a telegram in a foreign language comes out second best after an encounter with the system of Italy.

A breezy individual made his way through the smoke and the throng to the vacant chair, tipped it back and sat down in it. "I'm late, as usual, John," he said, "but that is one of my official prerogatives. So I won't apologise, but will make it up in beer, now that I am here."

"There is little use of being United States Consul at Naples if you can't do as you like, Jimmy. There isn't any too much money in the office, so one must seek compensation in other directions."

"Do as I like? That's exactly what I can't do. I'll be hanged if every citizen of the great Republic that blows in on me in Naples doesn't seem to imagine I'm a sort of man-of-all-work for him. And I'm expected to be polite, and to fetch and carry for all concerned. Truth to tell, Steele, I'm tired of it; I've a notion to chuck the whole outfit and go back. Now, to-night, I was kept at my office long after business hours by a persistent man who would not take 'No' for an answer—actually thought I was lying to him, and had the cheek to intimate as much."

"And were you?"

"Certainly I was; but it was not etiquette for him to throw out any hints about my lack of veracity. It was all on your account, and I'd indulge in any amount of fiction to oblige a friend. He wanted your address, and wanted it badly; but I didn't know that you were anxious to see him, so I prevaricated and told him that if he came in to-morrow morning I'd see if I could get it for him."

"That's singular. No one has been looking for me for years past. I thought and hoped I had been forgotten over in the States. What was his name?"

"Here is his card. Colonel Beck, of New York."

"Colonel Beck! Thunder!"

"Know him? Don't wish to see him, I take it."

"No, I don't, and I'm much obliged to you, Stokes, for holding him off. How long is he going to stay in Naples?"

"Said he was going to stay till he found you."

"In that case I'll strike for Calabria or Sicily or somewhere; get among the real brigands and avoid this pirate. He used to be a legal adviser to the Rockervelts and probably is yet. Supposed to be rich through fleecing innocent lambs like myself. The shorn lamb, however, avoids the wolf, so I'm off to-morrow morning."

"What's the use of leaving now if your fleece is gone? He can't hurt you. Did he shear you in days gone past?"

"It's a long story. What strikes me, however, is the coincidence of old Beck turning up at this moment. There is, in fact, a coincidence within a coincidence. Read that cablegram."

Steele shoved over to his friend the message he had received that day from New York. The Consul wrinkled his brows over the Italian-English of the despatch, and made out its purport to be as follows:

*John Steele, Naples.*

*Have you block Northern Pacific? If so, send me particulars and full powers to deal. Act at once. Stock booming, but expect a crash shortly. Come over yourself if you can, immediately. The block will make you rich if realised without delay.*

*Manson.*

"Who is Manson?" asked the Consul.

"Philip Manson was my chief on the Manateau Midland Railway before he went east to New York. I succeeded him on the Midland. He and I lost about all we possessed in the Rockervelt panic a few years ago. I was what you would call a 'quitter' and came to Europe. Manson was a 'holdfast' and so he is still in New York."

"Then why not go right over and see him, instead of taking that trip to Calabria?"

"Well, to tell the truth, I do feel a yearning for the States, but I think I'll wait until I hear how this deal turns out. Read my answer to his cablegram," and the young man handed to his friend the document he had written before the other came in.

Stock in Broadway Safe Deposit vaults. Drawer nine hundred seven. Mailed you ten days ago key and legal papers. Make what you can, and we will share even.

Steele.

"Oh, I was wondering where I had seen the name Man-son before!" cried the Consul. "Were those papers you signed in my office a week or two since the documents referred to?"

"Yes."

"That's very strange. You sent them across ten days before you got the request for them."

"Exactly. Those shares had rested for years in the Safe Deposit Vaults. Manson had never referred to them in his letters to me and I had never referred to them in my letters to him, yet I suddenly made up my mind to throw them on the market."

"Why, that almost makes a person believe there is something in this thought-wave theory—telepathy, or whatever they call it."

"I am afraid it has a much more prosaic origin. A fortnight since you told me there had been a tremendous rise in Northern Pacific stock. That set me thinking, and I remembered I had a number of shares hidden away in Drawer 907. The stock was of no use to me, so I thought I might as well discover how badly some other fellow wanted it. Thus I threw the onus of selling on my friend Manson."

"You must have a good deal of confidence in him to give him a free hand like that. What's to hinder him from bolting with the money?"

"Nothing at all, except that he won't do it."

"I love to meet this charming belief in one's fellow man these cynical times, but I thought you said you lost money with him. Was he your partner?"

"No. The losing of the money was through no fault of his. He had nothing to do with my speculation. We were merely in the same boat, that's all. Nipped by the same pair of pinchers."

"So that was what disgusted you with America. I am disappointed with your story. Wasn't there a woman concerned at all?"

"No."

"Where does our friend Colonel Beck come in?"

"Beck comes in owing to the fact that he persuaded me to undertake the speculation by which I lost several hundred thousand. He gave me false information, and I believe he knew it to be false."

"Any proof?"

"No. Circumstantial evidence, that's all. I believed him to be my friend, and in fact acted the tenderfoot to perfection. I was even green enough to go to him when the crisis came, believing that a loan of twenty thousand or thereabout would save me, but he refused to let me have the money, although I offered this same stock I am cabling about as security."

"Perhaps he didn't have the money, like the man who neglected to buy Chicago."

"He said his ready money had been swept away by the panic, which I doubt. I have never seen him since, and somehow have no particular desire to meet him now."

"I appreciate your feeling in the matter. By the way, Steele, there was a very pretty girl with Colonel Beck—a very pretty girl, and charmingly attired. She did not say a word all the time the Colonel was talking, but she looked unutterable things and was deeply interested in our conversation. I thought she was a trifle disappointed when I told the Colonel I didn't know where you were. I supposed she was the Colonel's daughter."

"The chances are," mused Steele, "that the young lady is Miss Sadie Beck, niece of the old gentleman. She was rather a handsome girl when I knew her."

"Ah!" drawled the Consul, "then there is no particular reason why she should be anxious regarding your whereabouts?"

"None that I am aware of."

"I see. Well, are you going back to America after all?"

"I haven't quite made up my mind what I shall do, Jimmy, except that I shall call at your office in the morning, and there mature my plans, with your assistance."

"If you call at my office, you are more than likely to run against Colonel Beck. I expect him there bright and early."

"By Jove! I had forgotten about the Colonel. Still, there is no hurry. I can drop in later, when the Colonel has moved on."

All arrangements, however, bow to Chance, and Chance now intervened to upset their plans. A burly, florid-faced man with white moustache loomed up before them, and a heavy hand smote Steele on the shoulder with a force that made him wince and bite his lip to restrain a cry of resentment. "Hallo,

John, old man!" shouted the stranger, "I am mighty glad to see you. Been searching the town for you; called on that stuck-up Consul of ours, but he pretended he knew nothing about you. I suppose he thought I believed him, but the undersigned wasn't born yesterday, and I had met talented prevaricators before. Oh by Jingo! this you, Consul? I didn't notice you at first. Well, I stick to all I said. You told me this evening that you didn't know where John Steele was, and now I find you sitting here with him. I think, by Jingo! that you owe me an apology."

"I owe you nothing, Colonel, not even my appointment. Every man who drifts in on me appears to think I am indebted to him for my place. I beg to inform you that it is no part of a Consul's duty to bestow addresses upon any stranger who happens to ask for them."

"That's all right, Mr. Stokes," replied the Colonel genially, drawing up a chair and seating himself uninvited at their table. "It isn't the habit of your uncle Ben to get left, and I knew I would find Steele ultimately if he was in town. Say, John, you ought to be in New York nowadays. Things are booming there."

"I have had enough of booms," replied the young man without enthusiasm.

"Nonsense! It's absurd for a capable fellow like you, and a talented man, too, if I may be allowed to say so before your face, to chuck things up the way you've done. And that reminds me, John, did you ever sell that block of Northern Pacific stock you had during the panic?"

"I never did."

"Got it yet, eh? Well, I congratulate you. Now, at the present moment that would form a very nice little nucleus to begin on, and you can count on me to help you till everything's blue."

"The stock wasn't much of a nucleus last time I tendered it to you, Colonel," said Steele dryly.

The Colonel threw back his head and laughed boisterously.

"Oh, you haven't forgotten that episode yet? Well, you bolted from Warmington so quickly that I hadn't any chance of giving you an explanation."

"No explanation was needed, Colonel Beck. You refused me the money I required, and were quite within your right in doing so."

"Yes, but why did I refuse you; why? Answer me that, John."

The Colonel, with great good nature, placed a hand lovingly upon the shoulder of the other.

"Your conundrum is easy enough," replied the young man nonchalantly. "You didn't want to let me have the money, that was all."

"Certainly I didn't; certainly I didn't; and you should be very thankful to me that I refused. I knew Wall Street a great deal better than you did, my dear fellow, and that money would just have followed the rest into the pit."

"I quite believe you."

"Yes; but you didn't believe me then; and you left my house in a huff, without ever giving me a chance to make my position clear."

"If you had been anxious to make it clear, Colonel, there was plenty of time to do it in. That was some years ago, and a letter to Naples costs only five cents."

"True, true," cried the Colonel, in the bluff manner of an honest but misunderstood man. "I might have expended the five cents, as you say, if I had known your address, but you had got on your high horse, and had said things which a younger man should have hesitated before applying to his elder. Now, I don't pretend to be any better than my fellows, and I admit I was offended. Such usage coming from you, John, hurt me, I confess."

The American Consul, finding himself an unneeded third in what was drifting into a private discussion, pushed back his chair and rose to his feet.

"I must bid you good-night, Steele," he said; "I have another appointment. I shall see you at the office tomorrow, I suppose?"

"Don't go, Stokes. The Colonel and I have nothing confidential to discuss," returned his friend, while the Colonel sat silent, as if he thought this was not a true statement of the case. The Consul, however, persisted in his withdrawal, and Colonel Beck heaved a sigh of relief as he watched him disappear.

"Yes, my boy," continued the Colonel, in a tone of tender regret, "I don't think you treated your friends very well. I don't think you should have jumped at the wrong conclusion as quickly as you did. I would willingly have let you have the money if I had not known it was certain to go where the rest of your cash had gone."

"It is quite possible I was mistaken, Colonel; I always was rather hot-headed, and if in this case I made an error, I now offer apology."

"It hurt me, it hurt me at the time," murmured the Colonel in reminiscent tones; "but if only myself were involved, I would never have said a word. I am a man of the world, and am accustomed to the ups and downs of the world. I make no pretence that your silent desertion caused me permanent grief. I resented your impetuous action, but would never have spoken if no one else had been concerned."

"No one else concerned? I do not understand you. Who else was concerned?"

"Well, to speak frankly, as between man and man, I think you treated my niece Sadie rather badly."

"You astonish me, Colonel. I never treated any woman badly."

"I have been all my life a very busy man," rejoined the Colonel, with more of severity in his tone than had hitherto been the case, "and I frankly admit that much went on in my own household of which I was not cognisant. During the first months of our acquaintance you visited us somewhat frequently."

"Well, what of it?"

"What of it? This much of it, that I did not know until you had left that the affections of my niece were centred upon you."

"You are quite mistaken, Colonel."

"Do you mean to say there was never anything between you two but ordinary friendship?"

"I mean to say nothing of the sort. It is not a question for two men to discuss; but since you have broached the subject, I may tell you what you probably know already, that the last interview I had in your house was with your niece. She received me with great coolness and parted from me without visible regret. To put it quite plainly, Colonel Beck, the niece seemed to share the uncle's feelings regarding me. Financially, I was broken, and consequently was of no further use either to man or woman."

The stout Colonel placed the tips of his fingers together over the most corpulent portion of his person, raised his eyes to the ceiling, and drew a deep sigh.

"My hasty young friend, I see exactly what happened. You left me enraged because I refused to lend you money. You said to yourself, 'This man in a crisis declines to befriend me.' That was no state of mind in which to visit a young lady proud and sensitive. Something in your manner must have jarred upon her. Girls are of finer texture than we brutal men. Her seeming coldness was merely offended dignity, and you left her presence under a misapprehension, as, indeed, you left mine. She expected your return, but you never came back. It was long before I even suspected that anything was wrong between you two, but I knew that Sadie had received offer after offer of marriage, some of them most advantageous, but all proposals she rejected. The utmost confidence existed between us. She is to me as if she were my own daughter. I expostulated with her one day, and to my surprise she burst into tears and then confessed her preference for you. I must say that for a time I was filled with resentment against you, but this feeling gave way to sorrow at seeing my girl waste her life through misplaced love. I have spoken to you with the utmost frankness. Sadie is dearer to me than everything else in the world."

For some moments after the Colonel finished his exposition of the case John Steele maintained silence. The Viennese band was playing a lively selection, and he appeared to be listening to the music, but with troubled brow. The place seemed rather unsuited for a confession of love, and the tidings brought no particular joy to the listener. At last the young man spoke.

"Does Miss Beck know—was she aware that you were going to speak to me on this subject?"

"Certainly not. I doubt if she would thank me for my interference, because, as I said before, she is a proud girl. I don't think she knew you were in Naples until she heard me ask the Consul about you. When I was questioning him, she seemed rather eager to hear his answers, but she said nothing until we were outside." This coincided with the account given by Stokes of the visit, and Steele became more and more perplexed.

"What did she say when you were outside?" he asked.

"Oh! she wanted to know why I wished to see you, and I told her it was on a matter of business. This didn't quite satisfy her, so, being pressed, I mentioned that block of Northern Pacific stock which you offered to sell to me once, and said I thought I could dispose of it for you to advantage, if you still possessed it. Sadie knows nothing of Wall Street affairs, so, of course, this explanation seemed quite reasonable. Besides, it is true enough, for I do wish to make a bargain with you about that stock whenever you feel inclined to come down from the clouds and discuss mundane affairs."

"What do you expect me to do? I don't mean about the stock, but about Miss Beck."

"It is not for me to make any suggestions in the premises, my dear fellow. You are a man of honour. You have made a mistake which involves the happiness of an innocent person. I have put the matter before you with a plainness which is, I think, exceptional. The next move must rest with you."

"Where are you stopping?"

"At the Grand Hotel."

"Then, with your permission, I shall have the pleasure of calling upon Miss Beck to-morrow afternoon at four o'clock, if that hour is convenient."

The stout Colonel, with visible emotion, clasped Steele warmly by the hand. "You are a good fellow!" he said. "When you meet my niece, you will let no hint escape you of this conversation?"

"Most assuredly not."

"I came to see you," continued the Colonel, "about the Northern Pacific stock, remember that, and, of course, you call on her for old friendship's sake on learning she is here with me."

"You may rely upon my tact, Colonel."

His mission accomplished, the Colonel seemed to hesitate between going or staying, his attitude that of a man wondering whether it is better to leave well alone or to proceed further. Finally he said: "By the way, Steele, in order that we may make our conference the more legitimate, how about that Northern Pacific stock of yours? I am willing to buy it outright, or to sell it for you, just as you choose."

"I am not quite in a position to sell at the present moment, Colonel."

"I thought you said that you still held the stock?"

"So I do, but I don't care to make any move regarding it just now."

"Delays are dangerous, John."

"I know they are," rejoined the younger man shortly, with a finality of tone which showed the elder that nothing was to be gained by continuing the discussion; so the good man rose and bade farewell to his friend with a cordiality that was almost overdone, and left the other to his thoughts, such as they were.

John Steele enjoyed little sleep that night. The ghost of an almost forgotten love haunted him, and the apparition, as is usually the case, was most unwelcome. He had certainly left the girl with brusque abruptness, thoroughly convinced that she was as mercenary as her uncle, ready to throw him over because he had failed financially. At that time he had possessed the eager confidence of extreme youth; now, it occurred to him that he had often been mistaken in his estimates of people. Might not an error have been committed in this case? The manner of Colonel Beck retained its ancient bluff heartiness, and there was certainly a show of reasonableness in his presentation of the case. Time had long since mitigated the sting of the refusal. At the moment of asking he had supposed that the granting of the loan meant salvation. The continuance of the panic, however, convinced him that the money would have melted ineffectually and vanished like the rest. If his estimate of the situation had been so far astray, might not his judgment of both uncle and niece have been equally erroneous? There was but one thing for a man of honour to do, and that was to stand the brunt of his mistake, no matter what the cost. He was not the first to pay, with interest compounded, an early debt.

Next day the problem presented no more alluring aspect than it had done during the troublesome night. As the hour of the interview approached, Steele's dejection increased. He did not visit the Consul as he had promised. In fact, he had entirely forgotten the appointment made the night before. He walked along the promenade by the sea-wall fronting the fashionable quarter of Naples, with haggard face and bowed head, striving to collect his thoughts, although, so far, those he had succeeded in collecting proved of little comfort to him. However, the hour was set, and, as it approached, he walked resolutely to the Grand Hotel to meet the girl, in a frame of mind almost as greatly perturbed as when he last saw her.

Time had passed lightly over the blonde head of Miss Sadie Beck, who greeted him with subdued sweetness; a touch of melancholy in her voice. As the Consul had very truly said, Miss Beck was an amazingly pretty girl, who dressed with an elegance that suggested Paris.

"Through a chance meeting with your uncle last evening, I learned that you were in Naples, and I asked permission to call."

"Yes, he told me he had met you," replied the girl simply. "It gives me great pleasure to see you again, because, if you remember, we parted rather in anger," and Sadie raised her blue eyes to his, only to sink them again to the carpet with just the slightest possible indication of a little quivering sigh;

indeed, the eyes themselves, large and pathetic, gave token of unshed tears.

"Miss Beck—" he began, but she interrupted him in tremulous tones; a crystal drop actually became visible on the long eyelashes.

"In the old days you used to call me Sadie."

"But the old days are gone forever."

These words were his last effort against the silken web which he felt entangling him, and he knew himself to be a brute for uttering them. Their effect upon the girl was instantaneous. She sank down by the table, flung her arms upon it, lowering her face upon them in a storm of weeping.

"Oh! not for me! not for me!" she cried between sobs. "You may forget the old days, and I see you have forgotten them. Leave me, then! leave me to my memories! Why, oh why did you seek to see me again?"

That settled it. He placed his hand upon her heaving shoulders and spoke soothingly to her.

Half an hour later Steele came out of the hotel and went direct to the American Consulate.

"Hullo, old man! what's the matter with you?" cried James Stokes. "You are white as a ghost."

"I'm all right. Didn't sleep very well last night. See here, Stokes! I just called to say that I wish you would forget part of the conversation we had yesterday."

"Easily done! Which part, for instance?"

"What I said with reference to Colonel Beck. I was mistaken about him. He has convinced me of that."

"Oh! has he? You mean, then, he didn't refuse you the twenty thousand?"

"He refused it from the best of motives. I was rather a strenuous fool in those days, and thought everything should come my way. If I didn't see what I wanted, I imagined all I had to do was to ask for it. I left the Colonel in a temper, and I realise now that I did worthy people a great injustice."

"Some one else was involved, then, as well as the Colonel?"

"Yes. I was engaged to his niece, and, as there is no secret about it, I may as well inform you that the engagement has been renewed to-day."

The Consul whistled and then checked himself, as if this indication of surprise were not quite appropriate to so serious an announcement.

"Well, John, I congratulate you. She is a very handsome girl."

"Extremely so," answered the happy man, as he gloomily and abruptly took his departure.

The frivolous Consul was now at liberty to whistle as long as he liked, and he did so. Then he took to muttering to himself.

"I don't admire the position of affairs a little bit. My friend John resembles a man who's just got a life sentence. He was thunderstruck when I mentioned Beck to him last night, and quite evidently didn't wish me to leave him alone with the Colonel. I distrust the Beck contingent. By St. Jonathan, I'll try a little ruse with the gallant Colonel, which at least can do no harm."

The friendly Stokes pondered deeply over the situation, until his meditations were interrupted by the entrance of the Colonel himself. He had come in quest of letters, for the Consulate was post-office-in-ordinary to various tourists from the States.

No letters bearing the name of Beck had arrived, and the inquirer was turning away when Stokes acted with quick heedlessness, which must be the excuse for what followed. In his own defence he used to say afterward that the presence of Colonel Beck so corrupted him with an atmosphere of Wall Street, that he couldn't speak the truth if he tried.

"Oh, Colonel, one moment. You are an old friend of Steele's, aren't you?"

The Colonel turned on his heel.

"Yes. Why?" he asked.

"I'd like to speak with you a moment about him, if you don't mind. I'm an old friend of his, too, but unfortunately I'm poor, and so, however willing, I can't be of much assistance to him. Did he speak to you last night about money matters after I left you?"

"No," said the Colonel, drawing down his brows. "Ah! that's just like him. I came away to give him the opportunity. I owe you an apology for my attitude when you first came to the Consulate. Of course, I knew Steele's address, but I thought you might be a creditor of his, and goodness knows the poor fellow has had enough of them."

"Why, what do you mean? If he owns that Northern Pacific stock, he's a rich man, richer than you have any idea of, if he sells at once. He can realise millions on that stock at the present moment."

"Then he hasn't told you what he did with it?"

The ruddy face of the Colonel seemed to become mottled, and he moistened his lips as he said:

"No. What has he done with it?"

"Well, in spite of all my advice, he sent it over to a friend named Philip Manson in New York. He hasn't even a scrap of writing to show for it. You know Wall Street, so I need say no more."

The Colonel apparently knew Wall Street, for he gasped: "The eternal fool!"

"Exactly. Still, Steele's a good fellow, and we mustn't let him sink. I thought, perhaps, you wouldn't mind stumping up a bit to help him out."

"Hasn't he any other resources?" asked the Colonel. "Not a cent, so far as I know. All his hopes were centred on that Northern Pacific stock, and now that's gone."

"Well, I must say, Mr. Consul, that you have a good deal of cheek to ask me, a complete stranger to you, to spend money on an idiot who doesn't know enough to take care of a fortune when he has got it."

John Steele passed another unrefreshing night, but solace came next morning in the shape of an early letter and an important cablegram.

*Dear Mr. Steele (the letter began).*

*How inscrutable is the human heart! Ever since you left America I have yearned to see you, and at last this desire was gratified. You were the idol of my younger days, and were my first love—my first and only love, I may say; and yet I write these words as calmly as if I were inditing an order to my dressmaker. I find what I should have known before, that we cannot light a fire with a heap of ashes. I know you will think me wayward and changeable, especially after my emotion when you spoke of the olden days. But am I to blame that I find myself changed, and fancy I see a change in you also? There can never be anything between us, John, but that pure friendship which becomes more and more of a solace as we grow older. I give you back your promise of to-day. It will be useless to call upon me, for my uncle and I will have left for Rome before you receive this letter. But believe me,*

*Always your friend and well-wisher,*

*Sadie Beck.*

"Well, by Jove!" cried the astounded man, as he finished the epistle. "The girl is honest, after all, and I have not been able to conceal my real feeling towards her. I am afraid I have kept faith in the letter, but not in the spirit. However, thank God for her decision! Her letter does not betray a broken heart, even if I had conceit enough to think I had caused her suffering."

It was a jubilant man who called upon the Consul in his office that morning.

"Any thing new this morning, Steele? You seem brighter than I have seen you look for a day or two."

"Yes, rather important news. It seems to be my fate to come into this office and contradict what I said the day before, so I am at it again. The Becks have left suddenly for Rome, and the young lady jilts me, so that engagement is off."

"Oh! What is the reason of their change of plan?"

"No reason at all, so far as I can make out. Surely a woman doesn't need to give a reason for preferring Rome to Naples?"

"No; I suppose not," murmured the Consul, wondering how much his hint that John was a ruined man had to do with the sudden withdrawal.

"And I've had a most important cablegram from Philip Manson," continued John jubilantly. "He has sold out my Northern Pacific at a price which more than recoups me for all my losses."

"John, you're a good deal merrier than you were this time yesterday. I expect the next announcement to be that you are returning to the States, to leave me here lamenting."

"That's it exactly. But there's no law compelling you to stay here when there's ten thousand patriotic citizens eager to take your place. Manson has been appointed general manager of the Wheat Belt Line, with offices in Chicago, and he offers me my old position of division superintendent, so I'll be singing that 'Fare-well to Naples' which I've heard so often since I arrived here. Jimmy, I'm going to be a sane and useful citizen hereafter. No more stock exchange for me. I shall plant my money in gilt-edged mortgages where the interest will be as secure as the eternal hills. Then I'll settle down to hard work and show old Philip Manson what an industrious person can do on the Wheat Belt Line."

John Steele arrived in America to learn that it was easier to make good resolutions than to keep them. He settled down in Chicago and found there was little difficulty in placing his money on mortgage at attractive rates of interest. He gave, however, his personal care to the securities offered, trusted no man's word, and always viewed the spot and made close inquiries before he drew a cheque for investment. He divided his money between city and country, not depending on any one lawyer to do the business for him, but seeking local advice and local watchfulness wherever a mortgage was drawn. His eggs were in many baskets, or hatching nests, with a different legal hen to sit on each. The only gentleman of the law he had heretofore known was

Beck, and his opinion of the profession seemed to be tinctured by his dislike of the gallant Colonel. He gave work to many legal experts, but never allowed the left-hand lawyer to know what the right-hand lawyer was doing.

He was shocked to find himself so suspicious of everyone except Philip Manson, but even more perturbed to learn that all his old delight in work was gone. Philip Manson was ambitious to make the Wheat Belt Line the model railway of the West, and in his quiet intense purposeful way was accomplishing that object. To John this ambition seemed trivial and above all futile, when it was possible for some speculator in New York or a combination of speculators to make the road a mere pawn in a gamble; to wreck it if its ruin suited the game, to discharge every employee at a week's notice. His liking for Manson, his reluctance to disillusionise the one man on earth who was friend and believed in him, held him for more than a year at his task of division superintendent and the work that was growing more and more irksome to him. Then an incident at Slocum Junction gave the necessary impetus which finally shifted him from a career of usefulness into the predatory class. The faithful watch-dog became the ravenous wolf.

## CHAPTER X—BUYING A RAILWAY

THE station-master said nonchalantly that he had nothing to do with it, and from out the telegraph office he brought a stout wooden chair which he set down in the dark strip of shade which ran along the pine platform under the eaves of the station. The back of this chair being tilted against the building, the station-master sat down in it, put his heels on the wooden round, took from his pocket a jack-knife, and began to whittle a stick, an occupation which the momentary pausing of the express seemed to have interrupted. There was nothing of the glass of fashion or the mould of form about the station-master. He was dressed in weather-worn trousers, held to his thin frame by a pair of suspenders quite evidently home-made, which came over his shoulders, and underneath this was a coarse woollen shirt, open at the throat because the button had gone. On top of all this there perched a three-year-old, dilapidated straw hat which had once possessed a wide brim, but was now in a state of disrepair in thorough keeping with the costume. Yet in spite of appearances he was a capable young man who could manipulate a telegraphic machine at reasonable speed, was well up in the business pertaining to Slocum Junction, and had definite opinions regarding the manner in which the affairs of the nation should be carried on. Indeed, at that moment he was an exemplification of the independence for which his country had fought and bled. No one knew better than he that the Greased Lightning Express would never have halted for an instant at Slocum Junction unless it did so to put off a person of some importance. But that important person had begun to give his opinion of the locality in language that was painful and free the moment he realised the situation, and the station-master signified his resentment by sitting down in the chair and assuming a careless attitude, which told the stranger plainer than words that he could go to the devil if he wished. For all he knew, the obstreperous person who had stepped from the express might be his chief, but the station-master made no concession to this possibility.

Opposite him in the blazing sunlight stood a dapper young man grasping a neat handbag. He might have posed as a tailor's model, and he offered a striking contrast to the unkempt station-master. He cast an almost despairing look at the vanishing express, now a mere dot in the horizon, with a trail of smoke, as if it were a comet that had run aground. Then he turned an exasperated face upon the nonchalant station-master.

"You are not responsible for the situation, eh? You don't seem to care much, either."

"Well, to tell the truth, stranger, I don't."

"You mean to tell me there's no train for two hours and a half on the branch line?"

"I never said anything of the sort, because there isn't any branch line."

"No branch line? Why, there it is before my eyes! There's a locomotive, of a kind, and a composite passenger and freight-car that evidently dates from the time of the Deluge. Noah used that car!" cried the angry stranger.

"Well, if Noah was here, he wouldn't use it for two hours and a half," said the station-master complacently.

"I don't understand what you mean," protested the stranger. "Is there, or is there not, a train in two hours and a half?"

"Of course there is."

"You said a minute ago there wasn't."

"I didn't say anything of the kind, and if you weren't adding your own natural heat to the unnatural heat of the day, you'd learn something. You were talking about branch lines; I said there is no branch line. That's all."

"Then what's the meaning of those two lines of rust running to the right?"

"There's five or six thousand people," droned the station-master, "who'd like to know what that object you're referring to really is. Leastways, they used to want to know, but lately they've given up all curiosity on the subject.

They're the shareholders, who put up good money to have that road made. We call it the Farmers' Road, and it isn't a branch, but as independent as the main line."

"Or as yourself," hazarded the young man.

"Well, it's independent, anyhow," continued the station-master, "and I've nothing to do with it."

"Haven't the cursed fools who own it the sense to make it connect with anything on the main line?"

"Of course, we're all fools unless we come from Chicago," said the station-master imperturbably.

"I didn't say that," commented the stranger.

"No, I did. If your dome of thought was in working order, I shouldn't need to explain these things; but as I've nothing particular to do, I may as well teach a man from Chicago his ABC. You stepped off the express just now owning the whole country, populated with fools, according to you. I've been station-master here for eighteen months, and I never saw that express stop before. I may be an idiot, but still I am aware that a man who steps off the Greased Lightning is one of two things. He is either a bigbug with pull enough on the railway company to get them to stop the Greased Lightning for him, or else he's a tramp who can't pay his fare, and so is put off."

"Oh, you've sized me up, have you? Well, which am I? The millionaire or the tramp?"

"When you stepped off, I thought you were the millionaire; but the moment you opened your mouth, I knew you were the tramp."

John Steele laughed with very good-natured heartiness.

"Say, old man, that's all right. The drinks are on me, if there were a tavern near, which there doesn't seem to be. I suppose there's no place in this God-forsaken hole where on a hot day like this a man can get a cooling beverage?"

"Stranger, you're continually jumping at conclusions and landing at the wrong spot. Allow me to tell you"—here he lowered his voice a bit—"that you don't raise no blush to my cheeks by anything you can say; but there's a lady in the waiting-room, and if I were you I'd talk accordingly."

The change in the cocksure attitude of John Steele was so sudden and complete that it brought a faint smile of gratification to the gaunt face of the station-master.

"Great heavens!" whispered the crestfallen young man, "why didn't you tell me that before?"

"Well, you've been kind of monopolising the conversation, and I haven't had much chance to speak up to now. One would suppose that if a man had a thinking-machine in his head at all, he would know that the little road couldn't connect with a train that never stopped here."

"Of course, of course," said John hurriedly, his mind running on the language he had used in the first moments of chagrin at finding himself marooned at this desolate junction, which might have been heard by the unseen lady in the waiting-room. He hoped his voice hadn't carried through the pine wall.

"Well, station-master, I apologise. And now, if you will kindly tell me what the Farmers' Road does connect with, I'll be very much obliged."

"The Farmers' Road runs two trains a day," said the station-master sententiously, as if he were speaking of some mighty empire. "The train consists, as you see, of a locomotive and a mixed car. The first train comes in here at nine o'clock in the morning, connecting with the local going east. It then returns to Bunkerville, and reaches here in the afternoon at three o'clock, to connect with the local going west. That little train doesn't know there are any flyers on our line; all it knows is that the eastern local comes in somewhere about nine o'clock in the morning, and the western local arrives anywhere between three and five in the afternoon. So a Chicago man can't step jauntily off the express he has managed to stop, and expect to get a train to Bunkerville whenever he chooses."

"Admirably stated," said John Steele. "And if you will condescend further to enlighten a beclouded intellect would you mind explaining what the deuce the little train is doing here at this hour? If I follow your argument, it should have returned to Bunkerville after the nine o'clock local came in, arriving here again just before three o'clock."

"Your befogged brain is waking up," said the station-master encouragingly. "The phenomenon to which you have called attention happens once or twice a week. If you cast your eye to the other end of the platform, you will see piled there an accumulation of miscellaneous freight. The Farmers' Road has just dumped that upon us, and to do so has taken a special trip. That stuff will go east on Number Eight, which is a freight train that will stop here some time in the afternoon when it sees the signal set against it."

"I comprehend," said Steele; "and I venture on my next proposition with great diffidence, caused by increasing admiration of yourself and the lucid mind you bring to bear on Western railway procedure. If I have followed your line of argument as unerringly as the farmers' train follows the Farmers' Road, his nibs the engineer must take the train back to Bunkerville so that he may return here on his regular trip to meet the three o' clock western local. If I am right, what is to prevent him from going now, taking me with him, and giving me an opportunity at Bunkerville to transact my business and catch the regular train back?—for I am going further west, and would like to intercept the local, which would save me spending an unnecessary night at Bunkerville, and wasting most of to-morrow as well."

"The reasons are as follows: His nibs, as you call him, is engineer, conductor, brakeman, and freight handler. When he came in, he had to carry that freight from his car to the platform where you see it. That takes time, even if the day were not so oppressively hot as it is. So, instead of keeping up his fire under the boiler, and burning useless coal, he banks the furnace as soon as he arrives. Then, at his leisure, he removes the boxes to the platform. If he returned to Bunkerville, they would give him something to do there; here he is out of reach; besides, he would have to draw his fires and start anew about two o'clock, and that he doesn't want to do. He has, therefore, curled himself up in the passenger car, put a newspaper over his face to keep off the flies, and has gone to sleep. When the proper moment arrives he will stir up his fire, go to Bunkerville, and then be ready to make the return trip on one expenditure of coal. Now do you understand?"

"Yes, thank you, I do; and this has given me an idea."

"That's a good thing, and I can easily guess what your idea is. But before putting it into operation, I should like to mitigate a slight you have put on Slocum Junction. You made a sarcastic remark about cool drinks. Now, I beg to inform you that the nine o'clock local from the west slides off on this here platform every morning a great big square cold chunk of ice. That chunk of ice is growing less and less in a big wooden pail in the telegraph-office, but the water that surrounds it is chilly as the North Pole. If you have anything in your hip pocket or in that natty little valise which mitigates the rigour of cold water, there's no reason why you shouldn't indulge in a refreshing drink."

"Station-master," said John, laughing, "you ought to be superintendent of this road, instead of junction boss. You're the wisest man I've met in two years."

Saying this, he sprang the catch of the handbag and drew forth a bulky, wicker-covered, silver-topped flask.

"I propose we adjourn to the telegraph-office," he added, "and investigate that wooden pail."

The station-master led the way with an alacrity that he had not heretofore exhibited. The result of the conference was cheerful and comforting.

"Now," said the station-master, drawing the back of his hand across his lips, "what you want is a special train to Bunkerville. A man from the city would get that by telegraphing to the superintendent at the terminus and paying twenty dollars. A man from the country who had some sense would go to Joe the engineer and persuade him he ought to wake up and return to Bunkerville at once."

"How much would be required to influence Joe?"

"Oh, a couple of dollars would be wealth. A silver dollar in front of each eye will obscure the whole Western prairie if placed just right."

"Very well, I'll go out and place 'em."

"You are forgetting your flask," said the station-master, as Steele snapped shut his valise.

"No, I'm not. That flask and its contents belong to you, as a reward for being patient and instructive when a darned fool let loose from the city happened your way."

And this showed John Steele to be a reader of his fellow-man; for while the engineer might accept the two dollars, the independent station-master certainly would not have done so. That glib official, however, seemed to have no particular words for this occasion, so he changed the subject and said: "If you persuade Joe to go, I wish you'd remember the lady in the waiting-room. She's a Miss Dorothy Slocum, and a powerful nice girl, that teaches school in Bunkerville. Fact is, this junction was named after her father. Used to be the principal man round these parts; but he lost his money, and now his girl's got to teach school. I never knew him—he was dead long before I came here. She's been visiting relatives. This is vacation time, you know."

"All right. You tell her there's a special leaving in a few minutes, and that she's very welcome to ride upon it."

With that John Steele went out into the furnace of the sun across the dusty road and entered the composite car. The Farmers' Road did not join rails with the main line, and so caused much extra handling of freight. The engine stood there simmering in the heat, both external and internal, a slight murkiness of smoke rising from its funnel, shaped like an inverted bell.

"Hallo, Joe!" cried Steele, as he entered the car. "Don't you yearn for home and friends?"

The man was sprawling on two seats, with a newspaper over his head, as the station-master had predicted.

"Hello!" he echoed, sitting up and shaking away the sheet of paper, "what's the matter?"

"Nothing, except that if the spirit should move you to get over to Bunkerville with this ancient combination, five dollars will be transferred from my pocket into yours."

"'Nough said," cried Joe, rising to his feet. "It'll take me about twenty minutes to get the pot boiling again. You don't happen to have the fiver about you, I suppose? I haven't seen one for a couple of years."

"Here you are," replied Steele, drawing a crisp bill from his purse.

The engineer thrust it into the pocket of his greasy overalls.

"I'll toot the whistle when I'm ready," he said.

This financial operation accomplished, John Steele returned to the station. The station-master was standing by the door of the waiting-room conversing pleasantly with someone within. When Steele entered the room he was amazed to see so pretty a girl sitting on the bench that ran round the bare walls of the uninviting apartment.

"Will you introduce me?" inquired the city man, handing his card to the station-master.

"Miss Dorothy Slocum," said the latter, "this is Mr. John Steele, of Chicago."

The young man removed his fashionable straw hat.

"Miss Slocum," he said, "I desire to apologise to you. I'm afraid that when I found myself stranded on the platform outside, I used language which can hardly be justified, even in the circumstances. But I had no idea at the time that there was a lady within miles of us."

"I was much interested in my book," replied the girl, with a smile, "and was not paying attention to what was going on outside."

She held up the volume, between whose leaves her fore-finger was placed.

"Well, Miss Slocum, it must have been a pretty absorbing story, and I am deeply grateful to it for acting as a non-conductor between my impulsive observations and your hearing. Nothing excuses intemperate language, as the station-master here has taught me through the force of a benign example. Still, if anything could exculpate a man, I should think it would be the exasperating conduct of this Farmers' Railroad, as they call it."

"Indeed," said Miss Dorothy archly, "the book had really no right to interfere, because I am one of the owners of the railway, and so perhaps it was my duty to listen to complaints of a passenger. Not that I have anything to do with the management of the line; I am compelled to pay my fare just like the rest."

"I shall be delighted if you accept a ride on your own road as free as if you carried a superintendent's pass. I am going to Bunkerville in my own private car, as it were, and shall feel honoured if I may extend the courtesies of the same."

"The station-master has just told me you were kind enough to offer a poor vagrant a lift to Bunkerville. I wished to buy a ticket, but this haughty official of the main line so despises our poor little road that he will not sell me one."

"Indeed," said the station-master, "I haven't the power, nor the tickets. They don't entrust me with any business so tremendous. Joe starts his rickety engine going, then leaves it to jog along as it likes, and comes through the car to collect the fares. They have no tickets, and perhaps that's why the road has never paid a dividend."

"Oh, you mustn't say that!" protested the girl. "Poor Joe has not got rich out of his occupation, any more than the shareholders have made money on their shares. If you will permit me to pay my fare to Joe, Mr. Steele I shall be only too happy to take this early opportunity of getting to Bunkerville."

"I couldn't think of it, Miss Slocum; in fact, I must prohibit any communication between Joe and yourself, fearing you, as an owner of the road, may learn by what corrupt practices I induced Joe to make the trip."

The girl laughed, but before she could reply, a wheezy

"Toot-toot!" outside announced that Joe had already got steam up.

"I'll carry your valise across," said the obliging station-master, while Miss Dorothy Slocum picked up her lighter belongings and accompanied Mr. John Steele to the shabby little passenger-car. Joe was leaning out of the cab with a grin on his smeared face, which was there probably because of the five-dollar bill in his trousers' pocket. The station-master placed the valise in the baggage section of the car, and raised his tattered hat as the little train started gingerly out for the open country.

It was a pretty landscape through which they passed, with little to indicate that the prairies were so near at hand. The line ran along a shallow valley, well wooded, especially by the banks of the stream that wandered through it, which even at this parched season of the year was still running its clear-water course, and Miss Slocum informed the Chicago man that it flowed from a never-drying spring some ten miles on the other side of the main line. The little road was as crooked as possible, for the evident object of its constructors had been to avoid bridging the stream, piling up any high embankments or excavating deep cuttings. The pace, therefore, was exceedingly slow; nevertheless John Steele did not find the time hang heavily on his hands. At first the girl seemed somewhat shy and embarrassed to find herself the only passenger except this gallant young business man; but he tactfully put her at her ease by pretending much interest in the history of the railway, with which he soon learned she was unfortunately familiar.

"Yes," she said; "the building of this road was the greatest financial disaster that ever occurred in this section of the country. My father was one of its chief promoters. When the Wheat Belt Line, by which you came here from Chicago, was surveyed through this part of the State, those interested in the neighbourhood expected it to run through Bunkerville, which would thus become a large town. The railway people demanded a large money bonus, which Bunker County refused, because Bunkerville was in the direct line, and they thought the railway must come through there, whether a bonus were paid or not. In fact, the first survey passed just north of Bunkerville. But our poor little village was not so important as its inhabitants imagined, and the next line surveyed was twenty miles away. For once the farmers were too shrewd. They thought, as they put it, that the new line was a bluff, and did not realise their mistake until too late. My father had been in favour of granting the bonus, but he was out-voted. Perhaps that is why the railway people called their station Slocum instead of Bunkerville, which was twenty miles distant. The next nearest railway line was forty-five miles away, and two years after the Wheat Belt Line began operations, it was proposed to organise a local company to construct a railway from Slocum, through Bunkerville to Jamestown, on the other line. Bonuses were granted all along the route, and besides this the State legislature gave a subsidy, and, furthermore, passed a bill to prevent competition, prohibiting any railway to parallel the Farmers' Road for sixty miles on either side."

"Does that law still stand on the statute books of the State?" asked Steele, with increasing interest.

"I think so. It has never been repealed to my knowledge."

"Well, I should doubt its being constitutional. Why, that ties up more than seven thousand square miles of the State into a hard knot, and prevents it from acquiring the privilege of further railway communication."

"In a measure it does," said the girl. "You may run as many lines as you like north and south, but not east and west."

"It's a wonder the Wheat Belt Line didn't contest that law," said Steele.

"Well, I've been told that this law is entirely in the interests of the Wheat Belt Line, although the farmers didn't think so when they voted for the Bill. You see, the Wheat Belt Line was already in operation east and west, and could not be affected by that Act, and, of course, the same Bill which prevented competition to the Farmers' Road also, in a measure, protected the Wheat Belt Line through the same district."

"By Jove!" said Steele, his eyes glistening, "this is a proposition which contains some peculiar points. Well, go on, what happened?"

"Oh, disaster happened. In spite of the legislation and bonuses, the road was a complete failure, and ruined all who were deeply interested in it. The farmers subscribed stock to the amount of something like a hundred thousand dollars, but this money, with the sum of the legislative grant and the bonuses, was all swallowed up in the first twenty miles, and in getting the rolling-stock and equipment, such as it is. The line was never pushed through to Jamestown, and there arose litigation about some of the bonuses that had been paid, and, all in all, it was a most disastrous business. It was hoped that the Wheat Belt Line would come to the rescue and buy the unfinished road, but they would not look at it. This section has never paid a dividend, and is supposed to be doing well when it earns enough money for expenses and repairs. The shares can now be bought for five cents on the dollar, or less."

"How much of it do you possess, Miss Slocum?"

"I own a thousand shares, and my father told me not to part with them, because he was certain that some day they would be valuable."

For a few moments there was silence in the car, and the girl, glancing up at her companion, found his ardent gaze fixed upon her with an intensity that was embarrassing. She flushed slightly and turned her head to look out of the window at the familiar scenery they were passing. It would have surprised the young man could he have read the thoughts that occupied the mind of this extremely pretty and charmingly modest girl who sat opposite him. Here is practically what she said to herself: "I am tired of this deadly dull village in which I live, and here, at last, is a way out. I read in his eyes the beginning of admiration. He shall be the youthful Moses to lead me into the Promised Land. Through this lucky meeting I shall attain the city if I but play my cards rightly."

It would have astonished the girl if she had known what was in the man's mind. The ardent gaze was not for her, as she had supposed. Although he appeared to be looking directly at her, he was in reality almost ignorant of her presence, and saw unfolded before him a scene far beyond her—the whole range of the Eastern States. The power that enabled him to stop the fast express at Slocum Junction gave a hint of Steele's position in the railway world to the station-master, but it conveyed no meaning to the girl. It was his business to be intimately acquainted with the railway situation in northwestern America, and that involved the knowledge of what was going on in the Eastern States. He knew that the Rockervelt system was making for somewhere near this point, and that, ultimately, it would need to cross the State, in spite of the opposition it must meet from the Wheat Belt Line. Whoever possessed the Farmers' bankrupt road held the right of way across the State, so far as a belt of one hundred and twenty miles was concerned. It seemed incredible that Rockervelt, this Napoleon of the railway world, should be ignorant of the obstacle that lay in his path. Rockervelt was in the habit of buying legislatures and crushing opposition; still, he never spent money where it was not required, and it would be infinitely cheaper to buy the Farmers' Road, and thus secure the privileges pertaining to it, than to purchase the repeal of the obstructing law. At that moment John Steele determined to camp across the path of the conqueror. If Napoleon accepted battle, John was under no delusion as to the result. The name of Steele would disappear from the roll of rising young men in Chicago, and he might be forced to begin at the bottom of the ladder again. However, he knew that Napoleon's eye was fixed on the Pacific coast, and that he never wasted time in a fight if a reasonable expenditure of money would cause the enemy to withdraw. Steele calculated that he could control the road for something under three thousand dollars, which would give him the majority of the stock at the price the girl had named. That was a mere bagatelle. Then he would withdraw from Rockervelt's front for anything between three hundred thousand dollars and half a million. If he succeeded, he would at least recover all the money he had lost in the panic which followed the trickery of Rock-ervelt, Blair and Beck. But success meant more than this. Aside from the joy of relieving Rockervelt of a substantial sum, there would also follow the practical defeat of T. Acton Blair, for the Farmers' Road was situated in that Western district on which the general manager was supposed to keep his eye, in the interests of the Rockervelt system.

A sigh from the girl brought him to a realisation of his neglect of social duties, and the brilliant vision of loot faded from his eyes.

"What pretty scenery we are passing!" he said. "The wooded dell, and the sparkling little rivulet running through it. It is sweet and soothing after the rush and turmoil of a great city. It must be a delight to live here."

"Indeed it isn't!" cried the girl; "it is horrid! Deadly dull, utterly commonplace, with little chance of improving the mind, and none at all for advancing one's material condition. I loathe the life and yearn for the city."

As she said this she bestowed upon him a fascinating glimpse of a pair of lovely eyes, and veiled within them he saw what he took to be a tender appeal for sympathy and, perhaps, for help. After all, he was a young man, and perhaps that glance had carried a hypnotic suggestion to his very soul; and, added to all this, the girl was undoubtedly beautiful.

"Really," he said, leaning forward towards her, "I think that might be managed, you know."

"Do you?" she asked, looking him full in the face.

At this interesting moment the car slowly came to a standstill at a wooden platform, and Joe thrust open the door and shouted: "Here you are! Bunkerville!"

Dorothy Slocum held out her hand shyly to John Steele as she bade him "Good-bye." She thanked him once more for allowing her to ride on the special train, and added: "If you ever come to Bunkerville again, I hope you will not forget me."

"Forget you!" cried the enthusiastic young man. "I think you entirely underrate the attractions of Bunkerville. It seems to me a lovely village. But I shall visit it in the near future—not because of itself, but for the reason that a certain Miss Dorothy lives here."

To this complimentary speech Miss Slocum made no reply, but she laughed and blushed in a manner very becoming to her, and somehow managed to leave an impression on Mr. Steele's mind that she was far from being displeased at the words he had uttered.

When she was gone, the traveller asked Joe where the office of Mr. Hazlett, the lawyer, was situated, and being directed, he was speedily in the presence of the chief legal functionary that Bunkerville possessed. Steele had a considerable amount of money lent upon Bunkerville business property, and his lawyer had written him that, as times were backward, there arose some difficulty in persuading the debtors to meet the requirements of the mortgages. If the mortgages were foreclosed and the property sold, Hazlett did not think it would produce the money that had been borrowed upon it, and so Steele had informed him that he would drop off at Bunkerville on his way west and consult with him.

The lawyer had been looking for him on the regular train, and so was not at the station to meet him. If Hazlett had expected a visit from a hard old skinflint, bent on clutching his pound of financial flesh, he must have been somewhat surprised to greet a smiling young fellow who seemed to be thinking of anything but the property in question.

"We will just walk down the street," said the lawyer, "and I'll show you the buildings."

"All right," assented Steele, "if it doesn't take too long; for I must catch the three o'clock local at Slocum Junction."

During their walk together Steele paid but the scantiest interest to the edifices pointed out to him, and the lawyer soon found he was not even listening to the particulars he recited so circumstantially.

"Do you know anything about the Farmers' Railway?" was the question Steele shot at him in the midst of a score of reasons why it was better not to foreclose at the present moment.

"I know all about it," said the lawyer. "I have done the legal business of the road from its beginning."

"Is there a list of the shareholders in existence?"

"I hold a partial list; but shares have changed hands a good deal, and sometimes no notification has been given me, which is contrary to law."

"I was told to-day that shares can be bought at five cents on the dollar. Is that true?"

"Many shares have been sold at that price; some for less, some for more."

"What is the total number of shares?'

"A hundred thousand."

"Could fifty thousand and an odd share be bought?"

"Do you mean to get control of the road? Yes, I suppose it might be done if you weren't in a hurry, and it was gone about quietly. Some farmers in the outlying districts refuse to sell, thinking the price of the stock will rise, which of course it won't do. Nevertheless, I imagine there should be no difficulty in collecting fifty thousand shares and one more."

"What would it cost?"

"Anywhere between three and five thousand dollars—all depending, as I said, on the thing being done circumspectly, for in these rural communities the wildest rumours get afloat, and so, if it became known that some one was in the market, prices would go up."

"Well, I have in my mind exactly the man to do the trick with discretion, and his name is Hazlett. I will lodge in the bank here five thousand dollars in your name, and I depend on you to get me at least one share over the fifty thousand, although, to be on the safe side, you may purchase at least a thousand in excess. Send the shares to me in Chicago as fast as you secure them, and I'll take care of them."

"Very well, Mr. Steele, I shall do the best I can."

"We will return to your office now, Hazlett, and I'll hand you the cheque. In these matters it's just as well not to lose any time."

"There's another building I want to show you, about five hundred yards down the street."

"We won't mind it to-day. I have determined to take your advice and not foreclose at the present moment. Let's get back to your office, for I mustn't miss Joe's train."

After Steele had returned to Chicago, shares in the Farmers' Railroad began to drop in on him in bulky packages, which he duly noted and placed in a safe. Presently the packages became smaller and smaller, but as the total had already reached forty-nine thousand six hundred and thirty, Steele was not alarmed until he received the following letter from Hazlett:

Dear Mr. Steele:

About two weeks ago I became suspicious that somebody else was buying shares of the Farmers. Road. I came across at that time several people who had sold, although they did not know to whom; and a few days ago a young man called upon me to know if I had any shares for sale. I told him I had none, and as I showed very little interest in the matter, I got some information, and find that a man named T. Acton Blair, of Warmington, is the buyer, and apparently he has agents all over the country trying to purchase shares. I would have telegraphed this information to you were it not for the fact that our telegraph-office is a little leaky, and also because I thought I had the game in my own hands. A young woman in this town, a teacher, Dorothy Slocum by name, possesses a thousand shares, which I felt certain I could purchase for a reasonable figure. I began at ten cents, but she refused, and finally raised to fifty cents, and then a dollar. Higher than that I could not take the responsibility of going without direct authority from you. To my amazement, she has informed me to-day that she has been offered ten thousand dollars for her stock. I obtained her promise that she will not sell for a week. She telegraphed her decision to Blair, and has received an answer from him saying he is on his way to see her. I learn from Miss Slocum that she is acquainted with you, and I surmise, without being certain, that you personally will prove the successful negotiator if you are on the spot. This letter should reach you in time to enable you to arrive here at least as soon as Blair, and I advise prompt action on your part if we are to secure that thousand shares. If you cannot come, telegraph me any one of the following words, and I shall understand I am authorised to offer the amount set down opposite that word.

Yours most sincerely,

James P. Hazlett.

There followed this a dozen words, signifying amounts from ten thousand dollars upwards.

Lawyer Hazlett received a telegram:

*Will reach Slocum Junction at twelve to-morrow. Arrange special train on the Farmers' Road to Bunkerville to be at Junction.*

*Steele.*

The moment Blair's name caught John Steele's eye in the lawyer's letter, he knew that Rockervelt was at last alert and of course could outbid him a thousand to one.

When the Greased Lightning Express stopped at Slocum Junction on this occasion, John Steele had ample time to reach the platform, because the express detached itself from a sumptuous private car before it pursued its journey further west.

"Aha!" said John to himself, "friend Blair travels in style."

The station-master greeted Steele with the cordiality of an old friend.

"Here is a letter which lawyer Hazlett sent out to be handed to you as soon as you arrived, and wished you to read it at once."

Steele tore open the envelope and read:

*I am sorry about the special train, but Blair had telegraphed from Warmington ordering it before your wire came. I have arranged, however, that Joe will return at once for you, as soon as he has landed Blair in Bunkerville. This will make no difference in the negotiations; Miss Slocum has promised to be away from home when Blair calls, and will see you first. I think you've got the inside track, although I surmise the young woman is well aware that she holds the key to the situation. I don't know if she's after all the money she can get, or whether there is something of friendliness in her action. I rather suspect the latter, and I think you can conclude negotiations before she sees Blair at all.*

*Yours most sincerely,*

*James P. Hazlett.*

John Steele gave no expression to the annoyance he felt at missing the special. He distrusted the lawyer's optimism, and like a flash resolved to be in Bunkerville as soon as his antagonist. Blair had stepped down from his private car, asked the station-master where the special was to be found, and quickly ordered his car to be placed on a side track. When he had entered the Bunkerville composition car, and Joe had started up his wheezy engine, Steele darted from the shadow of the station, caught the car and sat down on the rear steps outside, well concealed from the sight of anyone unless that person stood by the end window. All went well until they were about five miles from Bunkerville, when Steele thought he recognised a lady's figure on the highway ahead, and forgetting that he might expose himself to the sharp eyes of Blair, he rose to his feet, clutched the stanchions, and leaned forward. An instant later the rear door was thrown open, a foot was planted energetically in the small of Steele's back, and that young man went hurtling down the embankment, head over heels. There were no half measures with Blair in a crisis like this.

Steele sat up bruised and dazed, not knowing whether he was hurt seriously, or had escaped practically unscathed, which latter proved to be the case. It seemed to him, as he fell through the air, he heard a woman's scream. When he was somewhat stupidly debating whether this was real or imaginary, his doubts were solved by a voice he recognised.

"Oh, Mr. Steele, are you hurt? What a brutal thing for that stout villain to have done!"

"Why, Miss Dorothy, you of all persons! And here was I trying to sneak into Bunkerville to see you first. I thought you were teaching school?"

"Not on Saturdays, Mr. Steele," said the girl, laughing. "I see, after all, you are not injured."

"I'm all right, I think. Fortunately Joe doesn't run sixty miles an hour. Dorothy, I want you to marry me and come to Chicago."

Again the girl laughed.

"Dear me," she said. "I thought you were here to buy my stock. I couldn't think of taking advantage of a proposal that had been literally shaken out of a man. I'm afraid your mind is wandering a bit."

"My mind was never clearer in its life. What is your answer, Dorothy?"

She sat down beside him, still laughing a little. The rivulet was at their feet, the railway embankment behind them, the highway, shrouded by trees, in front.

"Suppose we talk business first, and indulge in sentiment after," said the girl, with a roguish twinkle in her eye. "I have been offered ten thousand dollars for my shares. Are you prepared to pay as much?"

"Yes."

"Cash down?"

"Yes."

"I imagine Mr. Blair would never have come all the way from Warmington to see me if he were not ready to pay a larger sum. I have therefore two further provisos to make. Proviso number one is that you will give me ten per cent, on the profits you make in this transaction. Of course, in spite of Mr. Hazlett's caution, I know there is something very large going on, and naturally I wish to profit by it."

"You are quite right, Miss Slocum, and I agree to the ten per cent, suggestion; in fact, I offered you a hundred per cent, in the beginning, and myself into the bargain, which proposal you have ignored. What is the second proviso?"

"I am told you have a great deal of influence in railway circles in Chicago."

"Yes, I have."

"Can you get a good place for a capable and deserving young man?"

"I think so. Does he understand railroading?"

"Yes, he is the station-master at Slocum Junction."

"Oh, the station-master! Certainly, I should be delighted to offer him a good position. He is a splendid fellow, and I like him exceedingly."

"I am charmed to hear you say so," said Dorothy, with downcast eyes, pulling a flower and picking it to pieces; "for that brings us to the sentiment, and I show my confidence in you and the great esteem in which I hold you, by telling you this strict secret—that I am engaged to be married to the station-master, and am anxious to get to Chicago."

## CHAPTER XI—THE TERROR OF WHEAT

ROCKERVELT settled with John Steele by drawing his cheque for three hundred and ninety-eight thousand six hundred dollars, and it was the circumvented Blair himself who carried through the negotiations. Steele asked half a million at the beginning, but had made up his mind to accept three hundred thousand dollars. As he wished to net this sum clear, he added to it the amount he paid for the stock, including Miss Slocum's ten thousand dollars, and the percentage, which came to nearly forty thousand more. Then he informed Blair he was forced to add ten thousand dollars for that kick, which he did. He told Blair that he remembered the kick on an average of once a day, and that this thought humiliated him. Therefore he would be compelled to charge one hundred dollars a day for thinking of the assault while negotiations were pending. Whether this time-penalty hastened negotiations or not will never be known, but it accounts for the odd figures on the Rockervelt cheque, and, after paying all liabilities, Steele found himself with more than his minimum sum in hand.

The station-master of Slocum Junction was given the position of travelling man on the Wheat Belt Line, at a salary of fifty dollars a week, which seemed to him princely. Miss Dorothy Slocum insisted on finishing her year at the Bunkerville school, but during the Christmas holidays she married the station-master, and they set up housekeeping in Chicago with a nice little bank account of nearly fifty thousand dollars. The young lady's dream of life was now realised. She enjoyed the privilege of being an inhabitant of the Western metropolis, in comfortable circumstances, with everything at her disposal that a large city had to bestow. John Steele, in the New Year, had the pleasure of escorting the young woman to a matinee, and when he asked her if the few weeks' experience of Chicago had changed her mind regarding the delights of the place, she replied that Chicago was heavenly; which called up a smile to the young man's lips as he remembered the story of a Chicago man who had died and gone to the other place, and told an inmate thereof that his new residence was preferable to Chicago. But John didn't tell the story to his companion. He complained pathetically that she had broken his heart by marrying the station-master, but she laughed and said she had broken his heart no more than Blair had broken his neck by precipitating him down the railway embankment from the running train—which, by the way, was true enough.

As time went on, he saw less and less of his Bunkerville friends. He was rising rapidly in the financial world, had resigned his position on the Wheat Belt Line, important as it was, and had set up an office for himself. The newspapers made a great deal of his encounter with old Rockervelt and his victory over the magnate, but Steele was a clear-headed man who indulged in no delusions on the score of that episode. He had spent some very anxious days while negotiations were pending, and no one knew better than he that if Rockervelt had decided to fight, it might have cost the great railway king more than he had paid, but Steele would have been bankrupt when the battle was ended. He resolved never again to combat a force so many thousand times stronger than himself. He would be content with a smaller game and less risk. John attributed the few grey hairs at his temple to those anxious days while Rockervelt was making up his mind, keeping silent and giving forth no sign.

But grey hairs do not necessarily bring wisdom, and so little does a man suspect what is ahead of him that a few tears from a pretty woman sent him into a contest without knowing who his adversary was, to find himself at last face to face with the most formidable financial foe that the world could offer.

He had almost forgotten his friends from the West, when one day the young woman's card was brought up to him as he sat in his office, planning an aggression which was still further to augment his ever-increasing bank account. He looked up with a smile as Dorothy entered, but it was stricken from his lips when he saw how changed she was. All colour had left her cheeks, and her eyes were red as if with weeping.

"Good gracious!" he cried, springing to his feet, "what is the matter? Have you been ill?"

"No," she said, with a catch in her voice, sinking into the chair he offered, "but I am nearly distracted. Oh, Mr. Steele! you said once that the country was sweet and soothing after the turmoil of the city, and I told you I was tired of the country's dullness. It was a foolish, foolish remark. I wish we were back there, and done with this dreadful town!"

"Why, what has happened? Is it your husband, then, who is ill?"

"No—yes, he is—or, rather, yes and no; for, like myself, he is at his wits' end, and doesn't know what to do; therefore I have come to seek your advice," and with this she broke down and wept.

John thought at first that her husband had been dismissed; and if that were the case, Steele, being no longer connected with the railway, would be powerless to aid. Still, he did not see why such an event should cause so much distress, for a young couple in good health, with fifty thousand dollars in the bank, are not exactly paupers, even in Chicago.

"My husband," sobbed the woman at last, "has invested everything we possess in wheat, and since that time the price of wheat has been falling steadily. Now we are on the verge of ruin."

"What on earth did he meddle with wheat for? It is more dangerous than dynamite."

"I don't know," wept the young woman; "but Tom thought it was sure to rise."

"Yes. They always think that. How much did he purchase?"

"One million bushels."

"Good gracious! Do you happen to know the price?"

"Yes, seventy-eight cents."

"Great Scott! Do you mean to say that you two silly young people took on an obligation of seven hundred and fifty thousand dollars, when you possess less than fifty thousand? When he made the deal, how much of a margin did he put up?"

"You mean the money he gave the broker? Ten thousand dollars."

"Ah, then a decline of a cent a bushel would wipe that out."

"Yes, it did, and ever since wheat has been falling, until now it is seventy-four and a quarter. We have given the brokers so far thirty-seven thousand five hundred dollars, and if wheat drops another cent, we have not the money to meet the call and will lose everything. These last three weeks have been the most anxious time of my life."

"I can well believe it. Now, what do you want me to do?"

"Mr. Steele, I want you to take over this wheat. It can't possibly go much lower, and Tom says it is bound to rise. This time last year it was eighty-nine, and if it went up to that now we would net over a hundred thousand dollars. You see, you would not need to take the risk we have done, for we bought at seventy-eight, and you will be buying at seventy-four and a quarter."

"But I don't see how my taking it over would help you."

"Why if it went up to over eighty—and Tom says it is sure to do that before many weeks are past—you would make a good profit and could give us back our money."

Serious as was the situation John could scarcely refrain from a smile at such a beautiful specimen of feminine logic. Of course, if he wished to dabble in wheat, he could buy at seventy-four now, and if it went to eighty, secure the whole profit without paying anything to anyone.

"Is Tom at home just now?"

"Yes."

"Well, you ask him to call this afternoon, and we will talk the situation over."

The young woman rose and beamed on him through her tears.

"Oh, I am sure you two will hit upon a plan. When I told Tom this morning of the scheme I have just outlined to you he scoffed at me; but you see its feasibility, don't you?"

"Yes, I think I do. Anyhow, Tom and I will consult this afternoon about it, and he'll let you know at what decision we arrive."

He shook hands with his visitor and was very glad to see her depart.

"Good gracious!" he said to himself when the door was shut, "how fatuously silly she is! And to think that a little more than a year ago I proposed to her! Poor girl! Beauty almost gone, too, at the first whiff of trouble. Still, the situation is serious enough; but it is easier to refuse a man than a woman. I'll tell Tom what I think of him when he comes. Imagine the cursed fool marching into Chicago like a hayseed from the backwoods, and losing fifty thousand dollars inside of three weeks. What he needs is a guardian; yet I'd like to help the little woman, too, although I don't see how I can. I wonder if wheat's going any lower. Hold up, Jack, my boy, don't get thinking about the price of wheat. That way madness lies. No, I'll confine myself to giving Tom a piece of my mind when I see him which will make him angry, so we'll quarrel, and then it'll be easy to refuse him."

At three o'clock the ex-station-master of Slocum Junction was shown into John Steele's private office. His face was so gaunt and haggard that for a moment Steele felt sorry for him; but business is business, and sympathy has no place in the wheat-pit. Tom shook hands and sat down without a word; all his old jauntiness had left him.

"Well, my Christian friend," began Steele in his severest manner, "when I was the means of getting you transferred from Slocum Junction to Chicago, and also had something to do towards endowing your wife-that-was-to-be with nearly fifty thousand dollars, hang me if I thought you would act the giddy farmer-come-to-town and blow it all away in the wheat-pit! God bless my soul! haven't you sense enough to know that the biggest men in Chicago have been crumpled up in the grain-market? How could you expect to win where the richest and shrewdest dealers in the city have failed? Don't you read the papers? Haven't you any brains in your head at all? Is it only an intellectual bluff that you are putting up before the public, pretending to be a man of sense? Why, a ten-year-old boy born in Chicago would know better! Wheat may be the staff of life when it leaves the flour-mill, but it's the cudgel of death in the speculative market!"

"So I've been told," said Tom quietly.

"Well, you haven't profited much by the telling. What in the name of all the saints made you speculate in wheat?"

"I didn't speculate."

"I understand you bought a million bushels?"

"I did."

"What's that but speculating, then?"

"Look here, Mr. Steele, are you quite done with your abuse of me? Isn't there something more that you could say? That I wear a woollen shirt, and haven't any collar; that my trousers are turned up, and there's mud on my shoes? Do you see any straw out of the farmyard on my hair? If you do, why don't you mention it?"

John Steele laughed.

"Bravo, Tom," he said; "that's quite your Slocum Junction manner. I supposed you were up a tree—that you had bought a million bushels of wheat, spent thirty thousand dollars odd upon margins, and that now you couldn't carry it any longer. Am I right?"

"Quite right. That's exactly the situation. Now, are you in the frame of mind to listen to the biggest thing that there is in America to-day? Are you in a financial position to take advantage of an opportunity that may not recur for years? If you are, I'll talk to you. If not, I'll bid you 'Good-bye,' and go to someone else."

"All right, Tom, I'm ready to listen, and willing to act if you can convince me."

"I can convince you quick enough, but are you able to act, as well as ready?"

"Well, to tell you the truth, Tom, if you mean going in for a big wheat speculation, I'm able, but not willing."

"I told you I wasn't speculating. Wheat will be over a dollar a bushel before three months are past."

"Is there going to be a war?"

"I don't know; but this I do know, that the wheat crop of the entire West is practically a failure—that is to say, late frosts this spring, and the wet weeks we have had since, will knock off anywhere from thirty to forty per cent, of the output. The Chicago wheat-pit is a pretty big thing, but it isn't the Almighty, neither is it the great and growing West. It can do many things, but it can't buck up against nature. Wheat now we'll say, is seventy-five cents a bushel, because of the belief that there's going to be an abundant crop; but if twenty-five per cent, of that crop fails, it means that twenty-five per cent, is going to be added to the present price of wheat. It means dollar wheat, that's what it means, and a man who knows this fact to-day can make unlimited millions of money if he's got the capital behind him. Of course, my mistake was in biting off more than I could chew. If I had gone in modestly, I could have carried it, and would have made a moderate profit; but I was too greedy, and too much afraid Chicago would learn the real state of the crops. I expected the news to be out long before now; but instead of that the papers are blowing about full crops, which either shows that they don't know what they are talking about, or there's a nigger in the fence somewhere."

"What makes you so very sure the crop's a partial failure?"

"Because it's my business to know, for one thing. I have travelled from Chicago clear through to the Pacific coast; south as far as wheat is grown; and up north into Canada. I don't need to ask a farmer what crop he expects; I can see with my own eyes the state of affairs. I was brought up on wheat; I ploughed the fields and sowed the grain, and I may say I was cradled in wheat, if you'll forgive a farmer's pun. Wheat? Why, I know all about wheat on the field, even if I don't recognise it in the Chicago pit. You see, my business is looking after freight, and the chief freight of our road is wheat. Therefore, wherever wheat grows I must visit that spot, and I have done so. I give you my oath that wheat is bound to be a dollar a bushel before two months are past. It's under seventy-five cents now, and it doesn't take much figuring to show the possibilities of the situation. Three things are wanted: knowledge, courage, money. I have given you the knowledge; do you possess the other two requisites?"

"Tom, I esteem you very much—more so now than when you came in; but, after all's said and done, I'd be simply banking on one man's word. Suppose I go in half a million dollars? You say that knowledge is the first requisite. Have I got that knowledge? I have not. I have merely your word that you have the knowledge."

"Yes, that's a good point to make," said Tom imperturbably. "You don't know me well enough to risk it. That's all right. Now, I see on your wall the big map of our road, which I suppose you have kept as a relic of your connection with the Wheat Belt Line. It's a lovely map, with the Wheat Belt Line in heavy black as the great thing, and the United States sort of hung around it as a background. There," continued Tom, waving his hand towards the huge map on the wall, "coloured yellow by Rand, McNally and Co., are the wheat-producing districts of the United States and Canada. Now, I've been all over that yellow ground. I assert that in no part of it is the wheat crop normal. You pick out at random five or six spots in that yellow ground, and I'll tell you just what percentage of failure there'll be in those places you select. Then get on the train and visit them, question the farmers, and find out if they corroborate my statement. If they do, the chances are strong I am right about every other district."

John Steele got up and began pacing the floor, his hands thrust in his trousers pockets, his forehead wrinkled with a frown.

"Tom, that's pretty straight talk," he said at last. "I haven't been following the wheat-market—it's out of my line; but I dimly remember seeing in the papers not very long ago an estimate that we were going to have the most profitable wheat crop of recent years. Of course, that may be newspaper talk; but if recollection serves, it was backed up by telegrams from all over the West. How do you account for that?"

"I don't account for it. I am merely stating what I know. If the papers made such an estimate they were wrong, that's all."

Steele stopped in his walk and touched an electric button on his desk. A young man appeared in response.

"Holmes," said Steele, "there was an account of the wheat crop all over the country in the papers the other day—occupied a page, I think. Go to the nearest newspaper office and get a copy. As you go out, tell Bronson to come in here."

When Bronson appeared, Steele said sharply: "Find out for me, from some reliable source, the lowest price of wheat for the last ten years."

In an amazingly short space of time Holmes reappeared with a newspaper a week old, and laid it on Mr. Steele's desk, and Bronson brought in an array of figures.

"Here we are!" cried Steele, jerking open the crackling sheet. "'Wonderful harvests ahead! Tremendous wheat crops!' Of course, it must be remembered that prophesying prosperity is always popular, and newspapers like that sort of news. Now, I shall select twenty-five places named in this paper. The useful Bronson will find out for me a reliable man in each place, and I will telegraph him. By to-morrow we should have replies from some fifteen or twenty of them; and if the majority say that the wheat crop is a failure, then I think we may rely on your forecast. Now, let us see what Bronson's figures are. Sixty-five, sixty-two and a half, sixty-four and an eighth, fifty-three and five-eighths, forty-eight and three-quarters—gee-whillikins, that's getting down to bedrock!—fifty, fifty-four and nine-eighths, sixty-nine and one-eighth, eighty-five—ah! that's something like—seventy-four and a quarter, and so on. Why, it seems from this that no man is safe in buying for a rise if he pays more than fifty cents a bushel, while you have bought at seventy-eight! Septimus Severus! I admire your nerve, but not your judgment. Well, drop in to-morrow, about two, and we'll see what the telegrams bring us."

"Suppose, meanwhile, wheat falls another cent or two, what am I to do?"

"Oh, they can't hurt you to-day—it's after four o'clock; and to-morrow we'll see what is best to be done. It is useless to conceal from you the fact that there is an unholy gulf between seventy-eight at which you bought, and fifty, to which wheat has on more than one occasion fallen. That means a little deficit of two hundred and eighty thousand dollars on your gentle flutter."

"The truth must come out soon, Mr. Steele, and it may be published any morning. When that happens, wheat will go up like a balloon."

"All right, Tom, I can say nothing further just now. To-morrow you will find me brimful of information, and quite decided as to the course I shall take."

With this the visitor had to be content. Next day he arrived at Steele's office in a more cheerful frame of mind. Wheat had closed the day before one-eighth stronger than it was in the morning. The conference this time was short, sharp, and decisive. Steele was thoroughly the man of business.

"I received seventeen replies," he said, "and they all corroborate your forecast. Now, what do you wish me to do with the little parcel of wheat standing against your name?"

"I thought that in return for the tip you might relieve me of three-quarters of it."

"I'll relieve you of it all. I've given orders to my brokers to buy a pretty large slice of the wheat crop. This purchase may perhaps send up the price to the seventy-eight at which you purchased. If it does, I'll sell out your lot and send you the money, which I advise you to invest in gilt-edged securities and leave wheat alone."

"All right," said Tom. "I know when I've had enough. Nevertheless, it's a sure thing, and I hate to let go."

"If it's a sure thing," said Steele, "I'll hand over to you a percentage of what I win, in return for the information you have given me. You go straight home, taking this newspaper with you. Write out a report similar in length to these Press Alliance telegrams, giving name of locality and the actual state of the crop in each district. Let nobody know what you are doing, and work all night, if necessary, until the report is complete. Then bring it to me, and

I'll have it typewritten in this office. Now, this is my busy day. Clear out. Goodbye."

Steele's buying took the market by surprise. No one knew, of course, who the purchaser was, but the price rose rapidly, point by point, until seventy-eight was again reached, and then Steele instantly gave orders for the sale of the million bushels that stood in Tom's name, for the double purpose of getting the man his money, and lowering the price so that his own purchases might be accomplished at a less figure than seventy-eight. The sale took place an hour before the closing of business, and chanced to be just in the nick of time. Orders to sell came in from somewhere—supposedly from New York, and wheat was offered in any quantity at practically any price the buyers liked to pay. Someone was hammering down the market. A fight was on between two unknowns, and pandemonium was let loose in Chicago. The pit went wild, and prices came down with a run. Steele had already stopped his buyers, and he stood from under. Closing prices for wheat were sixty-five, three-eighths. John Steele did some deep thinking and close figuring that night. In spite of his purchases of the day, he had still a million dollars left to gamble with.

"My friend the bear," he said to himself, "is very likely to keep up his antics to-morrow, to frighten the opposition. If he squeezes down prices to sixty, I'll buy five million bushels. Every cent of a drop will mean a loss of fifty thousand dollars. It reached fifty in '94, and next year a cent and a quarter less, but this price has never on any other occasion been touched in the last forty years. Even if it drops to that, I'll have lost half a million or so, but I can still hang on. I'm not trying to corner the market; so, Mr. Bruin, go ahead, and let us see what happens."

Next day the panic and the slump continued. Wheat fell to fifty-nine, and between that price and sixty-one John Steele secured his five million bushels.

Who were the operators? That was what the papers wanted to know. Was it, as surmised, a contest between New York and Chicago? All the well-known dealers were interviewed, but each and every one insisted he was merely an interested spectator, holding an umbrella over his head. There was going to be a blizzard, so everybody had his eye on the cyclone cellar. Experts said it was a good time to seek cover.

Of course, John Steele might have rested on his oars. He was reasonably safe—in fact, he was perfectly safe if he merely held on, which was a good position to be in. But he had a plan of his own, although he resolved not to buy further unless wheat reached the low limit of half a dollar. In that case he feared he would plunge. This night, however, he proceeded to carry out his plan, which led to amazing results. He put Tom's report of the wheat crop's condition, now nicely typewritten, into his inside pocket, and locked up his office.

All the upper windows of a commodious business block were aglow with electric light. It was the home of the Press Alliance, with telegraphic nerves reaching to the furthermost parts of the earth. Its business was to gather news, which it furnished to journals belonging to the Alliance. John Steele was acquainted with Simmonds, the manager, and resolved to pay him an evening call at what was certainly a most inopportune moment. The great hive was a-hum with activity. The wild day on the Stock Exchange was enough of itself to keep it throbbing. Simmonds was a busy man, but he received John Steele, who came in cool and self-possessed, with courtesy and respect.

"Well, Simmonds, I suppose you're just rushed to death, so I'll not detain you a moment. I want to see one of your men who is less busy, if, indeed, he is here to-night."

"We're all here to-night, Steele. I hope you've not been dabbling in wheat?"

"Me? No fear. Wheat's rather out of my line."

"Somebody's going to get badly hurt before the week is out."

"So I understand," said Steele nonchalantly, as if it were none of his affair. "By the way, talking of wheat, you gather statistics of the crops from all over the country, don't you—your company, I mean?"

"Oh, yes, several times a year."

"From what office is that done, New York or Chicago?"

"Chicago, of course."

"Who is in charge of that department?"

"Nicholson. Why?"

"I should like to have a chat with him if he's not too busy."

"Well, you've mentioned the one man who isn't busy to-night. You see, his work is a daylight job."

"What sort of a fellow is he?"

"He's a new man—at least, he's been with us only six months—that is, at this office. He came on from New York. Splendid fellow, though, and well up to his work."

"Good. May I see him?"

"I'll find out if he's in his room."

Simmonds spoke through a telephone, and then said:

"Yes, Mr. Nicholson will see you; but I say, Steele, don't meddle with wheat. If you want any information from him, remember he can't give it out, except to the morning papers."

"Oh, I shan't buy a bushel of wheat; don't be frightened."

"This boy will take you to Mr. Nicholson's room. Good night."

Nicholson proved to be a man of uncertain age. His hair was closely cropped, his face smoothly shaven, bearing a look of determination and power, which one might not have expected to find in a mere subordinate.

"Is this Mr. John Steele," he asked pleasantly, "the Napoleon of finance who stood out against Rockervelt?"

"Well, I don't know about the Napoleon part of it, Mr. Nicholson, but Rockervelt and I had a little negotiation a while ago which I trust ended in our mutual advantage. Now, Mr. Nicholson," continued Steele, sitting down in the chair offered him, "if you are not too busy I should like to ask you a few questions."

"I am not very busy, Mr. Steele, and shall be pleased to answer any question you ask, so long as the information sought belongs to me, and not to my employers."

"Who is your employer, Mr. Nicholson?"

"My employer? Why, the Press Alliance, of course."

"The Press Alliance is one of your employers, I know. Your nominal employer, let us say. It pays you to collect accurate information. Who pays you for disseminating false news in the daily journals of this country?"

If John Steele expected a start of guilty surprise or a flash of anger or a demand for explanation, he was disappointed. The impassive face remained impassive. The piercing eyes narrowed a little, perhaps, but he could have sworn that the faint glimmer of a smile hovered about the firm lips. The voice that spoke was under perfect control.

"They say that all things come to him who waits, and here is an illustration of it. The man for whom every reporter in Chicago is searching, and whom I am most desirous to meet, walks right into my office. How many million bushels of wheat did you buy to-day, Mr. Steele?"

John Steele was a much more genial person than this man from New York. He threw back his head and laughed.

"Mr. Nicholson, I am delighted to have made your acquaintance. Your wild guess that I am the buyer of wheat is really flattering to me. Yet your own reference to my little contest with Rockervelt should have reminded you that I deal in railways, and not in grain."

"The reason I wished to meet you," went on Mr. Nicholson, as if the other had not spoken, "is because I have a message to you from my chiefs."

"Yes, but you have not mentioned who your chiefs are."

"There is no need to mention them, Mr. Steele. When I tell you they own banks in every city in the United States; that the income of the head of our combination is fifty million dollars a year from merely one branch of his activity; that we have employees in the United States Treasury powerful enough to cause the funds of this country to be placed for safety in our banks; that my principals can, if they wish, gamble with the savings of the people of the United States deposited in their keeping; that they have agents in every part of the world, and that there is not a country in Europe, Asia, or Africa which does not pay tribute to them; when I have said all this, Mr. Steele, I think two things may be taken for granted—first: no names need be mentioned; second: you are opposed to a power infinitely greater than that of Mr. Rockervelt or any other financial force which the world contains."

"You are right in both surmises, Mr. Nicholson, and I experience that keen joy which warriors feel with foemen worthy of their steel—if you will excuse the apparent pun on my own name. I am really quoting from Scott, not the railway man of that name, but the poet. And now for your message, Mr. Nicholson."

"You admit, then, that you are the buyer?"

"I'll admit anything in the face of such a formidable rival."

"Very well. My chiefs are the most generous of men."

"Oh, we all know that."

"If you have lost money these last two days, they will refund it. They are even willing to allow you a reasonable profit, and I am empowered to negotiate regarding the figures."

"And all this for pure philanthropy, Mr. Nicholson?"

"All this if you will merely stand aside and not interfere in a market you do not understand, and complicate a situation that is already somewhat delicate."

"And if I refuse to stand aside?"

"If you refuse, they will crush you, as they have crushed many a cleverer man."

"Ah! that's not tactful, Nicholson, and I'm sure it would not meet the approval of your employers. Your last remark is apt to provoke opposition rather than compliance. Would it surprise you to know that I possess a more potent backer than even your distinguished chief?"

"More potent? Yes, it would surprise me. Have you any reluctance in mentioning the name?"

"Not the slightest—it's a lady."

"A lady?"

"Yes. Dame Nature—a charming old woman if you stand in with her; a blue terror if you go against her. The wheat crop in America this year will be only three-quarters of the normal yield, if it is that much. You can juggle with the fact for a little time, but you can't conceal it. Even the great firm on Broadway cannot make a blade of wheat grow where one has been killed by the frost—not in the same year, at least. So you may telegraph to your distinguished principals and tell them that John Steele and Dame Nature are going to dance a minuet with those two Corsican brothers of New York, and your fraternal friends will find some difficulty in keeping pace with the music. And so good-bye, Mr. Nicholson."

"Good-bye, Mr. Steele. I am very sorry we cannot come to terms."

Once outside, Steele hailed a cab and drove to the Chicago Daily Blade building. Here, as at the Press Alliance, everyone was hard at work; but Steele's name was good for entrance almost anywhere in Chicago, and the managing editor did not keep him waiting.

"Good evening, Stoliker," began Steele. "I have got in my pocket the greatest newspaper 'beat' that has ever been let loose on Chicago since the night of the Brooklyn Theatre Fire."

"Then, Steele, you're as welcome as flowers that bloom in the spring. Out with it."

"There's been a gigantic conspiracy to delude the Press and people of the

United States."

"Oh, they're always trying that," said Stoliker indifferently.

"Yes, but this time they've succeeded, up to this evening. Just cast your eye over this document."

A managing editor is quick to form an accurate estimate of the proportions of a piece of news submitted to him.

"If anyone else had brought this in," said Stoliker slowly, "do you know what I should have thought?"

"Yes, you would think it an attempt of the bulls to get in out of the rain."

"Exactly. You've hit it the first time. Can you vouch for the accuracy of this?"

"I can."

"You won't be offended, Steele, if I ask you one more question, only one?"

"I know what the question is."

"What is it?"

"You are going to ask if I have been buying wheat?"

"Well, you seem to know exactly what's in my mind. Conversation is rather superfluous with so sharp a man as you are. Have you been buying wheat?"

"Yes, I'm the person who caused the flutter in the market these last two days."

"If I publish this, the price of wheat will instantly jump up."

"No, it won't."

"Oh, that's the evident object of the whole thing. If I prove that the wheat crop of America is from twenty-five to thirty per cent, short, up goes the price of wheat."

"My dear Stoliker, your paper will sell like hot cakes, but no one will believe a word you say. Everyone on 'Change will think exactly as you do—that this is a device of the bulls, and so the price of wheat is likely to remain stationary for some hours. But this sensational and categorical statement is bound to make everybody uneasy, and there will be a good deal of telegraphing going on during the forenoon. By the time the evening papers are out, it will begin to dawn on commercial Chicago that you've done the biggest thing that's been done for years. After that, every moment will enhance your reputation."

"Quite so, if—and that 'if' is the biggest word in the dictionary just now—if this article is accurate. If it isn't, then the reverse of all you have predicted will happen."

"My dear Stoliker, I was quite prepared for this unbelief, I therefore took the precaution before the bank closed to get a certified cheque for a hundred thousand dollars, and here it is. Pay this into your bank tomorrow, and offer in your paper a hundred thousand dollars to anyone who will prove the report inaccurate. It has been compiled by a man I can vouch for, in the employ of the Wheat Belt Line, who has visited every spot mentioned in the report. Now, time is precious; I give you five minutes in which to make up your mind."

"I don't need them; my mind is made up. I'll print it."

Next day, events proved that Steele was no false prophet. Wheat fluctuated for a time up and down, then began to rise steadily, and at last shot up like a rocket, ending at eighty-three and a quarter. Before the week was out it was well over the dollar mark, and John Steele was richer by more than three millions of dollars. The night of the day in which he sold out he strolled into the Press Alliance offices and visited his perturbed friend Simmonds.

"I would like to see Mr. Nicholson again," he said.

"Oh, curse him!" cried Simmonds, "he's gone to New York; and I wish he had never left there. I suppose you don't know what a hole he put us into, because you're not interested in wheat."

"Really? Why, I was tremendously impressed by Nicholson's manner and appearance!"

"Oh, his manner and appearance were all right. He came here with the very highest recommendations—in fact, he was the one man in our employ of all the hundreds here that I had orders from headquarters not to dismiss on any account. I was as much taken with his looks as you were. I would have sworn he was true to his employers, yet I have not the slightest doubt he sold them as if they were a flock of sheep."

"You are mistaken, Simmonds. He was perfectly true to his employers."

## CHAPTER XII—THE EMBODIMENT OF MAMMON

THERE now projects across these pages the sinister shadow of a man. He was one seldom seen except by his immediate business associates, and yet seldom has a newspaper been issued that did not contain his name. This was Peter Berrington, the greatest financial brain the world had hitherto produced—the modern embodiment of Mammon. In early life there had occurred to him the obvious proposition that if any one man could control the manufacture and sale of some simple article in universal use, he would secure a fortune greater than that of all the monarchs on earth put together. Peter Berrington chose soap as his medium, and the world-renowned trust called Amalgamated Soap has been the outcome. His methods were as simple as his products. He offered what he considered a fair price to a rival for his business and if that rival refused, Peter crushed him by a competition the other could not withstand. Berrington seemed to act on one fixed rule in life, which was to avoid the law courts wherever possible; yet, nevertheless, he was haled to the bar on many occasions, but invariably he escaped unscathed, without a stain on his character, as if the soap he supplied to the universe had removed even the suspicion of dishonesty from himself. It pleases the world to buy soap under different titles, but it is all manufactured by the same company. Berrington's air-tight monopoly finally produced an annual income in excess of the fortune any man on earth possessed twenty-five years ago. With this ever-increasing income he bought banks, first in New York, then in every other great city, and finally in the larger towns. He purchased trust companies and insurance associations. He bought railways and steamship lines, also city councils and State legislators, judges, juries and senators. He was now the guardian and manipulator of the people's savings, and his banks had the handling of all the money the United States Government possessed. Magazines printed vivid articles exhibiting the dark points of his career. Peter never entered a protest. Powerful newspapers hurled vigorous denunciations against him, but Peter never replied. The few who knew him in private life described him as a quiet, timorous man, apparently without opinions of his own, who was withal deeply religious. Yet all the histories printed of him never contained the record of any man who had defeated him.

It was but natural, then, that the Chicago papers should make much of John Steele's encounter with this giant of the financial world. Steele had met him on the battle-ground of the Chicago wheat-pit, and had routed him, horse, foot and dragoons. The Daily Blade's exposure of the real wheat situation of the country had been so sudden that the barrels of money which Peter Berrington kept in readiness to buy the whole crop, when he had hammered the price low enough, remained unopened and unexpended.

Berrington would have made billions at one fell swoop had not this man Steele blindly, quite unwittingly, stumbled across his path and tripped him up. The newspapers exaggeratingly credited Steele with making many more millions than he had actually secured, and it was only when the anxious three days of panic had ended that Steele himself realised what a tremendous fortune had been within his grasp if he could have commanded the capital to manipulate the situation, or even if he had risked all he actually possessed. Indeed, Steele perceived when too late that he had blundered into the biggest deal ever projected upon this earth, and while he undoubtedly spoiled the game for its inaugurates, he did not himself profit nearly as much as might have been the case. He began to question his own judgment, and the uneasy thought came to him that if he had made terms that night with Nicholson in the office of the Press Alliance, he might have made from ten to twenty millions instead of three or four. Yet he was consoled by the belief that Peter would have been true to no bargain he might have made, and in the end would have robbed him of the agreed share. In spite of his religious reputation, Peter was accredited with no qualms of conscience in a business transaction.

The Western newspapers re-recited Steele's brief besting of Rockervelt, which was now utterly eclipsed by his victory over Berrington, and they jocularly advised New York rustics to stay at home and not venture into a real city like Chicago. In face of all this ridicule, and in spite of accusations and denunciations levelled against him for his efforts to mislead a free and incorruptible Press, Peter Berrington made no sign, and New York silently swallowed up the mysterious Nicholson. A few wiseacres in Chicago shook their heads as they read the laudations of Mr. John Steele, saying the young man was not yet done with Peter Berrington; and later events proved the correctness of their surmise.

Steele himself was not particularly frightened at the outlook, but neither was he extremely pleased. He was sorry that Fate had brought him into opposition with Peter Berrington, but he had learned that fact too late to withdraw. When he met Nicholson, and became aware that the Great Bear was Amalgamated Soap, he was already committed too deeply for half measures to aid him. He had acted at once, decisively and successfully, and would have been relieved had he merely got out even. It was his usual luck that he came away with large profits, and for that he thanked Fate, because he knew his enemy was ruthless. Success did not turn his head in the least. He was a cool thinker and detested all this newspaper notoriety. He knew fortunes were not made by the beating of drums, and he kept very quiet until the hubbub was over, refusing to see reporters or say anything about the matter, save to his most intimate friends. He hoped that some fresh sensation would speedily drive his name from the columns of the Press, and until that time came he sought shelter, doing nothing. He comforted himself with the thought that Peter Berrington, while merciless to an opponent, was merciless merely to acquire that opponent's business. He believed the great man to be entirely without sentiment, and therefore surmised he would not seek revenge when an act was once completed and done with. Nevertheless, he resolved to keep his weather eye open, which was wise.

The new celebrity he had attained brought all sorts and conditions of men to his offices. He began to think that every wild-cat scheme in the country was placed before him. Letters poured in from various parts of the world, and he was offered gold mines, patents, railways, steamship lines, industrial enterprises and what not. He took larger offices and protected himself from intrusion. He became a much more difficult man to see than even the President of the United States—or perhaps it would be more fitting to say than Mr. Peter Berrington, for Peter allowed no outsider to penetrate to his den.

There was one man, however, who succeeded in reaching the inner room of John Steele, and his card bore the name of William Metcalfe. This card had been preceded, however, by some excellent letters of introduction, and so John Steele made an appointment with him. He was favourably impressed by the appearance of Mr. Metcalfe, who did not look like a city man, but rather a cross between a bluff farmer and a shrewd manufacturer—which, indeed, he turned out to be. After seating himself, William Metcalfe plunged directly into the heart of his business, without preliminary, which also pleased John Steele.

"I know your time is valuable," he said; "so is mine. I have undertaken an operation that proves too big for me, and I want you to help me carry it out."

"I have three rules, Mr. Metcalfe, which I rarely break. In the first place, I never finance anything. If, for instance, you wish to build a factory, or to exploit a patent, it is useless coming to me expecting help."

"I have no factory to build and no patent to exploit," said Metcalfe.

"My second rule is that the man with whom I go in, must be prepared to put up dollar for dollar with me in hard cash, and not in future prospects."

"I am prepared to do that," rejoined Metcalfe.

"My third rule is that I must see for myself and understand the business offered. I do not give a hang for the opinions of experts. If the proposal is complicated beyond my comprehension, I don't go in."

"Quite right," commended Metcalfe. "None of your three rules will be in the least infringed by me. Do you know anything of the beet-sugar business?"

"I do not."

"Did you ever hear of Bradley, of Bay City?'

"I did not."

"Well, what Bradley accomplished may be understood by a ten-year-old boy. He went over to Germany, and came back with a parcel of seeds in his handbag, which seeds he planted. From that parcel has grown the beet root industry of Michigan. There are now factories in that State capitalised at ten millions of dollars. There are nearly a hundred thousand acres of Michigan land in beets. Ten years ago I hadn't a penny; to-day I think I could put as much money on the table as you, and all on account of those seeds Bradley brought from Germany. I own three big factories in Michigan, and four others in States further west. You hinted that you didn't wish to deal in probabilities; but, if you will forgive me for saying it, there is no industry in this country at the present moment which offers greater promise than the manufacture of sugar out of beetroot."

"I dare say," remarked Steele indifferently. "I am quite willing to applaud the excellent Bradley, who made millions of beets grow where none had grown before. I admire such a man exceedingly, even though unprepared to follow in his steps. You see, Mr. Metcalfe, I am not a useful citizen like yourself and Mr. Bradley. I simply make a raid at some project, filch what I can, and get back into my den. As I told you, I am not building factories, not even those that squeeze the succulent beet. I squeeze my opponents on the Stock Exchange. My motto is large profits and quick returns."

"I am here to offer you immense profits and immediate returns. I understand the sugar business down to the ground, and have realised its possibilities for several years past. Therefore I determined to combine all the big sugar factories at present existing in the United States. Rapidly as I myself have acquired wealth, the sugar business has been growing too quickly for me, and at the beginning of this year I saw I had to put my project into action, or else interest a body of financiers, which I did not wish to do, for my ambition is to control the sugar-beet industry of the United States, and ultimately of the world."

"Ah, you hope to become a sort of sweetened Peter Berrington," said Steele, with a smile, and he thought of this remark somewhat grimly later on.

"Exactly," said Metcalfe seriously, without duplicating the other's smile. "As I told you, I own outright seven factories. I secured options on all the rest, and in each case have paid down a forfeit, for I shall be compelled to buy outright within the next month if I am to hold them. Now, the total cost of all the factories in the States at present, built or building, comes to almost double the capital I possess. If you will put up dollar for dollar with me, we will purchase these factories outright. Then we will form the whole into a gigantic company. When this is done, you can withdraw your money, and probably as much more as you put in. If the public does not subscribe the full amount we demand, I will guarantee to relieve you at par of all the shares that may fall to your portion."

"How can you guarantee to do that when at the present moment you have not got more than half the necessary capital for forming the company?"

"I can guarantee it because I am certain the public will subscribe; but even if they do not, the moment the company is formed there is a bank in this city willing to advance me cash to the amount of three-quarters of our capital. Therefore I can guarantee that you will double your money within a month—that is, within a month of your putting it in. You say you care nothing for the opinions of experts; neither do I, therefore I propose that you become my guest for two weeks, and visit most of the factories now under my control. You can see the books and balance-sheets of my own concerns, and from what you learn under my tuition you will be able to form a very good estimate of how the other factories are placed."

"I understand very little about company promoting," said Steele dubiously.

"I understood just as little a short time since, but it was necessary that I should learn, and I have learnt. Besides, I have secured letters of introduction to Far-well Brothers, the most substantial and honest firm connected with that business in Chicago. The same people introduced me to them that introduced me to you. Suppose, for instance, the combined factories were to cost us ten million dollars. With such prospects as there are ahead, we would be quite justified in forming a company for twenty millions. If the public subscribed only half of what we demanded, we would have our factories for nothing, and still control the combination."

"How about your working capital?"

"We don't need working capital. Every factory is making money."

"Well, candidly, Mr. Metcalfe, that project seems too easy and simple to be entirely feasible. There must be something lying in wait to wreck it."

"Nothing so far as I can see," said Metcalfe confidently.

"What if the public do not subscribe a penny?"

"Oh, I've looked out for that. When I got the options, there was, of course, no longer any need for keeping the affair secret, and I have already been promised subscriptions to the new company to the extent of one-third the proposed capital of twenty millions. That one-third will be subscribed in Michigan and Wisconsin alone, without touching the State of Illinois or the capitalists of Chicago."

"Very well, Mr. Metcalfe, you appear to have thought of everything. I'll accept your invitation, so long as it binds me to nothing, and will go wherever you lead me, beginning, let us say, with one of your own factories. I understand figures, and I shall want to see the books and make a somewhat thorough search into the income of at least the principal factories. You have no objection to that, I suppose?"

"No, not in the least. Big as our capitalisation will be, this is a thoroughly sound industrial proposition, and before five years are over I am certain that we will be justified in doubling our normal capital if we wish to do so, and paying a mighty good percentage on the same. Of course, I stand by the business. I suppose you wish to pull out as quickly as possible."

"Yes, that's the idea. I hope you have not offered extravagant prices for these factories?"

"That's just the point. I have not. You see, as I told you, I am thoroughly acquainted with the business. A capitalist from New York or Chicago might have been deluded, but they cannot delude a practical man like myself. Indeed, to convince you of the confidence that others show in the proposed company, I may tell you that the capital promised comes largely from the present owners of those factories, who appreciate the economies to be inaugurated by combination, and who in some instances are putting back into the new company the entire amount I shall pay them."

"Do they know you intend to capitalise for double what the property has cost?"

"Naturally not, Mr. Steele. Of course they understand I am not in this business entirely for my health; but apart from that, anyone conversant with the progress the beet industry has made during the last four or five years is well aware that the developments of the next five or six will be something enormous."

"All right, Mr Metcalfe I'm ready to go with you to-morrow, if that is not too soon for you."

John Steele's visits to the beet-sugar district more than corroborated all that Mr. Metcalfe had told him. Quietly he studied his host and guide during the excursion, and the more he saw of him the better he liked him. If there was an honest man in the country, that man appeared to be William Metcalfe, in spite of his determination to capitalise the properties for double what he paid for them. John's own conscience was not supersensitive on this point, and his private opinion would have been that a man was a fool not to take all he could get. So, before they returned to Chicago, he had quite made up his mind to become a partner with William Metcalfe in forming the Consolidated Beet Sugar Company, Metcalfe having no domicile in Chicago, the headquarters of the new trust was the private office of John Steele and the apartments adjoining. These adjoining apartments were occupied by William Metcalfe, upon whose shoulders naturally fell the bulk of the work. It was he who saw the lawyers to whom he had been introduced; who negotiated with the bank and made such outside arrangements as were necessary in the launching of so gigantic a scheme. Steele was more and more impressed with the business capacity of his new partner as the days went on, and he congratulated himself on being in conjunction with so capable a man. Notwithstanding his increasing confidence he never for a moment relaxed his vigilance, nor was anything done without his sanction and approval, and he allowed no obscure point to pass without thoroughly mastering it. Towards the conclusion of preliminary arrangements, he saw with some apprehension that this project would involve every penny of capital he possessed, and this, of course, was cause for anxiety, though not for alarm, because all the omens were favourable. Yet his vigilance might have been of little avail had not chance played into his hands. Steele was constantly in the office; Metcalfe was frequently called elsewhere, and in one of his absences a telegraph-boy brought in a message.

"Any answer?" asked the lad.

Steele tore open the envelope and gazed at the telegram for a moment, uncomprehending. It was in cipher. Then he looked at the envelope and saw it was addressed to his partner.

"No answer," said Steele to the boy; "but look here, my lad, do you want to earn fifty cents?"

"Sure," replied the messenger.

"Very well, get me another envelope from the nearest telegraph-office. I see this is for my partner, not for me."

He threw half-a-dollar on the table, which the boy grasped eagerly.

"Be as quick as you can," cried Steele, before he reached the door.

The cipher telegram was a long one, but speedily Steele wrote it out on a sheet of paper. When the boy returned with the envelope, Steele placed the telegram within it, sealed it, and addressed it in imitation of the telegraphic clerk. Then he walked into the adjoining office and placed the resealed telegram on Mr. Metcalfe's desk.

"Now, why does honest William Metcalfe receive a long telegram in cipher from New York?" said Steele to himself, knitting his brows. "He has never even mentioned New York to me, yet he is in secret communication with someone there. Lord! one can never tell when the biggest sort of crank will not suddenly loom up as the most useful man in the world!" cried Steele, as he suddenly bethought himself of Billy Brooks, a jocular person who bored all Chicago with his knowledge of cipher, claiming there was nothing he couldn't unravel except the Knock Alphabet cipher of the Russian Nihilists. And Billy had his office in the fifteenth storey of the adjoining block. Steele shoved the copy of the telegram in his trousers' pocket, put on his silk hat, went down one elevator, and up another, in almost less time than it takes to tell about it.

"Say, Billy, I've got a cipher here that you can't decode, and I've got twenty dollars to bet on it."

"Let's see your cipher," cried Billy, his eyes sparkling. "All ciphers fall into seven distinct classes. These classes are then sub-divided into——"

"Yes, I know, I know!" cried Steele impatiently. "Here's the message."

Billy glanced at it.

"Hand over your twenty dollars, Steele."

"What! you haven't solved it already?"

"No, but I see at a glance it falls into division three and into sub-division nineteen. I'll decode it within an hour. Shall I bring it over to your office?"

"No, Billy, I'll sit down right here, even if you are six hours at it. I herewith place two ten-dollar bills on your desk, and if this proves important, which it may or may not, I'll multiply those bills by ten; and for that number of days, at least, I shall require the utmost secrecy."

"All right, John, sit down and keep quiet, and there's the latest evening paper."

There was silence in the room as Billy opened a bookcase and took down one bulky tome, two medium-sized books, and a number of smaller volumes that looked like dictionaries. Turning to his desk, he wrote the message in a variety of different ways, on as many sheets of paper. For nearly three-quarters of an hour no sound was heard but the scratching of a pen now and then, and the rustle of leaves. Then the stillness was broken by a war-whoop.

"Here you are, John, my boy; and I'll take my Bible oath on its accuracy. Couldn't be such a series of coincidences as to run so smoothly otherwise.=

````"Precious greenbacks! Loot divine!

````Twenty dollars, you are mine!"=

Billy jubilantly grasped the currency and shoved it into his pocket, handing the sheet of paper to Steele, who read: "I shall occupy room one hundred and fifty at the Grand Pacific Hotel on Thursday, the twenty-seventh, at eleven a. m. Do not ask for me at the office, nor take the elevator, but come up the stair, and rap twice. Wait two minutes, and rap a third time. Bring all documents with you."

There was no signature.

"Billy," said Steele rather seriously, "we will now burn all your figuring, if you don't mind, and then I wish you to obliterate this from your memory. I cannot tell until after Thursday whether it is important or not. I think, however, if you keep mum, this will be worth an extra two hundred dollars to you."

"You can depend on me, John. We're not all making money as fast as you are. Of course, I know that financial ciphers are usually important. Here's the débris; burn it on the oilcloth, near the register."

Steele's investigation of the Grand Pacific Hotel floor occupied by room one hundred and fifty showed him that this apartment was well chosen, for neither of the rooms on either side had a communicating door. However, he engaged room one hundred and forty-nine, on the opposite side of the hall, and before ten o'clock on the twenty-seventh he took up his position inside that apartment. When eleven o'clock approached, he locked his door, shoved the table against it, stood thereon, and looked through the transom into the hall. He darkened his own window so that he could not be observed by anyone glancing up outside. He heard the first knock, then cautiously peered down and recognised William Metcalfe standing there, facing the opposite door, with a bundle under his arm. After the third knock, Metcalfe entered, but opened the door so slightly that Steele could see nothing within, nor did he hear any greeting voice. A full hour passed with not a sound from the closed room, then Metcalfe came out again, with the bundle still under his arm, and walked quietly away, leaving his partner on watch at the transom. Time goes slowly for a man on tip-toe with eyes strained, but at last his patience was rewarded. The door opposite opened, and the head of Nicholson appeared. He glanced quickly up and down the hall, and as the way was apparently clear, stepped out and vanished. John Steele came down from the table, drew aside the curtains, and let the light into the darkened room. He poured some water from the carafe into a tumbler, swallowed the liquid at a gulp, then sank into the arm-chair beside the bed. He gave utterance to an uneasy laugh, then muttered a sentence which might be called unexpected: "Billy Brooks, my boy, you'll get your two hundred dollars!"

Drawing a deep breath, he then concentrated his mind on the crisis with which he was confronted. Metcalfe was probably the owner of the sugar factories, and was, as he had said, a well-known business man in Michigan; but, nevertheless, here was undoubted proof that he was a minion of Amalgamated Soap, a mere pawn in the hands of Peter Berrington and his strong colleague, Nicholson. Every penny John Steele possessed was sunk in Consolidated Sugar, and that these men meant to ruin him he had not the slightest doubt. The question was, How could they do it? Even if Metcalfe's books had been false, even if a hundred per cent, too much had been paid for the factories, there would still be something left for him out of the wreck. Yet from the moment he saw the face of Nicholson at that door, he knew Amalgamated Soap had determined to strip him of every sou he possessed. The first obvious suggestion that occurred to him was that here was the occasion for consulting a first-class lawyer, yet what could a lawyer do for him? He had no money to fight. The more he thought of the situation, the worse it appeared. No doubt Farwell Brothers were employees of Amalgamated Soap. No doubt the bank in which his funds were deposited belonged to the same all-embracing combination. There were a hundred perfectly legal methods by which the amount lodged there could be tied up, while, if he appealed to the law, the expense would be tremendous, and he might be dragged from court to court; new trial could follow new trial, and appeal tread on the heels of appeal until his millions had vanished into thin air. He was as entirely in the hands of Amalgamated Soap as if he had been tied in a bundle and presented to that celebrated company. Terror was imported into the situation by his uncertainty as to what method these financial buccaneers would adopt. Yet at that distressful moment his mind wandered to the comic opera of the "Mikado," and a smile came to his lips. Would it be long and lingering, with boiling oil at the end of it, or would it be the short, sharp shock of the executioner's stroke? His resentment turned more against the apparently honest Metcalfe than toward even Nicholson or Peter Berrington. He would have liked to throttle that man, but he knew that, whatever the outcome, he must retain his grip on himself and present an impassive exterior to his colleague and the world.

Next morning John Steele met his partner as usual with a smile on his face.

"Well, Metcalfe, how are things going?"

"Oh, everything's coming our way," said Metcalfe. "This trick will be done so easily that you'll wonder you ever doubted its success."

"Well, I hope so, I hope so," replied Steele, the possible double meaning of his partner's phrase striking him like a blow in the face; but the smile never wavered.

Technically the company had already been formed—that is to say, a number of clerks in Steele's office, together with the brothers Farwell, had constituted themselves the Consolidated Sugar Beet Company, with various powers duly set forth, organised under the laws of the State of New Jersey, and when officers were selected, the beet sugar factories were bought by this company at just double the price Steele and Metcalfe had paid for them. Then the officials resigned in a body, when cheques had been passed and everything done with beautiful legality, while Steele and Metcalfe and their nominees took their places on the board. It was arranged that there should be seven directors. Steele was to nominate two, and Metcalfe was to nominate two, while they were to agree mutually on the chairman. Metcalfe had proposed that the elder Farwell should be chairman, and he nominated the younger as his colleague on the board. Farwell, who knew every intricacy of company law, was accepted by Steele, and there was still one nomination open to Metcalfe, which name he excused himself at this time from proposing, as he was not well enough acquainted with business men in Chicago to fill the place at the moment. He even intimated that he was willing to accept a nominee of Steele's, and this seemingly friendly suggestion had prevented any suspicion of the board being packed against him, arising in Jack Steele's mind. He remembered this now with bitterness, when it was too late for remedy. Steele and his two colleagues could tie the vote of Metcalfe and his colleagues, but the chairman would have the casting vote. Since he had seen the determined face of Nicholson in the corridor of the Grand Pacific, he had no doubt that the Farwell brothers were the minions of Peter Berrington.

At last the trap laid for the public was sprung, and the public, as usual, was nipped. The success of the flotation was immediate, although applications did not come within a million of the sum asked for. After the flotation, Metcalfe's manner changed perceptibly. Steele watched him as a cat watches a mouse, and saw that he was now perturbed and apparently dissatisfied.

"Why!" cried Steele to him, the morning after the figures were known to them, "you don't seem nearly so happy as I expected. You surely did not look for the shares to be subscribed twice over?"

"No," said Metcalfe gloomily, "but the amount that has been subscribed shows what vitality there was in the scheme."

"Vitality!" cried Steele. "Bless my soul! you never doubted it, did you?"

"Oh, no, no," said Metcalfe hastily. "No. I told you we were dead sure of a third, and the actual subscriptions have more than justified my forecast."

"They have indeed!" cried Steele enthusiastically.

"I tell you what it is, Metcalfe, you're one of the first financiers of this country."

"Oh, nonsense!" cried Metcalfe, in no way cheered by the compliment.

"It isn't nonsense," said the genial Steele. "You've taken lessons from a first-rate master, for I look on Nicholson as one of the best men in the business."

When John Steele had plumped a similar pointed remark at Nicholson, not the slightest change of expression had disturbed that individual's calm visage. William Metcalfe kept his countenance under less perfect restraint. Steele's smile was gentle and friendly, but his keen eyes missed no note of the other's face. He watched a ruddy flush mount into his partner's cheeks. He noticed the embarrassed hesitation that accompanied his utterance.

"Mr. Nicholson! Ah, yes, certainly, certainly. He's not a friend of mine, of course, only a slight and recent acquaintance. Not the sort of man, Nicholson, to form friendships easily."

"Really?" asked Steele. "I met him only once, but he seemed rather genial."

"A great business man, a great business man," hurriedly muttered Metcalfe, obviously trying to get himself under control once more, playing for time, and not quite knowing what he was saying.

"So I have been informed," remarked Steele with easy carelessness. "One of the Amalgamated Soap group, I understand."

"Quite so," rejoined Metcalfe, his own man once more. "You see, Mr. Steele, I thought it would strengthen us tremendously if I could get a man like Nicholson to become interested in our project. The mere rumour that Amalgamated Soap was behind us would have been worth millions to us at the present juncture."

"I quite agree with you, Metcalfe. Amalgamated Soap is a name to conjure with. The public worship success, and there you have success in its most highly developed form. Why didn't you let me know? I might have been of some assistance to you."

"Well, in the first place, I did not wish to mention so important a matter until I was sure of carrying it through. No use of giving promises that you cannot make good. In the second place, I was not aware that you knew Nicholson."

"Oh, you were quite right; it was just a casual meeting, when we were introduced by a mutual friend. I don't flatter myself that my views would have any influence upon a man of Nicholson's standing in the financial world. But there is another part I don't quite understand. I admit the value of Nicholson's name to us, but why wasn't his connection divulged in time to influence subscriptions?"

"You see, it was like this," hesitated Metcalfe, for a liar must be a most agile person, and Steele's questions had a fashion of touching the spot. "It was like this. I did not really conclude my arrangement with Nicholson until this morning. He's a very difficult man to handle, and he knows as well as anyone his own value. I imagine he wished to see which way the cat was going to jump before he committed himself."

"Well, Metcalfe, the cat has jumped entirely our way, even if the leap did not reach the furthest mark we staked out. The success of the subscriptions, then, induced Nicholson to join us?"

"Quite so, quite so, with the proviso that he is to have the vacant seat at the board, unless you have any objection."

"Objection? Certainly not. I am highly delighted with our acquisition. Besides, the seat at the board is entirely in your gift. I have no right to object, even if I wished to do so."

This was said with such an air of childlike simplicity that the perturbed Metcalfe, who seemingly still retained some remnants of conscience, showed confusion.

"True enough," he murmured. "Still, I should not like to nominate anyone who might be personally distasteful to you."

"I cannot imagine, Metcalfe, why you should suppose Nicholson could be distasteful to anyone. He is a tower of strength. I am overjoyed that you have induced him to join us."

"I am very much relieved to hear you say so," rejoined Metcalfe, who seemed bewildered at the turn things had taken.

The preliminary meetings of the company had all been held in Steele's offices. This afternoon, however, the directors were to forgather at the board-room of the bank in which the deposits of the subscribers were lodged. Steele was thus to beard the lion in the lion's own den, for he now no longer doubted that this bank was owned by Peter Berrington, Nicholson and their colleagues. The appointed hour was three o'clock, and John Steele arrived on the stroke, the last man to appear. Nicholson stood in the centre of the group. Metcalfe, who had quite recovered his composure, said with a fine air of good comradeship:

"I think you two gentlemen have met before, so a formal introduction is not necessary between Mr. Steele and Mr. Nicholson."

"I had the somewhat chastened satisfaction of encountering Mr. Steele once under conditions I am not likely to forget," said Nicholson quietly, with impressive geniality. "I count myself one of Mr. Steele's numerous admirers."

"It is kind of you to say that, Mr. Nicholson," replied John, extending his hand, while that winning smile of his played about his lips. "On the occasion to which you refer, I was so unhappy as to be placed in opposition to Amalgamated Soap. I am the more gratified, therefore, to find myself in some measure a colleague of so distinguished a coterie, even if I am admitted into but an outer temple, as it were."

"Your gratification, Mr. Steele, is as nothing compared to my own at seeing you here amongst us."

John Steele bowed his acknowledgment. It was if the lion had begun by complimenting Daniel.

"Gentlemen, I think the hour has struck," said the grave Farwell senior, taking his seat at the head of the long table.

The directors ranged themselves on either side, Nicholson at the right hand of the chairman, Metcalfe next him, and the younger Farwell the third on that side. Opposite Nicholson sat John Steele, and beside him his two nominees. Thus quietly the lines of battle were formed and to all outward appearance the meeting resembled a love-feast. Bunches of papers were heaped before the chairman, while writing-pads, pens and ink were placed in front of each director. Steele, assuming a negligent, unconcerned air that was admirably put on, wondered what particular battery Nicholson would unmask. The latter's eyes were bent on his writing-pad, and he tried one nib after another, as if to find a pen to his satisfaction. The chairman, in droning voice, recited the history of the company up to its going before the public, read documents, and gave various figures which it might be supposed were familiar to all there assembled. There was silence around the table. Nicholson never looked up until the chairman announced the amount of public subscription.

"What's that, Mr. Farwell?" he asked quietly, raising his head. "What are the figures?"

Farwell repeated them.

"And how much do you say is the authorised capital of the company?"

Farwell named the sum.

"Then we are a million short?"

"Nearly so, Mr. Nicholson."

Nicholson's face became set and stern. Slowly he turned towards Metcalfe on his right hand, whose eyes shifted uneasily from one to another without ever resting on John Steele.

"I understood, sir," said Nicholson very slowly, as if weighing his words, "that all the money was in the bank?"

"I told you, sir," replied the hesitating Metcalfe, "that there was in the bank all the capital we thought necessary."

"Necessary?" echoed Nicholson, in cold, even tones. "We make a demand upon the public. We state that the value of our property is so much. The public responds by offering us a million less. Necessary? I have never yet had anything to do with a company whose capital was not over-subscribed. I have never yet sanctioned the sending out of letters of allotment unaccompanied by letters of regret."

John Steele had difficulty in keeping the smile from his lips. The tones of righteous indignation were not in the least overdone. The expression of virtuous disapproval at being tricked, on the splendidly chiselled, clear-cut face, was marvellous in its reserve; in its hint of unlimited power behind. Steele felt, rather than saw, the uneasiness of the two colleagues by his side, who realised, without exactly understanding why, that things were going desperately wrong, like an engineer who sees an open bridge in front of him, and finds the brakes will not work.

"Admirably acted," said Steele to himself. "We pay good money to visit the theatre, and yet there is such histrionic talent as this in the business world."

Then aloud, in a voice mildly protesting, he said: "Nevertheless, Mr. Nicholson, the million shares left on our hands are quite marketable. We have ample capital to go on with, and Mr. Metcalfe will assure you that the factories themselves are all on a paying basis. You cannot surely mean that having arrived at this stage, we are not to proceed to allotment, Mr. Nicholson?"

"That is exactly what I do mean," replied Nicholson, speaking as mildly as his opponent had done. "My colleagues would never consent to admit connection with a company formed in the circumstances now before us. Our duty to the public——"

"Mr. Nicholson, I quite appreciate your position, and that of your colleagues, Mr. Peter Berrington and the rest. The public would indeed be shocked to learn that Peter, one of our religious pillars, could be guilty of anything in the least oblique. As cleanliness is next to godliness, we are all aware that Amalgamated Soap stands close to the Pearly Gates, and the only thing we fear about Peter is that when he gets to heaven he shall find another saint of the same name there before him, which may lead to confusion of identity. I take it for granted, Mr. Nicholson, that you are about to move a resolution requiring all this money to be returned to the subscribers. If you will propose such a motion, I shall be very happy to second it."

An electric silence fell on the group, the kind of silence which on a hot summer's night precedes a clap of thunder. Nicholson drew a long breath and squared his shoulders. Metcalfe gazed in fascinated dismay at John Steele. Even the Farwells showed traces of human interest. Nicholson did not venture to challenge a vote. After a few moments of this embarrassing stillness he said gently:

"Perhaps Mr. John Steele has something else to propose?"

"No, I have not," said Steele; "but with the chairman's permission, there being no motion before the house, I should like to make a personal explanation which may save you future trouble."

The chairman nodded permission, and Nicholson said:

"We shall be interested to hear anything you say, Mr. Steele."

"To return the money is, of course, to wreck the company. Hitherto this company has been associated with the names of John Steele and William Metcalfe. Tomorrow the sensation of the daily journals all over the country will be the collapse of the big scheme which those two men undertook to float. Mr. William Metcalfe is unknown in Chicago; is but a stool-pigeon well paid for the part he has enacted, and he disappears from the scene. John Steele stands the brunt. All the funds he possesses are in Amalgamated Soap's bank. His affairs are in the hands of Amalgamated Soap lawyers. One legal difficulty after another comes up; there is a long fight over the remains, and at last Amalgamated Soap steps in and sweeps up the débris. They are in possession of valuable property scattered throughout the West in the beet-sugar line; they announce their possession and the reconstruction of the company, and everything is beautiful, but John Steele is mangled in the collision, with no insurance, even for his relatives.

"When I learned the other week that Mr. Nicholson was interested in this company, I felt like the man who had gone down into a cave and unexpectedly clutched a huge bear at the black bottom of it. That man did not stop to question the intentions of the bear; he simply got out. I followed his example. In the wheat deal Mr. Nicholson knows of, I made several millions, and ever since then certain capitalists in this city have begged me if I fell in with a similar good thing not to hug it all to myself, but allow them to come in on the ground floor, and I promised to do so. The moment I knew Mr. Nicholson was to have something to do with the beet-sugar project, I went directly to these capitalists, pledged them to secrecy, guaranteed that Amalgamated Soap was head and shoulders in this deal, and that no less a person than Mr. Nicholson himself would assume charge of the company. Gentlemen, they bit instantly. I sold out my share to them for the money it had cost me, and fifty per cent, additional; and, furthermore, I got the cash. Now I shall read you a letter which will appear in the Chicago newspapers to-morrow morning."

To the Editor:

Sir—The Consolidated Beet Sugar Company, with which my name has hitherto been associated, and which has been so splendidly supported by Western capital, as indicated by the subscriptions now in the bank, will hereafter be in charge of the eminent financiers associated with Amalgamated Soap. I am pleased to state that this will be almost entirely a Chicago enterprise, and that some of the best men in this city have bought out my interests therein. I have only to add that Mr. Nicholson himself is now a member of the board of directors, and nothing further need be said to assure all concerned of the immense prosperity which awaits this company, and the far-reaching advantages it will offer both to agriculture and manufacture in the West.

Yours sincerely,

John Steele.

"And now, gentlemen," said Steele, as he folded up the copy of this letter and placed it in his inside pocket, "nothing remains for me to do but to resign my seat on the board, as I have no longer the slightest interest in this company. But before handing in my formal resignation, I shall be pleased to second any motion Mr. Nicholson cares to propose."

"Mr. Chairman," said Nicholson, quite unruffled, "I move we now proceed to allotment."

"I have pleasure in seconding the motion," said John Steele, rising, bowing to the company, and leaving the room.

## CHAPTER XIII.—PERSONALLY CONDUCTED BY A GIRL

SUGAR is a fattening product, and the Consolidated Beet Sugar Company waxed fat and prospered. Its shares stood high on the Stock Exchange, and the members of the syndicate to whom John Steele had sold his portion were exuberantly grateful to the young man for the opportunity he had given them. His reputation of possessing a keen financial brain was enhanced by the forming of this company; for it was supposed that it was he who had induced Amalgamated Soap to take it up. It was erroneously surmised that the great Peter Berrington and his colleagues had been so much impressed by Steele's genius in the wheat deal, where he was opposed to them, that they now desired the co-operation of this rising young figure in the commercial world. No hint of the momentary death-struggle in the board-room of the bank had ever leaked out through the solid doors. Steele was now one of the men to be counted with in the large affairs of the Western metropolis. Everything he touched was successful. Personally he was liked, and great social success might have been his had he cared for society, which he did not. He was commonly rated as being worth anywhere from six to ten millions, and the world looked upon him as the most fortunate of men. It did him no harm to be thought to enjoy the backing of the powerful Peter Berrington, and probably not more than half-a-dozen men knew that such was far from being the case. He did not bask in Peter's smile, but, on the contrary, shivered in his shadow.

The one man who had no delusions on the subject was John Steele himself. For the second time he had been entirely victorious over Nicholson and the gigantic coterie behind him; but this, strange as it may appear, gave him no satisfaction. If he had won the determined fight through his own superior skill, or because of some great display of mental power, he might have rested more at ease. Had that been the case, he would have awaited the next onslaught with more equanimity than he at present possessed; but he knew that his victory came to him through chance; chance multiplied again and again. It was chance that his partner had been out of his room when the messenger-boy brought the telegram. It was chance that Steele had opened the envelope. It was chance that he knew a man who could decode the cipher before it was too late for him to take action on the information it carried. After these three lucky throws of the dice, he admitted to himself that he had handled the situation with diplomatic success; but it disturbed him to remember that all his vigilance would have proved unavailing, had not pure luck stood his friend. Yet, after all, the initial mistake was Nicholson's, who should not have sent a cipher telegram to the office of the man he intended to destroy. Nicholson presumably did not know that his agent was actually housed with Steele, and it was a mistake on Metcalfe's part not to have furnished his chief with this information. But even putting the best face upon the matter, he could not conceal from himself the large part that luck had played in compassing his salvation.

This never-lifted shadow of the silent Peter Berrington began to produce its effect upon him. He became timourous—afraid to venture in any large concern. He knew he was wasting time in pottering with small affairs—street railways in outside towns, the installing of electric light here and there, and such enterprises, which furnished only a moderate revenue to an enterprising speculator. Time and again he refused chances involving large amounts which turned out tremendously lucrative to the promoters, but which he had been afraid to touch, fearing the grip of Peter Berrington's unseen hand on his throat. He began to acquire the unexpected reputation of being an over-cautious capitalist, and finally well-known people, who formerly professed much admiration for him, ceased to come to his office with their schemes. Steele laughed uneasily to himself as he thought that Peter Berrington might perhaps accomplish his purpose by the gradual wearing down of his courage. Of course, the fact that a project became successful was no proof that the hand of Nicholson was not concealed somewhere within its intricacies to clutch at John Steele if he had become involved. He tried to shake off this depression, and once or twice plunged rather recklessly, only to become nervous before the climax arrived and sell out, sometimes at a small profit and sometimes at a loss.

At last he came to the conclusion that it was not Peter Berrington at all, or his shadow, that was affecting him, but the usual breakdown which afflicts strenuous business men in the stimulating atmosphere of a great American city.

"My nerve's gone; that's what's the matter with me," he said to himself. "I must go and rough it for a summer in the mountains, or else take a trip to some spa in Europe. If I keep on like this, I shall be utterly useless in a live city like Chicago."

He consulted several of his friends—many of them, in fact—and told them he was feeling far from fit. His complaint was common enough, and every man to whom he spoke suggested a remedy. Some advised the plunging into dissipation at a fashionable health resort, and some recommended various medicinal springs in Europe which would work wonders; but the majority counselled him to take rod and gun, and get into the Rocky Mountains, camp out, and live like an Indian.

"Then," they said jocularly, smiting him on the back, "you'll be all right, and come back yearning for scalps on the Stock Exchange."

The newspapers mentioned the fact that John Steele was going into the Rockies to hunt and fish and camp out for a month or more to recover tone.

It was at this interesting juncture that Alice Fuller called to see him. Now, John Steele was the most susceptible of men, and one reason he shunned society was because he knew he would surely fall a victim to the first designing pretty girl who laid a trap for him—if, indeed, pretty girls ever do lay traps for men said to possess from six to ten millions. His weakness in this line was exemplified by his impetuous proposal to Dorothy Slocum in the environs of Bunkerville, as has already been stated. But Alice Fuller was not the commonplace young person Dorothy Slocum had been. He often thought of his proposal to Dorothy with a shudder, and accounted it a narrow escape, which, indeed, it was not, for Dorothy was thoroughly devoted to her station-master, and never gave even a thought to Mr. John Steele of Chicago.

Alice Fuller was a blonde, and she brought in with her to the conventional private office of John Steele, with its extremely modern fittings of card indices, loose-leaf ledgers, and expanding office furniture, an air of breezy freshness that hinted of the mountainous West. Although dressed as any Chicago woman might be, there was, nevertheless, something about her costume which suggested the riding of mountain ponies and even the expert handling of a rifle.

The glory of a woman is her hair, and in truth Miss Fuller's golden tresses were glorious enough; but her eyes were the most distinguished and captivating features of a face sufficiently beautiful to attract attention anywhere. They were of a deep, translucent blue, darkening now and then into violet, like a pair of those limpid mountain lakes in the Rockies whose depths are said to be unfathomable. It was impossible to look into those honest orbs without trusting the clear purity of the soul behind them, and Steele, whose nerves were unstrung, almost shivered with apprehension when they were turned full upon him.

"Lord save me!" he thought with a gasp. "If this girl wants to sell shares in the most bogus company afloat, I'm her victim. John Steele, if your bank account is to remain intact, now is the time to play St. Anthony."

But aloud he said calmly enough: "Pray be seated, madam," and she sank gracefully into a chair on the opposite side of the flat-topped desk behind which he was entrenched, although small protection the barricade afforded him against such artillery as a handsome young woman might bring to bear upon the position.

"It is so good of you to see me," said the girl. "I have read much of you in the newspapers, and I know that your time is valuable, so I shall take up as little of it as may be necessary to explain my business."

Somehow this remark, although only introductory sparring, disappointed young Mr. Steele. Nearly every stranger he met said the same thing in almost identical words. They all referred to his newspaper reputation, of which he was exceedingly tired, and nearly everyone spoke of the value of his time, promised not to encroach upon it, and then stayed for hours if they were permitted.

"My time is of little value at the present moment, Miss Fuller, because

I am doing nothing. For some months past I have been rather out of health, and, in fact, within a few days I expect to leave Chicago."

"Yes," she rejoined, "I saw that also in the papers. I read that you intended to go West among the mountains. Is that true?"

"Such are my present intentions, but they are always liable to change. A man who is fighting his own nerves is rather capricious, you know."

"Like a woman," laughed Miss Alice. "Well, it is on account of the statement in the Press that I am here. I have been thinking of calling upon you for a long time, but it appears we have no mutual friends who could give me an introduction, and so, seeing you were about to leave the city, I said to myself: 'It's now or never.'The reference to the mountains struck me as a lucky omen. You know we women are rather superstitious, Mr. Steele, and I think it was that even more than your impending departure which gave me courage to venture up here."

"I am very glad you came," said John Steele gallantly, "and I shall be more than pleased if there is anything I can do for you."

"My father is the owner of a gold-mine in the Black Hills. Do you know anything of mines, Mr. Steele?"

John slowly shook his head. The mere mention of a gold-mine did something to clarify his brain from the glamour that was befogging it.

"I know nothing whatever about mines, Miss Fuller, excepting the fact that more gold has been sunk in goldmines than has ever been taken out of them."

"Oh, I'm sorry to hear you say that," replied the girl, with a slight tremor of apprehension in her voice, "and, furthermore, I do not in the least believe it to be true. Indeed, it cannot be true, because it is impossible to sink gold without first having mined it. Nothing can be more lucrative than a good gold-mine, for its product is one of the few things taken from the earth which do not fluctuate in value. With copper, or silver, or iron, you are dependent on the market; not so with gold."

"You are a very eloquent advocate, Miss Fuller. Where is your father?"

The girl looked up quickly at this sudden change of subject, and once more John fell under the fascination of those enchanting eyes.

"My father? He is in Chicago."

"Then, Miss Fuller, the best plan will be to have him call upon me, and we can discuss the mine together."

"Alas!" said the young woman, with a mournful droop of the head, "if that had been possible, I should not have been here. My father at the present moment is very ill and quite unable to discuss business with anyone. You are going from the city to the mountains in search of health. He has come from the mountains to the city on the same quest. The gold-mine is at once our hope and our despair. If it can be properly worked, we are certain it will produce riches incalculable; but it takes money to make money, and my father knows no wealthy people nor does he possess the necessary capital for the preliminary outlay. We are somewhat like King Midas, in danger of starving with gold all around us."

"Has the mine been opened, or is it only a prospective claim?"

"At the present moment there are from sixteen to twenty miners working upon it. The shaft, I believe, is something like a hundred feet deep, and one or two short galleries have been run. The ore assay is extremely rich; I have not the figures with me, but can easily bring them; and the reports are better and better as the miners proceed."

"If that be the case, Miss Fuller, I see no reason why you should lack for capital."

"There are a hundred reasons, but one is sufficient. Every capitalist shuns a gold-mine. They speak just as you spoke a moment ago. Then, you see, our lives having been spent in the West, we know very few Eastern people, and those few have no money. The great difficulty is not in proving the wealth of the mine, but in getting a capitalist to listen. If you promise to listen, I shall undertake to prove to you that this is one of the most valuable properties in the world."

"Well, Miss Fuller, I am listening; but, as I told you, I know nothing whatever about gold-mines, and, indeed, am rather afraid of them. If the mine is producing ore in paying quantity, why does not your father have that ore crushed?—I suppose they could do that in the neighbourhood, or at Denver, or wherever the nearest mining town is—and with the product keep himself and pay his men?"

"That is exactly what he has done, Mr. Steele, and a ruinous thing it is to do. If it were not for that, we should have had to give up the struggle long ago. But there are no mines within miles of us, and we are two days and a half's journey from the nearest railway. Ore is bulky and heavy, and the transport alone over those mountain roads, which are not roads at all, and scarcely even paths, is at once slow and expensive. Railway freight is high, and when the ore gets to the reducing-plant, we have to take exactly what is given us, because beggars cannot be choosers. We need machinery at the mouth of the pit, and whoever will furnish the money for that machinery is sure to reap a rich reward."

"Nevertheless—" protested John, but the girl interrupted him, her eyes aglow with fervour.

"You promised to listen, you know. There is another point I wish to put before you. The ore is very rich, and if we ship much of it, there is bound to be inquiry as to where it came from. Now, my father has been able to stake out only a comparatively small claim. If once it becomes known where this ore originates, there will be the usual rush. The rush is ultimately inevitable in any case, but my father is anxious to be fully secure before it comes."

"I'll tell you what I'll do, Miss Fuller," said John in a burst of enthusiasm, "I'll give you a thousand dollars; and if you make money out of your mine, you can repay me at your leisure."

Alice Fuller slowly shook her golden head.

"I could not accept money in that way," she said. "It is like the giving of charity when a pathetic tale is told. Besides, a thousand dollars would be of no particular use; it would not purchase the stamp-mills, or transport them to the mine. In two months, or three, we should be just where we are now, and the thousand dollars would be gone."

"What is it, then, you wish me to do, Miss Fuller?"

"I wish our transaction to be upon a sane business basis, and I don't want you to offer me a thousand dollars or twenty thousand dollars, or two hundred thousand dollars again."

"I beg your pardon. I had no thought of charity or anything of the sort when I made my proposal."

"I am sure you hadn't," said the girl, with a naïve confidence which Steele found very charming. "I'll tell you what I wish to suggest. You are going to the mountains in any case. Very well, go to the Black Hills; there you will find the air pure and bracing; there are wild mountains and sparkling streams, and everything that a tired city man could desire. I want you to camp near our mine and investigate it thoroughly. If you are so satisfied with it as to justify the risk, I ask you to be prepared to buy a half share for three hundred thousand dollars."

John Steele drew a long breath.

"My purpose in going to the mountains is to get away from business, and not to take upon myself a new anxiety; to fish and shoot, not to pore over gold-bearing ore."

"Are you an enthusiastic sportsman, then?"

"Not at all. I was too busy when I was young to indulge in such recreation, and too poor. Since then I have become busier still."

"And too rich?" suggested the girl, with a smile.

"A man is never too rich, I am afraid."

"If you are not an enthusiastic sportsman, a week in the woods will prove more than enough for you. After that comes boredom, and a yearning for the ticker and the morning newspaper."

"I more than half believe you're right," said Steele ruefully.

"Of course I am right. Now, if you camp out beside the mine, you have something to interest you. Don't bother about it for the first week. There is plenty of shooting and fishing in the neighbourhood."

"I hate to put two and a half days between me and a telegraph-wire."

"Then you had better leave mountains alone and stay in Chicago."

John laughed.

"You are a very clever young lady, Miss Fuller, and I wonder you haven't made that gold-mine a success on your own."

"I am doing it now," she said with a flash almost of defiance from her eyes.

Again the young man laughed.

"Are you?" he asked. "You women have us at a disadvantage when you talk business, but I am going to get right down to plain facts, and speak to you as if you were your own brother. You won't be offended?"

"Not in the least."

"Very well. Do you know what a salted mine is?"

"Certainly. I thought you said you knew nothing of mines? A salted mine is one in which rich ore has been planted for the cheating of fools."

"An admirable definition, Miss Fuller. Well, in the matter of mines I'm a fool, and a salted mine would take me in as a gold brick on State Street would delude an Illinois farmer."

"Then induce an expert to go with you—a mining expert who knows pay ore when he sees it."

"I am more distrustful of mining experts than of salted mines."

The girl sighed.

"I suppose all faith has left Chicago?"

"It has—in gold-mines."

"Now, Mr. Steele, I'll talk to you as if you were your own sister. Have you ever done a stroke of useful toil since you were born?"

"Oh, yes; I worked on a railway."

"Very well. Go to the Black Hills and take a miner's outfit with you. Become for the time one of my father's workmen—or, rather, boss of the gang, if you like. Go into that mine, and direct them where they are to run the next level, and follow that level for a month, working with the men and keeping clear of the blasts. After you have penetrated a month in any direction you please, take the ore from the last blast and have it assayed. A mine can't be salted under those conditions. If that whole mountain is salted with gold, you'd better buy it."

"No one can gainsay the honesty of that, Miss Fuller; but, to tell you the truth, I dread the two and a half days' journey from the railway."

"You don't need to. I will be your guide."

"What!" cried John, in amazement.

"I'll take you from the railway to the Hard Luck mine. Will you go?" she demanded with a touch of defiance.

"Go!" he cried, discretion struggling with enthusiasm. "Of course I'll go. Nothing would give me greater pleasure. But, then, on the other hand—you see—well—to speak quite frankly, for a young lady to—to, as one might say, journey across the plains——"

"Yes, I know, I know. You are talking now, not to my brother, as you remarked a while ago, but to my brother's sister. All my life I have had not only to take care of myself, but of my father as well. This project is a matter of vital importance to me, and I cannot allow it to fail merely because the rules of society would frown on what I intend to do. I shall take with me my own tent, and an old man who was in my father's employ long before I was born. This is a cold business deal, and no other consideration is going to enter into it. So let us brush aside every other consideration and come down to plain facts. You offered me a thousand dollars, and I refused it. If you will now give me the necessary money, which may be anything from two hundred dollars upwards, depending on what you want to take with you, I shall go at once to Pickaxe Gulch, which is the nearest railway station to the Hard Luck mine, and will collect what transport we need. There I shall await your coming. Do you intend to take any servants with you?"

"I shall be accompanied by Sam Jackson, a negro man, who is the best cook in this town."

"Very well, you will need a horse for him, and one for yourself; I shall need two horses; that's four. Then if you will give me an idea of the number of tents and boxes you require, I shall secure mules enough to carry them. We shall want two or three men to look after the mules, and you must give me a week at least to get this cavalcade together. Sometimes there are neither animals nor men at Pickaxe Gulch, but I intend to telegraph at once and secure whatever transport is available."

John Steele smiled his appreciation of the capability displayed by the fearless young woman, opened his drawer, and took out a cheque-book.

"Shall we say five hundred dollars?" he asked, looking across the desk at her. "You must leave some money with your father, you know."

"Five hundred will be ample," she replied decidedly, and he wrote a cheque for that amount.

Later on in his life Steele remembered that demand for money with admiration. It was just one of those little points where a less subtle person than Miss Fuller would have made a mistake, deluded by success in getting him to promise to make the trip. But the young woman was evidently shrewd enough to know that after she left he would wonder, she having pleaded poverty, where the money came from to pay for so long a railway journey and at the same time provide for an ailing father at home. He always regarded that request for expenses as the climax of a well-thought-out plan.

## CHAPTER XIV—AN IMPORTANT CHAMPAGNE LUNCH.

WHEN John Steele stepped down from the sleeping-car in the early morning at Pickaxe Gulch, he found Alice Fuller the sole occupant of the platform. She welcomed him with the cordiality of good comradeship. Her costume differed rather strikingly from the apparel she wore in his office. She reminded him of one of those reckless female riders he had seen at Buffalo Bilks Wild West Show, and he was forced to confess that the outfit suited her to perfection. She was even more attractive than when he had first seen her, and he could hardly have believed that possible. Before he ventured to compliment the young woman on her appearance, she complimented him on his.

"You are already looking very much better than you did in the city."

"Yes!" he cried jubilantly. "Your visit did me ever so much good; and, besides that, I am now out from under Peter's shadow."

"'Peter's shadow?'" she repeated. "What is that? The shadow of a mountain?"

"In a way, yes," laughed Steele, "and a gold-producing mountain at that. I have been a rather anxious person these many months past; but now, whether it is the exhilaration of the air in the West, or the prospect"—he hesitated a moment, then continued—"of this journey, I am quite my own man once more."

Without reply she led the way to the dusty road which ran between two rows of roughly built shanties.

"Did you breakfast on the train?" she asked.

"No."

"I thought you might not have an opportunity to get anything to eat on the train, as it stops here so early, and I have ordered a meal for you at the one tavern in this place, which is far from being first-class. However, possibly, you can endure such a repast for once and then we will get on our way as soon as possible."

"Oh, the cuisine of the West is no surprise to me," said Steele. "I've had a good deal of experience with it in my time."

They walked up the street together, the negro cook following and carrying Steele's valise. At the tavern the caravan was collected, and more than ever the resemblance to the Wild West Show impressed itself upon the young man. The boxes had been sent on some days ahead, and were now securely fastened to the backs of the mules. Four saddle-horses were tied to the rude pillars of the verandah. Steele went inside the building and partook of the breakfast, such as it was, and ten minutes later the procession started north.

Their route lay across the plain, and during the forenoon the party traversed a road of sorts, reasonably well defined. In the horizon loomed low mountains, which did not seem perceptibly nearer when a halt was called by the side of a stream to prepare lunch. Steele was more accustomed to a street-car than to the back of a horse; but the way was level, and the horse developed none of those buck-jumping peculiarities which John, in his Eastern ignorance, had always associated with the steeds of the Far West. His business heretofore had never taken him away from a line of railway, and where it had been necessary to make a road journey, the jaunt was accomplished in some sort of vehicle. However, he soon became accustomed to his new method of locomotion and succeeded better than he had anticipated.

Alice Fuller proved a most expert horse-woman, and her superb attitude in the saddle still further enslaved this ardent young man, who began to think he had never really lived until now. He was rather disappointed, but rendered none the less eager, to find that he was not getting as much of her company as he had hoped. In the beginning they rode side by side in front of the cavalcade, to be out of the dust which the mule train raised. But every now and then she wheeled her horse round and allowed the procession to pass her, scanning each animal and its burden with the eye of an expert, seeing that everything was in order. When Steele expressed admiration of her capability, Miss Fuller told him she had many times been in full charge of a similar expedition going or coming from the mine; and once when he complained of lack of companionship, she informed him that success depended a great deal on the first few hours of the march, and it was her duty to see that none of the animals fell lame, and that no burden shifted, thus causing a mule to lag behind its fellows.

"To-morrow," she said, "we shall be among the foothills, and even this afternoon we shall be free of the road and the dust. Then, if everything is going well, I may find plenty of time to talk to you, for I see you are anxious to learn more about the mine before you reach it."

Steele threw a free-hearted laugh on the echoless air. Any little incident seemed now a fit subject for mirth. The clear atmosphere seemed as exhilarating as wine, and there was the further intoxicant of the girl's alluring presence.

Lunch by the side of the stream more than made amends for the unattractive breakfast. The efficient Jackson had caused each of the numerous boxes to be numbered, and he began with Number One, which his master said was a very good thing to look after. He produced a portable stove, and a handful of coke performed miracles in the desert. It was soon evident that John Steele had no intention of starving while he wandered in the wilderness. He drew from its straw envelope a bottle of prime champagne, a drink which doubtless had never quenched thirst on that particular route before. Miss Fuller partook of the wine but sparingly, and lifted her glass when he proposed the toast of success to the expedition, thrilling him as she did so with those enthralling eyes of hers, and the young man began to wonder whether he actually saw heaven in their depths, or was looking at a desert mirage through an atmosphere of sparkling wine.

He persuaded her to linger after the cavalcade had moved on, saying they would overtake it at a gallop, and the young woman, with scarcely concealed reluctance, acquiesced. He threw himself full length at her feet and gazed up at her, while she watched, with the suggestion of a frown on her smooth brow, the procession lessening in the distance. He lit a cigarette, with her permission; and began the sort of conversation which a young man in the early stages of fascination is prone to indulge in. At first it seemed to him her thoughts were elsewhere, which was not in the least flattering to a person who was doing his best. On his chiding her for this, she drew a sharp breath and cast a glance upon him which he fancied was the reverse of friendly. It was veiled an instant after, and then, with something like a sigh, she appeared to accept the situation.

At this presaging of victory, John Steele's conscience began to trouble him. He guessed why she appeared so changeable. Her father's future and her own depended on the good-will of the young man stretched at her feet. She was anxious not to offend him, and yet her reluctance to remain alone with him, her absent-minded look, and the slight frown that now and then marred her brow, were hints that his attentions proved unwelcome. Steele surmised that any undue compliments or any too palpable indulgence in sentiment at this particular moment might prove disastrous to ultimate success. The resigned air with which she endeavoured to face a tete-a-tete not to her liking touched his pride, and also made him rather ashamed of himself for taking advantage of one who in the circumstances was helpless. He wondered if he could put this girl more at ease by telling her he had quite made up his mind to finance the mine, whether it proved all she said or the reverse. Yet she might regard this statement as merely an unblushing bid for her preference, for she knew that until he had examined the mine any such avowal would be made merely because he thought it would please her. While these thoughts ran through his mind, a silence had fallen between them, which, however, the girl appeared not to notice, for her eyes were fixed on the distant mountains. She was quite startled by the suddenness with which he sprang to his feet.

"Miss Fuller," he cried, "I see you are anxious to be off towards the hills, and it is selfish of me to detain you here."

He held out his hand to her and helped her up. She smiled very sweetly and said:

"I think it is time we were on our way again. We have further to go than you suspect, before we reach the regular camping-ground."

He had reason to congratulate himself on his intuition, for during that journey she was kinder to him than she had ever been before, as if anxious to make up for her former coldness.

The sun had gone down ere they reached the halting-station for the night. They were now on an elevated plateau among the hills, and an impetuous torrent near by gave forth the only sound that broke the intense stillness. Tents were pitched, horses and mules tethered, and Jackson set out a dinner which their keen appetites made doubly memorable. Night came down, and the moon rose gloriously in the east. Time and place were ideal for a lovers' meeting, but the adage which intimates that luck with gold does not run parallel with luck in love proved true in this instance. Immediately after partaking of the excellent coffee Jackson had brewed, the young woman rose and held out her hand, pleading fatigue.

"I must bid you 'Good night,'" she said shortly.

"Oh! won't you stay a little while and enjoy this unexampled moonlight? It seems as if I had never seen the moon before."

The young woman smiled wanly, but shook her head.

"I'm really very tired," she explained. "I have had a week of it at that awful hotel in the Gulch. It is fearfully noisy at night with drinking cowboys and miners, and so I have had scarcely any sleep for a long while. If I have proved a dull companion to-day, that is the reason, and I am sure you will excuse me now."

"Miss Fuller, you could not be dull if you tried. I am sorry you should have had so much trouble on my account at that terrible station. I should have sent a man, but I could not guess the horrors of the place before seeing it. Pray forgive my selfishness."

"Oh, that was really nothing. I am quite accustomed to the life; but, somehow, the first night in the mountains always leaves me stupid and drowsy."

"To-morrow night, then," he said very quietly, "we may perhaps view the moonlight together."

"To-morrow night," she murmured and was gone.

Steele threw himself into the canvas camp-chair, and, reclining, gazed on the moonlit plain below and listened to the roar of the torrent. Dreamily he fancied himself floating in the seventh heaven of bliss.

Next morning the camp was early astir, for a long day of mountaineering lay ahead. The party numbered seven, all told, there being three men of peaceable demeanour, but rough aspect, in charge of the pack-train. At no time during that day did Steele secure an opportunity of speaking with Alice Fuller alone. They could not ride together, as the mountain path was too narrow. After dinner, at the final camping-place, a wild spot in a profound valley, where John saw with dismay the moon would not be visible, the girl seemed loth to keep him company as had been the case the night before. She laughed somewhat harshly, he thought, when he complained that she must have known they could not see the moon.

"You can study its rays on the northern peaks," she said. "Who would ever have expected a modern financier to yearn for the moon?"

"A modern financier is but a man, after all," protested Steele.

"I have sometimes doubted it," replied the girl cynically.

"Well, Miss Fuller, if you will sit down again, even in the absence of moonlight, I think I can remove your doubts."

She stood there hesitating for a few moments, but it was too dark to see the expression on her face. Finally she sat down in the chair from which she had risen.

"I am seated," she said; "but not to talk of moonlight, merely to tell you that I intend to go no farther. To-morrow morning we bid 'Good-bye' to each other. You go north, and I go south."

"Oh, I say," cried John reproachfully, "that's contrary to contract. You promised to lead me to the mine."

"I know I did; but it is always a woman's privilege to change her mind. Perhaps you will understand I do not wish to influence you at all in the decision you may come to about the mine."

"Would it make you abjure your cruel resolve if I informed you that I have quite determined to invest in the mine if it gives any show of success, which I am sure it will do from what you have told me about it?"

"The mine must plead its own cause," she said, with an indifference that amazed him. "You have no real need of me as a guide, for the three men I engaged know the route as well as I do. They have been over it often enough. I am really very anxious about my father. He promised to telegraph me at Pickaxe Gulch, but has not done so. I sent a despatch the day before you arrived, but no reply came, and it may be waiting for me now at the office there."

"Why not send back one of the men?"

"Because of my own anxiety. I fear the telegram may call me to his side. I think you will understand now why I have been distraught while in your company."

"Miss Fuller, believe me, I am very sorry to hear that this worry has been hanging over you. If I had known, I should have proposed our remaining at Pickaxe Gulch until you had heard from your father. I fear my own conduct and conversation may have added to your discomfort."

"Oh, no, no," said the girl, quickly rising again.

"Will you accept this trifle from me?"

He spoke hurriedly, and took from his waistcoat pocket something that she knew to be a ring, for even in the dim light it sparkled as if fire were playing from its facets.

"I'd rather not," she replied, stepping back.

"It will bind you to nothing—nothing at all. It is simply to keep me in your memory until we next meet."

"Oh, I shall never forget you!" she cried, in a tone of bitterness that startled him.

"It is a mere trinket," he urged, "and I bought it for you before I left civilisation. If you do not accept it, I shall throw it into the darkness of the valley yonder."

"That would be foolish, even for you."

"Why, Miss Fuller, such a remark has a very dubious sound. What do you mean by it? Do you think I am foolish?"

"Oh, I don't think anything at all of either you or your folly. I tell you I merely want to get away."

"Won't you take the ring with you?"

She stood for a long time with head bowed.

"I don't suppose it makes any difference one way or the other," she said at last.

"Of course it doesn't. I told you it wouldn't."

"Very well, I shall take the ring, if you will accept a much cheaper and more significant present from me in the morning."

"I shall accept gratefully anything you like to give me, Miss Fuller, in the morning or at any future time."

"I wonder," was all her comment, as she took the ring and instantly disappeared.

Somehow this night held none of the glamour that distinguished the previous evening. The depth of the profound shadows surrounding him was merely emphasised by the touch of cold moonlight on the hilltops far away. John wondered if the exhilarating effect of the atmosphere had departed, leaving him sober again. He felt strangely depressed, and although he immediately entered his tent and flung himself, dressed as he was, upon his canvas cot, he found it difficult to sleep. It was after midnight before he dozed off, and then his slumber was troubled and uneasy. Towards morning, however, a kind of stupor descended upon him, leaving him dreamless and lost to the world. This was broken by a sharp and angry voice, whose meaning did not at first reach his consciousness; but the sentence lingered in his awakening mind and at last became clear to him, as an image comes out during the gradual development of a photographic plate.

"I tell you I will not leave until I bid 'good-bye' to Mr. Steele."

It was Alice Fuller's voice, and in an instant the young man was on his feet and out of the tent. Day had just dawned, gray and chill, but already the camp was astir and the young woman in her saddle.

"Did you call me?" he cried.

"No," she answered; but he seemed to detect a tremor of fear in her voice.

"I thought I heard you say you wished to bid 'goodbye' to me!"

"You must have been dreaming. But I do wish to bid you 'good-bye.'"

Two of the muleteers stood near, and the old attendant, mounted, had already started slowly on his way. John sprang to her side, and as he came to a stand by the horse, she stooped and slipped a small box into his coat pocket.

"Good-bye! good-bye!" she cried somewhat boisterously, with an exclamation that seemed to be half sob and half laugh. "Go back to your tent at once and brush your hair. It's enough to frighten anyone," and now she laughed with unnecessary vehemence, the near mountains echoing the peal with a strange mocking cadence that sent a chill up the spine of one listener.

"What does this mean?" he asked himself.

The man at the bridle turned the horse's head towards the distant railway, and the other smote the steed on the flank.

"Let go my horse!" commanded Miss Fuller savagely. The man slouched away. She touched the animal with her heel and galloped off, while Steele stood in a daze watching her. Only once she looked back, then made a quick motion to the pocket of her jacket and disappeared round the ledge of rock. Jack remembered the packet she had dropped into his pocket, and imagining her gesture might have reference to that, walked to his tent to examine the present so surreptitiously given him, remembering that she had said the night before it would prove more significant than the ring she had so reluctantly accepted. It was a little, square parcel, tied in a bit of newspaper with a red string. He whisked this off, and held in his hand a box of white metal. Opening the box he saw within it a simple cake of soap!

Steele held this on his open palm, gazing at it like one hypnotised.

"My God!" he groaned at last, "soap—Amalgamated Soap! Peter Berrington and Nicholson! Trapped, as I am a fool and a sinner! These muleteers are the real chiefs of this expedition. They saw Alice Fuller weakening; but she weakened too late, and now they have sent her away. What's the object of all this? It is too fantastic to imagine that Nicholson supposes he can exact all I possess as ransom. Even the Black Hills are not the mountains of Greece. What is it, then? Murder? That's equally incredible, and yet possible. Here am I unarmed, rifles in the boxes, no one with me but a cowardly nigger. Walked right into the trap with my eyes open, like a gaping idiot! Well, John Steele, you deserve all you will get! Let's discover what it is."

He strode out of the tent. The negro was preparing breakfast. The three men stood in a group together, talking, but they looked round and became silent as he approached.

"I have changed my mind," said Steele; "we're going back to the railway."

"Oh, no, we're not," said one of the men, stepping forward, and taking a revolver from his hip pocket; "we're going on to the mine."

"Is there a mine?" asked Steele, with a sneering laugh.

"Oh, there's a mine all right enough, and they're waiting for you there."

"Who?"

"You'll find out about twelve o'clock to-day."

"See here, boys," said Steele persuasively, "I'll make you three the richest men in this part of the country if you'll accompany me safely back to the railway."

"We've heard that kind of talk before," replied the man, "and have had enough of it. You tell that to the boss of the gang at the mine; and whatever he says, we'll agree to."

"Yes, but at the mine—How many are there, by the way?"

"You'll see when you reach the spot."

"Well, even if there's one more, he divides the loot with you. You can make better terms with me now than you can at the mine."

"Chuck it, stranger. There ain't no use giving us any more taffy. You're going on to the mine."

"All right," said Steele, turning on his heel. "I'll have breakfast first. Is the coffee ready, Jackson?"

"Yes, sir."

The prisoner sat down at the collapsible table and enjoyed a hearty meal.

At noon they reached the mine, and a dozen, gaunt, wild-eyed men, who were sitting round, stood up when the riders came into sight. They gave no cheer when they saw the captive, nor did their attitude of listless, bored indifference change a particle as Steele stopped his horse and dismounted.

"Here's the goods," said the leader of the muleteers, and the boss of the mining gang nodded, but made no reply.

"Good day, gentlemen," began Steele, a smile coming to his lips in spite of the seriousness of the crisis, as he thought that this sombre, silent gang in the midst of the mountains bore a comical resemblance to the gnomes in Rip Van Winkle when that jovial inebriate appeared amongst them. "I take it, sir, that you are leader here, and I think there has been some mistake. During today's journey I have been forced to travel to this mine against my will. You seem to have been expecting me. Now, what's up?"

"You'll be, in about ten minutes," replied the boss. "Dakota Bill, where's your rope?"

"Here it is," said Bill, stepping forward and exhibiting a slip-noose at the end of about thirty feet of stout line.

"Now, stranger, if you've got any messages to leave your friends, we'll give you ten minutes to write or say them."

"I've no messages, thank you, but I am disturbed by a lively curiosity to know what all this means."

"Oh, of course you've no suspicion about what it means, have you?"

"No, I have not."

"You never saw your mine before, did you?"

"It isn't my mine."

"I knew you'd say that. Well, now, we've been left here for four months without a markee of pay. For the last month we would have starved if it hadn't been for Dakota Bill's good work with a rifle; but even the game has fled from this accursed place and now we are starving. You're the man responsible, and you know it. We've sworn to hang you, and we're going to hang you."

"My dear sir, your statement is definite and concise, without being as illuminating as I should like. A mistake has been made, of which I am the innocent victim. You are the victims, too, for that matter; because, after all, it is not a mistake, but a conspiracy. I can see, however, that nothing I may say will mitigate the situation in the slightest degree. I shall, therefore, not indulge in useless declamation. Three things are fixed. I am the owner of this mine. I have cheated you out of your pay for four months, therefore I am to be hanged. There comes into my mind at this moment something I have read somewhere about hangings at Newgate prison in England. They drop a man, then all concerned go at once to enjoy what is called the 'hanging breakfast.' The gruesomeness of such a proceeding fastened the item in my mind. Let's have a 'hanging lunch.'"

"Stranger, as I understand your remarks, the person turned off didn't attend that breakfast."

"No, he didn't."

"Very well, stranger, we'll look after the lunch when you're strung up."

"But, excuse me, the victim had a hearty breakfast before he was hanged. Now, I beg to point out to you that I drank my coffee just about daybreak this morning, and since then I've travelled over the worst set of mountains it has ever been my privilege to encounter. I'm as hungry as a bear. I therefore insist on your lunching with me, and I shall give you a meal such as you wouldn't better at the Millionaire's Club. Before I left home, six manufacturers of portable stoves insisted on my accepting one each, in the hope of getting an unsolicited testimonial. I shall leave the stoves with you, and trust you will recommend them to your friends. I don't need them where I'm going."

"No," said one of the party, "they'd melt there."

"Now, Jackson," cried Steele enthusiastically, "set up the whole six stoves. You've got to cook dinner for the party. But, meanwhile, open some of those boxes of new sardines with the trimmings on, which they've just sent across to us from Brittany. A little caviare also may be a novelty in this district. I think we've plates enough to go round. If not, use saucers or the tins. Gentlemen, I take it you don't need an appetiser, but what will you drink before we begin?"

"I admit, stranger, you're a mighty plausible cuss, and we expected that; but you don't palaver this crowd. There's no drinking till after the ceremony."

For the first time there was a murmur of disapproval at this, but the leader held up his hand.

"See here, you fellows," he said, "we've got to deal with a pretty slippery customer. You know what them city men are. Now, there's no drinking till after the performance; you hear me. I'd string him up this moment, only we'd scare his cook white, and then we'd have to eat things raw."

Jackson handed round sardines and other tempting extras, while Steele put the collapsible table on its legs and opened various boxes, from one of which he took out a case of champagne, and another of Scotch whisky. Then, getting a large pitcher which had been intended as the water-holder of his tent, he poured two bottles of Scotch whisky into it, followed by bottle after bottle of champagne until the jug was full. Meanwhile the busy negro had got the six stoves ablaze, and the appetising smell that came from the utensils over the fires made the starving miners oblivious to everything else. The first course was devoured in silence.

"Although you may not care to consume intoxicating liquors, and I quite agree with you that it is best to keep sober, I hope you have no objection to temperance drinks. Who'll have some cider?"

"Cider?" said the leader. "Have you got any?"

"Here's a pitcher full."

"That's all right. Pour it out. I wish you had brought beer instead. We'd risk beer."

"Oh, well, you can risk the cider. I'm sorry I haven't any beer," and, hungry as he was, the young man himself poured out full glasses to each.

"By jiminy crickets!" cried the leader, "that's the best cider I ever tasted."

"It's the very best cider made in this country," said Steele earnestly, "and thank goodness, I've got plenty of it."

As course after course was served, and bumper after bumper was drunk, the geniality of the crowd rose and rose, until Steele at last saw he could possibly make terms with them, but he resolved not to chance that. He determined to leave them so drunk that none could move; then he would depart at his leisure. Under the exhilarating effects of the mixture he poured out, all objections to intoxicating liquor fled from the jovial assemblage, and Jackson now opened whisky bottle after whisky bottle. The miners were laughing, singing, weeping on one another's necks, utterly oblivious of mine owners, lack of pay, lynching, or anything else, when Steele and Jackson mounted their horses, the coloured cook leading one of the mules laden with provisions ample for a week's journey.

When Steele reached Pickaxe Gulch, he thought he never should be so glad to see a pair of rails again. He felt like throwing his arms round the neck of the station-master, but instead asked that rough diamond if there were any news.

"No, not much," replied the station-master, "except that Peter Berrington, the billionaire, is dead."

"Thank God!" fervently ejaculated Steele, to the astonishment of the station-master.

"Yes," said the official, "he's gone where his money won't do him no good. Found dead in his chair in his office in New York, two days ago. There's the paper, if you want to read about it."

Steele went in and possessed himself of the paper.

"By Jove!" he muttered, as he gazed at the big, black headlines. "He or his system sent a man to death when he ought to have been preparing for death himself. That's as it should be. Thank goodness the shadow has lifted!"

John Steele forgot the words of Shakespeare:=

\`\`\`\`"The evil that men do lives after them."=

## CHAPTER XV—AN ATTEMPT AT AN ARMISTICE.

JOHN STEELE'S friends were amazed to find him back in town almost within a week after he had left with such lavish preparations for a long stay in the wilderness. It was difficult for him to offer an adequate explanation, and it grew to be most annoying, once he had constructed his excuses, to be compelled to repeat them to every friend he met, and listen without cursing to the inane advice given by people who didn't in the least know what they were talking about.

"What! back already?" cried Philip Manson, who had offered to place a private car at his disposal if he would keep close to the railway. Manson held that camping out in a private car was the right way to do it, and that a canvas tent was a delusion and a snare. "Back already?" exclaimed the general manager. "Why, John, you look as haggard as if you'd been through a panic in the wheat market. Didn't the Black Hills agree with you?"

"No," said John shortly and truthfully; "threatened to develop throat trouble," and he tapped his neck significantly.

"How long were you in the mountains?"

"Five days."

"Oh, well, I told you how it would be before you left. That's what comes of sleeping in a cot-bed, over damp ground, under thin canvas. You should have taken both my advice and my private car then you could have carried all the comforts of town with you."

Now that the immediate tension of the crisis had relaxed, John Steele found himself very close to a mental and physical collapse. It was true that the great Peter Berrington was dead, but the elation which that startling piece of news had first caused subsided long before he reached the city. Men die, but systems remain. Had the shadow of Peter Berrington been lifted, after all, even though Peter himself was now a shadow? The grotesque uncertainty of the situation was making rags of John Steele's nerves. Even as he walked through the crowded streets he had to fight down an impulse to shriek aloud, raising his hands to heaven and crying: "In God's name, if you're going to do anything, do it now, and let's have it over!"

It was not that he shrank from ruin, or even from death, both of which he had faced within the past year. It was the uncertainty of when and how the blow was to fall. He began to fear that something worse than either ruin or death would overtake him. In the privacy of his own room he would sometimes march up and down with set teeth and clenched fists, saying to himself: "You must quit thinking of this, or you'll go mad," and yet with all his strength of mind he could not stop his planning to circumvent the unseen danger which threatened him.

The fantastic nature of the peril that surrounded him was such that if it were made public, he would be laughed at from one end of the country to the other. In a busy, practical, work-a-day world, it was incredible that a group of men, only one of whom he had ever seen, and that most casually, should sit in a sky-scraper in New York and actually plan the murder of a young man in Chicago; for this group of men were churchgoers, Sunday-school teachers, philanthropists who had founded colleges; bestowers of charity on a scale of munificence hitherto unexampled. And yet more potent than all these things was the fact that they were hard-headed business men, the most successful business men in the world, intent on their own affairs, and naturally far removed from any thought of revenge, for the simple reason that revenge is not business, and there is no money in it. It was quite true that this same group, in early days, had been accused of burning rival factories, of inciting riots, and of many other crimes against the peace and security of the commonwealth, but these things had never been legally proven or brought home to the group by irrefutable evidence. Where investigation had followed crime, and the inquiry was not quashed, it had always been shown that the rash acts were the work of over-zealous employees exceeding their instructions. The hands of the financial group in the tall building on Broadway were clean. No band of Quakers were more set against violence than these mild-mannered men in New York. If John Steele had told the story of the attempted lynching among the Black Hills, the incredulous public would have looked upon the affair as a practical joke played by humourous mountaineers on a tenderfoot from the East. No one knew better than John Steele that to connect Dakota Bill of the Black Hills with Nicholson of New York was an impossibility. He was certain the miners knew nothing of Nicholson; that they held a genuine lynching grievance against the owner of the mine, whoever he was, and that they were acting quite naturally according to their instincts when this supposed owner had fallen into their hands.

Alice Fuller, who led him so easily into the trap, as the tame animal in the stockyards leads its fellows to the slaughter-pen—she, of course, knew for whom she was acting, but John doubted if this knowledge led by any followable clue to Nicholson. When he thought of the handsome girl, he shuddered; and, for ten thousand reasons, that episode must never become public. To be hoodwinked by a pretty woman was merely to join the procession of fools that extended from the time of Adam to the year 1905.

It was difficult for Steele to cease his thoughts of the Amalgamated Soap combination, for the papers continued full of Peter Berrington and the financial upheaval which his sudden death was certain to cause. The imagination of the world was touched by the fact that this tremendous power which Peter Berrington had wielded in ever-increasing force for nearly half a century now lapsed into the hands of a girl, Constance Berrington, aged twenty-four, the only child of the billionaire. The newspapers printed column after column about this young lady, who appeared to be even more of a recluse than her father was. They published portraits of her, no two alike—pictures ranging from the most beautiful woman in Christendom to the most gaunt and ugly hag; which seemed to indicate that photographs of Miss Constance were unobtainable, and that the artists drew on their imagination as well as on their Whatman pads. She avoided society, was never seen at such resorts as Newport or Lenox; she took no part in the festivities of a great city, and believed that the door of a theatre was the gate of hell. Gossip said she was haunted by a fear of being married for her money, and so at this early age had become a man-hater. It was also alleged that she kept a conscience, a possession with which her father had never been credited even by the wildest imaginative writer. She was going to devote her life and her billions as far as possible to the undoing of the harm which her parent had accomplished.

"She is fanatically religious," proclaimed one newspaper.

"She is a plain, commonplace girl," said another, "whose father has bequeathed her his cash, but not his brains."

When John Steele found he could not cease thinking over his paralysing situation, which had entirely emasculated his initiative and wrecked his business career; when he feared lunacy awaited him, he resolved to meet this girl, and persuade her, if he could, to stop the huge, golden Juggernaut which threatened to crush the life or reason out or him. Yet it seemed cowardly for a grown man to make such an appeal to a young girl who was an entire stranger to him, and who, if he actually succeeded in reaching her presence, would most likely consider herself insulted that such crimes as he placed before her without the slightest proof, should be attributed to her father. Thus the interview would doubtless end with his being turned out of the house by the servants. Then again, even if she believed him—and the chances were only as one in ten thousand—did she possess the actual as well as the nominal power to stop the persecution? Was she like the Czar of Russia, helplessly at the head of an organisation over whose movements the supposed chief had no control?

Yet, after all, Steele had not gone so far towards insanity as to be in any error regarding the real mover in the conspiracies of which he was the victim. Nicholson was the man; there could be no doubt of that. Twice Steele had beaten Nicholson to the ground. In the great wheat deal he had exposed his treachery and dishonesty; had publicly shown him to be an unscrupulous scoundrel; had prevented him from making millions in a single coup, which was all prepared and certain to succeed had not Steele disarranged the machinery. He had humiliated the man personally, wounding his pride and crushing his self-esteem. Was it possible, then, ever to make terms with one naturally so embittered? Steele braced himself and resolved to try. Twice he had defeated him, and there remained in John's hand the powerful weapon of publicity. After all, could Amalgamated Soap risk such an exposure as it was in Steele's power to cast forth to the eager Press of the country? Was it so certain that the public would not believe the story he might tell regarding

Amalgamated Soap? Even though Nicholson was imbued with malice, his colleagues would be more reasonable, more amenable to persuasion. They would undoubtedly try to induce this angry man to refrain from tempting the avalanche. He resolved to propose a treaty of peace with Nicholson. Then came the doubt. Should Nicholson agree to such a pact, would he keep it? Would he merely use it as a sedative to lull his intended victim into false security? Such an outcome was very likely; still, a frank talk with Nicholson could do no harm, and Steele had not the slightest intention of being lulled into security by anything Nicholson might say. Recalling to his mind the stony countenance of that human sphinx, Steele could not delude himself that any appeal to conscience or any plea for mercy would have the least chance of success. Nicholson was as unemotional as the Pyramids; Steele could make no bargain with such a man unless he had something to offer. Therefore he did not go impetuously to New York and fling himself at the feet of Nemesis, the divinity of chastisement and vengeance. He set about the preparation of the goods he would trade with, this white Indian. It gratified him to think that after all these months of doubt and uncertainty he could at last come to a definite decision about anything.

There were no women in John Steele's office. His confidential stenographer was a quiet man, a little older than himself, named Henry Russell. Steele touched an electric button on his desk, and Russell came in, notebook in hand.

"Sit down, Russell. If I remember rightly, you were connected with a newspaper in your early days?"

"In a very humble capacity, sir; I was merely a reporter."

"Oh, don't say 'merely.' A reporter is ever so much more important than an editorial writer. Have you ever attempted a novel?"

"No, sir."

"Still, you know something of literary form and the way a book is put together, I suppose?"

"I know nothing about the writing of books, sir. I think I have a fair knowledge of how a sentence should read."

"Well, that's the main thing. Still, as a reporter you must have seen a good deal of the seamy side of life, and later you have had to do with important business affairs, ever since you came into my employ."

"That is very true, Mr. Steele."

"Don't you think you could concoct the plot of a novel? A novel of every-day business life, let us say, like one of those that have been so successful lately—a book pulsating with the greed of gold, and all that sort of thing, you know? Unscrupulous men, and perhaps an adventuress here and there, of perfectly stunning beauty. For instance, someone resembling that girl who came in to see me a fortnight ago."

"Yes, I remember her. She was good looking."

"An amazing beauty, I thought her," said Steele, thrusting his hands into his trousers pockets and marching up and down the room. "Well, couldn't such a belle of the markets as that inspire you towards the writing of a great work of fiction?"

Russell shook his head. "I'm afraid not, Mr. Steele."

"There's nothing much doing just now," continued the promenading man. "At this present moment I intended to be off on my vacation, but I found the mountains too exciting—er—too dull I mean—and so you see I am back among you earlier than I expected. Now, Russell, between ourselves, there is nothing more absurd than for a successful business man to attempt the writing of a novel. Yet I'm the sort of person who cannot remain idle, and there is nothing in sight to do for a month or two. I'm going to while away the time by composing a business novel, and I want you to assist me. I'll dictate the thing straight off to you, and you must invent the names and kick the sentences into shape."

"I'll do my best, sir."

"And remember, Russell, of all the confidential transactions you've been called upon to perform, this is the one in which I demand the utmost secrecy.

I should be the laughing stock of the town if it once got out that I were plunging into fiction instead of into wheat."

"I'll never breathe a whisper of it, sir."

"I am sure you won't, and that is why I trust you. Now, we'll just lock the doors and refuse ourselves to all comers. If a novel is to be a success nowadays, when people have so much to read and so little time for reading, it must be as sensational as possible, and I think I can do the trick. Anyhow, if it fails, there's no great harm done, and for a time we two will court that seclusion with which, I read in the papers, all true literary men surround themselves."

The two men worked together day after day, until the first draft of the history was completed and typed; then they revised this copy very thoroughly, and Steele directed that duplicates should be made, with blanks left for all proper names. He professed himself dissatisfied with the titles they had invented, and said that while the final manuscript was being prepared, he would concoct more suitable appellations for his main characters, and insert them with his own hand. This final revision was accomplished by John Steele alone, when he inserted the real names; then with his own hand he wrote the following letter to Stoliker, editor of the Daily Blade:

*My dear Stoliker:*

*If the accompanying manuscript ever comes into your possession, I want you first of all to remember that on a certain night I brought to you a most remarkable article regarding the wheat situation in this country, the truth of which you quite legitimately doubted. After-events proved the accuracy of my statement, and you were thus enabled to score a great triumph for your paper. Believe me, then, when I tell you that every word here typed is true; for when you read the accompanying pages, I shall not be by your side to use arguments in favour of its publication. I shall either have disappeared, or, more probably, I shall be dead. In either case, this manuscript, every name in which is real, will give you a clue to the disaster which has overtaken me. In the meantime I remain, Your friend,*

*John Steele.*

This letter and the manuscript he wrapped up into a parcel, which he securely sealed. On the outside he wrote instructions that in the case of his death or disappearance the package was to be handed intact to Stoliker, of the Daily Blade. The other package, with a duplicate of the letter to Stoliker, was placed in the vault of a depository, supposed to be the greatest strong-room in the city, which, he afterwards learned with some amusement, belonged to Amalgamated Soap. The thin key and the code word which opened this receptacle he placed in a sealed envelope which he left in the hands of his legal advisers, with instructions to forward the envelope to Stoliker in case of his death or disappearance.

All this accomplished to his satisfaction, he took the Limited to New York, and entered the tall building on Broadway which was body to the brain that directed the activities of Amalgamated Soap. Asking that his card should be taken to Mr. Nicholson, and replying to an inquiry that he had no appointment, he was taken into a small but richly furnished waiting-room, which he saw to be one of many on the eleventh floor, and there he rested for nearly half an hour before a messenger entered and announced that Mr. Nicholson would be pleased to see him.

Nicholson's room was large and sumptuous, with several windows opening on Broadway. The two financiers, big and little, met on the plane of ordinary politeness, without any effusion of mutual regard on the one hand, or evidence of mutual distrust on the other.

"I have called," said Steele, "to see if we can come to any workable arrangement."

"In what line of activity?" asked Nicholson.

"In a line of passivity rather than of activity," explained Steele, with a smile. "When I was a youngster, and engaged in a fight, it was etiquette that as soon as the under boy hollered 'Enough!' the fellow on top ceased pummelling him. I have come all the way from Chicago to cry 'Enough!'"

Nicholson's eyebrows raised very slightly.

"I fear I do not understand you, Mr. Steele."

"Oh, yes, you do. It will save time and talk, if we take certain things for granted. When we first met, I was so unfortunate as to find myself opposed to you. I admit frankly that I entirely underestimated your genius and your power. Since then, on one occasion you came within an ace of ruining me. On a second and more recent occasion you came within an ace of causing my death. Now, I have called at the captain's office to settle. In the language of the wild and woolly West, my hands are up, and you have the drop on me. What are your terms?"

For a few moments Nicholson regarded his visitor with an expression in which mild surprise was mingled with equally mild anxiety. When at last he spoke, his voice was perceptibly lowered, as if he addressed an invalid in a sick-room.

"You are not looking very well, Mr. Steele?"

"No, nor feeling well, either, Mr. Nicholson."

"I am sorry to hear it. What is the trouble?"

"Amalgamated Soap, I should say," said John, with a dreary laugh. "Excellent for the complexion, but mighty bad for the nerves."

"I shall make no pretence of misunderstanding your meaning, Mr. Steele," Nicholson went on with the patient enunciation one uses towards an unreasonable child. "You are hinting that in revenge for fancied opposition on your part, either I personally or the company with which I am associated, or both, have entered into a conspiracy, first to rob, and secondly to murder you. I hesitate to speak so bluntly, but, as you quite sensibly remark, we should be frank with each other."

"Your bluntness is more than compensated for by your accuracy, Mr. Nicholson. What you describe is exactly what you have done. Mere accident saved me from ruin in the Consolidated Beet Sugar formation. Less than a month ago I was led across the plains by one of your minions—a most charming, beautiful, and fascinating young woman—into a death-trap, from which I escaped largely through my own ingenuity. Now, I have written down a rather vivid and strictly accurate account of these doings. I have put in your name, and that of Amalgamated Soap, and my own, and there are three copies of this narrative in existence, two of them with a slow match attached which you can very easily light."

"Meaning that this interesting account will appear in print, Mr. Steele?"

"Quite so. Now, I ask you, Mr. Nicholson, is it worth while going any further with this feud? We're not illicit distillers in the mountains trying to pot-shot each other, but two supposedly sane men; and the world is amply wide enough for both. What do you say?"

"Really, Mr. Steele, it's rather difficult to know what to say without seeming impolite. Many things have been printed about Amalgamated Soap during the last twenty years, and so far they have never been replied to, nor have our dividends been adversely affected. A few of the articles I have read. Some were largely statistical, others of a defamatory character, others, again, contained the two qualities combined. But you, Mr. Steele, threaten to inject a most unusual and interesting quality—namely, that of an attractive young man journeying across the prairies with a beautiful and mysterious young woman. If I raised a finger to prevent the publication of a human document so well calculated to touch the better and more sentimental parts of our nature, I should consider that I was depriving my fellow-creatures of a source of pure enjoyment. I believe we sometimes unite beauty and soap in our advertisements. Attractive pictures they are. But this romance of the Black Hills——"

"How do you know it was the Black Hills?" asked Steele quickly.

"Didn't you mention that locality?"

"I said the plains."

"Then I beg pardon—this romance of the plains——"

"Now, stop a moment, Nicholson; just stop where you are. Do you see what a blunder you've made? For your own purpose, whatever it may be, you have been pretending that this human document of mine, as you call it, is a myth. Yet, in the calm and choice language with which you are describing it, you have suddenly given yourself away. You know the mine was in the Black

Hills, and, of course, I knew you knew from the very first. Now, let us quit sparring. I asked you what your terms were. I am not using threats at all. I am merely trying to come to an arrangement. Suppose, on the third attack, you succeed in driving me to the wall. What good will it do you?"

"None at all, Mr. Steele, and I assure you I have not the least desire to interfere even in the remotest degree with your affairs. You evidently attribute to me more-power than I possess. The undertakings of our association are all matters of mutual arrangement between the directors, of whom I happen to be one. We meet each day at eleven o'clock, and I trust you will believe me when I say that if I proposed to my colleagues either the robbery or murder of Mr. John Steele, I should be very promptly asked to resign my position, and deservedly so. Really, Mr. Steele, if I may make an appeal to your own common sense, you must admit that the building up of the prestige of this company, its successful carrying on, its increase of business in all parts of the world, are not accomplished by such bizarre devices as you ascribe to us."

"Do you mean to say that you did not, in my own presence, attempt to wreck the Consolidated Beet Sugar Company when you thought I would be ruined by it, and immediately go to allotment when you learned I had escaped the trap?"

"I am very glad you mentioned that, Mr. Steele, because a few simple words will show you that I am not the Machiavelli you suppose me to be. To wreck you I should have been compelled to wreck ourselves to at least an equal amount, and it is not the custom of Amalgamated Soap to purchase revenge at so excessive a price. It is one of our principles never to enter into any company put before the public unless the capital is fully subscribed. To my surprise I learned that we were a million short, therefore I could not agree to go to allotment."

"But you went to allotment all the same when you learned I was out."

"Pardon me, it was not learning that you were out of it which caused me to change my mind. It was knowing you had sent a letter to the papers informing the public that we were interested in the Consolidated Beet Sugar Company. The moment our good name was involved I proposed going to allotment; but before doing so I myself drew my cheque for a million dollars and bought the unsold shares. Your being in or out of the Company had nothing to do with my action."

"You will not come to terms, then?"

"There are no terms to come to."

"Is this your last word, Mr. Nicholson?"

"If you will pardon the liberty I take, Mr. Steele, I shall venture some last words on another subject. As I said when you came in, you are not looking well. Do you know what paranoea means?"

"I do not."

"Then, if you take my advice, you will consult a physician and ask him about it."

"I'll ask you, to save the physician's fee. What is paranoea?"

"It is a disease of the brain, and its symptom is fear. The victim imagines that someone, or everyone, is plotting against him. All the energies he possesses are directed towards the circumvention of conspiracies that are wholly imaginary. This disease, if not checked, leads to insanity or suicide."

John Steele rose to his feet.

"Does paranoea ever lead to murder, Mr. Nicholson?"

"Quite frequently."

"Then as I have been told that the directors of Amalgamated Soap are a most piously inclined body, please solicit their prayers that I may not be afflicted with the malady you mention. I thank you for giving me so much of your time, and now bid you 'Good day.'"

"Good-bye, Mr. Steele," said Nicholson, rising; then speaking in his suavest manner, he said: "If ever you entertain any project that requires more capital than you can command, I shall be most pleased to submit it to Mr. John Berrington, and perhaps we may be of assistance to you. As I told you before, I have the utmost admiration for your financial ability."

"Thank you, Mr. Nicholson; I shall bear your kind invitation in mind. However, I may inform you that I have entirely dropped out of all speculative business. I am one of the few men who know when they have had enough. I have accumulated all the money I shall need during my lifetime, and I intend to take care of it."

"A most sensible resolution, Mr. Steele; and once more good-bye, with many thanks for the visit."

John Steele walked up Broadway the most depressed man in New York. His attempted compromise had proven a complete failure; his journey East a loss of time. And yet of what value was time to him, who dared not undertake the most innocent project through fear of the developments that might follow? Nicholson had said that fear was the symptom of the malady he had so graphically depicted. Could it be possible, Steele asked himself, that he was actually the victim of a disease, every indication of which he seemed to possess? Nicholson had evidently planted that thought in his brain to his further disquietude. That man, who rarely allowed a smile to lighten his face, had inwardly laughed at him, flouted him, defied him! and all done with soothing, contemptuous insults.

Steele walked slowly up Broadway until he came to its intersection with Fifth Avenue, and then he followed the latter street, aimlessly making for his hotel. Nevertheless, when he came opposite the hotel he wandered past it and on up the Avenue. Suddenly he shook himself together and denied the cowardliness which he had hitherto attributed to the design forming in his mind. He would appeal to a woman, and if he could not thus circumvent the demoniac Nicholson, he would go out of business entirely, as he had threatened, and either travel or take up some interesting recreative occupation. He made inquiries, was directed to the Berrington residence, walked up the steps of that palace, and rang the bell. A servant in gorgeous livery opened the door.

"I wish to speak with Miss Berrington," he said.

"Not at 'ome, sir," was the curt answer.

Steele put his hand in his pocket and drew forth a twenty-dollar bill.

"I think the lady is in," he said quietly, handing this legal tender to the man in plush. Even in the residences of millionaires tips of this size are unusual, and the haughty menial at once melted. He pocketed the money.

"No, sir," he said, "she is not in town at all. Speaking confidentially, sir, Miss Berrington's that peculiar she don't like New York. Her ladyship—I beg your pardon, sir—Miss Berrington is at her country 'ome some distance out of town, sir."

"How far? Where is it?"

"On a lake, sir. I don't quite remember its name. Begins with a h'S, I think, sir."

"Lake Saratoga?" suggested Steele.

"It begins with a h'S, sir," repeated the man thoughtfully; then with a sudden burst of inspiration: "Oh, yes, sir, Superior—Lake Superior, sir."

"Great Heavens!" cried Steele, unable to repress a smile, "that isn't just exactly in the environs of New York. I suppose you couldn't tell me whether the house is on the Canadian or the United States side?"

"No, sir, I couldn't say, sir, being it's in Michigan, sir."

"Oh, well, that's near enough; I can guess the rest." The man in plush pronounced the name of the State as if the first syllable were spelt M-i-t-c-h.

"Yes, sir, her ladyship—beg your pardon—Miss Berrington owns a large estate there, so they tell me—thousands and thousands of acres, all covered with forests, and there's a big 'ouse full of servants; but her lady—but Miss Berrington receives nobody, sir. Not if you brought a letter from the King of Hengland, sir."

"Ha! rather exclusive, isn't she?"

"Yes, sir."

Thanking the man, Steele turned away and walked down the Avenue to his hotel, resolved to let the Berring-tons or the Nicholsons do their worst. He would attempt no further parley with any of the gang, and—probably inspired by the accent of the servitor in plush—gave serious thought to the investing of all his money in British Consols, small as was the percentage granted by that celebrated security. He took it for granted that the Government of Britain was probably free from the influence of the Berrington crowd, and he was rapidly coming to the conclusion that no other sphere of human activity was.

Arriving at his hotel, he found a telegram waiting for him. It proved to be from Philip Manson, and it ran:

*Congratulate me. Have just been appointed president of the Wheat Belt System. Important development. Great opening here that just suits you. Must see you immediately. If you cannot come here, telegraph me, and I will go to New York.*

"Ye Gods!" cried Steele, bracing back his shoulders, while the chronic look of anxiety vanished like mist before the sun, "just at the point when I don't know what to do, here comes my chance. I'll bet a farm Manson is going to offer me the vice-presidency of the road. I'll take it like a shot, and raise the freight rates on soap if Philip will let me."

He seized a telegraph blank and wrote:

*Heartiest congratulations. The right man in right place. You need not come to New York, as I am leaving for home to-night. I shall accept your opening, whatever it is.*

Before two days were past, John Steele was closeted with Manson in the president's room of the huge Wheat Belt building. The great, flat table in the centre was covered with broad maps taken from the civil engineer's department, maps unknown to the general public.

"Now, John," said his friend, "I'm in a position to offer you the absolute surety of doubling, trebling, or even quadrupling your money."

"Thunder!" cried Steele in a tone of disappointment, "I thought you were going to present me with the vice-presidency of the road."

Manson glanced up at him in surprise.

"Would you take it?" he asked.

"Take it? Of course. That's what I thought I was engaging to do when I telegraphed from New York."

"Why, no sooner said than done, John. I'd no idea you wished to get back into the railway business. I should think a man who can make millions outside wouldn't be content to sit here at a salary of ten or fifteen thousand a year."

"I am tired of making millions," said Steele.

"You don't mean to say," protested Manson with something like dismay in his words, "you don't mean to say you won't go in with us? I took your telegram as consent, and because I could thus guarantee the bringing in of a big capitalist, I have induced others to join and secured an extra slice for myself."

"Where there are millions to be made," said Steele dubiously, "there is always a risk, and I had determined not to accept any more chances."

"There is no chance about this, John; it is a sure thing, and the development of it rests entirely in my hands. You can double your money and pull out within ten days after I give the word, and I'll give the word whenever you say so."

"What's your project, Mr. Manson?"

"Well, you see, the Wheat Belt Line, which has been one of the most prosperous roads in the country for some years past, is going to build a branch running two hundred and seventy miles northwest until it taps the Wisconsin Pacific. This red line shows you where the road will run. The Wheat Belt Line has secured all the timber land on each side, but the former president, whose place I have taken, and myself have an option on the prairie and the stump-lands where timber has been cut. The president resigned simply to give his whole time to this land company, and that's why I am in his place. Now, we can get the property at prairie value just now; but the minute we begin surveying, up it will jump. You can trust me to keep my word. If you join us, I shall give the order for surveying the line the moment deeds of the land are in our possession."

"How much money do you expect me to put up, Mr. Manson?"

"You couldn't invest twenty millions, I suppose?"

"Twenty millions! Heavens and earth, no! It would practically clean me out to furnish nine."

"I mentioned the bigger amount simply because I am sure you will double your money within a month, and the more you put in, the more you're going to take out. You see, this is not a speculation, but a certainty."

For a few minutes Steele walked up and down the room, hands deep in his pockets, as was his custom, brow wrinkled and head bent. At last he said, with the old ring of decision in his voice:

"All right, Mr. Manson, I'll go in; but if I fail, you must give me the vice-presidency, as a sort of consolation prize."

"I'll give it to you now," said Manson. "But it can't fail. I tell you everything is in my hands. It is not as if this were any bluff. The proposed line is a road that is becoming more and more needed every day, and the land is good for the money, even if the road were never built. It's as safe as government bonds."

It would be going over ground already sufficiently covered to recount the history of the Western Land Syndicate. Steele had resolved not to invest more than half his fortune; but once a man is involved in an important enterprise, he rarely can predict where he will stop. A scheme grows and grows, and often the financier is compelled to involve himself more and more deeply in order to protect the money already ventured, and finally it becomes all or nothing. Besides this, every speculator is something of the gambler, and once the game has begun, the betting fever has him in its clutch. Before a month was past, Steele had not only paid over every dollar he possessed, but had also become deeply indebted to his bank. In borrowing from the bank he made his irretrievable mistake. As the president had said, the land was intrinsically worth the money paid for it; and if John Steele had merely risked his own assets, he might have been penniless for ten years, but he would ultimately have been sure of getting back what he paid, and probably a good deal more. But to borrow hundreds of thousands at sixty days, in the expectation that he would take profits enough to pay the loan before that time expired, was an action he himself, in less feverish moments, would have been the first to condemn. He felt the utmost confidence in his old friend, the new president, and it may be said at once that Manson throughout the history of what was known as the Great Land Bubble, was perfectly honest and sincere. He was merely a pawn on the board, moved by an unseen force of which he knew nothing.

On the afternoon of the day when the final payment on the land was made, the president of the Wheat Belt Line entered the room of his subordinate with a piece of paper in his hand. His face was white as chalk and he could not speak. He dropped into a chair, before John Steele's desk, and the latter, with a premonition of what was coming, took the paper from his trembling hand. It was a telegram from New York, and ran as follows:

*The Peter Berrington Estate has acquired control of the Wheat Belt system. The new Board of Directors yesterday resolved to abandon the Wisconsin Pacific Branch. If the branch is built at all, which is doubtful, it will begin a hundred and seventy miles West of the point formerly selected. You will, therefore, countermand at once any instructions previously given regarding the Wisconsin Pacific connection. The board also refuses to ratify the nomination of John Steele as vice-president of the road.—Nicholson.*

"Cheer up!" said John, with a laugh that sounded just a trifle hollow. "Cheer up, old man. I know all about this, and you're not in the least to blame. You acted in good faith throughout."

"It's horrible, John, horrible; but still, you know, you have the land, and before long that will realise all you've put in."

"Yes, Mr. Manson, I've got the land; that's one consolation."

But he knew perfectly well he hadn't. He knew that when the sixty days were up the bank would foreclose, which was exactly what happened. There were practically no bidders for so large a plot, and Nicholson purchased the property for the exact amount owing to the bank.

The ruin of John Steele was complete.

## CHAPTER XVI—THE RICHEST WOMAN IN THE WORLD

THE clearing in the primeval forest had been only partial, for several tall trees were left standing here and there, grouped around a log-house. The house itself, to a casual observer, resembled the dwelling of an ordinary pioneer, except that it was much larger than any residence a poor woodman ever erected. It was built of great pine logs, the ends roughly dovetailed together with a lumberman's axe. Where log lay on log, the interstices were plastered with clay. A broad verandah ran completely round the oblong building, a luxury which the pioneer usually denied himself. A settler would also have been contented to cover his roof with split oak clapboards, but here the refinement of yellow pine shingles was used, which not only kept out the weather better than the pioneer's economical device, but caused the tone of the broad roof to harmonise well with the hue of the bark on the logs; and as one approached the edifice from the forest, the whole structure standing out against the background of deep blue afforded by the lake and sky, formed a more pleasing colour scheme than might have been expected where contrasts were so vivid in that translucent air. Around the large log-house were grouped many other log-buildings, with no attempt at regulation and order. Each one appeared to have been put up as needed, and these ranged from an ordinary outhouse or shed to complete residences. A few hundred yards away from the verandah of the house, down a sloping lawn, lay sand of dazzling whiteness, and along these sands rippled the smallest waves of the largest lake in the world.

No such body of fresh water as Lake Superior exists anywhere else on earth. The water in bulk is blue; taken in detail, it is almost invisible; and this was strikingly illustrated by an adjunct of civilisation which no stretch of the imagination could attach to pioneer days. Anchored in the bay floated a large white steam-yacht, with two funnels and two slender, sloping masts. It seemed resting, not on the surface of the lake, but in mid-air, for the details of the twin screws, the long, level keel, and submerged part from prow to stern were as plain to the eye as the upper works or the funnels or the masts.

To the south and east and west, this little oasis of civilisation was walled in by the eternal forest. To the north, blue lake and blue sky blended together. On this day in late summer the place was a paradise of solitude. The great lake, which on occasion could raise a storm that might swamp an Atlantic liner, was now placid and on its good behaviour. The only sound was the gentle whisper of the leaves in the forest and the impatient pawing of a horse, which a groom held, saddled, by the southern verandah.

Through the open doorway there presently emerged a young woman, in a tight-fitting riding-habit, so short in the skirt that it looked like a walking dress rather than a costume for an equestrienne. The girl seemed very slight, and not as tall as the average woman. In spite of the frown on her brow, the face was redeemed from lack of amiability by some indescribable spiritual intellectuality which beamed from it. The whole figure gave an impression of gloom. The hair was black; the complexion almost that of an Italian woman. The eyes of velvet midnight could sparkle with dark anger, but at times they melted into a glance of appeal that was strangely pathetic, which partially redeemed the austerity of the other features. The costume was of unrelieved black, but the attention of a stranger invariably returned again and again to the face, puzzled by it. It seemed to stamp its owner as querulous, selfish perhaps, caring little for the feelings of others, yet nevertheless there sometimes fitted across it an expression indicating true nobility of character, that seemed to account for those many deeds of kindness, with which even a critical world credited the young woman.

She spoke with cutting sharpness to her groom, who had not placed the horse to please her. The man did his best, but the animal was restive from its long wait, and with a curt word of impatience at what she called the stupidity of the groom, the girl sprang with great dexterity into her saddle, gathered the reins in her left hand, and flecked the animal a stinging stroke on the flank with her whip. The horse snorted and reared, pawing the air, and again the whip descended. Now he tried to bolt, but she held him firmly, in spite of her apparently slight physique, and at last the frightened horse stood there trembling, but mastered.

"Shall I follow you, madam?" inquired the groom.

"Don't ask unnecessary questions!" snapped the girl, scowling at him as if she were in half a mind to hit him as well as the horse with the whip. "If I wished you to follow me, I should have told you so."

The cringing groom raised his forefinger to the peak of his cap and slunk away. The horse would have cantered, feeling the exhilaration of the air and the delight of the day in its supple limbs, but the girl appeared to take a grim pleasure in restraining the ardour of her steed and forcing him to a slow walk. The horsewoman certainly rode well and looked well in the saddle, but her face was marred by an expression of chronic discontent, which perhaps had a right to be there, for she was accounted the richest woman in the world, living what she supposed to be the simple life.

Constance Berrington was one of those unhappy persons whose every wish had been gratified almost before it could be expressed. Slight as she appeared, her health was excellent, and she had never yet come upon a crisis in life which money could not smooth away. It would have done her a world of good to be compelled to earn her living for a year, and meet a section of humanity she had never yet encountered, who cared not a rap whether she lived or died. But at this moment, when her ill-temper caused her to curb the eager horse to a slow walk, she was playing into the hands of the enemy in a manner that would have startled her had she but known.

Parallel with her course, a stooping man dodged from tree to tree. There was something of the stealthiness of the savage about him, and he took all the precautions of a savage to avoid observation—precautions that were unnecessary in this case, for the girl was absorbed in the conquering of her horse, and the horse's own hoofs in the pine needles made noise enough to render inaudible the footsteps of the pursuer. For more than a mile the conscious hunter and the unconscious hunted kept their course. The ground rose perceptibly all the way, but at last became tolerably level, and then the girl shook out the reins and settled herself for a gallop. But at that instant, the wary pursuer, who day after day during the past month had been baffled by the speed of the horse, sprang out from behind a tree and seized the bridle near the bit. The complexion of the woman became a shade less swarthy with the sudden fright of this assault, and although she did not cry out or scream, her inward panic was in no way lessened by the sight of the countenance turned upon her. It was the face of one in despair, and the fierce, vengeful light of the eyes betokened a mind perilously near to insanity.

"Let go my horse!" she said in a low, tense voice.

The man tightened his grip.

"Keep quiet!" he retorted.

She raised her arm and struck the animal with all the force at her command, then with both hands jerked the reins and tried to ride down her obstructor. The horse reared and for a brief second lifted the man off his feet; but he held on, and horse and man came to the ground together.

"If you try to do a trick like that again," he cried, "I'll throw both you and the horse! Drop that whip!"

Instead of dropping it she raised it again, leaning forward this time to strike the man; but he sprang towards her, holding the rein in his right hand, and with his left caught the whip as it descended and wrenched it rudely from her grasp. For a moment she thought he was about to strike her, and her arm rose waveringly to protect her face.

"Will you keep still?" he demanded.

"If you want money," she said in the quiet, semi-contemptuous tone with which she would have addressed a beggar, "you might have the sense to know that I carry none with me in the forest."

"I want money," he replied, "and I have the sense to know you carry none with you."

"Then how do you expect to obtain it by this violence?"

"That I shall have the pleasure of explaining to you a little further on."

She folded her empty hands on her knee, now that he was possessed of both whip and rein.

"I advise you, sir, to turn my horse's head in the other direction, and warn you that you will make less by threats than by trusting to my good will."

"I reject your advice, Miss Berrington. The philanthropy of your family is well-known and widely advertised. Your good deeds rise up and call you blessed; but I am not an object of charity, although I may look it. The sum which I demand I shall exact by coercion."

"Oh, very well. Set about it, then. Pray do not allow me to hinder you in the least."

"Thank you, Miss Berrington; you shall not." Placing the riding rein over his arm, he turned his back upon her and led the horse along the level towards the west for perhaps half a mile further, when he deflected to the right until they arrived at the top of a high cliff overlooking the lake. Neither had spoken a word during the journey, and Constance Berrington sat very rigidly on her led horse, like a clothed Lady Godiva, sans the beauty. The look of discontent, however, had vanished from her face, and the expression which took its place was not unpleasing.

At the cliff her leader stopped, swung round, and said gruffly, "Get down!" without, however, making any offer to assist her.

She sprang lightly from the saddle to the ground and stood there, as if awaiting further commands.

"Seat yourself on that log."

A fallen tree which one of the winter storms had uprooted lay with its branches far out over the chasm. The girl sat down on the trunk as she had been directed. "I am John Steele, of Chicago," he said.

"That does not interest me," replied the young woman. "Have you ever heard the name before?"

"No, and don't wish to hear it again."

"Six months ago I was worth ten millions."

"That does not interest me, either."

"You need not reiterate the statement, madam; I shall interest you before

I am done with you."

"I wish you were not so slow about it, then."

"Do you know a man named Nicholson?"

"Yes."

"Nicholson tried first to ruin me and then to murder me."

The young man paused, as if to allow this startling sentence to produce its effect. The young woman's eyes were upon the ground, but after a few moments of silence she glanced up at him with a languid air of indifference and said: "Is this the interesting part? Is any comment expected of me? If so, I can only say that Mr. Nicholson is usually successful in what he attempts, and I deeply regret the failure of his second project. It would have saved me from a most unpleasant encounter."

"Quite so," said Steele, tightening his lips. "I am glad you take it that way. Nicholson, as, of course, you know, was acting for the organisation which, I understand, contributes some fifty millions a year towards your support. In spite of your humane wish, he failed in his two attempts, but his third conspiracy succeeded."

"Ah! you were right, Mr. Steele, you do interest me. What did he endeavour to do on the third occasion? Consign you to a lunatic asylum?"

"No. To tell you the truth, madam, I feared that would come of itself. The fact that I have not gone mad under the silent persecution I was called upon to endure leads me to suppose that I shall hereafter be proof against any malady of the mind."

"I do not in the least doubt that. Nothing can damage a sanity already destroyed. If you are not a lunatic, you are worse—a cowardly hound who dares to offer violence to an unprotected woman."

Slowly the colour mounted in John Steele's pale face, and a glint of admiration came into his eyes. The little woman was absolutely at his mercy, yet she said these words with perfect serenity and turned upon him a gaze that was quite fearless. He noticed now for the first time the gloomy depths of those dark eyes, and thought how much more steadfast and beautiful they were than the blue orbs which had crazed his brain on the plains.

"Not such a coward as you think me, madam. Now that we are entirely free from any chance of molestation, when you must recognise your own helplessness, I beg to assure you that I shall treat you with the utmost courtesy."

"Thank you. But let us get to the point. You are John Steele. You were worth ten millions. Nicholson plotted against you and ruined you. Nicholson is one of the combination in New York from which I draw my money. In spite of what you say, you are too much of a coward to face Nicholson; therefore you have endeavoured to kidnap me and terrorise me into giving you a cheque for ten million dollars. How near am I right?"

"You are exactly right, madam."

"Very well. Although I am no admirer of Mr. Nicholson, nevertheless, it is easy to see why he defeated you. A man who takes so long to reach the kernel of his business may be all very well in Chicago, but he has no right to pit himself against a citizen of New York. I refuse to give you one penny."

"Don't say 'give,' madam, I beg of you. 'Restore' is the word. As I told you, I am making no appeal to the renowned philanthropy of the Berringtons. My ten millions, although lost to me, have gone into the coffers of your company. You have no more right to the money than I have to this horse. I own that amount because I made it without cheating anybody. I made it legitimately. I demand it back."

"I have already refused. What is your next move?"

"My next move will take some little time to tell, and you are so impatient of my loquacity that I almost fear to venture——"

"Oh, pray go on!" she cried wearily.

"Does the height make you dizzy? I should like to have you look over this cliff."

"It doesn't make me in the least dizzy. I know the cliff very well, and have been here many times. There are five or six hundred feet of sheer precipice, then a ledge of rock, then the lake."

"You have described it admirably, madam. Well, what I shall do is this. I possess, within a mile and a half of this place, a log cabin not so large or comfortable as your house. I intend to take you there and to hold you prisoner until I receive back what is mine."

"Mr. Nicholson would have mapped out a more feasible plan. How long do you think I shall remain captive without being found? To-morrow there will be a hue and cry after me—to-night, indeed, if I do not return. I shall be tracked by dogs, or an Indian will be got and put on the trail. Your scheme is absurd, Mr. Steele."

"You have forgotten the cliff, madam. I shall lead your horse to the edge of the cliff, strike him with your whip, and send him over. He will lie dashed to death on the ledge six hundred feet below. The Indian or the dog will trace the horse to this cliff. It will be naturally supposed that you have been flung into the waters of the lake, which are another six hundred feet deep. Then the search will end, madam. Lake Superior never gives up its dead, and to dredge at that depth is impossible."

"I beg your pardon," she said; "your plan is better than I thought. There is just the risk that the horse, poor creature, may bound from the ledge into the lake, and in that case the search would not end at the cliff."

Saying this, she rose and walked bravely to the very brink, looking over.

"Don't go so near!" cried John Steele, taking a step towards her. She paid no heed to him, and for a moment he held his breath in alarm as she walked along the extreme edge of the precipice. Then she turned listlessly.

"Alas!" she said, "the ledge is quite wide enough for your purpose."

"Oh, I have planned it all out," replied John, relief coming to his voice as she turned away from danger with her head lowered as if in deep thought. Then she took him entirely unawares. With a spring forward like that of a lynx, she jerked the reins from his unprepared hand. Striking the horse sharply with the loose leather, making him snort and shy with fear, she then smote him with her open palms on the flank, and away he galloped in a panic of fright. The face she turned to the astonished man seemed transformed. The black eyes danced with delight. She sank to the log again, shaking with laughter.

"Oh! I was wrong, Mr. Steele, when I said you didn't interest me! You do, you do! I have never met so interesting a man before. In twenty minutes, or thereabout, the riderless horse will gallop into my courtyard. Now, Mr. John Steele, of Chicago, what is the next move?"

"Well, logically," said John Steele, unable to repress a smile, grave as was his situation and quick his recognition of its seriousness, "logically the next move should be for me to throw you over the cliff."

"No, that wouldn't be logical. It seems, to the poor reason that a woman possesses, Mr. Nicholson is the man who should be thrown over."

"I am rather inclined to agree with you, Miss Berrington; but, alas! Nicholson is in New York, and you are the only member of the company now in my power."

"Are you quite sure I am in your power?" she asked, looking up at him.

"Frankly, I'm inclined to doubt it."

"I haven't laughed for years," she said, "not since I was a girl."

"Oh, you're nothing more than a girl now."

"I'm afraid I act like it," she replied, flushing slightly, and that evidently not from displeasure. "You are mistaken about Mr. Nicholson being in New York. Did you see that white yacht in front of my house?"

"Yes."

"Well, it belongs to Mr. Nicholson."

"Is he your guest?" asked John, the light of battle coming into his eyes.

"No, he is in Duluth. He went there a few days ago in his yacht, and sent the vessel back, in case I should wish a sail on the lake. Shall I arrange a meeting between you?"

"I suppose you will not credit me, Miss Berrington, when I tell you that I do not wish to meet Mr. Nicholson, and it is not cowardice which keeps me from the encounter. If I met him, I should kill him; then the law would hang me, and I have no desire to be executed."

"Oh, you are quite safe in Michigan," said the girl encouragingly; "there is no capital punishment in this State."

"I had forgotten about that, if I ever knew it. You see, I live in Illinois, and Nicholson lives in New York. In the one State they hang, and in the other they electrocute. It may be weak in me, but I shrink from either of those ordeals, much as I detest Nicholson."

The girl rose to her feet, put up both hands to her hair, and arranged the black tresses that had gone astray.

"How long have you possessed your log cabin, Mr. Steele?"

"About two months. One month I have spent round your house watching for you; but you have always left on a canter, or else that confounded groom of yours was following you, and I didn't want to hurt him. In truth, I didn't wish to hurt anybody."

"Poor man! have you been lingering in the forest all that time? No wonder you look like an escaped convict."

"Do I?" asked John in alarm, glancing down at his ragged garments. "I suppose I do. Since I came into the forest I have paid no attention to my personal appearance. Pray accept my apologies."

"Oh, don't mention it. I imagine you didn't expect to meet a lady."

"Well, I've been frustrated so often that I suppose I did not."

"You are, then, my nearest neighbour? By the rights of etiquette I should have made the first call, being the older resident. I think, however, Mr. Steele, that your methods of teaching me politeness to a new-comer were somewhat rough. So, if you will excuse me, I shall not go with you to your log-cabin this evening. It is getting late; see how low the sun has sunk, and how gloriously he lights up the lake."

"Yes," said Steele dolefully, "it reminds me of the copper situation here."

"It is copper that brings Mr. Nicholson to this district," she replied brightly, "although I suppose I should not tell that to an opposing speculator."

"Oh, damn Nicholson!" cried John hastily; then: "Really, I beg your pardon, madam. I have been a savage these two months past, as you very rightly remarked."

"I was going to say," she went on, "that if you will waive etiquette and come and dine with me to-night, I shall be very glad of your company."

"Ah, Miss Berrington, that is heaping coals of fire on this tousled head of mine. I could not venture into a civilised household in these rags. I am sure you will excuse me."

"Indeed I shall not. I make a bold appeal to your gallantry. I do not know my way; I am certain to get lost in the forest. You see, my horse has always been my guide, and, entirely through your fault, my horse is no longer here to lead me through the woods, so please be my pathfinder."

"Certainly, certainly, I'll lead you to the gates, but don't ask me to come in. I'm very much ashamed of myself, and I assure you that if your horse were here, I should help you to mount, and allow you to depart unscathed."

"You didn't help me to dismount," said the girl, glancing at him with eyes brimful of mischief, and laughing again.

With something of his old-time heartiness, Jack laughed at her readiness of repartee.

"You should not hold that against me. We were not acquainted then. It seems years ago, instead of minutes. I think if you and I had met when I first called on you, my later troubles would all have been averted."

"Oh, they did not tell me you had called."

"My visit was to your palace on Fifth Avenue, where I was received by a gorgeous individual with a cockney accent, whose knowledge of geography was such that he supposed Lake Saratoga and Lake Superior were neighbours and about of a size."

"Really? You met Fletcher then? Poor man, he is quite lost now, for I have him here with me in the woods. Nicholson brought him in the yacht. I rather suspect that the quiet Mr. Nicholson wishes to acquire this man's services; but, thank goodness, I can always outbid him, and Fletcher is peculiarly susceptible to the charms of money."

"Fletcher seems to be in demand, then?"

"Oh, he is most useful, but I fancy—which is a word he is very fond of—that he is very unhappy, for I have compelled him to abandon the gorgeous raiment you mentioned and dress as a northern farmer. I fear I shall need to restore his plumage, for he seems to think he has lost caste entirely. I am unable to convince him that he has gained it; but perhaps when he sees you in such raiment, and learns you were worth ten millions six months ago, he will be reconciled."

They were walking homeward through the forest, but at this remark John stopped and said ruefully: "Look here, Miss Berrington, if you are merely taking me with you to show Fletcher how badly a man may be costumed, I shall at once return to my cabin, for I have another suit there. I think that allusion to my clothes was most unkind, just as I was trying to forget them."

"Indeed I am going to turn you over to Fletcher, who will see that you are clothed, now that you are in your right mind. I think this is the spot where I first had the pleasure of meeting you, Mr. Steele."

"Now, that's another subject you are not to refer to."

"Dear me, I must get you to write out a list of them," and the sprightly little woman looked up at him with merriment sparkling in her fine eyes. No one would have recognised her as the Tartar who a short time before had browbeaten her servant and lashed her horse.

A cry rang out through the forest.

"They are looking for me," she said. "Answer the call."

John Steele lifted up his voice and gave utterance to a piercing scream that rent the silence like the soul-scattering screech of a locomotive.

"Bless us and keep us!" cried Constance Berrington, covering her small ears with her small hands, "is that an Indian war-whoop, that once used to resound in this wilderness?'

"No, it's the acme of civilisation; merely a college yell. If any of your people are graduates of Chicago University they'll recognise it."

The people who were not graduates of anything, except the college of hard labour, hurried to meet them with anxious faces.

"No, I am not in the least hurt," said Constance Berrington quite composedly. "I was merely compelled to dismount more rapidly than I usually do. Did the horse get home all right?"

"Yes, miss."

"Oh, then everything is as it should be. Luckily this gentleman was near by, and I came to no harm. Fletcher!"

The dejected, crestfallen man came slowly to the front, while she advanced a few rapid steps toward him, gave him some instructions in an undertone, and the search-party left under his leadership for the house, Steele and the girl following them at their leisure.

"How true it is that fine feathers make fine birds!" said John. "I should never have recognised Fletcher, whom I once took to be the finest specimen of our race."

"It's a poor rule that doesn't work both ways," laughed the girl. "Did you notice that Fletcher failed to recognise you?"

"Oh, I will go back and get that other suit!" cried John, coming to a standstill. "Don't wait dinner for me."

"Nonsense!" she said, letting her hand rest for one brief moment on his arm. "I didn't think men were so vain."

"I'm afraid you don't know much about them, Miss Berrington."

"I didn't until to-day. I've had my eyes opened."

"Well, I must make one proviso. You are to return my visit."

"Will you wear the other suit, then?"

"Yes, I will; and besides that, I have a negro cook who can prepare a meal that will surprise you, in our neck of the woods."

"A negro cook? Dear me, I thought you were ruined!"

"Oh, well, in a manner of speaking, so I am, now you mention it; but still, let us live by the way, you know."

When they reached the clearing, Fletcher was awaiting them on the verandah.

"If you will come with me, sir," he said, "I shall take you to the guest-house."

"Dinner at seven. Fletcher will show you the way to the dining-room. Until then, au revoir!" and the girl disappeared into the log-house, while Fletcher escorted Steele to a building near by and ushered him into a sumptuous bedroom facing the lake. On the bed was laid out a suit of evening clothes and all that pertained to it.

"I think you will find this about your size, sir. If not, I can get you one larger or smaller, as you wish."

"Good gracious!" said Steele, "do you keep a clothing store out here in the backwoods?"

"Well sir, for a country 'ouse situated as this is——"

"So far from London, eh?"

"Why, yes, sir, we are very well stocked, sir. And now sir, if you'd like a hair-cut, or your beard trimmed——"

"What! do you employ a barber, too? Thank Heaven!"

"Well, sir, you see, I used to be servant to General Sir Grundy Whitcombe, of the British Army, sir, and they do be particular."

"Do you mean to hint you can shave me, Fletcher, and cut my hair?"

"Oh, yes, sir."

"Well now, Fletcher, you don't like look an angel, but that's exactly what you are. I'll have the beard cut away entirely, but leave the moustache where it is; and if you give me the hair-crop of a British general, why, I've nothing more to ask in this life."

"Very good, sir," consented the admirable Fletcher.

When the task was finished, and John looked at the result in the mirror, he absent-mindedly thrust his hand into his pocket, but brought it forth empty. Fletcher was regarding him with admiration.

"By Jove!" cried the young man, "I haven't got a sou markee on me; but I won't forget you, Fletcher. I'll see you later, as we say out West, and you won't lose by it."

"Well, sir, I think I remember you now, sir; and if I may make so bold as to say it, sir, I'm already in your debt. Her Ladyship—I mean, Miss Berrington—being as she was thrown from her horse, sir, and you 'andy to 'elp 'er, you got the right kind of introduction, after all, sir."

"Ah, Fletcher, it seems like it, doesn't it?"

## CHAPTER XVII—TO THE SOUND OF THE SILVER CHIME

A GREAT deal of nonsense has been written about the inartistic qualities of the modern man's evening clothes. The truth is that no other costume so befits a stalwart, good-looking young fellow. It is in plain black and white, and affects none of the effeminacy of lace and ruffles and colour which made a fop of the dandy centuries ago. There is a manly dignity about dinner-dress which nothing else can give, except perhaps a suit of armour, but armour, unless it be chain mail, develops inconveniences at table.

When Miss Berrington entered the dining-room, and found her guest standing by the huge open log-fire, awaiting her, she stopped still for a moment in amazement, and then an expression of unqualified admiration came over her ever-changing face.

"Why—why—" she hesitated, as he came eagerly forward with a smile to meet her, "is this really Mr. Steele?"

"It is Fletcher's Mr. Steele, madam. You have tamed the bear, Miss Berrington, and Fletcher has groomed him, that's all."

"I remember, Mr. Steele, that you interdicted the topic of costume; but may I be permitted the vanity of congratulating Fletcher and myself on our collaboration?"

John laughed as he led her to the head of the table.

"In my youth I read once of an enchanted land, presided over by a fairy princess so gracious and so good that when outside barbarians wandered into her realm, they became what we would call civilised; but I never knew this land and this princess existed until to-day."

In the soft glow of the shaded candles the expressive face of the girl seemed almost handsome. She wore no jewels, but even the young man's uncritical eye could not mistake the richness and exquisite design of her evening gown, which indicated that if this young woman shunned society, she had nevertheless chosen an artist for her dressmaker.

The dinner was so excellent that Steele regretted he had mentioned his negro cook. White-fish from the icy waters of Lake Superior is unequalled by anything that swims, unless it be the brook-trout which the northern streams that enter Lake Superior produce. Wild turkey of the Michigan woods is world-renowned as the choicest of game.

Although Steele's hostess drank nothing but cold spring water, an ancient and renowned vintage sparkled at his right hand. It is little wonder that Jack, healthily hungry, was brilliant that evening as even he had never been before, and this poor, rich girl who listened, delighted and amazed, began to wonder if, after all, she had not missed a good deal in life by flouting smart society which she considered frivolous.

After dinner, Constance Berrington put a shawl over her shoulders and asked her guest if he would come outside and see the lake glittering in the moonlight. On the verandah he found the unique arrangement of an out-of-doors fireplace facing the platform, and in its depths roared a hickory fire, which burns with a flame bright as electric light, and leaves an ash white as flour. Two screens of sailcloth drawn like curtains along the roof of the verandah partially fenced in this snug spot, leaving it open only towards the lake. The pale yacht lay like a liner's ghost on the silver sea, bathed in the light of the moon, and now and then the phantom ship gave forth melodious sounds as it chimed the hours in nautical fashion, the peal sweetly mellowed by the intervening water. John laughed in boyish glee to find himself in such a Paradise.

"I never saw anything so beautiful," he said; "nor have I ever known so ambitious a fireplace, trying to warm all outdoors."

Two rocking-chairs awaited them, and between these chairs stood a round table, on which the silent servant placed coffee and liqueurs. The hickory fire kindled a gleam of ineffable satisfaction in the young man's eyes when a box of prime cigars was placed before him.

"May I really smoke?" he asked, taking one between his fingers.

"I believe that is what they are for," replied the girl, with a smile, rocking gently to and fro. Then, when they were alone she said seriously: "Mr. Steele, I want you to tell me the particulars of the conspiracies you referred to, that proved so disastrous to you."

"Dear princess," he answered earnestly, "do you think I am going to talk finance in the land of enchantment? Not likely. Do monetary centres exist in the world? I don't believe it. Are people struggling anywhere to defeat one another? This silver silence denies it."

"But the silence is not going to deny me," she persisted. "I must know. You said I was responsible."

"I said such a thing? Never! That is a mistake in identity. You are thinking of the barbarian whom you quite justly tried to ride down in the forest. He said many stupid and false things, for which I refuse to assume responsibility. Reluctantly I admit that that barbarian was my ancestor, but a thousand years have passed since he lived, and I say the race has improved."

He blew a whiff of smoke into the still air and, watching it waft upward, murmured softly:

"And yet those wretched comic papers say a woman cannot choose cigars."

"I am glad they are good. It was not I who selected them, but Mr. Nicholson."

If some of the icy water of Lake Superior had unexpectedly dropped upon him, he could not have appeared more startled than at the mention of this name.

"Ye gods!" he whispered huskily, "I had forgotten that man existed! For years he has never been out of my mind before."

The girl's eloquent eyes were fixed upon him.

"The smoke has disappeared into the blue," she said, "but that name has brought you to earth again. Now tell me what he did."

"Miss Berrington," he said solemnly, "you are no more responsible for what Nicholson did, than I am for the actions of the savage who seized your horse. Let me forget again that either the white Indian or the savage ever lived."

"No," she persisted, "you must tell me." And so he told her, sometimes puffing at his cigar like a steam-engine, again almost allowing it to go out. The narration was vivid, but possibly it might have been more interesting if he had not substituted the father for the daughter in the case of Miss Alice Fuller. When the recital was finished the girl shivered a little; and seeing that he noticed it she said: "I think it is getting cold, in spite of our fire. And now I shall bid you 'Good night.' I must thank you for the most interesting day and evening I ever spent in my life. Good night, and I hope you will not dream of Mr. Nicholson."

He rose and took the hand she offered, raising it, before she was aware, to his lips.

"Princess," he said, "I know of whom I shall dream."

She laughed a little and was gone.

When the maid had girded round her the soft and trailing dressing-gown, bidding her mistress "Good night," Constance Berrington opened the window, knelt down before it, placed her elbows on the low sill, with her chin on her open palms, and remained thus gazing at the moonlit lake. The ship of mist tolled the unheeded hours as on a silver chime. At last, with a sigh that seemed to end in a sob, she murmured: "Oh, how beautiful the world is, and yet I never appreciated it before!"

Then she closed her window.

The informative Fletcher told Steele that the breakfast hour was nine, and the grandfather clock was striking as he entered the dining-room next morning. The fragrance of the coffee-urn was stimulating to a man from the keen outer air, and the girl who presided over it turned towards him a smiling face, radiant as the dawn. Steele spread out his arms.

"What do you think of this?" he cried, jovial as a lad with a holiday.

"This is the other suit."

"Dear me!" replied Constance Berrington. "How came it here?"

"I was up this morning before five, donned my rags, tramped to my hut, comforted my negro, who was nearly white with panic at my absence, put on the other suit, and here I am."

"Well, if you do not enjoy your breakfast after that, I shall admit my cook inferior to your negro. Why didn't you take one of the horses?"

"Never thought of it. I seemed to be walking in midair."

"Then come down to earth, and buckwheat pancakes and maple syrup. Do you prefer tea or coffee?"

"Oh, coffee, of course. The aroma excels all the perfumes of Araby."

The breakfast was even more intimate and delightful than the dinner had been. Daylight had not removed the glamour of the moon from the land of enchantment. When the meal was finished, Constance Berrington rose and said: "Before you go, I wish to show you my library."

He followed her into this attractive room, its walls lined with books. Here and there were cosy alcoves and recesses, with leather-covered easy-chairs that might have graced a metropolitan club. A very solid table of carved oak occupied the centre of the room, and beside this the girl came to a stand, while he glanced around him in admiration.

"I never had much time for reading," he said, "and I do envy you this room. My own library is small, consisting mainly of books by friends of mine who kindly presented me with some of their writings."

"Then I wish you to accept a specimen of my works. My writings may not be very literary, but they are concise and to the point."

Here she placed a slip of paper before him, and glancing at it he saw it was a cheque for ten millions. Then he looked up at her, a slow smile coming to his lips, and shook his head.

"Princess, this is for the savage, not for me. The savage is dead."

"You are his heir, remember."

"No, we are too far removed from each other, the savage and I. Remember the centuries between us, and less than ten years outlaws all claim."

"You must accept it. It is mere transference, as you quite rightly pointed out. It does not belong to me, but to you."

The young woman spoke with tense eagerness, and the former frown came into her brow before she had finished. He picked up the cheque.

"That's right," she said, with a sigh of relief; but the smile broadened on his face as he slowly tore the signature from the cheque and placed her autograph in his pocket-book.

"Give me the hope that this may prove my return ticket to Paradise, and I am satisfied. Miss Berrington, you called me a coward yesterday, and you spoke the truth. I was, but I hope I am one no longer. I am young and reasonably ambitious. The world is before me. I shall begin where I began half-a-dozen years ago. I do not need your money."

"I shall write you another cheque—you must accept it."

"You dare not."

"Why?"

"Because I am your guest, and I forbid you. The rules of hospitality, madam, extend even to the land of enchantment."

"Is the guest so cruel, then"—there was a pathetic quaver in the voice—"as to leave his hostess to brood over this weight of obligation? Will he not thus, in the only possible way, lift that weight from her shoulders?"

"No!" cried John, coming swiftly round the table to her, "I shall lift her and the obligation together," and, suiting the action to the word, he picked her up as if she were a child and seated her on the table before him. "I'll not accept your cheque, but I ask you to accept me."

For an instant her eyes blazed up as if lighted from within, then dulled again. She did not in the least resent his boisterous action, but she shook her head and said:

"I shall never marry a man who is not in love with me, and I am too insignificant a woman for any man to love me for myself."

"Insignificant! Magnificent is the word! Why, Constance Berrington, you are the most beautiful woman I have ever seen. Your face makes every other in the world insipid. I'm not going to try and persuade you that I love you, because you know it. You knew it last night. You saw it in my eyes, and I saw the knowledge in yours. Curse the money! I'll make all the money I need if I have you by my side. What is money, anyhow? I've made it and lost it, and I can make it again and lose it again. Constance, let us take that yacht, go to Duluth, and be married before a magistrate for ten dollars, like a lumberman and his girl."

She looked up at him and smiled, then down again, then up once more, and he kissed her.

"Oh, don't!" she cried. "There is some one coming!" A knock sounded at the door, and Miss Berrington sprang down from the table.

"Your foot has touched the electric bell that is under the carpet," she whispered quickly, with a nervous laugh; then "Come in!" she cried, and the servant entered.

Steele was turning the pages of a magazine; Constance Berrington stood in the middle of the floor.

"Did you ring, miss?"

"Yes, tell the captain to get the yacht ready. I am going to Duluth."

**THE END**

# THE MUTABLE MANY: A NOVEL

*"For the imitable, rank-scented many, let them*

*Regard me as I do not flatter, and*

*Therein behold themselves?*

CORIOLANUS.

He that trusts you,

Where he should find you lions, finds you hares;

Where foxes, geese. You are no surer, no,

Than is the coal of fire upon the ice,

Or hailstone in the sun. Your virtue is,

To make him worthy, whose offence subdues him

And curse that justice did it.

Who deserves greatness,

Deserves your hate: and your affections are

A sick man's appetite, who desires most that

Which would increase his evil. He that depends

Upon your favours, swims with fins of lead,

And hews down oaks with rushes.. Hang ye!

Trust ye?

With every minute you do change a mind;

And call him noble that was now your hate,

Him vile, that was now your garland."

Coriolanus.

## CHAPTER I.

The office of Monkton & Hope's great factory hung between heaven and earth, and, at the particular moment John Sartwell, manager, stood looking out of the window towards the gates, heaven consisted of a brooding London fog suspended a hundred feet above the town, hesitating to fall, while earth was represented by a sticky black-cindered factory-yard bearing the imprint of many a hundred boots. The office was built between the two huge buildings known as the "Works." The situation of the office had evidently been an after-thought—it was of wood, while the two great buildings which it joined together as if they were Siamese twins of industry, were of brick. Although no architect had ever foreseen the erection of such a structure between the two buildings, yet necessity, the mother of invention, had given birth to what Sartwell always claimed was the most conveniently situated office in London. More and more room had been acquired in the big buildings as business increased, and the office—the soul of the whole thing—had, as it were, to take up a position outside its body.

The addition, then, hung over the roadway that passed between the two buildings; it commanded a view of both front and back yards, and had, therefore, more light and air than the office Sartwell had formerly occupied in the left-hand building. The unique situation caused it to be free from the vibration of the machinery to a large extent, and as a door led into each building, the office had easy access to both. Sartwell was very proud of these rooms and their position, for he had planned them, and had thus given the firm much additional space, with no more ground occupied than had been occupied before—a most desirable feat to perform in a crowded city like London.

Two rooms at the back were set apart for the two members of the firm, while Sartwell's office in the front was three times the size of either of these rooms and extended across the whole space between the two buildings. This was as it should be; for Sartwell did three times the amount; of work the owners of the business accomplished and, if it came to that, had three times the brain power of the two members of the firm combined, who were there simply because they were the sons of their fathers. The founders of the firm had with hard work and shrewd management established the large manufactory whose present prosperity was due to Sartwell and not to the two men whose names were known to the public as the heads of the business.

Monkton and Hope were timid, cautious, somewhat irresolute men, as capitalists should be all the world over. They had unbounded confidence in their manager, and generally shifted any grave responsibility or unpleasant decision to his shoulders, which bore the burdens placed upon them with equanimity. Sartwell was an iron man, with firm resolute lips, and steely blue eyes that were most disconcerting to any one who had something not quite straight to propose. Even the two partners quailed under these eyes and gave way before them if it came to a conflict of opinion. Sartwell's rather curt "It won't do, you know" always settled things.

Sartwell knew infinitely more about the works than they did; for while they had been at college the future manager was working his way up into the confidence of their fathers, and every step he took advanced his position in the factory. The three men were as nearly as possible of the same age, and the hair of each was tinged with grey; Sartwell's perhaps more than the others.

It was difficult to think of love in connection with the two partners, yet it is pleasing to know that when love did come to them at the proper time of life, it had come with gold in one hand and a rigid non-conformist conscience in the other. The two had thus added wealth to wealth by marrying, and, as their wives were much taken up with deeds of goodness, done only after strict and conscientious investigation, so that the unworthy might not benefit, and as both Monkton and Hope were somewhat timorous men who were bound to be ruled by the women they married some of their wealth found its way into the coffers of struggling societies and organizations for the relieving of distress.

Thus there came to impregnate the name of Monk-ton & Hope (Limited) a certain odour of sanctity which is most unusual in business circles in London. The firm, when once got at, could be counted on for a subscription almost with certainty, but alas! it was not easy to get at the firm. The applicant had to come under the scrutiny of those searching eyes of Sartwell's, which had a perturbing habit of getting right at the heart of a matter with astonishing quickness; and when once he said "It won't do, you know," there was no going behind the verdict.

A private stairway led from the yard below to the hall in the suspended building which divided the large office of the manager from the two smaller private rooms of the firm. This stairway was used only by the three men. The clerks and the public came in by the main entrance, where a watchful man sat behind a little arched open window over which was painted the word "Enquiries."

Outside in the gloom the two great lamps over the gateposts flared yellow light down on the cindery roadway and the narrow street beyond. Through the wide open gateway into the narrow stone-paved street poured hundreds of workingmen. There was no jostling and they went out silently, which was unusual. It seemed as if something hovered over them even more depressing than the great fog cloud just above their heads. Sartwell, alone in his office, stood somewhat back from the window, unseen, and watched their exit grimly, sternly. The lines about his firm mouth tightened his lips into more than their customary rigidity. He noticed that now and then a workman cast a glance at his windows, and he knew they cursed him in their hearts as standing between them and their demands, for they were well aware that the firm would succumb did Sartwell but give the word. The manager knew that at their meetings their leader had said none was so hard on workingmen as a workman who had risen from the ranks. Sartwell's name had been hissed while the name of the firm had been cheered; but the manager was not to be deterred by unpopularity, although the strained relations between the men and himself gave him good cause for anxiety.

As he thought over the situation and searched his mind to find whether he himself were to blame in any way, there was a rap at his door. He turned quickly away from the window, stood by his desk, and said sharply, "Come in."

There entered a young man in workman's dress with his cap in his hand. His face was frank, clear-cut, and intelligent, and he had washed it when his work was done, which was a weakness not indulged in by the majority of his companions.

"Ah, Marsten," said the manager, his brow clearing when he saw who it was. "Did you get that job done in time?"

"It was off before half-past five, sir."

"Right. Were there any obstacles thrown in your way?"

"None that could not be surmounted, sir."

"Right again. That's the way I like to have things done. The young man who can accomplish impossibilities is the man for me, and the man who gets along in this world."

The young fellow turned his cap over and over in his hands, and, although he was evidently pleased with the commendation of the manager, he seemed embarrassed. At last he said, hesitatingly:

"I am very anxious to get on in the world, sir."

"Well, you may have an opportunity shortly," replied the manager.

Then he suddenly shot the question:

"Are you people going to strike?"

"I'm afraid so, sir."

"Why do you say 'afraid'? Are you going out with the others, or do you call your soul your own?"

"A man cannot fight the Union single-handed."

"You are talking to a man who is going to."

The young man looked up at his master.

"With you it is different," he said. "You are backed by a wealthy company.

Whether you win or lose, your situation is secure. If I failed the Union in a crisis, I could never get another situation."

Sartwell smiled grimly when the young man mentioned the firm. He knew that there lay his weakness rather than his strength, for although the firm had said he was to have a free hand, yet he was certain the moment the contest became bitter the firm would be panic-stricken. Then, if the women took a hand in, the jig was up. If the strikers had known on which side their bread was buttered they would have sent a delegation of their wives to Mrs. Monkton and Mrs. Hope. But they did not know this, and Sartwell was not the man to show the weakness of his hand.

"Yes," said the manager, "I have the entire confidence of Mr. Monkton and Mr. Hope. I wonder if the men appreciate that fact."

"Oh yes, sir; they know that."

"Now, Marsten, have you any influence with the men?"

"Very little, I'm afraid, sir."

"If you have any, now is the time to exert it; for their sakes, you know, not for mine. The strike is bound to fail. Nevertheless I don't forget a man who stands by me."

The young man shook his head.

"If my comrades go, I'll go with them. I am not so sure that a strike is bound to fail, although I am against it. The Union is very strong, Mr. Sartwell. Perhaps you do not know that it is the strongest Union in London."

The manager allowed his hand to hover for a moment over a nest of pigeon-holes, then he drew out a paper and handed it to Marsten.

"There is the strength of the Union," he said, "down to the seventeen pounds eight shillings and twopence they put in the bank yesterday afternoon. If you want any information about your Union, Marsten, I shall be happy to oblige you with it."

The young man opened his eyes as he looked at the figures.

"It is a very large sum," he said.

"A respectable fighting fund," remarked Sartwell, impartially. "But how many Saturdays do you think it would stand the drain of the pay-roll of this establishment?"

"Not very many perhaps."

"It would surprise you to know how few. The men look at one side of this question only, while I am compelled to look at two sides. If any Saturday their pay was not forthcoming, they would not be pleased, would they? Now I have to scheme and plan so that the money is there every Saturday, and besides there must be enough more to pay the firm for its investment and its risk. These little details may not seem important to a demagogue who knows nothing of business, but who can harangue a body of men and make them dissatisfied. I should be very pleased to give him my place here for a month or two while I took a rest, and then we would see whether he thought there was anything in my point of view."

"Mr. Sartwell," said Marsten, looking suddenly at the manager, "some of the more moderate men asked me to-night a similar question to one of yours."

"What question was that?"

"They asked if I had any influence with you."

"Yes? And you told them——?"

"That I didn't know."

"Well, you will never know until you test the point. Have you anything to suggest?"

"Many are against a strike, but even the more moderate think you are wrong in refusing to see the delegation. They think the refusal seems high-handed, and that if you were compelled to reject any requests made, you ought not to let things come to a crisis without at least allowing the delegation to present the men's case."

"And do you think I am wrong in this?"

"I do."

"Very well. I'll settle that in a moment. You get some of the more moderate together—head the delegation yourself. I will make an appointment with you, and we will talk the matter over."

The young man did not appear so satisfied with this prompt concession as might have been expected. He did not reply for some moments, while the elder man looked at him critically, with his back against the tall desk.

At last Marsten spoke:

"I could not lead the delegation, being one of the youngest in the employ of the firm. The secretary of the Union is the leader the men have chosen."

"Ah! The secretary of the Union. That is quite a different matter. He is not in my employ. I cannot allow outsiders to interfere in any business with which I am connected. I am always willing to receive my own men, either singly or in deputation, and that is no small matter where so many men are at work; but if I am to open my office doors to the outside world—well, life is too short. For instance, I discuss these things with you, but I should decline to discuss them with any man who dropped in out of the street."

"Yes, I see the difficulty, but don't you think you might make a concession in this instance, to avoid trouble?"

"It wouldn't be avoiding trouble, it would merely be postponing it. It would form a precedent, and I would have this man or that interfering time and again. I would have to make a stand some time, perhaps when I was not so well prepared. If there is to be a fight, I want it now. We need some new machinery in, and we could do with a week's shut-down."

Marsten shook his head.

"The shut-down would be for longer than a week," he said.

"I know that. The strike will last exactly three weeks. At the end of that time there will be no Union."

"Perhaps there will also be no factory."

"You mean there will be violence? Very well. In that case the strike will last but a fortnight. You see, my boy, we are in London, and there are not only the police within a moment's call, but, back of them, the soldiers, and back of them again the whole British Empire. Oh no, Marsten, it won't do, you know, it won't do.

"The men are very determined, Mr. Sartwell."

"All the better. I like a determined antagonist. Then you get things settled once for all. I don't object to a square stand-up fight, but eternal haggling and higgling and seeing deputations and arbitrations, and all that sort of thing, I cannot endure. Let us know where we are, and then get on with our work."

"Then you have nothing to propose, Mr. Sartwell? Nothing conciliatory, I mean."

"Certainly I have. Let the men request that blatant ass Gibbons to attend to his secretarial duties and then let a deputation from our own workshops come up and see me. We'll talk the matter over, and if they have any just grievance I will remedy it for them. What can be fairer than that?"

"It's got to be a matter of principle with the men now—that is, the inclusion of Gibbons has. It means recognizing of the Union."

"Oh, I'll recognize the Union and take off my hat to it; that is, so far as my own employees are concerned. But I will not have an outsider, who knows nothing of this business, come up here and spout his nonsense. It's a matter of principle with me as well as with the men."

Marsten sighed.

"I'm afraid there is nothing for it then but a fight," he said.

"Perhaps not. One fool makes many. Think well, Marsten, which side you are going to be with in this fight. I left a Union, and although I was older than you are at the time, I never repented it. It kept me out of employment, but not for long, and they kept me out of it in the very business of which

I am now manager. The Union is founded on principles that won't do, you know. Any scheme that tends to give a poor workman the same wages as a good workman is all wrong."

"I don't agree with you, Mr. Sartwell. The only hope for the workingman is in combination. Of course we make mistakes and are led away by demagogues, but some day there will be a strike led by an individual Napoleon, and then we will settle things once for all, as you said a while ago."

Sartwell laughed, and held out his hand.

"Oh, that's your ambition is it? Well, good luck attend you, my young Napoleon. I should have chosen Wellington, if I had been you. Good-night. I am waiting for my daughter, to whom I foolishly gave permission to call for me here in a cab."

Marsten held the hand extended to him so long that the manager looked at him in astonishment. The colour had mounted from the young man's cheeks to his brow and his eyes were on the floor.

"Mr. Sartwell," he said, with an effort, "I came tonight to speak with you about your daughter and not about the strike."

The manager dropped his hand as if it had been red-hot, and stepped back two paces.

"About my daughter?" he cried, sternly. "What do you mean?"

Marsten had to moisten his lips once or twice before he could reply. His released hand opened and shut nervously.

"I mean," he said, "that I am in love with her."

The manager sat down in the office chair beside his table. All the former friendliness had left his face, and his dark brows lowered over his keen eyes, into which their usual cold glitter had returned.

"What folly is this?" he cried, with rising anger. "You are a boy, and from the gutter at that, for all I know. My daughter is but a child yet; she is only——" He paused. He had been about to say seventeen when it occurred to him that he had married her mother when she was but a year older.

Marsten's colour became a deeper red when the manager spoke so contemptuously of the gutter. He said slowly, and with a certain doggedness in his tone:

"It is no reproach to come from the gutter—the reproach is in staying there. I have left it, and I don't intend to return."

"Oh, 'intend'!" cried the manager, impatiently. "We all know what is paved with intentions. Why; you have never even spoken to the girl!"

"No, but I mean to."

"Do you? Well, I shall take very good care that you do not."

"What have you against me, Mr. Sartwell?"

"What is there for you? Perhaps you will kindly specify your recommendations."

"You are very hard on me, Mr. Sartwell. You know that if I came from the gutter, what education I have, I gave to myself. I have studied hard, and worked hard. Does that count for nothing? I have a good character, and I have a good situation——"

"You have not. I discharge you. You will call at the office to-morrow, get your week's money, and go."

"Oh!"

"Yes, 'oh!' You did not think that of me, did you?"

"I did not."

"Well, for once you are right. I merely wish to show you how your good situation depends on the caprice of one man. I have no intention of discharging you. I am not so much afraid of you as that. I'll look after my daughter."

Marsten said bitterly:

"Gibbons, ass as he is, is right when he says that no one is so hard on a workman as one who has risen from the ranks. You were no better off than I am, when you were my age."

Sartwell sprang to his feet, his eyes ablaze with anger.

"Pay attention, young man," he cried. "All the things you have done, I have done. All the things you intend to do, I have already done. I have, in a measure, educated myself, and I have worked hard night and day. I have attained a certain position, a certain responsibility, and a certain amount of money. I have had little pleasure and much toil in my life, and I am now growing old. Yet as I look back I see that there was as much luck as merit in what success I have had. I was ready when the chance came, that was all; if the chance hadn't come, all my readiness would have done me little good. For one man who succeeds, a dozen, equally deserving, fail.

"Now, why have I gone through all this? Why? For myself? Not likely. I have done it so that she may not have to be that tired drudge—a workman's wife—so that she may begin where I leave off. That's why. For myself, I would as soon wear a workman's jacket as a manager's coat. And now, having gone through all this for her sake—you talk of love! What is your love for her compared to mine? When I have done all this that she might never know what it means, shall I be fool enough, knave enough, idiot enough, to thrust her back where I began, at the beck of the first mouthing ranter who has the impudence to ask for her? No, by God, no! Now you have had your answer, get out, and don't dare to set foot in this office until you are sent for."

Sartwell in his excitement smote the desk with his clenched fist to emphasize his sentences. Marsten shrank before his vehemence, realizing that no workman had ever seen the manager angry before, and he dreaded the resentment that would rise in Sartwell's heart when the coldness returned. He felt that he would have been more diplomatic to have left sooner. Nevertheless, seeing that things could be no worse, he stood his ground.

"I thought," he said, "that it would be honourable in me to let you know——"

"Don't talk to me of honour. Get out."

At that moment the door from the private stairway opened and a young girl came in. Her father had completely forgotten his appointment with her, and both men were taken aback by her entrance.

"I knocked, father," she said, "but you did not hear me."

"In a moment, Edna. Just step into the hall for a moment," said her father, hurriedly.

"I beg of you not to leave, Miss Sartwell," said Marsten, going to the other door and opening it. "Good-night, Mr. Sartwell."

"Good-night," said the manager, shortly.

"Good-night, Miss Sartwell."

"Good-night," said the girl sweetly, with the suggestion of a bow.

The eyes of the two men met for a moment, the obstinacy of the race in each; but the eyes of the younger man said defiantly:

"I have spoken to her, you see."

## CHAPTER II.

We speak of our individuality as if such a thing really existed—as if we were actually ourselves, forgetting that we are but the sum of various qualities belonging to ancestors, most of whom are dead and gone and forgotten. The shrewd business-man in the City imagines that his keen instincts are all his own; he does not recognize the fact that those admirable attributes which enable him to form a joint-stock company helped an ancestor in the Middle Ages to loot a town, or a highwayman of a later day to relieve a fellow-subject of a full purse on an empty heath.

Edna Sartwell possessed one visible, undeniable, easily recognized token of heredity: she had her father's eyes, but softened and luminous and disturbingly beautiful—eyes to haunt a man's dreams. They had none of the searching rapier-like incisiveness that made her father's eyes weapons of offence and defence; but they were his, nevertheless, with a kindly womanly difference, and in that difference lived again the dead mother.

"Edna," said her father, when they were alone, "you must not come to this office again."

There was more sharpness in his tone than he was accustomed to use toward his daughter, and she looked up at him quickly.

"Have I interrupted an important conference?" she asked. "What did the young man want, father?"

"He wanted something I was unable to grant."

"Oh, I am so sorry! He did appear disappointed. Was it a situation?"

"Something of the sort."

"And why couldn't you give it to him? Wasn't he worthy?"

"No, no. No, no!"

"He seemed to me to have such a good face—honest and straightforward."

"Good gracious! child, what do you know about faces? Do not interfere in business matters; you don't understand them. Don't chatter, chatter, chatter. One woman who does that is enough in a family—all a man can stand."

The daughter became silent; the father pigeonholed some papers, took them out again, rearranged them, and placed them back. He was regaining control over himself. He glanced at his daughter, and saw tears in her eyes.

"There, there, Edna," he said. "It is all right. I'm a little worried to-night, that's all. I'm afraid there's going to be trouble with the men. It is a difficult situation, and I have to deal with it alone. A strike seems inevitable, and one never can tell where it will end."

"And is he one of the strikers? It seems impossible."

A look of annoyance swept over her father's face.

"He? Why the——Edna, you return to a subject with all the persistency of a woman. Yes. He will doubtless go on strike to-morrow with all the rest of the fools. He is a workman, if you want to know; and furthermore, he is going on strike when he doesn't believe in it—going merely because the others go. He admitted it to me shortly before you came in. So you see how much you are able to read in a man's face."

"I shouldn't have thought it," said the girl, with a sigh. "Perhaps if you had given him what he wanted he would not go on strike."

"Oh, now you are making him out worse than even I think him. I don't imagine he is bribable, you know."

"Would that be bribery?"

"Suspiciously like it; but he can strike or not as he wishes—one more or less doesn't matter to me. I hope, if they go, they will go in a body; a few remaining would only complicate things. Now that you understand all about the situation, are you satisfied? It isn't every woman I would discuss it with, you know, so you ought to be flattered."

Sartwell was his own man once more, and he was mentally resolving not to be thrown off the centre again.

"Yes, father, and thank you," said the girl. "The cab is waiting," she added, more to let him know that so far as she was concerned the discussion was ended, than to impart the information conveyed in her words.

"Let it wait. That's what cabs are for. The cabby usually likes it better than hurrying. Sit down a moment, Edna; I'll be ready presently."

The girl sat down beside her father's table. Usually Mr. Sartwell preferred his desk to his table, for the desk was tall where a man stands when he writes. This desk had three compartments, with a lid to each. These were always locked, and Sartwell's clerks had keys to two of them. The third was supposed to contain the manager's most private papers, as no one but himself ever saw the inside of it. The lid locked automatically when it was shut, and the small key that opened it dangled at Sartwell's watch-chain.

Edna watched her father as he unlocked one after another of the compartments and apparently rearranged his papers. There was always about his actions a certain well-defined purpose, but the girl could not help noticing that now he appeared irresolute and wavering. He seemed to be marking time rather than making progress with any definite work. She wondered if the coming strike was worrying him more than he had been willing to admit. She wished to help, but knew that nothing would be more acceptable to him than simply leaving him alone. She also knew that when her father said he would be ready to go home with her at a certain hour he usually was ready when that hour came. Why, then, did he delay his departure?

At last Sartwell closed down the lid of one desk and locked it as if he were shutting in his wavering purpose, then he placed the key from his watch-guard in the third lock and threw back the cover. An electric light dangling by a cord from the ceiling, threw down into the desk rays reflected by a circular opal shade that covered the lamp. The manager gazed for a few moments into the desk, then turning to his daughter, said:

"Edna, you startled me when you came in tonight."

"I am very sorry, father. Didn't you expect me?"

"Yes, but not at that moment, as it happened. You are growing very like your mother, my girl."

There was a pause, Edna not knowing what to say. Her father seldom spoke of his dead wife, and Edna could not remember her mother.

"Somehow I did not realize until to-night—that you were growing up. You have always been my baby to me. Then—suddenly—you came in. Edna, she was only four years older than you when she died. You see, my dear, although I grow older, she always remains young—but I sometimes think that the young man who was her husband is dead too, for there is not much likeness to him in me."

Sartwell had been drumming lightly with his fingers on the desk top as he spoke; now he reached up and turned off the electric light as if its brilliancy troubled him. The lamp in the centre of the room was sufficient, and it left him in the shadow.

"I suppose there comes a time in the life of every father, when he learns, with something of a shock, that the little girl who has been playing about his knee is a young woman. It is like when a man hears himself alluded to as old for the first time. I well remember how it made me catch my breath when I first heard myself spoken of as an old man."

"But you are not old," cried the girl, with a little indignant half sob in her voice. She wished to go to her father and put her arms around his neck, but she felt intuitively that he desired her to stay where she was until he finished what he had to say.

"I am getting on in that direction. None of us grows younger, but the dead. I suppose a daughter is as blind to her father's growing old, as he to her advancing womanhood. But we won't talk of my age. We are welcoming the coming, rather than speeding the going, to-night. You and I, Edna, must realize that we, in a measure, begin life on a new line with each other. We are both grown-up people. When your mother was a little older than you are, I had her portrait painted. She laughed at me and called me extravagant. You see, we were really very poor, and she thought, poor girl, that a portrait of herself was not exactly a necessity. I have thought since that it was the one necessary thing I ever bought. I had it copied, when I got richer, by a noted painter, who did it more as a favour to me than for the money, for painters do not care to copy other men's work. Curiously enough he made a more striking likeness of her than the original was. Come here, my girl."

Edna sprang to her father's side and rested her hand lightly on his shoulder. Sartwell turned on the electric light. At the bottom of the desk lay a large portrait of a most beautiful woman. The light shone down on the face, and the fine eyes looked smilingly up at them.

"That was your mother, Edna," said the father, almost in a whisper, speaking with difficulty.

The girl was crying softly, trying not to let her father know it. Her hand stole from the shoulder next her to the other, his hand caressed her fair hair.

"Poor father!" she said, trying to speak bravely.

"How lonely you must have been. I seem to—to understand things—that I didn't before—as if I had suddenly grown old."

They looked at the picture for some time together in silence, then she said:

"Why did you never show me the portrait before?"

"Well, my dear, it was here and not at the house, and when you were a small girl, you did not come to the office, you know. Then, you see, your stepmother had the responsibility of bringing you up—and—and—somehow I thought it wouldn't be giving her a fair chance. The world is rather hard on stepmothers." He hurriedly closed the desk. "Come, come," he cried, brusquely, "this won't do, you know, Edna. But this is what I want to say. I want you to remember—to understand rather—that you and I are, as it were, alone in the world; there is a bond between us in that, as well as in the fact that we are father and daughter. I want you always to feel that I am your best friend, and there must never come any misunderstanding between us."

"There never could, father," said the girl, solemnly.

"That's right, that's right. Now if anything should happen to trouble you, I want you to come to me and tell me all about it. I wish there to be complete confidence between us. If anything perplexes you, tell me; if it is trivial I want to know, and if it is serious I want to know. Sometimes an apparently trivial problem is really a serious one, and vice-versa; and remember, it is almost as important to classify your problem as to solve it. That's where I can help you; for even if I could not disentangle the skein, I could perhaps show you that it was not worth unravelling."

The girl regarded her father earnestly while he spoke, and then, as if to show that woman's intuition will touch the spot around which a man's reason is elaborately circling, she startled him by saying:

"Father, something has happened concerning me, that has made you anxious on my account. What is it? I think I should know. Has my step-mother been saying——"

"No no, my child, your step-mother has been saying nothing about you. And if she had I would not—that is, I would have given it my best attention, and would have no hesitation in letting you know what it was. You mustn't jump at conclusions; perhaps I am talking with unnecessary seriousness; all I wish to impress upon you is that although I am seemingly absorbed in business, you are much more important to me than anything else—that, in fact, since your mother died, you are the only person who has been of real importance to me, and so if you want anything, let me know—a new frock, for instance, of exceptional expensiveness. I think you will find that where your happiness is concerned, I shall not allow any prejudices of mine to stand in the way."

The girl looked up at her father with a smile.

"I don't think my happiness will be endangered for lack of a new gown," she said.

"Well, dress is very important, Edna, we mustn't forget that; though I merely instanced dress for fear you would take me too seriously. And now, my girl, let us get home. This is our last conference in this office, you know, and there has somehow entered into it the solemnity that pertains to all things done for the last time. Now if you are ready, I am."

"Not quite, father. You see, I like this office—I always did,—and now—after to-night—it will always seem sacred to me. All this talk has been about an insignificant person and her clothes—but what impresses me, father, is how much alone you have been nearly all your life. I never realized that before. Now after this you must talk over your business with me; I may not be able to help, at first, but later on, who can tell? Then it will flatter me by making me think our compact is not one-sided. Is it a bargain, father?"

"It is a bargain, Edna."

The father drew the daughter towards him and the bargain was sealed. He turned out the lights, and they hurried down the stair to the slumbering cabman. The fog had reached down almost to the top of his head.

"Waterloo Station, Main Line," cried Sartwell, sharply.

"Yessir," said the cabby, exceedingly wide awake, as he gathered up the reins. The porter opened the gates.

"Everything all right, Perkins?"

"All right, sir," answered the porter, touching his cap.

"Keep a sharp look-out, you know."

"Yes, sir."

The rapidly lessening rattle of the hansom down the narrow street came back to Perkins as he closed the big gates for the night.

## CHAPTER III.

As father and daughter approached Wimbledon a mutual silence came over them. Perhaps this was because they had talked so much in the office. When they passed the station gates, Sartwell said:

"We'll have a cab, Edna, and blow the expense."

"I don't mind walking in the least; there is no fog here."

"We're late, so we'll have a cab." Once inside, he added, reflectively: "I wonder why it is that a cab seems extravagance in Wimbledon and economy in London."

This apparently was a problem neither of them could solve, so nothing more was said until the vehicle drew up at the door of a walled garden in a quiet street near the breezy common. Sartwell put his key in the door, held it open, and let his daughter pass in before him. A square house stood about a hundred yards back from the street, surrounded by shrubbery and flower-beds. The two walked somewhat gingerly up the crunching gravel path, opened the front door, and entered a dimly-lighted hall. Sartwell placed his hat on the rack, pushed open the dining-room door and went in, this time preceding his daughter. There were many comfortable chairs in the room, and one that was not comfortable. On that chair sat a woman, tall and somewhat angular, past the prime of life. She sat exceedingly upright, not allowing her shoulders to rest against the chair back. On her face was a patient expression of mitigated martyrdom, the expression of one who was badly used by a callous world, but who is resolved not to allow its ill treatment to interfere with her innate justice in dealing with her fellows.

"I thought I heard a cab drive up and stop," she said mildly, in the tone of one who may be wrong and is willing to be corrected.

"You did," said Sartwell, throwing himself down in an armchair. "Being late, I took a cab from the station."

"Oh!"

Much may be expressed by an apparently meaningless interjection. This one signified that Mrs. Sartwell, while shocked at such an admission, bowed to the inevitable, recognizing that she was mated with a man not amenable to reason, and that, while she might say much on the influence of unnecessary lavishness, she repressed herself, although she knew she would have no credit for her magnanimity.

After a few moments of silence, during which Mrs. Sartwell critically examined the sewing on which she was engaged, she looked across at her husband, and said:

"I may ask, I suppose, if it was business kept you so late."

"Important business."

She sighed.

"It always is. I should know that by this time without asking. Some men make business their god, although it will prove a god of clay to call upon when the end comes. There is such a thing as duty as well as business, and a man should have some little thought for his wife and his home."

This statement seemed so incontrovertible that Sartwell made no effort to combat it. He sat there with his head thrown back, his eyes closed, and his hands clasped supporting his knee. This attitude Mrs. Sartwell always regarded as the last refuge of the scoffer—an attitude he would be called upon to account for, as a sinner must account for evil deeds.

"Father has had more than usual to worry him at the office to-day," said Edna. She stood by the table, having removed her hat and gloves.

A look of mild surprise came over Mrs. Sart-well's face. She turned her head slowly around, and coldly scrutinized her step-daughter from head to foot. She apparently became aware of her presence for the first time, which may be explained by the fact that the young woman entered the room behind her father.

"Edna," said Mrs. Sartwell, "how often have I told you not to put your hat and gloves on the diningroom table? There is a place for everything. I am sure that when you visit your father's office, which you are so fond of doing, you find everything in its place, for he is at least methodical. You certainly do not take your disorderly habits from him, and everybody, except perhaps your father and yourself, admits that you live in an orderly household. How did you get that stain on your frock?"

Edna looked quickly down at her skirt; the hansom wheel had, alas! left its mark. Two-and-six an hour does not represent all the iniquities of a hansom on a muddy day.

"You are my despair, Edna, with your carelessness, and no one knows how it hurts me to say so. That frock you have had on only——"

"Edna," cried her father, peremptorily, "are you hungry?"

"No, father."

"Sure?"

"Quite sure. I am not in the least hungry."

"Then go to bed."

Edna came around the table to where her stepmother sat and kissed her on the cheek.

"Good-night," she said.

"Good-night, my poor child," murmured Mrs. Sartwell, with a sigh.

The girl kissed her father, whispering as she did so, "I'm afraid I'm your little girl again by the way you order me off to bed."

"You will always be my little girl to me, my dear," he said. "Good-night."

Mrs. Sartwell sighed again as Edna closed the door.

"I suppose," she said, "you think it fair to me to speak in whispers to Edna when I am in the room, or you wouldn't do it. How you can expect the child to have any respect for me when you allow her to whisper——"

"Is there anything to eat in the house?"

"You know there is always something to eat in the house."

"Then will you ring, or shall I?"

"You can't expect servants to sit up all night——"

"Very well; give me the keys and I will get something for myself."

Mrs. Sartwell's lips trembled as she folded her work methodically, enclosing needle, thimble and various paraphernalia of sewing in the bundle, placing it exactly where it should be in the workbasket. The keys jingled at her waist as she rose.

"I am ready, and always have been, to get you what you want whenever you want it. Perhaps I expect too much, but I think you might ask for it civilly. If you treat your men as you do your wife, it's no wonder they strike."

Sartwell made no reply, sitting there with his eyes closed until his wife, with a quaver in her voice, told him his supper was ready. It was a plentiful spread, with a choice of beer or spirits to drink; for one of Sartwell's weaknesses was the belief that to work well a man must eat well. Although his wife did not believe in nor approve of this pampering, she nevertheless provided well for him, for is not a woman helpless in such a case? As the man of the house ate in silence, she looked at him once or twice over her sewing, and finally said, pathetically:

"I am sure Edna was hungry, but was afraid to say so, you were so gruff with her. One would think that if you had no feeling for your wife, you would have some for your only daughter."

Sartwell cut another slice from the cold joint, and transferred it to his plate.

"I am accustomed to it, I hope, by this time, but she is young and nothing warps the character of the young like uncalled-for harshness and unkindness. You are blind to her real faults, and then you are severe when there is no occasion for severity. What had the child done that you should order her off to bed in that fashion?"

There was a pause for a reply, but no reply came. Mrs. Sartwell was accustomed to this, as she had said, for there is a brutality of silence as well as a brutality of speech; so she scanned her adversary, as one does who searches for a joint in the armor where the sword's point will enter. Then she took a firm grasp of the hilt, and pressed it gently forward. Turning over her sewing, and sighing almost inaudibly to it, she remarked, quietly:

"As I said to Mrs. Hope when she called——"

"Said to whom?" snapped Sartwell, turning round suddenly.

"Oh, I thought you were never interested in my callers. I suppose I am allowed to have some private friends of my own. Still, if you wish me to sit in the house all day alone, you have but to say so, and I will obey."

"Don't talk nonsense, if you can help it. What was Mrs. Hope doing here?"

"She was calling on me."

"Quite so. I think I understand that much. What was her mission? What particular fad was on this time?"

"I should think you would be ashamed to speak like that about your employer's wife, when she did your wife the honour to consult her——"

"About what? That is the point I want to get at."

"About the strike."

"Ah!" A glint of anger came into Sartwell's eyes, and his wife looked at him with some uneasiness.

"Mrs. Hope is a woman who goes about doing good. She is much interested in the men at the 'works,' and thinks of calling on their wives and families to see for herself how they live. She thinks perhaps something may be done for them."

"Does she?"

"Yes. She wonders if you are quite patient and tactful with them."

"And came to find out? You told her, no doubt, that I studied tact from you and was therefore all right as far as that was concerned."

"I told her the truth," cried Mrs. Sartwell, hotly.

"Which was——?"

"That you were an obstinate, domineering man who would brook no opposition."

"You hit the bull's-eye for once. What did she say?"

"She said she hoped you considered the men's helpless families."

"And you answered that not having any consideration for my own, it was not likely I would give much thought to the wives and families of the men."

"I didn't say so, but I thought it."

"Admirable self-restraint! Now look here, Sarah, you're playing with fire and haven't the sense to know it. Mrs. Hope is a meddling, hysterical fool, and——"

"You wouldn't dare say that to your employer."

"Now that remark shows that a woman of your calibre can live for years with a man and not begin to understand him. The trouble is that I shall say just that very thing to my employer, as you delight to call him, the moment his wife puts her finger in the pie. Then what follows?"

"You will lose your situation."

"Exactly. Or, to put it more truthfully, I resign—I walk out into the street."

"You surely would do nothing so foolish."

"That follows instantly when I am compelled to give Mr. Hope my opinion regarding his domestic relations. Then what will become of your income? Will Mrs. Hope contribute, do you think? Do you aspire to a place on her charity list? Whatever your opinion has been of me, privately held or publicly expressed, you must admit that I have at least provided money enough to keep the house going, and you have surely the sense to appreciate that. You never could see an inch ahead of your nose, or realize that effect follows cause as inevitably as fate. How a woman can describe a man as obstinate and domineering, impatient of all control, and then deliberately wag her tongue to bring about the very interference that she must know, if she believes what she has said, he will not stand, passes my comprehension. The result of your gossip to-day may be that I shall be looking for another situation to-morrow."

Mrs. Sartwell had been weeping during the latter part of this harangue.

"It is always me," she sobbed, "that is to blame for everything wrong. Your hasty ungovernable temper is never at fault. If you made me more of a confidante in your affairs—other men consult their wives, better men than you, and richer than you will ever be. Mrs. Hope says that her husband——"

"I don't want to hear any more about Mrs. Hope."

"You insisted on talking about her. I didn't want to say anything, but you cross-questioned me till I had to, and now you blame me."

"Very well, let it rest there. Bring me a jug of milk, if you please."

"You are surely not going to drink milk after beer?"

"I claim the liberty of a British subject to drink any mortal thing I choose to drink. Don't let us have an argument about it."

"But you won't sleep a wink, John, if you do. It's for your own good I speak."

"Everything is for my own good, Sarah; perhaps that's what makes me so impatient."

"Well, you know how you are after a bad night."

"Yes, yes. I think I have earned my bad night anyhow. Get the milk or tell me where to get it." Mrs. Sartwell always rose when her husband offered to help himself from the larder. She placed the jug of milk at his elbow.

"I've got a number of things to think over," he said. "I want to be alone."

She stood by the table looking at him.

"Good-night, John," she faltered at last.

"Good-night," he answered.

She gazed at him reproachfully in silence, but he did not raise his head, so turning at last with a deep sigh, she left him to his meditations.

Sartwell sat there with deep anxiety on his brow. Silence fell on all the house. At last the master roused himself and turned to the table. He buttered two slices of bread and cut a piece of dainty cake, placing them on a plate with a drinking glass. Lighting a candle and turning out the gas, he set to himself the acrobatic feat of carrying plate, jug, and candle. First he softly opened the door and kicked off his slippers. Awkwardly laden, he mounted the stair with the stealthy tread of a burglar, but in spite of his precautions the stairs creaked ominously in the stillness. He noiselessly entered a room, and, placing the difficult load on a table, softly closed the door. When the light shone on the sleeping girl's face she opened her eyes very wide, then covered them with her hand, laughing a quiet, sleepy little laugh, and buried her face in the white pillow.

"H—s—sh," said her father.

Instantly she was wide awake.

"I was afraid you were hungry after all," he whispered.

"I wasn't then, really, but I am now a little."

"That's good."

He placed a small round gypsy table near the bed and put the plate and jug of milk upon it.

"You knew of course when I spoke, that—I merely wanted you to get a long night's rest. You were tired, you know."

"Oh, I know that, father."

"Then, good-night, my dear; perhaps it was foolish to wake you up, but you will soon drop off asleep again."

"In a minute, and this does look tempting. I just wanted a glass of milk. It's so good of you, father."

She drew his head down and kissed him.

"I hope you'll sleep well," she added.

"I'll be sure to."

At the door he stopped; then after a moment, whispered cautiously:

"Edna, you'll take the things down in the morning yourself, quietly. The servants, you know—well, they don't like extra trouble—sometimes."

"Yes, father, I understand."

Sartwell stole quietly out like a thief in the night.

## CHAPTER IV.

Barnard Hope, commonly known as Barney, never quite got over his surprise at finding himself the son of James Hope and Euphemia his wife. James Hope, the junior member of the firm of Monkton & Hope, was an undersized man with a touch of baldness and an air of constant apology. He seemed to attach a mental string to every hesitating opinion he uttered, so that he might instantly pull it back if necessary. Meeting him on the street, one would take him for a very much bullied, very much underpaid clerk in the City. In his office he lived in fear of his manager; at home he lived in fear of his wife. The chief characteristic of his wife was uncompromising rigidity. She was a head taller than her husband, and when one met them on the way to church, he had the meek attitude of an unfortunate little boy who had been found out, and was being taken to church as a punishment by a just and indignant school-mistress. Mrs. Hope joined in none of the fashionable frivolities of Surbiton, where she lived. She had a mission and a duty towards her fellow-creatures—that is, towards those who were poor, and who could not very well resent her patronage. She had an idea that if all the well-to-do did their duty, the world would be a brighter and a better place—which is doubtful.

We may all be more or less grateful that Mrs. Hope has not been intrusted with the task of making this world over again; many interesting features would in that case have been eliminated. Hope himself was not an example of unmitigated happiness. The lady always had a number of protégées on hand, whom she afterwards discovered, as a usual thing, to be undeserving, which discovery caused them to be thrown over for new cases that in turn went bad. She was also constantly in demand by organizations needing members with long purses, but Mrs. Hope had a wonderful talent for managing which was not always recognized by those with whom she associated. This often led to trouble, older members claiming, as they vulgarly put it, that she wanted to run the whole show, and one outspoken person advised her to ameliorate the condition of her husband's workmen, if she desired fit subjects for her efforts.

This remark turned Mrs. Hope's attention to the manufactory of Monkton & Hope, and led to her calling upon Mrs. Sartwell, in the neighbouring suburb of Wimbledon.

Now the son of these two dissimilar but estimable persons ought to have been a solemn prig, whereas he was in fact a boisterous cad, and thus does nature revel in unexpected surprises.

Barney was a broad-shouldered, good-natured giant, who towered over his shrinking father as the Monument towers over the nearest lamp-post. He was hail-fellow well-met, and could not shake hands like an ordinary mortal, but must bring down his great paw with an over-shoulder motion, as if he were throwing a cricket-ball, and, after the resounding whack of palm on palm, he would crunch the hand he held until its owner winced. Friends of the young fellow got into the habit, on meeting him, of placing their hands behind them and saying, "I'm quite well, thank you, Barney," whereupon Barney laughed and smote them on the shoulder, which, though hard to bear, was the lesser of two evils.

"Boisterous brute," his comrades said behind his back, but the energetic shoulder-blow or hand-clasp merely meant that Barney was very glad indeed to meet a friend, and to let the friend know that although he was very poor and Barney very rich this circumstance need not make the slightest difference between them.

It is possible that in the far West, or in the Australian bush, where muscle counts for something, there was a place yawning for Barney; perhaps there was a place for him even in London, but if there was, fate and Barney's own inclinations removed him from it as far as possible. Barney was an artist; that is to say, he painted, or rather he put certain colours on canvas. For some years

Barney had been the amazement of Julian's school in Paris. He had a suite of rooms at the Grand Hotel, and he drove to the school in the Rue du Dragon every morning with a coachman and footman, the latter carrying Barney's painting kit, while the former sat in a statuesque position on the box with his whip at the correct angle. Of course the art students were not going to stand that sort of thing, so they closed the gates one day and attacked the young man in a body. Barney at first thought it was fun, for he did not understand the language very well, and his good-natured roar sounded loud over the shrill cries of his antagonists. He reached for them one by one, placed them horizontally in a heap, then he rolled them over and over, flattening any student who attempted resurrection with a pat of his gigantic paw.

Whatever admiration they may have had for art at Julian's, they certainly had a deep respect for muscle, and so left Barney alone after that. He invited them all to dinner at the Grand Hotel, and they came.

When his meteoric career as an art student in Paris was completed, he set himself up in an immense studio in Chelsea. The studio was furnished regardless of expense; there was everything in it that a studio ought to have—rich hangings from the East, tiger-skins from India, oriental rugs, ancient armour, easels of every pattern, luxurious lounges covered with stuffs from Persia.

"There," cried Barney to Hurst Haldiman, with a grand sweep of his hand: "what do you think of that?"

Haldiman, one of the most talented students he had met in Paris, had now a garret of his own in London, where he painted when he got time, and did black and white work for the magazines and illustrated weeklies to keep himself in money. Barney had invited all his own old Parisian friends, one by one, to see his new quarters.

"Wonderful!" said Haldiman. "I venture to say there is not another studio in London like it."

"That was my intention," replied Barney. "They told me that Sir Richard Daubs had the finest studio in London. I said nothing, but went to work, and here I am. Have you ever seen Daubs' studio, Hurst?"

"No. He is not so friendly as you are, Barney; he has never invited me."

"Well, I'll get you an invitation, and I want you to tell me candidly what you think of mine as compared with his."

"Thanks, old man, but don't trouble about the invitation for me. I haven't any time to spare; merely came up here, you know, because we had been in Paris together. Daubs' studio has one great advantage over many others—it contains a man who can paint."

"Oh, yes, Haldiman, that's all right. That's the old Paris gag, you know. Ever since I heaped the boys one on top of the other, they have revenged themselves by saying I couldn't paint; but you should be above that sort of thing, Haldiman, you really should. You see I'm a plain, straight-forward fellow, and I've got what is admitted to be the finest studio in London; but does that make any difference between me and my old friends? Not a bit of it, and the fact that you are sitting there proves it. I'm a born Bohemian; I despise riches, and my very best friends are fellows who haven't a sou-markee. You know that, Haldiman."

Haldiman lit another of Hope's very excellent cigarettes. Barney imported them from Egypt himself, and said they were the same brand the Khedive smoked until one of the war correspondents informed him that the Khedive was not a smoker. Then Barney slightly varied the praise.

"Help yourself, dear boy. You'll find they're not half bad as cigarettes go. I get them direct, for you can't trust these rascally importers. The Khedive is not a smoker himself, still he keeps nothing but the best for his guests, and this is the identical brand, as supplied to him.

"Now about this painting business," continued Barney. "I venture to say that there was a time when Daubs was utterly unknown. Very well. Here also am I utterly unknown. The public won't buy my pictures. I don't conceal that fact. Why should I? I sent a picture to the Birmingham exhibition—I don't say it was great, but I do claim it had individuality. They rejected it!"

"You amaze me!"

"I give you my word of honour they did, Haldiman. Birmingham! Think of that! A town that manufactures nails and gun-barrels."

"Oh, art in England is going to the dogs," said Haldiman, dejectedly.

"Now I don't go so far as to say that. No; I laughed when my little effort came back, with regrets. I said I can bide my time, and I can. The people will come to me, Haldiman, you see if they don't."

"They do already, Barney—those who want to borrow money."

"Now look here, Hurst, don't throw my beastly cash in my teeth. Am I to blame if I am rich? Do I allow it to make a difference between man and man? We were talking about art, not money."

"So we were. About your pictures. Go on."

"I only wanted to point out to you that one must take things philosophically. Now if Birmingham had rejected one of your pictures it would have depressed you for a week."

"Birmingham has got me on the other alley, Barney. It has accepted two of mine. Hence my gloom after what you have told me."

Barney beamed on his visitor. Here was his argument clinched, but he repressed his desire to say, "I told you so"; still he could not allow the occasion to pass without improving it with a little judicious counsel.

"There you are, Haldiman, there you are. Does not the fact that you are accepted of Birmingham make you pause and think?"

"I'm staggered. It's a knock-down blow. I'll be into the Academy next."

"Oh, not so bad as that. You see, Haldiman, you have talent of a certain kind——"

"Now, Barney, you lay it on too thick. I like flattery, of course, but it must be delicately done. You are gross in your praise."

"I am not flattering you, Haldiman, 'pon my soul, I'm not. Most other fellows would be offended at what I'm going to say, but you're a sensible man——"

"There you go again."

"Listen to me. You have a certain talent—technique, perhaps, I should call it; a slight skill in technique."

"Ah, that's better. Now go on."

"You got the praise and the prizes in Paris because of your technique, and that set you on the wrong tack. You are merely only doing well what hosts of other men have done well before you. You are down among the ruck. Now I strive after individuality."

"You get it, Barney."

"That's not for me to say; anyhow, individuality and strength are what I want to see in my pictures, and there will some time come a critic with a mind unbiased enough to recognize these qualities. Then my day will have arrived. You mark my words, I shall found a school."

"Like Julian's?"

"No, like Whistler's. You know very well what I mean. That's your nasty way of showing you are offended because I'm frank enough to tell you the truth."

"I suppose none of us likes the candid friend, however much we may pretend to. Well, I must be going. I've got some technique to do for one of the magazines."

"Don't go just yet. I have not half finished. Here is what I have to propose. Give up your room and come with me. You see the great advantage I have over you is that I can wait. If a magazine asked me to do black and white work for it, I would say, 'No, go to those poor devils who must have work or starve. I'm working for the future, not for the present!' That's what I'd say. Now I'll give you a bedroom, rent free, and a corner of this studio. It won't cost you a penny—nor your board either. You can paint just what you like, and not what the public demands. Then you will be independent."

"We have different views about things, Barney. That would seem to me the worst form of dependence. It is very generous of you, but utterly impracticable; besides, you haven't thought of the danger of my becoming a mere copyist of you—a shadow of the new individualist. I couldn't risk that, you know."

"Better become the shadow of one man, than a shadow of many, which you are now."

"Perhaps; but we each must hoe our own row in our own way. Good-by, Barney."

Haldiman went down-stairs, not cheered as much as might have been expected by Hope's overflowing good nature and generosity. He met Barney's mother on the stairs, who gave him a head-to-foot glance of evident disapproval. She did not admire the set with whom her son had thrown in his lot, and feared their influence on him would not be beneficial.

"Oh, mater!" cried Barney, when she entered. "I did not expect you to-day. How did you find the place?"

His mother raised her lorgnette to her eyes and surveyed the room in silence.

"So this is the studio, Barnard," she said, at last. "I don't think much of it. Why is it all untidy like this?—or haven't you had time to get it in order yet?"

"This is the kind of thing we artists go in for, mater. It is as much in order as it ever will be."

"Then I don't like it. Why could you not have had a man in to lay one carpet as it should be laid? These rugs, all scattered about in this careless way, trip one up so. What's this old iron for?"

"That's armour, mater."

"Oh, is it? I don't see how any one can do useful work in a room like this, still I suppose it is good enough to paint in. I found the place easily enough. Trust a neighbourhood to know where there is any extra foolishness going on. Of course you have been cheated in everything you bought. But that's neither here nor there. I came to talk with you about the business."

"What business, mater?"

"What business? The business, of course. Your father's business and yours, for I hope the time will come when you will take more interest in it than you do now. The men, it seems, talk of going on strike."

"Foolish beggars! What are they going to do that for, and what do you expect me to do? Not to talk to the men, I hope, for I detest the workingman. He's an ass usually, otherwise he wouldn't work for the wages he gets. Then he spends what he does make on bad beer and goes home and beats his wife. I can't reason with the workingman, you know, mater."

"No, I don't suppose you can. I sometimes doubt whether you can reason with anybody. It is because the workingman labours that you can idle away your time in a place like this. There are many deserving characters among the working classes, although they are often difficult to find. The men have made-some demands which Sartwell, the manager, won't even listen to. It seems to me that he is not treating them fairly. He should, at least, hear what they have to say, and if their demands do not cost the firm anything; he should grant them."

"Mater," cried the young man, with enthusiasm, "what a head for business you have!"

"I am of a family that became rich through having heads for business," replied the lady, with justifiable pride. "Now, what I want you to do is to see this man Sartwell; he will pay attention to you because he knows that in time you will be his master, and so he will be civil to you."

"I'm not so sure of that," said Barney, doubtfully. "I imagine he thinks me rather an ass, you know."

"Well, now is your opportunity for showing him you are not, if he has the impertinence to think such a thing. You must see him at his own house and not at the office—here is his address. Tell him to receive the men and make a compromise with them. He is to make concessions that are unimportant, and thus effect a compromise. A little tact is all that is required."

"From me, or from Sartwell?"

"From both of you. I expect tact from you because you are my son."

"But why doesn't father talk to Sartwell? I know nothing of the business, and father does; it seems to be entirely in his line, don't you know?"

"Your father, Barnard, is a timorous man, and he actually is afraid of his manager. He thinks it is interference and doesn't want to meddle, so he says, as if a man were meddling in looking after his own affairs! He fears Sartwell will resign, but that kind of man knows where his own interest lies. I'll risk his resigning, and I want you to see him at his house, for it is no use bothering your father about these things."

"I don't like the job, mater; it does look like interference."

Mrs. Hope again raised her lorgnette by its long tortoise-shell handle, and once more surveyed the studio.

"This must have cost you a good deal of money, Barnard," she said, impartially.

"It did," admitted the young man.

"I suppose I shall soon have to be writing another cheque for you. For how much shall I make it?"

"It is such a pity to trouble you so often, mater," replied the young man, "that perhaps we had better say three hundred."

"Very well," said his mother, rising, "I will have it ready for you when you come to Surbiton after having seen Sartwell at Wimbledon. It is on your way, you know."

"All right, mater. But you mustn't blame me if I don't succeed. I'll do my best, but Sartwell's an awkward beggar to deal with."

"All I ask of you, Barnard, is that you shall do your best," answered the lady, rising.

## CHAPTER V.

When Mrs. Hope departed, Barney sat down on a luxurious divan in his studio, and rubbed his chin thoughtfully.

"I may as well have that cheque as soon as possible," he said to himself. "It is no use delaying important matters; besides, delay might injure the scheme the mater has on her mind. What a blessing it is father asks me not to mention the cheques he gives me. Between the two you manage to rub along, Barney, my boy. Well, here goes for Wimbledon!"

The young man arrayed himself with some care, jumped into a hansom, and was driven to Sloane Square station, where, in due time, a deliberate train came along that ultimately landed him in Wimbledon.

If Barney had been a man of deep thought, or experienced in the ways of working people, or able to reason from induction, he would have arrived at the fact that there was not the slightest chance of finding Mr. Sartwell in his house at that hour of the day. It must not be supposed that Barney was an unthinking person, for, when the servant informed him that Mr. Sartwell was never at home except in the evening or early morning, Barney at once accused himself mentally of heedlessness in having to come all the way from Chelsea to Wimbledon to learn so self-evident a fact. He thus admitted to himself his own ability to have reasoned the matter out, had his mind been unobscured by the shadow of a coming cheque.

He was not quick at grasping an unexpected detail, and he stood at the door hardly knowing exactly what to do next; while the servant watched him with obvious distrust, wondering whether he came to sell something or merely to ask for a subscription; however, the fact that he was keeping a hansom waiting at the gate told in his favour, so she broke the silence by saying:

"Any message, sir?"

He ignored this question, which raised him still higher in the servant's estimation, and ventured the perfectly accurate opinion:

"He will not be home for some hours, I suppose?"

"No, sir."

Barney pondered for a while, and suddenly delivered himself of a resolution that did credit to his good sense.

"Then I won't wait," he said.

"What name shall I say, sir?" asked the maid.

"Oh, it's of no importance. I will call again; still, here is my card. I am the son of Mr. Hope, one of the proprietors of the works."

The maid took the card, and Mrs. Sartwell appeared in the hall, almost as if she had been listening to the words of the speaker, which, of course, she had a perfect right to do, as one generally wishes to know who calls at one's front door.

"Did I hear you say that you were Mr. Hope?" she asked.

"I am his son, madam," said Barney modestly, and with that politeness he had learned in Paris.

"Won't you come in? I'm sorry my husband is not at home. Is it on account of the strike you come? I feel very anxious. Your mother called yesterday, and we had a long conversation about it."

"Yes, the mater takes a great interest in the workingman, although I can't say I do myself. I merely wished to have an informal chat with Mr. Sartwell on the situation, and that is why I called at the house rather than the office."

Barney stepped into the hall and kept his hat in his hand to show he had a hansom waiting. He had no intention of staying more than a moment or two. He had thought it best to have something to tell his mother about his visit to Wimbledon, for she was a relentless cross-questioner, and if he could have a conversation to report she might take the will for the deed and give him the cheque.

The door of the drawing-room was thrown open and when the two entered they found Edna Sartwell sitting there in a deep chair, reading a book with such interest that she evidently had not heard a word of the colloquy at the door. She rose in some confusion, colouring deeply as she saw a stranger come in with her step-mother. The latter said nothing to the girl, but directed a glance at her that, speaking as plainly as words, told her to leave the room.

Barney's first thought on seeing Edna was that she was about to escape from the room, and that this desertion must be diplomatically prevented. Barney's great burden in life, so he often told his friends, was that the young ladies of England were in the habit of throwing themselves at his head, which remark caused Haldiman once to say that they had a quick eye for his weakest point of defence. Now here was a "stunning" girl, to use Barney's own phrase about her, who was actually about to walk out of the room without casting a second glance at him. A young man always likes the unusual.

"Not your daughter, Mrs. Sartwell?" said Barney, in his most winning manner.

"My step-daughter," answered the lady, coldly.

"Ah, I thought you could not have a grown-up daughter," murmured Barney, delicately. He always found this particular kind of compliment very successful with ladies well past middle age, and in this case his confidence was not misplaced.

"Do not let me drive you away, Miss Sartwell," he continued. "I am Barnard Hope," he added, seeing that Mrs. Sartwell did not intend to introduce him, "and I called to see your father and talk with him regarding the strike. So, you know, it is a matter that interests us all, and I beg of you to join in the conference."

The moment he mentioned her father and the strike, he saw he held the attention of the girl, who paused and looked at her step-mother. That perplexed lady was in a quandary. She did not wish to offend Mrs. Hope's son, and she did not want her step-daughter to remain in the room. She hesitated, and was lost.

"Pray let me offer you a chair in your own drawingroom," said Barney, with that gallantry which he always found irresistible, "and you, Mrs. Sartwell. Now we will have a comfortable informal chat, which I know will be of immense assistance in my talk with Mr. Sartwell, for I confess I am a little afraid of him." Edna opened her eyes at this; she had several times heard people say they stood in awe of her father, and she never could understand why.

Mrs. Sartwell sat bolt upright and folded her hands on her lap, frowning at her step-daughter when she got the chance unseen by Barney. She did not at all like the turn events had taken, but saw no way of interfering without seeming rude to her guest.

"You see," chirruped Barney, "the mater takes a great interest in the workingman; so do I." He thought this noble sentiment would appeal to Edna Sartwell. "I think we all—we all—as it were—should feel a certain responsibility, don't you know. You see what I mean, Mrs. Sartwell?"

"Certainly. It does you great credit, Mr. Hope," replied the lady appealed to, although she uttered the phrase with some severity, as if it were an aspersion.

"Oh, not at all. I suppose it was born in me. I think it natural for all rightly brought up persons to take a deep interest in their fellow-creatures. Don't you think so, Miss Sartwell?"

"Yes," said Edna faintly, without looking up.

"For workmen are our fellow-creatures, you know," cried Barney, with all the enthusiasm of a startling discovery.

"Am I my brother's keeper?" said Mrs. Sartwell, in gloomy tones.

"Quite so, quite so," assented Barney, who took the remark as original. "I couldn't have stated the case better if I had thought all day about it. Now the mater imagined that perhaps Mr. Sartwell would consent to meet the men and talk it over, making perhaps some trifling concessions, and then everything would be lovely. You see what I mean?"

"It seems a most reasonable proposal," said Mrs. Sartwell, with a sigh; "but my opinion is of no value, especially in my own house."

"Oh, don't say that, Mrs. Sartwell. I am sure every one must value your opinion most highly—every one who has the privilege of hearing it. I assure you I do. Now, what do you think, Miss Sartwell?"

The young man beamed on the girl in his most fascinating manner, but his charming facial expression was in a measure lost, for Edna was looking at the carpet, apparently perplexed.

"I think," she said at last, "that father, who spends nearly all his time dealing with the men, must understand the situation better than we do. He has had a great deal of experience with them, and, as I know, has given much thought to the difficulty; so it seems to me our advice may not be of any real value to him."

Barney could scarcely repress a long whistle. So this was how the land lay. This demure miss actually had an opinion of her own, and was plainly going to stand with her father against the field. Heretofore everybody had always agreed with Barney, excepting of course those rascally students, who were no respecters of persons, and more especially had all women agreed with him, therefore this little bit of opposition, so decorously expressed, had a new and refreshing flavour. The wind had shifted; he must trim his sails to suit the breeze.

"There, Miss Sartwell, you have touched the weak spot in our case. Just what I said to the mater. 'Mr. Sartwell's on the spot,' said I, 'and he ought to know.' Almost your very words, Miss Sartwell."

An ominous cloud rested on Mrs. Sartwell's brow.

"Surely," she said, severely, "the owners of a business should have something to say about the way it is to be conducted."

"The tendency of modern times," cried Barney, airily, waving his hand, "appears to be entirely in the opposite direction, my dear madam. It is getting to be that whoever has a say in a business, the owners shall have the least.

And I am not sure but this is, to a certain extent, logical. I have often heard my father say that Mr. Sartwell was the real maker of the business. Why then should he be interfered with?" Edna looked up gratefully at the enthusiastic young man, for she not only liked the sentiments he was beginning to express, but she liked the manly ring in his voice. Barney had frequently found this tone to be very taking, especially with the young and inexperienced, and he knew that he appeared at his best when assuming it, if none of his carping comrades were present. He could even work himself up into a sturdy state of indignation, if his audience were sympathetic, and he were free from the blighting influence of pessimistic young men he met in Bohemia.

"And now, Miss Sartwell, I'll tell you what I propose Have a talk with your father; then, if Mrs. Sartwell will allow me, I will call again, and I can judge from what you say whether it will be worth while troubling Mr. Sartwell with our advice. You see, we have all the same object in view—we wish to help Mr. Sartwell if we can. If we can't, then there is no harm done. You see what I mean?"

Mrs. Sartwell rather grudgingly assented to this. Edna said nothing.

"You see, ladies, I am an artist—a painter of pictures. I work, as it were, in the past and in the future. I feel that I do not belong to the present, and these little details I know I ought to leave to those who understand how to deal with them. I told the mater so. But whether we are able to help Mr. Sartwell or not, you must allow me to thank you for a very charming afternoon. My studio is in Chelsea. It is said to be the finest in London; but of course I care nothing about that, to me it is merely my workshop. But there are relaxations even in artistic life, and every Tuesday afternoon from three o'clock till five I am at home to my friends. I expect the mater to receive my guests, and you must promise to come, Mrs. Sartwell, will you not? I will send you cards, and you will be sure to meet some nice people. May I count on you? I know the mater will be pleased."

"I shall be very happy to accept your invitation," said Mrs. Sartwell, softening under the genial influence of the young man.

"And you, too, Miss Sartwell?"

Edna looked somewhat dubiously at her stepmother.

"You will bring Miss Sartwell with you, will you not?" persisted the young man.

"I am always glad to do anything to add to Edna's pleasure," said Mrs. Sartwell, a trifle less cordially; "but it must be as her father says."

"Then you will use your influence with him, Miss Sartwell, won't you, and get him to consent. I am sure he will not refuse if you care to come."

"I should like very much to go," said Edna.

"Then we will look on it as settled."

When Barney stepped into his waiting hansom, he said to himself, "Ah, Barney, my boy, you light on your feet as usual. What a lovely girl! and a mind of her own, too, if she is so shy. Who would ever have suspected grim old Sartwell of having such a pretty daughter! I must persuade the mater to come off that particular hobbyhorse of hers, for it is easy to see the girl doesn't want anyone to interfere with her father. If I can bring the mater around and get the cheque too, I'm a diplomatist."

## CHAPTER VI.

From Wimbledon to Surbiton is comparatively but a step. An enterprising train, bent on accomplishing the feat, can do the distance in seven or eight minutes, and even the slowest of "locals" takes but twelve. Barney was an energetic young man, and, where a cheque was concerned, knew the dangers of delay; so he resolved, being in the neighbourhood, to go to Surbiton, see his mother, and settle the business. The young man often reassured himself by saying inwardly that he was no fool, and the few minutes he had to meditate on the situation, as he paced up and down No. 3 platform waiting for the train, enabled him to formulate a course of action.

Barney had a well-defined mental process by which he arrived at any plan of procedure. "The great thing, my boy," he used to say, "is to know exactly what you want, and then go for it." In going for it the young fellow trampled on anything that came in his path: truth, for example. His one object was success—the kind that succeeds. Having attained that, he was careless of the means.

In this instance what he wanted was to prevent any interference with Sartwell, and he knew, if he boldly opposed his mother's scheme, such opposition would inevitably bring about the meddling he desired to avoid, and at the same time place himself in her bad books, which was financially undesirable.

"It will take a bit of thinking," said Barney to himself, thus showing that he correctly estimated the difficulties of the situation, and realized the shortness of the distance between Wimbledon and Surbiton.

Surbiton is a most attractive Surrey suburb with an excellent service of trains. The houses are large, detached, and of the class known in the estate agents' vocabulary as "desirable." Stockbrokers in the city are attracted thither as much by the rapid train service as by the desirable residences; thus many of them live there. The rich and retired tradesman and the manufacturer in a large way have given the place an exclusiveness which it could never have attained if it had been a mere resort of noblemen, or a place for the housing of the working classes. It is the rich and retired tradesman who has given England its reputation as a cold and dignified nation. Nothing can compare with a first-class compartment from Surbiton—"Vaux-hall and Waterloo only"—for frigid exclusiveness. Sometimes an unfortunate duke or marquis, coming from his estates in the southwest, chances upon the Surbiton contingent, and makes an innocent and friendly remark. He is frozen into silence by the icy stare of the other five occupants of the compartment.

Surbiton, to a stranger, has the look of a sea-side place. Some of the streets are broad and divided by narrow railed-in parks. There are benches here and there, and trees everywhere, while an assembly hall in the centre of the town, and a sort of marine parade along the river, and a band-stand and military concert every Wednesday evening during the summer, give to this charming suburb the air of a coast resort, lacking only the long, spidery, cast-iron pier, which Surbiton may yet build over the river into the Hampton Court grounds, where in spring the waters lie like a broad yellow ocean. When that pier is built, the charge for admission will doubtless be fourpence—double the Brighton price, for Surbiton is prone to attest its exclusiveness in a manner that appeals to the financial imagination. It is proud of the fact that its local rates are high. The Surbiton improvement committee being elected to attend to that matter, and that a first-class season ticket costs two pounds more than to any other place an equal distance from London.

The Hope residence was a large, square, yellow house, rather old-fashioned—"an imposing mansion" was the phrase that caught Mrs. Hope's eye, in the Times, before she induced her husband to buy it—and it stood in extensive well-wooded grounds. Barney drove up to it in one of the open victorias which stand for hire at the station, a class of vehicle that adds to the sea-side appearance of Surbiton.

Telling the man to wait, he sprang up the steps and knocked, for there was nothing so modern as a bell at the front door. He found his mother in the drawingroom, and with her Lady Mary Fanshaw, who had driven over from her father's country place in the Dorking direction. Lady Mary was a nice girl, rather shy, who blushed prettily when Barney came in, and had a great admiration for the young man's hitherto unappreciated artistic talents, liking a painter better than a manufacturer. Her father, having ascertained definitely that Barney's possession of a studio would in no way interfere with his ultimate coming into the proprietorship of the remunerative factory, made no objection to the acquaintanceship between the Hope family and his own.

"How-de-do, Lady Mary," cried the young man, shaking hands with her. "How are you, mater?" he added to his mother, kissing her on the cheek.

"Barnard," said the elder lady, with a touch of severity in her tone, "I did not expect to see you in Surbiton so soon. I thought you would attend to the business I spoke of."

"It's all been attended to, mater. I don't let the grass grow under my feet—not that it's a good day for grass either," continued the young man cheerfully, warming his hands at the fire. "Beastly weather," he remarked to Lady Mary, who assented to the terse statement.

"Yes, mater; my motto is, what is worth doing is worth doing quickly—speedily done is twice done—I think there's a proverb to that effect, don't you know. If there's not, there ought to be."

Lady Mary rose to leave the room, as mother and son had evidently something to discuss together.

"Sit down, child," said Mrs. Hope. "It is nothing private. The men at the 'works' talk of going on strike. The manager is a stubborn, unyielding man, given even to browbeating his employers—"

"Bullying, I call it," interrupted Barney, who now stood with his back to the fire, his feet well apart on the hearth-rug.

His mother went on calmly, without noticing her son's interpolation—"So it seems to me that such a man, utterly lacking in tact, might not perhaps be mindful of the feelings of those under him. We all have our duties towards the working class, a fact many, alas! appear to forget."

Lady Mary said softly, with her eyes cast down, that this was indeed the case.

“So you saw Mr. Sartwell, Barnard?”

“Oh, yes, I saw Sartwell, and had a talk with some of the men—with the—ah—ringleaders, don’t you know.”

“You mean the leaders, Barnard.”

“Yes, something of that sort. I don’t pretend to understand the bally workingman, you know, but there’s lots of sense in what they say. They know what they want.”

“Did you find Mr. Sartwell obdurate?”

“Oh, bless you, no, mater. Sartwell’s the most reasonable of men.”

“Indeed? It never occurred to me to place him in that category.”

“Don’t you make any mistake about Sartwell, mater; you won’t find him stand in your way at all. He’s perfectly willing to do whatever you want done. ‘Barney, my boy,’ he said to me, when I told him what you thought about this trouble, ‘Barney,’ says he, ‘after all is said and done, it’s the women’s affair more than ours.’”

“The women’s affair!” said Mrs. Hope, drawing herself severely up. “Do I understand you to mean, Barnard, that the man was referring to Mrs. Monkton and myself?”

“Well, mater, you see we were talking freely together as man to man—and—hang it all! you know, it is your affair and Mrs. Monkton’s, more than old Monkton’s and father’s. I don’t suppose they care so very much.”

Mrs. Hope slowly raised her glasses to her eyes and stared at her son, who was looking at the hearth-rug now, resting his weight on his toes and then coming down on his heels.

“I haven’t the least idea what you are talking about, Barnard.”

“I am talking about the proposed strike, mater; about the demands of the men.”

"Requests, my son. The men request an audience with Mr. Sartwell, and he refuses it, as if he were Prime Minister."

"That's just what I said to Sartwell. 'Sartwell,' said I, 'you're high-handed with the men.' He admitted it, but held that if he had a conference with them, no good would be accomplished unless he acceeded to their dem——requests."

"He could compromise—he could make some concessions and then everything would go smoothly again. He has no tact."

"Quite so, quite so. But you see the men want only one thing, not several. They are perfectly logical about it—I had a talk with them and they were very much gratified to hear that you were on their side. There will be no trouble with them in future if Sartwell is only reasonable. They look at it like this: they work ten hours a day and get on an average a pound a week—or—ah—something like that—I forget the exact amount, although they had it there in shillings and pence. Now father and Monkton work four or five hours a day—not very hard either—and go to Switzerland in the summer and Algiers in the winter, yet they draw twenty thousand pounds a year each out of the business. This, the men claim, is unjust, and of course I quite agree with them. It's outrageous, and I said so. Well, the men are prepared to do the most generous things. In order to compromise, they will allow the partners ten times what the real workers get; Monkton and father are each to draw five hundred pounds a year out of the business, and the forty thousand pounds is to be divided among the workers. I thought that it was an exceedingly liberal proposal, and I told them so."

During this able, if mythical, exposition of the workmen's views, Mrs. Hope gazed at her son with ever-increased amazement. When he had concluded, she was standing up, apparently speechless, with an ominous frown on her brow. Lady Mary looked with timid anxiety from one to the other. There seemed to be a sweet reasonableness in the young man's argument, and yet something hopelessly wrong about the proposition.

"Five hundred pounds a year!—to me!" cried Mrs. Hope, at last.

"Well—to father, technically—same thing, of course."

"Five hundred a year! Barnard, if anyone had told me an hour ago that you were a fool I—five hundred a year!—how can people exist on five hundred a year?"

Barney looked reproachfully at his mother. He was evidently hurt.

"That's just the way Sartwell talks, and I suppose he thinks I'm a fool, too, merely because I'm trying to understand the labour problem. It seemed to me that if a workman with twelve children to support can live on fifty pounds a year, an elderly pair with but one child, and he about to make a fortune in painting, could get along on ten times that amount."

"Oh, I've no patience with you, Barnard."

"And then, Sartwell says, look at the capital invested——"

"Certainly. He is perfectly right, and anyone with a grain of sense would see that. There are thousands and thousands expended in the buildings and in the development of the business. The workmen never think of that—nor you either, it appears."

"You see, mater, it's out of my line. But what Sartwell said about investment made me think——"

"Think!" exclaimed his mother, with withering contempt.

"Yes," continued Barney, placidly; "so I went to the workmen to see what they had to say about it. They said at once that the capital had been refunded over and over again. I went back to Sartwell to see if this were true, and it was true. Well, then——"

"What then?"

"Under the circumstances it seemed to me that the workmen had made a most magnanimous proposal. If a man would paint a picture for me which I could sell for five hundred pounds and he was content to take fifty for it and leave me the other four hundred and fifty, I should think him the most generous of men."

"Stop talking nonsense, please. Is Sartwell going to receive the men?"

"I suppose so."

"Then you must instantly go back to the city and tell him he is to do nothing of the sort."

"But, mater—" protested the young man. He looked uneasily around the room and saw that Lady Mary had slipped away unperceived.

"Don't talk. You've done enough harm already. Try and undo it."

"But I say! It's rather rough on me, mater. When you promised me a cheque for three hundred, I didn't imagine I would have to see old Sartwell a second time and take back all I said. He would think me an ass then."

"He thinks it already. But it doesn't matter what he thinks. It is what he does that you have to deal with. You must see him at once and stop this nonsense about a conference."

Barney shook his head dolefully.

"I don't see how I can face him again, mater. I'd rather lose the three-hundred-pound cheque."

"The cheque has nothing to do with the question. I should hope you are not attending to this for the three hundred pounds. But I'll write you a cheque for five hundred, if that will satisfy you. Then I hope to hear no more about five hundred a year. Be consistent at least, Barnard."

"Thanks, mater, I'll try. And while you are writing out the cheque I'll have a word with Lady Mary."

"Very well," said his mother, rising. The request did not seem to displease her.

When the young lady came in Barney was wonderfully bright after his long discussion.

"I was afraid I was in the way," said Lady Mary, modestly, "I don't know much about work-people."

"The labour question," said Barney, "is an exceedingly intricate one, and

I'm afraid I don't quite understand it in all its bearings myself; but it's most interesting, I assure you—most interesting. I'm a labouring man myself, now. I've got my studio all fitted upland I work like a—let's see, is it a Turk—or a nigger?"

"I think a nailer is the simile you want."

"Very likely. I don't suppose a Turk works if he can help it. Oh, by the way, Lady Mary, I have 'At Homes' at my studio every Tuesday from three till five. I wish you would come. Get your father to bring you. I want a real live Lord, don't you know, to—well—to give tone to the gathering."

Lady Mary laughed.

"I should like to go very much. I was never in a studio since I had my portrait painted. I'll ask my father, but he doesn't go out very often."

"Oh, I know you can get him to come, so that's a promise."

In the hall his mother handed Barney a cheque.

"Be sure you go at once to Sartwell," she said, "and see that you don't bungle the business a second time."

And yet the poor boy had merely pretended that her former orders had been carried out! Barney made no remark about the inconsistency of woman. He kissed her on both cheeks, as a dutiful son should do, and departed.

## CHAPTER VII.

In almost any other country than England the name by which the evil-smelling cul-de-sac off Light Street was known might be supposed to have been given it by some cynical humourist. It was called Rose Garden Court. As there is a reason for almost everything in this world, the chances are that once upon a time a garden stood there, and that roses probably bloomed in it. The entrance to the court was through an archway, over which, on the Light Street side, was the name of the court. At the right hand of this tunnel stood the "Rose and Crown," locally known as the "pub," and the door of the jug and bottle department opened into the passage, which was convenient for the inhabitants of the court. On the left of the archway there was a second-hand clothing shop, the wares, exceedingly second hand, hanging in tattered festoons about the door.

A street lamp stood at the edge of the pavement, opposite the entrance to the court, and threw its rays under the archway, which somewhat feeble illumination was supplemented by a gas jet over the door of the jug and bottle department. At the blind end of Rose Garden Court stood another lamp post. The court was unevenly paved with large slabs of stone, sloppy, as a rule, from the overflow of a tap which supplied the inhabitants with water.

The court was walled about with five-story buildings, and in the oblong well, formed by these rather dilapidated edifices, the air hung dank and heavy, laden with many smells. Breezes blowing over London from the south, or the north, or the west, produced no movement of the noxious air in Rose Garden Court. "Come out," the gale from the Surrey hills might cry as it whistled merrily over the house-tops; "come out, and give the people a chance to breathe,"—but there was no answering rustle in the court—the air there was silent and sullen, as if it had taken its temper from the inhabitants of the place.

Sometimes, in early spring, the insistent east wind roared boisterously through the tunnel, catching the mephitic atmosphere unawares and flinging it headlong over the roofs, filling the court with a biting whirlwind, scattering loose bits of paper and rags skywards, but the inhabitants of the court didn't like it. They closed their windows, shivered, and wished the gale would cease. Next day the air would settle down quietly in the court, collect its odours once more, and then everybody felt that things were as they should be.

The court was a property that paid handsomely. No one residing there knew who owned the buildings or the ground. The man who collected the room rents did so promptly in advance, and he had once told the landlord of the "Rose and Crown" that the court was more lucrative as an investment than if it had been situated in the Grosvenor Square district. The owner was popularly supposed to have farmed the property to a company, and the rent-collector represented this organization. The company could not be expected to spend money on repairs, the owner could not be reached, and, aside from all that, the rooms were in constant demand; so if a tenant did not like the arrangement he could get out—there were a dozen others ready to take his place.

The people who lived in this human warren were not criminals. Most of them did something useful for the living they received. Criminals, when convicted, are housed in a much more sanitary manner, and they are sure of enough to eat—which the denizens of the court were not. If any prison in the kingdom were as fetid as Rose Garden Court, the great heart of the nation would be stirred with indignation, and some wretch in authority would feel the lash of righteous public scorn. The court was merely fairly representative of the home of the British workingman, in the wisest, largest, proudest, most wealthy city in the world, at the end of the nineteenth century, after a thousand years, more or less, of progress. Some homes of the workingmen are better; but then some are worse, for we must never forget that we have the "artisan's improved dwellings" amongst us. The occupants of the "improved dwellings" are hedged about with restrictions, but in the court was freedom: freedom to come and go as you liked; freedom to get drunk; freedom to loaf or work; freedom to starve.

The personal predilections of the courtites were much the same as those of habitués of first-class West End clubs. They liked to drink and gamble.

The "pub" was at the entrance, and there, or at the barbershop, they could place a little on a horse they knew nothing of. One of the advantages of a free country is that a man can get quite as drunk on beer as he can on champagne, and at a much less cost. The results are wonderfully similar. It is popularly believed that a policeman in Piccadilly is kinder to a client in a dress coat, than a fellow-officer on Waterloo Road is to a man in moleskins.

Rose Garden Court had little trouble with the police, although the court—especially the feminine portion of it—looked somewhat askance at the force. All a policeman asked of a drunken dweller in the court was, that if he wanted to fight he should fight in the court, and not on a busy thoroughfare like Light Street. In the court the wives of the combatants usually took charge of them before the battle had been fought to a finish, and sometimes a tall policeman watched over the separation of temporary foes, saying little unless one of the fighters resisted the wife who was vociferously shoving him towards his own doorway, when the officer would say: "Come now, my man, none of that," whereupon, strangely enough, it was the woman who resented the officer's interference for her protection, though when her man proceeded to abuse a member of the force also, she quickly told him to "shut his ——— mouth," using an adjective that was at once sanguinary and descriptive. Often a stalwart policeman would take by the scruff of the neck an inhabitant of the court staggering along Light Street, filling the air with melody or defiance, and walk him rapidly down the street, the man's legs wobbling about uncertainly, as if he were a waxwork automaton, until they were opposite the entrance of the court; then, having received the required impetus from the officer, the man shot under the archway and was presumably taken care of when he got inside: anyhow, once in the court he could not get out again except by the way he entered, and few ever became drunk enough to forget there was always a policeman in the neighbourhood. The thrust under the archway was merely the kindly Light Street way of doing the Piccadilly act of placing a man tenderly in a cab and telling the driver where to go. Few were ever actually arrested in the Light Street district, and their conduct had to be particularly flagrant to bring upon them this last resort of the force.

Along Light Street came Marsten, with the elastic springy energetic step of a young man in good health, who takes this world seriously and believes there is something to be done in it. He paused for a moment opposite the "Rose and Crown," and nodded to some men who were lounging there.

"Are you going to the meeting to-night, men?" he asked.

One shook his head, another shrugged his shoulders; it was evident at a glance that none of them had any interest in the meeting while the "pub" remained open.

"It's important," said Marsten. "The committee reports to-night, and 'strike or no strike' will likely be put to vote. You are not in favor of a strike, surely? Then come along and vote against it."

"I dunno' 'bout that," said one, removing his pipe. "Strike pay is as good as master's pay, an' less work to get it. I could do with a bit of an 'oliday."

"Strike pay may be as good as master's while it lasts, but it won't last," rejoined Marsten.

"When it gives out we'll go back to work," returned the man. The others laughed.

"Some of you won't get back," said Marsten. "That's always the way after a strike. Better keep a good job while we have it."

"Oh, I could do with a bit of an 'oliday," repeated the spokesman of the "pub" crowd, indifferently.

"My God!" cried Marsten, indignantly, "if you take no more interest in your condition than that, how can you ever expect to better it?"

"Well, I thort," answered the other, good-naturedly, "when I sees you a-comin' along, as 'ow you'd better it by arstin' us to 'ave a drop o' beer with you."

"You're muddled with beer already," said the young man shortly, as he turned and disappeared up the court.

The crowd smoked on in silence for some minutes after he had left them.

"Cocky young feller that," said one at last, jerking his pipe over his shoulder in the direction Marsten had gone.

"Oh, 'e knows a bit, 'e does," remarked another, sarcastically.

There was a longer pause, when the spokesman, who had been ruminating over the matter, said:

"Wot d' ye s'y t' 'avin another pint insoide? Then we go t' th' meetin' and wote for th' stroike. Larn 'im a lesson. I like 'is impidence, I do. Tork 'bout muddlin'; we'll show 'oose muddled."

This was unanimously agreed to as illuminating the situation. It is perhaps a pity that Marsten did not know the result of his brief conversation with his felow-workmen.

He was young and had to learn many things. He did not know that the desire for improving one's condition is not at all universal, and that even where there may be the germ of a desire, people do not wish to be dragooned into bettering themselves. Tact, as Mrs. Hope might have told him, goes farther than good intentions. A drop of beer and a friendly smite on the shoulder would have got him several votes against the strike. As it was, he had merely strengthened the arms of "that ass Gibbons," by making the mistake of supposing that the average human being is actuated by reason.

Meanwhile, the young man had passed under the archway and up the court, until he came to doorway No. 3. The hall, and the five pairs of grimy stairs, were only less public than the court, which in its turn was only less public than Light Street, because fewer feet trod thereon. He ascended the first flight of stairs and paused at one of the doors of the landing. From within came the droning notes of a harmonium, and Marsten forebore to knock as he listened to the sound. A slatternly woman came down the second flight with a water-jug in her hand. She stopped, on seeing a stranger standing there, and listened to the music also. The dirge being played did not soothe whatever savageness there was within the breast of the woman, for she broke out against the inmates of the rooms.

"Oh, yes," she cried. "Fine goin's on for the likes o' them. A harmonyum, if you please. Gawd save us! we ain't good enough for the likes o' 'im. A harmonyum! In Garden Court! No good can come o' 'stravagance like that. Wot's 'e, I'd like to know? Bah!"

The woman, with a wave of her hand, expressed her contempt for such goings on and departed down the stairs with her jug. Her husband spent his spare cash at the "pub," as a man should, and not in such vanities as a second-hand musical instrument. She had, very properly, no patience with extravagance.

Marsten rapped when the playing ceased, and Joe Braunt himself came to the door.

"Come in, my boy," he said cordially, and Marsten went in.

A tall girl, who might have been fourteen, or sixteen, or eighteen, rose from a chair at the harmonium. She was pale and thin, with large pathetic eyes that gave a melancholy beauty to her face. Shaking hands with her,— "How are you, Jessie?" said Marsten. "Is the cough any better?"

"I think it's always about the same," answered the girl.

"It is hard to get better in this hole," said her father, gruffly.

Braunt spoke with the accent of a Yorkshireman. He was a man who in stature and build did credit to his county, and it was "hard to believe that the slender girl was his daughter. However much Joe Braunt's neighbours disapproved of his putting on airs and holding himself and his slim useless daughter above their betters, they took good care not to express their opinions in his hearing, for he was a rough masterful man, taciturn and gloomy, whose blow was readier than his speech; not only prompt, but effective. The whole court was afraid of him, and it acted on the principle of letting sleeping dogs lie. The woman with the jug in her hand had good cause for resentment against Joe Braunt. She had been getting her "man" home one evening from the "pub" with difficulty, and in spite of many breakings away on his part. She had succeeded in pushing and hauling him as far as the first landing, when he, overcome by a sudden realization of her unnecessary cruelty in dragging him from the brilliantly lighted public bar filled with jollity, gin, and good comradeship, to the dismal back room two flights up, with nothing but her own bitter tongue for company, clenched his fist and felled her to the floor, the back of her head striking against Braunt's door as she went down. Braunt, pulling open his door, found the husband walking over—or perhaps it would be more accurate to say, staggering over—the prostrate body of his wife. Joe clutched the drunkard and flung him airily over the landing rail. The ill-used man rolled down the stair and out into the court, where he lay in a heap and groaned. Braunt lifted the woman and carried her up to her room. She had a dazed idea of what had happened, and at once, rather incoherently at first, began to give her rescuer her opinion of him. Who was he, she would like to know, to interfere between man and wife, great strong brute that he was. If her man had been sober he'd have given him what for, takin' advantage of a man wot 'ad a drop too much. Braunt went down stairs and picked up the "pore" man, who had certainly had one drop too much, carried him up, and laid him in his room with his wife.

"You've killed the pore man, as never did no 'arm to you," screamed the wife.

"No such luck," said Braunt; "he's too drunk to hurt."

Which was, indeed, the case. Joe drew the door shut behind him, and left them to fight it out if they wanted to.

Mrs. Scimmins had much sympathy from the court when she related the incident. The women were more indignant than the men. It was a fine state of things if a great, hulking, sulky brute like Braunt was to interfere in little matrimonial discussions that happen in all well-regulated families. Much as they disliked the police, it seemed that now, if ever, their aid should be invoked.

"If he'd tried to break every bone in my man's body, Mrs. Scimmins," said one bulky woman, "I'd 'a 'ad 'im by the 'air."

"I donno 'bout that, Sarah," said Mrs. Scimmins, who did not wish to rest under the imputation of not doing all she could, under the circumstances, for her husband in his comparatively helpless state. "Wot with bein' 'it in the 'ead, an' the face, an' the back, an' then my 'ead strikin' the door; an' one eye as I couldn't see out o', an' yer 'usban' a-tramplin' of yer, yer wouldn't 'ave breath enough to 'ave anybody by the 'air."

Mrs. Scimmins pressed tenderly the bruised and still swollen portion of her face under the eye, and felt that she had made out her case; in fact, her defence was accepted as a strong plea that only made Braunt's inhuman and uncalled for conduct stand out the darker by comparison.

The men were astonished, of course, but not so emphatic in their denunciation of Braunt as the wives had been. Scimmins bore no particular malice against his assailant, although what he had thrown him over the stairs for, he expressed himself as unable to conceive. In answer to sympathetic inquiries from his pals at the public bar of the "Rose and Crown," he informed them that, although shaky, he was still in the ring.

"Gawd 'elp us!" he went on, more in sorrow than in anger, "wot's this world a-comin' to? If you arsts me I gives it up. Wot with Braunt an' the police both on a chap's shoulders, if he raises 'is 'and to 'is own wife, the court's no fit place for a pore 'ard-workin' man to live in."

But nobody ventured to remonstrate with the York-shireman, least of all Scimmins, although the court as a community held more aloof from him than ever.

"Are you coming to the meeting to-night, Mr. Braunt?" asked young Marsten, when he had greeted father and daughter.

"Not me."

"Why not?"

"Why go?"

"Well, you see, Mr. Braunt, there is a crisis on. The committee is to report. Mr. Sartwell has refused to meet them, and this will likely anger Gibbons and the others. Strike or no strike will be put to vote, and I for one don't want to see a strike—at least not just now."

"No more do I," said Braunt.

"Then come on to the meeting and speak up against a strike."

"I'm no speaker. You speak."

"They won't listen to me, but they would pay attention to what you would say."

"Not a bit of it, my lad. But it doesn't matter to me, not a haporth."

"What doesn't? Whether there is a strike or not?"

"I'm not going to strike. They can do as they've a mind."

"But if the Union orders us out we'll have to go."

"Not me."

"Supposing the strike succeeds, as it may—the Union's very strong,—what will you do then?"

"Stick to my work, and mind my own business."

"But the Union won't let you. If the strike fails you'll merely get the ill will of all the men; if it succeeds they'll force you out of the works. There's no use running your head against a brick wall, Mr. Braunt."

"You speak; you've got the gift o' the gab," said Braunt.

"I'm too young. They won't listen to me now. But a day will come when they will—aye, and the masters, too. I'd willingly devote my life to the cause of the workingman."

Marsten spoke with the fire of youthful enthusiasm, and was somewhat disconcerted when the other took his pipe from his mouth and laughed.

"Why do you laugh?"

"I'm laughing at you. I'm glad to know there's some one that believes in us, but as thou says, thou 'art yoong; thou'll know better-later on."

"Don't you believe in yourself and your fellow-workers?"

"Not me. I know 'em too well. By the sweat of thy brow shalt thou earn thy bread. Them's not the right words, happen; but that's the meaning. It has been, is now, and ever shall be. Amen."

"I don't object to that, Mr. Braunt," cried the young man, rising and pacing the floor in his excitement. "Don't think it. But I want to see everybody work. What I object to is earning your bread by the sweat of the hired man's brow, as someone has said. Bless me! look at our numbers. We outnumber the loafers ten to one; yes, a hundred to one in every country in the world. All we need is an unselfish leader."

The elder man looked at him with a quizzical smile on his stern lips.

"Look at the number of the sands on the seaside. Will any leader make a rope out of them? Numbers are nothing, my lad. Take care of yourself, Marsten, and never mind the workers; that's the rule of the world. You may pull yourself up, but you can't lift them with you. They've broken the hearts—aye, and the heads too, of many a one that tried to better them. You think you have only the masters and capital to fight. The masters won't hurt you; it's the men you're fighting for that will down you. Wait till your head is an inch above the crowd, then you'll catch it from the sticks of every rotten one of them that thinks he's got as much right as you have to be in command. It isn't money that helps the masters, it's because they've the sense to know a good man when they see him, and to stand by him when they've got him. Don't be deluded by numbers. What's the good of them? One determined man who doesn't need to bother about his backing—who knows his principals will back him through thick and thin—will beat any mob. Why can a small company of soldiers put down a riot? It's because they're commanded by one man. When he says 'jump,' they jump; when he says 'shoot,' they shoot. That's the whole secret of it."

Braunt resumed his pipe, and smoked vigorously to get back to his usual state of taciturnity. Marsten had never heard him talk so long before, and he stood pondering what had been said. Braunt was the first to speak.

"Play the Dead March, Jessie," he said, gruffly.

The girl hesitated a moment, evidently loath to begin when Marsten was in the room, a slight hectic colour mounting to her cheek: but obedience was strong in her; her father was not a man to be disobeyed. She drew up her chair, and began Chopin's Funeral March, playing it very badly, but still recognizably.

Peace seemed to come over Braunt as he listened to the dirge. He sat back in the chair, his eyes on the ceiling, smoking steadily. Marsten sat down, meditating on what Braunt had said. He was not old enough to have his opinions fixed, and to be impervious to argument, so Braunt's remarks troubled him. He hoped they were not true, but feared they might be. The mournful cadence of the music, which seemed to soothe the soul of the elder man, wound itself among the younger's thoughts, and dragged them towards despair; the indifference of the men in front of the public-house flashed across his memory and depressed him. He wished Jessie would stop playing.

"Ah," said Braunt, with a deep sigh when she did stop. "That's the grandest piece of music ever made. It runs in my head all day. The throb of the machinery at the works seems to be tuned to it. It's in the roar of the streets. Come, my lad, I'll go with you, because you want me to, not that it will do any good. I'll speak if you like, not that they'll care much for what I say—not hearken, very like. But come along, my lad."

## CHAPTER VIII.

Braunt and Marsten passed from the dimness of Rose Garden Court into the brilliancy of Light Street, which on certain nights in the week was like one prolonged fair, each side being lined with heaped-up coster's barrows, radiant with flaring gasoline. Incense was being burned—evil-smelling incense—to the God of Cheapness. Hordes of women, down at the heel, were bargaining with equally impecunious venders—meeting and chaffering on the common level of poverty.

Turning into a side street and then into a narrower lane, the two men came to a huge building where the Salvation Army held its services—a building let temporarily to the employees of Monkton & Hope for the discussion of their grievances. The place was crowded to the doors, and the latest comers had some difficulty in making their way along one side of the walls, nearer the front platform, where they at last found room half way between the doors and the speakers.

Scimmins was in the chair, looking very uneasy and out of place, not knowing exactly what was expected of him, smiling a wan deprecatory smile occasionally as some of his pals in the crowd made audible remarks about his elevation, and the native dignity he brought to bear on his office. One gave it as his opinion ("if you awsked him") that Scimmins would have looked more natural with a pint pot in his right hand, instead of the mallet with which he was supposed to keep order.

On a row of chairs at the back of the platform sat the members of the committee, looking, most of them, quite as uncomfortable as the chairman. Several reporters were writing at a table provided for them. Sometimes one whispered a question to the chairman or a member of the committee, and received the almost invariable answer, "Blest if I know, arsk Gibbons."

Gibbons was quite palpably the man of the hour. He was on his feet by virtue of his position as chairman of the committee and secretary to the

Union, and was just finishing the reading of the committee's report as Braunt and Marsten found standing-room at the side of the hall.

"—And finally your committee begs leave to report that Mr. Sartwell, having rejected all overtures from your committee, refusing to confer with it either through its chairman, or as a body, it was resolved that this report be drawn up and presented to you in order that definite action may be taken upon it."

Gibbons, when he had finished reading the document, placed it upon the reporters' table for their closer inspection. He had drawn up the report himself and was naturally rather proud of the wording, and he hoped to see it printed in the newspapers. He turned to his audience, after saluting the chairman.

"Now, gentlemen, you have heard the report. The committee appointed by you, empowered by you, acting for you, vested in your authority, has done all in its power to bring this matter to an amicable conclusion; It has left no stone unturned, shrunk from no honourable means, spared no trouble, to bring about an understanding fair alike to employer and employee. But, gentlemen, your committee has been met at the very threshold with a difficulty which it could not surmount; a difficulty that has rendered all its efforts abortive. The firm of Monkton & Hope refers the committee to Mr. Sartwell, the manager, and Mr. Sartwell absolutely refuses to see the committee and discuss anything with it. This man, who was once a workman himself, now arrogates——"

Here one of the reporters pulled Gibbons's coat-tail, and a whispered colloquy took place. When it was over, Gibbons continued: "A gentleman of the press has asked me a question—and a very proper question it is. He asks if we threatened Mr. Sartwell in any way with a strike, as has been rumoured. Gentlemen, no threats of any kind whatever have been used." (Cheers.) "We have approached Mr. Sartwell with the same deference that we would have approached a member of Her Majesty's Government if we had a petition to present. The sum and substance of the whole business is that Mr. Sartwell absolutely refuses to treat with his own men when they have——"

"That is not true," said a voice, from the side of the hall.

The crowd turned their heads towards the sound, noticeably gleeful at the interruption. It promised liveliness ahead. There was a murmur of pleasurable anticipation. Gibbons turned sharply towards the point from which the voice came.

"What is not true?" he demanded.

"It's not true that Mr. Sartwell refuses to see his own men."

"Are you one of them?"

"Yes. Are you?"

There was a rustle of intense enjoyment at this palpable hit at Gibbons. The glib speaker himself was taken aback by the retort, but only for a moment.

"I thought," continued the secretary, "that it might have been some one sent here to interrupt this meeting. This may still be the case, but we will waive that point. We will not follow Mr. Sartwell's example, and if there is any friend of his present we shall be pleased to hear from him at the proper time. As I was about to say when I was int——"

"I answered your question; answer mine," cried the voice.

Gibbons glanced appealingly at the Chair for protection, and Scimmins rapped feebly with his gavel on the table in front of him, saying, "Order, order," but in a tone that he apparently hoped nobody would hear.

"What is your question?" asked Gibbons, with an angry ring in his voice.

"Are you an employee of Monkton & Hope?"

"I am secretary of the Union of which that firm's men are a part, and I may add, the strongest Union in London. I am chairman of this committee, composed of that firm's men. I did not seek the position, but was unanimously elected to it; therefore I claim that practically I am an employee of Monkton & Hope, and that no man here has a better right to speak for those employees—aye, or to stand up for them against oppression—than I have. And I will tell the man who interrupts me—I'll tell him to his face—that I am not to be brow-beaten from the path of duty, by him, or by Mr. Sartwell either, as long as I retain the confidence of the men who put me here. I acknowledge no other masters. If you want to address this meeting, come up here on the platform and face it like a man, and not stand barking there like a dog. Let's have a look at you."

There was wild cheering at this. The fight was on, and the crowd was jubilant. This was the kind of talk they liked to hear.

Braunt smote young Marsten on the back and pushed him forward.

"Take oop the challenge, lad," he cried. "Oop wi' ye. I'll follow ye, and give them some facts about the unemployed. We've got this meeting if we work it right. Oop wi' ye, mate."

Marsten went toward the platform, the crowd making way for him. Gibbons stood for a moment apparently surprised at this unexpected opposition, then walked back to his chair at the head of the committee. The good-natured gathering cheered when they saw the young man standing before them.

"Fellow-workingmen—" he began.

"Address the Chair," admonished some one in the middle of the hall, whereat there was a laugh. Scimmins himself indulged in a sickly smile. The speaker reddened slightly, and in confused haste said:

"Mr. Chairman and fellow-workers——"

The crowd cheered lustily, and it was some moments before Marsten could again get a hearing. A feeling of despair came over him as he stood before them. It was only too evident that they all looked upon the whole proceeding as a great lark, something in the way of a music-hall entertainment without the beer,—which was a drawback of course; but also without any charge for admission,—which was an advantage, for it left so much more cash to expend in stimulants after the fun was over. He wondered, as he looked at the chaffing jocular assemblage, whether he was taking too serious a view of the situation. There flashed across his mind a sentence he had heard in a lecture on socialism. "It is not the capitalist nor the government you have to conquer," the lecturer had said, "but the workmen themselves."

When the disorder had subsided so that his voice could be heard, Marsten went on:

"Mr. Gibbons asserted that the manager had refused to consult with his employees, and I claimed that such a statement was not true. Mr. Sartwell told me himself that he was willing to receive a deputation from the men of the works. He said——"

"What's that?" cried Gibbons, springing to his feet and taking a step forward.

"Don't interrupt the speaker," shouted Braunt, from the body of the hall.

"He interrupted me," roared Gibbons, now thoroughly angry. Turning to the young man who stood there silently, waiting for statement and retort to cease, the secretary demanded:

"When did Sartwell tell you that?"

"On Tuesday night."

"On Tuesday night!" repeated Gibbons, coming to the front of the platform. "On Tuesday night! and you have the brazen cheek to stand here and admit it."

"Why shouldn't I?" asked Marsten, with perceptible self-control, but whitening around his tightened lips.

"Why shouldn't you? I'll tell you why. Because you sneaked in behind the backs of the committee you had helped to appoint. That's why."

"I had no hand in appointing the committee."

"Every man in the works had a hand in appointing the committee. If you didn't vote, then you neglected your duty. If you voted against the committee, you were bound by the result just as the committee would have been bound, if they had been defeated. That's trade unionism—stand together or fall together. You, knowing a committee had been appointed to deal with this very business, must go crawling to Sartwell, and undermine the work of your fellow-unionists."

"That's a lie!" hissed Marsten, through his set teeth, in a low but intense tone of voice which was heard to the further end of the hall. The young man strode toward his antagonist, his right hand nervously clinching and unclinching. It was an electric moment,—the crowd held its breath. They expected the next move would be a blow.

Gibbons stood his ground without flinching. Not a muscle of his face moved except his eyelids, which partially closed over his eyes, leaving a slit through which a steely glance shot at Marsten; but his answer was not so truculent as his look.

"If it's a lie," he said calmly, to the evident disappointment of his hearers, "then the lie is not mine. I was merely putting your own statements in a little terser language; that's all."

Braunt, who had with difficulty kept his hot temper in hand during this colloquy on the stage, now roared at the top of his voice:

"Give t' lad a chance to speak and shut your silly mouth. He's called you a liar like a man and you daren't take him oop like a man. Sit down, you fool!"

"I must really ask the protection of the Chair," protested the secretary, turning to Scimmins. The latter, feeling that something was expected of him, rose rather uncertainly to his feet, and struck the table three or four times with his mallet.

"Order, order!" he cried. "If there is any more disturbance down there, the man will be put out of the meeting.

"What!" shouted Braunt. "Put me out! Egod! I'll give 'ee th' chance."

The big man made his way toward the platform, brushing aside from his path a few who, in the interests of law and order, endeavoured to oppose him. The majority of those present, however, were manifestly of opinion that the progress of the angry man should not be barred, so they cheered his intervention and made encouraging remarks.

Braunt sprang upon the platform, advanced to the chair, smote his clinched fist on the table, and cried:

"Here I am, Scimmins. Now put me out; d'ye hear?"

He paused for a reply, but there was none. Scimmins, shrinking from him, obviously prepared for flight if Braunt attempted to storm the position. The Yorkshireman glared about him, but those on the platform appeared to think that the time for protest had not yet arrived. Meanwhile, the audience was calling loudly for a speech.

"I haven't much to say, mates," began Braunt, calming down through lack of opposition, "and I'm no man at the gab. I'm a worker, and all I want is a chance to earn my bread. But I'll say this: I saw in t' papers not so long ago that there's twenty-seven thousand men of our trade out of work in England today. Twenty-seven thousand men anxious for a job. Now what is this man Gibbons asking you to do? He's asking you to chook up your jobs and have your places taken by some of them twenty-seven thousand. Sartwell has only to put an advertisement in the papers, and he can fill the shops five times over in two days. It's always easier to chook oop a job than to get a new one these times. I know, because I've tried it. So have most of you. Take my advice, and go no further with this nonsense. If Sartwell, as Mar-sten says, is willing to talk over grievances, then I say let us send him a deputation of our own men, with no outsiders among 'em. What's the Union done for us? Taken our money every week, that's all I can see. And now they have got so much of it they want to squander it fighting a strong man like Sartwell."

Marsten had sat down on the edge of the platform. We are always quicker to perceive the mistakes of others than to recognize our own, and he did not like Braunt's talk against the Union. He felt that it would be unpopular, besides he believed in the Union if it were properly led. His fight was against Gibbons, not against the organization.

Gibbons was in his chair, and he had rapidly taken the measure of the speaker. He saw that the address was having its effect, and that the crowd was slipping away from his control. It was a risky thing to do with such a powerful man, but he made up his mind that Braunt must be angered, when he would likely, in his violence, lose all the ground he had gained. So Gibbons quietly, with his eye, gathered up his trusty henchmen, who were scattered in different parts of the hall to give an appearance of unanimity to the shouting when the proper time came, and these men had now gradually edged to the front during the speaking. One or two had silently mounted the platform and held a whispered conference with the secretary, after which they and some others took their places behind the seated committee. When Sartwell was alluded to, Gibbons arose.

"Mr. Chairman," he said, "I cannot allow——"

Braunt turned on him like a raging lion.

"Don't you interrupt me," he cried, rolling up his sleeves, "or I'll bash you through that window."

"Order, order!" said the chairman, faintly.

"Yes, an' you atop o' him!" shouted the infuriated man. "I've done it before."

"Respect the meeting, if you have no regard for the Chair," said Gibbons, calmly.

"You talk to us as if we were a parcel of fools," cried a man in front. Braunt, like a baited bull, not knowing in which direction to rush, turned his eyes, blazing with rage, upon the last speaker. He shook his clenched fist and bared arm at the audience.

"What else are you?" he roared, at the top of his voice. "A parcel o' dommed fools, all o' ye. Led by the nose by a still bigger fool than any o' ye. Yes; a set o' chattering idiots, that's what ye are, with not enough brains among the lot o' ye to turn a grindstone. I know ye, a beer-sodden gang, with just enough sense to see that your pint mug's full."

By this time those in the hall were in a state of exasperation bordering on frenzy. A small door, to the right of the stage, connecting with an alley, had been opened, and a number of the more timid, seeing a storm impending, had quietly slipped out. The meeting was now a seething mob, crying for the blood of the man who stood there defying them and heaping contumely upon it.

Gibbons, his lips pale but firm, took a step forward. "We have had enough of this," he said. "Get off the platform!"

Braunt turned as if on a pivot, and rushed at the secretary. The latter stepped nimbly back, and one of his supporters, with a running jump and hop, planted his boot squarely in Braunt's stomach. The impetus was so great, and the assault so sudden and unexpected, that Braunt, powerful as he was, doubled up like a two-foot rule, and fell backward from the platform to the floor. Instantly a dozen men pounced upon him, and hustled him, in spite of his striking out right and left, through the open door into the alley. The door was closed and bolted in the twinkling of an eye—Braunt outside and his assailants within. It was all so neatly and so quickly done, that the police, who had been on the alert for some time, only reached the spot when the door was bolted. The crowd, with but the vaguest general notion of what had happened, beyond the sudden backward collapse of Braunt, raised a wild cheer for which Gibbons was thankful. He did not wish them to know that Braunt had been taken in hand by the police outside, and he had been very anxious, if an arrest were inevitable, that it should not take place in the hall, for then even Braunt's violent tirade would not have prevented universal sympathy turning towards him. While the cheer was ringing up to the roof, Gibbons had heard a terrific blow delivered against the door, a blow that nearly burst in the bolt and made the faces of those standing near turn pale. Another crashing hit shattered the panel and gave a glimpse for one moment of bleeding knuckles. Then there was an indication of a short sharp struggle in the alley, and all was quiet save the reverberating echo of the cheer.

Gibbons strode to the front of the platform, and held up his hand for silence.

"I am very sorry," he said, "that the last speaker made some remarks which ought not to have been made, but let us all remember that hard words break no bones. However, there has been enough talk for one night, and it is time to proceed to business. Gentlemen, you have heard the report of the committee—what is your pleasure?"

"I move," said a man, rising in the middle of the hall, "that we go on strike."

"I second that motion," cried several voices.

"Put the motion," whispered Gibbons to the bewildered chairman.

Scimmins rose to his feet.

"You have all heard the motion," he said. "All in favour say aye."

A seemingly universal shout of "Aye" arose. The chairman was on the point of resuming his seat when Gibbons, in a quick aside, said: "Contrary."

"All to the contrary," called out the chairman, hovering between sitting and standing.

There was no dissent, for Marsten had left to see what had become of his friend, and the timorous men had stolen away when they detected signs of disturbance.

"Motion's carried," said Scimmins, seating himself with every indication of relief.

"Unanimously," added Gibbons loudly, unable to conceal his satisfaction with the result.

## CHAPTER IX.

There are streets in Chelsea practically abandoned to studios. Long low buildings of one story, with many doors in front, and great broadsides of windows at the back, multipaned windows letting in from the north the light that artists love, lined these thoroughfares which Barney in his jocular off-hand manner called "aurora borealis" streets, because, as he always explained, they were so full of "northern lights." Such studios were all very well for the ordinary everyday artist who exhibited at the Royal Academy and places of that sort; but a painter with a soul (and, incidentally, a reliable bank account) desired something better than one of these barns, so Barney had taken a house and fitted it up to meet his requirements. Craigenputtoch House, as Barney called it in tardy recognition of the genius of Thomas Carlyle, was a building of three stories, standing back from the street in grounds of its own. The rooms on the upper floor were allowed to remain as they were, and gave Barney bedrooms for himself and his friends; his hospitality being unique and unlimited. All the partitions on the first floor had been torn away, so that this portion of the house was formed into one vast apartment, with the exception of a space for a noble landing, up to which, in dignified manner befitting a temple of art, arose a broad flight of stone steps that replaced the ordinary wooden stairway which had contented the former occupants of the house. To afford the support necessary for the upper floor, now that the partitions were taken away, huge square beams of timber had been put in, and these gave the ceiling of the roomy studio that barn roof appearance so necessary to the production of works of the higher art.

Barney's mother objected to the bare coldness of the uncovered stone stairs. Being inside the house, she said, and not the steps that led to the front door, they should have a carpet on them. Barney admitted that under ordinary circumstances this was so, and willingly offered to make a certain concession should the occasion arise. If Royalty visited him, he would put down the customary red carpet which the feet of Royalty were in the habit of treading. In fact, he admitted to his mother that a roll of red carpet had already been purchased, and was at that moment in the closet under the stairs, to be ready at a moment's notice. But for every-day wear the steps should remain uncovered, because the stone stairways of the Pitti Palace were always bare, and as Barney intended ultimately to make Craigenputtoch House quite as celebrated in the world of art as the Florentine gallery, he would follow its precedent so far as stairs were concerned. There is nothing like beginning right.

On the ground floor were dining-room and kitchen, below that a well-filled cellar. The hall was toned a rich Pompeiian red, and was lit by two windows of brilliant stained glass which had been put in when the building was transformed from a residence into a studio. "Oh, yes," Barney would say, when he was complimented on these windows. "They are all very well in their way, but not original, don't you know, not original. No, they are simply nicely executed copies of a portion of a window in Cologne Cathedral done in 1508. I placed them there temporarily, because I have been so busy that I have not had time to design anything better myself, which I shall do later on, don't you know."

But of all the ornamental appendages to this studio, perhaps the most striking was Barney's "man," attired in a livery of blue, crimson, and silver, which was exceedingly effective. Although Barney had not had time to design a stained-glass window which would excel those of Cologne, he had been compelled to sketch out this livery, for it was not a thing that one could copy from abroad, and the Hope family had not been established long enough to have a recognized livery of its own. Nothing gives character and dignity to a place so much as a "man" sumptuously fitted out in a style that is palpably regardless of cost, and if it may be plainly seen that the "man" performs no needful function whatever, then is the effect heightened, for few human beings attain the apex of utter inutility. The great hotels of this country recognize the distinction reflected upon them by the possession of a creature of splendour at their doors, who grandly wafts the incoming guests with a hand-wave towards the hall. But these persons of embellishment often demean themselves by opening the doors of cabs and performing other useful acts, thus detracting from their proper function, which was, Barney insisted, to content themselves with being merely beautiful.

When a visitor once complained that the man at the top of the stair had refused to direct him into the studio, Barney laid his right hand in friendly brotherliness on the visitor's shoulder, and said:

"He knew, dear boy, that I would discharge him instantly if he so far forgot himself as to answer a question."

"Then what is he there for?" asked the visitor, with some indignation. "I don't see the use of him."

"Quite so, quite so," answered Barney, soothingly. "If you did, I would have to get rid of him and engage another, and, I can assure you, that perfectly useless persons six feet two in height are not to be picked up on every street corner. No, dear boy, they are not, I give you my word. People are so unthinking that they will ask foolish questions. I intend to discourage this habit as much as possible. You want to know what he is there for? Now if I had placed a marble statue at the top of the stair, you would not have been offended if it did not answer your query, don't you know, and you would not have asked what it was there for, don't you know. There are so many useful things in this world that something untainted with utilitarianism ought to be welcomed by every thinking man, and if this deplorably proficuous country is ever to be redeemed, we artists must lead the way, don't you see."

The grand individual at the head of the stair had his uses, nevertheless; for when Haldiman and another, accepting Barney's effusively cordial invitations to attend one of his "At Homes," entered-the hall below, and saw this magnificent person standing like a resplendent statue before and above them, Haldiman gasped, "Great Heavens!" and groped his way out on the pavement again, followed by the no less astounded other, who was an artist also struggling along in the black and white line. The two exchanged glances when at a safe distance from the studio, pausing as they did so. Their amazement was almost too great for words, yet Haldiman remarked solemnly:

"I might have expected something of that sort. Imagine us dropping in there in these clothes! Lucky escape! I know a place on the King's Road where there are fluids to drink. Let us go there and see if we can recover from this blow. O Barney, Barney, what deeds are done in thy name!"

So the living statue silently warned off Barney's two Bohemian friends, who are all right in Paris, don't you know, but not at all desirable when a man settles down to serious work and expects nobility at his receptions.

The calm dignity of Barney's "man" was offset in a measure by the energetic activity of the boy in buttons who threw open the door with a flourish. "Buttons" might be likened to a torpedo boat, darting hither and thither under the shadow of a stately ironclad. While the left hand of the small boy opened the door, the right swept up to his cap in a semi-military salute that welcomed the coming and sped the parting guest.

It would be difficult to imagine a room more suitable for an artistic function like Barney's "At Homes" than Barney's studio. The apartment was large, and it contained many nooks and crannies that the Tottenham Court Road furnisher had taken excellent advantage of. There were neat little corners for two; there were secluded alcoves fitted with luxurious seats; there were most alluring divans everywhere, and on the floor were the softest of Oriental rugs. Eastern lamps shed a subdued radiance over retired spots that otherwise would have been dark, and wherever a curtain could hang, a curtain was hung. Barney's most important works, framed in gold and silver or the natural wood, were draped effectively, and to prevent the non-artistic mind from making a fool of itself by guessing at the subject, the name of each picture stood out in black letters on the lower part of the frame. There were "Battersea Bridge at Midnight," "Chelsea in a Fog," "Cheyne Row at Three A. M.," and other notable works, while one startling picture of the Thames in crimson and yellow showed Barney's power to accomplish a feat, which, if we may trust a well-known saying, has been tried by many eminent men, but has been rendered unsuccessful by the incombustible nature of that celebrated river.

Barney's "afternoon" was at its height, when the bell was rung by a young man who had not received a card; but "Buttons" did not know that, and he swung open the door with a florid flourish as if the visitor had been a duke. The incomer was as much taken aback by the triumph of nature and art at the head of the stair as Haldiman had been, but although he paused for a moment in wonder, he did not retreat. He had a vague notion for an instant that it might be Barney himself, but reflection routed that idea. He was entering a world unfamiliar to him, but his common sense whispered that the inhabitants of this world did not dress in such a fashion.

"Is Mr. Barnard Hope at home?" he asked.

"Yessir," answered the boy, with a bow and a wave of his hand. "This is his day. What name, sir?"

"Marsten."

"Mr. Marsten," shouted the boy up the stair.

The decorated sphinx at the top was uninfluenced by the announcement, but a less resplendent menial appeared, who held back the heavy curtains as Marsten mounted the stair, and, when he entered, his name was flung ahead of him upon the murmur of conversation within. The sight that met Marsten's eye as he entered the studio was rather disconcerting to a diffident man, but he was relieved to notice, after a moment's breathless pause beyond the threshold, that nobody paid the slightest attention to him.

The large room seemed bewilderingly full of people, and a row of men were standing with their backs against the wall, as if they were part of the mural decoration. Many of them held tea-cups in their hands, and all of them looked more or less bored. The divans and chairs had been arranged in rows, as if for the viewing of some spectacle, and every seat was taken, most of the occupants being ladies. Two men-servants were handing around tea and cake, while Barney himself flitted hither and thither like a gigantic butterfly in a rose garden, scattering geniality and good-humour wherever he went. The steady hum of conversation was brightened constantly by silvery laughter. It was evident that the gathering, with the possible exception of that part of it standing pensively around the walls, was enjoying itself.

As the throng slowly resolved into units before the gaze of young Marsten, his heart suddenly stopped, and then went on again at increased speed, as he recognized Edna Sartwell sitting on one of the front chairs, smiling at some humorous remark which Barney, leaning over her, was making. A moment before, Marsten had been conquering his impulse to retreat, by telling himself that all these idle persons were nothing to him; but now, when he had recognized one person who was everything to him, he had to quell his rising panic with a new formula. Although out of his depth and ill at ease, he knew that he would not quit the field in a fright before the task he had set himself was even begun. At the back of his nature there was a certain bull-dog obstinacy, the limitations of which had never yet been tested, although this unexpected meeting with a number of his fellow-creatures in an evidently higher social station than his own put a severe strain upon his moral courage. In vain he told himself that he was as good as any of them; for in his heart he did not believe that he was, so the assurance was of little value to him. Finally, he took his courage in his hand, and spoke to the servant who had held aside the curtains for him.

"Would you tell Mr. Hope that I wish to speak with him for a moment?"

Barney approached the new-comer with smiling face and extended hand.

"Oh, how-de-do, how-de-do? I am so glad you found time to come to my little affair. You are just in time—just in time, don't you know."

Barney's artistic eye rapidly took in the appearance of his guest, and all at once he realized that his clothes had not quite the air of Bond Street about them, in spite of the fact that they were flagrantly the best suit his visitor had. The smile faded from the artist's face.

"Oh, pardon me!" he added. "I thought I recognized you, but I don't think I've had the pleasure of——"

"No. We are not acquainted, Mr. Hope. I am one of the workmen in your father's factory."

"Really. You have some message for me, perhaps?"

"I came of my own motion. I wished very particularly to speak with you on business."

"Oh, but really, my good fellow, don't you know! This is my 'At Home' day. I never talk business on these days, never. If you want to buy any of my pictures, or anything, don't you know, you must come another day."

"I did not come about pictures, but about something vastly different and more serious."

"My good fellow—you'll excuse my interrupting you, won't you? There is no serious business except art, and to-day I don't even talk art."

"Human lives," said Marsten, hotly, "are more serious than art."

"Please don't raise your voice. You are certainly wrong about things, but I haven't time to correct you to-day, don't you know. All one needs to say about your last remark is that human lives are ephemeral, while art is everlasting Therefore is art the more important of the two. But we'll let that pass. Can't you come and talk another day? I'm sure I shall be delighted to see you at any time."

"Couldn't you give me five minutes out on the landing?"

"It is impossible. I cannot leave my guests. You see, we have the dancing Earl on in a few moments. His Grace is just now arranging his skirts. I really must go, don't you know."

"Then I will stay until the Earl has done his dancing, if that is what he is here for."

"Do, my dear fellow, do. A most excellent idea. I am sure you will like it, for though I have not seen the dance myself, I understand it is quite unique. Have a cup of tea. I would have sent you a card, if I had thought that any of my father's workmen were interested in the latest movements of art; but never mind the lack of invitation. If you care to stay without it, I shall be delighted. It is really very good of you to drop in, in this unexpected way; it is the kind of thing I like, so Bohemian, don't you know. You'll excuse me now, I'm sure," and Barney tripped away to see that all arrangements for the appearance of the Earl were complete.

The model-stand had been pushed to one end of the room fronting the audience; heavy curtains had been drawn across the big north window, leaving the place in semi-darkness; there was the hissing and sputtering of a lime-light in the gallery, causing inquisitive people to turn their heads and see what it was.

Marsten stood against the wall beside another man, who said to him in a weary tone:

"Who is this man, Barnard Hope?"

"He is an artist," answered Marsten, astonished that one guest should question a stranger regarding their mutual host.

"Evidently," replied the other "But who are his people, or has he any?

"His father is one of the richest manufacturers in London."

"Egad, I was sure of it. I knew there was a shop somewhere in the background, the fellow is so beastly civil."

Conversation was here interrupted by a figure leaping on the model-stand, while at the same instant a blinding white light was thrown from the gallery upon it. There was a ripple of applause and the Earl, a beardless youth of perhaps twenty, bowed. He looked like a girl in his clinging fluted skirts. He was a scion of an ancient noble family, founded by an affectionate dancer of the opposite sex in the reign of the second Charles, and it was quite in the regular order of things that there should be a recrudescence of terpsichorean ability in the latest member of the house.

The white light changed to red and the skirt dance began. As it went on it was received with tumultuous applause, for a London audience is always easy to please, especially when there is no charge for admission at the doors. Still it must be admitted that the sprightly little Earl deserved the warmth of his reception, for his exhibition was a model of grace and agility, while his manipulation of the voluminous skirts left little to be desired. The variegated colours thrown on the fluttering whirling drapery gave a weird unearthly effect to the rapid movements of his Grace, and the grand finale, where a crimson light was flung upon the flimsy silk waving high above the dancer's head, gave the agile young nobleman the appearance of one of the early martyrs wrapped in flames.

The curtains were drawn back, the entranced assemblage rose to its feet, and, gathering about the host, congratulated him upon the success of his afternoon. Barney received these felicitations with exuberant gratification, and the young Earl, finally emerging from behind the scenes, clothed and in his right mind, but a trifle breathless, accepted modestly his well-earned share of the compliments, for, let cynics say what they will, true merit is always sure of appreciation in the great city.

Edna Sartwell lingered for a moment on the outskirts of the throng that pressed around Barney and the little Earl, then leisurely made her way towards the door, waiting for her step-mother, who lingered to thank her host. The men who had stood along the wall were already in the street, and the other visitors had nearly all departed.

Marsten stood alone where he was when the entertainment was going on, gazing with beating heart at the girl he loved. She came slowly towards him, her head averted, watching her step-mother standing in the fast thinning group about Barney. There was a certain unconsciousness about her movements, as if the young man had hypnotized her, and was drawing her to him by mere force of will. At last her skirts touched him and his nerves tingled to his finger ends. Almost involuntarily, he murmured:

"Miss Sartwell."

The girl turned her head quickly, and for a moment met his gaze without recognizing him.

"My name is Marsten," he said huskily, seeing she did not know him. "I met you the other evening at your fathers office, when he and I were talking of the strike."

"Oh, yes," she replied; "at first I did not remember you. I—I did not expect to——" She paused and seemed confused, looking away from him.

"To find me here," said the young man, completing the sentence for her, and gathering courage as the delightful fact that he was actually talking to her impressed its almost unbelievable reality upon him. "I did not know there was anything like this going on. I came to consult with Mr. Hope on the same subject——" He flushed as the memory of one subject arose in his mind, and he felt his newly acquired courage beginning to ebb again. He pulled himself together and ended lamely, "—about the strike, you know."

"Oh," said Edna, instantly interested. "Is there anything new about the strike?"

"Yes; there was a meeting last night, and it was unanimously resolved to quit work."

The colour left the girl's cheeks.

"And are the men out? Is that why you are here to-day?"

"No; they do not go out until Saturday. I did what I could to prevent it, but without success. I applied to your father for this afternoon off, and he gave it to me without asking any questions. It seemed to me that in the few intervening days before the men go out, something might be done, when the enthusiasm of the meeting had died down. That's why I came, but I'm afraid there is not much to look for here."

"Does father know?"

"About the strike? Oh, yes."

The girl's winsome face clouded with apprehension. "I am so sorry," she said, at last. "I am sure it is not father's fault, for he is kind to every one. Even if he is sometimes severe"—she cast a shy upward glance at the young man that made his heart beat faster—"he is always just."

"Yes, I know that is true. He will beat the men, and that is the reason I want moderate counsels to prevail. The workingman is always the under dog. Most of his mouthing friends are fools, and he himself is the greatest fool of all."

"Don't you think you are a little hard on the workingman? Were you here in time to see the dancing Earl?"

She looked at him with a frank smile, and Marsten smiled in company with her—it brightened his face wonderfully, and established an evanescent bond of comradeship between them.

"I had forgotten the Earl," he said.

"I must go now. I see my step-mother looking for me. I hope you will be successful in averting trouble at the works."

She extended her hand to him and he took it tenderly, fearing he might grasp it too closely and betray himself.

Mrs. Sartwell and her step-daughter were the last to go.

Barney threw himself on a divan and lit a cigarette.

"Well, my young friend, here we are alone at last. Help yourself to the cigarettes and allow me to offer you something stronger than the tea with which we regale the ladies. We have several shots in the locker, so just name your particular favourite in the way of stimulant while I order a B and S for myself. You might not believe it, but one of these afternoons takes it out of a fellow more than a day's work at the factory. Not that I ever indulged in factory work myself, but I think you said it was in your line."

"Yes," said Marsten, after declining the offerings of his host. "It is about the factory I wish to speak with you. The men resolved last night to go out on strike."

"Foolish beggars."

"I quite agree with you. Their action is worse than foolish—that is why I came to see if you would intervene in any way so that a better state of feeling might be brought about."

"Well, now—let's see, I believe I have forgotten your name, or did you tell me? Ah, Marsten—thanks—so many things on my mind, don't you know. You see, Mr. Marsten, it's really no business of mine, although I must admit that your offer of the position of arbitrator flatters me. This makes twice I have been asked within a few days, so I think I must really be a born diplomat, don't you know. But you see, there's nothing I enjoy so much as minding my own business, and this strike is no affair of mine."

"I think it is. All the luxury you have here is surely earned by the men I am now speaking for."

"My dear fellow, you are not in the least flattering now; you are not, I assure you. You are saying in other words that my pictures do not sell."

"I had no intention of hinting anything of the kind. I have no doubt you can sell anything you paint."

"Ah, you are commending the artistic discernment of the British Public which—at present—is an honour the B. P. does not deserve. It will come round ultimately—the great B. P. always does—but not yet, my boy, not yet. Give it time, and it will pour cash in your lap. I regret that the moment—how shall I put it?—well, up to date, has not arrived. The workmen whom you honour by associating with, at present supply—as with perhaps unnecessary bluntness you state it—the financial deficiency. But the public will pay for it all in the end—every penny of it, my boy. You see these pictures around the walls? Very well; I hold them at two thousand pounds each. I find little difficulty in so holding them, for no section of the great British Public has, up to the present time, evinced any dogged desire to wrench them from me in exchange for so much gold. What is the consequence? I shall increase the price five hundred pounds every year, and the longer they hold off, the bigger sum they will have to pay, and serve them jolly well right, say I. Ten pictures twenty thousand pounds—this year. Next year twenty-five thousand pounds, and so on. With property on my hands increasing at that rate, I should be an idiot to urge people to buy. Ground rents in Belgravia are not in it with my pictures as investments. So you see, Mars-ten, when my day comes, the factory will be a mere triviality as an income producer compared with my brush, don't you know."

"But in the meantime?"

"In the meantime, I am getting along very nicely, thank you. The strike will not affect me in the least. The men may have to diminish the amount of shag or whatever awful mixture they smoke, but I shall not consume one cigarette the less. I have done nothing to bring on this struggle. If the men want to fight, then, by jingo! let them, say I."

"The fight is not yet actually on and won't be until Saturday. Now is the time for a cool-headed man to interfere and bring about an amicable understanding. Won't you at least make the attempt, Mr. Hope?"

"My dear Marsten, the way of the self-appointed arbitrator is hard. I was reading in this morning's paper about your charming meeting, last night, and I noticed that one man who interfered was kicked off the platform and thrown out into a side street. That is the workingman's idea of how an intellectual discussion should be terminated. I love the workingman myself, but I sometimes wish he would not argue with his hob-nailed boot. By the way, did you see this interesting episode? You were there, I suppose?"

"Yes. Braunt, who was kicked out, is one of the best workmen in the factory, but very hot-tempered. He lost control of himself last night, under strong provocation, and when he was outside tried to batter in the door. The police interfered, and he knocked down three of them. This was disastrous, for he was fined five pounds this morning, and I have been trying to raise the money so that he need not go to prison; but we are in the minority—he exasperated our fellow-workmen—and I am not getting on well with the subscription list."

Barney sprang to his feet.

"Knocked down three, did he? Goodman. That's something like. It's a most deplorable trait in my character that I somehow enjoy an assault on the police, and yet I recognize the general usefulness of the force. Five pounds did you say? Then there will be the costs; I don't understand much about these things, but I believe there are usually costs, on the principle of adding insult to injury, I suppose. Will a ten-pound note see him through? Good. Here it is. Three-pound-odd a policeman is not expensive when you think how much some of the luxuries here below cost, don't you know. No thanks, Marsten, I beg of you; it's a pleasure, I assure you."

As Marsten took the money a servant came in and said in a low voice: "Simpson wants to know if he may go, sir."

"Bless me, yes. I thought he had gone long ago. Simpson is my ornamental six-footer at the head of the stair; perhaps you noticed him as you came in. Poor fellow, he's not allowed to do anything but stand there and look pretty, so I suppose it gets wearisome. Imagine such boy-stood-on-the-burning-deck devotion at this end of the nineteenth century! I had forgotten him, absorbed in your interesting conversation. Well, Marsten, I'm sorry I can't arbitrate, but drop in again, and let me know how things go on. Good afternoon!"

## CHAPTER X.

On Saturday the men took their well-earned pay, one by one, and went out of the gates quietly, if sullenly. During the days that had intervened between the meeting and the strike, neither side had made advances to the other. If Sartwell had prepared for the struggle, these preparations had been accomplished so secretly that Gibbons failed to learn of them. The secretary of the Union issued a manifesto to the press, setting forth the position of the men in temperate phrase that had the effect of bringing public sympathy largely to the side of the workers. It was an admirable document, and most of the papers published it, some of them editorially regretting the fact that in this enlightened country and this industrial age, some hundreds of men, the bone and sinew of the land, willing to work, were forced to go into the streets in protest against a tyranny that refused even to discuss their alleged wrongs. The newspapers pointed out that whether their grievances were just or not was beside the question; as the point was that the manager had refused to see a deputation, and this high-handed conduct the papers expressed themselves as forced to deplore.

Both members of the firm thought this manifesto should be answered. The manager did not agree with them, so it was not answered.

Pickets were placed before the gates, and a few extra policemen appeared, as if by accident, in the neighbourhood; but there was nothing for either policemen or pickets to do. On Monday, some of the men lounging around the place looked up at the tall chimneys, and saw them, for the first time during their remembrance, smokeless. They had never noticed the smoke before, but now its absence created an unexpected void in the murky outlook. It was as if the finger of death had touched those gaunt lofty stacks, and the unusual silence of the place the men had always known to be so busy seemed to give the situation a lonely feeling of solemnity they had not looked, for.

On Tuesday some dray-loads of new machinery arrived at the works, and these the pickets attempted to stop, but without success. Gibbons was consulted, but he took a sensible and liberal view of the matter.

"Let them put in all the new machinery they wish. That will mean employment for more men when we go back. We will not interfere with Sartwell until he tries to fill the works with other employees."

For the remainder of the week the shops echoed with the clang of iron on iron, but no smoke came out of the tall chimneys.

"Call this a fight?" said one of the men, over his mug of beer. "I call it a bean-feast."

On Saturday, strike pay was given out at headquarters, each man getting his usual wage, for the Union was rich. It was indeed a bean-feast—all pay and no work.

The first week had enabled Sartwell to make repairs and to add machinery that had long been needed; but it had another effect which he considered more important still. It allowed Mr. Monkton and Mr. Hope to recover their second wind, as it were. These good but timorous men had been panic-stricken by the going out of their employees, and by the adverse comments of the press. As nothing happened during the week they gradually regained what they called their courage, and, although they perhaps did not realize it, they were more and more committed to the fight when it did come on. They could hardly with decency, after keeping silence for a week during which there was peace, give way if afterwards there should be violence.

The vigilance of the pickets perhaps relaxed a little as time went on and there was nothing to do. But one morning they had a rude awakening. When they arrived at the gates they saw smoke once more pouring from the chimneys; there was a hum of machinery; the works were in full blast; and the former workers were outside the gates.

The news spread quickly, and the men gathered around the gates from all quarters. Gibbons was early on the ground, like an energetic general, ready to lead his men to the fray. He saw that the fight was now on, and he counselled moderation when he spoke to the excited men. It was all right, he answered them; he had expected this, and was prepared for it.

The gates were closed, and when Gibbons asked admittance to speak with the manager his request was curtly refused. This refusal did not tend to allay the excitement, nor to improve the temper of the men. The police kept the throng on the move as much as possible, but the task became more and more difficult as the crowd increased.

At noon a wagon, evidently loaded with provisions, drove down the street, and when the mob learned that its destination was the works, a cry went up that the vehicle should be upset.

Again the pacifying influence of Gibbons made itself felt, and the wagon, amidst the jeers of the bystanders, drove in, while the gates were speedily closed after it.

Gibbons retired with his captains to headquarters, where a consultation was held. There was a chance that Sartwell, during the first week, when it was supposed he was putting in new machinery, had also been building dormitories for his new men, and that he was going to keep them inside the gates, free from the influence of the Union.

This plan had not been foreseen by Gibbons, and he was unprepared for it.

"The men must come out sooner or later, and when they do we will have a talk with them," said the secretary. "My own opinion is that they will come out to-night at the usual hour, and I propose to act on that supposition. If I find I am wrong, we will meet again to-night, and I will have some proposals to make. In a short time we shall be able to learn whether the scabs are coming out or not. Meanwhile, get back among our own men, and advise them not to make any hostile demonstration when the blacklegs appear; and when the scabs come out, let each man of you persuade as many as you can to come to the big hall, where we can have a talk with them. Tell the men that if there is any violence they will be merely playing into Sartwell's hands. We don't want the police down on us, and, until there is a row, they will at least remain neutral."

This advice commended itself to all who heard it, and, the details of the programme having been ar ranged, they all departed for the scene of conflict.

Promptly at six o'clock the gates were thrown open, and shortly after the "blacklegs" began to pour forth into the street. There were no hootings nor jeerings, but the strikers regarded the new-comers with scowling looks, while the latter seemed rather uncomfortable, many of them evidently apprehensive regarding their reception.

"Men," cried Gibbons, "who is your leader? I want a word with him."

The stream of humanity paused for a moment, in spite of the commands of the police to move along. The men looked at one another, and Gibbons quickly recognized the state of things—they were strangers to each other, coming as they did from all parts of England. This surmise was confirmed by one man, who spoke up:

"We've got no leader," he said.

"Then you be the spokesman," cried Gibbons. "Did you men know, when you came here, that there was a strike on?"

"Something of that sort," replied the spokesman, sullenly.

"Do you belong to a Union?"

"The Union never did nowt for us."

"Do you know that you are taking bread from the mouths of other workers?"

"We must put bread into our own mouths."

At this point the police captain touched Gibbons on the shoulder.

"I can't allow this obstruction," he said.

"Give me two minutes," pleaded Gibbons.

"No—nor one."

Gibbons turned savagely upon him.

"Look here," he said. "Have some tact and sense. Don't you know that

I have merely to raise my hand and this crowd will sweep you and your men off the face of the earth?"

"That won't prevent me from sweeping you into prison."

"Certainly not. But you can arrest me quietly, when you like, or I'll meet you at the police station any hour you name, but if you attempt to interfere now, you'll have a riot on your hands. I'm holding this crowd in check—it is not their fear of you. There's no traffic coming through this street nor likely to come. We're therefore obstructing nothing, and I'm as anxious as you are to keep the men within the law. Good heavens! you may have your hands full at any moment, so don't push patient people over the line. Remember, you are not in Sartwell's employ. I only want a few words with these men, then we'll leave the street to you."

The captain hesitated a moment. It was an ominous mob.

"Look sharp then," he said, and stepped back.

"Come with us," cried Gibbons. "We can't talk here. Come to the big hall, and, if, you don't like what we say there will be no harm done. This is a free country."

The secretary turned as if he had no doubt the crowd would follow, and the leaderless men walked after him. Gibbons' assistants mixed among them, and talked persuasively with the strangers. Before half an hour all the "blacklegs," were in the Salvation Army hall, signing the Union roll and being put on the strike-pay list.

It was a notable triumph for Gibbons; first blood, as a sporting-man would say.

Next morning, when the gates were opened, not a man entered, and Sartwell once more found himself without an employee. After the gates had remained invitingly open for half an hour, they were closed again, and a great cheer went up as the two big iron-bolted leaves came together.

Sartwell's resources, however, were not yet exhausted, for two days later the factory was thronged with workmen once more, and these also Gibbons bought from under the manager.

Thus the game went on, and it convinced the men that their secretary knew a thing or two, being more than a match for the manager. Gibbons carried himself confidently, and talked with grand assurance that he was perhaps far from feeling, for he became more and more haggard and anxious as the fight continued. He alone knew the seriousness of the increased drain on the resources of the Union, through the forced support of the new hands he had lured away from Sartwell's employ, and which had upset all his previous calculations. An attempt had been made to lighten the burden by trying to induce the new men to return to their homes, and this had been partially successful with the first lot, but the others obstinately insisted on getting their share of the strike pay, and refused even to consider the advisability of returning. They demanded what was promised them, or threatened to enter the works in a body, which action would have speedily put and end to the contest. Gibbons was well supported by that section of the press which gave more than a few lines each day to the progress of the strike. One morning the chief of these papers came out with an appeal to the public for aid. The case of the strikers, battling, it might be, at first for their own rights, but fighting in reality for all working humanity, was most convincingly and tersely put in a double-leaded editorial, and the journal itself headed the list with a handsome contribution. Would the people of England hold aloof, reduce these workers into slaves, using the weapon of grim starvation against them? The journal did not believe such apathy existed, and its belief was amply justified, for subscriptions poured rapidly in, together with indignant letters from all parts of the country, which were duly printed in its columns.

The first pinch of the strike came on the men when it was suddenly announced that strike pay would, the next Saturday, be cut down to one-quarter the amount they were then receiving. There was a good deal of grumbling and some inquiries as to what they were fighting for, but, on the whole, the disastrous proclamation was received quietly, if somewhat grimly.

"We are bound to win," said Gibbons, when he was reluctantly compelled to tell the men of the reduction. "The firm is losing nearly a thousand pounds a week by the factory remaining idle, and it is not likely they will stand that long, even to oblige Sartwell."

Gibbons had not the courage to add that even with this reduction the Union could not hold out more than a week longer; that it was practically at the end of its resources, and that future strike pay would have to depend on the subscriptions received from the outside, a most precarious source of revenue, for every one knows how short-lived enthusiasm is, and how the collection of hard cash destroys it.

There is much in good generalship, and one of its axioms is that you should endeavour to discover your enemy's weakest point. Never once did it dawn on Gibbons or any of his lieutenants, that the fortress they were attacking had only to be approached in one direction, when the walls would have crumbled like those of Jericho; never did it occur to him that Sartwell was fighting at the same time two battles—one with the men and one with the masters, and of the two contests he feared the result of the latter most. Sartwell was between two fires; he had urged both Monkton and Hope to quit England until the fight was over, and leave the conducting of it to him. They vacillated; in the evening Sartwell might have their promise, but in the morning they had changed what they were pleased to call their minds. They always feared the worst. They saw the factory in flames, and the mob shot down by troops. They implored Sartwell to come to some agreement with the men. He had said the strike would be over in three weeks, and here it was still dragging on, the men as determined as ever. If he were wrong about the duration of the fight, might he not be wrong also in his treatment of the men? Was no compromise possible?

This sort of thing Sartwell had to contend with, and it wearied him more than the strike itself. He opened the papers in daily fear that he would find there some letter from the firm, in answer to the strictures of the day before, which would show the public at once how the land lay.

Gibbons believed that the backbone of a fight was money, as in many cases it is; but a moment's reflection might have shown him that, if the fight was to be conducted on a cash basis, the strikers had not a ghost of a chance, because the firm of Monkton & Hope was much richer than the Union. He believed in fighting the devil with fire. Adages are supposed to represent the condensed wisdom of the ages, whereas they too often represent condensed foolishness. If one has to meet an expert swordsman on the field of honour, he should select a pistol if he has the choice of weapons. Fight the devil if you like, but never with fire. When Marsten had said to Gibbons, "Mr. Sart-well knows to a penny how much you have in the bank," the secretary had answered grandly that Sart-well might see the books of the Union for all he cared, and much good might it do him. The fact that a man like Sartwell thought it worth his while to find out what the enemy was doing, did not suggest to Gibbons that it might not be a bad plan to have a look over Sartwell's shoulders, and discover just how things were going in the privacy of the manager's office. When Marsten ferreted out various things as the fight progressed, and brought his knowledge to Gibbons, the latter waved it aside as of no consequence, treating Marsten throughout as an enemy in the camp.

Timid little Mr. Hope passed through the gates each day to his office, scarcely ever glancing at the crowd that hooted him and made remarks not pleasant to hear. He dreaded the moment of arriving and leaving, but thought it a courageous thing to do, imagining he would be neglecting his duties as a freeborn Briton if he deserted his post at this time of danger.

If Gibbons had been a shrewd man, he would have called upon Mr. Hope at Surbiton, and ten minutes' conversation there would have shown him the true state of affairs, for the timid little manufacturer was as transparent as crystal. If the secretary had lured one of the partners to the strikers' place of meeting, which might have been accomplished as easily as with the "blacklegs" from the country, he would in all probability have had a public statement which would have made Sartwell's resignation inevitable. Thus might Gibbons have led his army to victory, and at the same time have placed his enemy where his army then was—outside the gates.

And this was merely one of the methods by which a clever general would have triumphed. If Gibbons had taken the trouble to inform himself about the effect the few editorials had produced in the minds of the partners, he would have endeavoured to make arrangements for the publication of a series of articles on the well-known philanthropy of the firm, with some moral reflections about charity beginning at home. This undoubtedly would have caused the ground to crumble away beneath the feet of Sartwell, for Monkton & Hope were proud of the good their benefactions were supposed to do; and until this trouble had arisen, they had thought themselves just employers, who treated their men with fairness, as indeed they were, and as indeed they did.

Now they were in doubt about the matter, and had an uneasy feeling that they had been, perhaps, remiss in their duties toward their employees. Sartwell dominated them when he was in their presence, and they knew his value too well to run the risk of losing him. They knew, also, if they gave way to the men without his sanction, they would lose him, and they had rivals in London who would be only too glad to take him into their employ; yet in spite of this knowledge they wavered, and it required but a little tact and diplomacy on the part of Gibbons to win a victory all along the line.

## CHAPTER XI.

SARTWELL showed little sign of the wear and tear of the struggle. He walked from the station to his office every morning at his usual hour, as if everything were going on to his entire satisfaction. He was always dressed with scrupulous neatness, and he invariably carried in his hand a trimly folded umbrella, which no one had ever seen him undo, for when it rained he took a cab. The umbrella seemed a part of him, and a purely ornamental part; he was never met on the street without it. No man could say when Sartwell purchased a new suit of clothes; each suit was precisely the same as the one that preceded it, and it was always put on before its predecessor began to show signs of wear.

There was as little change in Sartwell's demeanour towards his men as there was in his clothes. He did not keep his eyes on the ground as he passed along the street to the gates, nor was there, on the other hand, any belligerency in his manner. The men had gone out; that was their affair; he nodded to them or bade them a curt "Good-morning," as had been his habit before the trouble. Few of them had the presence of mind to do otherwise than raise their fingers to their caps or answer, with the customary mumble, "Mornin', sir." Habit is strong in the human animal, as has often been pointed out.

No one of all those concerned was more anxious for the strike to end than Sartwell, but none the less was he determined that it should end his way. He saw the openings in his armour through which, with a blindness not understandable to the manager, Gibbons neglected to thrust.

Curiously enough, it was not Gibbons that Sartwell feared in this contest, but Marsten. He knew the young man had been strongly against the strike, but he also knew that he had thrown in his lot with the men; and although the leaders of the strike, up to that time, had held aloof from Marsten, pretending to look upon him as a covert traitor to the cause, still Sartwell feared they might take him into their counsels at last, and that he would show them the way out of their difficulties. The manager had made it his business to learn all he could of what was done by his opponents, and he had been amazingly successful. He knew of Marsten's visit to Barney and of the generally futile result of that conference; but he had so slight a confidence in Barney's good sense, that he feared some hint might have been dropped by the artist which would show the men how anxious Monkton & Hope were for a settlement on almost any terms. As time passed, and Sartwell saw that Gibbons still held Marsten at arm's length, he became less and less anxious. Affairs were rapidly approaching a crisis when Marsten's aid would be useless.

A few days after the announcement of the reduction in strike pay had been made, Sartwell, approaching the gates in the morning, saw Marsten standing alone at the street corner. The manager had almost passed him without greeting on either side, when the elder man suddenly stopped, turned half around, and said sharply:

"On picket duty, Marsten?"

"No, Mr. Sartwell."

"Not in their confidence, perhaps."

"I suppose I am neither in their confidence, nor in yours, Mr. Sartwell."

"Rather an uncomfortable position, is it not? I should like to be one thing or the other if I were in your place, Marsten."

"I am one thing. I am entirely with the men."

"Perhaps in that case you are afraid to be seen talking with me. Some of the men might happen to pass this way."

"I am not afraid to be seen speaking with anybody, Mr. Sartwell."

"Ah, you are young; therefore you are brave. I have known a smaller thing than this conversation to cost a man his life, but perhaps times and methods have changed since my early days. It is a pity you are on the wrong side for your bravery to be appreciated. The masters of this world always value talent and courage, and pay well for them. The men do neither. That is why they are usually beaten in a fight, and it is one of the many reasons why they should be. I have a few words to say to you; the street corner is not a good place for a private conversation; will you come to my office in an hour's time?"

"Do you wish to speak about the strike?"

"Yes," said Sartwell, looking with some intentness at the young man. "We have no other subject of mutual interest that I know of."

"Very good. I merely asked, because whatever you may have to tell me, I shall use in the interests of the men."

Sartwell shrugged his shoulders.

"You are quite welcome," he said, "to make what use you please of the information I shall give you. I am well aware that your advice is in demand by the men and their leaders."

The elder man walked briskly on; the younger reddened at the covert sneer in his last remark.

"My God," he said to himself, angrily, "I would like to fight that man."

Marsten turned and walked rapidly to the strike headquarters. There he found Gibbons and the committee in consultation, while a few of the men lounged about the place. The talk ceased as Marsten entered the room, the committee and its chairman looking loweringly at him.

"What do you want?" asked Gibbons, shortly.

"I met Mr. Sartwell a moment ago in the street and he said he had something to tell me about the strike; he asked me to call at his office in an hour's time. I promised to do so, but told him any information he gave me I should use in the interests of the men."

"And so you came here, I suppose, to get some information to give in return?"

Marsten had resolved not to allow himself to be taunted into anger, but he saw he had no easy task before him. He was going to do his duty, he said to himself, and help his comrades if he could; the situation was too serious for recrimination.

"No. I shall tell him nothing. If he wants information I shall refer him to you. I thought he perhaps might say something that would be of value for us to know, and so I came to tell you that I am going to his office."

"Us? Who do you mean by us?"

"The men on strike. I am on strike as well as the others. I have lost a situation, even if you haven't," retorted the young man, knowing as he spoke that he was not keeping to his resolution.

"Well," said Gibbons, taking no notice of the other's insinuation, "you don't need to come here for permission to visit Sartwell's office. I suppose you have often been there before."

"I have not been there since the strike began."

"Oh, haven't you?"

"No, I haven't. Do you mean to assert that I have?"

"I assert nothing. It merely seems strange to me that you should come bawling here, saying you are going to consult Sartwell. It has nothing to do with us. Go and come as you please, for all I care."

The members of the committee murmured approval of the chairman's firm stand, and Marsten, seeing there was little use in further delay, turned on his heel and left them. The men lounging around the door nodded to him in a friendly manner as he went out, and the committee presumably continued its deliberations, untroubled by the interruption.

The young man walked down the street, looking neither to the right nor to the left, sick at heart, rather than angry, with the fatuous pettiness of Gibbons's resentment, who would rather wound and humiliate a man he disliked, than accept help when it was freely offered.

"How different," said Marsten to himself, "is the conduct of Sartwell! He has more cause to detest me than Gibbons has, yet he asks me to confer with him. He does not despise the smallest card in his hand, while Gibbons may be throwing away a trump, if I were mean enough, and traitor enough to the men, to refuse to tell what I may learn. Sartwell, parting with me in anger, hails me on the street, merely because he thinks he can use me to serve his employers. That he likes me no better than he did when I left him, is shown by the sting in his talk, yet he puts down his personal feelings, hoping to win a trick; while Gibbons, the fool, although approached in a friendly way, does his sneaking little best to drive a man over to the enemy. I wonder what Sartwell wants to discover. I'll tell him nothing; but what a man he is to fight for—or against!"

"Hold hard, youngster. Where are you going?" cried the picket at the gate.

"I'm going to see Mr. Sartwell."

"Oh, no, you're not."

"It's all right, mate; I've just come from headquarters. I am going with the committee's consent and Gibbons's permission."

"What's on?" asked the picket in a whisper, while others of the strikers crowded around.

"Is the jig up? Are we going to give in?"

"There's nothing new. I'll know more when I come out. Perhaps Sartwell has something to propose; we haven't."

The men drew back, with a simultaneous sigh that may have indicated relief, or perhaps disappointment. The sternness of their resolution to hold out did not increase under reduced strike pay. Their organization was disintegrating, rotting; each man knew it and was suspicious of his comrades. The heart had gone out of the fight.

Marsten, crossing the deserted and silent yard, mounted the stairs, and rapped at the manager's door. He found Sartwell alone, standing at his desk, with some papers before him.

"Now, Marsten," began the manager brusquely, turning from his desk, "you think I've asked you here to learn something from you, and you have firmly resolved to tell me nothing. That's right. I like to see a man stick to his colours. We save the ship if we can; if she sinks we go down with her. You may be surprised then to know that I am not going to ask you a single question. That will relieve your mind and enable you to give full attention to what I have to tell you. I hope, however, that you will keep your word and remember the promise you made me a short time since on the street."

"What promise?"

"Have you forgotten it? Perhaps you thought it was a threat. You said you would give the men the information you received. I hold you to that. To tell Gibbons is not necessarily to tell the men. You said you would let the men know."

"I will repeat your conversation to Gibbons and the committee."

"Ah, that's not what you said. Neither Gibbons nor the committee were mentioned in our talk this morning."

"As near as I can recollect, I said I would use what information I received in the interests of the men."

"Quite so. I am as anxious about the men's welfare as you are, and what I have to say to you must reach them. If you tell it to Gibbons and the committee, and if they do not pass it on to the men, as they will take precious good care not to do, I shall then learn whether you are a man of your word or not. The strikers meet to-night at the Salvation Hall. If Gibbons does not inform them what he will then know, I shall expect you to stand up in your place and add to the enlightenment of the situation. When you were here last I showed you a sheet of paper, at the top of which was written the resources, for the moment, of the Union. The remainder of the sheet was blank, but it is now filled up. It shows the expenditure, week by week, up to the last payment made to those on strike. If you cast your eye over this sheet, you will see that the Union is now bankrupt."

"If that is all you have to tell me, Mr. Sartwell, it is no news. The men already know they are depending on public subscriptions."

"And they still believe in Gibbons as a leader?"

"Yes."

"Very good. Now, I come to what is news—news to you, to Gibbons, and to the men. Most of this money has gone to loafers from the east end of London. I had such unlimited confidence in Gibbons's foolishness and in the stupidity of the committee, that I have sent through the gates, not workmen like you, but such unfortunate wretches as were out of work and willing to absorb strike pay merely on condition that they would keep their mouths shut. It never seemed to occur to Gibbons that, if I were able to fill up the works with men transported to our river-steps on a steamer, I could either have fed and lodged them here, or taken them back and forth in the same way they came. He gathered them into the Union with a whoop, which was just what I expected him to do, but he never tried to find out whether they were genuine workmen or not."

"You mean, then, that by a trick you have bankrupted the Union."

Sartwell shrugged his shoulders.

"Call it a trick, if you like. A strike is war; you must not expect it to be fought with rose-leaves. But aside from that, I have borne in mind the real interests of the men. I could have filled the works with competent men—yes, ten times over. If I had done so, where would the strikers be at the end of the fight? Some would be in prison, some would have broken heads, all would be out of employment. I want my own men back here. I want them to understand they have got a fool for a leader. They have had a nice little play spell; they have eaten and drank their money—the vacation has come to an end. If they return to work now, there is work for them; if they delay much longer, I shall fill the shops with genuine workmen, and the Union has no money now to bribe them with."

"If I tell the men all this, there will be a riot. They will mob the bogus workmen who have taken their money."

"Oh, no, they won't. I have told the bogus workmen just how long the money would continue to be paid, if they held their tongues. With last week's reduced payment the loafers have scattered. The men may mob Gibbons, and I think he richly deserves it."

"They will be much more likely to attack you."

"They are welcome to try it. Now, I think that is all I have to say, Marsten. I have required no answers from you, and I imagine I have given you some interesting information. I am ready to get to work, with the former employees of the firm, or without them, just as they choose. The best friend of the men will be he who advises them to call off this foolish strike and buckle down to business once more."

## CHAPTER XII.

Albert Langly found himself compelled to search for a cheaper room. The thin young man bitterly regretted that good money had to be wasted on food, clothes and rent. A person cannot live without food; Langly had tried it, not as an economical experiment, but largely through forgetfulness, and he found, to his astonishment, that hunger actually forced itself upon his attention, after a sufficient lapse of time. The changeable English climate, not to mention the regulations of that moral body the police force, compelled him to cover himself; and a room he needed mainly to keep his stacks of music dry. The church of St. Martyrs-in-the-East afforded a very good living to its rector and a very poor one for its organist, although if people were paid according to professional efficiency in this world, the salaries of clergyman and musician might have been reversed. Those who entered the church door came, not to hear the sermon, but to listen to the music.

Langly never applied for more remuneration, because deep down in his musical soul he knew he was already taking advantage of the generosity of the church authorities, and he lived in constant fear that some day they would discover this and righteously dismiss him. To be allowed to play on that splendid instrument, erected at the cost of an unbelievable amount of money, was a privilege which he felt he ought to pay for, if he were the honest man the deacons thought him. He tried to soothe his troubled conscience, by telling it that he would refuse to take money were it not that sheet music was so dear, even when bought from the man who gave the largest discount in London, to whose shop Langly tramped miles once a week; but thus the guilty have ever endeavoured to lull the inward monitor, well knowing, while they did so, the sophistry of their excuses. The consciousness of deceit told on Langly's manner; he cringed before the rector and those in authority. Never did one of the kindly but deluded men accost their organist without causing a timorous fear to spring up in his heart that the hour of his dismissal had arrived. Yet, let moralists say what they will, the wicked do prosper sometimes on this earth when they shouldn't, while the innocent suffer for the misdeeds done by others. There was the case of Belcher, for example, and although it must in justice be admitted that Belcher's hard luck caused the organist many twinges of conscience, still of what avail are twinges of conscience when the harm is wrought? If, in our selfishness, we bring disaster on a fellow-creature, after-regret can scarcely be called reparation.

Belcher was the hard-working industrious man who pumped the organ in St. Martyrs, and, besides labouring during the regular service, it was also his duty to attend when the organist wished to practice the selections which afterwards delighted the congregation. This was Belcher's grievance. Langly had no "mussy," as the overworked pumper told his sympathizing comrades at the "Rose and Crown." He would rather follow the vestry-cart all day with a shovel, would Belcher, than suffer the slavery he was called upon to endure by the unthinking organist, who never considered that bending the back to a lever was harder work than crooking the fingers to the keys. Besides, Langly could sit down to his labour, such as it was, while Belcher couldn't. Naturally the put-upon man complained, and Langly at once admitted the justice of the complaint, at the same time exhibiting a craven fear that a rumour of his unjustifiable conduct might reach the ears of the church authorities. The honest Belcher now regretted that he had borne his burden so long, for the reprehensible organist immediately offered to compound with the blower by paying him something extra each week, if he would say nothing about the additional labour. It was Belcher's misfortune rather than his fault that mathematical computation was not one of his acquirements, and he failed to appreciate the fact that there was a limit to the musician's income; a limit very speedily reached. He was an ill-used man and he knew it, so he struck often for higher pay and got it, up to the point where Langly insisted that there was not enough left to keep body and soul together, not to speak of the purchase of music. Belcher yearned for the tail of the vestry-cart, and threatened to complain to the rector; which at last he did, not mentioning, however, that he had received extra remuneration, because he did not wish to exhibit the organist's culpability in all its repulsiveness. He told the rector that he would rather accompany the vestry-cart in its rounds than accompany an organist who had no "mussy" on a "pore" man. He was always ready to pump a reasonable quantity of air, but if an organist knew his trade so badly that he needed to practice so much, it was hard that the man at the lever should bear the brunt of his incompetence. The rector thanked Belcher for his musical criticism, and said he would see about it.

While the virtuous Belcher took his walks abroad with his chin in the air, as befits one who has done his duty, the transgressor crept along by-ways and scarcely dared to enter the silent church. He dodged the rector as long as he could, but was at length run to earth. The kindly old man put his hand on the culprit's shoulder, and said:

"You have been overworking Belcher, I hear."

"I shall be more thoughtful in future, sir," murmured the nervous organist in excuse. "I'm afraid I've been playing too much, but it is a difficult art——"

"Of course it is," interrupted the clergyman. "I have made arrangements to satisfy the ambition of Belcher, which appears to tend in the direction of a vestry-cart, and we are putting in a hydraulic blower which we should have put in years ago. You will find it a great convenience in your practice, Mr. Langly, for it is always ready and never complains."

The organist tried to thank the rector, but his throat seemed not at his command for other effort than a gulp or two. The good man smiled at the grotesque twistings of Langly's mouth and the rapid winking of his eyelids; then the organist turned abruptly and walked away, tortured afterwards with the fear that the rector might have thought him rude and ungrateful; but the old man knew the musician much better than the musician knew himself.

After that, when Langly chanced upon the indignant and gravely wronged Belcher, at the tail of his oft-mentioned but entirely unexpected cart, the young man shrank from the encounter, and felt that inward uneasiness which is termed a troubled conscience.

"Call that Christianity!" Belcher would say to his mate when their rounds took them near St. Martyrs,—"a-puttin' a squirtin' water-pump in there, to tyke th' bread out o' a pore man's mouth, an' a-cuttin' down o' 'is livin' wyge! Yus, an' the lawr a-forcin' us to support the Church too."

But Belcher was really of a forgiving spirit, and should not be judged by his harsh language towards the Establishment which, he was under the impression, rigourous legal enactment compelled him to subsidize; for he so far overlooked Langly's conduct as to call upon him occasionally, and accept a few pence as conscience-money.

"I don't blime 'im," said Belcher magnanimously, over his pot of beer, "as much as I do the mean old duffer wot preaches there. 'E put me on the cart."

Langly, as has been said, found it necessary to secure cheaper lodgings, and this was his own fault as much as it was the fault of his limited income. A London landlady in the more impoverished districts carries on a constant fight against circumstances. Her tenants pay her as seldom and as little as they can; sometimes they disappear, and she loses her money; while if they stay, there are no chances of extracting extras, those elastic exactions which often waft a West End boarding-house keeper to affluence. Terms are close and invariably inclusive. The organist's conduct towards his numerous and successive landladies admits of no defence. These good women, when he had taken his departure, spoke bitterly of his sneaky and deceptive ways, as indeed they had just cause to do. On first arriving at a new place, he was so apologetic and anxious not to give any trouble; so evidently a person who did not really live in bustling, elbowing London, but in some dreamy mental world of his own, that his good hostess, merely as an experiment and entirely without prejudice, as the legal man puts it, tentatively placed on his bill for the week some trifling item, that, strictly speaking, was merely placed there to be taken off again, if complaint were made, or allowed to stand if overlooked. Of course, under these circumstances, the landlady was in expectation of a row, during which epithets reflecting upon her financial probity might be hurled at her, when she, with voluble excuses for her unfortunate mistake, would correct the error and assure the lodger that such a thing would not occur again. After a few essays of this kind, all perfectly just and proper in a commercial country, and in fact the only means of discovering to what extent the lodger could be depended upon as an asset, life would flow on with that calm serenity which adds so much to the comfort and enjoyment of a furnished apartment in the Borough or a palace overlooking the Park.

But Langly never took a straightforward course with his landladies. Instead of finding fault at the proper time, he meekly said nothing and paid the bills as long as he was able—bills which mounted higher and higher each week. Thus the deluded woman had no chance, as she could not be expected to know when she had reached the limit of his weekly income. At last the organist would take his bundle of music under his arm, and would sneak away like a thief in the night, to search for a cheaper abode, after leaving a week's money in lieu of notice, wrapped in a piece of paper, in a conspicuous place, for he had never had the courage to face a landlady and baldly tell her he was going.

In Rose Garden Court there was more than one family that might be likened to an accordion, because of the facility with which it could be compressed or extended. The Scimmins household could occupy the three rooms it rented in the court, or it could get along with two, or even one if need be. The spare space was sub-let whenever opportunity offered, and here Langly found lodging that had at least the merit of cheapness. The policeman at the entrance of the court looked suspiciously after the new-comer, and resolved to keep an eye on him. The organist had a habit of muttering truculently to himself as he walked the streets, and his nervous hands were never a moment at rest, the long slim fingers playing imaginary keys or chords, inaudible outside of his own musical imagination.

When the already suspicious policeman at the entrance of the court saw the musician come out, clawing the empty air with the two forefingers of either hand crooked like talons, a fearful frown on his brow, and an ominous muttering in his throat, the officer said to himself:

"There goes a hanarchist, if ever there was one," not knowing that the poor little man was merely pulling the stops of a mythical organ, immense in size and heavenly in tone. The police always looked askance at Langly when he moved into a new locality, until they learned that he was the organist at St. Martyrs-in-the-East.

One night, shortly after he took the back room two flights up at No. 3,

Langly came down the common stairway, and paused in amaze at the landing opposite Braunt's door. He heard some one within, slowly and fearfully murdering Chopin's Funeral March, part first. The sound made him writhe, and he crouched by the door, his fingers mechanically drumming against the panel, repressing with difficulty a desire to cry out against the profanation of a harmony that seemed sacred to him. The drone stopped suddenly, and next instant the door was jerked open, causing the amazed listener to stumble into the room, where, as it seemed to him, a giant pounced down, clutched his shoulders, and flung him in a heap on the floor by the opposite wall. Then, kicking the door shut, the giant, with fists clenched and face distorted with rage, towered over the prostrate man.

"You miserable sneaking scoundrel!" cried Braunt. "So that's why you took a room with the Scimminses—to ferret and spy on me. I've seen you crawling up these stairs, afraid to look any honest man in the face. Because I took no strike pay Gibbons wants to know how I live, does he? I'm up to his tricks. You're Gibbons's spy, and he has sent you to live with that other sneak, Scimmins. Scimmins himself was afraid, for he knows already the weight of my hand. Now," continued Braunt, rolling up his sleeves, "I'll serve you as I did Scimmins. I'll throw you over the banisters, and you can report that to Gibbons, and tell him to come himself next time, and I'll break every bone in his body."

Jessie clung to her father, begging him in tears not to hurt the poor man. Braunt shook her off, but not unkindly.

"Sit thee down, Jessie, lass, and don't worrit me. I'll but drop the bag o' bones on the stairs, and serve him right for a sneak."

Langly, encouraged by his antagonist's change of tone in speaking to the girl, ventured to falter forth:

"I assure you, sir——"

"Don't 'sir' me, you hound," cried Braunt, turning fiercely upon him, "and don't dare to deny you are one of Gibbons's spies. I caught you at it, remember."

"I'll deny nothing, if it displeases you; but I never heard of Gibbons in my life, and I'm only a poor organist. I stopped at the door on hearing the harmonium. For no other reason, I assure you. I know I oughtn't to have done it, and I suppose I am a sneak. I'll never do it again, never, if you will excuse me this time."

There was something so abject in the musician's manner that Braunt's resentment was increased rather than diminished by the appeal. He had a big man's contempt for anything small and cringing.

"Oh, you're an organist, are you? Likely story! Organists don't live in Garden Court. But we'll see, we'll see. Get up."

Langly gathered himself together, and rose unsteadily to his feet. Every movement he made augmented the other's suspicion.

"Now," said Braunt, with the definite air of a man who has his opponent in a corner, "sit down at the harmonium and play. You're an organist, remember."

"Yes," protested Langly, "but I don't know that I can play on that instrument at all. I play a church organ."

"An organ's an organ, whether it is in church or out. If you can play the one, you can play the other."

The young man hesitated, and was nearly lost. Braunt's fingers itched to get at him, and probably only the presence of the girl restrained him so far.

"Have you any music?" asked Langly.

"No, we haven't. She plays by ear."

"Will you allow me to go up-stairs and bring some sheet music?"

This was a little too transparent.

"Now, by God!" cried Braunt, bringing his fist down on the table. "Stand there chattering another minute, and I'll break thy neck down the stair. Sit thee down, Jessie, an' don't interfere. The man plays or he doesn't. I knew he was a liar, an' he quakes there because it's to be proven. Now, coward, the organ or the stairs—make thy choice quickly."

The driven musician reluctantly took the chair before the instrument. He had played on the harmonium in his early days, and knew it was harsh and reedy at the best. But under his gentle touch the spirit of all the harmonies seemed to rise from it, and fill the squalid room. Braunt stood for a moment with fallen jaw, his hands hanging limply by his sides; then he sank into his arm-chair. Jessie gazed steadfastly, with large pathetic eyes, at their guest, who seemed himself transformed, all the lines of dismay and apprehension smoothed away from his face, replaced by an absorbed ecstacy, oblivious to every surrounding. He played harmony after harmony, one apparently suggesting and melting into another, until at last a minor chord carried the music into the solemn rhythm of Chopin's march; then the organ, like a sentient creature, began to sob and wail for the dead. The girl's eyes, never moving from the wizard of the keys, filled with unshed tears, and her father buried his face in his hands.

When at last the organist's magic fingers slipped from the keys, and the exultant light faded from his face as the dying music merged into silence, Braunt sprang to his feet.

"Curse me for a brutish clown!" he cried. "To think that I mishandled thee, lad, an' thou playest like an angel. I never heard music before."

He laid his huge hand on the other's shoulder gently and kindly, although the youth, hardly yet awake from his dream, timidly shrank from the touch. "Forgive me, lad? I misdoubt I hurt thee."

"No, no; it is all nothing. So you like the music?"

"The music! I shall never forget it; never. That march rings in my head all day. The whole world seems tramping to it."

The young man for the first time looked up at him, the light of brotherhood in his eyes.

"I feel it, too," he said, "that there is nothing around us but good music.

It smooths away the ruder sounds of earth, or uses them as undertones—as—as a background. I sometimes fancy that the gates of heaven are left ajar, and we—a few of us—are allowed to listen, to compensate us for any trouble we have, or to show us the triviality of everything else."

The young man's thin face flushed in confused shame at finding himself talking thus to another man, although what he said was merely the substance of many a former soliloquy. With a hasty apologetic glance at the girl, who regarded him like one in a trance, with wide unwinking eyes, Langly continued hurriedly:

"The march is a difficult one and should not be attempted except after many lessons. I shall be pleased to teach your daughter, if you will let me. She has a correct ear."

Braunt shook his head.

"We have no money for music lessons," he said.

"I have very little myself. I am poor, and therefore need none," said the organist, as if that were a logical reason. "The poor should help the poor. If they don't, who else will? The poor have always been kind to me." He thought of his many landladies, and how they had robbed themselves to sustain him, as they had often admitted, little thinking he would desert them one by one. "Aye, and the rich too," he added, remembering the hydraulic motor in the church, and of the continued endurance of the authorities with their organist.

"Well, lad," said Braunt, with a sigh, "come in when you can, and if nowt else, you'll be sure of a hearty northern welcome."

## CHAPTER XIII.

SARTWELL prided himself on being a man who made few mistakes. He was able to trace an event from cause to effect with reasonable certainty, and this slight merit made him perhaps a trifle impatient with others who could not be credited with similar foresight, as his own wife would not have hesitated to bear witness. It would probably have filled that just woman with subdued, if pardonable, gratification had she known how wide of the mark her husband was in his estimate of the result on the strikers of the news he had committed to the care of Marsten. Sart-well imagined that the men, in their fury at being outwitted, would turn on Gibbons and rend him. He believed that Gibbons would not dare tell his dupes, as Sartwell persisted in calling them, how the Union had been befooled into supporting for weeks the bogus workmen whom the manager had flung into its credulous lap. After wreaking their vengeance on Gibbons and deposing him, they must return to the works, reasoned the manager. Their money was gone, interest in the strike had all but died out, fresher events had compressed it into a two-line item in the papers, subscriptions had practically ceased; what then was there left but a return or starvation, that powerful ally of masters all the world over?

But Sartwell forgot that the Englishman knows how to starve. No Indian ever tightens his belt another notch with grimmer determination to compress hunger than an Englishman sets his teeth and starves, if need be. He has starved on the ice near the Pole, and under the burning sun in the desert.

He has met famine face to face in beleaguered fort with no thought of surrender, and has doled with scrupulous exactitude the insufficient portions of food on a raft in mid-ocean. The poet has starved in his garret, making no outcry, and the world has said, "If we had only known." In the forests and on the plains, in the jungle and on the mountains, and—perhaps worst of all—in the great cities, amidst plenty, the Englishman has shown he knows how to starve, saying with the poet:

> "I have not winced nor cried aloud."

When Gibbons heard what Marsten had to tell, he promptly said, "It is a lie"; but the committee looked one at the other with apprehension in their faces, fearing it was the truth.

"The question is," said Marsten, "are you going to let the men know this?"

"Certainly, if I find it is true; but I don't believe a word of it. Perhaps you want the pleasure of being the bearer of bad news to the men."

"I intend to tell them, if you do not."

"Of course. I'm sorry we can't gratify you."

The committee dismissed Marsten, and went into secret session; shortly afterwards separating, to meet again in the evening just before the large gathering in the Salvation Hall. In the interval, Gibbons and his fellow-members made active search for the alleged fraudulent workmen, but they found none; the birds had flown. It was evident the word had been passed, and that, fearing the vengeance of the legitimate claimants to the Union funds, the former "blacklegs" had taken themselves off, out of the reach of possible harm.

When the committee met for the second time that day, the members were divided among themselves as to the advisability of taking the men fully into their confidence. Some thought it best to break the doleful news gradually; others, that the worst should be known at once. Gibbons, however, said there was in reality no choice; the men must be told the whole truth, for if the committee tried any half measures, Marsten would undoubtedly rise in his place and relate what Sartwell had told him. So the whole truth and nothing but the truth was resolved upon.

When Gibbons faced his audience that night in the large hall, he saw he had to deal with a body of men whose mood was totally different from that of the crowd which light-heartedly voted, with a hurrah, to go on strike. There was now little jocularity among the men; they sat in their places in sullen silence. A feeling that something ominous was in the air seemed to pervade the hall, and, as Gibbons stepped to the front of the platform, he felt that the atmosphere of the place was against him; that he had to proceed with great caution, or his hold on the men was lost. He knew he was a good speaker, but he knew also that the men were just a trifle impatient with much talk and such small result from it all.

"Combination," he began, "is the natural consequence of the modern conditions of labour. A workingman of to-day may be likened to a single pipe in a large organ. He can sound but one note. He spends his life doing part of something. He does not begin any article of commerce, go on with it, and finish it, as did the workmen of former days; he merely takes it from a fellow-workman who has put a touch on it, puts his own touch on it, and passes it on to another; and thus the article travels from hand to hand until it reaches the finisher. The workman of to-day is merely a small cog on a very large wheel, and so, if he does not combine with his fellows, he is helpless. The workman of former times was much more independent. He began his work and completed it. If he was a cooper, he made the whole barrel, hooping it and heading it. If one of us may be compared to a single pipe in an organ, the workman of yesterday might be likeened to a flute, on which a whole tune could be played. He——"

"Ah, chuck it!" cried a disgusted man in front. "We don't want no philosophy; we wants strike pay or master's pay."

"'Ear, 'ear!" rang through the hall; the interrupter quite evidently voicing the sentiment of the meeting. Gibbons stood for a second or two looking at them.

"Yes," he cried, his voice like a trumpet call, "I will chuck it. This is not the time for philosophy, as our friend said; it is the time to act. When a man strips to fight, what does he expect?"

"A d——d good thrashing," was the unlooked-for reply.

It is never safe for an orator to depend on his audience for answers to his questions; but the laugh that went up showed Gibbons that the crowd was getting into better humour, which was what he most desired.

"When an Englishman takes off his coat to fight, he asks no favour from his opponent; but he does expect fair play, and if Englishmen are the onlookers he gets it, whether they like him or whether they don't. He doesn't expect to be struck below the belt; he doesn't expect to be strangled on the ropes; he doesn't expect to be hit when he is down. We stripped for a square and fair fight with Manager Sartwell, and we have fought as men should. We have broken no law; we have raised no disturbance. The police, always eager enough to arrest a striker, have laid hands on none of us. It has been a square, stand-up, honourable fight. It has been a fair fight on our side, and I am proud to have been connected with it. But in this struggle I have made one mistake. I made the mistake of thinking we were fighting an honourable opponent—with a man who would not break the rules of the ring. I was not on the outlook for foul play—for trickery. Knowing what I do to-night, I say—and I am ready to take the consequences of my words—that Sartwell is a thief, and a cowardly thief in the estimation of any honest man. He knew that the life of our fight was our money. He knew that starvation for the helpless wives and families of our men was his most powerful ally. He did not dare to break in and steal our money, because he was afraid of the law, but he took a meaner and more cowardly way of accomplishing the robbery. He appealed to the cupidity of men out of work—poor devils! I don't blame them; they were doubtless starving—and he told them that if they masqueraded as employees of his, the Union would take them in, and pay them wages, as long as there was no suspicion aroused—that is, if these men kept their mouths shut they could draw strike pay. Much as I have always despised Sartwell, I did not think he would stoop to a trick like this. A man who robs a bank has some courage, but a man who tempts poverty-stricken wretches to commit the crime, while he stands safely aside and reaps the benefit—there is no decent word in the language to characterize him. Now, men, you know what has been done, and the result is that our treasury is as empty as if Sartwell had broken into it with a jimmy. The manager is waiting expectantly for the reward of his burglary. He will throw the gates of the works open to-morrow for you to enter and complete his triumph. The question before the meeting to-night is—Are you going in?"

A universal shout of, "Never! We'll starve first!" rose to the rafters of the building.

When he first confronted the meeting that night, Gibbons feared he could not rouse the men from their evident coldness toward him; as the speech went on, increasing murmurs among the men and at length savage outbursts of rage showed him that he held them in the hollow of his hand; at the end, a word from him, and all the police in that part of London could not have saved the works from wreck and flames.

"To the works!" was the cry, and there was a general movement in response to it.

"No, men!" shouted Gibbons, his stentorian voice dominating the uproar. "Not to the works. Everyman home to-night, but be on the ground in the morning. We must not play into the enemy's hands by any attempt at violence. To-morrow we will intercept Monkton and Hope, and demand our rights from them in person. Let them refuse at their peril. We'll have no more dealings with Sartwell."

There was a cheer at this, and the meeting disbanded quietly.

Next morning the men were out in force at the still closed gates, and there were angry threats against the manager. It was all right enough, they said, for Gibbons to counsel moderation, but the time for moderation was past. There was an increased body of police, who kept the crowd moving as much as was possible, having for the first time during the strike a most difficult task to perform. The strikers were in ugly temper, and did not obey orders or take pushes with the equanimity they had formerly displayed; but the police showed great forbearance, and evidently had instructions not to use their truncheons except as a last resort.

Sartwell, knowing a crisis was at hand, had slept in his office, and the ever-increasing mob hooted when he did not appear at his usual time.

Gibbons, by word and action, moving about everywhere, tried to keep his men in hand and prevent a conflict. They cheered him, but paid little attention to what he said.

Shortly after ten o'clock, a hansom drove to the outskirts of the mob, and was received with a chorus of groans. Gibbons quickly stepped in front of it and addressed the occupant.

“Mr. Hope——” he began.

“Stand back there!” cried the officer in charge.

“Mr. Hope,” cried Gibbons, “I want ten words with you.”

Little Mr. Hope shrank into a corner of the hansom, speechless, his face as white as a sheet of paper.

“Stand back, I say!” The officer pushed Gibbons, striking him with some force on the breast.

“Let him answer. Will you speak for one minute with your men—the men who have made you rich?”

“Stand back!” reiterated the officer, pushing him a step further.

The hansom moved inch by inch nearer the gates. The crowd seethed like an uneasy sea, but every man held his breath.

“Listen to me, Mr. Hope. Your men are starving. They ask only——”

The officer pushed the speaker back once more. Gibbons's heel caught on a cobble-stone, and he went down backwards.

The crowd broke like a wave, submerging the police for a moment, flooding the street as if a dam had given way. The cabby on his lofty seat, trying to control his frightened horse, looked like a castaway perched on a buoy in an angry ocean. He made the tactical mistake of lashing around him with his whip. In an instant the hansom was over and down, with a crash of splintering glass. The police, edging together, struck right and left with a fury that quite matched the less disciplined rage of the mob. The officers fought their way until there was a ring around the prostrate cab; two of them picked up Mr. Hope, who was helpless with fear and horror, and these two, with the little man between them, surrounded by a squad that stood shoulder to shoulder, simply clove their way through the dense mass to the gates, where the small door in the large gate was quickly opened and shut, with Mr. Hope and one supporting policeman inside.

Gibbons, his hat gone, his coat in rags and his face smeared with blood, a wild unkempt figure, rose above the struggling mob, and stood on the top of the fallen cab.

"For God's sake, men," he screamed, "don't resist the police! Fallback! Fallback!"

He might as well have shouted to the winds. The police laid about them like demons, and the crowd was rapidly falling back, but not because Gibbons ordered them to. In an incredibly short space of time the police in a body marched down the street, and there was none to oppose them. The remnants of what a few minutes before seemed an irresistible force, lay on the pavement and groaned, or leaned against the walls, the more seriously wounded to be taken to the hospitals, the others to the police station.

In spite of their defeat in the morning, the men gathered once more about the works in the afternoon, and the threatening crowd was even greater than before, because the evening papers had spread over London startling accounts of the riot, as they called it, and the news had attracted idlers from all parts of the metropolis. The wildest rumours were afloat: the men were going to wreck the works; they were going to loot the bread-shops in Light Street; they had armed themselves and were about to march on Trafalgar Square. With a resolute and desperate leader, there is no saying what they might have attempted; but Gibbons, who had put another coat on his back, and much sticking-plaster on his face, moved about counselling moderation and respect for the law. They would forfeit public sympathy, he said, by resorting to violence; although some of his hearers growled that "a bleedin' lot o' good" public sympathy had done for them. "What we want, and what we mean to have," said Gibbons, "is a word with the owners. They are bound to come out soon."

They did come out ultimately together, and two more frightened men than Monkton and Hope it would have been hard to find in all the land that day. They were surrounded by a dozen policemen, whose resolute demeanour showed they were not to be trifled with. The gates immediately closed behind this formidable procession, and it quickly made its way up the street, the crowd jeering and groaning as it passed through.

"We've got nothing against them," shouted one. "Bring out Sartwell, and we'll show you wot for."

Hatred for the manager rather than the owners was plainly the dominant sentiment of the gathering. They cheered the remark, and gave three groans for the unpopular manager.

When the protected men disappeared, the vigilance of the force relaxed, and the crowd surged into the gap the police had cleared. With the masters safe and out of reach, the critical moment of the day seemed to have passed. The police could not be expected to know that the real resentment of the mob was not directed against the man whose cab had been overturned that morning.

"I hope Sartwell won't venture out to-night," said Marsten to Braunt. "It will take more than twelve policemen to guard him if he does."

"He has some sense," replied Braunt, "and will stay where he is."

Neither Braimt nor Marsten had been present during the morning's battle; but they, like many others with nothing to do, had come in the afternoon.

As Braunt spoke the small door in the gate opened, and Sartwell, entirely alone, stepped out. He had no more formidable weapon in his hand than his customary slim and trim umbrella. His silk hat was as glossy and his clothes as spick and span as if he were a tailor's model. He seemed to have aged a trifle since the strike began, but his wiry well-knit body was as erect as ever, and in his eye was that stern look of command before which, at one time or another, every man in his employ had quailed.

An instantaneous hush fell upon the crowd. The cry of a hawker in a distant street was heard. Every man knew that the flinging of a missile or the upraising of an arm even, would be as a spark in a powder-mill. Let but a stroke fall, and all the police in London could not have saved the life of the man walking across the cleared space from the gates towards the crowd. The mass of silent humanity had but to move forward, and Sartwells life would be crushed out on the paving-stones.

Sartwell, without pause and without hurry, walked across the intervening space with evident confidence that the men would make way for him. There was no sign of fear in his manner, nor on the other hand was there any trace of swaggering authority about him; but there was in the glance of his steely eye and the poise of his head that indefinable something which stamps a man master,—which commands obedience, instant and unquestioned.

The crowd parted before him, and he cast no look over his shoulder. Habit being strong, one or two raised hand to forelock as he passed, getting in return the same curt nod that had always acknowledged such salutation. The human ocean parted before him as did the Red Sea before the Hebrew leader, and the manager passed through as unscathed.

"God!" cried Braunt, towering above his fellows and shaking his fist at the unoffending sky, "I have seen in my life one brave man."

## CHAPTER XIV.

COME with me, Marsten," said Braunt. "Let us get out of this crowd. I want a word with you."

The two made their way to a quieter street, and walked together towards Rose Garden Court, talking as they went.

"This foolish strike must stop," began the York-shireman, "and now is the time to stop it. The men are tired of it, and the masters are sick of it; but neither will give in, so a way must be found out of the tangle, and you are the man to find the way."

"How? The men won't throw over Gibbons, and Sartwell will resign before he will confer with him. Remember how Gibbons swayed the men last night, in spite of the grumbling there had been against him before the meeting opened."

"Yes, I know. But, my lad, there is dissension in the other camp as well as in ours. Sartwell's coming out as he did just now was as much defiance of his masters as of his men. If we knew the truth of it, both Monkton and Hope wanted him to come with them and their bodyguard. He refused. From what I hear, Mr. Hope was so frightened this morning that he could not have spoken if his life had depended upon it. There must have been some hot talk between the three to-day. Sartwell underestimates the danger, and the two owners perhaps overestimate it. What I am sure of is, that there is division between Sartwell and the masters, and when they hear that he came out alone to-night, while they were guarded by twelve policemen, they'll be more angry than ever, if there's any spirit in either of them. Now, what you must do to-morrow is to meet either Monkton or Hope, or both if possible. You'll see they won't look near the works again until this strike's ended. I'd go to Mr. Hope first if I were you. He's had the worst fright. Tell him you want to end the trouble, and he'll listen willingly. Very likely he has some plan of his own that Sartwell won't let him try. If you get him to promise to give us what we want if we throw over Gibbons, we'll spring that on the meeting, and you'll see, if we work it right, Gibbons will be thrown over. Then there will be no trouble with Sartwell."

"It seems a treacherous thing to do," said Marsten, with some hesitation.

"God's truth, lad," cried Braunt, with some impatience, "haven't they been treating you like a traitor ever since this strike began? What's the difference, if it does look like treachery? Think of the wives and children of the men, if not of the men themselves; think of those that no one has given a thought to all these weeks, the women workers in the top floor of the works. They've had little strike pay; they have no vote at the meetings, and they have to suffer and starve when they are willing to work. Treachery? I'd be a traitor a thousand times over to see the works going again."

"I'll do it," said Marsten.

The young man had no money to waste on railway fare, so next morning early he set his face to the west, and trudged along the Portsmouth road the twelve miles' distance between London and Surbiton.

As he walked up the beautifully kept drive to the Hope mansion, he thought he saw the owner among the trees at the rear, pacing very dejectedly up and down a path. Marsten hesitated a moment, but finally decided to apply formally at the front door. The servant looked at him with evident suspicion, and, after learning his business, promptly returned, saying Mr. Hope could not see him. The door was shut upon him, but Marsten felt sure Mr. Hope had not been consulted in the matter; so, instead of going out by the gate he had entered, he went around the house to the plantation beyond, and there came upon Mr. Hope, who was much alarmed at seeing a stranger suddenly appear before him.

"I am one of your workmen, Mr. Hope," began Marsten, by way of reassuring the little man; but his words had an entirely opposite effect. Mr. Hope looked wildly to right and left of him, but, seeing no chance of escape, resigned himself, with a deep sigh, to dynamite, or whatever other shape this particular workingman's arguments might take.

"What do you want?" faltered the employer at last. "I want this strike to end."

"Oh, so do I, so do I!" cried Mr. Hope, almost in tears.

"Then, Mr. Hope, won't you allow me to speak with you for a few moments, and see if we cannot find some way out of the difficulty?"

"Surely, surely," replied the trembling old man, visibly relieved at finding his former employee did not intend to use the stout stick, which he carried in his hand, for the purpose of a personal assault.

"Let us walk a little further from the house, where we can talk quietly. Have you anything to propose?"

"Well, the chief trouble seems to be that Mr. Sart-well will not meet Gibbons."

"Ah, Sartwell!" said the old man, as if whispering to himself. "Sartwell is a strong man—a strong man; difficult to persuade—difficult to persuade." Then turning suddenly he asked, "You're not Gibbons, are you?"

"No, my name is Marsten. Gibbons was the man who tried to speak with you yesterday at the gates." The old man shuddered at the recollection.

"There were so many there I did not see any one distinctly, and it all took place so suddenly. I don't remember Gibbons. It was dreadful, dreadful!"

"I hope you were not hurt."

"No, no. Merely a scratch or two. Nothing to speak of. Now, what can be done about the strike?"

"Would you be prepared to grant the requests of the men, if they were to throw over Gibbons, and send a deputation to Mr. Sartwell?"

"Oh, willingly, most willingly. I don't at all remember what it is the men want, but we'll grant it; anything to stop this suicidal struggle. Does Sartwell know you?"

"Yes, sir."

"Of course he does. He knows every one in the works, by name even. A wonderful man—a wonderful man! I often wish I had more influence with him. Now, if you would go and see Mr. Sartwell—he lives at Wimbledon; it's on your way; I asked him not to go to the works to-day, so perhaps you will find him at home—you might possibly arrange with him about receiving a deputation. Perhaps it would be best not to tell him that you've seen me—yes, I'm sure it's best not. Then I'll speak to him about granting the men's demands. I'll put my foot down; so will Monkton. We'll be firm with him." The old man glanced timidly over his shoulder. "We'll say to him that we've stood at his back about Gibbons, and now he must settle at once with the men when they've abandoned Gibbons. Why will he not see Gibbons, do you know? Has he a personal dislike to the man?"

"Oh, no. It is a matter of principle with Mr. Sartwell. Gibbons is not one of your workmen."

"Ah yes, yes. I remember now. That's exactly what Sartwell said. Well, I'm very much obliged to you for coming, and I hope these awful occurrences are at an end. Good-by! There's a train in half an hour that stops at Wimbledon."

"Thank you, Mr. Hope, but I'm on foot to-day."

"Bless me, it's a long distance and roundabout by road. The train will get you there in a few minutes."

Marsten laughed.

"I don't mind walking," he said.

The old man looked at him for a few minutes.

"You don't mean to tell me you have walked all the way from London this morning!"

"It's only twelve or thirteen miles."

"Dear dear, dear dear! I see, I see. Yes, Sartwell's right. I'm not a very brilliant man, although I think one's manager should not say so before one's partner. Come with me to the house for a moment."

"I think I should be off now."

"No no, come with me. I won't keep you long; I won't take a refusal. I'm going to put my foot down, as I said. I have had too little self-assertion in the past. Come along."

The courageous man led the way towards his dwelling, keeping the trees between himself and the house as much as possible and as long as he could. He shuffled hurriedly across the open space, and went gingerly up the steps at the back of the building, letting himself into a wide hall, and then noiselessly entered a square room that looked out upon the broad lawn and plantation to the rear. The room was lined with books; a solid oak table stood in the centre, flanked by comfortable armchairs. Mr. Hope rang the bell, and held the door slightly ajar.

"Is there any cold meat down-stairs, Susy?" he whispered to the unseen person through the opening.

"Yes, sir."

"Well, bring up enough for two; some pickles, bread and butter, and a bit of cheese." Then turning to Marsten he asked, "Will you drink wine or beer?"

"Really, Mr. Hope," said the young man, moistening his lips and speaking with difficulty, "I'm not in the least hungry."

Which was not true, for the very recital of the articles of food made him feel so faint that he had to lean against the bookcase for support.

"Bring a bottle of beer, please," whispered the host, softly closing the door.

"Sit down, sit down," he said to Marsten. "Not hungry? Of course you're hungry after such a walk, no matter how hearty a breakfast you took before you left."

While Marsten ate, Mr. Hope said nothing, but sat listening with apparently intense anxiety. Once he rose and cautiously turned the key in the door, breathing easier when this was done.

"Now," said the old man, when Marsten had finished his meal, "you must go by rail to Wimbledon. Time is of importance—time is of importance. Here is a little money for expenses."

"I cannot take money from you, Mr. Hope, but thank you all the same."

"Nonsense, nonsense. You are acting for me, you know."

"No, sir, I am acting for the men."

"Well, it's the same thing. Benefit one, benefit all. Come, come, I insist. I put down my foot. Call it wages, if you like. No doubt you didn't want to strike."

"I didn't want to, but I struck."

"Same thing, same thing. You must take the money."

"I'd much rather not, sir."

Marsten saw the anxiety of his host, who acted as a man might over whose head some disaster impended, and it weakened his resolution not to take the money. He understood that for some reason Mr. Hope wanted him to take the money and be gone.

"Tut, tut," persisted the old man, eagerly. "We mustn't let trifles stand in the way of success."

As he was speaking, an imperious voice sounded in the hall—the voice of a woman. A sudden pallour overspread Mr. Hope's face, that reminded Marsten of the look it wore when the twelve policemen escorted him and his partner through the crowd.

"Here, here," said the old man, in a husky whisper, "take the money and say nothing about it—nothing about it."

Marsten took the money, and slipped it into his pocket. The voice in the hall rang out again.

"Where is Mr. Hope, Susan?" it asked.

"He was in the back walk a few minutes ago, mum."

Firm footsteps passed down the hall, the outside door opened and shut, and, in the silence, the crunch on the gravel was distinctly heard.

The anxiety cleared away from Mr. Hope's face like the passing of a cloud, and a faint smile hovered about his lips. He seemed to have forgotten Marsten's presence in the intensity of the moment.

"Clever girl, Susy—so I was, so I was," he murmured to himself.

"Good-by, and thank you, Mr. Hope," said Marsten, rising. "I will go at once and see Mr. Sartwell."

"Yes, yes. In a moment—in a moment," said the old man, with a glance out of the window. His voice sank into an apologetic tone as he added, as if asking a favour: "Won't you take some money with you, to be given anonymously—anonymously, mind—to the committee for the men? You see, the negotiations may take a few days, and I understand they are badly off—badly off."

Even Marsten smiled at this suggestion.

"I don't see how that could be managed. I shall have to tell the men I have been to see you, or at least some of them, and they might misunderstand. I think, perhaps——"

"I see—I see. There is a difficulty, of course. I shall send it in the usual way to the papers. That's the best plan."

"To the papers?" said Marsten, astonished.

The old man looked at him in alarm.

"I didn't intend to mention that. As you say, it might be misunderstood—misunderstood. The world seems to be made up of misunderstandings, but you'll not say anything about it, will you? I did it in a roundabout way, so as not to cause any ill feeling, under the name of 'Well-wisher,' Merely trifles, you know; trifles, now and then. Sartwell said the strike would end in a fortnight or three weeks. He's a clever man, Sartwell—a clever man—but was mistaken in that. We all make mistakes one time or another. I wouldn't care for him to know, you see, that I contributed anonymously to the strike fund; he might think it prolonged the strike, and perhaps it did—perhaps it did. It is difficult to say what one's duty is in a case like this—very difficult. So perhaps it is best to mention this to no one."

"I shall never breathe a word about it, Mr. Hope."

"That's right—that's right. I am very glad you came, and I'll speak to Sartwell about you when we get in running order again. Now just come out by the front door this time, and when you speak to Mr. Sartwell be careful not to say anything that might appear to criticise his actions in any way. Don't cross him—don't cross him. The easiest way is generally the best. If any one has to put a foot down, leave that to me—leave that to me."

The manufacturer himself let his employee out by the front entrance, and the young man walked briskly to Surbiton Station.

## CHAPTER XV.

When young Marsten reached the walled-in house at Wimbledon, he found that Sartwell had indeed paid little attention to the wishes of his chief, and had left for the works at his usual hour in the morning. Mr. Hope had evidently not put his foot down firmly enough when he told the manager not to go to his office next day.

Marsten stood hesitatingly on the door-step; not knowing exactly the next best thing to do. After the events of yesterday, there was some difficulty about seeking an interview with the manager at his office.

"Mrs. Sartwell's not home either," said the servant, noting his indecision; "but Miss Sartwell is in the garden. Perhaps you would like to see her?"

Perhaps! The young man's pulses beat faster at the mere mention of her name. He had tried to convince himself that he lingered there through disappointment at finding the manager away from home; but he knew that all his faculties were alert to catch sight or sound of her. He hoped to hear her voice; to get a glimpse of her, however fleeting. He wanted nothing so much on earth at that moment as to speak with her—to touch her hand; but he knew that if he met her, and the meeting came to her father's knowledge, it would kindle Sartwell's fierce resentment against him, and undoubtedly jeopardize his mission. Sartwell would see in his visit to Wimbledon nothing but a ruse to obtain an interview with the girl. Braunt had trusted him, and had sent him off with a hearty God-speed; the fate of exasperated men on the very brink of disorder might depend on his success. Women and children might starve to pay for five minutes' delightful talk with Edna Sartwell. No such temptation had ever confronted him before, and he put it away from him with a faint and wavering hand.

"No," he said, with a sigh, "it was Mr. Sartwell I wanted to see. I will call upon him at his office."

The servant closed the door with a bang. Surely he did not need to take all that time, keeping her standing there, to say "No."

The smallness of a word, however, bears little relation to the difficulty there may be in pronouncing it. Yet the bang of the door resulting from his hesitation brought about the very meeting he had with such reluctance resolved to forego. It is perhaps hardly complimentary to Sartwell to state that, when his daughter heard the door shut so emphatically, she thought her father had returned, and that something had gone wrong. Patience was not among Sartwell's virtues, and when his wife, actuated solely by a strict sense of duty, endeavoured to point out to him some of his numerous failings, the man, instead of being grateful, often terminated a conversation intended entirely for his own good, by violently slamming the door and betaking himself to the breezy common, where a person may walk miles without going twice over the same path.

The girl ran towards the front of the house, on hearing the noisy closing of the door, and was far from being reassured when she recognized Marsten almost at the gate. That something had happened to her father instantly flashed across her mind, She fleetly overtook the young man, and his evident agitation on seeing her confirmed her fears.

"Oh, Mr. Marsten," she cried, breathlessly, "is there anything wrong? Has there been more trouble at the works?"

"No; I don't think so," he stammered.

"I feel sure something is amiss. Tell me, tell me. Don't keep me in suspense."

"I think everything is all right."

"Why do you say you 'think'? Aren't you sure? You have come from the works?"

"No, I haven't. I've just come from Surbiton. I wanted to speak with Mr. Sartwell, but I find he's not at home."

"Oh," said the girl, evidently much relieved. Then she flashed a bewilderingly piercing glance at him, that vaguely recalled her father to his mind. "From Surbiton? You came from Surbiton just now?"

"Yes," he faltered.

"You have been to see Mr. Hope?"

Marsten was undeniably confused, and the girl saw it. A flush of anger overspread her face.

"If your visit was a secret one, of course I don't expect you to answer my question."

"It was not intended to be a secret visit, but—but Mr. Hope asked me not to mention it."

"Not to mention it to my father?"

"To any one."

Edna Sartwell gazed at the unhappy young man with a look of reproach in her eyes, and also—alas!—a look of scorn.

"I can see by your face," she said, indignantly, "that you don't want my father to know that you have been talking to Mr. Hope about the strike."

"My face does not tell you everything I think, Miss Sartwell," replied Marsten, with a burst of courage that astonished himself. "I saw Mr. Hope about the strike, and it was his wish, not mine, that Mr. Sartwell should not know I had been there. But I am wrong in saying it was not mine. I don't want Mr. Sartwell to know either."

"Well, I call that treachery," cried the girl, her face ablaze.

"To whom?" asked Marsten, the colour leaving his face as it mounted in hers.

"To my father."

"It may be treachery, as you say, but not to Mr. Sartwell. It is treachery to Gibbons, perhaps, for he is secretary to the Union and leader of the strike, while I am a member of the Union and a striker. I cannot be treacherous to

Mr. Sartwell, for we are at war with each other."

"You were not at war with him when you thought he could do you a favour," said the girl, disdainfully.

The young man looked at her in speechless amazement.

"Oh, yes," she continued, "he told me of it—that night I was last at the office. He refused you, and you were angry then. I thought at the time you were merely disappointed, and I spoke to him on your behalf; but he said I knew nothing about you, and I see I didn't. I never thought you were a person who would plot behind your employer's back."

"Miss Sartwell," said Marsten, speaking slowly, "you are entirely wrong in your opinion of me. I feel no resentment against Mr. Sartwell, and I hope he has none against me. You spoke of treachery just now; my treachery, as I have said, is against Gibbons. I mean to depose him, if I can get enough of the men to vote with me. Then the way will be smooth for Mr. Sartwell to put an end to this trouble, which I am sure is causing him more worry than perhaps any one else."

"But why, if that is the case, don't you want him to know this?"

"Don't you see why? It is so that he won't make the same mistake that you have made. You have kindly allowed me to explain; Mr. Sartwell might not have waited for explanations."

"I have not been very kind, have I?" said Edna, contritely, holding out her hand to him. "Please forgive me. Now I want to understand all about this, so come with me into the garden, where we sha'n't be interrupted. Standing here at the gate, some one might call, and then I would have to go into the house, for my mother has gone to Surbiton to see how Mr. Hope is. Was he injured yesterday?"

"No. I will go with you, Miss Sartwell, on one condition."

"What is that?" asked the girl, in some surprise. She had turned to go, expecting him to follow.

"That you will not tell Mr. Sartwell you have been talking with me."

"Oh, I cannot promise that. I tell my father everything."

"Very well. That is quite right, of course; but in this instance, when you tell him you talked with me, say that I came to see him; that the servant said neither he nor Mrs. Sartwell were in, and asked me if I would see you. Tell your father that I said 'No,' and that I was leaving when you spoke to me."

The girl looked frankly at him—a little perplexed wrinkle on her smooth brow. She was puzzled.

"You say that because you do not understand him. He wouldn't mind in the least your talking with me about the strike, because I am entirely in his confidence; but he might not like it if he knew you had been to see Mr. Hope."

"Exactly. Now don't you see that if you tell him you have been talking with me, you will have to tell him what was said? He will learn indirectly that I have been to Surbiton, and will undoubtedly be angry, the more so when he hears I did not intend to tell him. In fact, now that this conversation has taken place, I shall go straight to him and tell him I have talked with Mr. Hope, although I feel sure my doing so will nullify all my plans."

"And this simply because I talked with you for a few minutes?"

"Yes."

The girl bent her perplexed face upon the ground, absent-mindedly disturbing the gravel on the walk with the tiny toe of her very neat boot. The young man devoured her with his eyes, and yearned towards her in his heart. At last she looked suddenly up at him with a wavering smile.

"I am sorry I stopped you," she said. "Perhaps you don't know what it is to think more of one person than all the rest of the world together. My father is everything to me, and when I saw you I was afraid something had happened to him. It doesn't seem right that I should keep anything from him, and it doesn't seem right that I should put anything in the way of a quick settlement. I don't know what to do."

When did a woman ever waver without the man in the case taking instant advantage of her indecision, turning her own weapons against her?

"Don't you see," said Marsten, eagerly, "that Mr. Sartwell has already as much on his mind as a man should bear? Why, then, add to his anxiety by telling him that I have been here or at Surbiton? The explanations which seem satisfactory to you might not be satisfactory to him. He would then merely worry himself quite unnecessarily."

"Do you think he would?"

"Think! I know it."

"Yes, I believe that is true. Well, then, I promise not to tell him of your visit unless he asks me directly. Now come with me; I want to know all your plans, and what Mr. Hope said. I can perhaps help you with a suggestion here and there; for I certainly know what my father will do, and what he won't do, better than any of you."

Edna led the way down the garden path, stopping at last where some chairs were scattered under a wide-spreading tree.

"Sit down," she said. "We can talk here entirely undisturbed."

Marsten sat down with Edna Sartwell opposite him in the still seclusion of the remotest depths of that walled garden. He would not have exchanged his place for one in Paradise, and he thought his lucky stars were fighting for him. But it is fated that every man must pay for his pleasure sooner or later, and Marsten promptly discovered that fate required of him cash down. He had no credit in the bank of the gods.

"Now, although I have promised," began Edna, "I am sure you are wrong in thinking my father would be displeased if he knew we talked over the strike together, and if I have said I will not tell him you were here, it is not because I fear he will be annoyed at that, but because I would have certainly to tell him of your Surbiton visit as well, and, as you say, he might not think you were justified in going to Mr. Hope, no matter what your intentions were. But with me it is quite different. He would just laugh at our discussing the situation, as he does over the conversations I have with Mr. Barnard Hope in this very garden."

"Ah, Mr. Barnard Hope comes here, does he?"

"Yes, quite often, ever since the strike began. He takes the greatest possible interest in the condition of the workingman."

"Does he? It is very much to his credit."

"That's what I say, but father just laughs at him. He thinks Mr. Hope is a good deal of a—a——"

"Of a fool," promptly put in Marsten, seeing her hesitation.

"Well, yes," said Edna, laughing confidentially; "although that is putting it a little strongly, and is not quite what I intended to say. But I don't think so. He may be frivolous—or rather he may have been frivolous, but that was before he came to recognize his responsibilities. I think him a very earnest young man, and he is exceedingly humble about it, saying that he hopes his earnestness will make up for any lack of ability that——"

"Then he needs all the earnestness he can bring to bear upon the subject."

"Oh, he realizes that," cried Edna, enthusiastically. "If there is only some one to point him the way, he says, he will do everything that lies in his power to assist the workingman in bettering his condition. I have told him that his own vacillation of mind is his worst enemy."

"He vacillates, does he?"

"Dreadfully. He will leave here to-day, for instance, thoroughly convinced that a certain course of action is right. To-morrow he will return, having thought over it, and he has ever so many objections that he is not clear about. He says—which is quite true—that it is a most intricate question which one must look upon in all its bearings; otherwise mistakes are sure to be made."

"That is why he does nothing, I suppose. Then he is sure of not making any mistake."

Something of bitterness in the young man's tone caused the girl to look at him in surprise. Surely two people who had the interests of the workingman so much at heart as both Hope and Marsten ought to be glad of any help one could give the other; yet Marsten did not seem to relish hearing of the unselfish and lofty aims of Barney.

"Why do you say he does nothing?"

"Well, when I called upon him before the strike began, hoping he would use his influence to avert trouble, he showed no desire to ameliorate any one's condition but his own. He was comfortable and happy, so why trouble about the men? 'Foolish beggars,' he called them, when I told him they had voted to go on strike."

"Now you see," cried Edna, gleefully, "how easy it is, as you yourself said, for men to misunderstand each other. A few words of explanation will show you how you have thought unjustly of Mr. Barnard Hope. He did intend to use his influence on behalf of the men, and came all the way from Chelsea here to see father on the subject, just as you have done to-day, and father was not at home, just as he is not to-day. Mr. Hope talked it over with mother and me, and he quite agreed with us that it would not be fair to father if there was any interference. It was for my father's sake that he refused to take part in the dispute."

To this conclusive defence of Barney, the young man had no answer; but he was saved the necessity of a reply, for both talker and listener were startled by a shrill voice near the house, calling the girl's name.

Edna started to her feet in alarm, and Marsten also arose.

"That is my step-mother calling me. She has returned. I had no idea it was so late. What shall we do? She mustn't see you here, and yet you can't get out without passing the house."

"I can go over the wall. I wonder who lives in the next house?"

"It is vacant, but the wall is high, and there is broken glass on the top."

"I'll have a try for it, any way."

They passed through the shrubbery to the dividing wall.

"Oh, I am sure you can't do it, and you will cut your hands."

Marsten pulled off his coat; threw it, widespread, over the barbarous broken glass; stepped back as far as the shrubbery would allow him, and took a running jump, catching the top of the wall with his hands where the coat covered the glass. Next instant he was up, putting on his coat, while his boots crunched the broken bottles.

"You haven't cut yourself? I'm so glad. Good-by!" she whispered up at him, her face aglow with excitement.

"One moment," he said, in a low but distinct voice. "I haven't had a chance to tell you my plans."

"Oh, please, please jump down; my mother may be here at any moment."

The cry of "Edna!" came again from the house.

"It's all right yet," whispered Marsten. "But I must know what you think of my plans. I'll be here at this hour to-morrow, and if the coast is clear would you throw your shawl, or a ribbon, or anything, on the wall where my coat was, so that I can see it from this side?"

"Do go. If you are seen it will spoil everything. I don't know what to say about to-morrow. I'll think over it."

"Remember, I shall be on this side. You make everything so clear that I must consult you about this—it is very important."

"Yes, yes. I promise, but you are risking it all by remaining there."

Marsten jumped down into another man's garden and pushed his trespass ruthlessly over and through whatever came in his way, until he reached the gate and was out once more on the public way. The safety signal, "To be Let," was in the windows of the house and on a board above the high wall.

"Ah, Barney Hope," he muttered, clenching his fist, "all the good things of this world are not for you. Once over the wall is worth a dozen times through the gate. I fancy I need instruction on my duty to my employers quite as much as you require having your obligations to the workingman explained to you."

## CHAPTER XVI.

"Edna, where are you?"

"Here, mother."

"You heard me calling you; why did you not answer?"

"I have answered by coming to you. How is Mr. Hope?"

"In a dreadfully nervous state. He thinks he is not hurt, but I am sure he has been injured internally, which is far worse than outward wounds, as I told him. He seems to be strung on wires, and jumps every time his wife makes the most casual remark to him. I advised him to see a physician, and know the worst at once. And Mrs. Hope tells me he acts very queerly. He took scarcely any breakfast this morning yet before lunch he ordered into the study a simply enormous meal, and devoured it all alone."

"Perhaps that was because he had taken so little breakfast."

"No, child, you don't know what you are talking about. There are some things Mr. Hope can never touch without being ill afterwards. Mrs. Hope is very careful of his diet. There's pickles, for instance; he hasn't touched a pickle for sixteen years, yet to-day he consumed a great quantity, and drank a whole bottle of beer, besides roast beef and cheese, and ever so many other things. Mrs. Hope, poor woman, is sitting with folded hands, waiting for him to die. I never saw such a look of heavenly resignation on any human face before."

"As on Mr.. Hope's?"

"Edna, don't be pert. You know very well I mean Mrs. Hope."

"Really, mother, I didn't. I thought perhaps Mr. Hope was resigned. What does he say?"

"He says it hasn't hurt him in the least, but Mrs. Hope merely sighs and shakes her head. She knows what is in store for him."

"I'll warrant the poor man was just hungry, and tired of too much dieting. I hope he enjoyed his meal."

"Edna, you have too little experience, and, much as I regret to say it, too little sense to understand what it means. Mr. Hope's digestive organs have always been weak—always. If it had not been for his wife's anxious care, he would have been dead long ago. She allowed him out of her sight for a few minutes this morning, and refused all callers, except myself and one or two of her own very dearest friends, and you see what happened. She fears that the excitement of yesterday has completely ruined his nerves, and that he doesn't know what he is doing, although he insists he feels as well as ever he did; but I said to Mrs. Hope I would have the best medical advice at once if I were in her place. Who was it called here to see your father while I was away?"

"I have not been in the house since you left."

"What! In the garden all this time! Edna, when will you learn to have some responsibility? How can you expect the maids to do their duty if you neglect yours and never look after them?"

"You train them so well, mother, that I did not think it was necessary for me to look after them while you were away."

"Yes, I train them, and, I hope, I do my duty towards them; but you also have duties to perform, although you think so lightly of them. You forget that for every hour idled away you will have to give an account on the Last Great Day."

"I have not been idling, and, even if I had, one can't be always thinking of the Last Great Day."

They had by this time reached the drawing-room, and Mrs. Sartwell sat down, gazing with chastened severity at her step-daughter.

"Edna," she said, solemnly, "I implore you not to give way to flippancy. That is exactly the way your father talks, and while, let us hope, it will be forgiven him, it ill becomes one of your years to take that tone. Your father little thinks what trouble he is storing for himself in his training of you, and, if I told him you were deceiving him, he would not believe it. But some day, alas! his eyes will be opened."

"How am I deceiving him?" cried Edna, a quick pallour coming into her face.

Her step-mother mournfully shook her head, and sighed.

"If your own heart does not tell you, then perhaps I should be silent. You have his wicked temper, my poor child. Your face is pale with anger just because I have mildly tried to show you the right path."

"You have not shown me the right path. You have said I am deceiving my father, and I ask what you mean?"

Mrs. Sartwell smiled gently, if sadly.

"How like! how like! I can almost fancy it is your father speaking with your voice."

"Well, I am glad of that. You don't often say complimentary things to me."

"That is more of your pertness. You know very well I don't compliment you when I say you are like your father. Far from it. But a day will come when even his eyes will be opened. Yes, indeed."

"You mean that his eyes will be opened to my deceit, but you have not told me how I am deceiving him."

"You deceive him because you take very good care, when in his presence, not to show him the worst side of your character. Oh, dear no, you take good care of that! Butter wouldn't melt in your mouth when he is here. But he'll find you out some day, to his sorrow. Wait till your stubborn wills cross, and then you will each know the other. Of course, now it is all smooth and pleasant, but that is because you don't demand to know what he means, and do not tell him that you can't be bothered about the Last Great Day."

"Father never threatens me with the Judgment, as you so often do, nor does he make accusations against me, and so I don't need to ask what he means. I suppose I am wicked," continued the girl, almost in tears, "but you say things that seem always to bring out the bad side of my character."

"You are too impulsive," said the lady, smoothly. "You are first impenitently impudent to me, and then you, say you have a bad character, which I never asserted. You are not worse than your father."

"Worse? I only wish I were half as good."

"Ah, that's because you don't know him any better than he knows you. You think he takes you entirely into his confidence, but he does nothing of the sort. Why did he so carefully carry away the newspaper with him this morning?"

"I'm sure I don't know. Why shouldn't he? it's his own."

"His own,—yes! but he never did it before. He took it away the better to deceive his wife and daughter,—that's why. So that we shouldn't know how he braved and defied the men yesterday. Oh, I can see him! It was just the kind of thing that would gratify his worldly pride."

"Oh, what happened, mother?" cried the girl, breathless with anxiety.

"I thought he didn't tell you, and I suppose he did not mention that poor Mr. Hope, and Mr. Monkton too, begged and implored him not to go to the works to-day,—yes, almost on their bended knees; and he paid not the slightest attention to their wishes—and they his employers! If for no other reason he——"

"But tell me what he did? How did he defy the men?"

"Why do you not allow me to finish what I am saying? Why are you so impatient?"

"Because he is my father. Is that not reason enough?"

"Yes, my poor child, yes," murmured Mrs. Sartwell, in mournful cadence, "that is reason enough. Like father, like daughter. It is perhaps too much for me to expect patience from you, when he has so little."

"That is not my meaning, but never mind. Please tell me if he was in danger."

"We are all of us in danger every moment of our lives, and saved from it by merciful interposition and not by any virtue of our puny efforts. How often, how often have I made my poor endeavour to impress this great truth on your father's mind, only to be met with scorn and scoffing, as if scorn and scoffing would avail on the Last——Why are you acting so, Edna? You pace up and down the room in a way that is—I regret to say it—most unladylike. You shouldn't spring from your chair in that abrupt manner. I say that scoffing will not avail. Surely I have a right to make the statement in my own house! When I said to your father this very morning that he should not boast in his own strength, which is but fleeting, but should put his trust in a higher power, he answered that he did—the police were on the ground. What is that but scoffing? He knew I was not referring to the police."

Edna had left the room before her step-mother completed the last sentence, and when the much-tried woman, arising with a weary sigh, followed the girl into the hall, she found herself confronted with another domestic tribulation. Edna had her hat on, and was clasping her cloak.

"Where are you going?" asked her amazed stepmother.

"To London."

"To London! Does your father know of this?"

"He will. I am going to take a hansom from the station to the works."

"What! Drive through that howling mob?"

"The howling mob won't hurt me."

"Child, you are crazy! What is the meaning of this?"

"The meaning is that I am going to hear what danger my father was in yesterday, and to be with him if he is in danger to-day:"

The good woman held up her hands in helpless dismay. Was ever human being, anxious to do her duty to all, harassed by two such ungovernable persons since the world began?—she asked herself. But for once she made exactly the remark to cope with the situation.

"'The time has come sooner than I expected. Your father has forbidden you to go to the office, and, when he sees that you have disobeyed him at such a time as this, he will be furious. Then you will know what I have to stand."

The impetuous girl paused in her preparations.

"Then why do you exasperate me beyond endurance by refusing to tell me what happened?"

"I refuse! I refuse you nothing. Better would it have been for me if I had when you were younger; then you would think twice before you flung all obedience to the winds. You have only to ask what you want to know, and listen with patience while it is told to you."

"I have asked you a dozen times."

"How you do exaggerate! I call it exaggeration, although I might perhaps be forgiven for using a harsher term. Exactitude of statement is more——"

"Will you tell me, or shall I go?"

"Have I not just said that I will tell you anything? What is it you want to know? Your own ridiculous conduct has driven everything out of my head."

"You said my father had defied the men and was in danger yesterday."

"Oh, that! After seeing the police guard Mr. Hope and Mr. Monkton through the lawless mob, what must your father do but show how brave he was compared with his superiors. He came out of the gates alone, and walked through the mob."

"What did he say?"

"He didn't say anything."

"Then how did he defy the men?"

"Good gracious, child, how stupid you are! When men are driven to extremities, surely his coming out among them—and he the cause of it all—

was defiance enough. But a full account is in the paper I bought at the station; it is on the hall table, where you would have seen it if you could have kept your temper. Read it if you want to. It is not me you are disobeying when you do so. Remember, it was your father who did not want you to see the paper."

The day proved a long one to Edna Sartwell, and, when her father did not return at the usual hour, she became more and more anxious. Her step-mother said nothing about the delay, as the hours passed, but began to assume that air of patient resignation which became her so well. Dinner was served to the minute, and at the accustomed moment the table was cleared. Once or twice she chided Edna for her restlessness, and regretted she had to speak, but was compelled to do so because the good example she herself set was so palpably unappreciated. At last she said:

"Edna, go to bed. I will wait up for your father."

"He is sure to be home soon. Please let me wait until he comes."

There was silence for a few minutes.

"I don't wish to ask you twice, Edna. You heard what I said."

"Please do not send me away until father comes. I am so anxious! Let me sit up instead of you. I can't sleep if I do go to bed. Won't you let me sit up in your place?"

The martyred look came into the thin face of her step-mother—the look which told of trials uncomplainingly borne.'

"I have always sat up for your father, and always shall, so long as we are spared to each other. For the third time I ask you to go to bed."

The girl sat where she was, the red flag of rebellion in her cheek. The glint of suppressed anger in Mrs. Sartwell's eye showed that a point had been reached where one or the other of them had to leave the room defeated. The elder woman exhibited her forbearance by speaking in the same level tone throughout.

"Do you intend to obey me, Edna?"

"No, I do not."

Mrs. Sartwell went on with her sewing, a little straighter in the back, perhaps, but not otherwise visibly disturbed by the unjustifiable conduct of the girl. In each instance after Edna's prompt replies there was silence for a few moments.

"In the earlier part of the day, Edna, you permitted yourself to speak to me and act towards me in a manner which I hoped you would regret when opportunity for reflection was given. I expected some expression of contrition from you. Have you reflected, Edna?"

"Yes."

Mrs. Sartwell threaded her needle with almost excessive deliberation.

"And what has been the result?"

"That I was pleased to think I had said nothing harsher than I did."

The ticking of the tall clock on the landing echoed through the house. Edna listened intently for a quick, firm step on the gravel, but all outside was silent.

"Added to your—if I use the word insolence, it is because I can think of no other term with which to characterize the remarks you have addressed to me—added to your insolence is now disobedience. If I am overstating, the case, no one can be more pleased than I to be corrected, in the proper spirit."

"I have no desire to correct you."

After nipping the thread with her teeth and drawing a deep, wavering sigh, Mrs. Sartwell said:

"In every household, Edna, some one must command and others obey. When my time comes I shall gladly lay down the burden of what poor authority is delegated to me, but until that time comes I shall be mistress in my own house. Your father freely, and of his own choice, gave me that authority, and he, not you, is the proper person to revoke it, if it pleases him to do so. I shall therefore say nothing more until he returns. Then he must choose between us. If you are to be mistress here, I shall bow my head without a word, and leave this house, praying that peace and every blessing may remain within it."

Something of the self-sacrificing resignation breathing through these measured words must have touched the hardened heart of the girl, for she buried her face in her hands and began to weep,—a certain sign of defeat. But she evidently determined not to give her antagonist the satisfaction fairly won by so admirable a dissertation upon the correct conduct of a well-ordered household.

"It is always poor father!" she sobbed. "With all the trouble and anxiety already on his mind, he must be worried when he comes home by our miserable squabbles."

"I never squabble, Edna. Neither do I ever use such an undignified word. Where you got it, I'm sure I do not know, but it was not from me. If you wish your father not to be troubled, then you should act so that it would not be necessary to appeal to him. It is no wish of mine to add to his cares,—far otherwise. Are you ready to obey me now?"

"Yes."

The girl rose and went rather uncertainly to the door, her eyes filled with tears.

"You have not kissed me good-night, Edna."

She kissed her step-mother on the cheek and went to her room, flinging herself, dressed as she was, on her bed, sobbing. Yet she listened for that step on the gravel which did not come. At last she rose, arranged her hair for the night, and bathed her face, so that her father, if he came home and saw her, should not know she had been crying. Wrapping herself in her dressing-gown, she sat by the window and listened intently and anxiously. It was after midnight when the last train came in, and some minutes later her quick ear heard the long-expected step far down the street; but it was not the quick, nervous tread she was accustomed to. It was the step of a tired man. She thought of softly calling to him from the window, but did not. Holding her door ajar, she heard the murmur of her step-mother's voice and occasionally the shorter, gruffer note of her father's evidently monosyllabic replies. After what seemed an interminable time, her stepmother came up alone, and the door of her room closed.

Edna, holding her breath, slipped noiselessly out of her room and down the stairs. The steps were kind to her, and did not creak. She opened the door of the dining-room, and appeared as silently as if she were a ghost. Her father started from his chair, and it required all his habitual self-command to repress the exclamation that rose to his lips.

"Heaven help us, my dearest girl; do you want to frighten your old father out of what little wits he has left him?" he whispered.. "Why aren't you asleep?" She gently closed the door, then ran to him, and threw her arms about his neck.

"Oh, father, are you safe? You are not hurt?"

"Hurt! Why, what would hurt me, you silly baby?" He ruffled her hair, pulling it over her eyes. "You've been dreaming; I believe you are talking in your sleep now. Why are you not in bed?"

"I couldn't sleep till you came home. What kept you so late, father?"

"Now this is more than the law requires of a man. Have I to make explanations to two women every night I come home by the late train?"

The girl sat down on a hassock, and laid her head on her father's knee, he smoothing her hair caressingly.

"What is all this pother about, Edna? Why are you so anxious at my being out late?"

"I was afraid you were in danger; I read what was said in the paper about your defying the men, and—and——"

Sartwell laughed quietly.

"My dear girl, if you are going to begin life by believing all you see in the papers, you will have an uneasy time of it. I can tell you something much more startling which has not yet appeared in print."

"What is that, father?" asked the girl, looking up at him.

"That you have been a most unruly child all day, causing deep anxiety to those responsible for your upbringing."

Edna sank her head again upon her father's knee.

"Yes," she said, "that is quite true. I have been dreadfully wicked and rebellious, saying things I ought not to have said."

"And leaving unsaid the things,—ah well, none of us is quite perfect. It is a blessing there is such a thing as forgiveness of sins, otherwise most of us would come badly off."

"Somehow, when you are here, nothing seems to matter, and any worries of the day appear small and trivial, and I wonder why they troubled me; but when you are away—well, it's different altogether."

"That is very flattering to me, Edna, but you mustn't imagine I'm to be cajoled into omitting the scolding you know you deserve. No, I can see through your diplomacy. It won't do, my dear girl, it won't do."

"It isn't diplomacy or flattery; it's true. I'll take my scolding most meekly if you tell me what happened to-day."

"I refuse to bargain with a confessed rebel; still, as I must get you off to bed before morning, I will tell you what happened. An attempt was made to settle the strike to-day. The men had a meeting to-night, and I waited at my club to hear the outcome. I had a man at the meeting who was to bring me the result of the vote as soon as it was taken. A young man—one of the strikers, but the only man of brains among them—saw me this afternoon, and made certain proposals that I accepted. Gibbons was to be renounced, and a deputation of the men was to come to me. We should probably have settled the matter in ten minutes, if it had come off."

"Then he failed, after all his trouble?"

"Who failed?"

"The—the young man you speak of?"

Edna found her rôle of deceiver a difficult one. She was glad her father could not see her face, and bitterly regretted giving Marsten a promise not to tell of his visit.

"Yes, he failed. Of course there was not time to canvass the men properly, and at the meeting Gibbons, who is a glib talker, won over enough to defeat the efforts of the others. It wasn't much of a victory, but sufficient for the purpose. They had, I understand, a very stormy meeting, and Gibbons won by some dozen votes or thereabouts."

"And what is to be done now?"

"Oh, we are just where we were. I'll wait a few days more, and, if the men do not come back, I'll fill their places with a new lot. I don't want to do that except as a last resort, but I won't be played with very much longer. Now, dear girl, you know all about it; so to bed, to bed, at once, and sleep soundly. This dissipation cannot be allowed, you know."

He kissed her and patted her affectionately on the shoulder. The girl, with a guilty feeling in her heart, crept up stairs as noiselessly as she had descended.

## CHAPTER XVII.

Albert Langly found a new and absorbing interest in life. This interest was friendship, the pleasures of which the organist had never before experienced during his lonely and studious existence. He became a constant visitor at Braunt's rooms and began teaching Jessie the rudiments of music, finding her a willing and apt pupil as well as a very silent one. Her gaunt face and large sorrowful eyes haunted him wherever he went, while she looked upon him with an awe such as she would have bestowed upon a being from another world; which perhaps he was, for he had certainly little relationship with this eager, money-seeking planet. Joe Braunt was quite content to sit in his armchair and smoke. However small the money is for the housekeeping, a workingman will generally contrive to provide himself with tobacco.

As often as not, Braunt was absent when his daughter had her music lesson, for Mrs. Grundy has little to say about the domestic arrangements of the extreme poor. The entire absence of all world-wisdom in the young man would have made it difficult for any one to explain to him why two people who loved music should not be together as often as opportunity offered, had there been any one who took interest enough in him or in her to attempt such an explanation. The girl, who had even more than her father's worship of harmony, was fascinated by the organist's marvellous skill upon the instrument to which he had devoted his life, before her solemn eyes had lured his musical soul into their mystic influence. The two were lovers without either of them suspecting it.

Once Langly persuaded Braunt and his daughter to go to the empty church with him and hear the grand organ. The workman and the girl sat together in the wilderness of vacant pews, and listened entranced while the sombre rhythm of the Dead March filled the deserted edifice. Langly played one selection after another, for the love of the music and the love of his audience. It was a concert such as the mad king of Bavaria might have hearkened to in lonely state, but heard now by a man without a penny in his pocket and hardly a crust to eat in his squalid rooms. Whether the deft fingers of the Bavarian player soothed for the moment the demon that tortured the king, as the skill of David lulled the disquiet of Saul, who can say?—but the enchanted touch of the solitary organist on the ivory keys transported his listeners into a world where hunger was unknown.

The stillness of the great church, untroubled by outside sounds; the reverberation of harmony from the dim, lofty, vaulted roof; the awaking of unexpected echoes lurking in dark corners, added to the solemnity of the music,—gave the hearers and performer a sense of being cut adrift from the babel beyond. The church for the time being was an oasis of peace in a vast desert of turmoil.

Never again could Langly persuade Braunt to accompany him to the church. Some memories are too precious to be molested, and he who risks the repetition of an experience of perfect bliss prepares for himself a possible disillusion.

"Nay, my lad," he said, "we'll let that rest. Some day, maybe, if I'm ever like beginning to forget what I've heard, I'll go back, but not now. I would go stark music-mad if I often heard playing like yon; in fact, I think sometimes I'm half daft already."

But Jessie often accompanied the organist to the quiet church, neither of them thinking of propriety or impropriety; and luckily they were unseen by either the sexton or his wife, who would have raised a to-do in the sacred interests of fitting and proper conduct. Sometimes the girl sat with him in the organ loft, watching him as he played, but more often she occupied one of the pews, the better to hear the instrument in correct perspective. Jessie had inherited from her father the taciturnity which characterized him, and her natural reticence was augmented by her shyness. There was seldom any conversation between the two in the church; each appeared abundantly satisfied by the fact that the other was there. They might almost have been mute lovers, for any use spoken language was to them.

Once, on coming down the narrow stair which led from the organ-loft, Langly thought she had gone, so strangely deserted did the church seem.

Even in the daytime the gas had to be lighted when service was held; for the windows were of stained glass, and the church was closely surrounded by tall buildings. The atmosphere in that grim quarter was rarely clear, and the interior of the church was always dim. Langly peered short-sightedly through the gloom, but could not descry her. A feeling of vague alarm took possession of him, until, hurrying up the aisle, he saw she was in her place, with her head resting on the hymn-book board of the pew, apparently asleep. He touched her gently on the shoulder, and, when she slowly raised her head, saw that she had been silently weeping.

"What is the matter, dear?" he whispered, bending over her.

"I feel afraid—afraid of something—I don't know what. The church grew black dark suddenly, and the music faded away. I thought I was sinking, sinking down, and no one to save me." She shuddered as she spoke, and rose uncertainly to her feet, tottering slightly on stepping into the aisle. "It was like a bad dream," she added, with long-drawn, quivering breath.

He slipped his arm about her waist, supporting her as they walked down the aisle together.

"It's the darkness of the church," he said, "and perhaps the sadness of the music. I'll play something more cheerful next time you come. I play too much in minor keys."

At the door she asked him to stop a moment before going out. She dried her eyes, but ineffectually; for, leaning against the stone wall, she began to cry again in a despondent, helpless way that wrung the young man's heart within him.

"Jessie, Jessie," he faltered, not knowing what to do or say.

"I feel ill and weak," she sobbed. "I shall be all right again presently."

"Come, and we will have tea somewhere. That will cheer you up."

They went away together, and he took her to a place where tea was to be had. She sat there, dejectedly leaning her head on her hand, while the refreshments were being brought; he opposite her, in melancholy silence. She took some sips of the tea, but could not drink it, shaking her head when he offered her the buttered bread.

"I must get home," she said at last. "I can't eat. I shall be better there."

They walked slowly to Rose Garden Court, and at No. 3 he helped her up the sordid stair; she clinging breathlessly to the shaky railing at every step or two, he thankful there was but one flight to climb. Braunt sat in his armchair, an angry cloud on his brow. He was in his gruffest mood, looking at them when they entered with surly displeasure, but he said nothing. It was the evening after the men, with their small majority, had resolved to continue the strike, and Braunt's pipe was cold. Not another scrap of tobacco could he gather, although he had turned out every pocket in hope of finding a crumb or two. Jessie sank into a chair, her white face turning appealingly, alternately from her father to her friend, evidently fearing that something harsh might be said, for she knew her father was rough-spoken when ill-pleased.

"Jessie is not well," said the organist.

Braunt did not answer him, but crossed over to his daughter, and, smoothing her hair, said more gently than she had expected:

"What's wrong, lassie? Art hungry?"

"No, no," murmured the girl, eagerly. "We had tea before we came in. I'm not hungry."

Langly, slow as he was to comprehend, saw that Braunt, at least, had been without food, perhaps for long. He had several times offered him money from his own scanty store, but it had always been refused, sometimes in a manner not altogether friendly. The organist went quietly out, leaving father and daughter alone together.

"Would you like me to get some one to come in—some woman?" said Braunt, anxiously. "We don't know our neighbours, but one of the women would come in if she knew you were ill."

The girl shook her head.

"I want none—naught but just to rest a little. It will all pass away soon.

I need but rest."

The father returned to his chair, and they sat silent in the gathering darkness.

Presently the door was pushed open, and Langly entered with parcels in his arms. He placed a loaf on the table, with the rest of his burdens, and put on the empty hearth the newspaper that held a pennyworth of coals.

Braunt glared at him, speechless for a moment; then cried out, indignantly:

"I'll ha' none o' thy charity, my lad, d——d if I will!"

Before Langly could reply, Jessie rose tremblingly to her feet.

"Don't, father, don't!" she wailed; then, swaying as she attempted to walk towards him, she fell suddenly in a heap on the floor.

Langly sprang forward, but Braunt brushed him roughly aside, and, stooping over his daughter, lifted her slight form in his arms, speaking soothingly and caressingly to her. He carried her to the bed, and placed her lovingly upon it.

"Run!" he cried to Langly. "Run for a doctor. There's one down Light Street. There's something main wrong here, I'm feared."

The young man needed no second telling. The doctor objected to go to Rose Garden Court; he had his own patients to attend to, he said. He knew there was little to be got out of the court.

"I am organist at St. Martyrs," replied the messenger, eagerly. "I will see you paid."

"Oh, it's not that," said the doctor. "Who generally attends people in the court? There must be some one."

"I don't know," answered Langly, "and I have no time to find out. The case is urgent. Come!"

So the doctor, grumbling—for this kind of practice was out of his line—

went with him.

They found Braunt anxiously chafing the hands of the girl.

"You've been long about it," he cried, as they entered.

Neither answered, and the doctor went quickly to the bed, with the seemingly callous indifference of a man to whom such scenes are matters of hourly routine. He placed his fingers upon her wrist, bent his ear down to her breast, then put his hand on her smooth white brow.

"Has she been long ill?" he asked, sharply.

"Jessie was always weakly," answered her father, "and latterly has not been at all well, poor girl."

"Who has attended her?"

"No one."

"Oh, well, you know, I can't grant a death certificate under these circumstances. There will most likely be an inquest."

"Good God!" shrieked Braunt. "An inquest! You don't mean to say—you can't mean it!—Jessie is not dead?"

"Yes, she is dead. I can do no good here. I'll let the coroner know, and he can do as he pleases. I have no doubt it is all right, but we are bound to act according to the law, you know. Good-night!"

Braunt threw himself upon the bed in a storm of grief; Langly stood by the side of the dead girl, stunned. He took her limp, thin hand in his, and gazed down upon her, dazed and tearless. Her father rose and paced the room, alternately pleading with fate and cursing it. Suddenly he turned on Langly like a madman.

"What are you doing here?" he roared. "It was your interference that caused her last words to be troubled. Get you gone, and leave us alone!"

Langly turned from the bed and walked slowly to the door without a word, Braunt following him with his lowering, bloodshot eyes. The young man paused irresolutely at the door, leaned his arm against it, and bowed his head in hopeless anguish.

"Heaven help me!" he said, despairingly, "I loved her too."

Braunt looked at him a moment, not comprehending at first. Gradually the anger faded from his face.

"Did you so, lad?" he said gently, at last. "I didn't know—I didn't know. Forgive me my brutish temper. God knows it should be broken by this time. I'm crazy, lad, and know not what I say. I have not a penny-piece in the world, nor where to go to get aught. My lassie shall not have a pauper's funeral in this heartless town. No, not if I have to take her in my arms, as I ha' oft done, and trudge wi' her to the North, sleeping under the hedges by the way. Yes, that's what I'll do. We'll be tramping to the Dead March then. It will keep us company. We'll rest at night in the green fields under the trees, away from the smoke and din, alone together. Ah, God! I'll begin the journey now and tramp all night to be quit o' this Babylon ere the morning."

"No, no!" cried Langly, catching his arm. "You mustn't do that. You must hear what the coroner says."

"What has the coroner or any one else to do with me or her?"

"It is the law: you must obey it."

"What care I for the law? What's it done for either me or Jessie? I'll have no pauper funeral, law or no law."

"There won't be a pauper funeral. There are kind hearts in London, as well as in the North. Promise me you'll do nothing until I see if I can get the money."

"I promise," said Braunt, sinking into his chair. "I doubt if I could walk far to-night, even if I tried. But leave me now, lad, and come back again later. I want to be alone and think."

Langly left the room, and on the landing met Marsten, whom he did not know, but who he saw was about to enter.

"Don't go in," he whispered. "He wants to be alone."

"Is there anything wrong?" asked Marsten, alarmed at the tone of the other.

"Yes, his daughter is dead."

"Dead! Good God! How? An accident?"

"No. She has been ill for weeks, but no one thought of this. Jessie died about an hour since—unexpectedly. Are you a friend of his?"

"Yes."

"Then you must help me—tell me what to do. Come down into the court where we can talk."

The two young men descended the stair.

"Braunt has no money, and he will not have his daughter buried by the Parish. We must get money. I have promised it, but I have very little myself, although I will willingly give all I have. If it was more I would not ask help from any one."

"I have only a few shillings," said Marsten, "but we must get more somehow. None of the men has any, or they would give it. Yesterday I could have gone to Sartwell; but to-day, unfortunately, I have quarrelled with him, bitterly and irretrievably, I fear. Although he said nothing to me, I can't go to him. But there is Barnard Hope. Yes, he's the man. He helped Braunt when there was trouble with the police. I don't like to go to Barnard Hope—for certain reasons I don't care to be indebted to him. Would you mind going? He lives in Chelsea."

"No. I will do anything I can. I have promised."

"Then I would go to-night if I were you. Tomorrow is his 'At Home' day, and there will be a lot of people there. It will be difficult to see him then, and we can't wait until the day after. His address is Craigenputtoch House, Chelsea. If you fail, I will see his father, so one or other of us is sure to get the money."

"I will go at once," said Langly.

It was a long journey to Chelsea, and when the tired organist reached the place he found Barney had a theatre party on, with a dance to follow, and would not likely be home that night. It was uncertain when he would return in the morning, but he would be sure to be back at three o'clock, as his 'At Home' friends would begin to gather at that hour, so Barney's servant said. The wearied man tramped back, and reached Rose Garden Court about midnight. He rapped at Braunt's door, and, receiving no answer, pushed it open after a moment's hesitation. He feared the headstrong, impatient man might, after all, have carried out his resolution, and left with his burden for the North, but he found nothing changed. Braunt sat there with his head in his hands, and gave him no greeting.

"I am to have the money to-morrow," Langly said, feeling sure it would not be refused.

Braunt made no answer, and, taking one look at the silent figure on the bed, whose face seemed now like that of a little child, the young man departed as quietly as he had entered.

Mrs. Scimmins met him on the stair. She wanted to know all about it. She said that the women of the court, when they heard of the death, had offered their help, but Braunt had acted like a brute, and had driven them away with fearful oaths. She was sure something was wrong. The coroner had been there, and thought so too. There was to be an inquest at the Vestry Hall in the morning. A summons had been left for Langly to attend and give his evidence.

"But I'm going to Chelsea in the morning," cried the young man, aghast. "I know nothing, except that Jessie has been ill."

"You saw her die, they say. Braunt admitted that. You will have to attend the inquest, or they will send a policeman after you."

Langly did not sleep that night, and was gaunt and haggard in the morning. The coroner's jury trooped up the stair, and, after looking at the dead girl, adjourned to the Vestry Hall. Langly gave his evidence, and, leaving the room at once, hovered about the door, waiting for Braunt, who remained in the Vestry Hall. At last he came out, with white face, staring straight ahead of him.

"What did they say?" asked Langly; but the other did not answer, striding through the curious crowd as if he saw nothing.

"What was the verdict?" inquired a bystander of one of the jurymen as he came out.

"Starved to death," replied the man.

# CHAPTER XVIII.

On the day after Marsten's failure to win a majority of the men to his side in the strike controversy, the young man went to Wimbledon, hoping to find consolation for his defeat in the company of the girl he loved. He felt that he was perhaps taking a rather unfair advantage of Sartwell in thus making a clandestine appointment with his daughter, but he justified himself, as lovers have always justified themselves, by claiming that a man was a fool to lose a trick when he had the card in his hand to take it. It was evident that Sartwell had no objection to the visits of Barnard Hope, and that he would be quite willing to have his daughter marry the son of his employer. If Marsten had known this the day before, he would not have been so self-denying as to refuse to see Edna Sartwell, and now that fate had interposed in his behalf, giving him the knowledge that he had a rival, he was not going to be idiot enough to throw away his chance.

He entered the vacant plot surrounding the empty house, and looked anxiously along the glass-topped wall for the signal that Edna had promised, under compulsion, to display. It was not in sight. He wondered if, after all, the girl had told her father of his visit. Let Sartwell get but the slightest inkling of it, and Marsten was certain the whole particulars would soon be within the manager's knowledge.

He wandered up and down the wrong side of the wall disconsolately, not knowing what to do. Once he paused near where he had, on the previous day, jumped over. He thought he heard a slight cough on the other side. It might be a warning, or an invitation: the question was, which? She must know that he would be there, waiting for her signal; or perhaps—the thought was bitter—she might have forgotten all about him.

At the further end of the garden was a park fence, lower than the forbidding stone wall, which it joined at right angles. As anything is better than suspense, the young man resolved to take the risk of reconnoitering. He mounted the park fence and peered over the wall, but the trees and shrubbery were so thick that he could not see whether any one was in Sartwell's garden or not; even the house was hidden from his view. Faint heart never climbed a stone wall: Marsten hesitated but a moment, seized a branch of an overhanging tree, pulled himself up to the top, chancing the glass, and leaped down among the shrubbery on the other side. He listened intently for a while, but there was no sound; then he moved cautiously through the bushes to the open space under the trees where he had talked with her the day before. No one was there, but he caught his breath as he saw a red-silk scarf hanging over the back of one of the chairs. She had at least thought of him, for that was undoubtedly the unused signal.

He was now in a greater quandary than he had been on the other side of the wall. She had apparently intended to throw the scarf over the broken glass, otherwise why had she brought it to their rendezvous; but, as she had not given the signal agreed upon, might there not be a danger that her father was at home? The young man knit his brows as he pondered on what explanation he would give Sartwell if he were discovered standing under the trees.

Marsten had half made up his mind to return by the way he came, when he saw Edna approaching from the house. The girl held out her hand to him with a smile that went to his heart, but her words were not so reassuring.

"I was watching for you," she said, "hoping you would not come."

"Hoping I would not come?" echoed Marsten, with a suggestion of dismay in his tone.

"At least hoping you would not come, except by the gate. I don't like this. It seems secret and mean—as if we were doing something we were ashamed of. Now, we may not accomplish much good, talking about the strike, but we are certainly not doing anything either of us would fear to have the whole world know. There is no reason, now that your plans of yesterday have failed, why you should not have come to the front door like any other visitor, is there?"

"I suppose not."

"Of course not," cried the girl, eagerly, "and so I intend to tell my father all about this visit, even if I could not mention yesterday's."

"Oh, but you must not do anything of the kind," pleaded Marsten, thoroughly alarmed. "You will promise me, won't you, that you will not say a word of my being here to-day?"

The girl laughed and shook her head.

"I'll not make another promise so foolish as yesterday's. You see, my promise did no good."

"What! Did you tell Mr. Sartwell I had been here?"

"No. I said I wouldn't, and I didn't; but it made me feel wretchedly guilty when there was no occasion for it. What I mean is, that your plans did not succeed in putting an end to the strike, and so it would have made no difference after all, if I had told my father. Don't you see that? No, I won't make another such promise in a hurry again."

"Miss Sartwell," said Marsten, seriously, "you don't understand all the circumstances; there are reasons why your father must not know I have been here. Although negotiations have failed for the moment, they will come on again shortly. If Mr. Sartwell knew I was here yesterday——"

"Oh, I intend to keep my promise about yesterday. I shall not say a word about that visit: it is of to-day's I shall tell him."

"But don't you see? Yesterday's visit led to this one. They are inseparably joined: you cannot mention one without leading to the other. Please promise you will say nothing about to-day's either."

"I won't make any more promises. When my father came home late last night, he told me all that happened—what you had tried to do, and everything. I felt so guilty at having to keep anything from him, that I resolved to make no more promises to any one unless he knew of them and there was no need to feel guilty. I am sure he would have been glad to know we had talked about the strike, and were trying to help him; yet all because of that foolish promise I dared not say a word. I think, if you knew what I suffered, you would not ask me to keep anything from him."

"Dear Miss Sartwell," cried Marsten, with more of his affection for the girl in his voice than he was aware of, "I would not cause you suffering for anything in the world!"

Edna looked at him with wide-open eyes, surprised at his vehemence; then she laughed merrily.

"Why, how serious you are! After all, I shall soon forget about it; and although I won't make rash promises again, I'll think it all over, and if—— but then, what is the use of 'ifs'? I shall say to my father tonight that you came to see him, and that I talked with you about the strike."

"That wouldn't be true, Miss Sartwell. I didn't come to see him; I came to see you."

"Oh!"

"Yes, and you would have to tell him I climbed the wall. You can't go in for half-truths, you know, and we haven't talked much about the strike, have we?"

"Ah, but you came for that, didn't you?"

"Yes. Oh, yes, of course. Nothing else; but you see it wouldn't do to say anything about this visit to your father unless you told him everything. He would want to know why I came over the wall."

"And why did you? Iam sure you might just as well have come through the gate. It would have been much easier."

"I will next time I come. But you know the wall is there, and I came over it; so, without making any promise, I beg of you to say nothing about it to Mr. Sartwell, for he will want all sorts of explanations that I don't quite see how I can give."

"Well, then, I won't. Oh, dear! that's a promise, isn't it? And I protested I wouldn't. I suppose you'll think that it is just like a woman. But I'll never make you another promise—never."

"Oh, don't say that, Miss Sartwell. I would promise you anything."

"Very well. Promise me you will tell my father you were here."

The girl laughed as she saw his discomfiture when she so promptly took him at his word.

"There," she cried, gleefully, "you see, you didn't mean what you said. I really believe you are afraid of my father."

"I am."

"That's very funny. I should like to tell him that. I can't imagine any one being afraid of him."

"Perhaps you have never seen him when he is angry."

"Oh, yes, I have; but I just sit quiet and say nothing. He is never violent, when angry, as some men are, but his eyes half close, and his lips are set tight, and he doesn't care to be spoken to just then; so that's why I don't speak. He was angry with you that night, was he not?"

"What night, Miss Sartwell?" asked Marsten, almost holding his breath.

."The night at the office when I came in. The first time you ever spoke to me. Don't you remember?"

"I shall never forget it," Marsten said, in a hushed voice.

"Oh, you take things too much to heart, I can see that. You shouldn't mind a little disappointment, nor think my father hard because he refused you. I spoke up for you at the time, as I told you yesterday, and I'm afraid I didn't further your interests by doing so, for father thinks women shouldn't interfere in business."

They were seated opposite one another, the girl bending forward in friendly confidential attitude, the young man unable to take his eyes from her, listening, like one in a dream, to the entrancing murmur of her speech.

"You spoke up for me?" he repeated, as if soliloquizing.

"Yes, and father said——"

The girl paused, embarrassed, remembering that what had been said had not been complimentary to her listener.

"What did he say?" asked Marsten, breathlessly.

"Well, you know, he thought you too young and inexperienced for a responsible position, and you are not very old, are you? But by and by, when you have more experience, I am sure he will listen to you. The great thing is to gain his confidence,—at least that is what I should try to do."

"Yes, I should like to win his confidence," said Marsten, dolefully.

"Oh, it's not difficult. All that is required is to do your duty. I think it's nothing against a young man that he is ambitious. That ought to be in his favour, especially with a man like my father, because he has always been very ambitious himself: and I think the great drawback with workingmen is that they do not seem to care whether they better their positions or not. You can't do anything for a man who won't help himself: and you are ambitious, aren't you?"

"Very. Too much so, I sometimes think."

"Oh, one cannot be too ambitious, unless one is a man like Napoleon and thoroughly base and wicked. Then it's wrong, of course. Now, if you want my advice—but perhaps you think I know nothing about these things?"

"Miss Sartwell, I would rather have your advice than any one else's in the world, and I will follow it to the letter."

"You do take things too seriously. What a weight of responsibility you would place upon my shoulders! No, you must hear the advice first, and then judge whether it is best to follow it or not. I think you should work along quietly for a year or two, doing your very best and saying as little as possible. Father likes a man who does things, rather than one who says things. He doesn't believe much in talk. Then, when you see he trusts you implicitly, perhaps by that time he will offer you the situation; but if he doesn't, you let me know, and I will speak to him about it. Oh, I shall approach the subject very diplomatically. I shall begin by asking how you are getting on at the works, and if he speaks well of you, I will suggest that you be given a better position than the one you are in. How do you like my plan?"

"It is an admirable one, but—but——"

"But what? Where is the objection to it?"

"There is no objection, except that I may get rather discouraged as time goes on."

"Oh, that is nonsense. You are interested in your work, are you not?"

"Very much so, but if I could see you now and again, I—well—wouldn't become hopeless or despondent, you see. If that could be managed——"

Edna sat back in her chair, and looked straight at him with clear, wide eyes that seemed puzzled, trying to see beyond what was plainly in view. Marsten, burdened by the consciousness that he was not dealing honestly with her, yet afraid to awaken her too prematurely to the realities of the situation, was as confused as most single-minded persons are when placed in a false position from which there is no escape without risking disaster. For a moment there arose in his fast-beating heart an heroic determination to cast all caution to the winds, and cry out, "I love you, my girl, I love you; I am poor, and your father has forbidden me to see you;" but he feared a repulse from the girl, more fatal to his hopes than the check he had received from her father. He bent his gaze upon the ground and curbed his impatience. He realized that honesty had not been the best policy when he had inopportunely confessed his affection for the girl to her father, although he thought at the time he had taken a manly and straightforward course. Had he been less impulsive, and tried to win still farther the confidence of Sartwell, he might perhaps have ultimately gained a footing in his chief's house, and then who knows what would have happened! He had drawn upon the bank of confidence, and his cheque had been dishonored: he could not risk a second mistake of that kind.

"I don't like your word 'managed,'" said Edna at last, a little wrinkle of displeasure on her fair brow. "Your visits here do not need to be managed. You can come as any other friend of my father comes, and we shall have plenty of opportunities for talk. You persist in thinking that my father has some feeling against you, when I assure you such is not the case."

Before Marsten could answer, the silence was sharply broken by the emphatic click of the gate, and the young man was dumbfounded by seeing Sartwell enter, stride up the path leading to the house, stop, turn his head toward the spot where they sat, then cross the lawn directly to them. Marsten sprang to his feet; the girl arose more slowly, a roguish twinkle in her eye. Here was the solution of the problem right to her hand, at precisely the proper moment. The expression of the three faces would have interested a student in physiognomy. Anger, delight, confusion, were reflected from the countenances of Sartwell, Edna, and Marsten, respectively; but the elder man was the first to control his emotion, and, as he approached, his face became an impassive mask, revealing nothing of the passion within. He cast a brief quick glance at Marsten, who stood there pale, in the attitude of one who has been trapped, and who sees no avenue of escape. A longer, more searching look at his daughter showed him at once that she had nothing to conceal. Her evident undisguised pleasure at his coming was too palpable to be misunderstood. He drew a deep breath of relief, but recognized instinctively that the situation required very delicate handling if the girl's ignorance was to be maintained. Here the fates fought on his side, for each man, from directly opposite motives, desired the same thing: neither wished to have a conflict in Edna's presence; neither could run the risk of full knowledge coming to her at that time. Luckily Edna's eyes were all for her father, and she gave no look to the young man, in whose face and attitude were undeniably stamped both guilt and discomfiture. She was the first to speak.

"Oh, father, I am so glad you came; we were just speaking of you."

"Yes, Edna, there are one or two adages bearing on the subject: complimentary and the reverse."

Edna laughed brightly.

"We have been trying to settle the strike, and Mr. Marsten thought you would be angry if you knew he had been here—thought you might call it interference. I told him that was all nonsense, but I could see he was not convinced; so you come at the proper moment to solve the problem finally."

"I see I came just in time. I am only too glad to have assistance in unravelling this perplexing tangle, and I welcome help from any quarter."

"There!" cried the girl triumphantly, turning to her lover, who had by this time partially recovered his composure. "Isn't that just what I said?"

"Mr. Hope told me an hour ago, Marsten, that you had visited him yesterday, and had done me the honour to call at Wimbledon afterwards; so I came home, fearing I might miss a second visit. Mr. Hope spoke very highly of you, and I do not wish to be less cordial than he in expressing my own opinion of your most disinterested devotion to the welfare of your fellow-workmen."

Marsten moistened his dry lips, but made no attempt at reply. Timorous little Mr. Hope had not kept faith with him, then, and, after counseling him to silence, had blurted out all the particulars as soon as he came again under the influence of his masterful servant, and thus had precipitated this deplorable encounter. Edna looked from one to the other, a slight shade of apprehension on her face. The words of her father were all that she could ask, their tone was unexceptionable, and yet—and yet—there was frost in the air. She spoke with less buoyancy than before, still with confidence that all was as it should be.

"That was one of the very points which troubled us. Mr. Hope asked Mr. Marsten to say nothing about the Surbiton visit, while I felt sure you wouldn't mind."

"You did quite right, Marsten, in saying nothing about it when Mr. Hope asked you not to mention it, but Edna is right also in stating that it would have made no difference to me."

"Now," said Edna to the young man, "you see how groundless all your fears were, and how a few simple words of explanation clear away all difficulties. I hope you will visit us whenever you want to talk to my father—you would be pleased to have him come, wouldn't you, father? Mr. Marsten has done his best to settle the strike, even though he failed."

"I quite appreciate that, Marsten, and my house is always open to you."

Edna glanced with a smile at Marsten; his eyes were fixed intently on

Sartwell, who continued suavely:

"However, it is only right that I should let you know there will be no more need to discuss the strike. I have been played with long enough. It is now my turn to strike. On Monday the works will be going again. I have on file four times as many applications for work as I have vacancies to fill. My clerks are at this moment writing out some hundreds of telegrams, asking the receivers to report for duty on Monday morning. I shall have no more traffic with the Union."

"Oh!" cried the girl, in dismay.

"Won't you give me another chance with the men?" asked Marsten, speaking for the first time.

"There were only a few votes against us at the last meeting."

"You have from now until Friday night. I give you up to the latest moment, and that is why I pay six times as much and use the telegraph rather than the post. Letters would do quite as well mailed on Friday. The works open on Monday, with or without you, so you see you have little time to lose."

"I shall go at once to London and call a meeting of the men. May I see you at your office to-morrow?"

"Certainly. My office is always open: but remember, it is an unconditional surrender now. I'll have no more parleying."

"Good-by," said Marsten briefly, turning on his heel and hurrying to the gate, father and daughter watching him until he disappeared. Sartwell sank down in one of the chairs, murmuring as he did so:

"Thank God!"

"Why do you say that, father?"

"Say what? Oh! Because a certain tension has been relaxed. I have seen Hope and Monkton off together for Germany this morning, and they will be gone for at least a fortnight. This leaves me a clear field, and I will crush this strike as I would an eggshell."

Sartwell nervously clenched his right hand, as if the egg-shell were within it.

"I am sorry for the men, father."

"So am I, my dear, if they stand out; but it will be their own fault. Experience is said to teach a specified class of individuals, and they are preparing for themselves a bitter dose of it."

"Will you' not take him back, even if they hold out?"

"Him? Whom? Oh! Marsten. If they do not come back in a body, I will never allow another Union man to set foot in the works again. But never mind the men; I want to talk about yourself."

"About me?"

"Yes About the situation here at home. It is not exactly what I wish it to be, and I intend to try an experiment."

"Do you mean what happened yesterday between mother and me?"

"I mean the whole situation. What happened yesterday was merely an indication of the tendency—I don't know just how to put it, but it isn't satisfactory."

"I was at fault, father, as I said last night; I was worried and anxious—that is no excuse, of course—and then I said things I shouldn't have said. I was sorry at once, but I am more sorry now when I see I have troubled you. It won't happen again. I shall be very careful in future, and I am sure if you think no more about it I shall do better."

"My dear Edna, I am not blaming you in the least, nor do I think you were at fault; that is, not entirely. I am not censuring any one; we are as God made us, and there are differences of temperament which sometimes cause friction. You are not having a fair chance just now. I care very little about your mother's friends, and I have few friends myself; thus you have no companions of your own age whom you can have here, and whose visits you can return, as is right and proper. You are thrown too much on your mother and me for your friendship, and I am not sure that either of us is suitable. You are at an impressionable time of life, and I want to do my best for you; so I think I shall send you to some school where you will meet nice girls and form friendships that you will enjoy. Then you have a decided talent for music, which will be developed, and—there are many reasons for such a step."

"Do you mean that I shall have to leave home?" asked Edna, with a tremour in her voice.

"I think that will be best. In a year or two you will look upon life with perhaps more philosophy."

"A year or two!" cried Edna, as if she spoke of eternity.

Her father smiled.

"The time will pass very quickly," he said. "In a year or two, when you come home, both your mother and you will be glad to meet each other. We sometimes grow to think kindly of the absent."

The girl buried her face in her hands.

"Tut, tut, Edna, my own little girl!" cried her father, placing his chair beside hers and taking her almost in his arms. "One would think you were being sent off to Africa. I imagined you would be glad."

"It isn't that," she sobbed. "It shows how dreadfully wicked you must think me when you are compelled to send me away."

"Nonsense, Edna! It shows nothing of the kind. I can't send your step-mother to boarding-school, can I? Well, then! I don't think you wicked at all. I have not the slightest doubt but you said just what you were provoked to saying. There now; see what a hopeless admission that is to make to a rebellious daughter. No, no. I am not blaming you in the least. As I said before, I am blaming nobody. We are driven by circumstances, that is all."

"And am I never to see you except when I come home?"

"My darling girl, that is the delightful part of it. You will see me, and I will see you, practically more often than we do now. What do you think of that? I shall select some excellent school, situated in a bracing spot near the sea. I believe it will be cheaper for me to take a season ticket on the railway there, I shall go so often. We will take long walks on the downs entirely alone, and talk of everything. We will have delightful little dinners at the wayside inns we discover, and now and then a grand luncheon, at some very expensive place with a window that looks over the Channel. Edna, it will be the rejuvenating of your old father. He rarely gets a sniff of ozone as things are now, but then——"

Edna, with a cry of joy, flung her arms around his neck.

"Oh, father," she cried, "that is too good to be true! When can I go?"

"This very week, I hope. You see now how everything depends on the point of view."

## CHAPTER XIX.

With the words "starved to death" ringing in his ears, Langly walked to Chelsea. Bitterly he accused himself for his stupid blindness; all this had been going on for days, and he had had no suspicion of it. She had from the first undoubtedly stinted herself so that her father might not go hungry, and when, at last, the real pinch came, she was too weak to resist it. Her father, isolated by his temper from any friends who might have seen what was happening and given warning in time, had also been unconscious of what was passing before his eyes. His gruff independence had slowly famished his own daughter.

"Starved to death!" in the richest city in the world,—the granary of the nations, into whose ample lap pours the golden wheat from every country under the sun that ripens it.

At last Langly reached the studio, and might have known, had he been conversant with the habits of the great world, that a notable function was in progress thereabout by the numerous carriages, with fine horses and resplendent coachmen and footmen, that waited near by. In his earlier days Langly had hoped for pupils to instruct and thus increase his scanty income. He had cards printed—"Albert Langly," in the centre, and "Teacher of Music", in smaller type in the corner. These were never used, Langly not having the courage to push his inquiries for pupils and secure them. He, knowing Barney to be a fashionable man, had put some of these cards in his pocket, and, when the boy in buttons swung open the door, the bit of pasteboard was handed to him. The boy glanced at the card, dropped it into the receptacle that contained many others, and shouted the name up his stairway, wafting its ascent with a wave of his hand. The man who held aside the heavy drapery which covered the doorway bawled the name into the room, from which a confused murmur of conversation came, mingled now and then with a pleasing ripple of laughter. The ornamental living statue at the top of the stair gazed dreamily over Langly's head as he mounted.

Taking another card, the organist gave it to the man at the door.

"I have not come to the 'At Home,'" he said. "Would you give this to Mr. Hope and ask if he will see me for a moment. Tell him I called last night, and could not come earlier to-day."

The man took the card and disappeared behind the curtains. In an incredibly short time Barney came out, and his reception of the musician was bewilderingly effusive.

"My dear fellow," he cried, placing a hand on each shoulder of Langly, "can you play the piano? Of course you can. What a foolish question to ask! I always alight on my feet. Providence has dropped you down here, my boy, don't you know. Here we have just sent out to scour Chelsea for a pianist, and here you drop right down from the skies, don't you know. This is luck. Want to see me? Of course you do, and what's more to the point, I want to see you, don't you know! Now come right in. I've got the finest grand piano you ever fingered in your life—magnificent instrument—case designed by myself—told 'em to spare no expense, and they didn't, don't you know. Trust 'em for that. Now come in, come in."

"Mr. Hope, I did not come to play—I am in no condition for playing."

"Of course you didn't come to play. That's the beauty of it. You want something from me, now don't you?"

"Yes, and if you will give me a moment——"

"A thousand of'em, my boy, a thousand of'em, but not just now. Listen to me. You want something I've got, and I want something you've got Very well. All England's prosperity is based on just that position of things. Our commerce is founded on it. Our mutual country is great merely because she knows what she wants, and because she has something the other fellow wants, don't you know! Now, I want a man who can play dance music, and I want him now—not to-morrow, or day after, or next week. You see what I mean? Good. You come in and polish us off some waltzes on the new piano; then, when it's all over, I'll let you have what you want, if it's half my kingdom, as the story-books say. Then we will both be happy, don't you know."

"I am organist at St. Martyrs church. I can't——"

"That's all right. Don't apologize. You can play the piano as well as the organ—I know that by the look of you. Come in, come in."

Barney triumphantly dragged the reluctant musician after him.

"I've got him," he cried, at which there was a clatter of applause and laughter.

"Now, there," said Barney jubilantly, seating Langly before the grand piano, with its great lid like a dragon's wing propped up, "there's all the sheet music any reasonable man can want; but if you prefer anything else I'll send out for it; and there's the piano—'Come let us hear its tune,' as the poet says."

The rugs which usually covered the waxed floor had been cleared away; the chairs had been shoved into corners and against the wall. There was much laughter and many protestations that they had not come prepared for a dance, but all were quite noticeably eager for the fun to begin.

"You see, you are in Bohemia," cried Barney, beaming joyously on his many guests, "and the delight of Bohemia is unconventionality. I danced after the theatre till daylight this morning, and I am as ready as ever to begin again. Shall we not lunch because we have breakfasted, and because we dine at seven? Not so. I am ready for a dance any time of the night or day. Now, Mr. Musician, strike up. 'On with the dance, let joy be unconfined!' as the poet says."

Langly could not have played out of time or tune if he tried. The piano, as Barney had truly said, was a splendid instrument, and when the gay waltz music filled the large room, each couple began to float lightly over the polished floor. The musician played on and on, mechanically yet brilliantly, and in the pauses between the dances more than one of the guests spoke to their host of the music's excellence.

"Oh, yes," said Barney, with a jaunty wave of the hand, "he's one of my finds. The man's a genius, don't you know, and is in music what I am myself in painting."

"Barney, you always lay it on too thick," said one of the young men. "You'll turn the pianist's head with flattery, if he knows you consider him as clever as yourself."

"Perhaps you imagine I'm too dense to see through that remark," said Barney, with the condescension of true genius. "I know your sneering ways: but let me tell you what I meant was that both the musician and myself are unrecognized by the mob of commonplace people of whom you are so distinguished a representative." ("I flatter myself I had him there," whispered Barney, aside, to the lady on his right.) "Yes, my boy, the day will come when you will be proud to say you were invited to these receptions, which I intend to make one of the artistic features of London society."

"Why, Barney," protested the young man, "I'm proud of it now. I make myself objectionable in all my clubs by continually bragging that you smile upon me. I claim that you are in art what the Universal Provider is in commerce."

"Do get him to play something while we are resting," murmured the lady, thus pouring oil on the troubled waters.

Langly sat at the piano, a disconsolate figure, paying no attention to the hum of conversation around him. His thoughts were far away, in the squalid room where the dead girl lay. Barney bustled up to him, and the musician came to himself with a start on being spoken to.

"Here are several Hungarian mazurkas—weird things—you'll like'em. Just polish off a few for us while we have some tea, will you? They are all complimenting your playing—they're people who know a good thing when they hear it. Won't you have some refreshment yourself before you begin?"

Langly shook his head, and began playing the Hungarian music. Barney sat down again beside the lady, smiling with satisfaction at being able to pose as the patron of so accomplished a musician. The lady leaned her chin on her hand, and listened intently.

"How marvellously he does those mazurkas!" she whispered, softly. "He brings out that diabolical touch which seems to be in much of the Polish and

Hungarian music."

"Yes," assented Barney, cordially, "he does play like the devil, yet he is an organist in a church. Ah, well, I suppose Beelzebub looks after our music as he does our morals."

"Has he composed anything?"

"Who? Satan?"

"No, no. You know very well I'm speaking of the organist."

"Composed! Well, rather. He's an unrecognized genius, but I'm going to look after his recognition. I'm going to bring out some of his works, if he'll let me. He's a very modest man, and——"

"Another likeness to yourself."

"Exactly, exactly. I'm always pushing other people forward and neglecting my own interests; still, I'll arrive some of these days and astonish you all, don't you know. You see, our set doesn't produce men of genius like that organist. The 'upper ten' never produced a Shakespeare."

"I thought it did. Didn't Lord Bacon write Shakespeare?"

"No, he didn't. I've looked up that question, but there's nothing in it, don't you know. No, the really great men come from the common people. The world doesn't know where to look for them, but I do, and I find 'em just as I found this man. I go for my society to the aristocracy, but for my geniuses to the democracy."

"But if society does not produce great men, how do you hope to become the greatest of painters?"

"Ah, painting's a different thing, don't you know; it has always been the gentleman's art. Leonardo and all of those chaps were great swells. Rubens—or was it Titian?—one of them, anyhow, went as ambassador to the court of Spain in great pomp. Painters have always been the companions of kings. But I say, let us have another dance."

Once more the dreamy waltz music mingled with the swish-swish of silken skirts, sibilant on the polished floor. Langly nearly always lost himself in whatever music he played, but now it merely dulled his sorrow, and an undertone of deep grief lay beneath the frivolous harmony that rippled so smoothly and sweetly from the piano—an undertone heard by none save himself. Merry laughter, and now and then a whispered phrase as the dancers swung close to where he sat, fell on his unheeding ear, and he wished his task were done, so that he might face again the long walk lying before him. He chided himself as being ungrateful, when it seemed hard that at this time he should be called upon to minister to the amusement of a pleasure-loving party; for he remembered that the Hebrew had toiled seven years uncomplaining for the woman he loved: so why should he grudge an afternoon, when the object was practically the same, although hope cheered the longer task, and despair clouded the shorter. Each in his way laboured for his love, living and dead.

The heavy hand of Barney came down boisterously on the thinly clad shoulder of the player, and partially aroused him from his bitter reverie.

"First rate, my boy, first rate! You've done nobly, and every one is delighted—charmed!—they are indeed, I assure you. Now they're saying good-by, so give us a rousing march for the farewell—anything you like—something of your own would be just the thing; you know what I mean—a march with a suggestion of regret in it—sorry they're going, don't you know."

Barney hurried back to his guests, shaking hands, asking them to come again, and receiving gushing thanks for a most agreeable afternoon. Suddenly there knelled forth on the murmur of farewell the solemn notes of the Funeral March, like the measured toll of a passing-bell. The metallic clangour of the instrument gave a vibrant thrill to the sombre music, which was lacking in the smooth, round tones of the organ. Langly played like a man entranced, his head thrown back, his pale face turned upward, looking as if life had left it. An instantaneous chilling hush fell on the assemblage, as if an icy wind had swept through the room, freezing into silence the animated stream of conversation. Some shivered where they stood, and one girl, clasping her cloak at her throat, paused and said, half hysterically:

"If this is a joke, Mr. Hope, I must say I don't like it."

"Cursed bad taste, if you ask me," muttered one man, hurrying away.

"Oh, I say," cried Barney, as much shocked as any one at the inopportune incident, and striding toward the performer, as soon as his wits came to him, "we didn't want a dirge, don't you know."

The lady who had spoken in praise of Langly's music laid a detaining hand on Barney's arm.

"Hush!" she said gently, the glimmer of tears in her eyes, "don't stop him. Listen! That man is inspired. I never heard Chopin played like that before."

"Oh, it's Chopin, is it?" murmured Barney, apologetically, as if, had he known it, he would not have interfered.

The throng dissolved rapidly with the unwelcome chords ringing in their ears, leaving Barney and his guest standing there alone. Langly, on finishing the march, sat where he was, his long arms drooping by his side.

"Wouldn't you like to speak to him?" asked Barney.

"No, not now."

The lady stole softly out, Barney following her to the landing at the head of the stair.

"Please don't lose sight of him," she said, giving Barney her hand. "I want you to ask him here again, and let me invite the guests."

"I'll do it," said Barney, enthusiastically. "That will be awfully jolly."

"No, it won't be jolly, Mr. Hope, but we'll hear some enchanting music. Good-by!"

Barney re-entered the room, and found Langly standing beside the piano like a man awakened from a dream, apparently not quite knowing where he was.

"You must have something to drink," cried Barney, cordially. "You look fagged out, and no wonder. I never heard Chopin so well rendered before. I tell you, my boy, you get all out of a piano that's in it, don't you know. Now, will you have whiskey or brandy?"

Langly thanked him, but refused either beverage. He had a long walk before him, and was anxious to get away, he said.

"Walk!" cried Barney. "Nonsense! Why should you walk, and thus insult every self-respecting cabby you meet? I'll see about the walking; I hope I know my duty towards the hansom industry."

Barney touched an electric bell, and when his man appeared said to him:

"Just send Buttons to the King's Road for a hansom. When it comes, give the cabby ten shillings and tell him he belongs to his fare for four hours. Ask him to wait at the door till his fare comes, and meanwhile, bring in some whiskey and soda. Now, Mr. Organist—I always forget names—ah, Langly, here it is on the card, of course. Have you ever composed any music yourself? I thought so. Ever published any? I thought not. Well, my boy, we must remedy all that. You're too modest; I can see that. Now, modesty doesn't pay in London. I know, because I suffer from it myself. Heavens! if I only had the cheek of some men, I would be the most famous painter in Europe. If you bring a few of your compositions to me, I'll get a publisher for you. Will you promise? Nonsense! not worthy? Bosh! Compared with the great composers? My dear fellow, the great composers were all very well in their way, I've no doubt, but they were once poor devils like you. Because Raphael painted, is that any reason why I should not improve on him? Not a bit of it. You and I will be old masters in painting and music some few centuries hence—you just wait and see. The great point is to realize that you're an old master while you're young and can do something. If you don't recognize the fact yourself, you may be jolly well sure no one else will—at least, not in time to do you any good here below. Do have some whiskey; 'it's cheering and comforting,' as the advertisements say. Well, here's to you!"

"I came to see you, Mr. Hope," stammered Langly, diffidently, "because Marsten—one of your father's employees—told me he thought you might—that you were good enough to help once——"

"Oh. yes, I remember Marsten. He was here about some fellow knocking down a few policemen. Well—has he knocked down some more?"

"No, but he is in great trouble, Mr. Hope."

"Such a man is sure to be. How much is the fine?"

"His only daughter died yesterday."

"Oh, I'm very sorry to hear it—very sorry, indeed."

"He has no money, and none of the men have any. Braunt would ask no one for help, but I know that he fears there will have to be a——He doesn't want her to be buried as a pauper—and I thought——"

"Of course, of course. I see it all. I never could understand the feeling of the poor on that subject. They seem to like a fine funeral, as if that mattered. I confess that if you give me good company while I'm alive, you may do what you please with me when I'm dead. I would just as soon lie beside a pauper as a prince, but I prefer the prince when I'm above ground. Now, how much will be needed? Of course you don't know; no more do I. Let us say fifteen pounds; if more is wanted, just telegraph me and I'll send it by messenger at once, don't you know. No, you mustn't think of sending any of it back. Use the surplus, if there is a surplus, for some charity or another. But you must come back yourself, and we'll have a talk on music. Drop in any time—there's no ceremony here. And just write your address on this card, so that I may communicate with you. I promised a lady to have you here some day to play for a few friends. You won't disappoint me, will you? Thanks, I'm ever so much obliged."

"The hansom is here, sir," said the man, entering. "All right. I'll just see you into your cab, Mr.—er—Langly. No trouble at all; don't mention it. You can make this fellow drive you around for four hours, if you want to. He'd take you to Brighton in that time, so I suppose he'll land you anywhere in London in short order. Well, good-by, my dear fellow, and I thank you ever so much for your exquisite music."

## CHAPTER XX.

After the burial of his daughter, Braunt sat in his lonely room and pondered bitterly upon the failure his life had been, ever since he could remember. Hard and incessant toil he did not complain of: that was his lot, and it had been the lot of his fathers. He was able to work and willing; the work was there waiting to be done: yet, through the action of men over whom he had not the slightest control, he was doomed to idleness and starvation until the capricious minds of others changed, and the signal was given to pick up the tools that had been so heedlessly dropped.

"Ah'll not stand it!" he cried aloud, bringing his fist down on the empty table.

But after these momentary flashes of determination, the depression habitual to him settled down with increased density upon his mind, and, realizing how helpless he was, he buried his face in his hands and groaned in hopeless despair. It is difficult for a starving man to be brave for long. What could he do? Absolutely nothing. He might drop dead from exhaustion before he got a chance to earn a meal, though he tramped the huge city searching for work. The trade he knew was already overcrowded with thousands of men, eager for the place he had been compelled to abandon. Even the street crossings were owned by impoverished wretches who earned what living they got by sweeping them. If he were presented with a crossing, he had not the money to buy a broom. Gibbons, fool though he might be, spoke the truth when he said a workingman was but a cog in a large wheel: the wheel might get a new cog, or a new set of cogs, but the cog separated from the wheel was as useless as a bit of old iron.

Langly stole softly in upon his stricken friend, closing the door stealthily after him, with the bearing of a man about to commit a crime and certain of being caught. Braunt gave him no greeting, but glowered upon him from under his frowning, shaggy eyebrows.

"There is some money here that you are to take," said the organist timidly, placing a heap of coins on the table.

Braunt, with an angry gesture, swept away the pile, and the silver jingled on the floor.

"Ah'll have none o' thy money, as Ah've told 'ee before!" he roared. "Ah can earn ma money, if Ah boot get th chance."

Langly, with no word of remonstrance, stooped and patiently collected every scattered piece.

"It is not my money," he said, on rising. "It was sent to you, and is for you and for no one else. It belongs to you: I have no right to it, and this very money you yourself have earned. I don't know who has a better claim to it."

Again placing the silver and gold on the table, Langly tiptoed out of the room in some haste, before Braunt could collect his wits and make reply.

The Yorkshireman, with curious inconsistency, had accepted without question the money which had saved his child from a pauper funeral, although he must have known, had he reflected, that the expenses were paid by some one; yet charity which did not come direct awakened no resentment in his turbulent nature, while the bald offer of money or food sent him instantly into a tempest of anger.

He thought over the organist's words. How could the money be his? How had he earned the coins? His slow brain gradually solved the problem the money evidently had come from Hope or Monkton, or perhaps from Sartwell. He cursed the three of them, together and separate, and in his rage once more scattered the heap to the floor. The coins whirled hither and thither, at last spinning to rest on the bare boards. Braunt watched them as they lay there glittering in the dim light, his mind ceasing to cogitate on the respective culpability of employers or employed for the state of things under which he suffered. He had formerly thought of Monkton and Hope as purse-proud, haughty capitalists, until he saw their cringing, frightened demeanour when escorted out of the works by the policemen, and since that time he had been endeavouring to reconstruct his ideas concerning them. So, after all, why should he refuse to take money from them if one or other had sent it? He gazed at the coins on the floor, white splotches and yellow points of light, hitching round his chair the better to see them. He had heard that a man might be hypnotized by gazing steadily on a silver piece held in the palm. As Braunt watched the coins intently, he passed his hand swiftly across his brow, concentrating his gaze by half closing his eyes. He leaned forward and downward. Surely they were moving, edging closer to each other, the larger heaps attracting the various atoms of metal, as he remembered, with bewildered brain, was the case with money all the world over, which gave a plausible cause, such as one has in dreams, for the coins creeping together, although what was left of his reason told him that it was all an illusion. The sane and insane sections of his mind struggled for mastery, while Braunt leaned closer and closer over the money, sitting forward now on the very edge of his chair, breathing hard, almost wholly absorbed in the strange movement on the floor, and gradually losing interest in the mental conflict regarding the reality of what his strained, unwinking eyes told him was going on at his feet. At last he noticed that the heap was slowly but perceptibly sliding away from him. All doubts about the genuineness of what he saw vanished The money was trying to escape.

He sprang to his feet and jumped to the door, placing his back against it.

"Oh, no," he shouted, "you're mine, you're mine!"

Crouching down, never taking his eyes from the coins, he got upon his hands and knees, crawling towards them craftily; then pounced suddenly on the main heap, while the isolated pieces scuttled back to their former positions, pretending they had never shifted their places. He laughed sneeringly at their futile attempts to deceive him, poured the heap into his pocket, and captured each separate coin that remained, by springing upon it. He searched the whole room like some animal, nosing into' the corners, crouching lower and proceeding more cautiously when he spied a silver or gold piece that had rolled far, chuckling when he seized it and placed it with the others. At last he rose to his feet, slapping his pocket joyously, and making the money jingle. Once erect, the blood rushed to his head, making him dizzy. He staggered, and leaned against the wall, all his hilarity leaving him. The room seemed to swim around him, and he covered his eyes with his hands.

"Ah'm gooin' mad," he whispered. "Ah moost ha' summat ta eat—or drink."

Braunt staggered through the doorway to the passage and down the stair, out into the open air, which revived him and made him feel the nip of hunger again. Once on Light Street, he turned into the "Rose and Crown," and asked for a mug of beer. The barman hesitated. The credit of the strikers had long since gone.

"I'd like to see the colour of your money," he said, gruffly.

"Ah've no money. Ah'll pay thee next week; ah'm goin' to put a stop ta the strike to-day."

He brought down his open palm against his trousers pocket to emphasize his poverty, and was startled by the clink of coins. He thrust his hand down into his pocket, and pulled out some silver, gazing at it stupidly.

"Ma word," he gasped at last, "Ah thought Ah dreamt it!"

The barman laughed, and reached for an empty mug, grasping the beer-pump handle.

"That dream's good enough for the 'Crown,'" he said. "Better have some bread and cheese with it."

"Yes. Be quick, man."

Standing there, Braunt ate and drank ravenously.

"I can get you a plate of cold meat," said the barman, seeing how hungry the man was. The other nodded, and the plate, with knife and fork, was placed before him.

"So the strike's off, is it?" said the man, leaning his arms on the bar.

"It'll be off when Ah get there."

"Well, it's not a minute too soon. Our trade's suffered."

"More than your trade has suffered, worse luck. Dom little you'll do for a man, unless the money's in ta pouch."

"Oh, if it comes to that, neither will other people. We're not giving out-door relief, any more than our neighbours."

Braunt ate his food and drank his beer, but made no reply. The barman's attitude was commercially correct; no one could justly find fault with it. Money was the master-key of the universe; it unlocked all doors. The barman did not care how Braunt came by it, so long as he paid for what was ordered; and the workman now found that courage was taking the place of despair, merely because he had money in his pocket. He felt that now he had energy enough to cope with the strikers, simply because he had fed while they were hungry. He would wait for no meeting, but would harangue the men on the street, those of them that were assembled in futile numbers around the closed gates, and most of them were sure to be there. If Gibbons opposed, he would settle the question by promptly and conclusively knocking him down—an argument easily comprehended by all onlookers.

Braunt drew the back of his hand across his lips when he had finished his meal, and departed for the works. He found, as he expected, the despondent men standing there, with hands hopelessly thrust deep in their empty pockets. Their pipes were as smokeless as the tall chimneys of the factory, and that of itself showed that their condition was at its lowest ebb. They were listening with listless indifference to a heated altercation going on between Gibbons and Marsten, as if the subject discussed did not concern them.

"You might have played that card last week," Marsten cried, "but it is too late now. You can have no conference with the owners. I tell you they have left the country, and won't return for a fortnight, and by that time the works will be filled with new men. The new men are coming in on Monday. I demand that the committee call a meeting now and that a vote be taken."

"Don't mind him, men!" cried Gibbons. "He's in Sartwell's pay."

The men didn't mind him, and paid no attention to Gibbons either. What they wanted was something to eat and drink, with tobacco to smoke afterwards. If Marsten was in Sartwell's pay, they would gladly have changed places with him. Braunt made his way roughly through the crowd, elbowing the men rudely aside. None resented this; all the fight had gone out of them. Marsten seemed on the point of attacking Gibbons for the slanderous remark made, when he felt Braunt's heavy hand on his shoulder.

"The time is past for meetings, lad," said the big man, "and for talk too. The meeting's here, and Ah'll deal with it. Stop bothering with that fool, and stand among the crowd, ready to back me up if need be."

Marsten at once did as requested, while Braunt strode across the open space, in spite of the warning of a policeman to stand back.

Few of the force were on the ground; the authorities saw there was little to fear from cowed and beaten men.

"You'll have to stand back," said the officer, "or I'll take you in charge."

"Will you so?" cried Braunt truculently, rolling up his sleeves as he turned upon his opponent. "Then I warn you, send for help. You haven't men enough here to take me in charge. Ah've had a meal to-day."

After glaring for a moment, Braunt turned and strode unmolested to the closed gate.

The officer paid heed to the advice given him and sent for more men. He saw there was to be trouble of some sort.

Braunt smote his huge fist against the panels and roared at the top of his voice:

"Open the gates!"

A slight flutter of listless interest seemed to pass over the crowd. The men elbowed closer together, shuffling their feet and craning their necks forward. Those to the rear pressed towards the front, wondering what was about to happen. The few policemen looked on without interfering, waiting for reinforcements. Braunt beat with his fist against the sounding timbers, the rhythmic thuds being the only break in the stillness except when he repeated his stentorian cry, "Open the gates!"

The porter at the small wicket, fearing an attack, ran for Sartwell, and met the manager coming down the stairs.

"I'm afraid there's going to be another riot, sir," said the porter, breathlessly.

Sartwell did not answer, but walked quickly to the small gate, unbolted it, and stepped out.

"What do you want?" he said.

"We want our work!" cried Braunt. "Open the gates!"

Sartwell's glance swept swiftly over the men, who stood with jaws dropped, their gaunt faces and wolfish eyes turned towards the closed barriers. The manager quickly comprehended that it was no time for discussion or arranging of terms. What was needed was action, sharp and prompt. He turned towards the trembling porter, and said peremptorily:

"Throw down the bar!"

Whatever doubts the man may have had about the wisdom of such an order in the face of the hostile mob, he preferred to brave probable danger from the crowd rather than the certain wrath of the manager, and obeyed the command with haste. The heavy gates were slowly pushed open.

"Now, men, in with you!" cried Braunt, with a scythe-like swing of his long arm. "The man that holds back now—ah, God!—Ah'll break his back!" Some one stumbled forward, as if pushed from behind; then it was as if an invisible rope, holding the crowd back, had suddenly broken. The men poured through the open gateway in a steady stream. Gibbons, waving his hands like a maniac, cried:

"Stop! Stop! Listen to me for a moment!"

But no one stopped, and no one listened. Braunt, his face white with anger, struggled against the incoming tide, shouting:

"Let me get at him! Ah'll strangle the whelp!"

"Braunt!" said Sartwell sharply, his voice cutting through the din of shuffling boots. "Leave him alone, and get inside yourself. Gather the men together in the yard. I want a word with them."

Braunt's truculence at once disappeared. He turned with the men, and came to where Sartwell stood looking grimly at the moving throng. No one glanced towards his master, but each went doggedly forward, with head down as though doing something he was ashamed of. Braunt stopped at Sartwell's side and whispered:

"For God's sake, Manager, set them at work, and don't talk to them. They're beaten, and there's no more to be said. Be easy with them; there's been talk enough."

"I quite agree with you," said Sartwell, in kindly manner. "Don't be afraid, but gather them together. You have the voice for it. I heard your first shout at the gates in my office."

As the last man passed through, Sartwell heard Braunt calling them to halt. A few still remained outside,—Scimmins and his fellow-members of the strike committee, listening gloomily to Gibbons's frantic denunciation of the wholesale defection. The manager stepped inside, and ordered the wondering porter to close the gates.

As Sartwell walked briskly towards the works he saw the men huddled together like sheep, very crestfallen, and evidently ready to endure any censure the manager saw fit to launch at their defenceless heads. Braunt, towering over them, looked anxiously about him, with the air of a huge dog not quite certain how his flock would behave.

Sartwell mounted the steps leading to the door of the former office, and spoke.

"I take it, men," he said, "that this strike is off. I want to begin fair and square; so, if there is any among you unwilling to go back to work on my terms, let him stand out now and say so."

There was a short pause, during which the silence was unbroken. No one stepped out.

"Very well," continued the manager. "That's settled and done with. Now each man knows his place in these buildings; let him get there, and remain for further instructions. No work will be done to-day, as some preparation is required before we begin. You will come to-morrow at the usual hour, and, after arrangements for work have been made, you may each draw half a week's wages in advance from the cashier: I shall give orders to that effect. A number of telegrams were to have been sent out on Saturday which it is now unnecessary to send: I will spend the money thus saved in tobacco, of which each man shall get a share as he passes out through the small gate. The large gates will not be opened until to-morrow morning."

There was a faint wavering cheer as Sartwell stopped speaking and stepped down. The men then slowly filtered into the works.

## CHAPTER XXI.

GIBBONS knew that Monkton and Hope had gone to the Continent before Marsten shouted out this bit of information on the street in presence of the men. He saw that the game was up, and all he wanted was time in which to beat a retreat, posing, if possible, as the man who had brought about a settlement. As soon as Gibbons learned that the two nominal masters had gone, he tried to open communications with Sart-well, and sent a private letter to him, saying that, taking into consideration the privations of the men, and the large money loss to the firm, he was willing to sink all personal feelings and waive the proviso heretofore insisted upon regarding a meeting between the manager and himself. Gibbons expressed his willingness to withdraw from the conflict, and have a committee of the men appointed to wait upon Sartwell to arrange for the termination of the strike, but asked that his letter be regarded as confidential.

Sartwell, with perhaps unnecessary contempt, returned the letter to Gibbons, saying curtly to the bearer that there was no answer.

It is usually unwise to humiliate unduly a beaten adversary; but Sartwell was not versed in the finer arts of courtesy, and, when he hated a man, he hated him thoroughly, caring little for any reprisal his enemy might attempt.

Gibbons had ground his teeth in helpless rage when his letter was returned to him. He saw that no concession he could make would placate Sartwell; so, as the strike was doomed, he resolved to make the best of the inevitable retreat. The committee agreed that it was no longer possible to hold out, although they had refused Marsten's request that a meeting be called and a vote taken. It was resolved that they convene a meeting at once, not waiting for nightfall (hoping in this way to deprive Marsten of any credit that might accrue from the surrender), and march the men in a body from the hall to the works, where the committee, with the exception of Gibbons, would precede them, to induce the manager to open the gates. Gibbons would then be able to say that he, not Marsten, had ended the strike; and he might even enact the rôle of a benefactor, who had sacrificed his own feelings in the interests of the men.

But luck was against Gibbons that day. When he reached the works he found Marsten there haranguing his fellow-workmen, imploring them to give in before it was too late, assuring them the two buildings would be full of workers on Monday, and then all efforts to enter would be fruitless. It was very apparent that the young man was already angered at the slight effect his appeal was making on the seeming indifference of the men, and, if Gibbons had been less angry from the rebuff he had received from the manager, he might have taken advantage of the position and scored. As it was, he had little time for planning any new line of procedure. The moment he appeared, Marsten demanded that a meeting should be instantly called and a vote taken. Gibbons asked him to mind his own business, saying he had an appointment with the owners of the works, and there would be a meeting to consider their reply. Then Gibbons learned that his falsehood was useless and that Marsten knew the owners had fled.

At this point the unexpected advent of Braunt, and the results that followed, tumbled all schemes to the ground like a house of cards.

Braunt, if he had thought about the matter (which he had not), was revenged at the end of the strike for his ignominious ejection from the hall at the beginning.

Gibbons retired with the committee to consult over the new situation. It was a gloomy consultation. As the men came out of the small gate one by one, each with half a week's wages in his pocket and a packet of tobacco in his hand, Scimmins and another member of the committee stood outside, proclaiming that a meeting was called for that night, to discuss the events of the day in a friendly manner. No man answered; each hurried away to get something to eat or drink; nor did any appear that night at Salvation Hall. Next morning Scimmins and his fellow-committeemen applied to Sartwell for reinstatement, and were given their old places. Gibbons resigned the secretaryship of the Union, and his resignation was accepted, somewhat to his surprise; as he, knowing the men had been practically unanimous in bringing on the strike, expected to be asked to keep the office, with perhaps a vote of formal thanks. However, all blame for the failure was promptly placed on his shoulders, and he found himself suddenly called upon to seek another situation. His bitterness against Sartwell deepened into virulent hatred, and he heaped maledictions on the heads of the men whom so short a time ago he had swayed this way and that whenever he addressed them.

The morning after the surrender the gates stood invitingly open, and black smoke poured from the tall chimneys. The women and girls, who worked on the upper floors, were the first to come, and their pale faces turned in a look of mute thankfulness towards the banner of smoke flying above them like a signal of rescue. They had had no voice in bringing on the strike, and no voice in its cessation. No one during its continuance had been anxious to know whether they lived or died when strike pay ceased.

Before the day was done, work was going as smoothly as if nothing had happened. The men were at first afraid that Sartwell might pick and choose among them, and that some of them might be marked men because of what had been done on the day of the riot, but it soon became evident that no distinction was to be made.

Just as the men had settled down to a comfortable frame of mind regarding the point that had given them anxiety, they were startled from their complacency by an unexpected incident. Marsten was discharged. On the first regular pay-day the young man received what was due him, and a month's money besides. The cashier told him that his services would no longer be required in the factory. Marsten was so dazed by this unexpected intimation that he asked for no explanation, but walked away with his money in his hand. He knew well why he had been so unceremoniously dismissed, but it seemed to him unfair that the manager should use his power against him for what was entirely a personal quarrel, and not through any fault in his work. He counted the money automatically three or four times, without the process conveying to his mind anything definite about the sum that had been paid him. At last he noticed that Sartwell had apparently ordered four times as much to be given him as was legally his due with a notice to quit. Marsten went back to the cashier and said:

"There's a month's money here: I am only entitled to a week's notice."

"You'd better keep what you've got," replied the cashier. "I was told to pay you a month's wages and discharge you. The money isn't mine; it's yours, and you're a fool if you part with it for nothing."

"I'll take only what is my due," said Marsten. "Give the remainder to Mr. Sartwell, and tell him I want none of his generosity."

"It's no affair of mine," remarked the cashier. "I suppose you know what the trouble is—I don't. If you are wise you won't send any such message to the manager, but you will go quietly and see him. Perhaps a few words of explanation will set matters right; anyhow, nothing is to be gained by flying into a temper about it. That isn't the way to get back into the works."

"I'm not in a temper," replied Marsten, "and I'm not going back into the works—no, not if Sartwell asks me to. You may tell him that when I come back it will be as master of these shops, with his power broken—you tell him that."

"Oh, very well. If you think to frighten a man like Mr. Sartwell with great talk, you'll be disappointed."

Marsten turned away, and found Braunt standing outside the gates.

"Ah'm waitin' for 'ee, lad, and Ah thought thou might 'a gone oot wi' first lot, but porter said thou hadn't. Coom whoam wi' me, Marsten; Ah'm main lonely an' want some'un ta speak wi'. Ah donno what's wrong wi' me, but there's summat. Ma head's queer. Ah'm hearin' the Dead March night and day, an' it's soundin' solemner an' solemner till it frightens me. Will ye walk wi' me, lad?"

"Yes, willingly. Don't you find your work makes things easier? I thought that would help."

"Ah've been too long idle, lad. Work doesn't do what it used to. Ah used to lose maself in't, but now Ah just seem in a dream, thinkin', thinkin'; an' when one speaks ta me sudden, Ah have to pull maself back from a distance like, before Ah can understand what's said; an' all th' while the throb d' the machinery is beat in' out the Dead March. Once or twice Ah've seen Langly sittin' playin' at the far end o' the room wi' the machines all answerin' to his fingers, while Ah knew he'd ne'er been i' the shops in's life. Ah've stood there wi' ma jaw hangin' an' wi' people lookin' at me curious. Then when Ah'd rubbed ma eyes, Langly was gone, but the machinery kept on an' on."

"Oh, you mustn't think too much about what is past, Braunt. Everything will be all right in a little while. Stick hard at your work; that's the main thing. You are foreman of the upper room now, aren't you?"

"Yes. Sartwell's been kind ta me. Ah! he's a man, Sartwell is. There's no waverin' about him."

"That's true."

"He sticks by them as sticks by him, as a man should. Has he said anythin' to you, since the strike ended?"

"No."

"You're young, but your time'll come. You stand by Sartwell an' he'll see you through. He knows how you tried to end the strike, an' he'll not forget. Ah'll drop in a word for ye when Ah get the chance."

"I wish you wouldn't do that."

"Why? It'll do no harm."

"It will do no good."

Braunt paused in his walk and looked closely at his companion. "What's the matter wi' thee, lad? Ye seem cast down, an' here Ah'm talkin' away about maself, an' payin' no heed to aught else. What's wrong wi' ye?"

"Well, as you will have to know sooner or later, and there's no use making a secret of it, Sartwell has discharged me."

"No!" cried Braunt, incredulously, stopping short and turning to his friend.

"Yes, he has."

"In God's name, what for?"

"No reason was given. The cashier gave me a month's wages and told me to go. I gave back three-fourths of it, for I'm entitled to but a week's notice. I'll have no favour from Sartwell."

"Ah, lad, there ye were foolish. Never give back money when you've got your fingers on it. Ye hurt yourself an' not the others. Still, Ah'd very likely a' done the same thing; but then, Ah'm a fool, an' not to be taken pattern by. Have ye asked Sartwell the reason?"

"I have not seen him, nor will I."

"Wrong again, lad. Let's go back now, an' have it out wi' him before he goes whoam."

"No, no, I refuse to see him."

"Then Ah'll see him. A thing like that mustn't be. Discharged for no cause! Never! Ah've brought back the men, an' Ah can bring them out again. Ah will, too, before Ah'll let injustice like this happen!"

"What good would that do? The men are helpless, as you know; besides, they wouldn't come out, and, if they thought of doing so, I would myself beg of them to stay in their places. No, the proper thing now is to keep quiet; work hard; fill up the empty treasury; organize the trade—not locally, but universally; and see, when the next strike comes on, that we are not led by a fool like Gibbons."

"But lad, don't ye want to find out why you're paid off? It's rank injustice, but there must be some reason for't in Sartwell's mind. Ye've like said some foolish thing that's been misrepresented to him, an' Ah'm sure Ah can put it straight. Ah didn't think Sartwell was the man t' listen t' any jabber that was brought t' him, but one can never tell."

"You're quite right about Sartwell. He wouldn't pay attention to talk that came to him, no matter what the talk was. No, it's deeper than that. He knows my opinions about the proper organization of the men, but that wouldn't influence him for a moment. Because I said no reasons were given, you mustn't think I don't know why he turned me adrift. I do, but it's not a subject I care to talk about, even with you, Mr. Braunt. Only I should like you to understand that interference will do no good. I should like to drop out quietly and have nothing said. Remember that I, knowing all the circumstances, am not sure but that, were I in his place, I should have acted exactly as Sartwell has done. I'm not going to have this made into a grievance, for I don't want it talked about. The main fact to know is that Sartwell and I are enemies, and there can be no peace between us until one or other is defeated. If you could talk Sartwell into asking me to come back,—and you know the difficulty there would be in that,—I wouldn't go back. So you understand the uselessness of seeing Mr. Sartwell."

"But lad, how are ye t' live?"

Marsten laughed.

"Oh, I'll have no difficulty in making a living. Don't you fear. I'll stick by the Union too, and some day I hope to show Sartwell how a strike should be conducted."

"Right ye are, if that's the game!" cried Braunt, bringing his hand down on the other's shoulder. "Ah don't believe much in strikes, but Ah believe in ye! Ah'll see the men to-night, an' All'll have ye made secretary to th' Union. That will be our answer ta Sartwell. Then, lad, ye can have enough to live on, and ye can put the pieces o' th' Union together ta suit ye."

"I should like that," said Marsten, eagerly.

"It shall be done. The men will go in for it when they hear ye've got the sack. They still feel sore over the defeat, as if it wasn't all their own fault; and now their fear of Sartwell's packing some o' them off is over, they'll like to show a little independence by electing you, to prove to the manager that they're not afraid, which they are. Ah'll have to convince them that Sartwell won't strike back or take your appointment as a defiance."

"But perhaps he will."

"Not him. He was as sick o' the strike as any one. No. He'll shrug his shoulders, but he'll say nothing. Ah'm certain that if Gibbons had had the sense to go to the masters at the first, he would have broken Sartwell long since. An' that was what Sartwell was afraid of, Ah'll be bound. His greatest stroke was getting Monkton and Hope out of the country. It was your visit to Hope did that. Sartwell saw ye'd put your finger on the weak spot; an' Ah'll warrant, if we knew the ins and outs of it, Sartwell threatened ta chook up the whole business if they didn't leave, and they left. Ah! he's a man as can fight, is Sartwell."

They had reached the court shortly before their conversation had arrived at this point, and Marsten sat down with his host. The room was barer than such places usually are, for every pawnable or salable thing had been removed from time to time as the siege went on. The empty space where the old harmonium had stood made the room seem larger than it really was.

"Yes," said Braunt with a sigh, noticing Marsten's eye wandering to the vacant spot, "it was the last thing that went before Jessie died. We pawned it, thinking we'd get it back again, but Ah'll never take it back. Ah'm glad it's gone. Ah couldn't bear to look at it. But let's not talk of what's away, but o' what's here. Ye're still thinkin' ye can do somethin' for the workin' man by organization?"

"I'm sure of it."

Braunt shook his head.

"Ye won't, my lad, but Ah'll do my best to get ye the chance ta try. Just look at what has happened. They let Gibbons go without a word: he was a fool, perhaps, but he worked hard for them, an' they don't even say thankee. An' they'll do the same wi' ye. They'll do the same wi' any one."

"It all depends on how they are led. When men are foolishly led, they soon find it out and lose confidence. Think what a man like Napoleon might have accomplished if he had led workingmen instead of soldiers, and had turned his talents to bettering his fellow-men instead of butchering them!"

"Napoleon could have done nothin'. He could have done nothin' wi' soldiers, even, if it had not been for one power which ye can never have."

"What is that?"

"The power o' orderin' a man out o' the ranks, an' havin' him shot. If Ah'd that power Ah'd lead the men maself, an' get them anythin' they wanted. The State will let you slowly starve a hundred men to death and never interfere, but if ye shot even Gibbons there'd be a row about it. An' yet we think we're civilized! Ah say we're savages."

"Oh, that's wrong, Braunt!" cried Marsten, rising. "We're long past that stage. If I get the reorganizing of the Union, I'll try a fall with Sartwell some day, and will down him without shooting anybody."

"Very well, lad, Ah'll do ma best for ye, an' wish ye luck."

Braunt did his best, and the next week Marsten was unanimously made secretary of the Union by men who had looked upon him as a traitor only a few weeks before.

## CHAPTER XXII.

MARSTEN made no move to communicate with Sart-well. If the manager expected the young man to propose a compromise, he was disappointed; and when he heard Marsten had been elected secretary of the Union, he smiled grimly, but made no comment. It was to be war to the knife, and Sartwell always admired an able antagonist. He made no motion against the Union, although at that time he could probably have forced seventy-five per cent of his employees to withdraw from it, had he been so minded. Marsten gave him due credit for declining to use the weapon of coercion against the men, knowing Sartwell too well to believe that the thought had not occurred to him. Yet there was little of the spirit of Christian forgiveness about the manager, as his wife had with truth often pointed out to him: he pursued an enemy to the bitter end. Gibbons metaphorically prostrated himself before Sartwell, and begged for the place in the works from which Marsten had been ejected. He was starving, he said. Sartwell replied that he was glad to hear it, and hoped Gibbons would now appreciate the sufferings of the men he had so jauntily led astray; so Gibbons had again humiliated himself for nothing.

To do Sartwell justice, however, it must be admitted that the attempted management of Marsten had slipped out of his hands in a way he had never anticipated. He did not dislike the young man; in truth, quite the opposite: still, he had higher ambitions for his only daughter than to see her marry one of his own workmen. The incident of finding Marsten with Edna in the garden had disturbed him more than he cared to admit, even to himself. If this persistent young fellow managed, when half starved, in the turmoil of the strike, to attend so successfully to his love affair, what might not happen when he was at peace with the world and had money in his pocket? Sartwell could have forbidden his daughter to see Marsten, and doubtless she would have obeyed; but he was loath to pique her curiosity regarding the reason for the prohibition, and he could not baldly tell her the young man craved permission to pay his addresses to her: that might set her fancy afire, with disastrous results to her father's hopes. Sartwell only half expected Marsten would appeal to him against his discharge; but he knew that before the young fellow got another situation he must refer his new masters to his old manager, and, when that time came, or if Marsten made a move on his own account, Sartwell stood ready to make terms with him. If Marsten promised not to see the girl for two years, the manager would reinstate him, or would help him to secure another place.

All these plans went to pieces when the men unexpectedly chose Marsten as secretary of their Union. It was a contingency the manager had not counted upon, but he faced the new position of affairs without a murmur against fate.

Marsten thought his dismissal harsh and unjust, but he felt that it freed him from all consideration towards Sartwell. He now determined to meet the girl whenever and wherever he could; so, with this purpose strong in his heart, he went to Wimbledon, boldly presented himself at the front door, and asked to see Miss Sartwell. He knew her father did not dare tell her the true state of the case, and, if it came to that, permission to visit the house had already been given in Edna's own presence,—a permission which her father had probably not withdrawn when Marsten left them together in the garden, as such withdrawal would necessitate explanations which Sartwell would not believe it wise to make. Therefore, the young man resolved to see the girl, tell her frankly why he came, and plead his cause with her. Even if she refused to listen to him, he would at least cause her to think of him, and that of itself was worth risking something for.

The servant, on opening the door, recognized Mar-sten as the young man who on a former occasion did not know his own mind, and she promptly said to him: "Mr. Sartwell is not at home."

"I wish to see Miss Sartwell."

"The young lady is not at home either."

"Will she return soon?"

"I don't know. Miss Edna's gone away."

"Gone away?" echoed Marsten, visibly perturbed at this unexpected check in his advance.

The servant saw she was face to face with another case of mental indecision; so she promptly grappled with the situation by calling Mrs. Sartwell, who was in the dining-room: then, turning the embarrassed young man over to her mistress, she closed the door and returned to the more important work which Mars-ten's knock had interrupted.

"You wished to see Miss Sartwell?" began the lady, icily. "Why?"

It was not an easy question to answer, when suddenly asked by an utter stranger.

"Well, I can scarcely tell you, Mrs. Sartwell," stammered the young man, extremely ill at ease. "It is entirely a personal matter. I wished to have a few words with Miss Sartwell; that is all."

The lady sat bolt upright, with a look of great severity on her face. There was mystery here which she resolved to unravel before she allowed the unfortunate young man to depart. He speedily came to the conclusion that he had in the lady before him an implacable enemy, more to be feared, perhaps, than Sartwell himself. Each question shot at him led him deeper and deeper into the tangle.

"You are her lover, I suppose?"

"No. That is—I really can't explain, Mrs. Sart-well."

"Very well; I shall ask my husband when he returns to-night. He knows nothing of this, of course?"

"Yes, he does."

"He knows you are here?"

"He doesn't know I am here to-day. He knows I love his daughter."

"I thought you said you were not her lover. Young man, whatever else you do, speak the truth. All our earthly troubles come from shunning the truth, and from overweening pride. Avoid pride, and avoid falsehood. What did you mean when you told me just now that you were not Miss Sartwell's lover? I beseech you to speak the truth."

"I'm trying to, but you see it is rather difficult to talk about this with a third person, and——"

"I am not a third person. I am her step-mother, and responsible to a higher power for what I do regarding Edna. I must have full knowledge, and then trust to the guiding light from above. We are ever prone to err when we rely on our own puny efforts. Does Edna Sartwell know you love her?"

"No."

"And her father does?"

"Yes. I told him."

"Then I wonder he did not forbid you to see her."

"He did."

"Are you one of his workmen?"

"Yes. At least I was."

"Are you not now?"

"No."

"He has discharged you?"

"I have been discharged."

The stern look faded from Mrs. Sartwell's face. She drew a deep breath—a prolonged "Ah," with what might be taken as a quiver of profound satisfaction in it—and, for the first time during the conference, leaned back comfortably in her chair.

"My poor boy!" she said at last, gazing compassionately at him. "Do you mean to say, then, that you would risk your whole future for a girl to whom you have never spoken?"

"Oh, I have spoken with her, Mrs. Sartwell. I said I had never spoken about—that she doesn't know I care anything for her."

"But you know absolutely nothing about her disposition—her temper."

"I'd chance it."

Mrs. Sartwell shook her head mournfully.

"How well you reflect the spirit of this scoffing age! People chance everything. Nothing is so important to a man as the solemn, prayerful choice of a wife, for on that choice rests the misery or the happiness of this life. A woman's great duty—at least it seems so to my poor judgment—is to bring light, comfort, and joy, to her husband's home. Do you think Edna Sartwell is fitted by temperament or education for this noble task?"

"She'd make me happy, if that's what you mean."

"How little, how little you know her! But then, you know her father, and she's very like him. Of course, he will never permit you to marry her, if he can prevent it. You are a workingman, and he has no thought or sympathy for those from whose ranks he sprang. He has higher ideas for his daughter; I have long seen that. It is pride, pride, pride! Oh, it will have a terrible fall some day, and perhaps you, poor lad, who talk of chance, are the humble instrument selected by an overruling Providence to bring about the humbling of his pride, without which none of us can enter the Kingdom! I see it all now. I see why he sent Edna to school at Eastbourne, although he said it was because we could not get on together. How little prevarication avails! The deceiver shall himself be deceived! In your seemingly chance meeting with me I see the Hand pointing towards truth. Still," continued Mrs. Sartwell reflectively, as though speaking more to herself than to her hearer, "there is no doubt that, if you took Edna's fancy, she would marry you in spite of her father or any one else. I have long warned her father that such a time is coming; but alas! my words are unheeded in this house, and the time has come sooner than I expected. I have wondered for some weeks past what was in Edna's mind. I thought that perhaps she was thinking of Barnard Hope, but I see now I was mistaken. No, she was very likely thinking of you, and her father, discovering it, has packed her off to High Cliff School at Eastbourne, where he probably hopes you cannot visit her. She is a wayward, obstinate child, impulsive, and difficult to manage. She thinks her father is perfection, so you may form your own opinion of how defective her judgment is. Yes, I should not be at all surprised if, when you tell her you love her, she would at once propose to run away with you. Nothing Edna Sartwell would do or say could surprise me."

Marsten, who had been very uneasy while a forced listener to this exposition of the girl's character, now rose abruptly, and said he must leave; he had already, he said, taken up too much of Mrs. Sartwell's time.

"Our time is given us," replied the good woman, also rising, "to make the best use of, and if we remember that we must give an account of every moment allotted to us, we will not count that time ill-spent which is devoted to the welfare of others. I sincerely trust that what I have said will sink deeply into your mind, and that you will profit by it."

"I shall not fail to do so."

"You will understand why I cannot give you any information about Miss Sartwell, or arrange for any meeting between you. It would not be right. If she were now in the house, I could not permit you to see her, since I know you come without her father's permission. I hope you do not think me harsh in saying this."

"Oh, not at all."

"And whatever comes of your infatuation for her, will you do me the justice to remember that my last words to you were to implore you to cast all thought of her from your mind?"

"I shall remember it," said Marsten.

"If you attempt to meet her, you know you will be doing so against my strict wish and command."

"You certainly will not be to blame for anything that happens, Mrs. Sartwell."

"Ah, if I could only be sure of that!" said the patient woman, mournfully shaking her head. "But blame is so easily bestowed, and it shifts responsibility from shoulders certainly more fitted to bear it, and perhaps more deserving. No later ago than yesterday, Mr. Barnard Hope came here, and was surprised to find Edna gone. He told me he came to see me, but he could not help noticing how still and peaceful the house was. When he asked where Edna was, I replied to him as I reply to you. Her father is the proper person to answer that question. Yet Mr. Hope is the son of my best friend, a noble woman, whose benefactions shower blessings far and near. Well, good-by, and I'm sorry not to be able to assist you; but I shall remember you in my petitions, and will trust that your feet may be guided aright."

"Thank you, Mrs. Sartwell, and good-by."

As the young man walked away he kept repeating to himself, "High Cliff School, Eastbourne"; and when he got a sufficient distance from the house he wrote the name down on a slip of paper.

## CHAPTER XXIII.

On reaching the railway station Marsten's first regret was that he had not taken all the money offered him on the day of his discharge. He had no idea that his quest would lead him to a fashionable and expensive sea-side resort. Prudence proposed to him that he should defer his visit to Eastbourne until he had more money; but, he said to himself, if he did not go at once, Sartwell would be certain to learn from his wife of the visit to Wimbledon, and there might be increased difficulties in getting to see Edna at Eastbourne. As it was, he had no idea how the meeting he wished for was to be brought about, for doubtless Sartwell, when sending his daughter to the school, had given the lady into whose care Edna was entrusted, a hint of his object in placing her there. Marsten stepped out of the South Western carriage at Clapham Junction, and found he had but half an hour to wait for the Eastbourne train. He smiled when he remembered the care and thought he was giving to the Union, after having so frequently asserted that he was willing to devote his life to the work. It was a blessing that all the Union needed at the moment was to be let alone.

When he arrived at Eastbourne, he immediately set out in search of High Cliff School, thinking it well to reconnoitre the situation, hoping the sight of it might suggest some plan that was practical. He would have one thing in his favour, which was that Sartwell would not have warned his daughter against seeing him, fearing to arouse her curiosity or suspicions. If, then, he got one word with Edna alone, he had no fear but that he could arrange for a longer interview. He found High Cliff to be a large house, situated in extensive grounds, with a view of the sea, but with a wall that was even more discouraging than the glass-topped barrier at Wimbledon.

Marsten saw there was going to be more difficulty in getting an interview with his sweetheart than he had at first imagined. He thought for a moment of applying boldly at the front door for permission to see the young student, but quickly dismissed the plan as impracticable. He was certain that so shrewd a man as Sartwell would have more foresight than to leave arrangements at such loose ends that the first person who called to see his daughter would be admitted, even if the ordinary rules of the school allowed such a thing, which was most improbable. He realized that the place was not to be taken by assault, but rather by slow and patient siege; so, wandering down by the shore, he sat on the shingle, within sound of the soothing waves, and gave his whole attention to the problem.

If a man whose ambition it was to emancipate the worker, and change the whole relationship between capital and labour, was going to be baffled in seeking half an hour's talk with a young girl, not immured in a prison or a convent, but merely residing in an ordinary English school, then were his chances of solving the larger question remote and shadowy. Thus he came to bind the two enterprises together, saying to himself that success in the one would indicate success in the other. The first thing to do, then, was to secure some cheap lodging—if such a thing was to be found in this fashionable resort—and so hoard his money and bide his time, for he was convinced he would make haste only by going slowly. It was a case in which undue precipitancy would make ultimate victory impossible. He knew that some time during the day the pupils would walk, though guarded doubtless by vigilant governesses. It might be possible to pass this interesting procession, and, while doing so, to slip a note into Edna's hand; but even as Marsten thought of this plan, he dismissed it as impracticable, for Edna would be so surprised at such an inexplicable proceeding on his part that she would not have the presence of mind necessary to conceal the missive promptly enough to escape detection. He left the shore, still ruminating on the problem, and, searching in the back part of the town, found lodgings that suited his requirements and his purse. When this was done, he strolled on the promenade, still giving the great problem his whole attention.

Suddenly he received a staggering blow on the back which almost thrust him forward on his face. Recovering himself, he turned round breathless, alarmed and angry, to see before him the huge form and smiling face of Barney Hope, who genially presented the hand that had smitten him.

"Hello, old fellow!" cried Barney, laughing aloud at the other's resentful glare. "What are you doing down here? Has the strike taken it out of you so that you had to have sea air to recuperate?"

"No strike ever took it out of me like the blow you struck just now."

Barney threw back his head and roared; then, linking arms with Marsten in the most friendly manner, he said:

"No, my paw isn't light, as all my friends say, and it has got me into trouble before now. I had to thrash a fellow in Paris once, merely because I could not convince him that the gentle tap I gave him was in fun. He admitted afterwards that there was a difference, and that he would rather have my open palm on his back than my closed fist in his face,—but what can you expect? The French have no sense of humour, and yet they can't box well. It should occur to them, as a nation, that they ought either to know how to take a joke, or else how to put up their dukes, if they are going to take things seriously. But my slap on the back is nothing to my hand-shake when I'm feeling cordial towards a fellow-creature. Let's see, have we shaken hands this go?"

"Yes, thanks," said Marsten, with such eagerness that the other laughed again.

"Well, I'm delighted to meet you so unexpectedly, don't you know. Your name's Langton, if I remember rightly?"

"My name is Marsten."

"Oh, yes, of course. I'm the stupidest fool in the kingdom about names, and it's an awfully bad failing. People seem to get offended if you can't remember their names. I'm sure I can't tell why. I wouldn't care tuppence what I was called, so long as you don't say I'm no painter. Then I'm ready to fight. A man who won't fight for his art oughtn't to have an art. And, talking about art, I remember now that Langton was the fellow you sent me who can play the piano as if he were a Rubinhoff—that Russian player, don't you know. Well, I'm thundering glad to see you; I was just hoping to meet some fellow I knew. I'm dying for some one to talk to. It's a beastly dull hole, Eastbourne, don't you know."

"I was never here before. It seems to me a very nice place."

"Yes, it looks that way at first, but wait till you've been here a day or two. It's so wretchedly respectable!—that's what I object to in it. Respectability's bad enough on its native heath, but sea air seems to accentuate it, don't you know. I can't tell you why it is, but it's so; and respectability that you can put up with in London becomes unbearable down by the sea. Haven't you noticed that? And it's all on such a slender basis too: the third-class fare to Brighton is four shillings and tuppence-ha'penny, while to Eastbourne it's four shillings and elevenpence, so all this swagger is on a beggarly foundation of eightpence-ha'penny. You see what I mean? I wouldn't give a week in Brighton for a day in Eastbourne, although I should hate to be condemned to either, for that matter. London is the only town that's exactly my size, don't you know."

"Then why do you stop at Eastbourne?"

"Ah, now you come to the point; now you place your finger right on the spot. Why, indeed? Can't you guess? I can tell in a moment why you are here."

"Why?" asked Marsten, in some alarm.

"Oh, simply because some fool of a doctor, who didn't know any better, sent you down. You're here for the air, my boy: you don't come for the society, so it must be the air—that's the only other thing Eastbourne's got. You were told it would brace you up in a week, and it will, if your reason holds out for so long. I'd be a madman, sane as I am, if I were compelled to live in this place a fortnight; I would, on my honour! No, you don't catch me in Eastbourne for either air or the society, and yet, in a way, it is the society, too, only it doesn't seem to come off; and here I am stranded, don't you know, with a coachman and a groom, not to mention a valet, two horses, and one of the smartest carts that ever left London. That's my turn-out, there. I drive tandem, of course; it's the only Christian way to drive. Not that I care about the style of it,—I hope I'm above all that sort of thing,—and I'm not to be blamed because so many other fellows do it, don't you know; I love a tandem for itself alone. Ever drive tandem?"

"I never did," said Marsten, looking at Barney's handsome equipage, which was being slowly driven up and down the road by a man in livery. He had noticed it before, but now he gazed at it with renewed interest, as Barney modestly proclaimed himself the owner.

"Well, it isn't as easy as it looks. It's not every fool can drive a tandem, although I am said to be one of the first tandem-drivers in London, don't you know. I don't say so, of course; but there are those who do, and they are judges, too. But it's no fun driving about alone: to enjoy tandem-driving you need to have a pretty girl beside you."

"And are there no pretty girls in Eastbourne?"

"There are, my boy, and that's just what I want to talk with you about. Let's sit down here in this shelter, because I want your whole attention. Now, I did you a favour one day, even though it was for another fellow, didn't I?"

"Yes. You have done me at least two favours."

"Well, that's all right. I may be able to do you a third or a fourth,—who knows?—and I mention it because I'm about to ask you to do me a great one now. That's what made me so glad to see you, don't you know, as well, of course, as the pleasure of talking with you again in this dismal hole. I was just thinking about it, and wondering whom I could get, when I looked up, and there you were. Providence always helps me when I'm in a pinch—always, don't you know. I never knew it to fail, and yet I'm not what you'd call a devout man myself. You've got nothing particular to do down here I suppose?"

"Nothing but my own pleasure."

"Quite so. And, as there isn't any pleasure to be had here, you may just as well turn round and help me; it will be a great lark. You see, I want a man of intelligence, and I don't suppose one is to be found in Eastbourne,—for if he was intelligent he wouldn't stay. Then, too, he must be a man not known in the town—you see what I mean? Also, he must know something about the labouring classes and their ways; so you see, my boy, Providence has sent the very man I want, don't you know. Now promise that you will help me."

"If I can, I will."

"Right you are! You're just the individual who can, and no one else can do it half so well. Now, in the first place, have you ever seen Sartwell's daughter? He's only got one."

"Have I ever seen her?"

"Yes. She was at my reception the day you were there. I don't suppose you noticed her among so many; but she was the handsomest girl in the room, far and away."

"Yes, I have seen Miss Sartwell. She used to call for her father at his office quite frequently."

"Good again! That's a fourth qualification needed by the person who is to help me, so you see you are the man of all men for this job. Now it happens that this charming girl is at school in Eastbourne, which is, in a word, the reason I am here. I want to get a message taken to Miss Sartwell at the school, and I want you to take it."

"Oh, I don't think I should care to go on a mission of that sort, Mr. Hope. If Mr. Sartwell were to find out that I——"

"My dear fellow," interrupted Barney, placing his hand confidentially on Marsten's shoulder, "it's all right, I assure you. There is really nothing surreptitious about it. Heavens and earth, Langton, you don't think I'm that kind of a man, I trust! Oh, no! I've the parental consent all right enough."

"Then why don't you go to the school and see her?"

"Because, dear boy, the case is just a trifle complicated, don't you know. I can always get the parental consent; that's the money, you know. As a general thing the girls like me, and I won't say the money has all to do with that: no, I flatter myself, personal attractions, a fair amount of brains, and a certain artistic reputation come in there; but money tells with the older people. Now Sartwell and I understand each other. Not to put too fine a point upon it, you know, he says practically: 'Barney, you're an ass, but you're rich, and I don't suppose you're a bigger fool than the average young man of the present day, so I give you a fair field; go in, my boy, and win.' I say to Sartwell: 'You're a grumpy old curmudgeon, with no more artistic perception than the Shot Tower; but your daughter is an angel, and I've got money enough for the two of us.' You see, I never did care for money except to get what I want. So there we stand. Sart-well was coming down here with me; but, after I started, he telegraphed to my studio that there was so much to do in the shops, with all the men newly back, that he would like me to postpone my visit for a week. Well, I had to get the horses and trap down here; so I drove, and I left London a day earlier than I expected to. Hence the present complication. I called at the school, asked to see Miss Sartwell, saying I was a friend of her father's; but the lady in charge looked on me with suspicion,—she did indeed, my boy, difficult to believe as the statement is. The lady said she could not allow Miss Sartwell to see any person unless that person was accompanied by her father. She would take no message to the girl—and there I was. I wrote to Miss Sartwell from my hotel here, but the letter was opened by the dragon, who returned it to me, asking me not to attempt to communicate with any of the young ladies under her charge. So here is this stylish tandem, and there is that lovely girl, while I am wasting in the desert air, longing to take her out for a drive. That's the situation in a nut shell, don't you know, and I want you to help me by taking a message to Miss Edna."

"I don't see how I can do it. If you, with her father's permission, could not get a word with her, how can I hope to?"

"Oh, I have that all arranged. I thought first of getting some young man in as a carpenter or plumber; but, so far as I can learn, the pipes and the woodwork of the school are all right. Then an inspiration came to me,—'I am subject to inspirations. The man who looks after the garden lives in the town, and he is quite willing to assist me; in fact I have made it worth his while, don't you know. The trouble is that all his assistants are rather clodhoppers, and would be sure to bungle a diplomatic affair like this; however, I was going to chance it with one to-morrow when I saw you, and said to myself: 'Here is the very man!' When Providence sends the right man I always recognize him. That is the whole secret of a successful life, don't you know,—to be able to recognize the gifts Providence sends at the moment they are sent. Where most people go wrong, don't you know, is by not appreciating the providential interposition until afterwards. You will put on a gardener's smock, take a clumsy and unwieldy broom in your hand, and go to High Cliff School to sweep the walks, and that sort of thing, don't you know. Then, as the girls are walking about, seize the psychological moment and tell Miss Edna I am waiting down here with the tandem. The young ladies are allowed to walk out three at a time. Two of them can sit back to back with us, and Edna will sit with me. Tell her to choose two friends whom she can trust, and we will all go for a jolly drive together. If she hesitates, tell her I am down here with her father's permission, but don't say that unless as a last resort. I would much rather have her come of her own accord, don't you know."

"What I fail to understand about your plan is why—if you really have Mr. Sartwell's permission,—no, no, I'm not doubting your word,—I should have put it, as you have her father's permission,—why do you not telegraph him, saying you are here, and get him to send a wire to the mistress of the school, asking her to allow Miss Sartwell to go with you for a drive, with a proper chaperon, of course?"

"My dear Langton——"

"Marsten, if you please."

"Oh, yes, of course. My dear Marsten, what you suggest is delightfully simple, and is precisely what would present itself to the well-regulated mind, It would be the sane thing to do and would be so charmingly proper. But you see, Marsten, my boy, I understand a thing or two about women, which you may not yet have had experience enough to learn. I don't want too much parental sanction about this affair, because a young girl delights in an innocent little escapade on her own account,—don't you see what I mean? Of course, if the villain of the piece is baffled, he will ultimately appeal to the proper authority; but you know I have already seen a good deal of the young lady under the parental wing—if I may so state the fact; and although she is pleasant enough and all that, I don't seem to be making as much progress with her as I would like, don't you know. Now a little flavour of—well, you understand what I mean—thingumbob—you know—romance, and that sort of thing—is worth all the cut-and-dried 'Bless-you-my-children' in the market. You'll know all about that, as you grow older, my boy."

"Mr. Hope——"

"Look here, my boy, call me Barney. Few of my friends say 'Mr. Hope,' and when any one does say it, I always think he is referring to my father, who is at this moment giddily enjoying his precious self at Dresden, or thereabouts. You were about to——"

"I was about to say I would very much like to oblige you, but I have scruples about doing what you ask of me."

"Marsten—you'll forgive me, won't you?—but I'm afraid you're very much like the rest of the world. Fellows always want to oblige you, but they don't want to do the particular obligement that you happen to want—if I make myself clear. If you want to borrow a fiver, they will do any mortal thing you wish but lend it. Now it happens that, so far from wanting a fiver, I'll give you one—or a ten-pound note, for that matter—if you will do this, don't you know."

"Oh, if I did it at all, I wouldn't take money for doing it."

"But I don't want a fellow to work for love, don't you know. I don't believe in that. If I sell a picture I want my money for it—yes, by Jove, I do!"

"If I did this, it would be entirely for love and for no other consideration. But I don't think I would be acting fairly and honourably if I did it. I can't explain to you why I think this; my whole wish is to do what you ask me, and yet I feel sure, if I were thoroughly honest, as I would like to be, I should at once say 'No.'"

"My dear fellow, I honour your scruples; but I assure you they are misplaced in this instance. They are, really. Besides, I have your promise, and I'm going to hold you to it. It isn't as though I were going to run away with the girl, and marry her against her own wish and the wishes of her combined relatives. If I wanted to see the girl against her father's will—well, then there might be something to urge in opposition to my project; but I'm not,—and don't you see that fact makes all the difference in the world? Of course you do. Why, a man ought to do anything for the girl he loves, and he's a poltroon if he doesn't. That's why I'm taking all this trouble and staying in this town of the forlorn. If a girl doesn't find you taking some little trouble in order to see her, why she is not going to think very much or often about you; take my word for that."

"I believe you are right. I'll go."

"You're a brick, Marsten! yes, my boy, a brick!" cried Barney, enthusiastically, slapping his comrade on the shoulder.

"A brick of very common clay, I'm afraid, Mr. Hope. I suppose you believe in the saying, 'All's fair in love'?"

"Of course I do, dear boy; it is the maxim on which I regulate my daily life."

"Very well. I will not take a verbal message, for I may not have an opportunity to deliver it; besides, I might forget something, or give it a misleading twist. If you will write exactly what you want Miss Sartwell to know, and give it to me as a letter, I will deliver it if there is the slightest chance of my doing so."

"Right you are, old man! Now come with me, and I'll introduce you to the gardener person, and see if he has a blouse that will fit you."

## CHAPTER XXIV.

In the morning Barney took Marsten to the house of the friendly gardener, whose good will had been secured through the corrupting influences of wealth, and there the young man donned the blouse that was supposed to give him that horticultural air necessary for the part he had to play. Marsten was very serious about it; but Barney seemed to enjoy the masquerade to the utmost, and wanted to take the amateur gardener to be photographed, so that there might be a picture as a memento of the occasion.

At last Marsten got away, with the broom on his shoulder, and, presenting himself at High Cliff grounds, was admitted without question. He made no attempt to conceal from himself the fact that he did not like the fraud he was about to practise, but when his conscience upbraided him, he asked of it what better plan it had to propose, and to this there was no reply.

The grounds were empty when he reached them, and with his natural shrewdness he applied himself first to the walks that were in public view; so that, when the young girls came out, he might be in the more secluded portion of the plantation, where he was sure the rules of the school would require them to take the air. His surmise proved correct, and the young man felt more embarrassed than he had even suspected he would be, when he suddenly found himself in the midst of a fluttering bevy of girls, all chattering, but happily none paying the least attention to him. He had not counted on the presence of any of the teachers; but three of them were there, who, however, sat on a garden seat and did not seem overburdened with anxiety about the pupils under their care.

Edna Sartwell had a book in her hand, with a finger between the pages, but she walked up and down with another girl, talking in a low tone. Marsten hoped the book was an interesting one, and wished the girl would go into some secluded corner to read it; for he began to see that his enterprise was not going to be so easy of accomplishment as he expected, even though he had gained admittance to the grounds, which at first had seemed the most difficult move in the game. The book at last gave him the opportunity he sought: Edna and her companion stood together for a moment after their walk, then each went her separate way.

In a corner of the grounds was a secluded summerhouse, screened from the view of the school by a wilderness of trees and shrubs, almost out of hearing of the lively chatter that made the air merry elsewhere; and to this quiet spot Edna betook herself, reading the book as she walked, for the paths thither were evidently familiar to her. Marsten followed, slowly at first, then more quickly as the chances of observation lessened, his heart beating faster than the exertion he was making warranted. The girl was seated in the little châlet when Marsten's figure darkened the entrance.

"Miss Sartwell," was all he could say.

Edna sprang to her feet, letting the book fall to the floor, and looked at him with startled eyes that had no recognition in them.

"I see you don't know me, and no wonder; for I did not wear gardener's clothes when I stood last in your garden."

A bright flush of pleasure overspread the girl's face, and laughter came first to her eyes, then to her lips.

"How you frightened me!" she said, seeming anything but frightened, and quite unable to restrain her merriment, as her glance flashed up and down his uncouth apparel. "Have you become gardener here, then, or did you come over the wall?"

"The walls here are too high, or I might have attempted them. I am gardener for the day only, and merely to get a word with you."

"With me? I thought the strike had happily ended. Haven't you gone back to work? How did you get away?"

"Oh, there was no difficulty about that! I can always get a day off when I want it. Yes, I went back to work and have been busy ever since. I came here yesterday in the hope of seeing you. It was very important—for me, at least."

"Has the desired promotion come so soon, then, or do you think I must speak to my father about your position when I next see him? I expected him here before this, but he writes that there is so much to be done, now the men are back, that he will be unable to come for perhaps a week or more."

"I have not come here to beg for your father's favour, but for yours. I love you, Edna, and I have loved you ever since I first saw you! Don't imagine I am so—so conceited—that I have even a hope that you—you—care for me, for of course you don't and can't; but I wanted you to know. I wanted to tell you, and that is why I am here. I am poor,—I don't deny that,—but your father was also poor once, and he has got on in the world. I will get on; I will work night and day. Whoever my master is, I will serve him faithfully,—my God! I will serve him on my knees, if that will convince him of my earnestness to win confidence and a place of trust,—and all the time cheerfully and hopefully, with your picture in my mind, as it has been in my mind—for so long—from the first. You see, I have no chance to win you as another might. You are in this school for the very purpose of keeping me from meeting you as I might meet you if I were rich. I have no fair chance—none at all, except what I steal for myself, as I have done to-day. It means so much to me—everything!—that I did not dare to take the risk. I know I have spoken too soon—too abruptly—but I dared not set my face at what is before me unless you knew. Some one might win you while I was working for you—there will be plenty to try. I don't want you to say a word—I want neither hope nor discouragement—no promise—nothing! You know, and that is enough for me now. But I would like you to remember—sometimes—that there is no man striving as I shall strive. Think of that—when others speak. My darling—my darling—no man ever felt as I feel since the beginning of the world!"

Whatever diffidence Marsten hitherto experienced in Edna's presence melted in the fervent heat of his passion when he began to speak. The words rushed forth, treading on the heels of those gone before, in jumbled, breathless procession; his face was aflame, and his nether lip trembled when he ceased to speak. At first he seemed to be running a race against time—they might be interrupted at any moment; but he soon forgot his competitor, and, so far as he was concerned, no one existed in the world but himself and the trembling, confused girl before him.

She, after her first look of amazed incredulity, felt backward with her hand for the support of the wall, and then gradually sank upon the seat, an expression, partly fear, overspreading her now colourless face. As Marsten went impetuously on, her head dropped upon her hands, and thus she remained while he spoke.

A pause ensued, so deep and silent that Marsten, as he leaned his hand against the door-post, afraid to move forward or retreat, heard the distant girlish laughter, free from any thought of problems other than those of the schoolroom. He knew he should remember every trivial detail of the place all his life,—the broom that lay at his feet; the book which had fallen open-leaved upon the floor; even the title glittering in gold on the side, which sent no meaning to his mind except one word that caught his attention,—"Courtship" ("The Courtship of Miles Standish" was the whole phrase), and he wondered vaguely if the courtship had prospered. Rapidly as his wondering eye gathered up the accessories of the scene, it always returned to the bowed and silent figure before him, and something in the outlines of her drooping shoulders told him intuitively of a change—elusive, but real. His mind had been too much occupied with the hard realities of life to indulge in speculative analysis of any sort, but now it was uplifted, touched by the magic wand of love, and endowed with: a subtle perception unknown to him before. He saw that the girl, who, as a child, welcomed him, would, as a woman, bid him farewell.

At last she slowly shook her head.

"It cannot be—it cannot be!" she murmured.

"Not now. I know that—I don't ask that!" he cried, eagerly. "But—some time—some time?"

The girl did not look up.

"It can never be—never!" she said.

"All I want is a chance—a fair chance. Don't—oh, please don't say 'No' or 'Yes' now! Your father is prejudiced against me, I know; not against me personally, I think, but because I am poor: it is only another expression of his great love for you. He knows what poverty is, and he wants to shield you from it. He is right, and if I am as poor two years from now, or four years, I shall not ask—"

"Does my father know?"

"Yes. I told him that night—the night you first spoke to me. That is why he is angry."

"Then that is why you—that is the reason—when you were in the garden——"

"Yes, that is why I was afraid to have him find me there."

Again there was a long silence between them. The thoughts of the girl ranged back over her past life, from the time her father forbade her to come to the office until the present moment, flashing like a searchlight upon events hitherto misunderstood, making them stand out in their true proportions. All her father's actions, his words, had to be reconsidered. She saw meanings in former phrases that had been hidden from her: she had now the key that unlocked the room illumined by knowledge; and although her heart yearned towards her father, sympathizing with him when confronted by an unexpected problem, and fully condoning his apparent lack of trust in keeping her ignorant of a situation so closely concerning herself, feeling that she ought to stand by him and repel the stranger who had so daringly come between them with his preposterous claim upon her affection, yet from no part of her being could she call to her aid that emotion of just resentment against Marsten which she knew ought to be at her command.

"I am very, very sorry," she said at last, speaking slowly. "I like you, of course—I think you are a noble, earnest man, and that you will do good and overcome many difficulties; but I don't care for you in the way you wish, and it would not be right to be dishonest with you. I should like to see you get on in the world, and I am sure you will. Some day you will write to me and tell me of your victories, and I shall be glad. It will make me happy then to know you have forgotten—this. Now you must go. Good-by!"

She rose, holding out her hand to him, and he saw her eyes were wet.

"Good-by!" he said, turning away.

Edna sat down, but did not pick up her book. With her hands listless in her lap, she gazed out at the blue sky, thinking. Presently, to her surprise, Marsten returned.

"You have forgotten your broom," she said, with a wavering smile trembling on her lips.

"I had forgotten more than that," he said, "I had forgotten my mission."

"Your mission?"

"Yes; my false pretences do not stop at climbing walls. I am really a traitorous messenger; for the device by which I came here was arranged by another, who wished me to take a letter to you. He is in Eastbourne, and had written to you, but his letter was returned to him. He has written another—here it is."

"Of whom are you speaking?"

"Mr. Barnard Hope."

"Oh!"

She took the letter. Marsten lifted his broom and went away. He wanted to leave the place and get back to London; but the gardener had cautioned him not to return until the sweeping was finished, while Barney himself impressed upon him the necessity of allowing no suspicion to arise, as it might be needful to despatch another messenger on a similar errand. So he kept on sweeping the débris into little heaps by the side of the path. The schoolgirls disappeared into the house by twos and threes, until he found himself once more alone, and yet he did not see Edna come from the summer-house. He moved nearer and nearer with his work to the place where they had met, hoping to catch a parting glimpse of her as she walked towards the house. At last she came out; but instead of taking the direct path to the house she came towards him, with the thin volume she had been reading in her hand. There was a slight increase of the usual colour in her cheeks, but with that exception she had succeeded in suppressing all trace of her emotion. She looked at him with what seemed, at first, all her former straightforwardness; but, as he met her gaze, he saw it was not quite the same: a misty shadow of difference veiled her honest eyes, so like her father's, but so much kindlier.

"I have brought you this book," she said, holding it out to him, "and I want you to keep it. It is the story of a messenger who was true to the trust of the one who sent him, and yet who failed."

"But you have not read the book yourself?" he replied, taking the volume, nevertheless.

"Oh, yes, I have. I was reading it for the second time to-day."

As he hastily concealed the book under his blouse, he looked anxiously about him, fearing they might be observed, unwilling to compromise her in the least. The craft of a man is rarely equal to that of a woman, no matter how young she may be. Edna smiled as she noticed his perturbation.

"There is no one to see us," she said, "and if there were, it would not matter. They would merely think I was giving improving literature and good advice to an under-gardener—which, indeed, is exactly what I am doing when I tell him to work hard, and—forget!"

As Edna said this she opened her hand and allowed to flutter upon the heap at his feet the minute fragments of a letter, which floated down through the air like a miniature snowfall, and she was gone before he could say "Good-by" for the second time.

Marsten stood there looking down at the bits of torn paper scattered over the heap, the remnants, undoubtedly, of the letter he had brought; and although he had had no word of encouragement—which, in spite of his disclaimer, he had yearned to hear—each separate piece of white paper reflected upwards to him a ray of hope.

## CHAPTER XXV.

SARTWELL, as he had written to his daughter and telegraphed to Barney Hope, found himself very busy, now the men had come back. Although he dismissed none who had taken part in the strike, he rearranged, with a dogged ruthlessness, the whole service of the works. Few men got their old jobs back again, or their old wages. There were promotions and retrogradations, although no one was discharged. At first it seemed to the men that this was a mere brutal display of power, presided over by wanton caprice, but as time went on they began to see the glimmering of a method in the weaving of the web. Those who were degraded to the meanest and most poorly paid work the firm had to offer were the men who had been most hot-headed in bringing on the strike, and the most persistent in opposing its conclusion. The soberer heads among the men, who had been thrust into the background during the agitation, were in every instance given promotion and higher pay; and as these changes took place one after another—for Sartwell was not the man to disorganize the works by any sweepingly radical changes—the general conclusion was that the manager merely desired to show the men that those whom they had valued lightly were the workmen whom he prized. Yet it could not be denied, even by those who lost in the game of reorganization, that the more conservative men thus advanced were among the most capable workmen in the factory. They were the men who had most to lose by a strike, and had naturally been most reluctant to enter into a contest the end of which no one could foresee. By-and-by it began to be suspected that the manager must have in his possession a complete and accurate record of every action and speech during the strike, so entirely did his shifting about of the pawns, which he played with such cool and silent relentlessness, coincide with the doings of each piece during the trouble they thought was past and hoped had been forgotten. In some instances it seemed as if Sartwell had deliberately marked the contrast by bringing the degraded and the elevated into purposeful juxtaposition, so that his design in showing that he held the future of each man in his hand could not be misunderstood by even the most stupid of his employees. It was a grim object lesson, apparently intended to convey Sartwell's determination to stick by the men who, even remotely, had sympathized with him in the late struggle; for not a word was spoken, and when a man protested humbly against debasement, the manager made no reply, and the workman knew he had either to submit or to apply for his wages at the office.

In no instance was the evidence of Sartwell's silent wrath more manifest than in the cases of Braunt and Scimmins. The two men had been equal in position when the strike began, although Scimmins received rather more money than Braunt. Now Braunt was made superintendent of the upper floor, where most of the employees were women and boys, while Scimmins was given the work which one of the boys who did not return at the end of the strike had done. Scimmins had the double humiliation of being under the none too gentle orders of the big Yorkshireman whom he had flouted during the strike, and also of having to accept little more than boy's wages. He cursed Sartwell loud and often; but the manager was a man who paid little heed to the curses of others, and Scimmins was not in a position to refuse the small pay he received.

Sartwell had at last arranged the interior economy of the factory to his liking, and was just promising himself a few days free from worry down at Eastbourne, when a most unlooked-for disaster overturned all his plans. Shortly before the dinner hour he was coming down the stairs from the upper floor, when a shriek, which seemed to be the combined voices of those he had left a moment before, paralyzed him where he stood. The first thought that flashed through his mind was that Braunt had gone suddenly mad, and, perhaps, killed some one; for the manager had noticed, since Braunt's promotion, that he sometimes spoke wildly, while now and again there was a dangerous maniacal gleam in his eye which betokened latent insanity. Before he could turn around, two dishevelled, screaming women passed him.

"What's wrong?" he shouted after them.

"Fire!" they shrieked back at him as they fled.

As Sartwell bounded up the stairs he met no more coming down. He heard outside in the yard a man's deep voice hoarsely shouting, "Fire! Fire!" The manager's heart sank as he thought of the numbers on the upper floor, the narrow stairway, and the single exit. The other floors were reasonably safe, with broad stairways and wide doors; but the upper floor, which formerly had but few occupants, had long been a source of anxiety to him, fearing, as he did, just such a catastrophe as now seemed imminent. The remedying of this had often been agreed upon by both the owners and himself, and was among the good intentions which were at various times postponed to a more convenient season,—and now the cry of "Fire!" was ringing in his ears, and the narrow stair was the only means of escape!

He found the open doorway blocked by a mass of howling human beings, each wild to escape, and each making escape impossible. They were wedged and immovable, many too tightly compressed to struggle, while others farther back thrashed wildly about with their arms, trying to fight their way to safety. The dangerous aromatic smell of burning pine filled the air, and smoke poured up through, the lift shaft, and rolled in ever-increasing density along the ceiling. There was no flame as yet; but if the jam could not be broken, it would not need the fire itself to smother the life out of those in the hopeless contest.

"Stand back there!" cried Sartwell. "There is no danger if you but keep cool. All of you go back to your places. I'll go in with you and be the last to leave, so there's nothing to fear."

A red tongue of flame flashed for the winking of an eye amidst the black smoke, disappearing almost as soon as it came, but sending a momentary glow like sheet lightning over the rapidly darkening room. It was a brief but ominous reply to Sartwell's words, and he saw he might as well have spoken to the tempest. He tried to extricate one of the girls, whose wildly-staring eyes and pallid lips showed she was being crushed to death, but she was wedged as firmly in the mass as if cemented there. Sartwell, with a groan of despair, saw he was powerless in the face of this irresistible panic. He was attacking the wedge at the point, and so was at a tremendous disadvantage.

An angry roar, louder than his shout had been, called his attention to the fact that Braunt was making an assault on the wedge from the rear. The big man, using his immense strength mercilessly, was cleaving his way through the mass, grasping the women with both hands by the shoulders, and flinging them, with a reckless carelessness of consequences, behind him, fighting his way inch by inch towards the door.

"Stand back, ye villain!" Braunt roared to Scimmins, who, crazed by fear, was trampling down all ahead of him in his frantic efforts to escape.

"It's every one for himself!" screamed Scimmins. "I have as much right to my life as you have to yours."

"Stand back, ye ruffian, or Ah'll strangle ye when Ah get ma hands on ye! Stand ye there, Mr. Sartwell, an' catch them when Ah throw them t' ye. The women first. Fling them down past the turn o' the stair an' they'll be safe. Stand ye there; Ah'll be at the door this minute. We'll have them all out in a jiffy."

While he shouted Braunt tore his way through the crowd, and at last reached the knot in the jam where further progress was impossible. Here he stood, and by the simple power of his arms lifted girl after girl straight up, and hurled them over the heads of those in front into Sartwell's arms, who pushed them on down the stairs.

"For God's sake, Scimmins," cried Sartwell, who from his position could see the fear-demented man pressing the crowd on Braunt and hampering him, "be a man, and stand back! Don't fight! There's time for all to get out."

"Ah'll crack your skull for ye!" shouted Braunt hoarsely, over his shoulder. "Remember ye've to pass me before ye get to the stair, an' little good your fightin' 'ill do ye."

At last the knot dissolved, as a long jam on a river suddenly gives way when the key-log is removed. Braunt stood now with his back against the door-post, while Sartwell took his place at the turn of the stairs, strenuously flinging torn and ragged items of humanity into safety. Several of those who had been at the point of the wedge lay at his feet, senseless or dead—there was no time to discover which. Now and then a girl he hurled down the stair tottered, fell, and lay where she fell.

"Why doesn't some one come to carry those women out?" groaned the manager, who had asked one after another whom he had saved to send help to him.

At last two of his men appeared.

"It's a bad fire, Mr. Sartwell," said one.

"Yes, yes, I know. Take down two each, if you can, and send up more men. Tell the clerks to see that the iron doors between the buildings are closed. Are the firemen here?"

"Five engines, sir."

"Good! Get down as quickly as you can, and send up more help."

"Ye devil! Do ye think to sneak past me?" cried Braunt, seizing Scimmins, who had at last fought his way through.

"Don't waste time with that man, Braunt. My God, don't you see the flames! The roof will be in on us in a minute! Fling him down here!"

"He stays behind me till the last soul's out," snarled Braunt, between his teeth.

Sartwell said no more. It was no time to argue or expostulate, and Braunt, although pinning Scimmins to the wall behind him, continued to extricate the women as fast as the manager could pass them along. The knot was continually forming at the door, and was as continually unloosed by the stalwart, indefatigable arms of Braunt.

"You are smothering me," whined Scimmins.

"I hope so," said Braunt.

The situation was now hardly to be borne. The smoke ascending the stairway met the smoke pouring through the door, yet, in spite of the smoke, the room was bright, for a steady column of flame roared up through the shaft, making it like a blast-furnace.

"Are they all out?" gasped Sartwell, coughing, for the smoke was choking him.

"Ah think so, sir; but Ah'll have a look. Some maybe on the floor,"—and Braunt, as he spoke, hurled Scimmins into the room ahead of him, pushing the door shut, so that Sartwell would not hear the man if he cried out. The manager, strangling in the smoke, appeared to have forgotten that Scimmins was there.

"Down on your hands and knees, ye hound, and see if any o' the women ye felled are there!"

Scimmins was already on his knees.

"There's no one here. Open the door!—open the door!" he cried.

Braunt opened the door an inch or two.

"All out, sir!" he shouted.

"Thank God for that!" said Sartwell. "Come down at once. There's not a moment to lose."

"I'll be down as soon as you are, sir. Run!"

The manager stumbled down the crackling stair, not doubting but Braunt followed.

"Now, ye crawling serpent, I'm going to keep ye here till ye're singed. I saw your villainy, ye coward!" The terror-stricken man mistook the purport of Braunt's words, and thus lost all chance of life.

"I swear to God, I didn't mean it!" he cried. "The match dropped before I knowed it. God's truth, it did, Braunt!"

"What! Ye fired th' works! Ye! With the women here ye tried to starve! Ye dropped the match! Ye crawling, murderous fiend!"

Braunt crouched like a wild beast about to spring, his crooked fingers, like claws, twitching nervously. Breathing in short quick gasps, for the smoke had him by the throat, his fierce eyes glittering in the flames with the fearsome light of insanity, he pounced upon his writhing victim and held his struggling figure with arms upstretched above his head. Treading over the quaking floor, he shouted:

"Down, ye craven devil, into the hell ye have made!"

The long, quivering shriek of the doomed man was swallowed and quenched in the torrent of fire.

Braunt stood in the centre of the trembling, sagging floor, with his empty hands still above his head, his face upturned, and swaying dimly in the stifling smoke. A fireman's axe crashed in a window; a spurt of water burst through the opening, and hissed against the ceiling.

"Jessie! Jessie! Listen! the Dead March! My girl! The—real—march!"

With a rending crash the floor sank into the furnace.

## CHAPTER XXVI.

Barney Hope drove his tandem up and down the parade, to the glory of Eastbourne, but with small satisfaction to himself. He did not care for the admiration of those who were strangers to him. Although his state was princely, and had all the exclusiveness which attends princeliness, it was a condition of things not at all to the liking of so companionable a man as Barney. His magnificent plan, which gave employment to an amateur gardener, had apparently miscarried; for no word came from the girl at the school, and, whatever attractions the tandem had for other inhabitants of Eastbourne, it certainly seemed that Edna Sartwell did not share them, at least sufficiently to arrange for a drive with the young man and any of her companions who dared to break the rules of the school for the giddy whirl of his lofty vehicle. Barney cursed his luck and also his messenger. He was sure it was Marsten's fault; some clumsiness on his part had undoubtedly spoiled everything. Now that Barney thought over Marsten's demeanour when he returned, he saw—what he should have seen at the time, from the gruffness and shortness of the fellow's answers—that he had made a mess of it somehow and was ashamed to confess his failure. Marsten had merely contented himself by saying to Barney that he had delivered the letter unseen, and that the girl had given him no message to take back. Barney could get no satisfying particulars from him regarding the incidents of the meeting. Had he talked with her? Of course he had. It was necessary to explain how he came to be there. What had she said? She said very little. Had she seemed angry? She did not seem any too well pleased. And thus Barney, with industry and persistence, endeavoured to draw the truth out of a reluctant man, who appeared only too eager to get away and commune with himself, and who evidently did not appreciate the fact that it was the duty of a messenger to communicate full particulars of his embassy to his chief.

Now that Marsten had so hurriedly gone to London,—probably loath to admit his diplomatic failure, yet fearing to be sent on another mission of the sort,—Barney was convinced there had been some awkward hitch in the proceedings, which was all the more annoying as he could not discover what it was, and so he set about to remedy it with that unfailing tact of which he knew himself to be possessed. For once in his life Barney had to confess that he did not know what to do. He did not care to return to London and admit defeat even to himself. One of his favourite boasts was that he never knew defeat; for where—to use his own language—he could not pull it off himself, Providence seemed always to step in and give him the necessary aid. He began to fear that his customary accuracy in detecting the interposition had for once failed him, for he remembered he had looked on the unexpected advent of Marsten as a distinct manifestation that fortune still favoured him; but, as day after day passed and no answer came to the letter he had sent, Barney began to have doubts as to the genuineness of the intervention on this occasion. At last, in deep gloom, he came to the conclusion that life under the present circumstances was not worth living if it had to be lived in Eastbourne without knowing a soul, and reluctantly he determined to return to London. He ordered out his tandem for a final exhibition, remembering that, even though he took no pleasure in it himself, it would be cruel to deprive the loungers along the parade of their usual delight in watching the elegance of the turnout and his own skill in handling a team placed endwise. After all, the innocent frequenters of Eastbourne were not to blame for what had happened, so why should they be punished unnecessarily?—said the ever-just Barney to himself. They should be allowed to feast their eyes for the last time on the tandem and its master, and Heaven help them when he finally departed! Barney mounted his chariot with a sigh; for, aside from the fact that this was in a measure a last act,—and last acts always carry a certain amount of pathos with them,—it is depressing to have it proven that one is after all under no special protection, and to have doubt cast on former instances which heretofore have stood unchallenged.

Barney drove his spirited horses with perhaps less than his customary dash, a chastened dignity taking the place of the exuberant confidence which generally distinguished him. The bracing air, the rapid motion, the feeling of controlling destiny that a man has when he is driving a tandem, all failed to raise his spirits, as might have been expected; for the very fact that he was driving alone emphasized his disappointment, and made this world the hollow mockery it sometimes seems to the most cheerful of us. Yet how often has it been said, in varying forms, that the darkest hour is just before the dawn!—and how often will men forget that simple nocturnal fact!—a defect of memory the more remarkable in a person like Barney, who so frequently had had opportunity, while on his way home from a post-midnight revel, of verifying the phenomenon. Just when his despair was at its blackest—on the fourth drive down the parade—he was amazed and delighted to see Edna Sartwell coming down one of the side streets all alone. She had a newspaper in her hand, and was looking anxiously, and, as Barney could not fail to see, furtively, up and down the street, apparently expecting to meet some one, yet fearing that her intention might be divined. Barney understood the whole situation in a flash: she had been afraid to write or had been prevented from writing, and had stolen alone from the school in the hope of meeting him. Well, they all did it, so far as Barney was concerned; and, in the glow of exultation that came over him at this proof of success, and the assurance that, after all, his luck—or whatever it was—had not deserted him, there was just a faint, annoying tinge of regret that she was no more proof against his fascinations than all the others had been. Man is but an uncertain creature at best, and never knows just what he does want. A moment before, it would have seemed to him that nothing on earth could have given him greater pleasure than a sight of her; and yet, now that he saw her looking for him, he was actually sorry she had not been walking unconcernedly along the pavement like those who were strangers to him.

However, it must be added in Barney's favour that this feeling of being perhaps a trifle too much sought after was but transitory, and that it did not for a moment interfere with his action. He pulled up his team with a suddenness that caused the front horse to turn round and face its driver, threw the reins to his groom, and jumped down with a grace and celerity as charming in its way as was his driving. The groom disentangled the horses as Barney accosted Edna with that urbanity which was perhaps his distinguishing characteristic. The girl seemed surprised to see him, and was plainly more than a little embarrassed.

"I am so glad to meet you!" cried Barney. "Why, the very sight of you makes this dull old Eastbourne smile like a rose, don't you know. I haven't had a soul to speak to for ages, and I began to fear I should lose the use of language. I give you my word, it's the truth! I do think—that is, I did, until I saw you—that Eastbourne is the dullest spot on earth."

"Then why did you come here?" asked the girl.

"Oh, now, I say, Miss Sartwell, that's rather too bad! It is, I assure you. You know I said in my letter I came solely for the pleasure of seeing you."

"So you did. I had forgotten."

"Yes; and you never even answered my note, Miss Sartwell. I call that rather hard, don't you know."

"You see, Mr Hope, we are not allowed to write letters from the school; that is one of the strictest rules."

"And are you so afraid of breaking a rule as all that? When I was at school the delight of being there was the breaking of all rules—and of most other things as well. I thought perhaps you would not mind breaking a rule for once, even if only out of pity for a friend stranded on this inhospitable coast."

Edna blushed when he spoke of the breaking of rules; then she lifted her honest eyes to his and said: "I am afraid I pay too little attention to the rules after all my pretence of regard for them. I am breaking a rule in being here now; but I was so anxious to see a newspaper that I stole out to buy one. That is why I am here, and I should not stand talking to you, but must go back at once."

"But I say, Miss Sartwell," protested Barney, "if you break a rule merely to buy a paper, surely you will break another, or keep on fracturing the same one, when you know how much pleasure it will give me to take you for a little drive."

"Oh, I couldn't think of such a thing, Mr. Hope—I couldn't, indeed, and you must not ask me! I wanted the paper to see if there was anything more about the fire. I should never have known about it had my father not sent me a short telegram that gave no particulars. I suppose he did not have time to write."

"What fire?"

"The fire at the works."

"Bless me! Has there been a fire?"

"Didn't you know? There has been a terrible fire; the east wing is destroyed, and two men have lost their lives—two of the workmen. There would have been a frightful loss of life had it not been for one of the men who is dead. It is supposed, so the papers say, that in trying to save the life of the other he lost his own."

"Dear me! how perfectly awful! I wonder why Mr. Sartwell didn't wire me, as neither father nor Monkton is there. You see I never read the papers myself—never have any interest in them. If a fellow could only know when there is to be something in them worth while, it wouldn't be so bad; but one can't go on buying them every day, in the hope there will some time be something in them, don't you know. Besides, people generally tell me all the news, so I don't need to read. I hear even more than I want to hear, without looking at the papers; but, you see, I know nobody down here, and so am slightly behind in the news of the day."

"I must go now," repeated Edna, who had listened to his remarks with ill-disguised uneasiness.

"Oh, but that's just what you mustn't do!" cried Barney, with great eagerness. "Have pity, if not on my loneliness, at least on my hopeless ignorance, don't you know, in a matter that I, of all others, ought to be interested—vitally interested—in. You see there may be no insurance, and perhaps I'm a beggar—may have to sell my tandem, don't you know; sacrifice my pictures, and all that sort of thing. I must hear about the fire, and all about it. It's of more importance even than the condition of the workingman, to me at least, dear as that subject is and—all—interwoven—as I may say, with my very—ah—being,—the workingman, don't you know."

"But," protested his anxious listener, "I know nothing about the insurance,—nothing whatever. You should go at once to London, by the very first train. There has been an inquest, and I expect to find a report of it in this paper. You can buy a paper at the station, and then you will learn everything that is to be known until you reach London."

"I say, Miss Sartwell," said Barney, in an injured tone, "you surely can't expect me to understand what's in the paper! I never could, don't you know. They seem to me to print such rubbish. Now you can explain it all to me in a very short time—you always make everything so clear. If you will just step into this cart of mine, I'll drive out of town and around behind the school; then no one will see us, and you can reach there much more quickly than if you walked, don't you know."

The girl frowned, and Barney saw with surprise that she perhaps had, after all, some of her father's impatience. He felt he was not progressing quite as favourably as he could wish; but a few words would put that right, if he could get her to go with him for a drive.

"Mr. Hope," she said, severely, "you will pardon me if I say that, under the circumstances, you should be busy in London rather than idling at Eastbourne. An unexpected calamity has happened; the business is deranged, and men are out of work just now when they need it most; yet here you stand idly talking of tandems and driving!"

Barney opened his eyes wide with astonishment. Here actually was censure, plain and undisguised. He had never encountered it before from any lady, except perhaps from his mother—and she did not count; for, as he knew, she would be the first to resent blame placed upon him by any one else.

"But—but what can I do?" stammered the unfortunate young man, with strong emphasis on the personal pronoun.

"I, of course, don't know; but that is what I should find out, if I were in your place."

"Nobody pays the least attention to what I say: they never did, and it's not likely they're going to begin now. Your father didn't even take the trouble to telegraph, although he knows I'm here."

"He knows you are here?"

"Of course. He was coming with me, and both of us were going to call upon you; but, unluckily for me, he couldn't come, and here I am stranded; and I must say, when you talk like that, I think fate is a little hard on me."

As the girl looked at him, her expression softened; she felt she had been unfair to him, and she had a keen sense of justice.

"I had no intention of saying anything harsh," she replied. "I merely told you what I thought any one in your position would do. Don't you agree with me?"

"I always agree with you, Miss Sartwell. I'm rather a blockhead, at best, don't you know; but I usually recognize the right thing when some one points it out to me. That's one great fault I find with myself: I don't see things till after every one else has seen them; then they all seem so plain that I wonder I didn't notice them before. People are so impatient with a fellow like me, that sometimes I feel sorry for myself,—I give you my word I do! If they would take a little pains,—but then, of course, no one ever cares whether a fellow goes right or wrong."

"Oh, yes, they do!" cried the girl, quickly. "I'm sure I care very much."

"You think you do," replied Barney, dejectedly; "but you won't even risk a slight scolding at the school to give me the advice I need at the time I need it most. But that's the way of the world," continued the ill-used young man, with a deep sigh. "All I want you to do is to take a short drive with me, and tell me what you know of the disaster, and what you think I ought to do under the circumstances. I brought this turnout from London on purpose to take you out. It isn't as if I were suggesting anything clandestine, for I came with your father's approval. I wrote to the mistress of the school, telling her so, but she answered with a sharp reprimand. Then I wrote directly to you, but my letter was returned with an intimation that I was trying to do something underhanded. So you see, I made every effort to be square and honest, but the honest people wouldn't have it. That's the sort of conduct that drives men to crime. Then I took to more questionable methods, and got that young fellow—I forget his name—to carry a letter to you. That offended you——"

"Oh, no!"

"It's nice of you to say so," Barney went on, mournfully; "but I am so used to disappointment that a little extra, more or less, doesn't matter. I see now I was wrong to send that letter in the way I did—I always see those things after; but I was forced into it. I expect to end up in prison some day, and never realize my crime until the judge sentences me. I suppose I ought to be above the need of an encouraging word now and then, but I don't seem to be."

"What do you wish me to do?" asked the girl, a shade of perplexity coming over her face.

"All I wish is a little straightforward clear-headed advice. Art beckons me in one direction, and advises me to leave business alone. You said just now that my place was at the works, and that I shouldn't be idling here when there was so much to be done. Mr. Sartwell quite evidently hopes I shall keep out of the way, or he would have told me of the fire. I seem to be a superfluous person, not wanted anywhere—not even by the police. What do I wish you to do? I wish you to let me take you for a little drive into the country, and tell me how I can help your father at this crisis."

"One is so conspicuous up there," she said, glancing with distrust at' the waiting tandem. "No; let us walk to the end of the parade. There we can sit down, and I will tell you all I know about the fire, and, if my advice is worth anything, you shall have it. After that you must let me walk to the school alone." Barney was forced to content himself with this, and he reluctantly ordered the groom to take the horses to the stables.

The two walked along the parade to the most sheltered seat, where they sat down together. The young man's mind was in a whirl; the coldness of his reception excited him, and made him fearful of losing what he had thought, up to that time, was his for the asking.

He proposed to the girl, and was rejected.

## CHAPTER XXVII.

There is an idea prevalent that the young women of our land welcome addresses which the golden youth of the opposite sex urge upon their consideration, and that a girl's happiness augments in proportionate ratio as the number of the proposals bestowed upon her increases. This, however, is merely a supposition, and there are unfortunately no statistics to which an historian, anxious to be accurate in statement, may turn in order to substantiate or overthrow this almost universally held opinion. It is to be regretted that the census, which gathers together in tabulated form so many interesting facts pertaining to the race, gives no attention to this particular subdivision of human data; and that, so far from being able to form any definite estimate of the feeling with which a girl welcomes the undoubted compliment of a marriage offer, we are left in the dark as to the average number of proposals a woman receives, say, between the ages of seventeen and thirty-seven. An inquisitive government which does not hesitate to ask a woman every ten years to set down her age in black and white seems, strangely enough, to shrink from inquiring into a vital question on which the future well-being of a nation largely depends; thus no one can positively state that matrimonial advances are held in high estimation by their recipients, clinching the proposition by referring the doubter to Blue Book such a number and such a page.

It being thus impossible to generalize, the careful writer is compelled to fall back on individual instances, and it must be set down that Edna Sartwell, so far from being happy or elated over the fact that two young men within one week had asked her to share their varying fortunes, walked hurriedly back to the school, filled with terror and dismay. On the very threshold of womanhood she had suddenly and unexpectedly been brought face to face with a state of things which made her wish to shrink back into the untroubled tranquillity of the life she had hitherto led. These two disquieting events, following one so closely on the other, loomed up in undue proportion to their importance, and threatened to overshadow the future. It seemed an appalling thing that the fate of two men should be placed at her disposal; that on her shoulders should be cast the great responsibility of deciding, unaided, a momentous question with far-reaching consequences. And if the first two young men with whom she became acquainted acted thus, what was to be expected from the numerous host she was still likely to meet? A pathway strewn with broken hearts offered no allurements to the feet of the young traveller; a life lived in an atmosphere of deep sighs was intolerable. The girl was frightened at the outlook, which was all the more bewildering because only partly understood. "It is often as important to classify your problem as to solve it," her father had once said to her; but solution or classification appeared equally difficult to her.

Barney had taken his rejection badly. He made no attempt to conceal the fact that his life was blighted; that he would re-enter the world a changed man, but heroically determined to make the most out of the wreck. The austere, rugged road that now lay before him, unbrightened by love or human sympathy, he would walk with grim, if sombre, resolution; brushing aside the frivolities of existence; setting his face with sullen but dogged persistence towards the cheerless journey of life; hoping for no recompense except that perhaps he might have the consolation of knowing that he left the world a trifle better for having lived in it.

Inexperienced as she was, Edna could not help contrasting the actions of Hope and Marsten, not altogether to the disadvantage of the latter. There was no question in her mind that Marsten had in reality an up-hill road to travel; yet he had gone into no heroics about it, and he asked nothing but that she should remember him. She had been sorry she could give no encouraging word to Marsten; but Barney made her feel somehow that she was to blame in his case, and that he was an ill-used man. Then, it was difficult to realize the serious nature or hardship of Barney's future career, when every one knew he had more money than was good for him. Some thought of this seemed to occur to Barney himself at the time, for he spoke bitterly and contemptuously of his wealth, and of how it handicapped him; however, he was going to give it all away when he came into his full fortune, and start the world afresh, winning his laurels and what little cash would suffice for his frugal needs, with his good right arm, assisted presumably by his paintbrushes; so in the face of this noble resolution it would have been unfair to censure him for the possession of riches he had had no hand in accumulating.

Edna hurried towards the school, thinking little of the reprimand in store for her, and much of the contrary conditions of this world. She, like Barney, needed advice, yet had no one in whom she might confide. She thought of writing fully to her father, remembering her promise to tell him everything that troubled her; but she shrank from the thought almost as soon as it took form in her mind. Besides, both complications were settled finally and forever, so why worry him unnecessarily about a page of her life on which was written the word "Finis"? There surged up in her heart a deep, passionate yearning for the mother she had never known, and whom she now missed as she had never missed her before. As she thought of the portrait of the beautiful, sweet-looking woman in her father's office, whose pathetic eyes shone so tenderly and lovingly upon her, the tears which had been near the surface suddenly blinded her, and she sobbed:

"I am alone—alone!"

On reaching the school, Edna went directly to her room, where she found a letter from her step-mother awaiting her; and this helped more than anything else to drive away the sad thoughts which filled her mind. The letter ran thus:

"My Poor Dear Edna:"

"You will doubtless have heard of the dreadful calamity that has overtaken the business of Monkton & Hope, a calamity from which I fear it may never recover; although your father, as usual, scoffs at what I predict, and says they are fully insured—as if an insurance policy could cover the far-reaching effects of such a disaster! There seems little doubt that the fire was caused by some of the disaffected men, exasperated, probably, by the treatment they have received, although that is no excuse tor the crime. But we are all short-seeing, misguided creatures here below, with the taint of original sin in each of us; unable, unless directed by a Higher Power, to take even the slightest action that will be acceptable; and prone ever to slip and stumble if we neglect those warnings which for our benefit are showered on the just and the unjust alike: but if warnings are passed by—or, worse still, scoffed at—how can we hope to profit by them and mend our ways, as an ever-indulgent Providence—eager to forgive, if we but exhibit a desire for forgive-ness—intended they should?—and when I asked your father in a most gentle and respectful (I hope I know my duty as a wife by this time!) way if the fire had not pointed a great moral to him, he said with most regrettable flippancy—which I have sometimes attempted to correct in you, my poor child!—that it pointed the moral to be well insured and to have fire-escapes from the upper floors; as if ribaldry like that was not very much out of place in speaking of a solemn event where two immortal souls went to their last account without a moment's warning—going, for aught we know, through perishable fire to flames that are never quenched! The usefulness of this thought makes no impression on your father, who is as stubborn as ever, and I fear no more just to his men than before all this happened. A poor young man named Marsten has been ruthlessly discharged by your father, and may now be wandering about the streets, looking for work and starving, for all any one knows or cares. Ask your father why he was discharged if you want to know, but don't ask me. It is nothing but pride—pride—pride! My child, take warning while there is yet time, for the night cometh. Harden not your heart.

"I shall continue to petition for you both, for the mercy is unfailing and unlimited.

"Your loving but sorrowing mother,

"Sarah Sartwell."

The benevolent intentions of this letter were in no wise frustrated, and Mrs. Sartwell would doubtless have been pleased had she known that the reading of, it did the recipient a world of good. It acted as a tonic, and gave Edna something to think about, preventing any morbid reflections on the wreck she had made of Barney's life.

The discharge of Marsten was a great shock to the girl, and for the first time in her life she thought her father had acted unjustly. At first, in pondering over the unexpected bit of information, she thought her father had, in some way, heard of the young man's visit to Eastbourne; but as she turned the subject over in her mind she came to the conclusion that his dismissal was the result of their meeting in the garden at home and the finding of Marsten there by her father. The reason, then, the young man had time to come to Eastbourne, was because his time was now his own. And yet he had said nothing about it, even when she asked him how he got away from duty. He had spoken well of her father, although he must have felt he had been unjustly treated. She had thought nothing of his good words at the time, but now they came back to her. She determined to write to her father, and tell him all about Marsten's visit and its result; but when she sat down with the paper before her, she found she did not know how to begin. She wished to ask him to repair the unnecessary wrong he had done Marsten, for there was not the slightest chance of her ever marrying the young man; but somehow, when she came to put this all down on paper, the task seemed very difficult. The difficulty was increased by the knowledge that her father must at that moment have as much on his mind as any one should be called upon to bear, and she pictured the silent man sitting at home, tired out with the work and worry of the day, while the monotonous voice of his wife drew moral lessons from every new obstacle he had to surmount. No; she would not add a single care to those already on his shoulders.

The girl sat with her elbows on the desk, her chin in her hands, gazing with troubled eyes into vacancy, as if the problems that beset her were in the air before her and could be hypnotized into solution. A bewildering feature of the case was that she had continually, of late, to readjust her ideas, and bring them into correct relationship with some new fact which came within her cognizance. All the conversations she had held with her father, many of his actions, bore quite a new significance when she learned that he knew Marsten loved her. Again, the fact of Mars-ten's dismissal lent a sharp poignancy to her remembrance of his fervent declaration that, for her sake, he would strive to please any master placed over him, as no man had ever striven before. Edna did not share her step-mother's fear that the young man was starving; but her imagination kindled at the thought of his impassioned words, his resolute determination to succeed, addressed to the daughter of the man who a day or two before had turned him into the streets. The more she thought about her father's action, the more unjust it seemed. A dozen times she began a letter, and as often relapsed again into reverie. Barney and his mythical woes faded entirely from her memory. Gradually she came to the conclusion that, if she did not intervene in Marsten's interests, she would be making herself responsible for the continuance of the injustice; and, although she wished to relieve her father from all anxiety regarding her feelings towards the young man, still she was ashamed to touch upon that part of the subject. It might be possible some time, when she sat at her father's knee, to tell him about it, with averted face; but to write it, she could not.

At last she succeeded in drafting a letter, which she hurriedly posted, fearing that longer meditation upon the question might result in its not being sent at all.

"Dear Father:

"I am sure you must be very busy, and perhaps very much worried at the present moment. You know I do not wish to add to your burden, and would rather lighten it if I could; but in that I am as helpless as you are strong. We made a compact a while since, and that is why I write. Something has happened for which I feel partly responsible. In a letter received to-day from my step-mother she says you have discharged Mr. Marsten, and she thinks he may now be looking in vain for employment. I am afraid you were not pleased at finding him talking to me in our garden, but that was my fault and not his. If that was the reason, won't you please reconsider and invite him back?

"Your loving daughter,

"Edna."

The answer came almost before she thought her letter had time to reach London.

"My Dear Little Girl:

"I should have written days ago, but unfortunately I cannot dictate an affectionate letter through my shorthand clerk, and the older I grow the more

I dislike writing with my own hand. Worried? Oh, dear no! Why should one worry? I'm afraid your belligerent old father still loves a fight, whether with circumstances or with men. Before the fire was out, telegraphic orders were despatched to three machinery firms in the North. While the fire-engines were still flinging water on the ruins, I had secured a lease of the four houses that adjoin the works, had compounded with the tenants, and sent them packing. That night men were at work knocking doorways through the partitions and strengthening the floors. Happily the engines and boilers were not injured, being in a separate building, and already such machinery as we could get is in place, and a long, sagging, wobbling iron rope carries the power across the yard. The new secretary of the Union proposed a conference with me to discuss what the firm was willing to do for the men thrown out of work by the fire. I refused to discuss anything with the new secretary, he not being an employee of mine. He is a shrewder man than Gibbons; so he at once got up a deputation of my own men and sent them to me. I received them, of course, and they asked me if I would give them fifteen per cent of their wages while out of work. 'No,' said I, 'I can always do better than the Union. There will be paid one hundred per cent of the wages, not fifteen; I expect you all back at the works on Monday.' I fancy I made the men open their eyes a bit. Work will be going on as usual within a week, and we won't be behind with a single order. The new factory which is now begun will be built in accordance with modern ideas, and I expect to be able to increase our business so that the four houses leased will be retained when the new building is ready for occupation. Forgive this patting of myself on the shoulder, but a man must brag now and then to some one, and you, my dear Edna, are the only one to whom I can boast.

"Yes, the compact is still in operation, and I'm glad you wrote about your step-mother's letter, although I hope you will not take too seriously any half-hysterical comments on my tyrannical conduct, A man must act, and one who acts is bound to make mistakes. Perhaps the discharge of Marsten was a mistake. I don't think so, but of course your step-mother does, and, as facts always embarrass her, she sees instant starvation and all the rest of it. Everything, Edna, depends on the point of view. A lighted match is dropped by accident or design, and, falling on inflammable material, certain chemical changes take place; carbonic acid gas is produced, and a factory goes down in ruins to supply the materials for combustion. All this seems perfectly natural to me, and in accordance with established scientific research. But your stepmother's point of view is different. She sees the finger of Providence, and because I don't, I'm a scoffer. Now, I've as great a belief and trust in Providence as any one, but to me Providence works sanely. It doesn't destroy a factory and kill two men merely to show me I'm in error, because it could accomplish its purpose at much less expense and trouble. I can't think that Providence is less sensible than my little girl, and she takes the right method. She says in kindly fashion, 'Father, I think you are wrong, and I want you to reconsider.' She doesn't try to prove me a heartless despot. I would at once reconsider, and would invite Marsten back, but it is not necessary. He is the new secretary of the Union, with a salary larger than the wages he had here, with his time practically his own, and with ample opportunity for mischief if he chooses to exercise his power. I feel it in my bones that in one or two or three years I shall have to fight him. It will be an interesting struggle, but I shall win. So with this final bit of brag I close my long letter. I hope to run down and see you on Saturday, and meanwhile all the sympathy you have to spare, lavish on that iron-handed tyrant,

"Your Father."

## CHAPTER XXVIII.

Barney abandoned his tandem to the tender care of his man, and went up to London by train. He sat gloomily in a corner of a first-class smoking-compartment, and cursed the world. Nevertheless he was able to consume a great number of cigarettes between the sea and Charing Cross, and, as he smoked, he made stern, heroic resolutions regarding his career. He would now take it seriously in hand. He would business-manage himself. He saw in the clear light of a great disappointment that he had hitherto paid too much attention to the production of masterpieces, and too little to the advertising of them. It was evidently hopeless to expect the appreciation of a stupid and uncritical public to come to his work, and the great critic whom he had confidently looked for had not yet put in an appearance. If, then, the critic would not come to Mahomet, Mahomet would go to the critic. He would purchase the most expensive art-critic there was in the market; then the tardy public would learn that a genius had lived among them unrecognized.

As his comprehensive plans took final shape the train ran into the glass-roofed tunnel at Charing Cross. Barney sprang into a hansom, and drove directly to the works. "Beastly hole!" he said to himself, as he gazed round at the ruin the fire had wrought. The ground was covered with cluttering heaps of burnt and twisted iron, and piles of new building material were scattered everywhere. The apparent confusion and ugliness of it all offended his artistic sense, and he thanked his stars it was not necessary for him to spend his days there. He accosted Sartwell, who had been discussing some question with the architect, and shook the manager's hand with energy and cordiality.

"Mr. Sartwell," he cried, "I came the moment I heard of the fire."

"Ah," said the manager, dryly. "Have you been in America?"

"No," laughed Barney, "not quite so far away as that; but, don't you know, I never read the papers, and so heard of the conflagration purely by accident. Now, I am here entirely at your disposal, and am ready to do anything and everything you want done. I would rather not carry bricks, if there is anything else I can do; but I am ready to help in any way I can. I don't mind telling you, Mr. Sartwell, that, in placing myself at the disposal of the firm, I do so at considerable sacrifice; for art is long and time is fleeting, and I have work to do in my studio that you, perhaps, might not think worth doing; but I hope posterity will not agree with you, don't you know. Still, I am here. Command me."

"Indeed, you do me wrong," said Sartwell, with a grim smile. "I consider you of much greater value in the studio than here. I have no doubt posterity and I will quite agree in our estimate of your labour. Artists are few and labourers many. It would be a real disaster if our present crisis were to interfere with your artistic work. Therefore, although I am flattered by your generous offer of help, I could not think of availing myself of it. No; the studio is your place, Mr. Hope."

"It's uncommonly kind of you, Mr. Sartwell, to say so many nice things about my efforts, and I assure you I appreciate them, for I don't have too many encouragements—I don't, I assure you. This is such a beastly materialistic world, don't you know. Has my father got home yet?"

"Yes; he returned last night."

"Ah, I didn't know that. Terribly upset, I suppose?"

"A trifle worried."

"Naturally he would be. Well, there's nothing I can do for you then?"

"Nothing, unless you undertake the decoration of the new factory, and thus send it down to posterity with the Vatican frescoes. Still, that question won't arise for a month or two yet."

"Quite so. I'll think about it. Well, if you need me, you know my address. A wire will bring me at any time."

"It's generous of you to stand ready to leap into the chasm in this way, but take my advice and stick to the studio. Nevertheless, I'll remember, and let you know if a crisis arises with which I am unable to deal single-handed."

"Do," cried Barney, again shaking hands with good-natured effusion. "Well, good-by!"

He picked his way to the gates, and stepped into his waiting hansom, a well-merited feeling of having answered the stern call of duty cheering his heart as he drove away.

It was a long drive to Haldiman's studio, and Barney, telling the cabman he might have to wait an hour or two, dashed up the steps and rang the bell. Being admitted, he asked if Haldiman was at home; then sprang up the stairs, struck one startling knock on the studio door with the head of his stick, and entered.

Haldiman stood at his easel, a black pipe in his mouth, an old jacket on his back, and a general air about him of not having brushed his hair for a week. A half-finished drawing in black and white decorated a great sheet of cardboard placed on the easel.

"Hello, Barney!" he cried. "I thought that was your delicate way of announcing yourself. You look as trim and well-groomed as a shop-walker. Haven't given up painting and taken to that line, have you?"

"No, old man, I haven't!" shouted Barney, slamming the door behind him and coming into the room like a cyclone. "And I'm not trim, for I have just had a railway journey, and went from Charing Cross to the works, and from the works here. I've had no time to go to the club and make myself pretty; I was in too much of a hurry to see you. So don't be sarcastic, Haldiman."

"Everything is comparative, Barney, and to me you look like a radiant being from another and a better world, where a man has unlimited credit with his tailor. Sit down, won't you?"

"That's what I came for. I say, Haldiman, where do you keep your exhilarating fluid and the syphons? I'm tired out. Be hospitable. You see I've a load on my mind these days. The works were partly destroyed by fire, and we're rebuilding and all that sort of thing, don't you know, which rather takes it out of a fellow, looking after workmen and seeing that no mistakes are made."

"Oh, I saw about that in the papers, and was wondering if it was your shop," said Haldiman, placing a small table beside his friend, and putting a bottle, a syphon, and a glass upon it. "Help yourself, my boy. You don't mind my going on with my work?"

"But I do!" cried Barney. "Sit down yourself, Haldiman. I want to talk to you seriously."

"I am behindhand with this picture now, Barney. I can work and listen. Fire away."

"Look here, Haldiman, how much do you get for a smear like that?"

Haldiman stood back and looked critically at the picture, then said with a drawl:

"Well, I'm in hopes of looting four guineas out of the pirate who edits the magazine this is for. It's a full page, you know."

"Great heavens! Imagine a man doing a picture for such a sum as that! I wouldn't draw a line under a hundred pounds."

"I've often thought of putting my price up to that entrancing figure," replied Haldiman, reflectively, "but refrained for fear of bankrupting the magazines. One must have some consideration for the sixpenny press." Barney thrust his hand deep into his trousers pocket, drew out a fist-full of coins, selected four sovereigns and four shillings, and placed them on the table, saying: "There, Haldiman, there's your guineas. I buy that picture. Now sit down and talk to me. I want your whole attention."

Haldiman stood for a moment looking alternately at the money and at the man. At last he spoke, slowly and quietly:

"Some day, Barney, you'll do a thing like that, and get smashed in consequence. I'm unfortunately unable to throw you out of the window myself; but there is a cabman loitering about in front, and I will call him in to assist me if you don't at once put that money in your pocket. Don't make me violate the sacred rules of hospitality."

"You have violated them, Hal, already, by getting angry. I see you're angry, so don't deny it. Besides, the cabman wouldn't come; I own him, and if he did I could put you both out."

"You can't hire me, like a cabman, you know, Barney."

"Of course not, of course not. I'm not trying to, dear boy. Do sit down and be sensible. I've come to you as one friend to another, for I'm at a crisis in my career. I need help, so be good to me. I take a serious view of life now, and——"

"Since when?"

"Since this morning, if you like. The 'when' doesn't matter. I've come to the conclusion that I'm wasting my existence. You'll scoff, of course, but I know I have genius—not talent, mind, but genius. There's no use of making any bones about it, or pretending false modesty: if a man is a genius, he knows it. Very well, then, why not say so?"

"I see no reason against it."

"Quite so. Now, Haldiman, how much money do you make in a year?"

"You mean, how little?"

"Put it any way you like. Name the figure."

"What's that got to do with your genius?"

"Never you mind. What's the amount?"

"Now, Barney, if you're cooking up some new kind of financial insult, I give you fair warning I won't stand it."

Barney had gulped down his stimulant, and now paced up and down the room, clearing a track for himself by kicking things out of the way. Haldiman sat in a deep armchair, his legs stretched out, and his hands in his pockets, watching his friend's energetic march to and fro.

"The artistic profession," cried the pedestrian, "has been held up to the scorn of the world since painting began. Read any novel, and you will see that, if the heroine is to make a doocedly bad marriage, she invariably falls in love with an artist—invariably."

"Well, she generally marries us."

"Yes, and lives in misery ever after."

"Oh, we're generous, and share it with her."

"You see what I mean. The artist is held up to contempt, and all respectable people in the book are aghast at the girl's choice. Now, why is this?"

"Ask me a harder one. It is because fiction is notoriously untrue to life. The wives of the Royal Academy live in a splendour and luxury undreamed of by the ordinary lady of title."

"Nothing of the sort. It's because the artists don't business-manage themselves. They have no commercial sense. Therefore they are poor. Now, if a man invents a soap, what does he do?"

"Washes himself."

"He advertises it. He becomes rich. Why, then, if a man writes a great book, should he not advertise himself and his book in every way that is open to him?"

"I believe he does, Barney. Where have you been living this while back to be so ignorant of the approved modern methods in art and literature?"

"Isn't a great picture of more value to the world than a much-advertised soap?"

"Well, if you ask me, I should say, no. I'd back the soap as a civilizer against the Louvre any day."

Barney stopped in his walk, raised his arms above his head, and let them drop heavily to his sides.

"I haven't a friend in the world!" he cried, in tragic tones. "Not one—not one!"

"Barney, this conversation is bewildering. What are you driving at, anyhow? Art, soap, literature, advertising, friendship, marriage—what's wrong? Who is the woman?"

"Don't talk to me about women! I hate them!"

"I thought you were most successful in that line. I believe I have your own authority for the statement."

"Success! One is successful up to a point; then there is a disappointment that shows what a sham success has been. I'll never speak to a woman again."

"I've been there myself—several times. Still we always return—if not to our first love, to our fourth, or fifth. As for friends, I don't know any man who has more."

"Not true friends, Haldiman. I haven't one, I tell you. I did think you were a friend, and you do nothing but sneer at me. You think I don't see it; I do, all the same. I'm the most sensitive of men, although nobody appears to appreciate it."

"I don't sneer at you, Barney. What put that in your head? I think you sometimes fail to appreciate other people's sensitiveness. You are a trifle prone to flaunt Bank of England notes in the faces of those not so well provided as you are with them. Then the sensitive soul rises in rebellion."

"That's my unfortunate manner, Haldiman. I don't really mean to do so. If I had a game leg, or a club foot, and came thumping in here with it, you wouldn't make fun of my defect, would you? Of course not. Well, why should you resent a defect of manner when you know my intentions are good?"

"I don't resent anything about you, Barney—at least only spasmodically."

"You know I'd go to the end of the world to serve a friend—I would, honest! Yet I've no luck. Here is a poor devil of a musician I am trying to befriend. I can see he dislikes me intensely. I got a publisher to bring out some of his music—paid all the expenses—yet it was like pulling teeth to get that organist to allow me to help him, and he's a genius if ever there was one. I got a select and appreciative audience together to hear him play. He didn't come, although he promised to do so, and the people thought I was trying to make fools of them. It must be all my accursed manner. Now you always know the right thing to say: I don't. My genius doesn't run that way. I'm an artist."

Haldiman threw back his head and laughed. Barney stared at him, displeasure on his brow.

"What the deuce are you laughing at now?"

"Forgive me, Barney; I'm laughing at the thumping of your club foot, although you did not believe me capable of it."

"What have I said?"

"Nothing—nothing. Barney, I love you! You are the one and only Barnard Hope; all others are base imitations. Now listen to me. I haven't the faintest idea what it is you want. This conversation has been simply encyclopaedic in the amount of ground covered; but I'll do for you what you would do for me, short of abduction or assassination. I'd prefer not to land myself in prison, if you don't mind, but I'll even run the risk of that. What do you want? Out with it!"

"But the moment I begin, you'll say your insulted. You terrorize me, Haldiman,—'pon my soul, you do!"

"Go on. For ten minutes insults are barred. Will you go on?"

"Very well. I asked you how much you made in a year, and you jeered at me."

"I never keep accounts, and never pay a debt until the brokers come in, so I really haven't the slightest idea. You can guess at the amount just as well as I can.. Guess and proceed."

"All right. I want to pay you double your yearly income for your help in this matter."

"That isn't friendship, that's commercialism again. I beg pardon, I forgot. Don't look daggers, Barney; I accept. Can I have the money in advance?"

"Of course you can," cried Barney, gleefully, making a dive for his inside pocket; then, as the other went into a fit of laughter, the joyful look faded into an expression of intense indignation, and Barney, with a curse, strode to the door. Haldiman sprang to his feet and grasped the offended man by the shoulders.

"None of that!" he cried. "Come back, you villain! You are not going to offer me a fortune and then sneak off in that fashion. Sit down, Barney; sit down and go on with the pretty talk!"

"Oh, it's no use!" said the other, in tones of deep dejection. "I said I hadn't a friend in the world, and I haven't."

"Bosh! You're harder to humour than a baby. If a man may not smile in his own room, where may he? I'm intensely interested, and want to know what crime I'm expected to commit. Never mind the money, but state your case."

"The money is part of the case. I pay or I don't play."

"Certainly. That's understood. I accept. Fire away!"

"Well, you know all the editors of the illustrated weeklies and magazines."

"For my sins I do—alas!"

"Then, to come right to the point as between man and man, I want to buy a first-class critic, and the editor of a first-class illustrated periodical."

"You mean you want to buy a going magazine?"

"I don't mean anything of the kind. I mean just what I say."

"Then I don't quite understand you. Explain."

"What I want is this: I want a first-class art-critic to write an article in a first-class periodical saying Barnard Hope is the greatest artist the world has ever seen."

"Oh, is that all?"

"No, that's not all. I want the article superbly illustrated—in colour if possible—with, reproductions of my chief paintings."

"Ah! I wouldn't do that, Barney, if I were you. The pictures would be rather a give-away of the great critic's eulogy."

"Yes, I knew you would say that. The obviousness of such a remark would commend itself to you. But you see I'm perfectly frank with you. Now, could you manage this for me? Remember, I don't care how much money I spend."

Haldiman removed the black pipe from his mouth, knocked the ashes out of it, and thoughtfully re-filled it.

"Well, for brazen cheek, Barney," he said at last, "that proposal——"

"Yes, I know, I know, I know. But these things happen every day—or, not to exaggerate, let us say every second day. It is simply doing for me what Ruskin did for Turner. Turner painted away all his life; nobody recognized him, and he died in Chelsea. Now I'm living in Chelsea, and I want recognition during my life. Of course my Ruskin will come along after I'm dead; but, like the fellow who was to be executed, I won't be there to enjoy it. Things rarely happen at the right moment in this world, and my brazen proposal is merely to take events by the coat collar and hurry them up a bit. You see what I mean? Besides, I'm infinitely greater than Turner, don't you know."

Haldiman smoked and meditated for some moments; then he said:

"I'm not sure but the trick may be done, although I doubt if brutal barefaced bribery will do it. How would a magazine like 'Our National Art' suit you?"

"Nothing could be better."

"And would a French art-critic like Viellieme be satisfactory?"

"Perfectly. What he says is taken for gospel all the world over."

"Well, I happen to know that the editor of 'Our National Art' has been trying for a year to get Viellieme to write about English art; but the Frenchman won't come over to London, even for a day, at any price. Viellieme is great as a writer, but greater still as a money-spender. I'll run over to Paris and sound him. You couldn't bribe the editor of 'Our National Art,' but he will print anything Viellieme will write for him. Now I know the Frenchman doesn't care what he writes for England, although he is rather particular about what appears in Paris. He thinks there is no art in England."

"He's right, too, as far as his knowledge goes; but he's never seen anything of mine."

"Just so. Then, if Viellieme agrees, you would be willing to send some of your immortal works over to Paris for his inspection."

"All of them, my boy, all of them."

"Then we'll look on that as settled. I'll do my best."

"God bless you, my dear fellow! God bless you!" cried Barney with deep emotion, crushingly wringing the hand of the wincing man, whom he now declared to be his one friend on earth. He clattered noisily down the stair like a stalwart trooper, sprang into the waiting hansom, and departed.

## CHAPTER XXIX.

MARSTEN went to work with an energy and singleness of purpose which probably no organizer of labour ever felt before. Chance, or destiny, had placed him in exactly the position he had long hoped to attain. At first there was little to be done but wait until the Union had recovered from the wounds received in the late fruitless struggle; nevertheless, while he waited, he planned and gradually developed the scheme which he hoped would revolutionize the labour of the world. He saw in the future one vast republic of workers—not bounded by nationality, but spreading over the entire earth—with its foothold wherever one man toiled with his hands to enrich another. He had no delusions regarding the immediate success of his project, and did not flatter himself that his ideas would spread with anything like the rapidity of the cholera, for example; but he hoped first to place the Union on a firm footing in England, and then, with a brilliantly successful strike—conducted as a general of genius conducts a battle—to show what might be done by a thoroughly well-organized force against a rich and powerful firm like that of Monkton & Hope. He looked forward to the time when every worker in England would be a member of the Union; after that he hoped to affiliate all the workers in all English-speaking countries; finally, the benighted foreigner would be included. Then, when the whole was united like an electric installation in a city, the unfortunate capitalist who placed a finger on one point would receive the combined current of the entire system, and die without knowing what hurt him. The equipment of the workers would be so complete that strikes would become fewer and fewer, and finally cease; just as war will cease when weapons of offence reach such a state of perfection that no nation will dare to pick a quarrel with another.

This great republic of labour would be divided into various states, and these states would be again subdivided into as many sections as experience showed to be most practicable. Each section would elect its secretary, the secretaries would elect a governor of the state, the governors would elect a president of the whole organization. Every official should be paid a salary, sufficient, even in the lesser offices, to keep the incumbent and his family without the necessity of manual labour, so that each officer's whole time could be given for the benefit of the Union.

Marsten gave much thought to the problem of reconciling deserved promotion with popular election, and, perhaps, if he had known more of the results of universal suffrage in a city like New York, he might have reconstructed his whole plan; but he had full belief in the adage that the voice of the people coincides with that of the Almighty, and so, perhaps, did not quite appreciate the practical difficulties which lay in wait for a scheme that looked beautiful on paper.

Early experience convinced him that he could hope for no active assistance from the men themselves, and he promptly eliminated that factor from his calculations. He thought of beginning his fight with an educational campaign, using in this way the time which must elapse before the treasury of the Union was once more in funds; but he found he could never get more than half a dozen of the men together at one time, and those who came to the meetings he called seemed to take but slight interest in what he had to say. This did not discourage him, as he was, in a measure, prepared for the indifference he met; and he remembered that his great model, Napoleon, took no one into his confidence. Napoleon struck unexpectedly,—struck quick and struck hard,—and Marsten resolved to do the same the moment he had the power. Failing to interest the men collectively in the desirability of a close and universal Union, Marsten tried to win their separate confidence; but he soon discovered that in attempting this he was travelling a dangerous road. He was amazed to find that there existed a latent sullen opposition to him; that many of the men seemed to regret the generous impulse which had caused them to place him where he was. They could not see what he did to earn the money he received; some thought they were giving him too much, as he had no work to do; and more than one advised him to keep quiet and leave the men alone, to know when he was well off, and not to turn the thoughts of the members to the fact that they were supporting him in idleness and luxury.

Marsten resolved to let nothing stand in the way of success. He believed he could more than earn any salary they gave him, and no man in London had a greater incentive for making and accumulating money than he had; nevertheless, he desired above all things to hold the good opinion of the men and to convince them that he was working for them and not for himself. He realized that alone he was powerless, but with their united support he was invincible.

He called a meeting to reconsider the salary of the secretary, and that meeting was well attended; for the subject to be discussed had more interest than his abandoned educational campaign, the purpose of which was to teach them the principles of combination. Most of the men thought him a fool in not knowing his own good luck.

Marsten, addressing them, said that his whole object in taking the secretaryship was to bring about an amalgamation of labour which would make the results of future strikes a certainty. All the rights mankind possessed had been won by battle; but the battles must be successful, and success was only possible when there was no dissension in the camp. He frankly stated that he had learned there was some dissatisfaction because he got more money than was earned by many who laboured in the ranks, and he had made an estimate of how little he could live upon, which was less than the poorest paid employee of the works received. He was willing to accept this sum, and would devote his whole time and energy to the cause of labour as faithfully as if he were given ten times the amount.

Gibbons, who had at last found employment in the neighbourhood, here rose to his feet. He said he thought the office of secretary could be still more economically filled. He was sure they had men among them, now in employ, who would act as secretary without salary from the Union, and perform all the duties quite acceptably to the majority of the men.

"Why didn't you propose that when you were secretary yourself, Gibbons?" asked one of the audience, at which there was some laughter.

"I did not do so because I was at that time out of work," replied Gibbons, warming to his theme. "I don't wish to say a word against the present secretary, but I would like to ask him a question or two. He seemed once of opinion that Sartwell was a very shrewd, far-seeing man. I would like to know, Mr.

Marsten, if you are still of that opinion?"

"I am," answered Marsten.

"Then can you explain to the meeting why Sartwell has taken no further steps to cripple the Union, which we all know he desired to smash, and in fact did threaten to smash? Why did he not, in taking back the men, make it a condition that they should leave the Union?"

"How should I know? I may say, however, that I believe Sartwell to be an essentially just man, although he may be mistaken in some things, and I don't think he would interfere with the personal liberty of his employees."

"It is very generous of the secretary of our Union to speak well of the honesty of a man who looted our treasury, and we won't forget that Sartwell has at least one friend among us. It is a little remarkable that that one friend should have been the only man, of all Sartwell's employees, who was suddenly dismissed, and, as far as we know, without cause. One more question, Mr. Marsten. Do you know why Sartwell discharged you?"

Marsten was silent, the colour rising in his face.

"Of course," continued Gibbons, calmly, "you are not compelled to answer. I am merely asking what many of us have been thinking. You either know, or you do not. You have called this meeting, and I think you should have the courtesy to answer any question—any reasonable question—asked you. You say you want the support of the men, whose servant you are. That is a reasonable desire; but to bestow that confidence we must have full knowledge of our man. I ask for the second time, do you know why Sartwell discharged you?"

"I do."

"Why?"

"On account of a personal quarrel between him and me with which this meeting has nothing to do."

"Oh, indeed! Then you had personal dealings with the man we were fighting, which you would prefer us to know nothing about. I will not press for a more specific answer. No man is bound to incriminate himself. I have given Mr. Marsten a chance to explain certain obscure points that have puzzled some of us, and I think the answers wrung from him, with only too evident reluctance, have not bettered his position, nor made any thinking man among us the more ready to bestow that confidence which our secretary seems so much to desire. I would like now to call your attention to one or two points. Rightly or wrongly, the committee with which I acted had grave doubts of the loyalty of Mr. Marsten during our late contest. Before the strike began, he himself admitted that he had been closeted with Sartwell, and we know that while the fight was on he was the only man who had a conference with the enemy, and the only man who was able to tell us of the enemy's plans—unfortunately when it was too late to make that knowledge useful to us. Whenever there was a crisis we found Mr. Marsten eloquent on the side of giving in—all through affection for the men, of course. I am making no accusations; I am merely stating facts that Mr. Marsten himself admits, and if I am mistaken in anything I say, the young man is here to set me right. These facts had a certain influence with the committee, causing a distrust to arise in their minds—a feeling that Mr. Marsten, for some reason, was more anxious to please Sartwell than to see his fellow-workers win. Now, what happens? The strike ends, and we are surprised to see that the only man dismissed is Mr. Marsten. The next move is that the young man is made secretary of the Union by a practically unanimous vote. I say that vote was to the credit of the men, and, had I been present, I would have voted for Mr. Marsten. But let us look into the matter a little closer. Who agitated the election of our new secretary? I now come to a difficult point, and I want to make myself perfectly clear, and to speak with absolute justice. 'Say no ill of the dead' is a noble motto, and I have nothing but good to say of that hero, Braunt. Greater praise hath no man than this, he gave his life to save others."

There was tremendous cheering at this, and it was some time before Gibbons could proceed. Marsten sat silent in his chair, with the helpless feeling of a criminal in the dock. He felt the chain of circumstance tightening around him.

"Braunt was a hero in death and a hero in life. He was frankly and honestly against us from the first, and he fought us with an uprightness that I wish Sartwell had emulated. He took no strike pay, and used language against us which I hope has been forgotten, and which I know has been forgiven. There was nothing underhand in his opposition, and he broke the back of the strike by hitting from the shoulder when we had reached the desperation of utter exhaustion. But, while giving full credit to the splendid character of Braunt, we must not forget that he was throughout our staunch opponent, and that it was he who elected Mr. Marsten secretary of this Union.

"Now, gentlemen, I am a plain man, who does not think himself any better than the average. I do not look for angels with wings among my fellow-workers; I look for plain, every-day motives when trying to trace cause from effect. It is not natural for a man to beg for a reduction of his screw unless that man is an angel, or unless there is some hidden cause for his doing so. We strike to increase our wages, and I have never heard of a deputation of workingmen waiting on an employer to ask for a reduction. Mr. Marsten does what we know to be most unusual, and what we believe to be unnatural. What is his motive? Who is going to make up the deficiency in his salary? These are questions for you to answer. I have tried to state nothing but facts, and no statement I have made has been contradicted. The result is a chain of circumstantial evidence that would convict a man in any court in the land. Men have been hanged on evidence less complete."

Gibbons sat down amidst universal applause. Marsten rose to his feet slowly. He knew the meeting was solidly against him, and that he had to bring it around in his favour or lose the race before it began. There flashed through his mind the sentence, "It is not the capitalist who will defeat you, but the men you are fighting for." He remembered Braunt's utter lack of faith in the rope of sand. Then he spoke:

"I have listened attentively to what has been said, and I have listened without interruption because I have sat spellbound by the cleverness of the speech, admiring its force and logic, and deeply regretting the fact that I have not the eloquence and gifts of the speaker who has just sat down. Two things are at this moment uppermost in my mind. First, that if some stranger were in my place, and I were sitting among you, I should believe him guilty.

Second, there has come over me a feeling of sympathy with any man who has been condemned on circumstantial evidence. I know now, as I never did before, that many a poor wretch has gone to an undeserved death. Gibbons, you have throughout referred to me as Mr. Marsten. I disclaim the 'Mr.' as doubtless you do, so I shall call you plain Gibbons. Gibbons, you have defeated me. The meeting I have called together is against me and for you."

There were cries of dissent at this.

"Oh yes, it is. I will prove it in a minute by putting it to vote, if you like."

"Hold on!" cried Gibbons; "that is not fair. I protest against a vote being taken after such a declaration."

"I am going to take no unfair advantage, and only spoke of a vote because my assertion seemed to be doubted. Now, Gibbons, you asked me several questions; I claim the right to put a few to you, and I charge you to answer as honestly as if you were on oath. Do you actually believe that I am in the pay of Sartwell?"

"I didn't say so."

"Do you believe I am?"

"Yes, I do."

"What object could Sartwell have in buying me?"

"Oh, that's too self-evident. If he controls you he controls the action of the Union."

"Please explain how. No action can be taken without a majority vote."

"That's it exactly. That's why you are begging for our confidence and support, so that when the time comes you can deliver to Sartwell what he pays for."

"I see. Did Sartwell ever offer to buy you?"

"He never did. He knew better."

"Did you ever offer to sell yourself to Sartwell?"

"What's that? What do you mean?"

"I'll put the question in another way. Did you write a private letter to Sartwell a few days before the strike ended?"

Gibbons rose to his feet in such evident confusion that several of the crowd laughed, and all were in a state of tense excitement. This was the kind of thing they liked. Marsten was carrying the war into Africa.

"What are you accusing me of?" cried Gibbons.

"Like yourself, I am making no accusations. Did you send such a letter or not?"

"As leader of the strike I may——"

"No, no. Answer, yes or no."

"Let me explain. I say——"

"First answer the question, Gibbons."

"I refuse to be coerced in this manner. I am willing to answer anything, but I must be allowed to answer in my own way."

"No man is bound to incriminate himself, Gibbons, as you remarked a while ago. Since we cannot get an answer to that question, I will ask another. Will you give me permission to read your Sartwell letter to this meeting?"

Gibbons was dumbfounded, and forgot entirely, in his agitation, that the letter had been returned to him, remembering only that its contents were not for the general public. His attitude was that of conscious guilt.

"Read it, read it!" cried the crowd, and the shouts seemed to rouse Gibbons to a sense of the situation.

"I protest against the reading of a private letter in public," he stammered.

"And quite right, too," said Marsten. "I protested against the public discussion of a private quarrel; and the protest was held against me. Now

I have no desire to push my opponent to the wall, and I will say at once that the letter in question may be as innocent as 'Mary had a little lamb.' I never read it and never saw it. I heard of it through a chance remark, but I know nothing of its contents. You see now how easy it is to ask a question a man may hesitate to answer, and you see of how little value circumstantial evidence is. Now, Gibbons, we are quits, and I am willing to let bygones be bygones if you are. I give you my word—and that is all I have to offer, for I'm the poorest among you—that I am not in the pay of any one on earth except yourselves. I swear to you that I have only one object in view, and that is the bettering of our condition. All I ask is fair play. Perhaps I can't do what I think I can, but I want to try. If I fail, then let the next man come on and have his try, and he will have no more earnest supporter than I will be. With dissension in our ranks, nothing can be done; so I want the backing of every man in the Union, and more especially of the man who thinks I have been a traitor,—which I declare to him and to you I was not. Now, Gibbons, this has been an open question-and-answer meeting. There has been a free-for-all give and take here tonight. I have a last question to ask you: are you going to be my friend or my enemy?"

There were cries of "Toe the mark, Gibbons!"

"Time!"

"Speak up, my boy!"

"Show your hand, Gibbons!"

Gibbons, who had now recovered his equanimity, rose to his feet, and said: "I move, gentlemen, that Marsten be confirmed in his secretaryship of the Union, and I hope the vote will be unanimous. We will give him what he asks—a fair chance—and as long as he deals squarely with us, we will deal squarely with him. As far as my friendship or enmity is concerned, I may say that I'm a friend to any one who is loyal to the cause, and an enemy to those who are against it. I think that is all that can be asked of me or any other man present."

The motion was seconded and carried unanimously, and the object for which the meeting was convened was lost sight of entirely.

Marsten went on with his work of organization, and met with much encouragement from the societies with which he entered into correspondence. Whatever opposition there was to him in his own Union, it at least did not show itself openly; but Marsten did not make the mistake of thinking Gibbons was his friend.

## CHAPTER XXX.

Ingenious persons have shown that a five-pound note rightly guided will liquidate an almost unlimited amount of liability. Let it be granted, says the mathematician, that A owes B; B owes C; C owes D, and D owes A,—one hundred shillings in each case. A gives a five-pound note to B, who gives it to C, who gives it to D, who gives it to A. The peregrinations of the same note wipes out twenty pounds of debt, and A has the original bit of paper he started with.

In like manner a clever person can bestow a great favour upon another and at the same time accommodate several others, leaving all under obligations to him; while a blunderer, instead of making everybody happy, would have accomplished nothing beyond creating enemies for himself.

The shrewd Haldiman, bringing some promised work to the editor of "Our National Art," casually mentioned that Barnard Hope had been invited to send some of his paintings to Paris.

"What! Do you mean the Chelsea giant? Why, that ass doesn't understand the rudiments of drawing, and as for colour—great heavens! there isn't a pavement chalk artist who is not his superior."

Haldiman looked puzzled; then he said with some hesitation:

"I confess I used to think that; but of course we studied together in Paris, and we students always underestimate each other. There is something in Barney's paintings that I don't pretend to understand."

"Understand! Bosh! There's nothing in them but the vilest and most ignorant smearing ever put upon canvas."

"Then how do you account for the fact that some of the most advanced critics are beginning to consider Barney seriously, as a new factor in the art world?"

"I hadn't heard of it. Who, for instance?"

"Well, I'm told that Viellieme simply raves over his work—says it's a distinctive new note, and that Barney is the only original genius England has ever produced."

"You amaze me! It can't be true! Whatever any one may say of Viellieme's morale nature, no one can deny that he knows a picture when he sees it."

"Of course; I'm simply giving what I have heard. As I say, I don't admire Barney's work myself. However, I'm just off for Paris, and I'll find out for you, on the quiet, just what Viellieme thinks. If Barney is a coming man you'd want to know it, and at least give the first inkling of the new craze, if there is to be one, wouldn't you?"

"Certainly. But I can't believe it!"

"I'm not sure that I ought to mention it, but I know that a number of Barney's paintings are going over to France, and I believe especially for Viellieme's inspection."

"I say, Haldiman, just find out for me all you can, will you? It seems incredible! Still, art is full of surprises, and I should like to know. If it is true, try to induce Viellieme to write an article on the new era in art for me."

"Would you print an article on Barney, if I get Viellieme to write it? I thought you didn't care for Barney's work."

"I don't, but I'll gladly print anything Viellieme will sign. Of course, among the different schools I endeavour to maintain absolute impartiality. I believe in letting every side be heard."

"Well, I'll do my best."

"Thanks, Haldiman. I'll be very much obliged to you, and any expense you——"

"Oh, don't mention it. I'm going to Paris anyhow, so there won't be any extra expense."

The article, marvellously illustrated, appeared in due course. The result quite justified Barney's expectations and expenditure, and the Barnard Hope boom raged up and down the land. He was interviewed, and photographed, and paragraphed. For a time it was hardly possible to pick up a sixpenny illustrated weekly without seeing the latest photograph of Barney in it, for the young man developed a genius for posing before a camera that would have done credit to our greatest actor. The picture representing him standing with arms folded across his breast, a stern commanding expression upon his countenance, was the one perhaps most sought after by young ladies, although the one in which he looked like Rembrandt was also very popular. Exhibitors begged for his paintings, nabobs bought them, and nobody understood them, which fact made the boom a permanency. Real painters looked at each other in amazement, and asked, "What is this world coming to?"—a question often propounded and never adequately answered.

His great fame did not change Barney a particle; he was the same hail-fellow he had always been, and an invitation to his "At Home" became a distinction. America was especially lavish in its purchases of his work, and he was offered fabulous sums to go there and lecture. The adulation he received would have turned the head of almost any man; but it had little effect on him, because he never had the slightest misgiving that his great reputation was entirely undeserved, and he had looked upon himself as the foremost man of the age long before the world had recognized the fact. He received letters from all parts of the country, whose writers, in most gushing phrase, said they had been privileged to look upon his work at such and such an exhibition, and they hoped to live better and nobler lives in consequence. Some of these epistles affected Barney almost to tears, and he read them to his friends, humbly thankful that the gift of bestowing such pleasure, and wielding such an influence for good upon his fellow-creatures, had been granted him.

Imitators arose, of course, but they did little to tarnish his reputation; for, as Haldiman had said, there was only one Barney, and it is never given to two men in any one generation to paint as badly as Barney did. Art-critics scored the imitators mercilessly, and were in the habit of saying that if Barnard Hope had not lived such and such a picture would not have been painted,—which statement was probably quite true.

Barney's people were naturally very proud of him. His father had always admired him with the intense admiration which a very little man has for a very big relative; his mother referred to him as, "My son, Barnard Hope, the celebrated painter."

To all appearances Barney was a man greatly to be envied, but, alas! how little does the public know the inner life of even its greatest favourite! All may be fair to outward view, while within sits brooding care. Barney had a secret trouble which he confided to no one, and it caused him serious mental dissatisfaction. He had told Edna Sartwell that she had blighted his life, and he fully believed this at the time he made the gloomy statement. He sombrely pictured himself in the future as a disappointed man—successful, perhaps, but cynically bitter with existence, living the life of a recluse, and cherishing his broken heart. As the victim of a hopeless passion, he pitied himself, and yet took a melancholy pleasure in ruminating over the wreck of what might have been a joyful career. To his dismay he found it impossible to live up to his ideal. The forced laugh; the pessimistic smile; the dark mantle of a great reserve which he hoped to fold around himself, did not come natural to him, and he was continually backsliding into being his own hilarious boisterous self, and having a good time, when he should have been moping alone over an aching void. Above all things he expected himself to forswear ladies' society, and never again indulge in the light, flippant, and complimentary talk in which he had been an acknowledged master; but it grieved him to discover that he still took a keen delight in their presence, while they, poor dears! unblushingly adored Barney as they had always done. His arrival in any room immediately brightened the occasion, and he was by all odds the most popular young man in his set. His failure in the tragic rôle he had marked out for himself at first worried Barney, and led him to suspect that he was not so deep as he had imagined; but this disquieting thought gave way under his ultimate realization that the taciturn recluse of fiction and the drama was merely a melancholy humbug who did not exist in real life. This comforting discovery did much to place Barney once more on good terms with himself, and by-and-by he abandoned the attempt to pose as a stricken victim of woman's inappreciation, and was once more the genial host and the welcome guest.

As time went on, and his fame continued to spread, he fell more and more under the gentle influence of Lady Mary Fanshaw, who was a modest, refined, and altogether charming girl. She had an unbounded admiration for Barney's strength and manliness; and his many deeds of kindness and lavish generosity, which he himself was at no particular pains to conceal, won her deep regard. She did not pretend to understand his paintings, but was quite willing to believe what appeared to be the universal estimate, that they were works of the very highest genius.

In the company of Lady Mary, Barney's heroic determination to lead a monastic life became fainter and fainter. When Barney saw whither he was drifting, he held a serious consultation with himself. Six months had elapsed since the episode at Eastbourne, and this half year had been the most fateful in his whole existence. Even though there was a lingering disappointment over the now self-admitted fact that his life had not been wrecked, yet he felt he owed it to his dignity not to propose to Lady Mary until a year at least had intervened between the two matrimonial excursions. To propose sooner would be to admit that he did not know his own mind—and he particularly prided himself on his strength of mind. An action that is indecent haste in six months may be the epitome of calm deliberation in twelve. Instances are on record where a man's most cherished political convictions have changed completely within a year, and a grateful country has testified its appreciation of the honesty of the transformation by bestowing a peerage or a knighthood upon the man. Why, then, should not a great painter be deeply in love with two charming girls, if a reasonable interval separated the declarations of affection? Barney said to himself that it was undoubtedly wrong to be in love with two or more at the same time, and he had to admit that in former days he had come dangerously near that complicated condition; but he was young at the time, and youth is an excuse which covers a multitude of errors. "This day six months," said Barney, definitely, "I shall ask Lady Mary to be my wife." Having thus reached finality in his meditations, he felt that sense of satisfaction which a man always experiences when a perplexing problem is authoritatively settled one way or another. Nothing is so demoralizing as indecision. Hitherto he had been almost afraid to meet Lady Mary, much as he delighted in her companionship; but now there was no reason why he should hold aloof from her. Therefore, having written down the date on which the momentous proposal was to take place, he arose with a joyful exuberance of spirits, and resolved to celebrate his decision by driving down to the pretty Surrey village near which Lady Mary's father lived. The tandem was a thing of the past.

He found that the sight of it brought up painful recollections of Eastbourne; so he sold it, and acquired a most stylish four-wheeled vehicle which he called his "growler," drawn by two spirited black horses. He spoke to his friends apologetically about his growler, and said it gave no particular scope for a man's driving powers, but would serve until the coach which he had ordered from the most noted builders in London was finished. A four-in-hand, he held, was the only thing a man could drive with credit to himself and satisfaction to all beholders. So with the black span dancing before him, held by a firm hand, he rattled across Chelsea bridge and made for the interior of Surrey.

## CHAPTER XXXI.

It is a pleasant thing on a beautiful day to drive through Surrey lanes, with a fine pair of horses in front and a liveried menial with folded arms on the seat behind. Barney, who knew the country well, chose the by-roads rather than the main thoroughfares; for he had a keen love of nature and an appreciation of landscape, as became a man who had placed on canvas so many amazing reproductions of natural scenery.

As he neared his destination he turned into the particular lane which he knew to be Lady Mary's favourite walk, and he kept a sharp look-out ahead, hoping to descry the girl in the distance. He also looked at his watch, and slowed the horses when he saw he had arrived at the head of the lane somewhat in advance of the time he had set for himself. Barney was, above all things, a practical man, and he knew that, outside the drama, coincidences rarely happened unless they were touched up a bit; so before leaving Chelsea he took the precaution to telegraph Lady Mary, telling her that at a certain hour he would be at the head of the lane, and that if he met there any one who lived in the neighbourhood who would extend to him a cordial invitation to visit a certain country house, he would accept with all the heartfelt gratitude of a homeless man perambulating the country with two horses and a wagon. It was one of Barney's habits rarely to write a letter, and to depend almost entirely on the telegraph as a means of communication with his fellows. He delighted in sending a friend a ten-page telegram on some perfectly trivial subject, and to the numerous people all over the country who now wrote to him asking for his autograph, he invariably sent it in a long telegram, explaining in the message that, as he never wrote letters, any signature of his at the end of an epistle was sure to be a forgery, and no autographs were genuine unless they came by wire. Barney's electrical autographs now bring good prices at auction sales.

As he entered the lane, then, he looked ahead for the fulfilment of the coincidence he had arranged; and was presently rewarded by seeing the fine figure of the girl coming towards him, an ebony stick in her hand, and three big dogs following her. Barney threw the reins to his man, told him to drive on, and sprang down.

The girl's cheeks were as rosy as the dawn, either with the exercise in the pure air or the pleasure of meeting him.

After greeting her, he cried:

"You got my telegram, then?"

"Yes. Have you any money left after sending it?"

"Oh, I'm in funds to-day. I sold a picture for a thousand pounds yesterday to a Chicago man. They know how to buy, those Western fellows! He took one of the burnt-umber night scenes, made me sign my name on it in scarlet with letters three inches long, and then told me with a chuckle, after it was done, that he would have given a couple of hundred extra for the signature if I had held out. Thus are we poor artists imposed upon! Still, the scarlet lettering completely killed the half-tones in the painting, and ruined it, in my opinion; but he said it was the signature he wanted, so we are both satisfied. He was a perfectly frank heathen: said he could buy better paintings in Chicago for five dollars each, with a discount off if he took a quantity, but that people over there wouldn't have the work of the native artists at any price. He proudly claimed to know nothing about art himself—tinned goods was his line. I said I supposed that was all right as long as the goods brought in the tin, and he replied that that was what he was after."

"Well, I'm sure I congratulate you."

"Me? Now, Lady Mary, I call that hard lines. I thought you were a friend of mine—I did, indeed."

"I am. May I not congratulate you on selling a picture?"

"No, your ladyship; no, m'um! But you might congratulate the Chicago man. I feel that he did me out of two hundred. Oh, he's got a bargain, and he knows it! I tell you what it is, my pictures are getting so expensive that I am beginning to realize it is reckless extravagance for me to have so many of them hanging in my studio. It looks like ostentation, and I hate that. That's why I took the thousand, merely to get rid of it."

"Did it take you long to paint?"

"Yes, a good while. Of course I can't tell just how long, for one does not do a masterpiece like that right off the reel, don't you know. I suppose I must have spent as much as six hours on it, off and on. You see you have to wait until the groundwork dries before you can go on with the rest. I first, with a big brush, covered the whole of the canvas with burnt-umber, and then let it dry. That's night, as it would appear if there were no lights anywhere. Then you put in your high lights—little dabs of white paint. That seems easy, but I tell you it requires genius. Then, if there is water, even though unseen to the general eye, you put in little wabbly lines of grey paint under the dots of high light, and there you are, don't you know. It all seems simple enough to talk about, and plenty of fellows are trying it, now I have shown them the way; but somehow they don't hit it off, don't you know. But sink the shop in a Surrey lane; I hate talking shop, anyhow! Now, am I going to get my invitation, or am I not?"

"Of course you are. My father is most anxious to meet you."

"That's very nice of him. But, I say, Lady Mary——"

The young man stopped suddenly, and the girl looked up at him. She read in his eyes such honest, undisguised admiration of herself, that she dropped her own and blushed still more rosily.

"What is it?" she asked. "Have you forgotten something?"

"No," he said eagerly, taking the unresisting fingers of her two hands in his, as they stood there. "No, I have just remembered. I ought to have something to say to your father, don't you know. We can't talk about painting, and——well, Mary, we should have some topic of vital interest to us both to discuss, shouldn't we?"

The girl laughed a little, but did not reply. The three dogs stood some distance off, regarding the pair with suspicion; and a low growl from one of them indicated that the situation was unusual and must not be carried too far.

"What shall I say to him, Mary?" cried the young man, with a tender thrill in his deep voice. "May I tell him I care more for his daughter than for any one else in the world? May I?"

The girl made no attempt to withdraw her hands, nor did she do more than give him one swift, brief glance.

"If it is true," she murmured, "I see no reason why you should not tell him so."

"True!" cried Barney, fervently. "There's nothing on earth so true, Mary, my darling, as that I love you! And do you—do you care in the least for a big blundering fellow like me?"

"Always, always!" said Lady Mary. "Ever since I first met you. And long before the world recognized your genius, Barney, I did."

The jubilant young man, suddenly abandoning the hands that were thus promised him, clasped the girl to him and kissed her. It is a remarkable thing that a man often attains celebrity for doing something that hundreds of others do better, while the world remains ignorant of performances that are really entitled to fame. As Barney threw one arm around Lady Mary's waist, he saw, out of the corner of his eye, the big dog spring at his throat. Yet the young man kissed the girl as tenderly and as gently as if nothing particular were happening on the other side of him; and Lady Mary, closing her eyes for the moment, rested her head against his breast and breathed a deep sigh of contentment. She was awakened from her momentary dream by savage, mouthing growls, and, remembering the dogs, jumped back in alarm. With rigid muscles Barney held at arm's length, his strong hand grasping the collar, a brute only slightly smaller than a pony, whose angry fangs were tearing at his coat-sleeve. The other two dogs looked on, snarling, but apparently waiting for their mistress to give the word of attack. The girl shrieked at the sight.

"Down, Nero, down!" she cried. "How dare you, sir!"

"Oh, it's all right," said Barney, nonchalantly. "Don't scold him. 'Tis his nature to, don't you know. He'll find out two things in about a minute: first, and most important, that I'm going to be one of the family; and second, that he's met his match. I say, Mary, this wouldn't be a bad scene for the Aquarium, don't you know,—Sampson defying the lightning, or was it Ajax? I never can remember those classical allusions."

"Down, sir!" commanded the girl. "Come here and apologize!"

Barney relaxed his grasp on the collar, and the huge dog cringed up to Lady Mary with a most crestfallen air. It was evident that, although he deferred to his mistress's authority, he was still unshaken in his opinion that such goings on as he had just beheld were entirely out of order; and although he humbly licked the girl's hand, he cast side looks at Barney that were anything but friendly, yet the truculent glance was mitigated by that respect for proven strength which one strong animal feels when he meets a stronger. The girl, crouching, patted his shaggy coat, and, alternately scolding and petting him, explained the situation as well as she could, beseeching Nero to treat Barney as a brother.

When she stood up again—blessed are the peacemakers!—Barney said:

"Let's see if he understands?"

"Now, Barney," cried the girl, "you must behave yourself! You can't tell who might come into view any moment."

"We'll risk the chance comer—purely for the dog's benefit, you know, Mary."

The big dog made no move this time; but his angry eye lighted up with a dangerous lurid gleam, and the corners of his heavy lips quivered, showing the teeth.

"Oh, it's a case of pure jealousy," said Barney. "I can see that. Nero and I never can be friends." They walked together slowly along the lane, the dogs in front. Nero seemed exceedingly dejected, and strode with offended dignity, taking little notice of the other two dogs; who, with a levity that met his sullen disapproval, indicated now and then by deep, low growls of rebuke, futilely chased imaginary rabbits by the hedge-rows, tumbling over each other in their frivolous, headlong career.

"Do you know, Mary, I think we should join hands and swing our arms as we walk along. I want to shout and whoop like a red Indian—and yet calm reflection tells me it isn't good form. I believe I'm hopelessly plebeian, and yearn for a Whitechapel expression of my happiness. If I weren't afraid of the dog—that is, morally afraid, for I can throttle him physically—I'd pull the pin out of that most fetching hat of yours, and put the hat on my own head, giving you mine. Actually, I'd like to dance, don't you know!"

The girl laughed.

"I shouldn't mind a dance myself," she said.

"Oh, then it's all right! I was beginning to fear I had a costermonger for my ancestor; but, if you're not shocked, I may, for all I know, be descended from the Conqueror."

"Well, if you want to shout, do it now; for I want you to be very circumspect and proper when we walk up the avenue."

Barney did not shout, but he placed his arm around her, and——and felt it was most delightful to be thus taken in charge and told how to behave.

## CHAPTER XXXII.

It was Barney's habit, now that money flowed in upon him, to deal liberally with his cabmen. He would hand to the man two or three sovereigns, or even a five-pound note if there happened to be one loose in his waistcoat pocket, and say to him:

"Now I may need you only twenty minutes, or I may need you all the afternoon; but I want you to feel happy while you're driving me, don't you know, so here's all I'm going to give you, and I wish to have no dispute about fares at the end of the journey." There never was any dispute, and Barney was extremely popular with the driving fraternity.

When the date of the wedding was fixed, Barney, on his return to London, took a cab at ten pounds in honour of the forthcoming event. He said to himself that he couldn't give less and retain his self-respect, as he intended using the cab in completing the necessary arrangements for the ceremony. He drove first to the residence of the clergyman who was in charge of St. Martyrs-in-the-East; for he had determined that the marriage should take place in this church, because it was the nearest sacred building to his father's works and was surrounded by a population largely in the employ of the firm, directly or indirectly. Besides this, Barney took a particular delight in the thought that all the newspapers would be compelled to send representatives to this unfashionable locality; for the wedding would be a notable one, and he was now so famous that should he marry or die in the most unknown spot in the British Isles, his doing so would forever bestow distinction on the place.

The genial old clergyman was undeniably impressed by the fact that so celebrated a man chose St. Martyrs for such an important ceremony.

"Of course," said Barney, airily, "I shall have a bishop or two to assist you, and perhaps a few lesser dignitaries. If you will just give me the names of any you prefer, I shall put myself into communication with them."

"You mean that I shall assist the bishop," protested the reverend gentleman, mildly. "His Lordship, as of course you know, takes precedence."

"Oh, well, you'll arrange all that among yourselves. I don't understand these matters, you know: I was never married before, and I leave every detail in the hands of those experienced. What I wish is to have everything well done, regardless of expense. If you will allow me I would like to send you a cheque for a thousand pounds, to be distributed among the poor, don't you know, and that sort of thing, in honour of the occasion. I suppose it can be managed."

"We shall be very grateful indeed for it. A plethora of money has never been one of the obstacles with which we have had to contend in this parish."

"Then that's all right. Now, have you seen your organist lately? What's his name? It has slipped my memory for the moment."

"Langly. I am sorry to say he has not been at all well lately. Not ill, exactly, for he has been able to attend to his duties, but still far from well. I think he needs some one to look after him. He is an absent-minded man—a dreamer—and I fear he neglects himself."

"I have tried to help him," said Barney; "but he shrinks from assistance of any kind as if it were infectious. He never will call on me, and I have had so many demands on my time lately that I have not looked him up, as I intended to do. Could you give me his address? I had it once, but I've mislaid it."

"He lives in wretched quarters—No. 3 Rose Garden Court, off Light Street. I don't think he would like you to call upon him. It would be better to write. It is very difficult to do anything for him, as you say, except indirectly. When I visited him, on hearing he was not well, I could see that my presence discomposed him."

"I wanted to speak with you about helping him indirectly. You all appreciate his abilities, of course."

"Oh, yes."

"And yet, as you say, you are not a rich parish. Now here is a cheque for a hundred pounds. I would make it more, but that would arouse his suspicions, very likely. Would you take this, and increase his salary by that much yearly?—I will send a similar cheque once a year—and put it to him that the increase is because of the general admiration there is felt for—well, you know what I mean? So that he will be encouraged, don't you know."

"It is very generous of you, Mr. Hope, and I shall see that your wishes are carried out."

When the interview with the kindly vicar was finished, Barney jumped into his hansom and drove to Light Street. It was impossible to take the cab into Rose Garden Court; so Barney, securing as a guide one of the numerous ragged urchins who thronged the place, made his way up the rickety stairs and knocked at Langly's door. A faint voice from within told him to enter, and on going in Barney saw the organist sitting on the bed. Langly had evidently been lying down, and now, with noticeable difficulty, sat up to greet his unexpected visitor. Thin as he had been when Barney saw him last, he was still thinner now, and a ghastly pallour overspread his face.

"I say, old man!" cried Barney, stopping short. "You're not looking first-rate, don't you know. Have you been ill?"

"I've not been well, but I'm better now, thank you," replied Langly, a shadow that would have been a flush in a healthy man coming over his cheeks.

Clearly he did not like the intrusion; and Barney, remembering the vicar's words, saw that.

"Now, Langly," he said, "you mustn't mind my coming in this unceremonious way, because I'm here to beg a great favour of you. I'm the most dependent man on my friends that there is in all London—I am, for a fact. It seems to me I spend all my time getting other fellows to do things for me, and they do them too, by Jove! in the most kindly way. This is a very accommodating, indulgent world, don't you know. Now you just lie down again—I see I've disturbed you—I'm always disturbing somebody—and let me talk to you like a favourite uncle. I'm going to be married, Langly!—what do you think of that? And I'll bet you a sixpence you can't tell where."

Langly, who still sat on the edge of his bed, ignoring Barney's command, smiled wanly and shook his head.

"I knew you couldn't. Well, the ceremony is to be performed with great éclat, as the papers say, at St. Martyrs-in-the-East. First time old St. Marts has ever seen a fashionable wedding, I venture to say. I have just been to see the vicar, arranging all the details. What a nice old man he is!—and I say, Langly, you ought to have heard him praise you and your music! It's very pleasing to be appreciated,—I like it myself."

Langly, in spite of his pallour, actually blushed at this, but said nothing.

"Now, that brings us to the music on the wedding-day—and that's why I'm here. You will play the organ, of course."

"I shall do my best," murmured Langly.

"There is nothing better than that. But here is what I want, and I know it's a great favour I'm asking. I want you to compose a wedding march for us. I'll have it published afterwards, and I know, when you see the bride, you won't need any begging from me to get you to dedicate it to her."

"I'm afraid——" began the organist.

"Oh, no, you're not," interrupted Barney. "You are such a modest fellow, Langly, I knew you'd be full of excuses; but I'm not going to let you off. I've set my heart on having a special wedding march. Any pair of fools can be married to Mendelssohn, don't you know; but we want something all our own. It isn't as if a fellow were married every day, you know."

"I was going to say that I feel hardly equal——I don't think I could do justice——but there is a march I composed about a year ago—it has never been played or heard by any one but myself. If you liked it——"

"Of course I'll like it. That will be the very thing."

"I would compose one for you, but I am sure I could do nothing so good as that, and I want to give you my best."

"I'm sure you do. So that's all settled. Now, Langly, here comes the uncle talk. I told you I was going to talk to you like an uncle, you know. You must get out of this hole, and you must get out now. It's enough to kill the strongest man to stay in this place. I've got a hansom waiting in the street; so come with me and we will look up a decent pair of rooms with a motherly old woman to look after you."

Langly was plainly embarrassed. At last he stammered:

"I can't afford a better place than this. I know it may not seem very comfortable to you, but it's all I really need."

"Afford it! Of course you can afford a better place! Oh, I had forgotten. They haven't told you, then?"

"Told me what?"

"Well, I don't know that I should mention it. The fact is (it all came out quite incidentally when I was talking to the vicar—I told you he was saying nice things about you! ), I imagine they're preparing a little surprise for you; so never say I spoke of it, but I don't like surprises myself. I always tell the boys that if they've any surprises for me, to let me know in advance, so that I may prepare the proper expression. What I don't like about a surprise is to have it sprung on me without being told of it beforehand. Well, as I said, I shouldn't mention this; but the churchwardens and the vicar and a number of the parishioners have resolved to increase your salary by one hundred pounds a year. I was very glad to hear it, and I said so. 'To show our appreciation of his music,' were the exact words of the vicar. Splendid old chap, the vicar!—I like him."

Barney walked up and down the room as he talked, never glancing at his listener. Langly's eyes filled with tears: he tried to speak, but he could not. Then he lay down on the bed and buried his face in the pillow. His visitor chattered on, pacing to and fro, taking no notice of the other's emotion, until Langly, recovering himself, said, gratefully:

"It is very, very good of them. They have always been exceedingly kind to me."

"Oh, it's merely a matter of business. They don't want some other church to lure you away. Trust a churchwarden! He's always up to snuff. Now, Langly, you must come with me. If you resist, I'll pick you up in my arms and carry you down to my hansom as if you were a baby. Brace up, old man, and come along!"

Faintly protesting, but in his weakness making no resistance, Langly staggered down to Light Street, leaning on Barney's arm. In about half an hour a comfortable domicile was found near the church, and a porter was sent back to Rose Garden Court to fetch the musician's' belongings.

The wedding ceremony was all that the best friends of the happy pair could wish. Never had old St. Martyrs seen such a brilliant assemblage. The splendid Wedding March was a triumph, filling the resonant church with its jubilant, entrancing harmonies, and it was played as no march had ever been played before.

Barney stole a moment or two, while friends were pressing around the bride, and drew Betson, the chief press man present, into a corner.

"Now, Betson," he said, "you heard that music."

"It was glorious!" replied the journalist.

"Of course it was, and composed specially for this occasion, remember. You may abuse me in the papers, if you like, Betson; if there's anything wrong—although I don't think there is—lay the blame on me; but one thing I beg of you, and please tell the other fellows this, won't you?—give a line or two of deserved praise to the organist and the music. Do, if you love me, Betson! The man's a genius!—I'm not the only one who says so, although I was the first to recognize the fact. You'll put in something nice about him, won't you? and give the others the tip to do the same."

"I'll go and see him; then I can do a special article on him."

"I wish you would; but remember he's very shy, and if he suspects your purpose you won't get anything out of him. He's a recluse. Talk to him about organs and music, and let him think you're merely a fellow-enthusiast."

"Never fear. I'll manage him."

For a week Langly had feared he would not be equal to the ordeal that faced him. He was anxious, for Barney's sake, to acquit himself well; but he was scarcely able to totter to the church and back to his rooms, although, when once seated before the banks of keys, renewed life seemed to animate his emaciated frame; but when the enthusiasm of playing passed away, he was left more deeply depressed than ever. Music was now a stimulant to him, and the longer the intoxication of sound lasted, the greater the reaction after.

His whole frame trembled when he saw how large an audience was to listen on the wedding-day, and he prayed that strength might be given him to perform his part flawlessly. When at last the supreme moment came, he looked with breathless fear at his shaking hands hovering over the keys; but when he touched them, he heard the sweet, pure, liquid, low notes come firm and sustained, like tones from a mellow flute, and his whole being thrilled when he became conscious of the instantaneous hush that fell on the vast assemblage, as though all had simultaneously ceased to breathe, fearing to miss a single golden thread of melody, or the enchanting mingling of them into the divinest, most subdued harmony, as if a choir of nightingales were singing far off, almost, but not quite, beyond hearing distance. When the music, swelling from its soft beginning, rose towards its climax, Langly knew he was master of the instrument as he had never been before. All fear left him, and a wild exultation took its place. It mattered nothing whether one or a thousand listened. As he gazed upward, with rapt ecstatic face, it seemed to him that the sounds took the form of an innumerable host of angels, flying about the beetling cliff of pipes that towered above him, and his own soul floated there also. Marvelling at this aerial vision, he yet played with his almost miraculous skill to the end; and as the last notes died away he saw the angels drop their wings one by one and fade into the empty air. He pushed in the stop that shut off the bellows motor, and for a moment his nerveless fingers touched the silent manual from which the breath of life had departed. A mist lowered before his eyes, his head sank slowly forward, and Death pillowed it gently on the soundless keys.

## CHAPTER XXXIII.

The building erected on the site of the wing destroyed by fire was larger than the one it replaced, and its plan was so well thought out that its convenience far excelled that of its companion factory, and increased the output of the firm by a much greater proportion than its greater size seemed to warrant.

"All we need now," said Sartwell, to little Mr. Hope, "is the other wing to burn down; then we could have a model establishment."

Mr. Hope looked up at Sartwell in alarm, as if he expected to see his manager apply the torch to the old building. He never quite fathomed Sartwell's somewhat grim style of humour.

The four houses that had been leased, to form a temporary annex to the works during the erection of the new wing, were kept on, and never in the long history of the firm was so much profitable business done, nor so large a dividend declared as during the months that followed the completion of the new building. The firm had good cause to be grateful to its manager. Both Monkton and Hope recognized that their constantly increasing prosperity was due to this resolute, self-reliant man, and they rewarded him as capitalists usually reward those who serve them well. Not only was his already large salary increased, without any demand on his part, but, when the business was formed into a private company, they allotted him a block of stock of the nominal value of a thousand pounds, the income from which, should the welfare of the company continue at its then level, would be sufficient to make Sartwell independent for life; and at the first meeting of the new board he was made managing director.

This meeting took place a little more than a year after the new wing had been opened, and Sartwell, addressing his fellow-directors, said:

"I am not good at returning thanks—by words at least; but, as you know, I shall try to make the stock you have given me a good investment for the new company. It might seem, under the circumstances, that I ought to be well content; yet human nature is hard to satisfy, and I am about to ask for further powers. I want an understanding that I am to have a free hand in case we should have another strike. I also want the power of increasing the wages of the men—not to exceed, say ten per cent—at any time, without the necessity of consulting the board."

"Why?" asked Monkton. "The board can be convened at any moment."

"As a matter of fact it cannot. By your articles of association there must be seven days' clear notice, and the object of the meeting must be stated when the call is made. Now, it may become necessary to act at once, and I want the power to do so."

"Surely there is no danger of another strike," said Mr. Hope, anxiously. "The men had such a severe lesson——"

"A lesson lasts the workingman just so long as his belly is empty, and rarely influences him after his first full meal. The Union is already working up to a demand for increased wages. Times are good, and they know it. We must face an increase of wages, and I want that increase to come voluntarily from the company, and not under compulsion. You may depend upon me to do nothing rash, but I want the power to announce such increase at any moment."

The power to act promptly was given him, and he was assured that, in the event of another strike, the whole strength of the company would be behind him; but he was besought by Mr. Hope to avoid trouble if it were possible to do so.

After the meeting Sartwell went down to Eastbourne, and, with his daughter, took a long walk on the breezy downs.

"Well, girlie," he said, after telling her of the firm's generosity, "you are an heiress now, on a small scale. I have made over that thousand pounds to you, and as it is really worth ten thousand, I think it is a good deal of money for a little girl like you to accumulate before she comes of age."

"But I'm not going to accept it, father!" cried Edna. "I'll make it all over to you again."

"Then we shall play battledore and shuttlecock with the stock. I generally have my own way, Edna, so you may as well give in gracefully to the inevitable. Besides, this comes as a sort of windfall; I didn't reckon on it, so you don't leave me a penny poorer than I was a month ago. I've laid by a bit of money in my time, and have at last got rid of a fear that has haunted me all my life—the fear of a poverty-stricken old age. That's why I draw such deep, satisfying breaths of this splendid air from the sea. Grey hair came, Edna, before the goal was in sight, but it's in sight now, my girl."

"I'm so glad, father," she said, drawing down his head and kissing him.

"Then you will take the windfall, Edna?"

"I will take it on one condition, father."

"And what is the one condition?"

"That if I ever do anything you disapprove of, you will let me give it back to you."

The girl was gazing far out at the line where the blue sky and the bluer sea met. Her father glanced at her sharply for a moment.

"Put into English, what does that mean, Edna?"

"You never can tell what a woman will do, you know."

"Granted, my dear. But you're not a woman; you're merely my little girl."

The little girl sighed.

"I feel very much grown up, and very old sometimes."

"Oh, we all do at eighteen. Wait till you're forty; then you'll know what real youth is. If you were a boy now, instead of being a girl, you would have serious doubts about the existence of the Deity, and the most gloomy ideas regarding mankind generally. Why should I disapprove of anything you do?"

"Oh, I don't know. Mother always predicts that our stubborn wills will cross some time, and——"

"Of course, of course. And false prophets shall arise. Don't let that trouble you, Edna. If our wills become seriously opposed, we will come here to the downs and talk it all over. I'll warrant we'll hit on a compromise."

"But suppose a compromise were not possible?"

"Dear me, Edna, what's on your mind? You are talking in generalities and thinking in particulars. What is it, my girl?"

Edna shook her head.

"I don't know why it is," she said at last, "but I feel afraid of the future. It seems so uncertain, and I should never like anything to come between us."

"Nonsense, Edna. What should come between us? All that is merely a little touch of the pessimism of youth, accentuated by the doleful fact that you are now a woman of independent means. Suppose our stubborn wills come into collision, as you fear, do you know what will happen?"

"What?"

"Well—it's an awful thing for a father to say to a daughter—but I'll give way. Think of that! What a humiliating confession for me to make!—a man who has refused to budge an inch before the united demands of some hundreds of men, backed by the pathetic entreaties of my own employers. If that isn't a victory for a small girl, what is?"

"Oh, no!" cried Edna, her eyes quickly filling. "I'll give way—I'll give way—even if it breaks my heart!" Her father stopped in his walk, and grasped her by the shoulders. The girl's head drooped, and she put one hand over her eyes.

"Ah, Edna, Edna, there's something at the back of all this; I won't ask you what it is, my pet, but some day you'll tell me, perhaps." He drew her to his breast, and, pushing aside her hat, caressed her fair hair lovingly. "If your mother were alive, dearest, we—well, there is little use of either grieving or wishing. We must make the best of things as they are. But don't bother about the stubborn wills, Edna; we'll cross that bridge when we come to it. You see, we are both competing to see who shall give way first, and there's nothing very stubborn about that. Now, my girl, I've disarranged that pretty hat, and a stranger who didn't know might think you had been crying. This will never do. Let us talk sensibly, for I imagine that before long I'll have all the fighting I need to keep me in form, without having a contest with my only daughter."

"What do you mean, father?"

"Oh, there's the usual ferment among the men. They are seething and foaming and vapouring, and I feel it in my bones that we will have another strike before long."

"Led by Mr. Marsten?"

"By him, of course. But I'll beat him! I'll crumple him up so that he will wonder why he ever started the fight. It's a pity to see him waste his energy and his brains in a hopeless struggle. He's clever and indefatigable, but a visionary and an enthusiast, and when he stops dreaming of impossibilities he will be a most valuable man."

"What impossibilities, father?" asked the girl, almost in a whisper, gazing at the ground.

"The impossibility of men hanging together on any one subject for more than a week. The impossibility of warding off treachery within the ranks. The impossibility of keeping down the jealousy which they always feel towards a man who is their evident superior in education and ability. However he got them, Marsten has the manner and instincts of a gentleman. The men are not going to stand that sort of thing, you know, and they will fail him when it comes to a pinch."

"If you think so well of him, why don't you offer him a good position in the works, and let him turn his ability towards helping you?"

"My dear girl, you have guessed one of the cards that is up my sleeve. I intend to make Marsten my assistant manager—but not now. He will be a valuable man when he awakes, but not while he is dreaming. He must be taught his lesson first, and only hard knocks can teach him that. The boy thinks he is going to be a leader of men, whereas he is merely serving his apprenticeship to become assistant manager of Monkton & Hope, Limited."

"But suppose he, succeeds? Suppose the next strike does not fail? The men held together more than a week last time."

"That was because they were led by a demagogue of like calibre to themselves. There is a large faction among them who hate Marsten, and Gibbons is their leader. I have fought Gibbons, beaten him, insulted him, trampled him under foot, yet, to-day, Gibbons loathes Marsten while he respects me, as such a man always respects one who has knocked him down. Now you will be surprised to hear that I have taken Gibbons into my employ, and am giving him better wages than he has ever received in his life before. More than that, when he recommends a man, I promote that man, and it is getting to be generally understood that Gibbons has much influence with the manager. This strengthens his hold on his faction."

"And what will be the result?"

"That we cannot tell, but it is always good politics to promote a split in the ranks of the enemy. I am playing a game, and I move the pawns about to suit my board. There is a sharp line now cleft between the two factions, and the gap will widen as soon as the trouble begins. Gibbons will likely go out with his crowd, if a strike is ordered; but they will be a source of weakness rather than of strength to Marsten, and the moment he makes a false move—which he is reasonably certain to make, not being infallible—there will be a defection."

"Have you a secret understanding with Gibbons, then?"

"Oh, bless you, no! One doesn't have a discussion on moves with a pawn. The pawn produces certain effects merely because it is placed in a given position, and not through any will of its own. Now Marsten is quite well aware of Gibbons's supposed influence with me, and will likely commit the error of thinking I have some arrangement with the ex-secretary. In the heat of a discussion he may give voice to his belief, and that will be an error, for no man is so righteously indignant at such a charge as the virtuous individual who would have sold himself if he could. It's going to be an interesting struggle, Edna."

"Poor Marsten!" sighed the girl.

"Yes, I am sorry for Marsten myself, but the lesson will do him a world of good. He is thoroughly unselfish, and Gibbons is as thoroughly selfish. The unselfish man almost invariably goes to the wall in this self-seeking world. Now let us get back, my girl. I think your old father has settled the whole universe to his satisfaction, so there's no more to be said."

## CHAPTER XXXIV.

The year's work had been most encouraging to Marsten. He had come to a cordial understanding with many of the Unions, not only at home, but in America and the colonies, and had formed an active alliance with several societies of workingmen in the United Kingdom. Times were good, business brisk, and comparatively few men were out of employment. All this inspired confidence in the success of a strike, for the demands of men are more certain to be listened to with attention when the market is rising than when it is falling. There would now be much difficulty in filling the shops with competent hands, as employment was more general throughout the country than had been the case for years before.

Marsten had been secretary of the Union for eighteen months before he made up his mind to begin the contest. He resolved to make a demand for a ten per cent increase of wages all round, and, if it were refused, to call out the men at once. The committee met in secret session and the demand was formulated. A gathering of the men was ordered for Saturday night, but the subject to be discussed was not stated. Marsten impressed on his committee the necessity for secrecy, although Gibbons, who was one of the members, said he failed to see the object of this, as their desire was to obtain the increase, and that desire could not be attained except openly. However, he added, Marsten was conducting the campaign, and it was but right he should be allowed to conduct it in his own way; therefore Gibbons merely stated his objection but did not insist upon it.

A deputation was appointed to seek an interview with the directors and make the demand on Saturday afternoon. After their conference they were to draw up a report to present to the meeting of the men.

On Friday Sartwell gathered his employees together and announced to them that, in view of the state of business, the company had voluntarily come to the conclusion that an increase of wages to the extent of ten per cent should be given, adding that he hoped the amicable relations between employers and employed at the works would long continue. This announcement was received with cheers, and the workers, who knew nothing of the meeting of the committee, dispersed well satisfied with the outlook.

It was too late to countermand the gathering ordered for Saturday night, and when it took place some inkling of what had happened was spread abroad; the general opinion being that in some way Marsten had been too clever by half, and had met with an unexpected check.

The young man, however, faced the meeting in good fettle, and congratulated them on the increase offered. The men were in jubilant humour, and they cheered everything that was said with the utmost impartiality. Marsten told them frankly why the meeting had been called, and he exulted in the fact that the recent unexpected turn of events had made any discussion unnecessary.

"I have heard it hinted," he continued, "that I have been out-generalled by Mr. Sartwell, but we can stand a lot of beating on these lines. Mr. Sartwell is evidently afraid of the Union now. If the mere rumour that we were about to make a demand induces so stiff-necked a man as the manager to capitulate before a gun is fired, it goes to show the tremendous influence we can wield by all standing firmly together."

It is said that the misplacing of a comma in an act of Parliament once cost the country a hundred thousand pounds. The one word "now," spoken quite unthinkingly by Marsten, made Gibbons grind his teeth in helpless rage. He saw Marsten triumphant and his own administration discredited. He determined to make that small word of three letters cost Marsten dear, if an opportunity of upsetting the confident young man offered itself. However, Gibbons said nothing, and the meeting dispersed with cheers.

Sartwell had no delusion regarding the advance he had made the men. He knew he had merely postponed the fight, but he wanted to be in a position to show the directors that he had done everything possible to avoid a conflict. Six months later Sartwell called the directors together.

"I desire to place before you," he said, "certain information I have received. There is reason to believe that a further demand of ten per cent will be made. If you are going to grant it, I would like to know; if we are going to make a stand, I would like to know. I will then arrange my plans accordingly."

"If we grant it," said Mr. Hope, "what do you think will be the result? Will it avert trouble, or will it be made the basis of fresh exactions? We cannot go on making concessions indefinitely."

"Giving the increase will probably postpone the trouble for another six months. I am certain that Marsten wants to force on a fight; he has been preparing for more than two years. What I want to impress on you is that the struggle, when it comes, is going to be a severe one, and if you enter upon it, you must do so with your eyes open, resolved to fight it to the very end. You may go on conceding until wages are doubled, and every fresh concession will merely make an ultimate fight the more inevitable."

"Then you think we had better make a stand now?"

"Yes; if, having made the stand, you refuse to capitulate on any terms."

"But if we find, when the strike has lasted a few weeks, that we cannot hold out, it would be folly to continue."

"Exactly. You know your own resources, and I know the resources of the men. You are therefore in as good a position to make up your minds now as two weeks hence, or a month, or a year. If we enter into a contest we must win, or I must resign."

"It is a most perplexing situation," sighed Mr. Hope.

"Oh, the situation is simple enough. You either give in or you don't. Which is it?"

"What are the chances of filling the works with new men, should it prove impossible to come to terms with our present employees?"

"They are not so good as they were. We could do it gradually, but it would be some time before we were in full force again."

"That would mean the refusal of new orders, and perhaps the cancelling of many now on hand."

"Undoubtedly. That is the cost of war. We must face it if we fight. We might be crippled for six months to come."

"That is very serious. Is no compromise possible? Could you not confer with Marsten and find out what he wants?"

"I know what he wants."

"And you think compromise impossible?"

"Frankly, I do."

"Have you the same objection to meeting Marsten that you had to meeting Gibbons?"

"As a matter of principle I object to discussing our business with any outsider. Marsten has never raised that point. When it was necessary to confer with me he always sent a deputation of our own men. He is a much more dangerous opponent than Gibbons was."

"Would you be willing, then, in the interests of peace, to arrange a conference with Marsten, talk the matter over, and come to an understanding, if that be possible?"

"Yes. I will send for him at once; but I don't think it will be of the slightest use, and it forms a bad precedent."

It was unanimously agreed that such an action on Sartwell's part would strengthen his hands, and that the fight, if it proved inevitable, could be gone into with greater spirit when all knew that everything possible had been done to avoid hostilities.

Sartwell invited Marsten to meet him at his office at seven o'clock in the evening. When the young man entered his first words were:

"You told me I was not to set foot in this office unless I was ordered to do so; I must apologize, therefore, for coming on a mere invitation."

"Ah, you haven't forgotten that yet!" said Sartwell, with a laugh. "But you do forget apparently that you were here on invitation before,—during the strike, you know."

"Yes, so I was."

"Now, Marsten, to begin with, have you any personal ill feeling against me for your summary dismissal?"

"Not the slightest. I should probably have acted as you did under the same circumstances."

"It is generous of you to say that, but I doubt if you would. However, not attempting to excuse myself at all, I may say that the event did not quite turn out as I expected. I hoped that you would call on me, and that we would—well, arrange an armistice, as it were."

"I thought you knew me better than that."

"I didn't, you see. But let the dead past bury its dead. Let us give our attention to the present and to the future, and I shall begin by asking if you have any suspicion that you are a fool?"

"A most diplomatic and soothing beginning, Mr. Sartwell. However, I suppose we are all more or less tinged with folly, so we won't quarrel about terms; but we seem to see the defects of others rather clearer than we see our own."

"That is undoubtedly true. It strikes me, then, that you are wasting your life, and I would like to convince you of that before it is too late."

"Yes?"

"Yes. I want an assistant manager. He must be a man of ability and a man I can trust. I am getting on in years, and will soon stand aside. My assistant, if he has the right stuff in him, will take my place, and the future will belong to him. I offer you the position."

"I cannot accept it."

"Why?"

"Because I have devoted my life to the men."

"But you will have an opportunity of doing more for the men in that position than you can possibly do for them in your present office, where they grudgingly pay you barely enough to keep body and soul together."

"I don't mean the men in these works, but all workingmen everywhere."

"Rather a large order, Marsten."

"I know it is, but I feel equal to filling it."

"I don't suppose you imagine I make you this offer because I am afraid of you as secretary of the Union."

"Oh, no. I am well aware that you want to avoid a fight, and I know you are afraid of nothing except that your directors will not back you through to a finish."

"Do you imagine that your own backers are as adamant?"

"No. My weakness is Gibbons and his gang. Yours is the board of directors. One neutralizes the other, so it will be an interesting fight."

"Make no mistake, my boy; a capitalist will back his man ten times as long as a worker will his."

"I haven't your intense admiration for the capitalist. Mr. Hope promised me, almost with tears in his eyes, to look after my future when he found I was working to settle the other strike which so terrorized him. I and my friends succeeded in breaking up the strike, yet you discharged me a week after, and I doubt if Mr. Hope ever gave a thought to his promise from that day to this. Your capitalist is notoriously timid and thoroughly selfish. The workingman has his faults, of course, and he is himself the greatest sufferer from them; but in generosity he is miles ahead of any capitalist that ever lived."

"Then you are determined to fight, Marsten?"

"Oh, no! Not if you give in."

"How often shall we have to give in?"

"Until such time as the compensation given to the workers is at least equal to the amount taken out by the so-called proprietors of the business."

"Ah, that is Utopian, which is simply another word for nonsense. Now, why not be perfectly frank and say you are resolved to fight us?"

"My position is this, Mr. Sartwell: I don't want to fight for a fight's sake, and I have no revengeful desire to humiliate you or to defeat the firm for the mere glory of victory; but I am convinced the men will not get the fair share of what they make until there is a fight and a decisive victory. A few years ago the very right to combine was Utopian and nonsensical in the mind of the capitalist, yet that right is one of the undisputed facts of to-day. The capitalist won't concede anything until he is forced to do so. Therefore there must be a struggle, and I am bound to choose my own time and my own battle-ground. We are ready to fight now, we are going to fight, and I believe we are going to win."

"Exactly. That is what I wanted to know. As to winning, we shall see. I quite agree with you that there is nothing so satisfactory in the long run as a square, stand-up fight, and let the best man win. The combatants have a mutual respect for each other afterwards. The trouble is that the contest is rarely free from the side issues that affect the final result. In this case you are not sure of your backers; neither am I. If I were the owner of this establishment I would bring on the war instantly, carry it through with the relentlessness of a Barbary pirate, win it, of course, and have the most contented men in England in my employ ever after. As it is, the trouble is not going to be decided by either your generalship or mine, but by the relative constancy of our backers. If the men round on you before my directors get a trifle more frightened than they are now, then you will be defeated. If the directors get panic-stricken first, then I shall go under. It will be a hollow victory either way, and will not be decided on the merits of the case at all. It is a toss-up, and, if we were sensible men, we two would settle it now by twirling a penny in the air; besides, if you do win, it will be a barren triumph, for you will lose everything you gain the moment there is a pinch in trade. The only reason you have a show of winning is because business is brisk, and the directors naturally wish to make hay while the sun shines. They don't wish to be crippled and have a fuss on while their trade rivals are reaping the benefit of their embarrassment. The moment trade becomes dull again, down will go the wages, and no power on earth can prevent the fall. It is all a question of supply and demand. On the other hand, I give you fair warning that, if I win, not another Union man will ever set foot in these works again. So if you really have the interests of the men at heart, Marsten, you will reflect a bit before you bring on the fight."

"Do you doubt that I have the interests of the men at heart?"

"No, I don't. I believe you are thoroughly unselfish, but I also believe you are needlessly sacrificing yourself. You see it is difficult for us to come to an agreement, for we look out on the world from entirely different standpoints. You are at the foot of the hill, and the mists of the valley of youth are around you, distorting your vision, and destroying correct proportion. I am up towards the top of the mountain, where the air is clearer. You see men heroic and noble; I see them small and mean. You believe in the workingman; I do not. The chances are that neither of us sees with absolute accuracy, and the truth lies between the two extremes. Nevertheless, I think the day of chivalrous, unselfish action is past, and it is every man for himself in these times."

"I can't understand why you talk like that, Mr. Sartwell. I have seen heroic things done even in my short life. I saw a man come out of these works alone and unprotected, when he knew the mob outside was howling for his blood, yet there was no trace of either fear or bravado about him. The same man nearly lost his life in saving others when the factory burned, and Braunt, an unlearned workingman, did unselfishly and chivalrously go to his death in the same cause."

"Ah, Braunt was one of a thousand! Well, perhaps there is something worth preserving left in human nature after all, and may be I am merely growing old and pessimistic. Anyway, the main point at present is that there must be a trial of strength; so I suppose there is nothing for us to do but shake hands like a pair of prize-fighters before the performance begins. I think you are foolish, you know, not to take the sub-managership."

The two men shook hands, and Marsten departed into the night. Sartwell sat in his office for some minutes thinking over the situation.

## CHAPTER XXXV.

The second strike was as clean-cut as the first: that is to say, no laggards remained behind in the works; there was apparent unanimity among the men, and apparent determination on the part of the masters. To all outward seeming it was to be a straightforward, brutal trial of strength between Capital and the Union. Marsten cared little for public sympathy, which Gibbons had considered of great importance; and Sartwell cared for it nothing at all. The public took small interest either way. It was known that the company had voluntarily advanced the wages of the men a short time before, and employers generally said that this showed the folly of sentimentality in business; that no master should advance wages until he was forced to do so. There was no gratitude on the part of the workingman, they averred, and some of the newspapers took the same tone. But even those journals favourable to labour had qualms about the wisdom of the strike under the circumstances, although they hoped it would succeed.

Marsten, however, paid small heed to the comments of friend or foe; he knew that success or failure did not lie in what the papers said, but in perfect organization and in hitting hard. He knew that, if he won, most of the praise would go to the determination of the men and the opportuneness of the strike; while, if he lost, he would have to shoulder all the censure that had to be bestowed. He picketed the works in the usual way, choosing for that duty the staunchest of his friends among the men. He asked the remainder of the employees to keep away from the gates and leave the conduct of the fight entirely to him and those he had chosen as his lieutenants.

Once the fight was on, Sartwell determined to give no quarter. He resolved to fill up the works, if possible, with men from outside, and to take back none of the old employees who did not sign a paper promising to abandon the Union. In the former strike he had been anxious to get his men back in a body, and had made no real attempt to fill their places. He knew in the beginning of the second struggle that he was fighting for his life, and that if he suffered defeat he would resign, and the place that had known him for years would know him no more. He had no fear that the company would discharge him if he lost the battle,—in fact he knew they would use every effort to induce him to remain; but it was his own stubborn pride, as his wife called it, that he felt he could not overcome even if he had wished to do so. Sartwell, like certain swords of finely-tempered steel, would break, but would not bend. Years of unflinching determination in what he thought was right had made him a man over whom he himself had but slight control; and he sometimes recognized with grim humour that while he could persuade all his confrères to take a devious but safe course upon any given problem, he could not induce himself to follow anything but the straight line. He worked night and day at the task of filling the factory with new men. He scoured the country for them, and his telegraph bills alone were enormous; but men were scarce—good men are always scarce, and now even indifferent workers were hard to find. Gibbons had once said that the workingman of modern times suffers from the fact that he is merely a cog in a big wheel, but this truism tells also against the employer who is trying to fill his shops. If a cog is useless by itself it must not be forgotten that the wheel is also useless until the cog is replaced. It is easy for an employer to supply the place of a single cog; but when the whole wheel is cogless, ninety-nine cogs are of no avail if the hundredth necessary to complete the circle cannot be found.

It was here that Sartwell had the first touch of his opponent's quality, and his anger was lost in admiration for the young man's shrewdness and knowledge of the business. The fight had been conducted so quietly that no one in the neighbourhood would have known, from any sign of disturbance, that war was in progress. Marsten made no attempt to buy off the new men, who came and went from the works unmolested by the pickets. Marsten sometimes talked with the strangers, telling them of the strike, and asking where they came from; advising them to get work elsewhere, but never making any attempt either to coerce or to bribe them. Sartwell wondered at this, and hoped Marsten would continue such a mild and harmless warfare; nevertheless its very mildness made him anxious, and he cautioned his new employees to give no information to the strikers, though he was well aware of the uselessness of trying to inculcate secrecy—for men will talk. In fact Marsten kept himself well informed of what was going on inside the works, and saw that the manager was quite shrewdly concentrating his attention to one branch of a department, instead of trying to fill the whole factory at one time. He was gradually collecting his hundred cogs from all points of the compass, and by and by would have one big wheel and pinion, out of the many wheels and pinions, revolving. One day at noon, when the men came out, Marsten, rapidly running his eye over them, saw a new man, and at once he recognized that here at last was the hundredth cog.

"You're a new-comer?" he said, accosting him.

"Yes," answered the man; "I came this morning."

"I'd like to have a word with you," said Marsten, keeping step with him.

"It's no use. I know there's a strike. I'm here to work, and I don't give a hang for the Union!"

"Well, it will do no harm to talk the matter over."

"It'll do no good. I didn't come out to talk; I came out for my dinner."

"Of course. I'm on the same lay myself; come with me. We can talk and eat."

"I can pay for my own dinner."

"Certainly; I'm not offering to pay for it. I don't suppose I get a tenth part of the wages you do; I can see by the look of you that you are a good workman. I'm secretary of the Union, and I get but a few shillings a week. I would tell you how few, but you probably wouldn't believe me, for I could get much more at my trade."

"The more fool you, then, for working for less."

"Perhaps. I want to raise the wages of men all over the kingdom, so I'm content to work for little if I can do that. Where do you come from?"

"I'm a Bolton man."

"Is your family here?"

"No."

"Why?"

"What's that to you, I'd like to know?"

"It's a good deal to all of us, because it shows that you are not sure of your situation."

"It shows nothing of the kind. I am guaranteed my situation."

"Guaranteed! What does a master's guarantee amount to? We're going to win this strike, and then where will you new-comers be? You know what happens when the men go back. Not one of you will be left in the shops. Suppose you do get good wages for a few weeks, what will be the benefit in the end? A permanent situation at even lower wages would be better."

"Who says it wouldn't? But I haven't the permanent situation, you see."

"Now you are talking sense. Are you a member of the Union?"

"I was. I had a row with the foreman, and he gave me the sack."

"In whose shop was that?"

"At Smighden's."

"I don't know it. What wages were you getting there?"

"Thirty shillings a week."

"Do you know Markham, Sarbury & Company, of Bolton?"

"Yes."

"Would you be satisfied with thirty shillings a week there?"

"Yes; if I could be sure of getting it."

"You can be sure of it. I will telegraph to the foreman this minute, and we'll have an answer before we finish eating. He has promised to find me places for three men, and I haven't sent him one yet. But don't say a word to any one here, for I want to keep the other two places for Bolton men if they come."

"I'll not go back to this shop at all if I can be sure of a place in Bolton."

And so it came about that Sartwell lost his hundredth cog, and the cog never thought it worth his while to give his late master even a word of explanation. He left on the first train for Manchester.

This kind of thing happened several times before Sartwell fully realized the method in Marsten's action. He thought at first that Marsten had been merely lucky in buying off a man at the very time when such a purchase would block all progress. It was like pulling the linchpin from one of the axles of a wagon. The manager wrote to his fellow-managers in different parts of the country, and warned them that their foremen were giving places to employees from the works of Monkton & Hope, and he received answers saying they would do all they could to prevent such transplanting; but, as it was difficult to trace where a man went, when so few of them were deported, the warning came to nothing. If a wholesale exodus had been attempted, Sartwell, with the aid of his fellow-managers, might have done something to prevent its success; but the very homoeopathic nature of Marsten's remedy made it difficult to cope with. By this time the feeling that he was a beaten man came over Sartwell, and, although he said nothing and sought sympathy from no one, it aged him more than years of toil had done. His daughter, now home from school, saw with helpless grief the deep lines care was ploughing in his rugged face.

Curiously enough, Marsten's quiet but effective methods, which convinced so far-seeing a man as Sartwell that they were ultimately to be successful, had the very opposite effect on the strikers themselves. They did not understand the game, and they saw with increasing uneasiness that the works were apparently filling up while nothing was being done to prevent it. Marsten did not call meetings and enthusiastically show his hand with an outburst of eloquence, as had been the habit with Gibbons. The men thought he was doing nothing merely because he was saying nothing, and even Marsten's own friends began to feel dubious about the result. There was no sign of giving in on the part of the masters, and they saw every day an increased number of men come out of the gates. In spite of Marsten's prohibition the strikers began to gather about the gates, hooting the new employees when they came out; for hoots and groans seemed to accomplish something, and were at least a relief to the pent-up feelings of the idle men. Marsten saw these signs of revolt with uneasiness; but he thought, as the men this time were not starving, and as they all knew the Union was still in ample funds, he could keep the strikers in hand until a decisive blow would show Monkton & Hope the futility of further resistance. He had quietly prepared such a blow, and he expected that when it fell the strike would triumphantly end.

A deputation of the strikers, headed by Gibbons, waited on him, and demanded that public meetings should be held—as had always been done before—so that the men might be kept informed of the progress of a struggle that vitally affected their interests. Gibbons spoke strongly and feelingly on the subject, as one who speaks from the heart, and the deputation was correspondingly impressed. It was not right, Gibbons held, that they should grope longer in the dark; they wanted to know where they were, and what measures were being taken to bring Sartwell to terms.

"But, don't you see," protested Marsten, "that any information I give publicly to my friends at once becomes known to the enemy? I never knew anything to be accomplished by talk. There is generally too much of it in a contest of this kind."

"I quite agree with you," said the glib Gibbons; "but in the absence of talk we would like to have some evidence of action. This sort of thing cannot be kept up for ever. Sartwell is gradually filling the factory, and we are all getting a little restive. We must know what is going on, for it will be no consolation to be told in a week—or two—or three—that you find you have no chance of succeeding, and that we must make the best terms we can. You must remember that, although you lose no situation, we do. Will you call a meeting and explain to the men what the chances of success are?"

"I will do nothing of the sort. A general does not call his army together and explain to them what he intends to do next. I am leader of this strike, and I am going to lead it my own way or not at all. You say the factory is filling up, but I tell you that not a stroke of work has been done since the strike began. All I will promise to do is to let you know two weeks before we come to the end of our funds; then, if you do not think we will succeed, you will have time to make what arrangements you please, and depose me."

"Oh, that kind of high-handed business does not do in this age. You are not an autocrat, remember. The men have every right to demand an account of what you are doing with them and their money."

"When you were leader, Gibbons, they were at the end of their funds before you let them know anything about it. There was talk enough in those days, and precious little information went with it. I won't conduct a strike with my mouth, and I won't stand any interference."

"You are our servant, I beg you to remember, and it is no interference when we simply ask to know what is being done and what you intend to do. Now you will either call a meeting of the men at the Salvation Hall or we will. Which is it to be?"

"I shall not call a meeting. If you call one, then you take the responsibility of meddling in a matter you don't understand. It is quite possible that you may be able to embarrass, or perhaps defeat me; but if you do, the time will come when the men will curse you for your intervention. I tell you we are bound to win this strike if you keep your hands off. Calling a meeting will merely show Sartwell that we are getting anxious, and his whole hope is centered in a division among us. He was frank enough to tell me so himself."

"When did he tell you that?"

"Before the strike began."

Gibbons looked significantly at the deputation, and one or two of the members nodded sadly, as much as to say they wouldn't have believed it; but it was now only too evident, from their secretary's own admission, that he had secret communications with the enemy.

"I think," said Gibbons, solemnly, "that, after what you have said, there is all the more reason why you should call the men together, and explain to them how you came to be discussing with Sartwell the probable failure of the strike even before it began. You knew that was a tender point with us long since; and if Sartwell is your enemy, as you said he was, I can't see for the life of me why——"

"Oh, there is no need of any secrecy about it, Gibbons. In fact there is little mystery about anything we do, and that is one reason I don't want to call a public meeting. Things are bad enough as they are. I have found that Sartwell generally knows what we are about to do before many of us know it ourselves. I went to Sartwell because he asked me to go. He knew this strike was coming on, although I had imagined it had only been discussed between myself and some of the others. He offered me the assistant managership of the works if I would resign my position as secretary. I refused, and he told me this strike was bound to fail because the men would not be true to me. You can give the men the whole particulars of my talk with Sartwell, but there is no need of calling a meeting to discuss it."

"That may all be true, but I confess it sounds rather fishy. I doubt if Sartwell is so much afraid of you as that comes to. Anyhow, there is no harm in finding out just where we stand. I will do my best to calm the apprehensions of the men, but I give you warning that if nothing more encouraging than we have had lately turns up within a week, there will be trouble. The men will call a meeting themselves if you don't."

"If nothing happens within a week, I will call a meeting and give them an account of what has been done so far; but I don't approve of meetings, and I shall call one practically under compulsion. You are forcing my hand, Gibbons, and you promised me fair play."

"It seems to me you have had a good run for your money, and I think we are very patient in consenting to wait a week when we are being led we don't know where."

The deputation then withdrew, and Marsten paced up and down the room, wondering if the directors were giving Sartwell as uneasy a time as the men were giving him. As was the case during the former strike, the

Salvation Hall had been placed at the disposal of the men. Marsten had called no meetings except the one that had ushered in the strike. He made his headquarters, however, in a room that opened upon the platform, and which also communicated with a narrow lane that led along the outside of the hall to the street. Here his pickets reported to him, and here the work made necessary by the strike—the bookkeeping and the correspondence—was done. Here also letters and telegrams were received. It was a bare room with only two or three chairs and a rough table as its furnishing. Several religious and moral mottoes were tacked on the boards that formed the walls. "Love one another" was the sentence that met Mars-ten's eye whenever he looked up from his seat at the table. He sometimes smiled sadly as he gazed at it. Marsten paused in his walk, and sat down at the table on hearing a knock at the outside door. A telegraph messenger entered and handed him an envelope. Marsten tore it open, and read the single word "Stopped." The word had come from the other side of the earth, travelling from Sydney, New South Wales, to London. A gleam of savage joy lit up the eyes of the young man, and, to the amazement of the messenger, he brought his fist down heavily on the deal table.

"There is no answer," he said to the waiting boy, suddenly recollecting that he was not alone; "and," he added to himself, "there will be no answer but one from Monkton & Hope."

Once more he paced the room up and down, his frame quivering with the delight of battle and the fore-knowledge of victory. The motto, "Love one another," shone peacefully, but unnoticed, on the wall.

## CHAPTER XXXVI.

When the two years' educational course at Eastbourne was finished, Edna Sartwell returned to Wimbledon, and again took up her position in her father's house. As time went on, Sartwell was quietly pleased to see that there was an absence of that friction between his women-folk which had been his ostensible reason for sending Edna away. He had had but faint hope that the interval of two years would soften his wife's only partially concealed dislike for the girl; but, now that peace reigned over the household, he did not inquire too closely into the cause of the welcome change. He did not know his daughter now bore uncomplainingly what she had before rebelled against. Mrs. Sartwell's attitude towards education in general was one calculated to discourage the friends of learning. She looked upon a course in school as a sinful waste of time and money. The Apostles, she held, had never even gone to a Board school, and who among present-day people were to be compared with the Apostles? Education was merely a pamperer of that deplorable pride which was already too great a characteristic of this conceited nation. She had many texts at her command which went to prove that too much learning was a dangerous thing, and these quotations she frequently presented to Edna, in the hope that many repetitions of them would mitigate, in some measure, the evil that was sure to follow a period spent at a fashionable and expensive school. Overweening pride was Mrs. Sartwell's especial bugbear; it, more than anything else, was driving modern nations rapidly to perdition. She told Edna, sorrowfully, that she noticed an unwelcome change in her manner since her return from Eastbourne. The pride which aped humility was ever the most baneful variety of that detestable fault, and Edna's silence in the face of good counsel showed that her pride had assumed the sullen type which is so difficult for a good woman to deal with. It was only when Mrs. Sartwell—offended by absence of retort and cheated out of her just due of argument by the silence of her adversary—threatened to lay before her husband the appalling results of over-education upon an already haughty nature, that some glimmer of the old rebellion flashed out between them;

yet the rebelliousness, like the hauteur, had been changed by the two years' residence at Eastbourne. That Edna was angry at this proposed appeal to her father, was evident; still there was a reserve and restraint in her indignation which Mrs. Sartwell could not fathom. The girl stood for a moment looking at her, then said very quietly:

"My father has enough to worry him without being bothered by our small affairs. He thinks my two years' absence has made you like me better than you did before I went away, and I wish him to continue thinking so."

"Like you better? My poor child, it is the love I have for you that causes me to endeavour, in my humble way,—praying that my efforts may be blessed by a Higher Power,—to correct those faults that will be your undoing some day."

"I am speaking of what my father thinks. The moment he finds things are just as bad as they ever were, then all your hold over me is gone. I am now trying to bear patiently and uncomplainingly all I have to put up with in this house, and I do so for no other reason than to save my father unnecessary trouble. You say I am proud, resentful, stubborn, and all that. I am far worse than even you have any idea of. It makes me shudder to think of the kind of woman I shall become if I am much longer under your sway. I feel like a hypocrite when I remain silent under your taunts, for I think such things that if I were to put them in words——well, we won't talk of that. If you imagine that I have learned meekness because I have lived in a really Christian family for two years, you are very much mistaken; but I have learned that true Christianity does not consist in nagging, with a text at the end of every exasperating sentence. Now, being a woman, I understand you very much better than my father does. You said once that, if he chose me to be mistress of this house, you would lay down your keys and depart without a murmur. You would do nothing of the kind. You would fight for your place. Therefore I want you to understand thoroughly what you may expect if you appeal to my father. The moment you complain of me in any way, or lead him to think there is the least friction, I shall go to him and say that I must be mistress here. What will happen then?—you know as well as I do. So long as he is not troubled with our affairs, I shall say nothing, and will try to be as dutiful and obedient as if I were your own daughter."

Mrs. Sartwell sat down, buried her face in her hands, and wept softly, as one does whose tenderest feelings are wounded. It was hard that, after having a lifelong contest with one stubborn person, resulting in a most uncertain and unsatisfactory victory,—if it could be called a victory at all,—she should be called upon to face the same problem over again. She knew that if Edna appealed to her father anything might happen. He would be brute enough to take another house somewhere, and live in peace with his daughter. The man was capable of anything, in spite of all the precepts she had flung away upon him. However, there was still the consolation that she might save the girl by earnest and devoted persistence in well-doing, and she knew Edna would not protest so long as her father was unmolested: so Mrs. Sartwell agreed that her husband should not be made the referee between them, and Peace once more folded her white wings over the happy home.

Edna had developed into a beautiful woman; more beautiful, indeed, than she herself had any idea of. She was more sedate and reserved than when she had left home, and more prone to sit thoughtfully, chin in hand, and ponder, with her dreamy eyes trying to peer into the future. Resolutely as she had set herself to put Marsten forever out of her thoughts, she never succeeded, and his vibrant, deep-toned voice often came back to her. Although she had been brought up in a democratic way, and theoretically held that one person was technically as good as another, yet she lived in a country where a grocer's daughter considers it quite beneath her dignity to be seen in company with a green-grocer's daughter; while the daughter of a draper, from her serene social altitude, would have some difficulty in distinguishing the relative status of the other two, although she would be well aware that the adjective "green" carried comparative degradation with it. Edna was the daughter of a man who had been a workman; yet, when she thought over the proposal she had received in the school garden, she was slightly shocked to think that a workman should aspire to the hand of his master's daughter. She had conversed with Marsten, and discussed the problems that had interested them both, yet never for a moment had the thought of equality between them entered her mind. He was merely a workman, and, when that was said, a gulf yawned. But love levels all ranks, as a distinguished man has sung, and, as the young woman meditated on the subject in all its bearings, the social barriers seemed to become less and less tangible. She remembered that no thought of social inequality had ever occurred to her while in his presence. She got no further in the understanding of her own feelings than the conclusion that she liked him very much indeed, and had a strong admiration for his manliness and his determination to succeed.

When the strike came on, and she knew that her father and her lover were opponents, her state of mind was one of great perplexity. It was hard that one or the other must be defeated, and she sighed when she thought of the relentlessness of fate in bringing into savage opposition the two men who were now dearer to her than all the world beside.

As the contest went on and she saw her father bending under the storm, ageing perceptibly day by day, becoming more and more silent, her strong affection for him grew stronger; she yearned towards him, wishing she could comfort him, yet knowing she was helpless. Sometimes a fierce resentment against Marsten would spring suddenly up in her heart. He had all the world to fight against, yet he must choose as his antagonist, out of the many millions, her father. It disconcerted her to perceive that this resentment never lasted long; that she found herself sympathizing too with the younger of the combatants, and making excuses for him. A partisan has an easy time of it in this world, compared with one who sees that all the good or all the bad rarely rests with one side solely, but is interwoven like the cotton and the wool in a piece of cloth. Sartwell and Marsten each believed he was fighting for the right; but Edna saw wrong on both sides and right on both sides, although—once the fight was started—she had not the courage to say this to her father.

But, as war goes on, the original right or wrong almost invariably sinks out of sight, and we choose our side from other considerations than those which appeal in times of peace to thinking beings. He who holds aloof is branded as a traitor: and yet man, with his marvellous capacity for self-esteem, flatters himself that he is a reasoning animal.

Sartwell generally came home late, sometimes returning by the last train. It had come to be recognized that it was Edna's privilege to sit up for him, and, although he faintly protested once or twice when he found her there after midnight, it was quite evident that her presence was a comfort to him. She had a soothing, restful way with her, moving silently about the room, anticipating a tired man's needs without unnecessary fuss, and with no irritating questions to ask; yet she was a sympathetic and receptive listener if there was anything to be told. In the wake of some women inanimate nature seems to clash: doors bang, plates fall, cups and saucers clatter, and chairs upset, jangling nerves sensitive to sound; but Edna could deftly set out a supper without so much as a chink of china. She knew the value of trivialities,—the setting of the arm-chair at just the right angle so that the light fell over the shoulder as it should, the placing of the slippers where the stockinged feet fell into them without effort; and, when her father was too much fatigued to care for the formality of sitting up to the festive board late at night, a small gipsy table, covered with spotless linen and some dainty that might tempt the appetite of a Lucullus, would appear at his right elbow as if they had come noiselessly up through the floor. All this came under the general head of "pampering" in Mrs. Sartwell's vocabulary, and the good woman, finding that her example was of no effect in putting a stop to it, retired early to rest, so that she might not countenance such proceedings by her presence. There was a time to eat and a time to drink, and if a man presumed to be hungry at midnight, it was a sin that should be punished by dyspepsia in this world and goodness knows what in the next.

In spite of the compact between them, Sartwell told his daughter little about the progress of the strike; and she, seeing him indisposed to speak, forbore to question him, feeling that no suggestion she might have to offer could be of any value to him, contenting herself with protecting him from annoyance at home, and cheering him as much as possible whenever she had him to herself. But it wrung her heart to see him failing perceptibly day after day, his step, which she eagerly listened for, losing more and more its selfreliant tread.

One night she sat in his arm-chair waiting for him, thinking deeply. She looked suddenly up with a start, and saw her father standing beside the table gazing down at her. His face was white, gaunt, and haggard, and the gloom of his countenance was deepened rather than relieved by the sombre smile that parted his lips as he regarded her. He seemed like a man on the verge of a serious illness, and so startled was the girl, that for a moment she looked at him with wide-open eyes, fearing that an apparition stood before her.

"Father!" she cried at last, springing to her feet. "What has happened?"

"Nothing, my girl, except that you have been asleep in the chair when you should have been in bed long ago."

"I don't think I have been asleep, yet I didn't hear you open the door. But you are ill."

"I'm right enough. A little tired, that's all. No, I won't have anything to eat, thank you. It's after closing hours, I know; but I'm a traveller, and I'll have something to drink, if you don't mind."

He tried to laugh a little over this attempted pleasantry, but his laugh sounded dismal, and it frightened the girl still more, instead of reassuring her, as was his intention. The neck of the decanter clattered against the glass like chattering teeth, which seemed to annoy Sartwell; for he muttered something, and shot a glance at his daughter to see if she had noticed his unusual nervousness. Then he grasped the vessel more firmly, pouring the liquor with a steadier hand, but the effort made him tighten his lips. He drank off the liquid and set down the empty glass. Edna stood opposite him; he looked up at her with a wan smile on his lips.

"Well, my girl," he said, "the game's up."

"Has the strike ended, father?" she asked, her voice quavering.

"Actually, no; practically, yes. The firm will give in to-morrow, and I shall resign. Sorry?"

"I am sorry if you are, father," said Edna, kneeling beside him. "I am not sorry that the tension has ended, for I think anything is better than the anxiety you have been undergoing for the past few weeks. And you look positively ill to-night."

"Yes. A man hates to be beaten. Well, I'm fairly knocked out, and if there is any comfort in a decisive beating, I have it."

"What has happened?"

"You see, Edna, in the pictures of a battle, we always have the horses galloping, the men firing, or being shot, or cutting down their enemies with the sword; but we rarely get a view of the background, and so people sometimes do not know that it exists: yet the picture shows merely the front of the fight, as it were, while battles are often won by perfect arrangements in the rear,—the supply of ammunition, the food and water carriers and all that sort of thing. Well, a strike is like a battle; there are other things to consider than the actual fighting, and these things often decide the day. The direct loss in a struggle of this kind is nothing to the indirect loss. We see trade slipping away from us and going to our bitterest rivals. Some of our customers may come back; others won't. Then we are unable to fulfil contracts we have made, and, as a strike can hardly be called an act of God, we are liable to have damages awarded against us where no strike clause has been inserted in the agreement. All this I have had to fight as well as the strikers themselves. Then there is great difficulty in filling up the shops—much more than I expected. During the last week I have been slowly losing ground with the directors. They haven't said very much, but I have felt it. It was in the air somehow that we were fighting a losing battle, and so things have been on the balance, and the only reason the directors did not give in a week ago was they knew I would resign if they did so. It only required a straw to turn the scales against me. Some time before the strike began, a steamer sailed for Sydney, New South Wales. It had a large quantity of our goods on board. To-day I received notice from the owners that the ship lay there and could not be unloaded because of our strike. They propose to hold us responsible for the delay, and that will mean an expensive lawsuit whichever way the verdict goes. This is serious enough in itself, but the fact that we have been struck from the remotest ends of the earth while being paralyzed in London will make the directors give in at once. So, my girl, I'm a beaten man."

"But might you not have been beaten in any case?"

"No; another week would have seen the men back—I am sure of it.

They are seething with discontent, and have called a meeting for to-morrow night, in spite of the protests of Marsten. There is sure to be a split, and all I need is a slight defection to set the works going again."

"Why need you resign, father? You have done your best, and the directors know it."

"Ah, my girl, you are sleepy; I can see that, or you wouldn't ask such a question. But now you know all about it, so off you go."

In the morning Edna walked with her father to the station.

"Is there to be a meeting of the directors to-day?" she asked.

"Yes. It is called for five o'clock this evening."

"Do you think the strike would end if they gave you another week?"

"I feel morally certain it would. There is sure to be a split at to-night's meeting of the men. You see it is called in direct opposition to Marsten's wishes, and that shows he is losing whatever hold he ever had on the strikers."

"Then wouldn't you be justified in saying nothing about this communication from the shipowners until the next directors' meeting? You would know by that time what the result of the strikers' meeting was."

"My dear Edna, you make proposals that take away a man's breath. No, that wouldn't do. The directors must have full information. I could not take the responsibility of holding back anything that bore on their interests, whatever might be the result to myself; but I can't help wishing the message had gone astray for a day or two."

"I am going to the office at six o'clock to-night, father."

Sartwell laughed, but in a mirthless, despondent manner.

"Hadn't you better come at five and give the directors your opinion of them? I'm sure it wouldn't be very flattering."

"You mustn't make fun of me, father. The situation is very serious, and I couldn't bear the suspense of waiting until you came home. I must know what happens, so please don't forbid me. Besides, it may be your last night there, and I should like to bring you home with me."

"Oh, it won't be my last night. I shall not leave the old firm like that. I shall stay until the new manager is installed and everything running smoothly. Even though a man is defeated, Edna, he owes it to himself to retreat in good order, and sometimes a masterly retreat is as good a bit of generalship as a victory. As everything is perfectly quiet, you may come if you are anxious, as of course you are; or I could telegraph you, if you would rather. But it is a foregone conclusion, I am sure of that. Whenever they see this message, and learn there has been little progress made in filling up the works, they will succumb—and I don't know that I can blame them. They have vast interests at stake, and they have backed me well up to the present, when, if it hadn't been for me, they would have given in long ago. Then I shall look for you at six, my dear. Take a hansom from the station, and ask the man to wait in the yard of the works. Wait for me in my room if I happen to be absent when you come. I shall tell the commissionaire to look after you."

The girl watched the train come in and leave; then, turning, she walked towards her home with a heavy heart. She went past the house and on to the Common, unconsciously imitating her father, who, when troubled in mind, sought its breezy expanse. Several times she paused, and thought of sending a telegram to Marsten, asking him to meet her in the old garden at Wimbledon at once. There she fancied herself appealing to him to put an end to the strike; but she feared the anger of her father should he discover what she had done, even though it had been done for his sake. It did not occur to her that perhaps the appeal might be in vain, for she knew she would do anything asked of her for one she loved, and she had little doubt that the young man had a true and lasting affection for her. What, she asked herself, if Marsten made conditions? Would she be willing to accept a great favour and grant nothing in return? What would he think if she telegraphed him to come? The answer was obvious, and, in searching her own heart, she for the first time admitted to herself that her reply would be different from what it had been at Eastbourne.

But when it came to the point, she could not bring herself to the length of sending a message. She shrank from playing so dangerous a card; for, if it failed to win the trick, how could she face the after-humiliation? Something in the self-reliant ring of Marsten's voice, something in the dogged determination of his manner, something in the compelling glance of his eye, warned her that not even to please the girl he loved would he be untrue to the flag under which he fought—and something in her own heart told her that she herself would think less of him if he did. Yet, if he refused, she could never speak to him again; she was certain of that. Having made an appeal in vain, she could never grant one of his own, or even listen to it. She thought of the pleasure it would be to her to have him plead his cause once more, and read his answer in her willing eyes before her lips could speak it; but if he refused her when she begged him to spare her father the impending humiliation of defeat, there could be no more friendship between them. Edna at last returned to her home, bewildered in mind and hesitating to act, and listened to a homily on the sinfulness of wasting one's time, although she heard or understood but little of the admirable discourse.

As evening drew on the girl became more and more anxious, and impatiently awaited the hour that was to take her to London. She half expected a telegram from her father, but as none came she knew the situation had not changed for the better. Shortly after six o'clock her hansom drove into the yard of the works; the gatekeeper was evidently on the watch for her, and had the gates open, closing them after her. The silent, deserted air of the huge place had a most depressing influence on her as she mounted the stairs that led to her father's office. He was standing at his desk as she entered, entirely alone, and looked round absent-mindedly when he heard the door open.

"Well, my girl," he said, "you have come to help pack, after all."

"If there must be packing, I am ready to help, father."

"I'm afraid that's all there's left to do, dear. But we're not going to show the white feather, are we? I've just been planning a lovely little tour on the Continent for you and me, where we shall forget, for a time, that there is such an ugly thing as a strike in the whole world. You'll be a princess, and I'll be the old dethroned king; they always went to the Continent, you know, after a defeat."

Sartwell's attempt at banter was a gloomy failure, and he avoided his daughter's eye, pretending to be sorting out some papers. She saw how hard hit he was, and the tears came into her eyes.

"Is the directors' meeting over?" she asked at last.

"No. They are in there yet, arranging the terms of surrender—or hardly that, for there are no terms. They simply give the men all they ask—which, of course, they might have done a month ago, and saved all this bother. I knew how it would be when they heard about the ship lying unloaded in Australia. There was not an ounce of fight left in them, and I felt sure a blow dealt so far away would appeal to what little imagination any of them has. It seems to them decisive, but of course it is nothing of the kind. It is merely a theatrical bit of by-play that should have no bearing on the result. But there is little use in kicking against fate. They are at this moment engaged in writing out their letter of capitulation—as if it made any difference how you worded an acknowledgment of defeat and a surrender of your interests to a lot of ignorant, beer-drinking boors who don't——but what is the use of cursing? Another week of this indecision would have demoralized me; in fact, I think it has done so already, for I don't generally growl."

"Will you come home with me, father?"

"No, my dear. I shouldn't have let you come all this distance merely to hear what we both knew this morning. Run along home, like a good little girl, and don't sit up for me to-night. I'll be late. Of course, in spite of my scolding, I'll stay till the last dog's hung. I'll see the thing through, and wave the white flag myself. It wouldn't be quite the thing, you know, to have all the fun of the fight and then funk the submission. I merely came into this room because you were due at six, and to rest my nerves a bit. I'm going back to the directors, and will write the letter of surrender myself; for they will never summon up courage enough to do even that if I am not at their elbows. I'm going down with the ship, my girl, pretending I like it; so off you go, Edna, and we'll feel all right about it next week——perhaps."

Haggard as he looked the night before, Edna now noticed, with a thrill of fear, that for the first time he seemed an old man. His usually well-set shoulders were bent, and even his neatly-fitting clothes hung loosely about him. The hesitation and the tone in which he said the last word, "perhaps," showed her like an electric flash what was in his own mind, and what had never occurred to her before,—that when he was suddenly wrenched away from the task that had been his life's work, he would break up in idleness like a useless hulk on the rocks.

"Father," she cried, "don't let them send that letter till to-morrow. A day more or less makes no difference, and they will keep it back if you ask them to."

Sartwell shook his head.

"There is no use in delay," he said. "It has always been my habit to do quickly what had to be done, and I am getting too old to change my habits. If you must walk the plank, walk it, and get it over."

The girl did not urge him further, but kissed him and said, "Good-night." He saw her into the hansom, and told the cabman to drive to Waterloo. At the first turning Edna pushed up the little trap-door in the roof of the cab.

"Do you know where the headquarters of the strikers are?" she asked.

"Yes, miss. At the Salvation Hall, miss."

"Well, drive me there as quickly as you can."

The cabby turned his horse and in a short time was making his way through the crowd of men who were gathering from all quarters to the meeting. He drew up at the kerb in front of the hall. Edna stepped out, flushing as she saw the men looking curiously at her. She said to one:

"Where can I find Mr. Marsten?"

"He's in his room at the back of the 'all, ma'am. This wye, ma'am. I'll show you the door."

Edna followed the man down the long, narrow passage at the side of the hall.

"For God's sake, mates, what's the meaning of this?" cried Gibbons, in amazement, taking his pipe out of his mouth.

Some of the men laughed, but Gibbons looked serious, and they saw that there was more in the incident than appeared on the surface.

"Who is it she wants to see?" cried Gibbons, as the man appeared who had led the girl down the passage.

"She arsked for Marsten. She's in with him now."

"Look here, mates," cried Gibbons. "What have I been telling you? We're sold, or I'm a Dutchman! That girl is Sartwell's daughter, and I'll warrant she has come direct from him. I say, cabby, did you drive that young lady here from the works?"

"What's that to you? You're not paying my fare," answered the cabman, with characteristic disregard of the threatening crowd.

"He came from the works; I saw him," said one of the men.

"Let's get inside, and call this meeting to order," cried Gibbons, decisively.

## CHAPTER XXXVI.

Edna rapped lightly on the door at the back of the Salvation Hall, and heard Marsten's voice shout "Come in." After a moment's hesitation she opened the door and entered. The young man was alone, sitting at the rough board table, with some papers before him, writing rapidly with a pencil. He seemed absorbed in his work, and kept his head bent over it, saying shortly:

"Well, what is it?"

Edna stood with her back against the door; she tried to speak, but could not. Her heart was beating so rapidly that it seemed to choke her, and her lips were dry. The murmur of numerous voices came through the thin board partitions from the main hall, with the noise of the shuffling of many feet. Marsten continued to write quickly; then suddenly he lifted his head with a jerk, stared incredulously in the gathering darkness, and sprang to his feet.

"My God—Edna!" he cried, and seemed about to advance towards her; but she raised her hand, and he stood by the table with his knuckles resting upon it.

"I came——" She spoke in a whisper, so husky and unnatural that it seemed to her the voice belonged to some one else. "I came——to speak to you——about the strike."

"Yes?"

"It must stop."

"It will stop within a day or two. Monkton & Hope are defeated."

"You mean that my father is defeated. It is killing him, I can see that, although he tries——He does not know I have come here. I came of my own accord because you——If you will get the men to go back, I give you my word that he will grant all you are fighting for. All I ask is that you will not make it hard for him. The men do not care as long as they get what they want. Will you do this?"

"Do you mean I am to call the strike off and pretend that the men are defeated?"

"Yes. It will be all the same in the end."

"Oh, I cannot do that."

"Why? The men do not care as long as they get what they ask. With my father it is different. He is breaking down. I know I am asking a great deal of you, for you feel as he does, and want to win as badly as he does; but he is old, and you are young. You have all the world before you. What need you care, then, whether you win this strike or not? There are other strikes for you to win, but he—he is fighting his last battle."

Her voice had become clearer and more like itself as she earnestly pleaded for her father. Some one in the main building had started a rollicking music-hall song then as infectious as an epidemic on the streets of London. The whole house had joined in the swinging chorus, beating time with the tramp of many feet. Neither of the two appeared to hear the song, but both raised their voices slightly to make themselves heard above the sound.

"I care nothing for any personal triumph—nothing at all," said Marsten. "If I could change places with your father and accept defeat for him I willingly would. But the men have trusted me——"

"The men!" cried Edna, the scarlet chasing the whiteness from her cheeks as her eyes flashed and her voice rose. "What do the men care? Listen to them!" She waved her hand toward the hall. "They would sing and shout like that if their best friend was dying. Who has done more for his men than my father? He risked his life for them at the fire, and would do so again. He has built up the works that have given them employment. He has kept the shops full at a loss when times were bad, so that they might not starve. Every man was sure of his place as long as he deserved it, and no master in London was more loath than he to discharge a man." She cast down her eyes as she suddenly remembered that one man had been discharged without cause by her father; then, without raising them, she pleaded again: "Why will not a real victory, without the name of it, satisfy you?"

"Because it is not for these men alone who are now shouting that I am fighting. The eyes of all England are on this strike. An acknowledged victory over so strong a firm as that of Monkton & Hope will mean an easier victory for every man who is now earning his bread in this country, when he is compelled to strike for his just due. It will hearten every workingman and be a warning to every employer."

The chorus in the hall was broken by three sharp raps of a mallet on a table. The sound of the singing subsided, and the voice of some one calling the meeting to order was heard.

Edna slowly raised her eyes and looked at him, with a flash of fearing defiance in them. She spoke in an agitated whisper.

"You remember what you said to me in the garden at Eastbourne. If you will do what I ask of you, I will do as you wish when—when you ask me."

The young man, his trembling right hand clenching and unclenching nervously, strode a step forward.

"No, no!" she cried. "Stay where you are. Answer me, answer me!"

"Oh, Edna," he whispered, "God knows I would do anything to win you,—anything,—yes, almost what you ask!"

"Yes, or no?" she cried. "Answer me!"

"I cannot be a traitor to the men!"

As if in approval of this sentiment, a cheer rose from the hall. Some one was speaking, and even in his misery Marsten recognized the voice of Gibbons.

Edna turned without a word and opened the door. Marsten followed her out.

"Stay where you are," she said, with a sob.

"I will see you to the station."

"No; you must not come near me. I hope never to see you again."

"I will see you to the station," repeated Marsten, doggedly.

The girl said nothing more, but walked hurriedly down the narrow passage, the young man following her. She sprang into the waiting hansom, crying, "Waterloo; quick!"

The cab whirled away, leaving Marsten standing bareheaded on the kerb. He remained there for some moments, gazing in the direction the cab had taken, then turned with a sigh and walked slowly up the passage to his room. It seemed more bare and empty than ever it had been before, and he could hardly realize that, a few short moments since, she had stood within it. He heard, without heeding, the noise from the hall, like the low growl of some wild beast. He looked at the papers on the table, wrinkling his brow trying to understand what they were all about. It appeared ages since he sat there writing—now he heard nothing but the words "Answer me!" ringing in his ears. He was startled by another knock at the door and sprang towards it, throwing it eagerly open, hoping she had returned. Monkton & Hope's tall, grizzled commissionaire, in his uniform, with the medal dangling from his breast, stood there, perhaps astonished at the sudden opening of the door, but not a muscle of his face showing his surprise. He saluted gravely.

"A letter from the firm, sir."

"Ah! Step inside. Any answer required?"

"I don't know, sir," answered the commissionaire, standing as straight and as rigid as if on parade.

Marsten tore open the envelope, and the reading of the letter brought him to his senses. It was a terse communication, and informed him that Monkton & Hope agreed to the terms of the men. Mr. Sartwell would wait at his office until ten o'clock to meet M Marsten and arrange for the opening of the works in the morning.

Marsten dashed off an official reply, and said he would wait on Mr. Sartwell in half an hour's time. Giving this note to the commissionaire, who again saluted and withdrew, Marsten, with the letter in his hand, opened the door that communicated with the platform and stepped out in the sight of the meeting. A howl of derision greeted his appearance, and the howl of an angry mob is a sound that, once heard, a man never wishes to hear again.

"There he is," shouted Gibbons, whose speech Marsten's entrance had evidently interrupted. "There he is, and let him deny it if he can!"

"Deny what?" cried Marsten.

"Deny that you have been in communication with the enemy! Deny that Sartwell's daughter has only this moment left you!"

"That has nothing to do with you, nor with this strike. England is a free country; a man may talk with whom he pleases."

"He can't deny it!" shouted Gibbons, at the top of his voice. "There were too many witnesses this time. She didn't know that a meeting was gathering. Where now is the man at the back of the hall who cried out it was a lie? I told you I would prove it by Marsten himself."

"Let me read you this letter," cried Marsten, waving in his hand the letter from the firm, to command attention. He saw the crowd was in that dangerous state of excitement which requires but an injudicious word to precipitate a riot. His own friends, evidently abashed by his admission, were at the back of the hall, silent and disconcerted. The Gibbons gang were massed in front, wildly gesticulating, and vociferous with taunts and threats. They were loudly calling upon him to get down from the platform. He saw, too, that the old committee and others of Gibbons's partisans were on the platform behind him, many standing up with their eyes on Gibbons, and the situation reminded him of the time when Braunt had been kicked off the platform and thrust outside.

"Let me read this letter," he repeated.

"Presently, presently," said Gibbons. "You will have your opportunity later on. I have the floor just now."

"I am secretary of the Union," persisted Marsten, "and I demand a hearing. After that you may do as you please."

Here the chairman rose and called loudly:

"Order, order! Mr. Gibbons has the floor. I may add for Mr. Marsten's information, since he chose to absent himself from the meeting knowing it was in session, that Mr. Gibbons has been made secretary of the Union by a practically unanimous vote, and I ask Mr. Marsten to leave the platform until he is called upon to speak."

"I have a letter from the firm!" shouted Marsten, trying to lift his voice above the uproar.

There was a chorus of howls, and roars of "Chair, Chair!" "Come down!" One of the men behind Marsten pushed him toward the edge of the platform, crying, "Obey the Chair!" This was the signal for a general onset, and, Marsten grappling with the foremost of his assailants, both went down together to the main floor. Instantly the meeting broke into an unmanageable mob, while Gibbons roared, "No violence, men!" and ineffectually waved his arms over the turbulent, seething, struggling mass. His appeals were as futile as Canute's commands to the sea. The chairman pounded unheard on the table with his mallet. Once Marsten shook himself free and rose to his feet. His right hand, with the tattered letter still clenched in it, appeared above the heads of the combatants for a moment, then it suddenly disappeared, and he went down finally under the feet of the maddened, trampling horde.

The police struck in promptly and with effect. The side door was thrown open, and Marsten was dragged out through it, accompanied by several struggling, torn, and bleeding rioters who had been nabbed by the law. Gradually the pounding on the table became audible, and Gibbons's voice, now hoarse with useless calling for peace, could be heard.

"I am sorry," he began, "that there has been even a semblance of a disturbance here to-night. It will be used by our enemies against us; but, as you know, it all came about through disobedience to the Chair. I want to say nothing against an absent man, and I am sure we all hope he has not been hurt [cheers]; but if our ex-secretary had calmly bowed to the will of the meeting, and had refrained from laying hands on the man who merely requested him to obey the Chair, this deplorable event would not have occurred. When, after the last strike, you lost confidence in me, I bowed to the will of the majority without a murmur, and, as you all know, I have done my best, ever since, to assist my successor; and now that I have been called again to this position, through no wish of mine, I have but to obey the mandate thus given. I take it that it is your pleasure that this strike shall now cease. Although I have never said so, I always looked upon the present strike as an unnecessary one, and unjust. The firm, a short time since, voluntarily increased our wages, and this struggle has consequently never had the sympathy of the public, without which no great struggle can succeed. I do not venture to offer suggestions, but if any one here has a suggestion to make, I now give place to him."

Gibbons did love the sound of his own voice, and it apparently gave pleasure to the majority present, for they loudly cheered all his noble sentiments.

A man promptly arose to his feet, and said it had lately been only too evident that Marsten had brought on this strike to further his own advancement, using the men, who trusted him, as tools for that purpose. Gibbons had said nothing on this point, but they all felt sore about it nevertheless; and although he admired Gibbons's good heart in refusing to say a word against a fallen enemy, still the matter ought to be referred to. He moved that Gibbons be appointed to meet Sartwell as soon as possible and arrange terms for going back, getting, if he could, a promise that the "blacklegs" be discharged. There would be general satisfaction if this promise could be secured.

This was seconded, and carried unanimously. Once more Gibbons rose to his feet.

"A messenger I sent off a few moments ago reports that Sartwell is still in his office. He has been staying late for some time past, so it struck me he might be there now. I will go at once and confer with him, and will return as soon as possible and give you the result of the conference. Meanwhile you can transact any other business that may come before the meeting."

Sartwell, alone in his office, expecting Marsten, was naturally surprised when Gibbons entered instead but he greeted the new-comer without showing that his visit was unlooked for.

"Mr. Sartwell," began Gibbons, going straight to the point, "I have again been made secretary of the Union. If I end this strike will you make me assistant manager?"

Sartwell's eyes partially closed, and he looked keenly at his visitor through the narrow slits for a moment or two before answering.

Gibbons fidgeted uneasily.

"We all play for our own hand, you know," the new secretary added, laughing uncomfortably, "and I know that with you it is better to say out what one means."

"We all play for our own hand,—yes," said Sartwell, slowly. "Can you end the strike?"

"I think so."

"You only think so. Well, Mr. Gibbons, come back to me when you are sure, and I will talk to you."

"I am sure, if it comes to that."

"Ah, that is a different matter. The meeting, then, after making you secretary, passed a resolution to end the strike?"

"Hardly that, Mr. Sartwell. It has authorized me to negotiate with you. Now, if you promise me the assistant managership, I will bring the men back tomorrow."

"The strike was bound to end soon without any promises from me. I sent a communication to Mars-ten to-night regarding it. Do you mean to hint that he has not read it to the meeting?"

"He did not. He tried to, but the men had enough of Marsten, and they refused to listen."

"Quite so. Then it is with you alone I have to deal? Marsten is out of it?"

"That is the state of the case."

"Well, I am sorry I cannot offer you the assistant managership; although, of course, I hope the strike will end as speedily as possible."

"Marsten said you offered it to him; is that true?"

"I think Marsten generally speaks the truth. Let us stop beating about the bush, Gibbons. The men to-night have either resolved to come back, or they have not. If they are coming back, they will come whether I deal with you or not. If not, then I don't see how you can say more than that you will do your best to bring them back. Now, all I shall promise is this: if you bring the men back to-morrow, I will see that your position in the works is improved."

"That's rather hard lines, Mr. Sartwell. Marsten brought on the strike, and you offer him the assistant managership. I end the strike, and you will make no definite terms."

"I offered Marsten the position before the strike began. Once the fight was on, it had to be fought to a finish. The finish has come, and I think you had better accept the only terms I can offer. Don't you see that, if I were not a man of my word, I could easily promise you anything, and then discharge you a month hence?"

"Well, I'll trust to your generosity, Mr. Sartwell. Now, what will you promise to the men?"

"What do they ask?"

"They wish you to discharge all the blacklegs you have engaged."

"I'm afraid, Gibbons, I cannot promise that either. I will, however, send home all who want to go and can find situations, but your men will not suffer on account of the new employees. I have work enough for you all; there will be plenty to do to make up for lost time."

"You practically offer us nothing, Mr. Sartwell."

"Oh yes, I do; I am conceding more than you think. I said in my wrath, when the men went out, that I would never again allow a Union man to set foot in the works: but now that they have chosen a moderate, sensible secretary, I am willing to have them come back, allowing them still to remain in the Union. Is that nothing? I think I have been most conciliatory under the circumstances."

"The meeting is still in session, Mr. Sartwell. Would you mind coming with me and telling the men that you will guarantee every one a place, and that you will not interfere with their membership of the Union?"

"I don't mind going with you, but you can probably make more out of the concessions than I, for you are more eloquent on your feet. I will simply corroborate what you say, and tell the men the gates will be open for them to-morrow. Meanwhile, just wait for me at the gate. I have a few orders to give my commissionaire."

The uniformed man answered Sartwell's call, and stood like a statue to receive his orders. The manager closed the door.

"I am afraid there is not much sleep for you tonight, Commissionaire," he said, in a low voice, "but we will make that up to you in some other way, and when the men come back to-morrow you may sleep the whole of the following week, if you like. As soon as Gibbons and I are away, and you have closed the office, I want you to search for Marsten. You will likely find him in his room. I don't know where he lives, but that you will have to find out—quietly, you understand. Ask him from me to give you back the letter you brought to him this evening. If he refuses, ask him not to show it to any one until he sees me in the morning."

The commissionaire brought his heels together sharply, and presently went forth on his vain search; for Marsten, unconscious, had been taken in an ambulance to St. Martyrs' Hospital, with the remnants of the letter firmly clutched in his clenched fist.

## CHAPTER XXXVIII.

Again it was the last train to Wimbledon; but Sartwell, tired as he was, strode home from the station with the springy step of a young man. Edna, waiting for her father in spite of his prohibition, heard the step with a thrill of hope. When he came in, there was a smile on his face such as she had not seen for weeks.

"Ah, my girl," he cried, "you can never guess what has happened!"

"Yes, I can," she answered; "Marsten has ended the strike."

"No, the strike has ended Marsten. He has been deposed, and Gibbons has been elected in his place. Gibbons, unselfish man, at once came to me to make terms for himself. So the works will be open to-morrow; and when the next strike comes, let us hope, unlike John Gilpin, I won't be there to see."

"And what does Mr. Marsten say to this sudden change?"

"I didn't see him. I suppose he has gone to his room to meditate on the mutability of the workingman."

"I am glad you didn't send that letter."

"Ah, but the funny thing about it is that I did send it. My commissionaire is probably at this moment scouring London to find Marsten and get it back. It would be rather a turning of the tables if Marsten, in revenge, were to publish the letter. I don't think he will do it, but one can never tell. I confess it would be a strong temptation to me, were I in his place; however, I hope for the best, and have charged the commissionaire to get him to do nothing about it until after he has seen me."

"Do you still intend to offer him a place in the works?"

"That will depend. If his experience has driven all the visionary nonsense about the regeneration of the workingman out of his head, he will be a most valuable man for any firm to have in its service. I will see how the land lies when I talk with him."

"You have no feeling against him then, father?"

"None in the least. Just the opposite. I have the greatest admiration for the way he conducted the fight."

"You will not resign, will you?"

Sartwell laughed.

"I think not. There will be a lot to do, and I shall want to be in the thick of it. No, our Continental trip is postponed, Edna. Why, my girl, you've been crying, all alone here by yourself! Tut, tut, Edna, that will never do! I thought you had more courage than myself—not that I've had any too much these last few days. Go to bed, girlie, and have a good sleep. I want to be off early in the morning, so you may have the privilege of being my sole companion at breakfast. Good-night, my dear," he added, kissing her, "and here's luck to all our future battles!"

Edna was the first afoot in the morning, and the night's sleep, short as it was, had smoothed away all traces of the emotion of the night before. Youth has a glorious recuperative power, and Sartwell, when a little later he came wearily down the stair, showed that sleep had not dipped him in the fountain of it. Even the conqueror has to pay some tribute for the victory. He seemed tired as he took his place at the breakfast-table and unfolded the morning paper. Years of not too congenial married life had developed in him the reprehensible habit of reading his paper while he sipped his coffee, and not even the presence of his daughter opposite him could break him of the vice; although he had the grace to apologize, which he sometimes forgot to do when his wife was pouring the coffee.

"I just want to see if the paper has anything to say about the ending of the strike, my dear."

She smiled at him, and asked him to read what the paper said. A moment later she was startled by an exclamation from him.

"Good heavens!" he cried. "I had no idea of this! There seems to have been a riot at the meeting—five men arrested, and two in the hospital—Marsten—by Jove!—trampled under foot—never regained consciousness—life in grave danger! I say, Edna, this is serious!"

There was no reply, and Sartwell, looking up, saw Edna, standing with pallid cheeks and lips parted, swaying slightly from side to side.

He sprang up, and supported her with his arm.

"My girl, my little girl!" he cried. "What is the matter? What is this to you?"

Her head sank against his breast, and she said in a quavering whisper, broken by a sob:

"It is everything to me, father, everything!"

He patted her affectionately on the shoulder.

"Is it so, my darling, is it so? I was afraid once that was the case, but I thought you had forgotten. There, don't cry; it is sure to be all right. The papers generally exaggerate these things. Come, let us have breakfast, and we will both go to the hospital together."

Edna's desire for breakfast was gone, but she made a pretense of eating and then hurried to get ready and accompany her father. It was so early that they had a first-class compartment to themselves, the travel city-wards not having begun for the day.

Edna was silent, and nothing had been said from the house to the station. When they were in the train, her father spoke with some hesitation.

"Edna, have you seen Marsten since the time when I found you together in the garden?"

"Yes, father; twice."

"I don't want you to answer, my dear, unless you care to do so. Where did you meet him?"

"I will tell you everything; I was willing to tell you any time——if you had asked me. I didn't speak of him to you because——I didn't like to."

"Of course, girlie. I understand. You needn't speak now, if you would rather not."

"I should like you to know. The first time was at Eastbourne, shortly after I went there. He managed to get unseen into the school garden, and he told me that——he said he hoped——we would be married some day. I told him it was impossible. I thought so——then."

"That was two years ago?"

"Yes."

The ghost of a smile hovered about the firm lips of Sartwell; but the corners of Edna's mouth drooped pathetically, and she seemed on the verge of tears. She kept her eyes on the floor of the carriage.

"There was not much use of an angry father's precautions, was there, Edna?"

"I did not know, until he spoke, that you objected to my meeting him. If you had told me, I would not have spoken to him at Eastbourne."

"Of course you wouldn't, my dear. Don't think I am blaming you in the least. I was merely thinking that I am not nearly as far-seeing as I thought. And the second time, Edna?"

"That was last night. I drove to the Salvation Hall and asked him to stop the strike. I told him——"

Edna began to cry afresh. Her father, who had been sitting opposite her, crossed to her side, and put his arm about her.

"Don't say another word, my dear, and don't think about it. I'll not ask you another question. You mustn't make people think you have been crying. They will imagine I have been scolding you, and thus you will destroy my well-won reputation for being the mildest man in London."

The girl smiled through her tears, and nothing more was said until they reached the hospital door.

"How is Marsten, who was brought here last night?" inquired Sartwell, of the doctor who received him.

"Oh, getting on very well, under the circumstances."

"The papers say his condition is dangerous."

"I don't anticipate any danger, unless there are internal injuries that we know nothing of. Some of his ribs are broken, and he got a nasty blow on the back of his head. He seems rather weak and dispirited this morning, but his mind is clear. I was somewhat anxious about that, for he was a long time unconscious."

"There," said Sartwell to his daughter, who stood with parted lips listening intently to what the doctor said. "I told you the papers made the case out worse than it was. Might we see Mr. Marsten?"

"Yes; but I wouldn't make him talk very much, if I were you."

"We shall be very careful. I think, you know, it will cheer him up to see us, but you might ask him if he would rather we came another time. My name is Sartwell."

Word was brought back that Marsten would be glad to see them. They found him in an alcove, curtained off, like other alcoves, from the rest of the ward. His face was not disfigured, but was very pale. He cast one rapid glance at the girl, shrinking back behind her father, then kept his gaze fixed on his old employer.

"Well, my boy," said Sartwell, cheerily, "I'm sorry to see you on your back, but I'm glad to learn from the doctor that you will be all right in a few days."

"Have the men——have they——gone back?" Marsten asked, in a faint whisper.

"Don't bother about the men. I'm looking after them. Yes, they've come back."

Marsten tried feebly to lift his head, but it sank back again.

"The letter," he whispered, "what is left of it——is under the pillow, I think."

Sartwell put his hand under the pillow and pulled forth the tattered document.

"You intend me to have this?"

Marsten, with a faint motion of his head, signified his assent, and Sartwell, with some relief, placed it in his pocket.

"Now, my lad, you must hurry up and get well. There will be stirring times at the works, and I shall need the best help I can get. I'm depending on you to be my assistant, you know."

The young man's eyelids quivered for a moment, then closed over his eyes. Two tears stole out from the corners and rolled down his cheeks. His throat rose and fell.

"I'm a bit shattered," he whispered at last. "I'm not quite myself——but, I thank you."

"That's all right, my boy. Here's a young person who can talk to you more like a nurse than I can. I must see about your having a private room and all the comforts of the place while you are here."

Edna took his hand when her father had left the room. Marsten looked up at her, standing there beside him.

"It came to the same——in the end——didn't it?" he said, with a faint, wavering smile.

For answer she bent over him and kissed him softly on the lips.

THE END.

# About Author

**Robert Barr** (16 September 1849 – 21 October 1912) was a Scottish-Canadian short story writer and novelist.

**Early years in Canada**

Robert Barr was born in Barony, Lanark, Scotland to Robert Barr and Jane Watson. In 1854, he emigrated with his parents to Upper Canada at the age of four years old. His family settled on a farm near the village of Muirkirk. Barr assisted his father with his job as a carpenter, and developed a sound work ethic. Robert Barr then worked as a steel smelter for a number of years before he was educated at Toronto Normal School in 1873 to train as a teacher.

After graduating Toronto Normal School, Barr became a teacher, and eventually headmaster/principal of the Central School of Windsor, Ontario in 1874. While Barr worked as head master of the Central School of Windsor, Ontario, he began to contribute short stories—often based on personal experiences, and recorded his work. On August 1876, when he was 27, Robert Barr married Ontario-born Eva Bennett, who was 21. According to the 1891 England Census, the couple appears to have had three children, Laura, William, and Andrew.

In 1876, Barr quit his teaching position to become a staff member of publication, and later on became the news editor for the Detroit Free Press. Barr wrote for this newspaper under the pseudonym, "Luke Sharp." The idea for this pseudonym was inspired during his morning commute to work when Barr saw a sign that read "Luke Sharp, Undertaker." In 1881, Barr left Canada to return to England in order to start a new weekly version of "The Detroit Free Press Magazine."

**London years**

In 1881 Barr decided to "vamoose the ranch", as he called the process of immigration in search of literary fame outside of Canada, and relocated to London to continue to write/establish the weekly English edition of the Detroit Free Press. During the 1890s, he broadened his literary works, and started writing novels from the popular crime genre. In 1892 he founded the magazine The Idler, choosing Jerome K. Jerome as his collaborator (wanting, as Jerome said, "a popular name"). He retired from its co-editorship in 1895.

In London of the 1890s Barr became a more prolific author—publishing a book a year—and was familiar with many of the best-selling authors of his day, including :Arnold Bennett, Horatio Gilbert Parker, Joseph Conrad, Bret Harte, Rudyard Kipling, H. Rider Haggard, H. G. Wells, and George Robert Gissing. Barr was well-spoken, well-cultured due to travel, and considered a "socializer."

Because most of Barr's literary output was of the crime genre, his works were highly in vogue. As Sherlock Holmes stories were becoming well-known, Barr wrote and published in the Idler the first Holmes parody, "The Adventures of "Sherlaw Kombs" (1892), a spoof that was continued a decade later in another Barr story, "The Adventure of the Second Swag" (1904). Despite those jibes at the growing Holmes phenomenon, Barr remained on very good terms with its creator Arthur Conan Doyle. In Memories and Adventures, a serial memoir published 1923–24, Doyle described him as "a volcanic Anglo—or rather Scot-American, with a violent manner, a wealth of strong adjectives, and one of the kindest natures underneath it all".

In 1904, Robert Barr completed an unfinished novel for Methuen & Co. by the recently deceased American author Stephen Crane entitled The O'Ruddy, a romance.Despite his reservations at taking on the project, Barr reluctantly finished the last eight chapters due to his longstanding friendship with Crane and his common-law wife, Cora, the war correspondent and bordello owner.

**Death**

The 1911 census places Robert Barr, "a writer of fiction," at Hillhead, Woldingham, Surrey, a small village southeast of London, living with his wife, Eva, their son William, and two female servants. At this home, the author died from heart disease on 21 October 1912.

## Writing Style

Barr's volumes of short stories were often written with an ironic twist in the story with a witty, appealing narrator telling the story. Barr's other works also include numerous fiction and non-fiction contributions to periodicals. A few of his mystery stories and stories of the supernatural were put in anthologies, and a few novels have been republished. His writings have also attracted scholarly attention. His narrative personae also featured moral and editorial interpolations within their tales. Barr's achievements were recognized by an honorary degree from the University of Michigan in 1900.

His protagonists were journalists, princes, detectives, deserving commercial and social climbers, financiers, the new woman of bright wit and aggressive accomplishment, and lords. Often, his characters were stereotypical and romanticized.

Barr wrote fiction in an episode-like format. He developed this style when working as an editor for the newspaper Detroit Press. Barr developed his skill with the anecdote and vignette; often only the central character serves to link the nearly self-contained chapters of the novels. (Source: Wikipedia)

## NOTABLE WORKS

In a Steamer Chair and Other Stories (Thirteen short stories by one of the most famous writers in his day -1892)

"The Face And The Mask" (1894) consists of twenty-four delightful short stories.

In the Midst of Alarms (1894, 1900, 1912), a story of the attempted Fenian invasion of Canada in 1866.

From Whose Bourne (1896) Novel in which the main character, William Brenton, searches for truth to set his wife free.

One Day's Courtship (1896)

Revenge! (Collection of 20 short stories, Alfred Hitchcock-like style, thriller with a surprise ending)

The Strong Arm

A Woman Intervenes (1896), a story of love, finance, and American journalism.

Tekla: A Romance of Love and War (1898)

Jennie Baxter, Journalist (1899)

The Unchanging East (1900)

The Victors (1901)

A Prince of Good Fellows (1902)

Over The Border: A Romance (1903)

The O'Ruddy, A Romance, with Stephen Crane (1903)

A Chicago Princess (1904)

The Speculations of John Steele (1905)

The Tempestuous Petticoat (1905–12)

A Rock in the Baltic (1906)

The Triumphs of Eugène Valmont (1906)

The Measure of the Rule (1907)

Stranleigh's Millions (1909)

The Sword Maker (Medieval action/adventure novel, genre: Historical Fiction-1910)

The Palace of Logs (1912)

"The Ambassadors Pigeons" (1899)

"And the Rigor of the Game" (1892)

"Converted" (1896)

"Count Conrad's Courtship" (1896)

"The Count's Apology" (1896)

"A Deal on Change " (1896)

"The Exposure of Lord Stanford" (1896)

"Gentlemen: The King!"

"The Hour-Glass" (1899)

"An invitation" (1892)

" A Ladies Man"

"The Long Ladder" (1899)

"Mrs. Tremain" (1892)

" Transformation" (1896)

"The Understudy" (1896)

" The Vengeance of the Dead" (1896)

"The Bromley Gibbert's Story" (1896)

" Out of Thun" (1896)

"The Shadow of Greenback" (1896)

"Flight of the Red Dog" (fiction)

"Lord Stranleigh Abroad" (1913)

"One Day's Courtship and the Herald's of Fame" (1896)

"Cardillac"

"Dr. Barr's Tales"

"The Triumphs of Eugene Valmont"

CPSIA information can be obtained
at www.ICGtesting.com
Printed in the USA
LVHW030501140720
660560LV00012B/561

9 789390 209019